Gone Whalin'

Gone Whalin'

Conor Lastowka

ISBN 978-1492966852

Edited by Lauren Lastowka
Cover illustration by Adam Koford
Illustrations by Cason Moore
Jacket layout by Jaime Robinson

For Mom and Dad,
who always encouraged me
and Lauren,
who always inspires me

All factual inaccuracies about the whaling industry and/or the 1800s are intentional and for the sake of comedy. They are not in any way due to an utter lack of research on the part of the author.

DAY ONE

The day before Cormac McIlhenney woke up aboard a nineteenth-century whaling ship, his electric bill came in the mail.

Technically, the bill was for the electricity used by both Cormac and his roommate, Vance. But since it bore his name, the responsibility fell to Cormac. Were the bill to go unpaid, his credit would be damaged beyond repair and his hopes of eventual home ownership would be dealt a devastating blow. Even worse, the goons from the electric company might decide to come out and cut off the power, forcing him to eat all of the frozen entrées in the freezer before they spoiled. Finding the opportune window of time when the entrées had warmed to a palatable temperature but not yet spoiled would be difficult under normal circumstances; success would be almost unimaginable with no lights on.

Cormac furrowed his brow at the bill and hoped it wouldn't come to that. The amount due this month was $63.21, nearly four dollars more than the previous month. This was most assuredly due to Vance's ill-fated attempt at growing marijuana in his bedroom closet, an endeavor that required heat lamps to shine on the plants twenty-four hours a day. This had almost caused a fire when Vance attempted to warm his bath towel on one of the lamps while he was in the shower. Cormac hadn't approved of the plan, which required a naked Vance to sprint from the bathroom to the weed closet at hours when Cormac might be around to witness it, but Vance assured him that the luxury provided by the hot towel would outweigh any potential awkwardness it might cause.

The house nearly burnt down the first time Vance tried it. Cormac put his foot down once it happened two more times after that.

Yes, obtaining Vance's share of the electric bill would prove unpleasant, but Cormac was used to it. They'd been living together for three years. Assigned to each other as random roommates when they enrolled at Harrington State, they got the boot from the freshman dorms when a rat that Vance had been feeding bit their resident advisor. The RA had been a pleasant, forgiving fellow, and likely would have laughed the matter off, but it turned out that he was allergic to rabies. Cormac knew that the school couldn't let them stay in the dorms after that, but he sometimes wondered if the RA wasn't being a bit of a drama queen. How does one measure something like "percentage of mobility loss on your right side" anyways? It sure looked like less than 90 percent every time Cormac saw him wheel by.

After the rat expulsion, Cormac and Vance rented the place on Craymore Street, and had lived there ever since. A decrepit two-bedroom house far enough off campus to discourage regular class attendance, it suited their needs (mostly the need to not make the effort to find a better place). The paint flaked, the faucet dripped, and, should they ever need to access the attic, the landlord strongly discouraged them from breathing while up there. The rat had died twenty-four hours after Vance transported him there from the dorm. Cormac told himself it was a coincidence.

Holding the bill, Cormac walked out of the living room and down the short hall that led to Vance's room. He didn't like coming down here, and not just because rodent-induced paralysis had a non-zero probability of occurring. Cormac and Vance had never been particularly close. If asked, Cormac would probably describe their relationship as "by default." They'd had some laughs over the years, tried a few penny-ante get-rich schemes, and their band, Uncle Jemima, was actively seeking out their fifth-ever gig. But as Cormac steeled his nerve to knock on his roommate's door, he realized that he didn't even know Vance's parents' names. Vance had never mentioned them, but then again, Cormac had never asked. He hoped they were still alive.

Cormac banged on the door, intending to right this wrong and turn the corner in his relationship with his roommate. Vance eventually opened the door in his boxers, squinting, his hair matted on one side of his head and sticking straight up on the other.

"Are your parents dead?" asked Cormac.

Vance's eyes widened in terror, and he vomited on Cormac's shoes.

* * *

"I'm sorry about your shoes, Mac," Vance said as he entered the living room wearing just a towel around his waist. Cormac glanced at the shoes drying on the windowsill and scooted over on the couch, allowing Vance room to plop down next to him. The shoes would be fine in the long run, but the matter of the towel-clad figure next to him had quickly become a much more pressing concern.

Vance glanced down and made a minor adjustment to the towel. "You have to see it from my point of view, buddy: I really had to puke."

Cormac tried to size up what response might end the conversation the fastest and result in at least another layer of material between him and his roommate. He decided the direct approach was best.

"And what's all this 'dead parents' nonsense?" Vance continued. "You know my folks are alive; my dad got held in contempt of court when he testified during RatGate and told the bailiff to—"

Cormac cut his roommate off. "Vance, you didn't just take a shower, why the hell are you wearing a towel?"

"Ah, I wondered if you would ever ask. New strategy, buddy," said Vance. "This sucker's my ticket to dealing with these hot nights we've been having."

Cormac sighed and opened a beer as Vance continued.

"Pure comfort. Air flow. Easy access in the can. One size fits all."

"That's a dress, Vance. You're describing a dress."

"That's ridiculous! Do they make dresses with the Seahawks' logo on them?"

Against his best instincts, Cormac took a closer look at the towel. Vance had drawn a crude Seattle Seahawks logo on it with a black marker. *Seattle* was missing a *t*, and Cormac was fairly certain that in the real football team's logo, the bird was not shedding a single tear.

Vance turned and stared at Cormac. The towel shifted alarmingly. "You know what the best part of my day is, Mac? Getting out of the shower in the morning and wrapping this towel around my waist. I'm fresh, I'm clean. Sure, it'd be nice if the towel had been pre-heated . . ."

Cormac glared as he took a pull from the beer.

"But it's still a great experience. I've got the whole day ahead of me. You know what the worst part is? When I take this towel off and get dressed. It's all downhill from there."

Cormac was aghast. Vance had really given this towel pitch some thought. He hadn't expected this plea to his emotions. If he didn't act decisively, the situation could quickly escalate out of control. Towels could become the de facto wardrobe at the Craymore Street house. Traditional clothing would be hauled off to the homeless, and any non-towel items found squirreled away would be burned on the spot. Vance's reign as towel lord would be a cruel one.

"But Vance," Cormac protested. "That's not because of the towel. It's because you don't study and do poorly in school. You don't have a job, you can barely pay your bills. Today you were lying in bed hungover until four in the afternoon."

"And you know what brought me back? Gave me a second wind?" Vance asked.

"Purging your stomach of toxins by vomiting onto my shoes?"

Vance smiled coyly, shook his head, and tapped his finger on the towel.

Cormac rolled his eyes and was preparing to drain the rest of his beer when he noticed something. On the towel, right next to where Vance was tapping, were two letters. Vance hadn't sharpied them on; they were monogrammed in orange thread: *CM*.

His initials.

* * *

Cormac navigated his ancient Volvo through traffic as Vance sat in silence in the passenger seat. It had been an ugly scene. Words had been exchanged. Threats had been made. When tempers died down, the situation was at a stalemate. Cormac had banned Vance from ever wearing his towel in the future, but he knew in his heart he would never be able to use it again either. Knowing it had touched Vance's bare skin was more than enough reason to avoid it, but Cormac also wasn't certain that the ink from the marker Vance had used was something he wanted coming into contact with his skin. Vance was itching his waist and thighs at the present moment. For the time being, the monogrammed "Seatle" Seahawks towel that Cormac's grandmother had given him as an off-to-college present lay crumpled in a corner of the living room. Cormac would deal with it after band practice.

Band practice was the last thing Cormac wanted to be doing at the moment. Uncle Jemima's practice sessions usually revolved around having a few beers and talking about how awesome the last show was. But with the last show having happened nearly two months ago, that particular discussion topic had begun to wear a bit thin. Also, the long gap between shows was very much related to their dismal performance the last time they'd taken the stage. Vance had misrepresented both their musical genre and talent level to the sorority that had hired them. "BAND RUINS FORMAL," screamed the headlines of the *Harrington School Paper* the next day; "DEVASTATED SORORITY FOLDS," the day after that. The reporter who penned what ended up being a special eight-part investigation into the incident received a letter of commendation from Bob Woodward. Vance considered the gig one of the highlights of his life.

Cormac pulled into a parking spot outside the abandoned Chinese restaurant that Uncle Jemima used as a practice space. He put the car in park and looked over at Vance, who was absentmindedly scratching his leg.

"Look, Vance," said Cormac, as he turned off the ignition and pocketed the keys. "I'm sorry I got upset about the towel. It's just the—"

"The principle of the thing," finished Vance. "Yeah, I know. You've got principles. Everyone's got principles. I just don't know if the Mac I met three years ago would have gotten upset if I'd borrowed his towel, drawn a sweet Seahawks logo on it, and occasionally wore it around the house."

"He would have, I can assure you of that."

"All my towels are burnt, Mac! What am I going to do now? Dry myself with a sleeping bag? Haul a sleeping bag into the bathroom and dry myself with it every time I take a shower? Where, pray tell, would I hang that up to dry?" The frustration in Vance's voice was escalating rapidly. Clearly, the wound left by the confiscated towel was going to take some time to heal. He was now raving about surface area and goose down, and Cormac knew he had to put a stop to it.

"OK, Vance! Shut up! You can use the damn towel!"

Vance stopped shouting. He was breathing heavily.

"But only after you shower, OK?"

Vance nodded.

"Good. Now can we go inside? If you put some of that energy towards the drums, we may be able to have a semi-decent practice."

Vance itched his leg.

Entering the practice space, Cormac was dismayed to see Uncle Jemima's bassist, Joey, on all fours, mopping up some sort of spill with a bath towel. Cormac was wondering how on earth his day had taken such a towel-based turn when Vance piped up from behind him.

"Joey, the hell are you doing?"

Joey looked up, noticing his two bandmates for the first time.

"Hey guys," Joey said in his half-stoned monotone. "Yeah, I spilled a beer and couldn't find the sleeping bag, so I'm cleaning it up with this towel."

Cormac strapped on his guitar and wondered if he'd been transported to a parallel universe. Vance supervised the final seconds of Joey's cleanup efforts approvingly, then went to the fridge to grab beers. He popped the caps off with a lighter and handed one to Cormac. A peace offering of sorts. Cormac took a swig and wondered if maybe he was too hard on his roommate. Then he glanced down at his shoeless feet and abandoned that line of thinking. When he looked up, Vance had taken a seat on his drum stool. He was scratching his stomach with one of his sticks.

Willie, the singer, showed up a few minutes later, and practice commenced. Cormac had once observed that an Uncle Jemima performance was not unlike a livestock auction: loud, frenzied, and with many more losers leaving than winners. The comparison had only grown more apt after the sorority show when a goat had bit the chapter president. Nobody was sure how it had gained admittance, but, in retrospect, everyone agreed that the show would have been stranger if a goat *hadn't* bitten someone.

The band had mastered a handful of crowd-pleasing covers. These were designed to lull the audience into a false sense of enjoyment, as well as reach a previously agreed-upon contractual minimum set length. Once these milestones had been checked off, Vance would bang his drum sticks together three times, announcing a switch to a lineup of all-original tunes. The happy spectators who had been dancing to a Motown cover seconds earlier would find themselves assaulted by the rapid-fire guitar-driven histrionics of Uncle Jemima's surprisingly deep catalogue. Rending of garments and gnashing of teeth soon followed. God help him, Cormac loved it when they gnashed their teeth.

Songwriting duties were shared amongst all four members. Willie penned songs that spotlighted his pipes. Typically these were about wizards and demons, with occasional forays into how awesome BMX biking was. Joey exclusively wrote songs about partying. His songs were intricately woven tapestries of good times, willing babes, endless booze and drug supplies, celebrity pop-ins, go-karts, and swimming pools. Cormac didn't like to speak in absolutes, and he had only known Joey for a couple of years, but he was certain that the man had never attended a party that was 10 percent as fun as the ones he described in such great lyrical detail. At most of the parties Cormac had attended with Joey, the bassist ended up quietly sneaking off and locking himself in the room where the video game system was. The most recent song he'd penned was about setting a UPS van on fire and driving it off the roof of an orgiastic celebration into a fountain of beer. Cormac worried about him.

Vance wrote songs about rock and roll, more specifically how great it was to be in a band that played rock and roll. Pounding verses gave way to quick, shoutable choruses, and he always left plenty of room for Cormac to shred. Cormac never felt comfortable setting aside time for extended guitar solos in his own songs, but Vance always insisted on it. Cormac's guitar playing was one of the few high points of an Uncle Jemima performance. Of course, the band had lowered the bar for "high points" to pretty much "anything done on stage that was not an arrestable offence." The only other two items that might be considered high points were the eventual end of a show and the fact that so far the band had a flawless track record of not exposing their genitals mid-song. Of course, it had only been four shows.

An increasingly boozy practice concluded with a run-through of a new song Cormac had brought in. Cormac knew that his strength lay in his musicianship and not his lyrical prowess, but the thought of a set list that merely extolled the virtues of dragons, parties, and the band itself had inspired him to take a renewed interest in songwriting. He was proud of the latest tune he'd brought in, a more abstract, psychedelic number that had been inspired by a camping trip he'd taken the summer before. Of course, by the time they got to it, Vance's drumming was a half step behind, Joey had found his missing sleeping bag and was playing from inside it, and Willie was indicating his drunken hunger by replacing the lyrics with the names of the Mexican food items he currently desired. The plug was pulled on the practice quite literally when Joey attempted to stand up in the sleeping bag and immediately crashed forward, pulling the PA's power cord out of the wall and leaving an unamplified Willie channeling his inner Robert Plant to shriek an off-key "Burritoooooooooooooooooo" for about six seconds before noticing the cacophony behind him had ceased.

* * *

Cormac sat in the driver's seat in silence as he waited for Vance to lock up. The band rented the practice space under one condition: that the owners of the practice space never find out that they were using a stolen key to access it without paying any rent. Vance had spearheaded this campaign, and like most of Vance's ideas, illegality was a definite, though not isolated, concern. The few times they had arrived for rehearsal to find another band already booked in the space, they had been forced to participate in an elaborate ruse, pretending to be janitors and tidying up the space while the paying customers shot them glares. Cormac found this annoying, even though the mess they were cleaning up was usually their own. But what irritated him more was that his bandmates seemed to somehow enjoy the act. Cormac blew up one day when Vance brought everyone press-on "janitor mustaches." Cormac didn't associate mustaches with janitors and was surprised someone out there was manufacturing them as an official product, but that was the least of his worries. He accused Vance of deliberately scheduling their practice sessions when he knew another band had the studio booked so they'd get to pretend to be custodians again. Vance had acted hurt, but since then there hadn't been another mix-up.

Vance got in the car and Cormac started the engine. In theory, the night was still young, but Cormac didn't feel like doing anything with the clowns in his own band and especially not with Vance.

"What do you feel like doing, buddy?" asked Vance. "I don't know if he mentioned it to you, but Willie was planning on getting some Mexican food . . ."

Cormac wordlessly put the car into reverse.

"Maybe we should meet him over there?" Vance continued. "At the Mexican place? Mac?"

"Vance," Cormac said quietly as they took an illegal right turn on red out onto Main Street. "I've had five beers. I'm going to go home, take two shots of vodka, and go to bed."

"Sounds fun," said Vance. His tone was devoid of sarcasm.

Cormac didn't reply, but maintained a steady course homeward at a sly five miles an hour below the speed limit. After a few minutes Vance broke the silence.

"Mac, in the interest of full disclosure, I should probably let you know that I drank all the vodka in the house last night."

Cormac gripped the steering wheel tighter.

"Yeah, that's why I threw up on your shoes this afternoon. But you know I'm good for it, buddy. The vodka, I mean, not the shoes. The shoes are still wearable, was the consensus, right? Oh check it out, there's Willie."

Willie's pickup was stopped at a red light and as Cormac slowed to a halt in the lane next to him, Vance leaned out the window to try to get his attention.

"Willie! Hey Willie! Willie! Dammit, Willie!"

Willie eventually stopped pretending he couldn't hear the driver next to him and looked over. Realizing it was his bandmates and not a driver he had recently and drunkenly wronged, he smiled and waved. Cormac rolled his eyes when he noticed Willie was wearing his janitor mustache. As Vance tried to ascertain whether Willie had stopped for Mexican yet, Cormac looked forward, willing the red light to change so he could get home before the day got any crappier.

It stayed red.

In the car seat next to him, Vance was trying to negotiate a trade for some food. Cormac looked to his left, where an elderly woman was crossing the street. She must have hit the crosswalk button, triggering an extra-long red light. In the passenger seat, Vance had applied his own janitor mustache to his upper lip in an attempt to sweet-talk Willie. Cormac heard honking behind him. He glanced in the rearview mirror and saw Joey waving. Next to him, Vance launched into a raucous duet with Willie of the alternate, Mexican-food-based lyrics to Cormac's song. The old woman inched across the street. Joey yelled something unspeakable at her and she shot him the finger. Cormac was considering blowing through the empty intersection when suddenly, the light turned green.

Dreaming of his quiet bed, Cormac stepped on the gas. His tires squealed, Vance yelled in protest, and Cormac realized that his roommate was still halfway out of the window, reaching for something. Cormac hit the brakes, the old woman dove to the ground in terror, Vance slumped back inside, and the burrito that Willie had reared back to heave at Vance splattered all over the side of Cormac's car.

Vance looked out the window at the explosion, then back at Cormac. The jolt from the sudden car movement had knocked his janitor mustache loose, and it hung vertically from his right cheek.

"Dammit, Mac!" Vance cried. "My burrito! Stop the car, I can still scrape some of it off."

Cormac envisioned Vance tied to the side of a mountain while buzzards in janitor mustaches pecked at his liver. "Vance," he said, as calmly as he could manage. "Your share of the electric bill is $31.60. I want you to slide it under my bedroom door. It had better be there when I wake up tomorrow morning." Without another word, Cormac stepped on the gas and guided the Volvo home in silence.

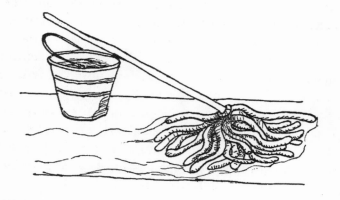

DAY TWO

Ziro stood on the bow of the *Levyathan* and surveyed the ocean. The sea was calm. In a few moments, he would embark on a day of backbreaking labor, but this was his time to enjoy.

Life was not easy for a slave on a whaling ship, let alone what was potentially the worst whaling ship currently operating on the seven seas. As the sun began to peek up over the eastern horizon, Ziro looked around at the variety of tasks that awaited him that day. Nets required mending. Harpoons had to be sharpened. The plank needed to be extended by a foot and a half for some reason. But looming large, as it always did, was a seemingly endless swath of deck that needed swabbing.

Swabbing the decks had occupied the majority of Ziro's hours ever since he was promoted from galley slave to regular slave. The promotion came with no added benefits and greatly increased responsibility. In fact, the total number of slaves on the *Levyathan* had been, and remained, one. Still, it was nice to have your performance recognized.

Ziro had been a slave on the *Levyathan* for nearly five years. The ship's captain had discovered him at a slave auction while they were unloading in New Orleans. Ziro wasn't actually up for auction; he was only there because some sailors had told him it was a good place to meet women. As lady after lady threw themselves upon the auction block rather than continue to endure Ziro's advances, he took to the bottle. The captain had found him, barely able to stand and attempting to bid on a soup bone that a stray dog was gnawing on. Deciding to save himself a few bucks, the captain stole the bone from the dog, then clubbed Ziro over the head with it and dragged him aboard his ship. Months later, it dawned on Ziro that the sailors had been messing with him.

Since then, he'd lived the seafaring life. Ziro wasn't exceptionally bitter about the hand he'd been dealt. Back on dry land, he didn't so much have "friends and family" as he had "an increasingly large and angry group of people he owed money to." Now, aboard the *Levyathan*, his food and lodging were free, plus he had a chance to see the world, meet interesting people, and learn several new types of knots. Sure, he wasn't getting paid. But lately, that was a problem for more people on the ship than just the resident slave.

Ziro took one last look at the horizon and went to retrieve his mop. As he wandered toward the small cabin that doubled as the supply closet and slave's quarters, he tried to recall the last time the crew of the *Levyathan* had actually caught a whale. It had been weeks, maybe even a month since they hauled one of the great beasts out of the water. There were many reasons that the *Levyathan* had become a laughingstock in the whaling community: out of date equipment, ugly whalers, misspelled ship's name. But most damning of all of them was the crew's plain inability to catch whales.

No whales meant no pay. No pay meant angry whalers. Angry whalers liked to blow off steam by carving scrimshaw. Scrimshaw— artistic patterns and pictures carved into whale bones and teeth— was difficult to carve when faced with a lack of whales. This made the whalers even angrier. Even angrier whalers drank, vomited, and then Ziro swabbed.

Ziro didn't understand why the other men needed to decorate bones, let alone whale bones. There was always plenty of driftwood floating around that would be great for carving and engraving, but nobody ever seemed interested. Once, when a dolphin had become ensnared in their nets, Ziro suggested a whaler carve its bones instead. The enraged man had to be physically restrained from hurling Ziro overboard. After that incident, Ziro kept his mouth shut about scrimshaw.

Ah well, Ziro thought to himself as he pumped sea water into his bucket. Maybe today will be the day. The sky the night before had been full of shooting stars, and Ziro, like many of the men on board, believed they were a good omen. Superstition was common on board the *Levyathan*. Finding a dead seagull meant the crew should buckle down for a fearsome storm. Red clouds as the sun went down meant that good luck would greet a sailor the next time they went ashore. Just last week, they'd seen a pod of whales breaching in the distance. Rather than pursue them, the captain decreed it a sign that they'd have a record haul the *next* day. Instead, they caught nothing and one of their sails accidentally got set on fire. Ziro sometimes thought the superstitions went a bit too far.

Even so, he was excited to see what the day would bring. Five years into his forced journey on the *Levyathan*, small details still thrilled Ziro. The creak of the masts. The salty spray of ocean water. The vulgar shouts of a poorly trained whaler who'd once again mistaken port for starboard and thrown his harpoon into the wide open sea, missing out on a sure kill. You never knew what life at sea would bring next.

Out of the corner of his eye, Ziro saw movement near the entrance to the whalers' quarters. Somebody else was awake. He quickly shoved the mop into the bucket to wet it and started swabbing, hoping it would look like he'd been at it for a while. Ziro didn't fear any direct reprisal if he was caught slacking. If anything were to happen to him, someone else would have to perform his duties and most people on board, though only dimly aware of what their own responsibilities entailed, were reluctant to take on any additional ones. This person would probably head off to get some breakfast without taking any notice of him or decide they were too hungover to be up and go back to sleep.

But this figure in the doorway wasn't doing either. He was just kind of standing there. Ziro stole a glance at him over his shoulder. The person looked confused. Squinting as if still half asleep, he looked to his left and then his right several times in a row. Ziro stopped swabbing and leaned on his mop, taking a closer look at the man. He had never seen him before in his life.

* * *

Captain Anson liked to start his day with a rundown of the *Levyathan*'s numbers. Today, like the day before and the day before that, this rundown took him about two seconds. Zero. That was the number of whales his supposed whaling ship had landed yesterday. The Captain glanced at the slate he had mounted on the wall of his cabin that displayed the quarterly goals he had laid out for the ship. They were still within reach. They'd just have to catch thirty-four whales a day for the next nine days, without breaks to sleep or eat. He supposed that many whales would pose a bit of a storage problem. Captain Anson jotted down a rudimentary sketch of a stack of whales, held in place by a quickly devised harness system. They'd need something like that once the whales started biting again. He'd have Ziro work on a prototype.

Anson pulled out his pocket watch and sized up the rest of his morning. He still had about an hour until most of the crew got up. As the streak of whaleless days grew longer, he'd been emerging from his cabin later and later. It gave the men confidence, he knew, to see that their leader had sequestered himself to remain deep in thought. He'd taken to ignoring the pounding on his cabin door, no matter how vigorous it grew. Whatever petty dispute the men needed him to settle on the deck was secondary to his current mission: devising a plan for the biggest whaling haul the world had ever seen.

He picked up the drawing of the harness system, and walked it over to the wall that the slate was mounted on. The harness system was just one of many innovations he'd devised during these early-morning brainstorming sessions. Tacked around the slate were drawings of catapults and flying machines, and one piece of paper that just said "ELECTROWHALES" in cool-looking letters. He grabbed the bottom of that one and took a closer look. He didn't remember writing it, or what it even meant. He debated tearing it down, but decided that he must have thought it was a good idea at some point in time, so it should stay. After all, he didn't want to toss what could end up being the missing piece to the whole puzzle just because it sounded kind of crazy. He moved ELECTROWHALES to a more prominent position in the center of the wall and tacked up the harness system diagram next to it.

Yes, the entire operation was shaping up nicely. Captain Anson stepped back to admire his work from a distance and nearly tripped over a stack of papers. It was an assortment of mostly maintenance requests from the crew with a few bills thrown in for good measure. He'd thought that forcing requests for repairs and new equipment to be submitted in writing would be an easy way out of having to fix or buy things. Instead, far more of his men had turned out to be literate than he'd anticipated, and demands had increased substantially. The captain eyed the top request with disgust as he gathered the papers together. "Think bigger, men," he said out loud. "'Functional life jackets' aren't going to solve our problems!" He dumped the papers into his garbage bin and slumped back in his desk chair.

"If I could run the ship by myself, I'd do it. I'd do it in a second!" Anson lamented. Every day, there were complaints from his sailors to deal with. The captain raised his voice to a nasal pitch and mocked them to himself: "The sails have holes in them! This hardtack tastes like dog food! A wharf rat bit me and inside the first aid box there were just more wharf rats! For the love of God, captain, when are we going home?"

Home. That was a complaint he was hearing more and more often. He'd hoped that the weeks without pay might light a fire under the men, make them work a bit harder to haul in a whale. Instead it had just served to remind them that the shift they had signed on for had ended nearly a year ago, and that they just might be happier surrounded by their wives and children than living aboard a rundown whaling boat. He wished the men could be more like Ziro. Ziro kept his mouth shut and did what he was told, and he sure seemed happy. Anson often tried calling attention to this. He'd wander over to Ziro while he was swabbing and loudly say, "Boy, Ziro, how do you stay so happy? Maybe not having any material possessions or freedom is something we all ought to consider, huh boys?" Then he'd look around at the whalers and point at Ziro while grinning broadly, but nobody was fooled. Some of the men just pulled out their scrimshaw etchings of their families and wept.

Unfortunately, a trip home was not currently on the *Levyathan*'s agenda and would not be added any time soon. For the rest of the men on board, returning to Nantucket meant a loved one's embrace and a warm bed. But only one thing awaited Captain Anson there: divorce papers served up by his harpy of a wife, Eleanor. Those divorce papers would mean the loss of half of everything he owned: the house in Nantucket, the summer cottage, the horse-drawn carriage. But most importantly, the *Levyathan*. And also, if you really wanted to get technical about it, *only* the *Levyathan*.

Purchasing his dream whaling ship had necessitated mortgaging the Anson's house. Stocking it with equipment meant the same for the summer home. Raising capital to hire a crew meant putting up pretty much everything else the couple owned as collateral. They'd actually gotten a fairly good loan rate, since before he took control of the whaling ship, Captain Anson had worked as a VP at a bank. Quitting his high-paying job had been another sore spot with his wife. That all of these events occurred spontaneously within a four-hour period on what he had forgotten was Eleanor's birthday did not help either. Nor did the fact that when he brought her down to the marina to surprise her with the christening of the ship, his brother-in-law, Wellington, was already there, presenting *his* wife, Gertrude (Eleanor's twin), with a pristine new sailboat he had secretly spent all year crafting by hand for *her* birthday.

Anson was still confident that he could have emerged unscathed if his overcompensating jerk of a brother-in-law hadn't gone and named his boat after his wife. *Gertrude*—what the hell kind of a name for a boat was that? Sadly, Anson not naming the boat after Eleanor was underscored by the fact that he had misspelled the name he had chosen instead. On the card that accompanied the boat, he had somehow managed to combine the two naming faux pas. "Dear Ellenore," it read. "With every whale I haul aboard to render blubber down for lamp oil, I shall think of you. Happy anniversary. Please call me Captain from now on. Love, Captain Anson."

When the Captain sobered up the next morning and realized what he'd done, he decided he'd better smooth things out. Eleanor wasn't home, so he hustled down to the florist to buy her the deluxe "I'm sorry" package. Stopping off at a tavern on the way for a hair of the dog, he noticed his wife across the street. She was walking quickly, with her head down, clearly trying not to attract attention. Without even pausing, she turned into the office of the town's most prominent attorney, a man who specialized in quick and devastating divorce settlements. Anson quickly came to a horrifying realization: he didn't have any money to pay for his beer.

Knowing that a divorce was fully justified and would rob him of his new boat, Anson fled to the harbor. There, he convinced his crew to leave several days early, by using a shrewd bargaining technique known as "making promises he had no intention of keeping." He came to regard the technique as a patented Anson trademark.

The *Levyathan* hauled up her anchor and set sail in less than an hour. As the Nantucket harbor faded from view, he swore he could make out the silhouettes of his shrieking wife and the furious tavern owner he'd stiffed cursing his name from the dock. Captain Anson turned to his first mate and dramatically said, "First mate! Let's go catch us some whales!" Then he snapped his fingers and said,

"Hey! First mate! Hey! You!" Eventually he explained to the person whose attention he was trying to get that he had the great honor of being deemed the first mate of the *Levyathan*. The guy didn't speak English. The Captain decided he didn't need a first mate.

They hadn't been back to Nantucket since. Anson knew the minute they docked there, he'd be served with divorce papers and he'd lose the boat. He couldn't give Eleanor that satisfaction. Unfortunately, she seemed very determined to see the divorce through. Her attorney had started turning up in other towns where the *Levyathan* was docked. Anson wasn't sure who was tipping her off, so he started keeping the crew in the dark about their destinations. He'd tell them they were sailing to Bermuda for shore leave, then dock at an industrial port in Halifax. These trust games worked both ways. His men grumbled that maybe someday it would be nice if he told them they were going to Halifax and instead sailed to Bermuda. Anson would just reply that the average high for Halifax in February was thirty degrees, so they had better change out of those swim trunks and goggles.

Even when the *Levyathan* arrived at a destination that he'd kept the men in the dark about, Captain Anson was reluctant to leave the boat. He started sending Ziro ashore wearing his clothes as a decoy. The ruse played out the same way every time. Ziro would step off the dock and be swarmed by legal underlings and process servers, all trying to hand documents to the wrong man, while Anson watched the scene unfold from his cabin, protected by the law of the sea. "If only Eleanor could see me now," he'd think as he squinted through a dirty port hole at the man he'd captured into slavery while wearing only his underwear.

The next trip ashore wouldn't be happening anytime soon though. There was no point until they had whales to unload and sell. Captain Anson decided he'd strategized enough for this morning. It was time to join his men on deck. He picked up his lucky spyglass and clipped it to his belt. If those shooting stars last night meant what he thought they did, today would be a busy and fruitful day for the entire crew. The damn decks had better be swabbed to hell and back.

When Cormac had woken up, he'd been confused and scared. This was fairly normal. During his three years at Harrington, he'd woken up in some confusing and scary places. Usually there'd be a clue nearby that would fill him in on where he was. A sorority pin on a nightstand, or a sanitation company logo on the interior of a dumpster. That would allow him to get his bearings and stumble home bleary-eyed, where Vance would fill him in on the rest.

Today, however, he wasn't finding anything. He'd woken up in a bunk bed, one in a tight row of a dozen or so, all of them full of snoring men. His first thought was that he was in the top-secret sleeping shed that the Harrington groundskeepers all slept in, where they were bathed in positively charged ions in order to dilute the harmful effects of the insecticide the dean forced them to use to keep the campus pristine. His second thought was how weird that first thought was. Seeing no immediate clues and not wanting to wake any of the men up, Cormac decided to head outside. Harrington was a fairly small campus; he'd hopefully be able to spot a landmark nearby and figure out where he was.

What the hell had happened to him? He didn't think he'd been that drunk when he went to bed, certainly not drunk enough to go wandering in his sleep. Maybe his frustration with Vance had focused him, made him feel more sober than he really was. But even as he made his way to the door, his feet felt unsteady beneath him, like the entire world was tilting from side to side. Maybe Vance had drugged him as revenge for the towel argument. If dosing your roommate's drink with powerful psychoactive drugs was now on the table as a legitimate response to a minor quibble over towel ownership, things were about to get a lot more interesting in the house on Craymore Street.

Cormac was pondering when he might have his first opportunity to fix Vance a reverse-revenge spiked drink when he pushed open the door and saw the ocean.

He stopped dead in his tracks. Either Vance had engineered a prank of colossally stupid magnitude or he was dreaming. And though Cormac was almost certain it was the latter, part of him kind of hoped Vance had pulled it off. The ocean was over five hours away from the Harrington campus. If Vance had somehow managed to transport him here, it would mean he was an actual supervillain. Cormac and his roommate had their differences, but he had to assume he'd be welcomed in on the ground floor of whatever diabolical enterprise Vance the supervillain had planned. It would sure beat finding a job after college.

But that wouldn't be necessary because this was definitely all a dream. And not a bad one, Cormac noted. The morning air was cool and there wasn't a cloud in the sky. Who knew, perhaps some sea wenches would make an appearance? Cormac immediately tried to concentrate really hard to get some sea wenches to make an appearance. Soon he felt dizzy, so he stopped before he burst a capillary. That was when he noticed he was not alone on the deck.

A man with a mop was twenty feet away, pretending not to look at him. Usually upon encountering a person whose profession involved mops, Cormac would respond in the same fashion and be delighted with the arrangement. But since this was dreamland, he figured he should be a bit friendlier. After all, you never knew when a mop-wielding deckhand was going to morph into a busty sea wench.

Cormac gave it just a few more seconds in case that moment was now, then decided to proceed with an introduction.

"Ahoy matey!" he shouted, raising a friendly hand as a greeting.

Cormac didn't know it was possible to convey disgust with a sweep of a mop, but the stranger did an admirable job of it. He was going to have to try another strategy.

"I just woke up in that room with a dozen other guys!" he said jovially as he walked toward the stranger. "Not a very comfortable bed, let me tell you! And man, how do you deal with the snoring in that place?"

"I don't sleep in that room. I sleep in there." The man pointed toward a rickety closet that appeared to be only slightly larger than a gym locker. A faint chemical haze appeared to emanate from it.

"It looks . . . cozy," Cormac lied, as a rat staggered out of the closet and died. He had two strikes. It was time to turn on the McIlhenney charm and make a new friend. "I'm sorry if you took any offense to that, not that you should, it's really not my business where anyone sleeps on this ship and who knows, maybe you choose to sleep there, it's certainly possible that you'd prefer to be in there than you would in a room with a dozen smelly guys in it, after all . . ." It was at this point in his panicked ramblings that Cormac realized he had walked through the section of the boat deck that the man had just mopped and left a trail of dirty footprints. He stopped himself midsentence and tried another tactic. "Look. I'm having a dream. I'm really sorry about ruining your mopping, but if it's any consolation, I'm sure I'm going to wake up soon anyways. My name's Cormac."

He stuck out his hand for the stranger, who looked at him with an uncertain expression before eventually shaking it. "Ziro," he replied.

"Nice to meet you, Ziro," said Cormac. "Is this your ship?"

"No. I'm a slave."

"A slave! Cool!" Cormac exclaimed. Ziro looked at him like he was the dumbest person he had ever encountered. "What I meant was, that's terrible. Humanity has a long way to go. One summer I worked as a busboy. That was pretty crappy, too."

Now Ziro was giving Cormac a look that he recognized. It was the same half-amused, half-horrified expression that professors would use after he was called on to talk about reading he hadn't done, and the professors realized this was the case and wanted to see how much further he would embarrass himself.

"But I was only a busboy for a couple weeks before I got fired. I suppose if you do a crappy job you don't get fired."

"They would starve me if I did a bad job."

"Right."

"And what is a busboy?"

Cormac started to describe his summer job to Ziro. While he explained the duties of a busboy to the slave on the deck of a large boat, he wondered what twisted part of his subconscious was conjuring up such a simultaneously bizarre and mundane dream.

"So the main thing to remember was, if you volunteered to take the garbage out to the dumpster, you'd have two or three minutes to sift through it for leftovers before anyone noticed you were missing," finished Cormac.

"That job sounds terrible," replied Ziro, as he lowered his head and started to mop again.

Cormac followed behind him, determined to force his dream in a more interesting direction. "So what do you guys do on this boat? Are you pirates?"

"Of course we're not pirates. The *Levyathan* is a whaling boat."

Cormac was taken aback. "Whaling? Like hunting whales? I didn't know people did that anymore."

Ziro didn't take his eyes off the ship's deck. "You're probably thinking of the scare a few years ago when people thought that blubber was making whalers go mad. It turned out that was just syphilis. A very popular and very filthy prostitute nearly shut our whole industry down."

Cormac mentally reversed his previous stance on sea wenches. The ravages of dream syphilis were not something he had any desire to experience. "I hadn't heard about that," he said. "But I thought killing whales was wrong? Aren't they endangered?"

"I don't know what that word means," Ziro responded, not looking up from his mopping.

This poor slave has lived such a sheltered life, Cormac thought. Perhaps his mission in this dream was enlightening this uneducated rube. Maybe doing so would unlock something that his subconscious had hidden away. Like he had been a "slave" to routine, and the "whales" were actually his unrealized potential. He wasn't sure exactly how this dream stuff worked; he'd been pretty stoned the time he watched *Inception*.

"Endangered means there aren't many of an animal left. We've got a list of endangered species that people aren't allowed to hunt or eat anymore." Cormac assumed what he considered a fairly important-sounding tone. "I know you and your fellow whalers may think you can hunt these animals forever, but the truth is, there aren't many of them left."

Right as Cormac finished his sentence, a giant whale leapt out of the ocean and crashed back down into the water about three hundred feet in front of the boat.

Cormac continued, undeterred. "Indiscriminate whaling has decimated the once-thriving population of these noble animals."

On the starboard side of the boat a pod of five or six happy whales surfaced to shoot water out of their blow holes.

"Ziro, it's important to preserve these creatures, because when an animal goes extinct . . . they're gone forever," he lectured as two female whales on the port side simultaneously gave birth, one of them to twins.

Cormac abandoned his ecology lesson and bitterly surveyed the sudden activity in the frothing ocean. "Or maybe hauling one or two of them out every so often wouldn't hurt anybody," he conceded.

Ziro didn't hear him. He was already on his way to alert the captain.

* * *

Ziro didn't know what to make of the strange new passenger on the boat. Even though he wasn't formally filled in on many of the matters that transpired aboard the *Levyathan*, Ziro was aware of just about everything that was going on. Swabbing the decks let a man observe things on the ship he wouldn't normally be allowed near. Due to the undignified circumstances of his joining the *Levyathan*, most of the men took Ziro for an idiot and freely discussed sensitive matters while he was within earshot. He overheard important stuff like rumors of other ships' record hauls and which men were scheming to go AWOL the next time the *Levyathan* docked. He was also privy to a wide variety of trivialities: who was planning on getting a new tattoo or which of the men had bet each other a week's worth of salt pork to see who could go the longest without changing their underwear. One time, he was able to piece together that one of the other men had called out in his sleep for Ziro to save him. From then on, he was always sure to swab the other side of the deck when that guy was around.

But Ziro couldn't recall any mention of new crew members joining up. Plus, the *Levyathan* hadn't docked in weeks. This Cormac fellow couldn't have been out of sight the whole time. And why the hell did he keep talking about how he was dreaming? The whole thing struck Ziro as an ominous portent. More importantly, it increased the odds of something happening that he would get blamed for. But then again, Ziro hadn't seen so many whales in months. Maybe this combined with the meteor shower meant something special really was afoot.

But it didn't matter what Ziro thought, it mattered what Captain Anson thought. Ziro reached out and knocked three times. The door swung open almost immediately. The captain grimaced when he saw Ziro.

"Dammit, Ziro!" barked the captain. "I don't like seeing you before I eat!"

"I'm sorry, Captain," Ziro responded. "I didn't want to disturb you, it's just that—"

Captain Anson cut him off by thrusting some papers toward him. "No time for that. Take these plans—I want to see a prototype for this whale harness system by the end of breakfast."

"Sir, if you didn't want to see me until after breakfast, how were you going to ask me to construct the prototype that you want done by the end of breakfast?" Ziro asked.

The captain's eyes narrowed. "You think you're pretty clever, huh Ziro? Make it *two* prototypes by the end of breakfast."

"Sir, I think by very definition, there can be only one prototype at a time. The Greek root *proto* means first, it would be more accurate to refer to the second version as a—"

"Dammit, Ziro!" the captain shouted. "Give me those designs back!"

Ziro handed the captain back his papers, not without noting that in each of the crude drawings, the whales were all smiling. Captain Anson crumpled the papers into a ball and threw it in Ziro's face.

"Now swab that up!" sputtered the captain.

"Sir, I can pick it up and dispose of it, the mop isn't really needed."

"You're really pushing your luck, Ziro," Captain Anson growled.

"Can I put it in your wastebasket?" Ziro asked, slightly crouching to pick up the wadded papers. "It's closer than the main garbage can."

"It's full. Full of paper. Full of ideas, Ziro, big ideas. Been doing a lot of thinking. You've got to be ready when inspiration hits." The captain looked proud.

"Sir, I empty your basket every night and last night the only thing in it was a banana peel, and I can see it right now and it's still empty."

Captain Anson glared at Ziro.

"Can I toss it in?" Ziro asked. "I'm pretty sure I could make it from here."

"Give me that!" shouted the captain, grabbing the wadded-up ball from Ziro. "I won't have you throwing garbage all over the captain's quarters!"

Anson tossed the ball toward the wastebasket, coming up short by nearly three feet. He shot Ziro a look, then walked to pick it up. He threw it at the wastebasket again, falling short a second time. He finally picked it up from the floor and dropped into the empty basket. He turned around and stared at Ziro.

"Why are you still here?" he bellowed.

"Sir, I actually have some news that you may want to hear."

"Well let's hear it, dammit. I'm very busy!"

"It's the whales, sir. There seem to be a lot of them very close by."

"Whales!" shouted the captain as he strode through the doorway onto the ship's deck. Outside, he pulled his spyglass off of his belt and peered through it. "How many did you see?" he demanded as he scanned the horizon.

"There had to have been at least ten."

"I'll be the judge of that," barked Captain Anson. Ziro watched him sweep the spyglass back and forth while the spray from the whales frolicking a mere twenty feet from the boat continuously stung his face. Eventually the captain lowered the spyglass. "It's just as I thought," he announced grimly. "Whales."

The captain launched into one of his trademark whale-based tirades. Ziro had learned to tune him out as soon as his language grew theatrical and he began spouting spittle-flecked invectives that contained phrases like "foul hellbeasts of the sea" or "cruel Poseidon's abominations." Usually these rants reached a climax with the captain scaling the crow's nest to shake his fist at the "detestable living embodiments of the tyranny of the seven seas" and informing them that he would "pluck them from the briny deep by the tines of Neptune's own triton." Ziro thought the more effective course of action would be to provide level-headed leadership to the often confused and directionless whalers, but the captain preferred to stick with his own methods.

Knowing that once Captain Anson got ramped up about the whales it would be difficult to get a word in, Ziro cut him off as soon as he could. "Captain, if I may . . . Shouldn't we wake the rest of the crew up? Get the whales while the getting is good, so to speak?"

The Captain had been ready to hurl his wastebasket overboard in whale-provoked frustration, but Ziro's words brought him back down to earth. He dropped the receptacle to the deck and looked at Ziro. "You're right," he panted, already winded. "There's not a moment to lose."

With that, Captain Anson strode off toward the bow of the ship. Ziro realized he hadn't had a chance to tell him about the other bit of news, the strange stowaway aboard the *Levyathan*. "Captain!" he called after him. Captain Anson turned and stared at him, his hand twitching impatiently as it gripped his spyglass.

Ziro hesitated. "Good luck," he shouted. Anson would find out on his own soon enough.

* * *

Rousting the rest of the crew out of their sleeping quarters proved difficult, as always. A crew of a dozen whalers was a dismal thing to deal with under any circumstances. If the dozen whalers had crippling hangovers, no scrimshaw to carve, *and* you were attempting to get them to do more of the same backbreaking manual labor that they hadn't been compensated for in weeks, the encounter could prove deadly.

Fortunately, Ziro had a weapon at his disposal: his ukulele. Or rather, the latest in a string of ukuleles that had suffered gruesome fates at the hands of irritated whalers. Ziro didn't take it personally. He knew that scorn was to be expected when you played the ukulele in public. Once, while busking in the French Quarter, he had asked a nun who was passing by if she had a request. She asked him if he knew "fuck you and that pussy guitar" without missing a bead on her rosary. Believing that Ziro had insulted the nun, a street performer on stilts ambled over and smashed the ukulele against one of the Quarter's trademark wrought iron balconies. When the stilt walker guys started disrespecting you, it confirmed your place at the rock bottom of the busking totem pole.

As the broken ukuleles started stacking up, Ziro became quite handy at fashioning them out of found objects. Old cans, cigar boxes, even a wooden shoe that a Dutch sailor had hurled at his head. Even in its dilapidated state, the *Levyathan* had an abundance of raw materials he had learned to mold into ukuleles. Ziro had created this latest model out of an old tin of tobacco and some fishing wire before he went to bed last night. He knew it wouldn't last long once the whalers discovered it, but he hadn't thought it would be put to the test this quickly. Suffice to say, the burly crew members of the *Levyathan* were not fans of his music.

Ziro flung the door open and instantly remembered that every day he vowed to remember to hold his breath the next time. There was nothing in the world quite like the smell of the whalers' quarters. Almost daily in New Orleans, Ziro had experienced depravity, vice, and the smells that resulted from the twisted mixture of both of them. But this was on an entirely different level. It smelled like sweaty beards and diseased mules. Half of a rotting fish lay on the ground near the door. Ziro turned and looked at the endless expanse of ocean not twenty feet past the door. Never mind what half of an uncooked fish was doing in the whalers' quarters to begin with, even the most scurvy-ridden of the men would have easily been able to throw it overboard without leaving the room. Instead, it lay there, making its own valued contribution to the horrifying potpourri.

Ziro wasn't sure how the stench of the quarters wasn't incentive enough to wake up at a reasonable hour, but the whalers seemed to be used to it. Even the bright rays of the early morning sun couldn't elicit a reaction other than louder snoring. Getting the men up to reap the ocean's bounty was all up to him. Reluctantly, he fingered a chord on the ukulele. As the strings vibrated ever so slightly, Ziro could have sworn that he saw the closest whaler stir in his sleep.

Ziro began to strum the ukulele. The only song he ever played anymore was a sea shanty he had written called "Treasures o' the Sea." It was long and bawdy, and had never been successfully performed in its entirety. The whalers hated the song, and as soon as the familiar melody drifted toward them, their eyes popped open, almost in unison. Groans and angry curses emerged from the cabin as Ziro began to sing from where he'd left off the last time.

On Christmas day I gave my wife some brand new underwear,
"Put these on and prance around for me my lady fair!"
She opened the box and then my wife she turned and ran and hid,
"That's not some underwear," she screamed, "It's just a giant squid."

"It works as both," I told my bride, "Just let me demonstrate."
"You tie the tentacles like this, a basic figure eight."

Just then my neighbor popped on by, it gave him quite a shock
To see his friend a-standin' with a squid around his—

OHHHHHH
You can keep your diamonds, and you can keep your gold,
My wife don't care for any of them, those treasures leave her cold.
She might get them from other men, but won't get them from me,
The only gifts I give my wife are treasures o' the sea.

On New Year's Eve I gave my wife—

At this point in the shanty, a grumpy whaler seized the tiny ukulele from Ziro's hands and bashed it against the cabin doorframe. The strings snapped instantly and the tobacco tin was dented beyond recognition. The bleary-eyed man tossed the remains of the ukulele over his shoulder and lumbered past Ziro. His fellow whalers followed close behind, grunting their approval at their colleague's action. Ziro was surprised he'd made it through the chorus.

"Go get 'em, guys," offered Ziro. "Lots of whales out there, lots of chances for a big score."

Upon hearing this encouragement, the last whaler to leave the cabin turned and stared at Ziro. Wobbling slightly, he walked back toward the cabin entrance, where he stomped up and down on the former ukulele. When it had been flattened to a thin strip of tin, he picked it up, walked to the edge of the ship, and dropped it into the ocean. He looked back at Ziro, spit over the side while maintaining eye contact, and walked to the bow of the ship to start his day. The half fish still lay less than a foot from where he'd been stomping.

* * *

Before Cormac really knew what happened, he went from being the only man on the bow of the ship to ducking thrown coils of rope and avoiding sweaty whalers. The hungover crew of the *Levyathan* seemed surprisingly adept at springing into action. Whether any of that action would effectively capture any whales had yet to be determined. After two of the whalers hoisted sails pointed in different directions and the entire shipped creaked as the wind threatened to tear it apart, Cormac noted that leadership appeared to be lacking aboard the whaling vessel.

A man whom he presumed to be the captain (based on the fact that he had a spyglass and wasn't doing any work), seemed to be out of touch with the rest of the whalers. He had been the first person to emerge after Ziro abandoned him, and Cormac had attempted to introduce himself. But it was as if the captain hadn't even seen him. He just walked past him with a wild look in his eye, assumed a dramatic stance near the bow, and starting shouting things at the whales. Cormac thought he looked similar to George Washington crossing the Delaware in that famous painting. It was a good look. Powerful. Not that anybody seemed to be paying him any attention.

Cormac figured it couldn't hurt to pick this guy's brain. He navigated the maze of busy whalers and stood next to the captain. Cormac eyed the man and attempted to imitate his stance: one leg forward and slightly bent, left hand on hip. It felt incredibly unnatural. Cormac tried to address the captain.

"Hi! I Cormac. Whales . . . out there today. Ocean?" Dammit! It was impossible to talk when you were standing like this. All your concentration went into the posing. Cormac relaxed and assumed a more natural posture, but he quickly realized that the captain hadn't even noticed him.

"Harpoons shall pierce their flabby hides and the full force of the heavens will tear them asunder!" the captain was shouting.

Cormac attempted to engage him again. "You must be the captain," he said. "My name's Cormac. I'm having a really weird dream."

The captain laughed, but the crazed nature of it let Cormac know it wasn't at him, but rather at the whales that continued to swim all around the boat. As the captain raised his spyglass to his eye to survey the sea, Cormac thought about the last thing he'd said.

It was by far the weirdest dream he'd ever had. Not just the content of it, which was growing stranger by the minute, but the dream as a whole, which just *felt* different. He couldn't put his finger on why, but standing on a whaling ship in the middle of the ocean felt more real than any other dream he'd ever had. Plus, he'd also remained in the dream once he realized he was dreaming. That never happened to him. Usually he'd realize he was dreaming just as two cheerleaders were about to do something to him that could result in prison time for all three of them. But when he was aboard a smelly whaling boat and realized it was all in his head, then the dream kept on going just fine.

I should get someone to pinch me, Cormac thought to himself. Obviously, the captain was in his own world. The closest whaler to Cormac was a muscular fellow who was sizing up a breaching whale with his harpoon gun. Cormac sidled over to him, and was about to tap him on the shoulder when the whaler pulled the trigger. Unfortunately, the man was still half-asleep, and had somehow managed to load the harpoon in backwards. This caused the gun to fly overboard and gently glance off the frolicking whale while the confused and angry whaler was left holding a harpoon in his hands. Cormac thought better of asking this guy to pinch him.

Wandering through the rest of the activity on the *Levyathan*, Cormac was amused and astounded at the level of ineptitude he saw. Whalers heaved when they should have hoed. The man at the helm was using a sextant to stir an early morning cup of rum. Fistfights broke out over the right to harpoon a whale within point-blank distance, only to have the whale dive and emerge on the other side of the boat, causing another fight to break out over there. It became quite clear that even though they were in the center of a gigantic cluster of carefree whales, there was a solid chance that the *Levyathan* might not land a single one.

In the midst of all the chaos, Cormac found Ziro, calmly swabbing a quiet corner of the deck.

"It doesn't look like they're going to catch anything," remarked Cormac.

Ziro looked up at him. He paused for a second before responding. "That wouldn't surprise me. It's been quite a while since they've hauled one in."

"Do they ever let you take a shot with a harpoon?" Cormac asked.

"No. That doesn't really fall under a slave's duties. The closest I ever get is sharpening them."

"That's great," Cormac said dismissively. "Hey would you mind pinching me?" He stuck out his arm. Ziro looked at him, then looked around to see if he was being set up.

"It might wake me up," Cormac offered. "From my dream."

Ziro was torn. The last thing he wanted to do was pinch someone. But if there was a chance it could get this guy to disappear, he was all for it. Reluctantly he stuck his hand out, closed his eyes, and pinched Cormac's arm.

"Dammit, Ziro!" an irritated voice bellowed. Ziro's eyes popped open. Cormac spun around to see that the captain had left his perch at the bow and was now standing five feet behind them.

Cormac looked down at his arm. The spot Ziro had pinched was red with indentations from his fingernails. He suddenly realized that it had really hurt. But he was still here on the ship, and now the captain looked pissed.

"Did you sharpen these harpoons?" shrieked the captain.

"Of course I did," stammered Ziro. "I sharpen them every night."

"Well they can't be *that* sharp! Because one of the men just shot another man with a harpoon and it just bounced off his chest!"

"Is that a bad thing?" Ziro asked. "Are you upset that it didn't impale him?"

"Don't get smart with me, Ziro!" snapped the captain. "I'm starting to think that the reason we're not catching any whales on this ship is because you're not keeping the equipment in shape. Look me in the eye and tell me you sharpened this harpoon last night!"

Cormac felt obliged to intervene. "That's not a harpoon. That's a loaf of bread."

The captain looked down at the long baguette he held in his outstretched hand, not comprehending. Cormac let him stand there for a second, then took it from him.

"Yeah it's definitely bread," Cormac said. He tried to take a bite of the end of it, but it was well beyond stale. "Jeez! This thing is rock hard! The guy who got shot is lucky he didn't bruise a rib."

Cormac banged the loaf against the port-side railing. "How did he load this into the harpoon gun?"

"That particular harpoon gun is now quite broken," explained the captain as the baguette eventually shattered. Half the loaf fell into the sea where an eager whale gulped it down and swam off merrily.

"Vile scavengers! The vultures of the sea! Dine on carrion while you can, you miserable behemoths, for the day of reckoning shall—" The captain abandoned his ravings as quickly as he had lapsed into them. He turned from the sea and stared directly at Cormac. For the first time on the ship, Cormac felt slightly uneasy.

"Ziro!" shouted the captain, not breaking eye contact with Cormac. "Who the hell is this?"

"That is Cormac, sir," replied Ziro. "He says he's dreaming."

"Dreaming? That some sort of stowaway talk? You stowaways think you're so big, with your fancy slang terms and stowaway code." Cormac wasn't sure what the stowaway code was, but he didn't care for the captain's tone, which was quickly ramping back up toward crazy again. He appeared to dislike stowaways almost as much as he did whales. "Life's just one big pleasure cruise for you stowaways. Hiding in cargo hulls and eating free hardtack as you get sailed from port to port without doing a lick of work!"

"Captain . . . Er, sir . . . I'm not a stowaway. As a matter of fact I've never been on a boat before." Wake up, Cormac, wake up! he thought to himself. A hungover morning with Vance was quickly becoming his more desired reality.

"Where'd you come aboard? Charleston? Up Canada way during that nor'easter? I know what the word is on the stowaway circuit. They're saying my ship's cursed, that I've taken desperate measures to turn things around. That one clear June night in a Louisiana port I found a crazy voodoo priestess who took me out to the bayou and told me the only way to restore my ship's honor was to let three swamp pirates have their way with me, first the tall one, then the short one, and finally the Haitian."

That was an awfully specific rumor, thought Cormac.

"Well, you stowaways can trade tales all you want on the rest of the circuit. But when you come aboard my ship, you're at my mercy."

That didn't sound good. Cormac nervously looked around for any signs of the Haitian.

"You two!" shouted the captain. Two whalers who had given up on the day's catch and were now passing a jug of rum shot him surly glances. Cormac noticed that Ziro had quickly grown concerned.

"It appears we have a stowaway. As your captain I order you to seize him."

"Captain," Ziro tried to interject. "Is this really necessary?"

"Shut up, Ziro, this doesn't involve you in any capacity," the captain snapped, before pausing dramatically. "We'll make him walk the plank. Ziro, go set up the plank."

* * *

Cormac noted that the same whalers who had been unable to pull off the whaling equivalent of shooting fish in a barrel had proved quite nimble at organizing a plank walking. They had grouped into rudimentary seating rows and one of them appeared to be selling concessions of some sort. Looking closer, it became apparent that it was just rum, which seemed redundant as most of the whalers were either clutching or being passed a jug of rum. Still, Cormac noted at least two sales while his wrists were being bound.

Ziro had been assigned that lowly task. In fact, he was the only one who was really doing any work at all. The two men who had seized him had stood by menacingly for a while, but eventually wandered back to their fellow whalers. The captain was striding around, waving his spyglass and shouting about "the fate that will befall any vagrant who is caught stowing away on this courageous vessel!" In the water all around the boat, the whales were more active than ever, but nobody seemed to care anymore. A plank walking was evidently quite a big deal.

"I'm sorry to see this end this way, Ziro," said Cormac. "You seem like a nice guy. I hope in my next dream you get dealt a better hand than slave."

"Cormac," Ziro replied in a low voice. "I'm not sure who you are, where you came from, or why you keep saying that you're dreaming. But because I feel sorry for you, I purposely bound your wrists very loosely."

"That's very kind of you, Ziro."

"It should delay your drowning by about three minutes," the slave informed him.

"Why does a whaling ship even have a plank in the first place?" demanded Cormac, but the time had come. Ziro pretended to give the knots a final pull and then stepped back. He gave Cormac one last bewildered nod, then retreated to the back of the crowd. The captain issued a few final grand pronouncements, then made his way toward Cormac. The rowdy whalers quickly settled down.

Cormac was very frustrated. Dreams were not supposed to be this crappy. He seethed as he imagined the restful night's sleep Vance was getting. Vance . . . Vance didn't even have a bedframe, he just threw his mattress on the floor! Cormac had mocked him for this once, but Vance had deftly countered by asking him what purpose, exactly, a bed frame served. Cormac had been stymied. When he got out of bed the next afternoon, Vance made a big show out of how easily he could reach over and grab his shoes from the floor while he was still in bed. Cormac had never considered being unable to reach his shoes from bed to be too much of a burden, but once Vance had gotten it under his skin, their inaccessibility was all he could think about for a week.

There was no time to get worked up about that again, though. As drawn-out and strange as this dream had been, Cormac was fairly certain that it was all going to end once he took the plunge from the plank. You always woke up when you were falling in a dream. It was a reassuring thought, and as Cormac accepted that he'd be back in his bed in a couple of minutes, he realized he hadn't really seized the opportunity he'd been presented with. Here he was, having an entirely lucid dream, in a completely foreign setting, and he'd just gone about it like it was a normal day. He essentially had a get out of jail free card. Nothing he did here actually mattered. If there was anything he'd been eager to try in real life but feared the consequences of, now was the time to do it.

The captain took a final few steps toward Cormac and turned to speak to the crew. "My friends," he began. "We've been through quite a bit together. We've seen the glory of the Southern Cross on a clear night, and witnessed the majesty of the northern lights. We've also traversed the treacherous Bermuda Triangle, and heard the distant moan of sea monsters we feared would destroy us. Throughout it all, one thing has become certain: we are a tightly knit band of brothers here on the *Levyathan*."

A jug of rum whizzed through the air, narrowly missing the captain's head and exploding when it hit the railing.

"Dammit, who threw that?" Captain Anson shouted. "You miserable sons of whores aren't fit to crew a rowboat! I'd trade the lot of you for a dozen Chinese the first chance I—" The captain stopped midsentence and regained his composure. "As I was saying, we're a tightly knit group here, and the one thing we cannot abide is outsiders. Intruders. Stowaways." With this last word he turned and leered at Cormac, who rolled his eyes and hoped that on the off chance that Vance had woken up before him, he wasn't picking the marshmallows out of the Lucky Charms.

"Do you have any last words before you go to see Davy Jones?" the captain asked Cormac.

Cormac was surprised. He hadn't expected to be given a platform. Unfortunately, he didn't think it was the type of crowd who'd appreciate being kept waiting while he hemmed and hawed trying to come up with something profound. Luckily, just then, he had a flash of inspiration. May as well leave dreamland with a bang, he thought.

"I have only one thing to say," Cormac intoned solemnly. He paused and looked at the crew and the captain. A big smile broke out onto his face right before he yelled out "can openerrrrrrrr!" As Cormac shouted his final words, he turned to run toward the plank, already envisioning the titanic splash he was going to make. Within two steps he completely lost his balance due to his bound wrists, and on the third he hit a wet patch of the deck that caused him to skid and spin around 180 degrees. Cormac tried to keep running as he slid, but now he was trying to go in the opposite direction his momentum was carrying him. It was like he'd jumped onto a treadmill that was already running at top speed. His strides got longer and longer until he was essentially running in place on the wet deck. With his hands still tied behind his back and shrieking a noise that sounded like "BLAGARRRRRGH," he was quite a sight.

The whole debacle lasted about ten seconds before his legs slipped out from under him and he crashed to the deck on his stomach. There was a brief window of silence where Cormac thought there was a chance that nobody had seen him. Then he realized the silence had happened because he'd hit the left side of his head on the deck and blacked out. As he regained consciousness, it became quite clear that the crew of the *Levyathan* had just witnessed the funniest thing any of them had ever seen in their lives.

The gathered whalers had erupted into hysterics. The men were doubled over, wheezing with laughter, pounding each other on the back. The already-prodigious rum consumption had somehow managed to triple, as whalers tilted back jugs to guzzle in between fits of giggles. Two blurry faces leaned into Cormac's field of vision.

"Dammit, Ziro . . . Dammit . . . Damn . . ." The captain sounded irritated, but had trouble getting more than two words out without snorting. As Cormac's eyes gradually focused, he saw tears of laughter streaming down the captain's face. Ziro looked slightly more concerned, and Cormac wondered if the wetness from the constant deck swabbing had been partially responsible for his spill.

"Are you OK?" Ziro asked him.

The captain didn't wait for a response. "Oh man," he chuckled, "That was spectacular. I haven't laughed that hard since Ziro thought that narwal was a mermaid."

"Can you remember your name?" asked Ziro, as he helped Cormac roll over onto his side.

"You guys remember when Ziro tried to have sex with that narwal?" the captain yelled to the crew, who roared even louder with laughter.

"I'm Cormac," groaned Cormac.

"And do you know where you are?" asked Ziro.

"No I don't know where I am!" shouted Cormac. "I went to sleep in my bed, and when I woke up I was on a godforsaken ship in the middle of the ocean! There're whales jumping around out there, slaves swabbing decks, I've got my wrists tied, and I probably just got a concussion, which is not something that should be happening to you in a dream!"

"Whoa, whoa, easy there," said the captain. "Let's not bring down the mood."

"Go to hell!" snapped Cormac. His head hurt, his clothes were wet, his wrists were bound, and he wanted off the damn boat.

"Now there's no need for that kind of tone." The captain sounded hurt.

"Can you stand?" asked Ziro.

"I think so," said Cormac. "I'll probably need a hand though."

Ziro reached out to grab Cormac's arm, but the captain smacked his hand away. "That will do just fine, Ziro, we don't need any more incidents today. You two!" he yelled at no two whalers in particular. "Get over here and help the stowaway to his feet!"

Two whalers who had failed to pretend not to hear the captain eventually stumbled over to where Cormac was sprawled and hoisted him to his feet. Standing made him feel lightheaded, and he leaned on one of the whalers for support. The captain stood and addressed everybody again.

"Well, I guess we were lucky enough to have a little pre-show entertainment. It's too bad; in better circumstances, this stowaway might have made a fine sea clown, cavorting for our entertainment. Unfortunately, our policy is what it is, and I'm afraid you're still going to have to walk the plank." The captain paused for some obligatory hooting from the crew. Once it died down, he quipped, "Maybe take it a bit slower this time, though." He then began to mimic Cormac's tumble, taking long, exaggerated strides and sputtering like an idiot.

Cormac was furious. As the captain milked the laughs from the crew a bit longer, Cormac looked over at the whaler who was supporting him. His harpoon gun hung from his belt on the same side that Cormac was leaning on. Cormac looked back at the captain and, for a split second, he saw Vance in the captain's outfit, running in place and making a stupid face. He closed his eyes and shook his head and the vision disappeared. But by then he'd already made up his mind.

He wriggled his hands behind his back and, true to Ziro's word, the bindings easily slipped off. Quickly, Cormac grabbed the harpoon gun from the whaler's belt and took a couple steps away from him.

"Hey, captain!" he shouted. The captain paused his impression and turned to look at Cormac. His face fell when he noticed the harpoon gun pointed directly at him. Nobody moved. After a few seconds, people started to look confused. Cormac realized that coming up with a clever quip on the spot was not that easy when you'd just suffered head trauma. He fidgeted with the trigger of the harpoon gun.

"Um . . . I may be the one walking the plank . . . but *you're* the one who's going to drop the anchor . . . in the crow's nest . . . the next time the ship full of tea comes into the harbor . . ."

"What?" asked the captain.

Just then a huge whale breached right off the side of the ship. It let out a tremendous roar as it leapt out of the water, and a startled Cormac pulled the trigger before he could finish his meandering quip.

The captain flinched as the harpoon shot out of the gun. At less than ten feet away, it should have easily pierced his skull, but out of all the poorly maintained equipment on the *Levyathan*, the harpoon gun Cormac had seized was quite possibly the shoddiest. The shaft was bent and the tension was set far too high. As the stock of the gun splintered into a dozen pieces, the harpoon shot out at nearly a ninety-degree angle. It sailed over the side of the ship where it struck the breaching whale directly in the blowhole, killing it instantly. The dead whale fell back to the surface with a gigantic splash, soaking all who had gathered to observe the plank walking.

Cormac looked down at his hands, which held what was left of the harpoon gun. He glanced over at the captain, then quickly tossed the remains overboard. May as well dispose of the evidence, he figured. They landed directly in the center of the floating corpse of the enormous dead whale that everyone was already staring at. Dammit.

Cormac had never tried to murder someone before, so he wasn't sure what the proper etiquette was if the attempt failed. Was it "forgive and forget"? Or maybe "laugh it off over beers, then bash their head in while they're accepting your apology and telling you how they had always liked you"? It was probably one or the other. Cormac looked around and tried to spot a couple of beers.

The captain was making his way toward Cormac through the crowd of dripping sailors. His soaking face was blank. Cormac instinctively clenched his fists and hoped he wouldn't have to punch anybody. He glanced over at Ziro, who shrugged and took two steps backwards. As the captain approached him, Cormac felt his entire body tense up, but he quickly realized the captain was staring past him. Cormac stepped out of the way as the captain made his way to the side of the boat, where he stared at the dead whale.

In a low but determined tone, he spoke.

"If the sea's stomach be o'ercharg'd with gold," the captain intoned solemnly. "'Tis a good constraint of fortune it belches upon us."

Cormac felt like his attempt on the captain's life was being ignored. He was kind of irritated about that, but immediately decided to try to capitalize on it with some well-timed ass kissing.

"That's a beautiful verse, sir," he offered.

"Thank you, Cormac," the captain said, using his name for the first time. "I guess I just . . . Well, I guess I just felt inspired."

"Shakespeare," chimed in Ziro. "It's a line from *Pericles*. I made him flash cards."

The captain slowly raised his eyes from the whale and turned in Ziro's direction. They looked at each other for a few seconds before Ziro broke the silence.

"I'll go get my mop."

* * *

The remaining hours in the day all blurred together for Cormac. As easy as killing the whale had been, hauling it onto the boat and butchering it proved to be a colossal ordeal. The whalers were out of practice and their equipment was either misplaced or in disrepair. One of the whalers had been using the main hauling harness as a blanket and was reluctant to give it up. The stains on the harness looked too fresh to have been caused by a whale, and Cormac felt slightly seasick for the first time all day.

The process of hauling the whale out of the sea and onto the *Levyathan* reminded Cormac of a carnival game. Specifically, one of those carnival games that was rigged so that you could never, ever win it. Sure, in theory there was a great big prize just sitting there for the taking. But everyone who saw you trying knew you were a sucker for attempting to win it. And you were drunk. And your partners, who presumably had the same goal as you, would occasionally drop what they were doing and fight you.

All it was missing was an annoying kid pestering his dad to keep trying, just one more time, because he really, really wanted the prize. The captain filled this role ably. He had been giddy as a kid on Christmas from the moment they started hauling the whale aboard. He skipped around the deck, barking orders to whalers who weren't listening and peeking through his spyglass at the mammoth creature. Every so often he'd rush over to a side of the ship and shout at the rest of the whales that this was just the beginning of what he had planned for them, and that they should fear the sight of the *Levyathan*, which represented grim death rolling toward them on every white-capped wave.

Once the men had finally pulled the beast out of the ocean, they began the even messier process of slicing it up. Cormac had never seen a chicken being butchered, let alone a giant whale, but even he could identify some inefficiencies in the crew's process. For example, one whaler took a machete and climbed into the whale's mouth. He hacked away for about twenty minutes and finally emerged dragging the whale's tongue behind him. Quickly, he walked over to a fellow whaler who he evidently had a dispute with. He tapped the other man on the shoulder, then swung the hefty tongue at his head with all his might. It connected with a squishy thump, and the second whaler fell to the ground, out cold. Satisfied, the first whaler dropped the tongue, downed half a jug of rum, and leaned up against one of the masts for a nap.

The rest of the men were slicing off huge chunks of blubber and stacking them like gym mats. Rather than cut off reasonably sized pieces, the men insisted on trying to carve off as large a piece as possible in a macho display of their whaling prowess. This meant that instead of a nice, speedy process of blubber stacking, there were multiple times when a whaler would slice off a chunk that he had no possible way of manipulating on his own, not realize this until it was too late, and have the blubber topple over on top of him, pinning him beneath it. The whalers found this uproarious every time it happened, even though it looked to Cormac like some of them were temporarily losing consciousness down there.

The captain though, was delighted with the crew's progress. At one point in time he demanded Ziro bring him the whale's heart so he could messily devour it to intimidate the remaining whales that he presumed were listening to him just below the surface of the water. Ziro and four other whalers attempted to push the heart over to the captain, but it was substantially bigger than any of them and all the blood made it difficult to get a firm grip on it. Eventually the captain clumsily ascended the heart with a boost from Ziro, and rather than eat it, sort of just stomped on it while he shouted for a while, eventually slipping off and landing on the deck with a thud.

By the time it got dark, the whale carcass had been rendered unrecognizable and hauled off to the ship's cold storage area. The satisfied whalers were covered with blood, guts, and rum. Having helped themselves to the newfound abundance of bones, they were happily carving scrimshaw.

The captain appeared to have yelled himself out, and was wandering between the busy men, complementing their work like a proud grade-school teacher. "Ooh, look at the scary shark on that one! Well, how about that, what a nice detailed map you've carved! Huh, is that . . . is that *me*, screaming in terror while the giant squid drags me below the surface? Hey, what's that tentacle doing!?"

Cormac walked over to the final patch of deck Ziro had left to swab. Cormac was exhausted after the eventful day, but Ziro, who was the only one on board who'd actually been working non-stop, showed no signs of tiring. This time, Cormac was careful to avoid walking in the recently swabbed area. Ziro stopped mopping as Cormac approached.

"Hey Ziro," he said. "Still swabbing the decks, huh?"

Ziro involuntarily glanced over at a spare mop leaning against his shack that had gone unused all day long. "Yes, Cormac," he sighed. "Still swabbing. How are you?"

"Well, the captain seems to have forgotten that he wanted me to walk the plank. I suppose that's a step in the right direction."

They both glanced over at the captain, who was tugging on a piece of scrimshaw, attempting to wrest it away from a whaler who had carved a picture of himself engaging in sexual relations with a mermaid who strongly resembled the captain. Cormac wasn't sure who it made look worse.

"You really were trying to kill him, weren't you?" asked Ziro.

"Well, yeah. I mean, not *really*, really. But sure, as much as you can in a dream, right?"

"A dream, right. This is all a dream." Ziro dropped his voice into a serious tone. "Have you ever killed a man before, Cormac?"

Cormac looked around to see if Ziro was setting him up.

"It's OK," Ziro reassured him. "You can trust me. Have you?"

"Er . . . Yes?" Cormac lied.

"Really?" Ziro grinned. "What happened?"

Ziro had put Cormac on the spot. His mind raced.

"I . . . I shot a guy."

"You shot him?" Ziro was skeptical.

"Yes. I shot him. Um, with a harpoon gun. Yeah, he was this mean captain."

What the hell was that, Cormac? he thought to himself. Stupid, stupid!

"Are you sure you're not just thinking of what happened a few hours ago? But with the harpoon actually hitting the captain?"

"Maybe . . ."

"Cormac, had you ever even *seen* a harpoon until today?"

That was it. Cormac's frustration boiled over. "No I hadn't seen a harpoon until today! I'd never been on a boat until today! And then I wake up on board some rundown whaling ship, where the only person who doesn't want to drown me is the slave, and I attempted a murder, and shot a whale, and I don't know what the hell's going on!"

"OK, OK," said Ziro. "Don't get too worked up. We're going to find out what's going on and get you where you want to be." Ziro resisted the urge to add, "Or perhaps eat you if the going gets rough." The last thought got Ziro thinking. "You must be hungry. Have you eaten at all today, Cormac?"

"Yeah, one of the whalers gave me some hardtack and salt pork."

"What'd you think of the salt pork?"

"It was terrible."

"Yeah," said Ziro. "It's the worst."

"It *sounds* good," said Cormac. "I mean, I like salt. I like pork. I usually put salt on my pork. How'd they screw that up?"

"I know what you mean, I know what you mean." Ziro chuckled. Then he quickly turned serious again. "But seriously, we often go for months where we don't eat anything else, so you probably ought to get used to it." He picked up his mop again and resumed swabbing. Cormac realized their conversation was over.

Not sure what else to do with his night, Cormac wandered to the bow of the *Levyathan*. The sky was clear and he could see more stars than he had ever seen in his life. Suddenly, he felt very alone. A sound carried over the calm ocean, a drawn out, mournful cry. Cormac wondered if it might be the mate of the whale he'd killed that morning.

"I'm sorry!" he yelled at the blackness of the night. "I didn't mean to do it! I'm so sorry!" He was scared, tired, and hungry, and wanted more than anything than to close his eyes and wake up in his bed. The cry persisted and Cormac found himself fighting back tears. That was when he realized that the sound wasn't coming from the ocean in front of him, but from the deck of the boat behind him.

A drunken whaler had whacked another whaler in the crotch with a sizeable whale bone. The unfortunate recipient was lying on the ground emitting a low groan, while holding himself and trying to catch his breath. It appeared that he had vomited. The other whalers were cackling with joy and passing jugs of rum.

Cormac took one last look at the beautiful night sky and went to find an empty bunk to lie down in.

DAY THREE

A loud crash woke Cormac. His eyes popped open. He quickly scanned the room. Hendrix poster on the wall. Beer bottle on the bedside table. Better yet, *existence of* bedside table. He sat up and silently rejoiced as his hopes were confirmed. He was definitely in his own bed in his own room. Cormac sighed and lay back down, about as relieved as he'd ever been in his life.

It wasn't that he doubted that he'd wake up back home. It was just that as his dream aboard the *Levyathan* had dragged on and on, he had begun to grow uncertain that he would wake up at all. But here he was. He could pull the blankets up tight, rest his head on his cool pillow, and . . . Dammit! Another crash? What the hell was going on out there?

"Vance!" Cormac shouted. "What the hell is going on out there?"

There was a quick sound of something being hastily pushed across the floor and then Vance's footsteps made their way down the hall. He appeared in the doorway, not wearing a shirt. Thankfully a pair of jeans covered his lower body instead of Cormac's towel.

"Holy shit," said Vance. "He lives."

Cormac reached over for his phone and hit the lock button. The display said it was 10:40.

"What do you mean 'He lives'? It's only 10:40, what are you doing up? What are you doing in general? It sounded like the floor was going to cave in."

"Well, for your information *your majesty*, I am doing a little bit of home improvement."

A chill ran down Cormac's spine.

"Though if you're not interested in stadium seating couches," Vance continued, "I can put away my hammer right now. Jeez, I thought you'd be a little less cranky after thirty hours of sleep."

Everything that Vance had just said confused Cormac.

"What are you talking about?" he asked, as he pushed off his covers and spun around to dangle his legs off the bed. He looked over at his shoes, just out of arm's reach. Vance noticed too, and was smirking at Cormac the whole time he got up to retrieve them and sat back down to put them on.

"Stadium seating couches," Vance explained. "Just like at the movies, but with our couches. Going to put one up on blocks behind the other so when we watch TV, we can—"

Cormac cut him off. "I didn't mean the couches, Vance! You said I slept for thirty hours!"

"Well, yeah," replied Vance. He seemed confused. "You slept through the entire day yesterday."

"What?" Cormac was floored.

"I didn't know you'd had that much to drink, buddy! Probably shouldn't have driven home!" Vance headed down the hall back toward the living room. "Ol' Mac Van Winkle, ha!"

Cormac hit the lock button on his phone again. Band practice had been on a Tuesday. His phone screen said that it was currently Thursday. Cormac's head was spinning as he jumped out of bed and dashed over to his desk. Actually, it was more like it was throbbing, specifically on the side of his head that had hit the deck when he'd slipped on the *Levyathan*. He reached up and rubbed it as he waited for his laptop to wake up. It felt like there could be a small goose egg beneath his hair, but no, that was impossible.

The computer clock confirmed that it was indeed Thursday. He'd slept through all of Wednesday.

"Vance!" he shouted as he got up from his desk chair. He stepped over the check for Vance's share of the electric bill and hurried out the door and down the hallway.

When he got to the living room, Cormac came face-to-face with the full madness of Vance's home improvement project. The couch was about a couch-length back from where it normally sat. Vance had raised it off the ground about four feet, precariously balancing it on cinder blocks, old newspapers, an overturned laundry bin, and Vance's desktop computer tower. Vance was attempting to climb onto the couch by stepping on a plastic tub of pretzels and gripping an extension cord that had been stapled to the ceiling. Several empty beer bottles were scattered around the project site.

"Just . . . gimme . . . a sec here, Mac," Vance said through gritted teeth, focusing all his concentration on trying to keep his balance. Cormac tensed instinctively, fearing a titanic crash, but couldn't look away. The couch wobbled as Vance managed to raise a knee onto it, then pulled himself up using the extension cord and swung around so that he was sitting down. An electronic whirring noise came from the computer tower, which Cormac realized was still running. Vance let go of the extension cord and looked very pleased with himself.

"Pretty sweet, huh?" he asked.

"It's ridiculous," said Cormac. "We don't even have a second couch! It's not stadium seating, it's just a couch up in the air!"

"I took care of the hard part first, Mac! You can always get a second couch. People just leave them on their porches when they're done using them. This is going to revolutionize things!"

A gentle breeze blew in through one of the living room's open windows, causing the entire structure to wobble uncontrollably.

Vance looked terrified for the few seconds it lasted. "We should probably keep that window closed from now on," he said once it had stopped.

"Look, terrific, I don't care." Cormac cut to the chase. "What the hell happened yesterday?"

"You were out, Mac! I couldn't wake you up! Shook you by the shoulders and everything. You were just zonked."

"Jesus . . ." muttered Cormac.

"I know," said Vance. "It was kind of wild. I'm glad you're up though, I think after like forty hours of sleep you're legally in a coma or something."

"Well I'm glad you were concerned enough to put our couch up on cinder blocks," snapped Cormac.

"Whoa, whoa! What are you so upset about? You missed some class, big deal! I didn't go yesterday either. Actually, I probably won't go today either—I think once you're up here, you're here for a while."

This failed to reassure Cormac.

"Look, Vance," he said. "I just had a really weird . . . dream."

"Do you have any pulleys, Mac? I'm thinking they're the answer to how you get beers up here."

"No I don't have any pulleys! Why in God's name would I have pulleys!? I've never needed a pulley in my life!"

"That's because you don't think big, Mac."

"Listen to me, Vance! I don't think I was asleep yesterday. This is going to sound really weird but . . . I think I had an out-of-body experience or something."

Vance pondered this as he adjusted himself to a lying-down position, a process that required intense concentration and precise movements. Cormac knew that what he had just said sounded crazy; in fact, he still didn't entirely believe it himself. He didn't expect Vance to answer right away, let alone believe him, but after nearly a minute had passed, it became apparent that his roommate had just fallen asleep.

"Dammit, Vance!" Cormac shouted. Vance woke up with a start, causing the whole couch structure to shake violently beneath him. Vance flailed his arms trying to get a grip on something stable. The only thing within his reach was the extension cord, which he reached out for, but it was too late. The couch toppled over with a gigantic crash, and Vance was left grasping the extension cord, which supported his weight for about two seconds before it too crashed to the ground.

Vance groaned. "Five minutes. I think that's a new record."

* * *

Frampton Q. Bickerstaff paced in his office, preparing to face the board. He had a feeling this meeting wasn't going to be pretty. Encounters with the board rarely were. As dean of Harrington State, Bickerstaff was constantly butting heads with the board. The differences were mainly philosophical. Whereas the board pushed for a multi-tiered approach to education involving student/faculty relations, alumni involvement, and maintaining their national reputation, Frampton Q. Bickerstaff took a multi-tiered approach toward keeping his goddamn cushy job at any cost.

Dean Bickerstaff looked at his watch. The meeting was supposed to have started fifteen minutes ago. Perfect. He was right on time as far as he was concerned. Keep them waiting, the dean figured, make them think your time is more valuable than theirs. This was made sort of difficult by the glass wall of his office that looked directly out into the meeting room where the board was gathered. He knew the board members were staring at him as he paced—he'd accidentally made brief eye contact with several of them already. They'd pointed at their watches and tried to wave him over. Dean Bickerstaff had responded by pretending to be on the phone and making the "roll your window down" gesture that drivers give to one another. This had confused them. Good. One of the board members actually had the nerve to come over and knock on the glass of his office to try to get his attention, a move that Frampton deftly deflected by kicking over his garbage can so he could kneel down on the floor and put the contents back in it.

No doubt about it, Dean Frampton Q. Bickerstaff would address the board when he was damn ready to do so. And that wasn't going to be the case until he'd lit up one of his pride and joys, a big fat *Romeo y Julieta* Cuban cigar. He pulled one out of the humidor and took a long whiff, making sure to turn just enough so the board could see him through the glass. He had started smoking them to try to distract people from the fact that he was a quite un-deanlike five feet tall with shoes on. In reality, the huge cigar and constant cloud of smoke only called further attention to how strange the balding little man looked as he reigned over the Harrington campus. "Like a troll whose mom got knocked up by a chimney," one student wrote in his final editorial in the *Harrington School Paper* shortly before disappearing.

Dean Bickerstaff lit up the stogie and took an enthusiastic puff. He'd been the dean at Harrington for twenty-two years. His performance in each of those years had been adequate enough to allow him to return for another one. Along the way he'd become firmly entrenched in the university, establishing a web of bureaucracy and inefficiency that assured it would be a costly, difficult ordeal should the board ever decide to replace him. In case this wasn't enough, he'd attempted to assemble healthy blackmail files on all of the board members and most of the faculty. Where he couldn't find any actual wrongdoing, he'd planted evidence and committed entrapment. Keeping his job had become Frampton's top priority. Everything else, including actually *doing* his job, was a secondary concern.

The phone on Dean Bickerstaff's desk rang. He glanced over at it instinctively. Instantly, he realized he'd fallen into the board's trap. Those bastards were crafty. He looked out at the meeting room where they were assembled and sure enough, one of them was on his cell phone, looking at the dean and appearing mighty pleased with himself. Well, two could play at this game, the dean thought to himself. He walked over and picked up the phone.

"Dean Frampton Q. Bickerstaff," he said with a noble air.

"Yes, Frampton, we've been waiting for twenty minutes now," replied the irritated voice on the other end of the line.

"I'm sorry, who might I be speaking to?" Frampton said, looking the man who'd just finished speaking directly in the eye.

The board member sighed. "Look, if we could just—" but Frampton cut him off before he had a chance to win his sympathy.

"I'm sorry," the dean said through the cigar that was clenched in his teeth. "I've got an incredibly important meeting with the board starting any minute now." He spoke in his most patronizing tone as he reached over to pick up his beloved oak shillelagh, which was resting against his desk. "I'll have to transfer you over to my secretary."

The aggrieved board member started to protest, but before he had a chance, Dean Bickerstaff hung up the phone. Without hesitation, he raised the shillelagh up over his head and slammed the knobby end of it down, shattering the handset into pieces. He smashed the shillelagh into the broken phone several more times, making sure to look out at the stunned board members while he delivered the final few blows.

When he was finished, the dean swept the pieces of the phone off the desk with his shillelagh. They landed in a pile of other assorted objects that had been reduced to debris by means of shillelagh beating. Finding himself surprisingly winded after the exertion of repeatedly lifting the cudgel, which was nearly the same height as him, he paused for a few seconds to catch his breath. When his panting had died down, Dean Bickerstaff looked out at the board with steel-eyed determination. "Sheila," he quipped to an empty room as he took a puff on the cigar. "Hold all my calls."

The dean was ready to address the board.

Gripping the shillelagh that had been in the Bickerstaff family for generations in one hand and holding his cigar in the other, Dean Bickerstaff walked out his office door, across the narrow hallway of the faculty building, and into the meeting room where the Harrington State board of directors was gathered. The board had five members, three men and two women, and Frampton held all of them in differing levels of contempt, ranging from "sputtering" to "outright." In his opinion, a board, with all its voting and discussion, was no way to run a school. As far as Frampton was concerned, only the iron fist of an all-powerful dean could get any results. Never mind that the board had been established as a direct response to the myriad abuses of all-powerful Dean Frampton Q. Bickerstaff.

Frampton had become dean after a brief stint heading the Commerce School at Harrington. He'd taken the job hoping to shape future titans of business, who would one day fondly reminisce from their opulent penthouse apartments about the dean who had given them their start, and then would give him a bunch of money or something. He hadn't really planned out many of the details, but he knew that all it took was one student from one class to be wildly successful, and he'd be ready and willing to ride their coattails.

Sadly, he had overestimated the quality of the students who he would be supervising. It turned out that Harrington's Commerce School had a bit of a reputation as a *"party* commerce school," which was not a concept that Bickerstaff had realized existed. Students enrolled in it looking for a good time, not an eventual job with a Fortune 500 company. This baffled Bickerstaff, as the Commerce School degree required an extra fifth year of study and had a substantially higher tuition than the regular undergraduate program. Nevertheless, the hard-partying Comm School students continued to shuffle into class late, reeking of last night's booze, at least when they made it to class at all.

Not only this, but the role of dean was evidently not as important in the day-to-day lives of the students as movies had led Frampton to believe. Hungover students interacted with professors and grad student TAs every day. But the average student had no reason to ever encounter the dean, who was in charge of higher-level issues for the school such as hiring faculty and appearing at fund raisers. This frustrated Bickerstaff, who quickly realized it would be difficult to take advantage of successful former students if none of them knew who the hell he was. He decided to undertake a major image-enhancement campaign, which mainly involved hanging out in front of the Comm School building and trying to chat up students who were too nauseous to make it into class. After a few weeks of making his presence felt, an article ran in the *School Paper* demanding that school security do something about the "gross little creep" who was "harassing Comm School students and is almost certainly a sex offender." "Alleged pervert actually dean, we guess," read the correction published months later on page C-17.

Commerce School Dean Bickerstaff was thus forced to rethink his long-term career path. The Comm School was a lost cause. Its reputation was a bright scarlet letter to any student of actual promise, and its presence on his résumé wasn't going to do him any favors either. Bickerstaff knew he'd have to make his own luck, and by luck he meant "fraudulently successful results." So the dean began an extensive campaign of cooking the books, adjusting test scores, threatening professors so they wouldn't fail students who had passed out while taking their final exam. The written-off status of the Comm School meant that he was able to operate without the interference of anyone who might question his unethical and at many times illegal tactics. When Bickerstaff's first year on the job ended and the numbers had soared in every single category, he was the new darling of the Harrington State faculty. With the impending retirement of the university's beloved but ancient dean, he was fast-tracked to replace him. He'd taken over after one more year at the Comm School and now he never intended to leave.

Unfortunately, the only opposition to this plan now sat directly in front of him. Frampton shot the room a big grin, not bothering to take his cigar out of his mouth. He twirled his shillelagh as he took his seat at the head of the table and tried to think what trap the board might be trying to ensnare him in today. Hush-money payments were up to date and all faculty complaints had been suppressed. A shipping container of dead zoo animals that one of Harrington's shell corporations was responsible for had been intercepted that morning by customs officers in Seattle, but Bickerstaff had been assured by his contacts that it was being handled and could not be traced back to him. Puffing his cigar, he eagerly awaited countering whatever his adversaries had to throw at him.

A man at the far end of the table spoke first. "Thank you for joining us, Dean Bickerstaff. We're sorry for the impromptu nature of this meeting, but we just needed to—"

The dean interrupted him. "Did you leave a message?" The board looked confused. "With Sheila?"

It eventually occurred to the man what the dean was talking about. "Do you mean just now, sir?"

How thick were these idiots? the dean thought to himself. "Yes, just now."

"That must have been what he was saying when we saw him talking to himself after he broke the phone," said a man sitting next to the first man.

The first man started to catch on. "Sir, if you made some sort of quip about leaving a message with your secretary, we had no way of hearing it in here! You had just broken the phone into pieces and these glass walls are very thick, so I'm afraid that—"

"I'm sorry, I don't recall your name," Frampton said apologetically.

"It's George," the man said. "For God's sake, Frampton, we've worked together for over a decade. I invited you to my daughter's wedding last year!"

"Of course!" Dean Bickerstaff said warmly. He knew it was George. "The wedding was such a lovely affair."

"You didn't come!"

"Why, that doesn't sound like me!" The dean did his best to sound hurt.

"You said you were undergoing treatment for esophageal cancer!"

"Well, I trust she got my present?"

"You never sent a present!" George shrieked. Clearly he was bearing some sort of grudge. "*We* sent *you* a present, because we thought you had cancer!"

"Well clearly you were misinformed," said the dean, as he took increasingly aggressive puffs of his cigar while he waited for George to drop the subject. Eventually another board member spoke up.

"Dean Bickerstaff," said one of the female board members, the one who had not been serving as long as the other. Frampton truthfully didn't know her name, but he did know that he had her husband in his pocket. After months of being bugged about it, the poor man had done a coworker a favor and accompanied him on a midnight mission to poach clams from a nearby wildlife preserve. Little did he know that the coworker was a plant in the employ of Dean Frampton Q. Bickerstaff. When they arrived at the preserve with shovels and gunny sacks, men posing as federal agents "gunned down" the coworker with blanks and were prepared to do the same to the sobbing husband when who should appear but the dean. Frampton explained to the man how much trouble he was in, but he also reassured him that he was a man who was able to make his problems disappear. All the husband would owe him was a few small favors. The devastated man quickly agreed, an event that was framed on either end by two distinct pants-soiling incidents.

Since then, his wife the board member had demonstrated an alarming tendency to not receive messages or emails alerting her to emergency board meetings regarding the dean's actions. She couldn't explain her absences, except when they were caused by flat tires, which happened surprisingly frequently. Since board by-laws required all members to vote in order for a motion to pass, many key proposals had to be scuttled. The dean would always express dismay that the board would yet again be unable to impeach him, but he would insist that as much as he'd like to, he was far too respectful of the school's by-laws to tolerate any deviation. Then he'd slowly drive by the board member's home and make a throat-slashing gesture to the petrified man as he looked out the window. He loved being dean.

The woman continued. "We need to talk to you today about the *College Review* quarterly rankings. The new issue is coming out in just a few weeks."

Ah, the *College Review*, thought the dean. Bane of the existence of any higher education administrator, the magazine was the definitive resource for ranking colleges. High school students and their parents pored over it when deciding where to apply. The magazine rated every accredited college in the country on a rubric of dozens of factors. So established was the power of the *Review*'s rankings that alumni donations and applications could sway dramatically based on moving up or down just a spot or two.

"As you know," droned the woman, "the board takes these independent rankings very seriously. They're one of the only concrete ways we have of evaluating your performance, and the performance of our entire university."

Frampton wasn't hearing anything new. He gestured with his cigar for her to pick up the pace. The board member waved some smoke away from her face and continued.

"Now, per your original employment contract with the university, falling in any of the *College Review* rankings is sufficient grounds for your dismissal."

Frampton tried to look serious, but the effort of suppressing his smile was too difficult. He let a broad grin creep across his face as he made himself comfortable in his chair. He knew what was coming next.

"But," sighed the board member, "due to renegotiations that have taken place throughout your tenure, we are now no longer allowed to exercise our right of dismissal for performance in the following categories: Job placement. Class size. Faculty-to-student ratio. Number of classes taught by grad students."

As the board member rattled off the list, Dean Bickerstaff thought back on his masterstroke of hardball negotiating. He had no choice but to agree to the *College Review* provision when he signed his initial contract. The school wouldn't budge on it and at the time he had no leverage. But as soon as he took office, Frampton began searching for ways to whittle away at the power the magazine's rankings held over him. Massaging the numbers for the whole university proved as easy as it had for the Comm School, but he couldn't risk losing his job over a five-point drop in something as trivial as the "percentage of students who graduate."

"Extracurricular activities," continued the board member. "Student volunteer opportunities. Alumni giving."

Just when the dean had thought he was stymied, an opportunity had presented itself in the most unlikely of places. After several years on the job, he'd amassed a wide network of puppet regimes and informants throughout the school. Unfortunately, in the early days he didn't have time to properly vet all of his underlings, and a few wild cards who had trouble taking directions caused some problems. When cars began exploding in the Classics Department parking lot, questions started getting asked, and the dean soon found his new autonomous reign being threatened before it had a chance to ever truly thrive. The solution demanded by the *School Paper* was the establishment of a board of directors that the dean would report to. Everyone had been stunned when Frampton quickly agreed to the new policy.

With just one little catch . . . The chagrined dean had appeared before the tribunal that was overseeing the board creation with his hat in his hands. How could he, the dean, assure the faculty that the car they had parked at the aquatic fitness center would not explode when he was forced to devote all his attention toward making sure Harrington's *College Review* rankings weren't dipping? Surely micromanaging the school's ranking in "legacy admissions" was not as important as making sure another laughing-gas leak didn't happen in the Econ Building, right? And dammit, if losing a point here and there in "handicapped accessibility" meant that he could avoid another incident like the plane carrying the Women's Studies Department getting hijacked to Panama, he should by all means lose that point!

This confused the tribunal, and Frampton realized that this particular incident was actually not due to occur for five more hours. He excused himself to make a frantic phone call in Spanish to an airborne contact, and that embarrassment was avoided. The Women's Studies Department could be dealt with later.

When the meeting eventually adjourned, Dean Bickerstaff had successfully convinced the tribunal to amend his employment contract so that nine of the thirty-seven *College Review* rankings were no longer grounds for dismissal. And he was just getting started. As the years passed, whenever the newly established board had needed his cooperation, he'd negotiate another ranking off of the list. Before anybody knew what had happened, despite the terms of his original contract, the dean had eliminated every *College Review* ranking from the list of fireable offenses, one by one.

As the board member neared the end her list, Frampton was silently tallying them up in his head. Thirty-five, thirty-six, and finally, thirty-seven. She stopped reading and looked up at Dean Bickerstaff.

The dean yawned without removing the cigar from his mouth. This was the latest contemptuous gesture he'd been working on, and he pulled it off mightily.

"That was real nice, darling, I appreciate the refresher," Dean Bickerstaff chuckled. "But in the future, it might not be the best use of everyone's time to tell them what I can't be fired for. Right Gary? I'm sure you'd rather be planning your daughter's wedding, am I right?"

George bit his lip and fumed.

"Well Dean Bickerstaff," the woman said in a tone the dean didn't like one bit. "I was hoping we could focus not on what you *can't* be fired for, but more on what you *can* be fired for. Specifically the part I touched on earlier, the part that says 'Falling in any of the *College Review* rankings is sufficient grounds for your dismissal.'"

Why was she mentioning this again? Frampton didn't care for this roundabout manner of bringing up her original point. It was a rhetorical device he himself had used many times, usually before someone who had wronged him was about to be chloroformed.

After a second of uncertainty, the dean collected himself. "Well, yes, of course, but we've already established that none of those rankings can be used to—"

The smiles that had begun to creep onto the faces of the five board members made him stop in his tracks. What was about to happen?

"You can't be fired for any of those thirty seven rankings, you're quite right, Frampton. But the board has received advance notice from *College Review* that for the first time in over fifty years, they are introducing . . . a new ranking."

Frampton sucked in too hard on his cigar and choked on a puff of smoke. He coughed so violently that his forward momentum caused his wheeled chair to push back from the table. Still sucking wind, Frampton tried to grab onto his shillelagh to steady himself, but he only succeeded in pushing the staff farther away. Reaching out to try to prevent it from falling, he found himself tipping forward out of the chair while it was still moving backward. The dean completely lost his balance at the same time the shillelagh toppled over, and as his chair shot out from under him and he fell to the ground, the bottom of the oak staff clipped him on the chin.

Frampton lay on the ground, wheezing as he tried to catch his breath. He pawed around for his shillelagh and after several missteps that involved grabbing George's foot and leg, he finally got a grip on the end of it. Pushing himself to his feet with the assistance of the shillelagh, he only now managed to draw a full breath. He unsteadily waddled over to his chair, which had only stopped rolling when it hit the wall. Pushing it back to his seat at the table, he leaned up against it and gasped for a few seconds more to make sure the room had stopped spinning, then crawled back into the chair.

The board looked about as amused as a group of unamused people could.

"A new ranking?" he asked, casually wiping away a string of drool that had nearly stretched down to his waist.

"Why yes, Frampton, a new ranking!" the board member said. It was her turn to be patronizing now. "The steadfastly traditional *College Review* has decided to get with the times and will now be ranking schools on a combination of 'online buzz, social media presence, and assorted high-tech miscellany.' They're calling it the X-Factor."

The X-Factor! Frampton was totally blindsided. "Well," he sputtered. "I'm sure we're pulling in great X-Factor numbers. After all, we've got a website."

"We *had* a website, Frampton," said George. "For the past three years it's just shown a picture of you eating a sandwich. And our social media presence is laughable. The 'HarringtonState' twitter handle is owned by a German construction worker who only posts when he's on the toilet."

"At least we *hope* that's when he's posting," interjected the newer woman. "The point is, *Dean*," she said with an audible sneer, "Harrington is going to debut at dead last in *College Review's* X-Factor ranking. And if we don't see some improvement in this ranking by the time the next issue comes out, we're well within our rights to fire your ass."

Frampton was floored, but he tried not to let it show. He extinguished his cigar on the table, stood up out of his chair, and gripped his shillelagh. The board had bested him with their broadside, but Dean Bickerstaff had a lot to throw back at them. He was happy to go without dignity, but he certainly wouldn't go without a fight. He walked over to the door and swung it open, but stopped and turned to face the board before leaving the room.

"Who do I talk to," Dean Frampton Q. Bickerstaff asked, "about getting a new phone?"

* * *

For the rest of his afternoon, Cormac had tried to explain to Vance that there was a decent chance he had spent the previous day aboard a whaling ship. He told him about almost walking the plank and trying to kill the captain and how he had been able to reach out and touch a whale that he himself had shot. Not surprisingly, Vance was not even close to sympathetic. It turned out that describing your out-of-body experience to someone was, for them, about as interesting as hearing you talk about your dream, only you sounded a lot crazier. The fact that Vance kept shooting longing glances at his incomplete stadium seating couch setup did not make the task any easier.

Cormac finally got him to stop by promising to help him buy or steal a second couch the next day. Vance's theory was that couches were more of a "weekday purchase" for most people, so that by waiting until the weekend, they'd catch sellers when they were desperate. The biggest-ticket item Cormac had ever seen Vance buy was a seventy-three pack of beer, which Cormac was fairly certain was a result of a massive assembly line malfunction and probably not fit for human consumption, so he didn't know where his roommate was getting this info about couch purchasing from.

Talking to each other about a matter of such importance was not the sort of thing either of the roommates were prepared to do without beer. Unfortunately, due to Vance's head start, they ran out before three o'clock in the afternoon. By this point in time, Cormac was feeling a bit stir-crazy, so he suggested they go to Mickey's, where Thursday was three-dollar pitcher day. Vance thought this was a great idea, but insisted that he needed to shower first. This made Cormac raise his eyebrow. Vance wasn't necessarily the showering type, and internally he questioned whether Vance just wanted a chance to strut around in his ill-gotten Seahawks towel.

But Cormac decided to take the high road. After all, turnabout was fair play, and he couldn't imagine a less pleasurable scenario than Vance starting to comment on *his* showering schedule. He sat on the front porch until Vance was done, then hopped in the shower himself. He'd forgotten that it had been two days since he'd last showered, and while that wasn't all that uncommon, it felt really good to clean up. His skin had that tacky, gritty feel that comes from exposure to salt water, but Cormac tried to convince himself that it might just be caused by not getting out of bed all day. Yeah, maybe he was lucky and it was just some sort of horrible rash brought on by his filthy, unwashed bedding? Cormac briefly imagined a smiling, happy five-year-old version of himself being told that one day he would have that thought. This caused him to turn off the water and stand staring in silence at the shower wall for about five minutes.

After the shower, Cormac drove the two of them to Mickey's, the one bar in the college area that, as a matter of policy, did not care if you were twenty-one or not. Vance and Cormac had been coming here regularly since freshman orientation, but they rarely encountered many of their fellow students. Sure, Mickey's wasn't the friendliest place, and it definitely wasn't the cleanest place. But it had character! For example, Cormac had never seen a three-legged dog before he started coming to Mickey's, but by now he didn't even bat an eye when one of the several that hung around Mickey's limped over to his table.

"Three-dollar pitchers! The best deal in town!" Vance crowed as they walked in the door. The bartender was a man with an eye patch who was sharpening an ax behind the bar, and the only other patrons in the place had the bleary-eyed look of hostages being forced to renounce their motherland on camera.

They were ignored by the bartender for a long time until they realized they were just in his patch zone. Once they repositioned themselves where his good eye could see them, they quickly got served a pitcher and two glasses, then claimed one of the sticky vinyl booths that lined the walls. They made small talk for a while, trying to remember which classes they were enrolled in and where Uncle Jemima might get another gig. Anything to avoid rehashing Cormac's day aboard the *Levyathan* for the tenth time. It was only after they'd sucked down their first pitcher and Cormac sprung for a second one that Vance got a serious look in his eye, a look that Cormac instantly feared the repercussions of.

"Mac, buddy," Vance said while looking around to make sure nobody could hear him. "I've gotta ask you . . . Have you been doing any drugs that I don't know about?"

An eavesdropper might assume that a concerned roommate was attempting to start an intervention, but Cormac knew differently. Vance had asked him this question dozens of times before, when he wanted to do drugs and suspected that Cormac had some he wasn't telling him about. Sometimes, when Vance had already been doing drugs, he asked Cormac more than once in a night.

"No, Vance," Cormac sighed. "I haven't been doing any drugs without you."

From the look on Vance's face, he wasn't entirely convinced. "You sure?" Vance asked, then looked around the bar again before leaning forward and confiding, "Because the time I did coke, I felt some pretty crazy stuff too."

Jesus! Cormac nearly choked on his beer. Vance had done coke?! Vance was a lunatic when completely sober, who the hell thought it was a good idea to give him coke!

"Coke! Vance, when did you do cocaine?" Cormac sputtered.

"It was sophomore year, buddy. I would have offered you some but you were home for fall break. Besides, the guy who sold it to me ripped me off. It ended up being mostly borax or something."

"Good God, Vance, you snorted a bunch of borax?"

"What? Snorted?" Vance scoffed with derision. "Psh, what is this the '70s? No, no . . . Man that would have probably killed me, huh? No, I did the thing where you just roll up some foil then you heat the coke from underneath it and smoke that. It's chill, you just put on some *Planet Earth*, pack up the alleged cocaine—"

"Freebasing, Vance!" Cormac shouted. "You're talking about freebasing cocaine!"

"One, as I've explained to you, it wasn't actually cocaine," Vance lectured. "Two, what's the big deal? People do it in movies all the time."

"*Homeless* people do it in movies, Vance! Drug addicts in movies do it in apartments where babies die! Montages of a character's descent into misery routinely end with someone freebasing as the haunting final image!"

"Anyways," Vance said as he refilled his glass. "It made me feel like I was in a cartoon helicopter."

"Well, I didn't end up on the whaling ship because I freebased cocaine. Or borax, for that matter," said Cormac.

"Well maybe it's just all the subliminal messages I've been pumping through the house without you realizing it," Vance chuckled. "Cormac, you're on a boooooooat!"

Cormac felt the hair on the back of his neck stand up. Vance couldn't actually do that, could he? He hoped to God Vance was drunk enough that he wouldn't remember that he'd had that idea.

Vance continued to ponder the matter. "Maybe you've got whales on your mind. Have you read anything about whales lately?"

"Vance, why would I be reading about whales?"

"I dunno, maybe you got assigned that book, what's it called, the famous one about the whale?"

"*Moby Dick*?"

"No, that's not the one I'm thinking of," Vance replied as he reached for the pitcher.

How the hell was Vance already refilling his glass again? "You asked me what the famous book about the whale is called and you're not thinking of *Moby Dick*?"

"Look, I don't know what the hell the whale book is called, Mac."

"Pretty sure it's *Moby Dick*. In fact the full title is *Moby Dick or, The Wha*—"

Vance pounded the table with his fist. "*Moby Dick* is about a lot more than a whale, Mac! It's about the limits of man's knowledge, the universal struggle between good and evil—at times Melville even delves into the nature, nay the very existence, of God himself! Now how about another pitcher?"

Cormac was floored. All he could do was nod.

Still bristling from his defense of the greatest American novel, a wobbly Vance stood up to get the pitcher refilled and immediately tripped on his own shoelace and collapsed to the ground. One of the three-legged dogs hobbled over and started licking the beer from the inside of the pitcher. Eventually a second dog wandered over and started to hump the first dog, who had moved on to licking Vance's cheek. It was an amazing display of dog agility, and one of the most hilarious things Cormac had ever seen. But after twenty seconds of Vance lying there motionless, Cormac thought that maybe it was time to go.

Vance was in and out of consciousness the entire ride home so his line of conversation tended not to be linear. At least he wasn't begging for Mexican food this time.

"When're we goin' to practish, Mac," Vance slurred.

"Band practice isn't until tomorrow, buddy, just relax," Cormac assured him.

"We're gonna rock it, I swear to God. An' we're gonna get another couch?" Vance asked as he fiddled with the left/right balance of the stereo.

"Vance, could you cut that out? Yes, we're gonna get a couch, it's gonna be stadium seating, whatever you want."

"Aw, you're the best, man. I can't believe you went sailing yesterday and didn't invite me," Vance said tenderly. Instantly this quiet wistfulness turned to rage. "I can sail, Mac! I've got a life preserver, dammit!"

"Ssh, ssh, I know you do, buddy. Here, play with the balance knob again, we're almost home."

As they pulled into the driveway, Cormac gave a little fist pump that they had made it home without incident. This was probably due to the fact that it was not yet 8:00 p.m., the sun was just starting to set, and most cops did not suspect that drivers currently on the road had already had nearly a dozen beers.

Cormac got out of the car and walked around to Vance's side. He opened the door and helped Vance to his feet. It wasn't a long distance to the front door, but it took them longer than it should have. Once they got the door open, Cormac led Vance down the hall to his room, where he lowered his roommate into his floor bed fully clothed. Vance let out a loud snore, and Cormac saw the monogrammed initials of the Seahawks towel peek out from inside Vance's lumpy pillow case. That really seemed like an odd place to keep it. Cormac was nearly out the door when he heard Vance mutter, "Hey, Mac?"

Cormac turned and looked at Vance, who was still lying facedown in bed. "Yeah, Vance?" he replied.

"How did it feel when you shot that whale?" Vance asked.

Cormac thought it over for a second. "It was pretty cool," he said as he flicked off the lights.

It seemed pretty early to go to bed, considering that the sun was up and he'd slept for the entire previous day, but Cormac figured a good night's sleep could only help things. After all, they had a big Friday planned: songs to practice, couches to obtain, classes to avoid. Get some rest and start the weekend with a bang, that was his plan. Cormac lay down and tried to ignore the sun's final rays shooting in through the window. His last thought before he drifted off to sleep was, it really *was* pretty damn cool, wasn't it?

DAY FOUR

When Cormac woke up the next morning, his thoughts were the exact opposite.

"No, no, uncool, uncool, very uncool!" he shouted as soon as his eyes opened. He was back in the dank bunk room of the *Levyathan*. Whalers were snoring all around him and his bunk was rocking gently from side to side. A few inches from his face, the thin mattress of the bunk above him strained under the weight of the burly whaler sleeping on it. Flecks of sawdust stuffing sprinkled down from the mattress, and Cormac blew them away before they had a chance to land on his face. The sawdust floated back up toward the mattress, then slowly descended again a few seconds later. Cormac blew it away again. This was actually kind of fun. He kept blowing the sawdust away for a few more cycles until the whaler in the bunk above him shifted in his sleep, causing a lot more sawdust to fall into Cormac's open mouth. Coughing and sputtering, he rolled out of bed and made for the exit.

He burst through the door of the whalers' quarters and was greeted by the exact opposite of his first day aboard the *Levyathan*. A steady wind was blowing and low grey clouds covered the horizon in every direction. With no sun shining, it was much cooler than it had been two days ago, and the spray of water in the air stung Cormac's face. Toward the bow, he saw Ziro swabbing the deck. Apparently, he was the only other person awake.

"Ziro!" Cormac shouted. He rubbed sawdust off of the corners of his mouth as he jogged toward the former slave.

The slave looked over his shoulder and did a full-body double take as Cormac approached, nearly dropping his mop.

"Ziro, I don't know what the hell is going on. What am I doing back here? Why am I here?!" Cormac yelled.

Ziro stared at the disheveled, shrieking figure who was flailing his arms in front of him. Not saying a word, he set down his mop and slowly reached inside his shirt. He pulled out a small vial from a hidden pocket, and as soon as Cormac took a breath from his ranting, Ziro uncorked it and threw the liquid contents into his face.

"Gah!" Cormac sputtered. "What the hell, man?" He wiped the liquid off of his face, looked down at his hands, then wiped them off on his pants. "What was that?"

"Holy water," replied Ziro, once he realized that there wasn't going to be any smoke or melting skin.

"You threw holy water in my face? Why would you do that!" demanded Cormac, who actually thought it was one of the cooler things that had ever happened to him.

"Cormac, I'll be honest," Ziro said. "All signs point to you being some sort of a lesser demon, or at the very least a witch."

"A witch?" Cormac asked, ignoring the lesser demon comment, which again, he thought was a pretty cool thing for people to suspect. "That's ridiculous."

"Well, you just appeared here out of nowhere," said Ziro. "You killed a whale singlehandedly. And then yesterday, you were nowhere to be found! I searched the entire boat. I found some warring tribes of rats that I pray never learn how disorganized and weak the crew is, but you weren't here! But then here you are again today! Do you have a better explanation?"

Cormac did not have a better explanation. "Look, Ziro, I don't know what's happening either. But yesterday I was back at school. I spent the day . . ." Cormac paused and thought better of describing how he had actually spent his day. "I read to some sick kids at the hospital, went for a run, and had a salad for dinner. But when I woke up this morning, I'm back here on the ship! But I can assure you, I'm not a witch. I mean, really, witches? What is this, the sixteen—"

Cormac stopped mid-sentence as a realization hit him. He glanced around at the deck as it dawned on him that he hadn't seen a computer or motor or one of those weird radar things that supposedly tell you when fish are beneath your boat the entire time he'd been on the *Levyathan*.

"Ziro, what year is it?" he asked.

Ziro recorked his holy-water bottle and picked up his mop. He looked at Cormac and quietly said, "I'm afraid I can't tell you that, Cormac."

Off to the east, a bolt of lightning flashed and a few seconds later, distant thunder rumbled across the sky.

Ziro, noticing the look of abject terror that had crossed Cormac's face, adopted a more reassuring tone. "But you're not dead or in purgatory or anything! I honestly don't know. You just sort of lose track of time when you've been at sea for a long time, and as a slave, they keep me in the dark about a lot of stuff to begin with. Frankly it doesn't really matter what the date is when you've got a job to do. Speaking of which, I should probably go and get the captain, this storm looks like it's headed our way."

Cormac had just realized that his situation was even weirder than he previously thought, but he turned and walked with Ziro toward the captain's quarters.

"I'm glad you showed up again," said Ziro as he glanced at the darkening skyline. "It looks like we're going to need the extra help today."

Captain Anson sat in his office scanning a map, more excited than he'd been in weeks. Hauling the whale on board his ship had rekindled his hatred of whales and his love of harpooning them and carving them into chunks suitable for rendering into lamp oil. But now a unique problem tempered his excitement. He had the whale chunks, he just needed to find a place to unload and sell them. And more importantly, it couldn't be a place where his wife and her lawyer would be expecting him. He was going to have to plant misinformation among his men to throw her off his trail. Now that his fortunes had taken a turn for the better, he was more determined than ever not to lose his beloved boat.

Charleston seemed like a good false destination. The men loved spending shore leave with the top-notch prostitutes in Charleston, so they'd work extra hard to get there. It wouldn't be until they dropped anchor that they'd realize they were in . . . The captain closed his eyes and waggled his finger above a map before dropping it to a random location. Greenland.

"Oh, goddammit," Anson said. His hatred for Greenland was nearly as vitriolic as his hatred of whales. If given the choice between sailing to Greenland and sailing to a port where he knew his wife and her lawyer awaited him, he would have to think about it for a long time, then pull the trigger to send a harpoon through his neck. Captain Anson closed his eyes, did another quick waggle and dropped his finger on St. John's, Newfoundland. That would do. It would take a little over a week to sail to St. John's, where they'd unload their wares, relax with some R&R, and then get the hell out of Newfoundland because the captain disliked it almost as much as Greenland.

The captain was folding up the map when there was a knock on his door. He glanced at his pocket watch. It was 9:45, far too early for any of the men to be up besides Ziro.

"Swab the decks, Ziro!" he shouted to the closed door. "I think I saw a dirty spot on the port side!"

Ziro's response was muffled by the door. "Sir, please open the door. It looks like we're going to have a bit of a weather situation."

The captain rolled his eyes. "That's impossible, Ziro! I'm looking at my barometer right now!" The captain pulled open his desk drawer and furiously rooted through it until he found the barometer that the crew had given him as a gift when the *Levyathan* had caught its first whale. It was still in the box. "Says we're in the clear for sunny sailing and fun times at sea!" Turning the box over in his hands the captain noticed that printed on it were the words "Made in Greenland." He frowned.

"Sir, I don't mean to contradict your barometer, but you really should come take a look at the sky. I'm afraid that—" Ziro's words were drowned out by several booming thunderclaps in succession. They sounded like they were happening directly over the *Levyathan*.

"Dammit, Ziro!" the captain shouted when he'd crawled out from under his desk. "Are you OK?"

"Yes," came the muffled reply.

"Then go swab the deck," said the captain with an air of finality.

"Captain Anson, sir, this may be out of place but I think Ziro is right, this really doesn't look too—" The captain had flung the door open before Cormac could even finish his sentence.

"Cormac, my boy!" he shouted warmly, enveloping Cormac in a bear hug. "We thought we'd lost you! Guess Ziro was just screwing around during that 'exhaustive' five-hour search, huh?" The captain shot Ziro a look.

"I toiled for twenty-three hours yesterday," replied Ziro.

"Good God, the sky is black!" the captain noticed. "Come inside, you're as good as dead out there." He motioned Cormac into his chambers and shut the door in Ziro's face.

"We missed you yesterday," boomed the captain, as he walked over to his desk and uncorked a jug of rum. "Didn't haul in any whales without that eagle eye of yours manning the harpoons!"

"Really?" said Cormac as the captain poured rum into two tin cups and handed one to him. "It seemed like there were dozens of whales out there, many of them within arm's reach of the ship. This *is* a whaling boat, right?"

The captain laughed and downed his cup of rum. "Ha! 'Is this a whaling boat?' We need more people with that attitude, son!"

"You do?" asked Cormac. Confused, he sucked back the rum and set the tin cup down, where the captain promptly refilled it.

"So, just between you and me, where were you yesterday when Ziro couldn't find you?" the captain asked conspiratorially. "Lemme guess, you went down to the cold storage area and surveyed your kill, huh? I knew it! Sometimes I'll spend all day down there after I land one of those hellbeasts, just strip off all my clothes and climb to the top of the blubber pile and just stand there in the nude and really show them who's boss."

Cormac could hear the captain growing more animated describing this scenario so he cut him off before he could get any weirder. "No sir, I wasn't hiding. I was back home yesterday. I don't know why, but I've been going to sleep in one place and waking up in another. I don't know why it's happening, but I'm trying to figure it out and I'll do my best to stay out of your way when I show up on board your ship."

"Nonsense!" yelled Captain Anson. "I like the cut of your jib, and I want you manning my front lines for me! You've got a natural whaler's look to you, my boy. To be honest, I see a little of myself at your age in you. Now, let's toast to the destruction of all whales in our lifetime!"

Cormac wasn't sure that anybody wanted or needed that, but he felt a little flattered by the captain's compliments, so he slugged the second pour of rum and tried to ignore the burning in his throat.

"So what did you need to tell me, boy?" asked the captain. "That whaling sense of yours tell you which way to sail today?"

"Well, no, sir. Seeing as how I woke up only fifteen minutes ago and still am not sure where I am exactly, I don't really have anything to tell you. Ziro seemed to think it was very important to talk with you, though."

"Dammit, Ziro," muttered the captain. "I'll tell you, if it weren't for his bad attitude . . ." Cormac didn't hear him finish his sentence as he trailed off walking to the door. But as Cormac glanced around the captain's quarters, he noticed the same lack of any modern-looking equipment. The captain had a quill pen and inkwell on his desk and a block of sealing wax for letters, and his globe just had a sea monster where Cormac expected to see Africa. Cormac also noticed that a frowny face was scrawled across what was either Iceland or Greenland. He could never keep those two straight.

The captain opened the door and barked for Ziro to get in. It had started to rain in the few minutes Cormac had been inside, and Ziro stepped inside, dripping, as the captain closed the door.

"Dammit, Ziro! I'm trying to talk to Cormac!" Captain Anson shouted.

"I realize that, sir, it's just that there's a storm outside."

"I can see that!" said the Captain, gesturing at Ziro's soaking clothes. "Cormac and I were just working out a strategy. We were thinking we'd head to Charleston." He turned and winked at Cormac, who was suddenly terrified of what his new biggest fan had planned for him in Charleston. He hoped it did not involve the Haitian.

"Sir, this storm is pretty much upon us right now. We're going to have to take some evasive maneuvers if we don't want the ship to sink," said Ziro.

"Well, I should consult with my whale honcho number one," said the captain as he turned back to Cormac, who was absentmindedly spinning the globe. "What do you think, son?"

"Sir, if you don't mind me asking," Cormac said. "What year is it?"

"Why do you want to know that?" snapped the captain, his tone shifting abruptly.

"That . . . doesn't seem like a very reasonable response," said Cormac.

"You leave all those big-picture details to me," said the captain. "You're here to whale, and right now the captain is asking for your opinion on whaling matters."

"Well, I'm not really sure," said Cormac. "But Ziro seems to have a pretty good grasp of these matters, so if he says we're in trouble, I'd be inclined to listen to him."

"Ziro's a slave!" bellowed the captain. "He is here to swab decks! The day the captain starts taking orders from a slave is the day I hand this boat over to my wife and her lawyer!"

The captain continued to rant, but Cormac had seen something that made him stop listening. Sitting on the captain's desk was a rough piece of parchment that the captain had started composing a letter on. The captain's handwriting was sloppy, but Cormac could make out the opening words: "Dear Eleanor, Go to hell." It sounded like he was off to a good start, but what intrigued Cormac was not the content but the date, scrawled in the top right corner: May 21st, 1867.

"It's 1867?" Cormac asked, half astonished and half realizing that this made a lot of sense. After all, being transported to a whaling ship while he slept wasn't made *that* much stranger by the fact that the ship was sailing well over a century before he was born.

"Give me that!" shrieked the captain as he pulled the letter away from Cormac. "How much did you see?"

"All five words?"

"Don't be smart with me, kid," said Captain Anson. "I knew you were trouble. Ziro! What did you hear?"

Ziro was looking out the porthole of the door nervously and hadn't been paying attention. "Hear what?" he asked.

"Good," said the captain as he touched the corner of the letter to a candle and let it go up in flames. "You were right, Ziro, this is a fearsome storm. We'll need all hands on deck if we're going to survive. Go wake up the rest of the men, I'll gather my thoughts on how best to address them."

Cormac's head was spinning. There was something off about this situation, but he couldn't put his finger on it. He glanced from the captain to Ziro and back again. The situation seemed to call for some real leadership, not just dictating orders to a slave. To a slave! That was it! Cormac spoke up before he realized what he was saying.

"Lincoln freed the slaves!"

The captain stopped his instructions midsentence. He turned to look at Cormac and mouthed the words "Shut . . . up . . ."

"He totally did!" said Cormac. He'd taken a class about the civil war during his first semester at Harrington, back when he'd been attending class more regularly, and he was delighted to be putting knowledge from school to practical use. He was only about 65 percent sure he had his historical timeline correct, which was not coincidentally the same percentage of answers he'd gotten right on the final exam. "Lincoln made slavery illegal! You're free, Ziro!"

"Psh! Free?" snorted the captain. "What does that even mean?"

"It means not a slave."

"But can a man ever *truly* be free? You know?" countered the captain.

The unexpected 'you know' nearly convinced Cormac that the captain was right, but he regained his philosophical footing and deftly replied, "Well, he can if he's not a slave. Right?"

Captain Anson appeared at a loss for words and Cormac knew he had won. Ziro continued to display no emotion other than ever-increasing panic about their impending deaths.

"Alright!" the captain finally hissed. "Slavery's been illegal for years! That damn Lincoln . . . If we had just made James K. Polk king like I wanted to . . . Ziro! Come here."

Ziro reluctantly shuffled over to stand near both men. Captain Anson clasped him on the shoulder in an attempt at a friendly gesture.

"Ziro," the captain said. "I've not been entirely truthful with you. If you must know, slavery was made illegal soon after you joined up with the *Levyathan*. Of course there are many grey areas . . ."

"There really aren't," interjected Cormac.

"Many people feel that there is a difference between nautical slaves and the more traditional kind. You know, the ones that go like," and here the captain launched into a full-body pantomime of a slave picking cotton in a field. Cormac had obviously never been in a pre-Civil War cotton field before and didn't know what things were actually like in one, but he immediately recognized the captain's impression as one of the most offensive things he'd ever seen in his life. However, he did silently note that being back in the mid-1800s was going to afford him a lot more social leeway with his casual racism.

The captain straightened back up and resumed talking in his normal voice. "But, until President Johnson does the right thing and reverses this whole emancipation unpleasantness, technically, you're free. God forbid nothing happens to prevent that brave man from serving out his entire term. Ziro, if you want to leave the ship when we unload in St. John's, I'll understand."

"I thought you said we were going to Charleston," said Cormac.

"You shut up," Captain Anson snapped. "I knew you were trouble and now you've cost me my most valuable slave! What the hell are you doing on my boat anyways, I mean look at that outfit you're wearing! You look like you should be crabbing on some skiff in Delaware!"

"President Johnson gets impeached!" shot back Cormac.

Ziro, keeping one eye on the door, piped up for the first time as a free man. "If it's all the same, sir, I'd like to stay on as a crew member. This ship is the only life I know."

"Ah, see, Cormac?" The Captain slung his arm around Ziro and pointed at him with his other hand. "Dedication! We don't see slaves and free men on the *Levyathan*, we only see brothers and less important, less wealthy brothers who don't have a say in matters. On this ship we take care of our own. Of course Ziro, we won't be able to pay you any back wages and we'll take all the free hardtack and salt pork you've eaten for the past five years out of any future earnings."

"What are 'Electrowhales'?" asked Cormac, noticing the papers tacked to the wall.

Ziro spoke up before anybody could start shouting at anyone else. "I'm glad we've settled this, but can we please go outside? I think the mast just floated by."

* * *

The good news was that Ziro's broken-mast sighting had been a false alarm. The bad news was that a broken mast would have

86

been the least of their worries. From the moment they left the captain's quarters, there was chaos on the deck of the *Levyathan*. A steady torrent of rain pounded down from above and the heavy winds made it hard to hear anyone who wasn't standing right next to you. Huge waves rocked the ship continuously and the thunder and lightning were terrifying. Cormac was fairly certain that he was going to die.

He wasn't happy about this. It meant that he wasn't going to have much time to revel in the morning's good deed. It had felt pretty good to help Ziro gain his freedom. Cormac imagined old Honest Abe must have felt the same way after he made his big "four score and seven years ago" speech. Although, and Cormac felt like a dick to nitpick, it seemed like helping one slave *directly* was a lot braver than just making a big blanket statement about the *concept* of slavery as a whole. Sort of like how it was more important to give a quarter to a homeless guy who had passed out in an alley than to give money to those African famine charities where you didn't know who was actually getting your money. Cormac made a promise to himself and to whatever god was up there to never be swindled by an anti-hunger charity again if he just made it out of this storm alive.

The rest of the crew of the *Levyathan* was doing everything in their power to keep the boat from capsizing or snapping in half. As far as Cormac could tell, this mostly involved pulling on lengths of rope that were as big around as a fire hose. He wasn't sure what they were connected to or how the whalers kept track of them, but every now and then the captain would yell something like "lower the boom!" and the whalers would drop the rope they were currently pulling on and race to another one. Then Ziro would yell "no, RAISE the boom, RAISE it! Lowering it will kill us all!" and the men would race to the other end of the rope and start pulling it in the opposite direction.

Cormac tried to be of assistance, but a lifetime of not being on a whaling boat had left him ill-suited for being a productive crew member of a whaling boat. He discovered that he could barely lift one of the bulky ropes, let alone grip and pull it. He quickly figured out that he could best serve the crew by making sure the men were constantly supplied with rum. Cormac ran back and forth from the rum storage area with jugs like a one-man bucket brigade. As soon as he handed a jug to a sailor, he turned around to get another one. Occasionally he'd take a small nip from the jug himself. It was helping him stay warm and the adrenaline of trying not to die seemed to counteract any of the intoxicating effects of the booze.

Every so often, Cormac would have a moment where the strangeness of his situation really hit him. Here he was, on the deck of a whaling boat, just after the civil war had ended, handing rum jugs to burly sailors who were struggling to keep the ship afloat. He didn't have any time to collect his thoughts and wonder how or why he was in this position. The only thing that kept running through his head was "Why couldn't this have happened to Vance?"

On what seemed like his fiftieth trip back to the surprisingly well-stocked rum storage area, Cormac noticed a small spurt of water shooting up through the floor. A leak. He put his foot over it, hoping in vain that this would solve the problem. Cormac and Vance had never been the "DIY home repair" types. Their method of dealing with a maintenance issue such as a dripping faucet or dead light bulb was to slowly back away from it, close the door, and really, really hope that it was the type of problem that could be solved by drinking in an adjacent room. Unfortunately, when he removed his foot the water only seemed to shoot up more forcefully.

But just then Cormac had an idea! He popped the cork out of a jug of rum and tried to press it into the hole that the water was spurting out of. No dice. The cork was much wider than the hole and the water was now spurting up twice as fast.

Cormac took a swig of rum and went to find someone who knew what they were doing.

Outside, the rain continued to pound down and the winds seemed to be picking up. The *Levyathan* had held up well to the storm so far, but the creaking noises she kept making were constant reminders of her poor craftsmanship and spotty upkeep history.

Cormac figured if he told any of the whalers that the rum was in danger, they might abandon their posts altogether. He squinted, trying to pick out Captain Anson or Ziro through the blinding rain. That blurry thing down near the bow might be Ziro, but it also could be a sack of minerals used to preserve whale blubber. Cormac waved at it trying to get its attention, but just then a huge wave washed over the bow of the boat, taking the object along with it. Cormac hoped it had been a sack of blubber preservatives.

While he was futilely scanning for someone to help him, something bumped into his back rather forcefully. Cormac spun around and saw Captain Anson, who was dragging a large coil of rope and wasn't looking where he was going. The captain frowned when he realized he'd bumped into Cormac.

"Hello, traitor!" said Captain Anson. "Betrayed anyone else lately?"

Cormac wondered how someone who had kidnapped and deceived a man into slavery for half a decade could question another person's morality, but he let it slide.

"Captain Anson," he started. "This is an emergency." But the captain cut him off before he could say another word.

"Save it for your best friend, Ziro!" yelled Captain Anson as he angrily gestured toward something in the distance. "I'm sure he's got plenty of time to help you now that he's lying around free all day!"

Cormac looked to his right and could just make out a soaking wet Ziro manning the ship's helm with one hand as he deftly tied knots with the other hand, all the while shouting instructions to the whalers. The captain sulked off with his rope and Cormac went to talk to Ziro.

"Ziro!" he yelled. "There's a leak in the rum room! You gotta help me, or the boat's gonna sink!"

Ziro stared at Cormac in amazement. "My God, Cormac, how much have you had to drink?"

Cormac hadn't realized it until that moment, but his occasional sips of rum over the course of the morning had added up. What he had thought was a frantic plea for help to Ziro had instead come out a slurred, unintelligible rambling. Cormac looked at Ziro and hiccuped.

"Look, Cormac," shouted Ziro as the rain beat down on both of them. "It's great that you're trying to help, but for your own safety, ease up on the booze! Keep bringing the crew rum, but don't you have any more—you're liable to fall overboard."

Cormac was overpowered by a strong desire to tell Ziro how great he thought he was, no matter what anyone else says, but instead he turned to go back to the whalers. The whalers . . . what a great bunch of guys! Not like that Captain Anson. Where the hell was that dick, he was a guy who needed someone to tell it like it is right to his face. Maybe a bit of rum for courage and then Cormac would . . . The rum!

Cormac wheeled back around toward Ziro, nearly losing his balance as a wave rocked the boat at the same time. Focusing on each syllable, he tried to eke out a coherent sentence.

"Ziro . . . A leak . . . We're all gonna die . . . I'm from the future!" No! Stupid! You're losing him! "Rum room! Leaking!" Cormac gestured wildly to emphasize how serious he was and nearly hit Ziro in the face a few times. It got the message across.

"OK, OK! Look, show me what you're . . . Ow! Stop flailing, you idiot! Show me what you're talking about!"

Ziro handed off control of the helm to a nearby whaler, then followed Cormac down to the rum storage area. When they opened the door, Ziro gasped in horror. The water was surging through the hole much faster than it had been before, and six inches of water now covered the rum storage area. Cormac turned and looked at Ziro with a satisfied expression. Who was the drunken buffoon now?

"What the hell are you smiling at, you idiot?!" shouted Ziro. "We need to get this fixed right away. Go tell the captain to send three men down here with the patch kit. We don't have much time."

Before Cormac could protest or even take a fortifying swig of sweet, sweet rum, Ziro had stripped off his shirt and was rooting around beneath the standing water to try and plug the leak. Cormac walked back out into the storm and promptly forgot what he was supposed to be doing. Whatever it was, in his overconfident state, he now felt it was probably more important that he give steering the boat a try. How hard could it really be? After all, he had done things these nineteenth-century idiots had never even *heard* of, like microwaving a Hungry-Man dinner and downloading pornography onto his phone at a red light. Rubes! He'd show them all.

Cormac was wobbling his way toward the general direction of the helm when he happened to look over the side of the boat. Something in the choppy waters caught his eye. He stopped and reached out to balance himself on the railing and peered closer. In the rolling, spraying ocean, not thirty feet off the side of the *Levyathan*, there was a lone whale. No doubt it had been separated from its pod during the storm and was now confused and lost.

"Stupid whale," muttered Cormac. "You're a moron! Way to get lost in the middle of the storm!" Cormac was now shouting at the whale. "Nobody knows where you are and nobody cares! You're all alone! You don't belong here but there's nowhere you can go! You're powerless and pathetic and the worst part is, you're too arrogant and stupid to realize it!"

Alone. Lost. Powerless. Pathetic. As he was yelling, Cormac came to a realization: he had to kill this whale.

He'd seen some of the whalers lay their harpoon guns down when they took up the ropes in an effort to save the ship. He made his way back toward that part of the boat, turning every so often to make sure the whale wasn't getting too far away. It seemed to be swimming close to the boat, the only other familiar shape in the ocean.

The busy whalers came into sight as Cormac stumbled closer to the heart of the ship. Captain Anson saw him approaching and yelled something at him, but Cormac was focused on the abandoned harpoon guns that the whalers had strewn about the deck. He picked one up and shot the captain a look. He meant it to be a "remember what almost happened the last time I got my hands on one of these" look, but to Captain Anson it looked a lot more like a "if asked to recite the alphabet, at this point I would probably include several numbers" look.

Confident that his message had gotten across, Cormac lurched back toward the side of the ship where he'd last seen the whale, unaware that Captain Anson had decided to trail behind him. The captain wanted to make sure Cormac didn't cause any further damage, and maybe give him a shove over the side if circumstances permitted.

Cormac's unintentionally indirect path back to the whale eventually took him past the rum storage area. Inside, Ziro was still futilely attempting to plug the leak. The water was now up to his waist and was rushing out the door in a steady stream. Cormac strode past the room without giving the leak a second thought, but as much as he wanted to follow, Captain Anson was unable to resist finding out what the hell was going on.

"Dammit, Ziro!" he shouted. "What the hell is going on?"

Ziro turned around, soaking and shirtless. In between deep breaths, he managed to gasp out "Sir . . . there's a leak."

"A leak!" the captain fumed. "You get your freedom and the first thing you do is sabotage the ship that housed and fed you for the duration of your lengthy enslavement? How dare you!"

"Sir, it's only getting worse. We need to plug it. I can stop it with my little finger but only if I submerge my head below water."

"Figure it out on your own, Ziro! In case you haven't noticed, I'm trying to keep a ship afloat! I've got bigger things to worry about! Now where the hell did that drunk idiot go with that harpoon gun . . ."

The captain hurried after Cormac and Ziro was left behind in the rapidly filling rum storage area.

Captain Anson spotted Cormac leaning up against the railing on the side of the ship. The wind was blowing in his face, whipping rain and gusts of sea water at him, but the kid stood his ground. The tentative, awkward way Cormac gripped the harpoon gun reminded Anson of the way Eleanor used to empty their horse's dung sacks, a task that fell to her because Anson had told her he was allergic to burlap and would break out in hives if he got near one. Eleanor demanded to know why they couldn't get a cloth dung sack like her sister's husband used, and Anson would angrily gesture at the lifetime supply of burlap dung sacks that he'd scoured a three-town area to find and shout, "And let these go to waste? And let these perfectly good burlap dung sacks go to waste? Who do you think you are?"

There was no way in hell she was getting his ship.

It didn't even seem worth it to try to figure out what this buffoon was aiming at, but Captain Anson wasn't about to let Cormac waste a perfectly good harpoon. He mentally prepared an airtight excuse along the lines of "he tripped, who cares," and got ready to shove Cormac overboard.

He was about five steps away when Cormac pulled the trigger. The harpoon shot out of the gun straight and true, and Captain Anson instinctively followed its path. He watched it sail out over the water, then arch downward into the dark and angry sea.

"Great job, idiot," said the captain. "Why don't you let the professionals—"

He was cut off by the sound of an injured whale leaping out of the water with a harpoon embedded just below its eye. Even with all of the rain, thunder, and wind, it was the loudest thing the captain had heard all day.

"Holy mother of God!" Captain Anson shouted. "A direct hit!"

Cormac gave no indication whether he was satisfied or not. He just stood there, watching as the whale begin to thrash in the water. Eventually he turned and seemed to notice the captain for the first time.

"I'm not having sex with *any* of you in Charleston," Cormac slurred.

Captain Anson found this statement concerning, but not nearly as worrisome as the idea that this whale might get away.

"Cormac, my boy," he reassured him. "Don't worry, nobody's going to Charleston. Why don't you hand me that harpoon gun and we'll haul in this whale."

Captain Anson reached out to take the gun, but Cormac snatched it back.

"Look, Cormac, you've got to hand me that gun. We've got to tie the cord off or else that whale's going to pull the gun out of your hands and we'll lose him for good."

Cormac turned toward the whale and pulled the trigger on the gun again.

"No, you have to load another harpoon in there before you can fire it again. No, that's not a harpoon, those are your pants!"

Cormac put his pants back on somewhat reluctantly.

"Look, dammit, son," said the captain, trying to remain calm. "I'm not about to let that accursed sea bitch become crab food instead of lamp oil. You're going to give me that gun or I'm going to take it from you."

Cormac grabbed his crotch.

Captain Anson lunged at him and easily grabbed the harpoon gun out of Cormac's unsteady grip. In the sea, the whale appeared to have gotten over the initial shock of the non-fatal but painful wound, and was focused on getting as far away from the *Levyathan* as possible. The rope attached to the harpoon gun was unspooling as it swam farther and farther away.

Captain Anson raced over to the nearest cleat, untied the rope from the harpoon gun, and started tying it onto the steel cleat. This was made quite difficult by the fact that Cormac was clawing at his back, grabbing at the rope, and generally just making a nuisance of himself.

"Dammit, Cormac, get off of me! It's going to get away!"

"It's stupid to have your couch up in the air!" Cormac deftly retorted.

Anson looked down at the spool of rope. It was quickly getting smaller. Without assistance, they were going to lose the whale. He didn't have a choice.

"Ziro!" he yelled. "I need your help!"

Ziro poked his head out of the rum storage area. After sizing up the struggle between Cormac and the captain, he ran over to them. Water continued to rush out of the storage room and onto the ship's deck.

"What's going on!?" Ziro shouted, trying to be heard over the storm.

"Cormac shot another whale," said the captain. "We don't have much time; tie this off while I punch him!" He handed Ziro the end of the rope and began to swing haymakers at Cormac. Ziro turned his back on the two of them and quickly threaded the rope around the cleat. He tried to ignore the sounds of a struggle that sounded much more evenly matched than it should have.

Skilled with knots, even in adverse weather conditions, Ziro quickly pulled the hitch tight and spun around. He was horrified to see Captain Anson on the ground, panting. Standing above him was a defiant-looking Cormac, holding the bundle of the last few feet of rapidly unspooling harpoon rope in his hands.

"Oh God, Cormac, put that down!" Ziro shouted, but it was too late. The whale had swam as far as it could, and the rat's nest of rope went taut with a vicious snap. A small object fell to the ground at Cormac's feet. The pinky finger of his left hand had been stuck in a loop in the harpoon rope, and as it pulled tight, the rope cut right through the bone, severing the finger.

"Dammit, Ziro! What the hell did you do?" shouted Captain Anson as Cormac's finger fell to the deck.

Cormac stared at the place where his pinky finger used to be while Captain Anson and Ziro started running around and shouting. It had been a clean cut, and though blood was spurting out of his hand, at the moment he didn't really feel any pain. Thank God I'm so severely inebriated, Cormac thought, otherwise that might have really hurt or been avoided altogether!

Soon, a team of whalers arrived. Ziro told them to help deal with Cormac's injury and Captain Anson told them to start hauling in the whale. The whalers didn't do so well with conflicting orders and several fights broke out. Eventually Ziro calmed them down and instructed half of them to haul in the whale.

The rest of the whalers circled around Cormac. Ziro pointed to one holding a jug of rum and got him to pour some over the place where Cormac's pinky used to be in an effort to sterilize it. Cormac gestured that he wanted some in his mouth and the whaler gave him the "open up" gesture. When he did, two more whalers slipped a long wooden dowel in between his teeth and held it there. When Cormac saw Captain Anson coming toward him with a long iron fire poker with a glowing orange end, he figured it was about as good a time as any to pass out.

The last thing Cormac saw before losing consciousness was Ziro picking up his pinky finger off the floor and running off to the rum storage area.

* * *

Cissy Buckler needed to talk to her editor. She sat outside of his office with a copy of Friday's *School Paper* in her lap. It was turned to page A-6, which featured a prominent above-the-fold article by one student reporter Cissy Buckler. "New Options at Dining Hall" screamed the thirty-six-point headline, next to a stock photo of the Harrington dining hall. So far, so good. Cissy's concern lay with the actual content of the article, which had been redacted. Entirely redacted.

When Cissy opened the paper that morning, she had expected to see her latest muckraking triumph. Instead, her allotted thirty column inches were filled with the word "REDACTED" over and over. Cissy was furious. Then she realized that it didn't say "RETARDED" and calmed down a bit. God, she was hungover.

Beneath the article was the italicized disclaimer, "*The* School Paper *has been unable to vet the contents of Ms. Buckler's article. We apologize for the inconvenience.*" Even in her hungover state, Cissy had recognized the haughty editorial tone of *School Paper* Editor in Chief Scott Brixon. Cissy had immediately decided to blow off the classes that she hadn't already skipped and had marched down to the *School Paper*'s office. She had now been waiting for over two hours.

Eventually the door to Brixon's office opened and he walked out into the *School Paper*'s common area. Cissy leapt up from the bench she'd been sitting on and quickly marched over to confront him.

"Scott!" she snapped. "Thanks for keeping me waiting."

Scott Brixon did a quick double take and stopped in his tracks.

"Cissy!" he said, obviously surprised to see her. "How long have you been here?"

"Two and a half hours. Going to act like nobody told you I was here? That's really professional of you, Brixon."

"Look, why didn't you just knock?" Scott was confused. "Who would have told you I was here? I don't have a secretary—this is a college newspaper!"

Typical Brixon, Cissy thought. Resentful of the people who were out there doing the real work. Here he was, the great editor, sitting way up in his ivory tower down here in sub-basement C of the Harrington gym. Cissy knew Scott Brixon had had it in for her ever since she'd contested his run for *School Paper* editor in chief last year. She'd tried to paint him as the elitist paper establishment and herself as the outsider who would shake things up, but somewhere along the way her message got misinterpreted and police got word that she was going to bomb sub-basement C on election day.

This would have been enough on its own to disqualify her from the ballot, but it turned out Cissy had forgotten to actually file the paperwork to enter the race, so it didn't really matter. Brixon received 100 percent of the vote and Cissy was asked to leave the election night party after she tried to make a concession speech in the men's bathroom.

"I don't have time to play these games, Brixon," said Cissy as she strode past him, into his office.

"No, I was about to go to . . . Of course, Cissy," Scott sighed. "Would you like to take a seat?"

"Spare me the patronizing attitude," Cissy said, taking a seat. "You killed my article and I want to know why."

Scott sat back down behind his desk, leaned forward and spoke in a calm voice.

"Cissy, you really let us down today. You told us for weeks you'd been working on a big exposé about the school's food-service contracts, and then you submitted an article about some changes they're making to the menu."

Cissy snorted indignantly. "You don't think Harrington's students deserve to know about changes the dining hall is making? Their tuition dollars pay for that food!"

"OK, you're right, it is of interest," conceded Scott. "But the changes you detailed were all fairly basic menu rotations that the cafeteria makes at the beginning of any given month. In some cases, it was just introducing a different topping option or new type of cheese."

Cissy made the "Blah, Blah, Blah" gesture with her right hand.

"I'm sorry you feel that way," said Scott. "But regardless of whether or not this menu information, which is readily available online, is newsworthy, your article had other problems! Cissy, you published numerous quotes from dining hall personnel that you said were from interviews conducted off the record!"

"Well, that's how you get the best quotes, right?" Cissy winked. "Nobody's going to serve up the juicy stuff if they know you're going to print it!"

Scott looked exasperated. "Disregarding that wildly unethical tactic, I followed up with your interview subjects. The workers you quoted said that they hadn't talked to you at all! On *or* off the record!"

He had Cissy there. "They were always closed when I went by," she admitted.

"When did you go by? The dining hall opens at 6:00 a.m. and serves meals all day long until they close at ten."

"I'm sure you know how it is, Brixon," Cissy said knowingly. "You get so caught up working a beat, you don't have time to eat a sit-down meal in the dining hall. It's the life of a reporter."

Brixon stared at Cissy for a solid ten seconds before continuing. "On top of all of this, you obviously oversold the amount of content you had. You didn't have thirty inches; you didn't even have ten.

Most of your article is just reprinting the Wikipedia entries for the various food items that the cafeteria is introducing to the menu this month! For example," Scott picked up a printed copy of Cissy's article and began to read from it.

"Another addition to the breakfast menu will be scrambled eggs with cheddar cheese melted on top. Wikipedia defines scrambled eggs as: 'One of the most common ways of preparing eggs. The yolk and the whites are beaten (or scrambled) together, then heated in a pan with butter [Citation Needed] or oil. Usually a serving consists of two or three scrambled eggs, though some people prefer to eat more or less.'"

"Excuse me for citing my sources," Cissy said with pride. "Some of us take journalism more seriously than others."

"Well, I appreciate your attention to bibliographic detail, but the thing is, none of these entries were even from Wikipedia!" The pitch of Scott's voice was rising as he got more frustrated. "I think you just wrote them for your article and *said* they came from Wikipedia!"

"Brixon, Wikipedia's an always-changing document," said Cissy. "It reflects the zeitgeist."

"What zeitgeist!? The scrambled egg zeitgeist?"

"Look, all of those things in the article could be on Wikipedia in a couple hours," said Cissy.

"You're right, they could be. But if I go on and see them there, I'll know that you just went in and added them as soon as you got home."

"Well maybe you wouldn't see them," countered Cissy. "Maybe I made the changes and some other people came in and edited them out right away."

"I don't know . . . I could always look at the change logs," said a defeated-sounding Scott Brixon, realizing his lunch break was quickly nearing its end.

"How many past entries would you review before you decided you were wasting your time?" Cissy asked, hoping it wasn't going to be more than twenty. That was a lot of Wikipedia editing she'd have to do.

"Look, Cissy," said Scott. "My point is, the *School Paper* just can't print stuff that is this far below our standards. Now, I want to give you a chance. I feel like I owe it to your family. But if you turn in another article like this one . . . I really don't think we're going to be able to keep you on the staff any longer."

Cissy felt like she should quit while she was ahead. She stood up, nodded at Brixon, and turned to walk out the door. Before she left the room, she spoke up with her back still turned to her editor. "Those statues on your desk. Those are real nice."

"Ah yes, my Buckler Awards," said Scott. "I know you've seen a few of those in your day, Cissy."

The Buckler Award was one of the more prestigious awards in college journalism. It was named after Cissy's great-grandfather, who had helped found the *School Paper* and gone on to work at the *New York Times*. When he retired after a distinguished career, the *Times* had honored him by naming an award after him. The Buckler Award was presented by the *Times* to recognize excellence in student journalism. The winner received a substantial scholarship as well as a summer internship at the *Times* that usually led to a staff reporting job. It had been awarded to just three Harrington students: Cissy's father, her older brother, and Scott Brixon. Brixon was the only two-time winner in history.

"Yep, the days I won those were two of the greatest days of my life," he continued proudly.

"Two? You won twice?" Cissy asked coyly. "Because I only saw one award statue on your desk."

She waited for his reaction.

"No, there's definitely two here. One, two," Scott counted. "Two awards."

Cissy wheeled around to see Scott pointing at both his Buckler Awards. Dammit! She had meant to slip one into her purse, then taunt him before fleeing sub-basement C. She had remembered to taunt, but had forgotten to actually steal.

Not breaking eye contact with her editor, Cissy started inching toward the award statues. As she slowly got closer, Scott looked down at the awards, then back at Cissy. He frowned. Trying to look inconspicuous, Cissy gradually lifted her arms and began to reach toward the statues.

"Cissy, what are you . . . Are you trying to take my awards?" He picked them up and clutched them to his chest. "Please don't touch them. They mean the world to me."

Cissy stopped in her tracks and straightened.

"Fine," she said indignantly. "I have to go anyways. I have a couch to sell."

DAY FIVE

The good news was that on Saturday morning, Cormac McIlhenney woke up in his own bed in the house on Craymore Street. The bad news was that he had fewer fingers than he'd gone to bed with. Cormac decided that anyone who'd ever drank out of an "I don't do mornings" coffee mug while still possessing all of their fingers on the morning they claimed not to be "doing" could go fuck themselves. He decided this, of course, after he screamed in terror at the top of his lungs for a solid minute and a half.

His left hand was now missing its pinky finger. In its place was a charred, black area of scar tissue where, presumably, once Cormac passed out, Captain Anson had cauterized the wound with a red-hot poker. This must have killed the nerve endings, because other than a hangover headache, Cormac didn't feel any pain. He thought for a moment that he might be having phantom limb syndrome, but that turned out to just be a boner.

Cormac did some preliminary tests on his mangled hand. He reached over and picked up his phone. It seemed that phone use wasn't really affected, since it mainly just required index fingers and thumbs. He spun around in bed, grabbed his pillow, and attempted to fluff it. But Cormac had never fluffed a pillow in his life, so he couldn't tell if his performance was impeded in any way. He got out of bed and walked over to his laptop. Aha! Typing! Finally, he'd found something that his handicap was going to make more difficult! Cormac instantly wondered why he had felt triumphant about this discovery.

While at his desk, Cormac took the chance to check his email and mark everything from professors and TAs as read. Obviously, he was dealing with extenuating circumstances. It was in poor taste and possibly downright offensive for them to send emails with subject lines like "abysmal attendance" or "you have never turned in an assignment." Cormac decided to forward them to the dean with a description of all he'd been through over the past few days.

With a bit of difficulty, he started to type: "I was unable to complete my midterm paper because when I go to sleep I get transported back in time to a whaling . . ." Cormac stopped typing midsentence and deleted the email draft. He would have to work on his excuse. He leaned back in his desk chair and held up his mangled hand. If it had been on someone else, say a grizzled miner showing it to him in a bar (but not in a terrifying, threatening way), Cormac would have thought it looked pretty cool.

What had happened on Friday while he was getting rained on and mutilated on the deck of the *Levyathan*? There was only one man who could answer that question and he was currently asleep lengthwise on his floor bed with one foot stuck inside a crumpled bag of Doritos.

"Wake up, Vance!" shouted Cormac from his roommate's bedroom doorway.

Without raising his head, Vance flailed his right arm around until he knocked a lamp off the stolen milk crates he used as a bedside table. It crashed to the floor, and, contented, Vance settled back into sleep. It was his equivalent of hitting the snooze button.

Waking Vance up was not going to be easy. He was immune to loud noises and Cormac didn't want to touch him. Cormac decided to take some smelly garbage out of the kitchen trash can and put it in bed next to Vance. Surely that would do the trick. But as he was leaving for the kitchen, he noticed that the garbage can was *already* in a far corner of Vance's room for some reason. It smelled ungodly and Cormac was fairly certain he could hear something rustling in it. Vance snored loudly.

Disgusted, Cormac decided to pour a glass of water on Vance's head. He turned to leave, when he noticed the Seahawks towel on the floor. He gave his former towel a sharp kick, and it sailed across the room.

"Don't kick my towel," came the muffled reprimand from his facedown, half-asleep roommate.

"Christ, Vance, wake up!" yelled Cormac. "Meet me in the living room, it's really important!"

Cormac left Vance to pull himself together. There was a decent chance he would emerge from the bed without any clothes on. Cormac had been through a lot recently, but seeing Vance nude might be the thing that pushed the week's exploits from "crazy shit" to "Lovecraftian descent into madness."

He walked to the living room, where their couch stood elevated. The entire project looked even less stable than before. Vance had replaced the stack of old newspapers that raised one leg of the couch with an enormous block of ice that, judging by the puddle of water on the ground next to it, used to be substantially bigger. For a second, Cormac thought about scaling the structure, but opted to sit on the floor. He scooted to avoid the puddle whenever it inched closer to him.

Eventually Vance came out of his room. Fortunately, he was wearing shorts, but he was also eating Doritos. Cormac hoped with all his soul it was a different bag.

"My, my," said Vance, spraying Dorito crumbs everywhere. "If it isn't my dependable old roommate."

Before Cormac could respond, Vance grabbed the electrical cord and vaulted himself onto the airborne couch with gymnast-like agility. Clearly, he had been practicing the maneuver. The couch wobbled, but Vance appeared not to notice.

"You look impressed, Mac," said Vance, not attempting to conceal his scorn. "Turns out a guy has a lot of time to practice getting onto an airborne couch when his fellow band members bail on practice."

"Look, Vance," Cormac tried to respond, but Vance wasn't through yet.

"Oh, I'm sure you've got a great explanation for missing band practice. Why don't you climb onto the lower half of our stadium seating couches and explain it all to me. Wait, what's that? You can't climb onto the lower half of our stadium seating couches because it's not here, because Vance couldn't pick it up without the help of his loyal roommate? The roommate who swore he'd help him get it from the chick Vance negotiated a great deal with? My, that is a predicament!"

Cormac stood and silently walked out of the room. He retrieved Vance's blow-dryer from the bathroom and walked back to the living room. Vance had never grown his hair long enough to warrant a blow-dryer, but he liked to keep it around for the winter. He called it his "portable sauna." Cormac was certain that from the moment the poor blow-dryer had been unboxed, it had been pointed exclusively at Vance's crotch.

Vance's eyes narrowed as Cormac walked back into the living room.

"What the hell are you doing, Mac?" he asked, turning gingerly on the couch as Cormac walked behind him. Cormac bent over and plugged the blow-dryer into a wall socket.

"Mac, all kidding aside, I would strongly advise not getting too close to the business end of that dryer," Vance cautioned.

Cormac silently flipped the blow-dryer to high and stepped over to the corner of the couch that was elevated by the block of ice. He pointed it at the ice, then raised his gaze to meet Vance's.

"Oh, come on, Mac," Vance protested. "There's no reason for that. Look, so you missed a practice and maybe let the deal of a lifetime on an auxiliary couch slip away, I can forgive tha—"

Vance was cut off as the melting ice suddenly dropped the couch leg a half inch. Vance tensed as he tried to rebalance to compensate.

"Dammit, Mac! I've been working on that block for a month!"

Cormac waved the blow-dryer back and forth to ensure even melting.

"OK, OK, I'm sorry!" panicked Vance. "It's not a big deal, it's just a couch! Look, put the dryer down, man!"

Cormac flicked the dryer off and let it drop to the floor. Staring squarely at Vance, he held up his left hand with his four remaining fingers outstretched. Vance looked uncertain. Cormac waggled his hand around and emphatically thrust it at his roommate. Looking over his shoulder to see if he was missing anything, Vance tentatively raised his own left hand and started to lower it toward Cormac's. Very gradually, he moved it closer and closer to Cormac's until it was only an inch or two away. He paused before quickly smacking his palm against Cormac's.

"Oh, goddammit, Vance, I didn't want a high five!" Cormac yelled. "I was on the whaling ship yesterday and one of my fingers got cut off!"

"Oh phew," said Vance. "Without any context that little gesture of yours seemed a little—"

"I lost a finger!" Cormac shouted even louder.

"Well I can see that now!" Vance yelled back. "How on earth did that happen?"

"A rope from a harpoon gun coiled around it and severed it. Then some whalers held me down while the captain burned the wound shut with a red-hot poker."

"Jesus," said Vance. "That's . . . that's terrible, buddy."

"I know," said Cormac as he stared at his hand. "It doesn't even feel real. Like, I know it's my hand. I know part of me is permanently altered, and that it's going to affect the rest of my life in ways I can't even imagine. It's probably the worst thing that's ever happened to me. But in a way, that makes me realize how fortunate I've been. There hasn't really ever been any hardship that I've had to deal with, and in the light of that, I feel like I've gained—"

"Can you still move a couch?" Vance interrupted.

* * *

Cormac drove the Volvo in silence as Vance navigated. There had been another round of shouting before they left the apartment. Cormac had expected that a crippling loss of limb might elicit a bit more sympathy from his roommate. Vance felt that his request had not been out of line, as apparently Cormac wasn't in much pain and due to his lack of insurance, wasn't planning on visiting a doctor. Plus, the girl who was selling the couch had just texted to say that in spite of being stood up the night before, she would still sell them the couch if they could come get it right away.

"It's weird, man," said Vance. "You were just lying there all day again. I played music, shook you by the shoulder, blew hot air in your face with the blow-dryer . . ." Cormac winced. "But nothing! I don't know what else to try, man, I think this may, turn left up here, I think this may be a matter for a professional."

Still not saying anything, Cormac turned left onto a residential street.

"And the guys on the boat said you just disappeared on the day you were back here? So you're probably not there right now. But you're lying in bed when you're on the boat . . ." Vance's attempt to make sense of the situation was severely irritating Cormac.

"Do you think your finger is still in your bed somewhere? We probably should have looked. You've got to put body parts on ice right away if you're planning on reselling them on the black market. Go right at the next stop sign."

The last disturbing statement aside, Vance was offering no new insights into the new metaphysics Cormac was evidently now subject to. He'd been excited to hear about the second whale Cormac had killed, was envious of the well-stocked supply of rum, and called Cormac a pussy for freeing a slave. But other than that, all of his suggestions and ideas had been fruitless.

"Frankly, I'm stunned that you've been on a major seafaring vessel twice in the past seventy-two hours and cannot say definitively whether you've been on the poop deck or not," Vance said with a touch of irritation in his voice. "The Cormac that I thought I knew would have made seeking out the poop deck his top priority. Third house on your left here. Because frankly, it seems like the poop deck is going to be where the action is happening, and a savvy whaler would stake that out as his turf. And here you are, saying that 'maybe' you've been on the poop deck and 'maybe' you haven't. An opportunity wasted is what it is, Mac, and I for one—"

Cormac slammed on the brakes in front of the third house and put the car in park. He turned to look at Vance.

"I lost a finger, Vance. I'm going back in time to the 1800s and have no idea what the hell is going on. I know it may be hard for you to understand from up on your stupid airborne couch, but I've been eating hardtack and hoping I don't encounter the Haitian and that a whale doesn't drag me overboard! So finding the poop deck is pretty damn far down on my list of priorities!"

For the first time that Cormac could remember, Vance looked speechless. Without a word he unbuckled his seatbelt and got out of the car. Before he closed the door, Vance leaned back in. "You probably can't play the guitar either with that finger missing," he added. Vance flashed Cormac an incredibly fake smile, pulled his head back out, and slammed the door.

* * *

Cissy heard a car door close outside her house and peeked out the window. A disheveled guy was making his way up her driveway with a slightly more irritated-looking disheveled guy trailing ten feet behind him. Cissy took the last swig of her mimosa and set the glass down. Then she thought better of her decision and poured herself another one. She needed to find inspiration somewhere today if she was going to redeem herself in the Sunday edition of the *School Paper*.

So far, her attempts at tracking down a scoop had been unsuccessful, mainly because Scott Brixon had caught her sneaking around his backyard the night before. Cissy had been certain that if she could just get inside her editor's house, she'd be able to track down evidence of his impropriety and wrongdoing at the *School Paper*, or at the very least break something valuable. But Brixon had heard her rustling around in his bushes and turned the garden hose on her. Apparently he had thought she was a raccoon rummaging through his garbage cans. He'd been stunned when a grown woman emerged from the juniper bushes, tipsy and soaking. Cissy had tried to yell something in Spanish as she fled, to throw him off her trail, but all she could remember was how to count to six.

The entire thing never would have happened if these two idiots had picked up the couch when they said they were going to. Cissy had waited around her house for over four hours until she realized that they weren't coming. Unfortunately, the two bottles of wine she'd consumed while waiting led her to believe that breaking into her editor's house was an excellent and feasible idea.

But that morning she'd decided to see if they were still interested and, lo and behold, here they were. Cissy needed the couch out because she had a new one coming on Monday. Well, it was new to her. It had previously belonged to her brother, but it wouldn't fit into the elevator of the new apartment building he was moving to, and so he had offered it to her.

Cissy resented the offer, which she perceived as charity from her big shot reporter brother. She had made her feelings clear with a cutting, profanity-laced email that she had written, then immediately deleted and replaced with a new one graciously accepting the gift. After all, her couch was in terrible shape.

Cissy ran her hand along the fabric of one of the couch's arms. It felt like polyester, but the tag indicated it was a Russian textile that she was unable to pronounce. The tag also had a skull and crossbones on it, with pictographs indicating that babies, senior citizens, and cats should not be exposed to it. She'd also spilled several glasses of wine on it over the years, so the couch looked like it had suffered multiple bruises that had healed poorly. One morning she'd woken up to discover that an animal had gnawed away a portion of one of the cushions. She hoped, but couldn't be certain, that whatever toxic material the cushion was stuffed with had killed the animal before it was able to make the inside of the couch its home.

So yes, the couch was horrible and needed to go before it caused her any irreparable harm. But as she looked around the living room, Cissy realized it was the only thing remaining that she'd picked out herself. Everything else—the art on the walls, the TV, the rug—had been either a gift from her father or a hand-me-down from her brother. She'd accepted all of them, because they were much, much nicer and less dangerous than anything she owned, but she hadn't wanted to. Trying to follow in their footsteps and win the Buckler Award was bad enough; she didn't want to be reminded of their achievements every time she had to sleep on the couch because she was too drunk to make it from the front door to her bedroom.

Just then, something inside the couch emitted a strange, strangled groan. Cissy decided that she was OK with living in her brother's shadow in this particular aspect of life.

A knock came from the front door and Cissy went to open it. On the way, she glanced in the hallway mirror to see how she looked. Her hair was ruffled and her shirt was grass stained from when she'd tripped on a raccoon in Scott Brixon's yard. She thought about changing it and brushing her hair, before realizing that impressing the kind of guys who were about to willingly make her couch a part of their home probably shouldn't be her goal.

Cissy opened the door. "You guys here for the couch?" she asked.

"We're here for *a* couch," said Vance.

"What?"

"Vance, just give her the money and let's get out of here," said Cormac.

Vance chuckled. "Don't mind him . . ." He paused, waiting for Cissy to introduce herself.

"Cissy," she offered.

"Don't mind him, Cissy," said Vance. "He's just angry because he's now unable to do the one thing he truly enjoyed and excelled at, due to a freak accident. Now where's this couch?"

Cissy gestured with her mimosa for the two of them to come inside.

"Would either of you like a mimosa?" she asked. "I'm going to top mine off."

"I'd love one," said Cormac.

"A little too early for me, thanks," said Vance, as he made a beeline for the couch. "I'll just take a glass of champagne."

Cissy walked to the kitchen. She refilled her drink, fixed one for Cormac, and poured some champagne for Vance. When she came back, Vance was flopped on the couch, running his hands along the top of the backrest.

"Yes, this is nice" Vance said, sounding impressed. "What is this, Naugahyde?"

"No, it's some sort of horrible Russian fabric that you shouldn't—"

"I've always wanted to own something Naugahyde," said Vance, not listening.

Cissy handed Cormac and Vance their drinks. Vance downed his in one sip from his prone position and quickly fell asleep. Cormac rolled his eyes and thanked Cissy.

"I guess he wanted to test it out," he said. "I'm Cormac."

"It's nice to meet you, Cormac," said Cissy.

"This is a good mimosa."

"Thanks. I've had four already." Cissy instantly wondered why she had told him that, and also why she had lied and said she'd had four instead of the actual number, seven.

"Yeah, I feel like it's going to be one of those days, too," said Cormac.

"Don't let Cormac bum you out, Cissy," said an evidently now-awake Vance. "He's been a bit of a grump since his finger got severed."

Cissy looked at Cormac's hand and noticed his missing finger for the first time. She let out an involuntary gasp.

"I'm sorry," she said, kind of embarrassed. "It's just . . . well it looks like that probably hurt. What happened?"

"Look, before we get into that, we will take this fine piece of furniture," said Vance, popping up from the couch. "Don't want to risk her giving us the heave-ho once she hears your crazy story, Mac. The ad said ten dollars?"

"Right," said Cissy, taking the crumpled bill that Vance was offering her. "Crazy story? What kind of a crazy story?"

"Well, you're probably not going to believe this," sighed Cormac.

"Cissy, have we met before?" interrupted Vance. "Maybe you were in my . . ." Vance trailed off as he tried to remember a class he'd taken. "I dunno, you look familiar."

"Sorry, Vance, I don't think so. Cormac, you were saying?"

Cormac downed the rest of his mimosa and handed Cissy his glass. She looked uncertain what to do with it.

"Well, ever since Wednesday, every time I go to sleep I wake up in the nineteenth century on a whaling ship called the *Levyathan*. Spelled with a *y*."

Cormac related all the events of the past few days to Cissy: Ziro, Captain Anson, the two whales he'd successfully killed, the rum, the scrimshaw, the ocean, the stars, the storm, and, finally, his unfortunate accident.

"So that's why we couldn't pick up the couch last night," Cormac explained sheepishly. "Because I was in the 1800s and Vance was . . . Well I don't know what Vance was doing last night."

"If you must know, I was engaged in a turf war with some raccoons over a particularly choice garbage can at this guy Scott Brixon's house."

Cormac was irritated that he didn't find this shocking.

Vance stopped talking and his eyes widened. He pointed at Cissy. "That's where I know you from! I saw you hiding in the bushes!"

"Look, never mind that," said Cissy. She turned her attention back to Cormac. "Cormac, this story is fascinating. I know this may put you on the spot, but I'm a reporter for the *School Paper*."

Vance suddenly appeared between them. He slung an arm around Cissy's shoulder. "A reporter, eh? Well there's a certain construction project going on in a living room on Craymore Street that I think is the very definition of newsworthy. While this guy here sails the seven seas, yours truly has been building stadium seating couches."

"Stadium seating couches?" Cissy said, intrigued. She couldn't believe her luck! She was staring down what could be her final deadline, and two scoops had just fallen into her lap. When it rains, it pours! "Well if it's OK with you two, I'd love to come by the house and interview both of you sometime."

"How does now work for you?" asked Vance.

"Perfect," said a relieved Cissy.

"Great!" said Vance.

Cormac faked a smile. Cissy chugged the rest of her mimosa. Something inside the couch groaned.

* * *

Later that evening, Cormac found himself sitting next to Cissy on the airborne section of the completed stadium seating couches. He dangled his legs off the ledge, and, for the first time all day, felt relaxed.

Moving the couch had been surprisingly uneventful. They hadn't brought any rope with them, so after they balanced the couch on top of the Volvo, Vance volunteered to lie on top of it while Cormac drove. He claimed that this would weigh the couch down and prevent it from flying off the car's roof. Cormac doubted the physics of that claim, but couldn't articulate a reason that Vance shouldn't risk his life for a ten-dollar couch.

Cissy had proven to be a major asset during the journey home. Fueled by journalistic pride and booze, she drove ahead of Cormac, honking at oncoming traffic to make sure that they allowed the

Volvo ample clearance. At one point in time, she tried to lead them on a shortcut through a city park. Cormac didn't think the couch could handle an off-road journey, so he stuck to the road. Cissy later confirmed that she'd actually just nodded off at the wheel. She said that she'd hit a goose, and would prefer not to discuss it.

Once they arrived home, Cormac and Cissy simply got out of Vance's way and let him complete his masterpiece. He had singlehandedly hauled the couch to the front door before Cormac could take the keys out of the ignition. Cormac had heard of mothers who performed adrenaline-fueled feats of strength when their children were in danger, and Vance appeared to be operating in a similar gear. Cormac wondered where this power had been during the time sophomore year when they'd seen an *actual* child pinned underneath a car. Instead of helping the mother, who was futilely trying to lift her SUV, Vance had pointed out to Cormac that when the panicked mom bent over, you could see the top of her thong.

Once Vance had the new couch positioned, he had to address the issue of the ice block, which was no longer large enough to hold up the airborne couch. He asked Cissy if she could mop up the melted water, and gestured for Cormac to move the ice block outside. When Cormac came back inside, Vance was propping the couch up on a full-size blacksmith's anvil. Baffled, Cormac asked him where he had obtained the anvil, and Vance just said, "I know a guy." Cormac wanted to snap that a back-alley anvil dealer might be the lamest illicit connection he had ever heard of, but instead he just quietly acknowledged that it was indeed a more permanent solution than a block of ice.

When it was done, they opened beers to celebrate, and Cissy offered to spring for pizza with the money they'd given her for the couch. When it arrived, they tried to offer Vance a slice, but he politely declined. He'd spent the rest of the afternoon lying on the grounded couch with a far-off, contented expression on his face, slowly sipping his way through six or seven beers. From his seat on the airborne couch, Cormac thought that this might be the happiest he had ever seen his roommate.

"So," said Cissy as she flipped through the pad she'd been jotting down notes on. "I think I've got the basics down. But maybe I could ask you some more personal questions about your experience on the *Levyathan*?"

"Shoot," said Cormac as he took a sip from his beer. "As long as they're not about the damn poop deck."

Cissy crossed out the first question on her list.

"OK," she continued, undeterred. "Well how about this: I think that for most people, if they went back in time, their first thought would be how they could make some money out of it. Do you think there's any way for us, I mean for you, to profit from all of this?"

"I'm certainly not opposed to it," said Cormac. "But I'm not really sure what's feasible."

Cissy chewed on her pen and thought it over. "What if you put some money in the bank and let it collect a hundred and fifty years' worth of interest?"

Cormac shook his head. "There're no banks at sea. And if we ever do get a day of shore leave who knows if there will be time in between all the prosti—" He cut himself off. Stupid! "Prosti-thetic legs. Prosthetic legs, you know, peg legs, that we have to replace for the whalers. Lots of peg legs on nineteenth-century whalers."

"Good save," said Cissy with a smile. "Well what if you bet on something? A sporting event that you already know the outcome of?"

"I don't know how I'd do it from the middle of the ocean. And what would I bet on? Fisticuffs? Velocipede racing? Basketball won't even be invented for twenty years!" lamented Cormac.

"What if you bet the whalers that it was going to be invented?" Cissy wondered.

"Look, I'm constantly in danger of being thrown overboard by these guys as it is. I can't go around acting like I'm smarter than them!"

Cissy was stumped. "Well . . . can you bring anything back with you? If you went to sleep with some doubloons or pieces of eight in your pocket, would they still be there when you woke up?"

"I don't know," sighed Cormac. "I don't think the whalers have been paid in weeks. I'm not sure if there's any money on the ship."

"Well, congratulations, Cormac," said Cissy, exasperated. "You've found the one situation where going back in time gives you no financial advantage whatsoever."

"It's probably for the best, Mac," said Vance from down below. "Now that we've got things just the way we like them here, we don't need you screwing them up by disrupting the space-time continuum." Vance blew his nose on a McDonald's bag that he had found under a couch cushion and threw it on the floor.

"So . . . I've noticed you keep glancing over at that guitar in the corner," said Cissy. "When are you going to pick it up and find out if you can still play?"

Cormac had been putting this off ever since he woke up. He already knew the answer, but was hoping that if he never picked up a guitar again, he might be able to coast by on a whispered reputation as a legendary "one that got away" for the next three decades, upon which point in time he'd get inducted into the Rock and Roll Hall of Fame and be issued a supermodel.

But now his hand was forced. He gestured for Vance to bring him the guitar. Vance rolled off the couch, retrieved the instrument, and handed it to Cormac with a solemn look on his face. Cormac strapped it over his shoulder and took a deep breath. He looked at Cissy, then Vance. Vance nodded.

Cormac launched into the solo he had debuted at Uncle Jemima practice the night before he woke up on the *Levyathan*. Fingering the strings, once the most natural thing in the world, felt foreign to him. His ring and middle fingers had to stretch to reach places his pinky once controlled. The physical strain, combined with the severe concentration this new technique required, was intense, and Cormac soon found himself sweating.

But something was happening. He was missing some notes, sure, but he was still *playing*. Slowly at first, but as he grew more comfortable, he was able to play at something resembling a normal speed. Cormac found himself getting lost in the music, the way he always used to when he was playing guitar. Soon, he wasn't even hearing the solo, he was just *feeling* it. And as he wrapped up after a minute or so, he was filled with a renewed energy, a passion he hadn't felt toward music in years.

"Wow," said Vance. "That was really terrible."

Cormac looked over at Cissy, who looked like she'd just seen a car accident.

"I was trying to figure out a way to tell you this earlier, Mac," continued Vance. "But we voted you out of the band when you missed practice yesterday. To be honest, this makes it a lot easier. For us, of course. Certainly not for you."

Vance tugged suggestively at the waist of his pants and pointed his chin toward Cissy. "Cissy, I'm up for it if you are. My room's at the end of the hall."

"Thanks, Vance," she said, as she carefully lowered herself down from the airborne couch. "But I'm going to need to pound out this article tonight."

"Consider it a standing offer," said Vance. "Mac? Enjoy the boat tomorrow." Vance walked down the hall toward his bedroom.

Cissy looked at Cormac. He was still sweating and his feet dangled off the couch at her eye level. Cormac had been planning to propose the same thing to Cissy but felt kind of sleazy about it now.

"You really think you're going to wake up there again tomorrow?" Cissy asked.

Cormac silently nodded his head, then looked down at the guitar he held in his hands. He attempted to fret a C7 chord, but stopped short of actually strumming it when he saw Cissy wincing.

"If it's any consolation," Cissy said, "I really think my editor's going to hate this story."

"Why the hell would that provide me with consolation?" asked Cormac.

"Well, we don't get along."

Cormac didn't understand.

"So, me turning in a really good story would irritate him because he doesn't want to see me succeed."

Cormac stared.

"And I think this is a really good story."

Cormac strummed a C7 that was so off-key, one of Vance's empty beer bottles shattered.

"I should probably go," said Cissy. "Do you need any help getting down?"

"Sure," said Cormac. He sat there for a second. Cissy didn't move.

"So should I get Vance or a ladder or something?" asked Cissy.

"You know what, don't worry about it," said Cormac. "I'm not really in a rush to fall asleep anyways."

Cissy made her way to the door, stepping around beer bottles, pizza boxes, electrical cords, and the anvil. It had certainly been one of the more interesting days, not only of her journalism career, but of her whole time at Harrington. But now the hard part was going to be writing it all down before the *School Paper* went to press. Usually this close to a deadline, she'd plagiarize something similar that she found online, but this time she figured the odds were against anything turning up about travelling back in time to nineteenth-century whaling ships.

Before Cissy opened the door, she turned to Cormac. "This was fun. Will you let me know if there are any further developments? I'm sure our readers will be interested in how you're doing."

Cormac nodded. "I hope any future updates are a bit more mundane," he said, waggling his mangled hand.

Cissy was halfway out the door before she turned to say one last thing. "Hey Cormac . . ."

Cormac looked up at her.

Cissy made an awkward shooting gesture with her right hand. "Harpoon one of them whales for me," she said. "For ol' Cissy."

"Are you trying to steal our DVD player?" Cormac asked.

Cissy sheepishly set the DVD player down in the doorway and ran to her car.

DAY SIX

At 4:55 a.m., Dean Bickerstaff rolled out of bed and lit a cigar. He took a long, satisfying puff, then walked to his bedroom window. The dean's house was on a hill that overlooked the entire Harrington campus. From his bedroom window he could gaze down on the entirety of his domain. He could watch the tiny campus slowly begin to pulse with life in the morning, and he could watch it extinguish its lights one by one at night. And best of all, he could do it naked.

The dean had been rising earlier than usual ever since the board issued their ultimatum. Upping the school's X-Factor ranking was not something that was going to be accomplished by working nine to five. He would have to rise with the chickens, go to bed with the alcoholics, and think with the mental dexterity of some sort of alcoholic superchicken. The dean was worried he was getting a touch sleep deprived.

Outside, the Harrington campus was lit by streetlights and porch lights. Come finals week, this time of night would see car headlights and the activity of cramming students, but for now, the night belonged to Frampton Q. Bickerstaff.

Actually, that wasn't entirely true. A small subset of the Harrington student body shared this ungodly hour with him. A band of outsiders that Frampton loathed. A desperate, degenerate group that insisted on disturbing the serenity of his mornings with their braying and lies. A collective of snake oil peddlers and flim-flam men that had posed one of the only checks to his autonomy in all his years at Harrington. And if his watch was set correctly, they were about to subject him to another bout of their harassment right about . . . now.

Frampton heard a thump on his doorstep and went to retrieve his copy of the *School Paper*.

He grabbed his shillelagh on the way out of the bedroom and was halfway to the door before he realized he'd forgotten his robe. The dean stopped in his tracks. This was a mini crisis. Turning around would cost him precious seconds of berating the *School Paper* paperboy. But doing so in the nude was not something he could afford to do again, not when the board was watching him like a hawk.

The dean waddled back to his room and threw on a robe. He cinched it around his waist and shuffled back to the front door. He threw it open, and sure enough, a copy of the bulky Sunday edition of the *School Paper* was lying on his front doorstep. The dean scanned the darkness until he saw the bright, flickering LED light of the paperboy's bike. Frampton shook his shillelagh at his distant adversary. Regardless of whether the paperboy could see it, the dean felt it helped his berating.

"Dump your lies elsewhere you media jackals! I'm cutting all funding for your muckraking rag! I got your fourth estate right here!" To emphasize this last remark, the dean turned and bent over. He lifted the back of his robe and repeatedly thrust the shillelagh toward his bare butt. After a couple seconds of this he realized that to any passersby, it would look like he was just sodomizing himself with a stick instead of taking a stand against yellow journalism. He quickly covered up and turned around.

"Did anybody see that?" he yelled to the darkness. Somewhere near the end of his driveway, a bicycle bell rang in affirmation.

"Dammit," muttered the dean as he picked up his copy of the paper and walked inside. He shuffled down the hallway to the kitchen, where he threw the paper down on the table and popped a pod into the coffee maker. Frampton impatiently puffed his cigar as the coffee brewed and snatched up the mug the second it was done. He inhaled deeply, then took a seat at the table.

This was where Dean Frampton Q. Bickerstaff had spent most of his time since his meeting with the board. He'd established a command center with everything he needed within reach: coffee, cigars, brandy, shillelagh, TV remote, and his laptop. So far, he was having quite a bit of trouble formulating a plan to increase Harrington's X-Factor ranking.

The X-Factor! Dean Bickerstaff snorted with contempt. Obviously, *College Review* had cooked it up as a desperate attempt to appear relevant to a new crop of applicants who had lived with the internet their entire lives. The fact that something as laughable as "online buzz, social media presence, and assorted high-tech miscellany" rankings could decide where a parent would send tens of thousands of tuition dollars sickened Bickerstaff. Did *Chinese* universities give a damn about their social media presence? Of course they didn't! They were too busy stringing up nets to prevent their overworked students from leaping to their deaths! Bickerstaff didn't much care for the nets (he thought they indicated softness), but he admired the conditions that led to them becoming a necessity. Also, social media was outlawed by the state there.

But like it or not, Bickerstaff's job now depended on his ability to increase Harrington's X-Factor. Bickerstaff interpreted this to mean their online reputation. When MIT students designed a robot that could play Skee-Ball, a video of it went viral, and the school's reputation as a hotbed of innovation increased. When protestors at Berkeley got maced, the entire internet's attention seemed focused on their campus. A kid might read some blog post about schools like these and decide that's where he wanted to go to college. Somehow, Bickerstaff had to get Harrington's name out there.

And as far as Dean Bickerstaff was concerned, if you were going to conquer the online world, there was no better way to start than by reading the newspaper.

The dean took a final puff from his cigar and stubbed it out as he eyed the Sunday edition of the *School Paper*. Frampton hated few things in life more than the *Harrington School Paper*. Because of this hatred, he had read every issue cover to cover for the past two decades. He perceived personal slights in every column inch and challenges to his power in every headline. He believed the single-panel comic *Marvelous Mr. Yux* to be the most treasonous thing he'd ever read, at least since the previous day's *Marvelous Mr. Yux*.

The hatred for the paper was based on the irreconcilable schism between Dean Bickerstaff's desire to operate corruptly and the *School Paper*'s tendency to call attention to the fact that his actions were beyond the reach of his power and often a federal crime. After a few of his schemes had been foiled by *School Paper* editorials, Frampton had begun to detect a hidden anti-dean agenda in every issue. He'd taken to writing letters under assumed names, blasting the paper's biased journalism, scolding their communist leanings, and demanding the resignation of Mr. Yux. Unbeknownst to him, these screeds were collected in a folder labeled "Dean B. Letters," which had been passed down over the years from one amused editor to the next.

Dean Bickerstaff reached out and picked up the paper. He unfolded it with a snap and began to scan the front page for insubordination. The lead story was about repairs to a footbridge that, due to worker illness, would be completed three days behind schedule. The footbridge would continue to remain open to pedestrians, as it had for the duration of the minor repairs.

The dean was instantly furious. He had campaigned to have that bridge torn down eight years ago, and now here was the *School Paper*, rubbing this engineering triumph in his face. He made a note of the author's name in a journal he kept. Next to her name, he put three tally marks. Three marks meant a reporter had committed an egregious offense, resolvable only by the student's resignation, then a public apology followed by a flogging. It was the lowest-level violation in the dean's eight-tier system.

Scanning the rest of the front page revealed the *School Paper*'s standard array of hidden agendas and propaganda. Unable to help himself, Frampton flipped to *Marvelous Mr. Yux* on page A17. The downtrodden Mr. Yux was attempting to return a light bulb. Disgusted, Dean Bickerstaff tore the comic out of the paper, crumpled it into a ball, and threw it across the kitchen.

With a sigh, he dropped the paper to the table and lit up another cigar. It was as bad an issue as he could remember; even worse, so far there was nothing in it that he could possibly leverage toward upping Harrington's X-Factor ranking. Frampton got up and made another pod of coffee. It was 5:50 a.m.

When the coffee finished brewing, the dean walked back to the table and picked up the rest of the paper. Perhaps one of Harrington's pathetic sports teams had finally abandoned all pretenses of dignity and started suiting up a chimp. Something like that would certainly generate some "social media buzz."

Scanning the B section revealed no such acts of desperation from the Harrington athletic department. Bickerstaff turned the page to the "Student Life" section and almost flipped past it as a force of habit. But below the fold in the corner, an odd picture caught his eye. It was of a grubby looking student, wearing shorts and a t-shirt, sitting on a couch that was elevated several feet off the ground. Something about the kid's expression intrigued Dean Bickerstaff. The headline read: *Gone Whalin': Harrington Student Experiences Life Aboard Nineteenth-Century Whaling Ship. Seriously.* It was written by Cissy Buckler.

The dean read on.

Have you ever wanted to have an adventure on a whaling boat? Cormac McIlhenney (Junior, Undeclared) thought he might never get the chance, but lately this Harrington student has been setting sail on a journey that puts the Moby Dick in Moby Ridiculous!

The dean nearly set the paper on fire with his cigar after the first paragraph, but he forced himself to keep reading.

For reasons unexplained, this modern day Jonah has been waking up aboard the Levyathan *[sic], an 1800s whaling ship, every other morning. The strange journeys back in time, which McIlhenney swears are really happening, started Wednesday morning. McIlhenney's body remains in his bed, but he apparently exists on a separate plane in the past while his body lies in a comatose state.*

"It's crazy," said McIlhenney's roommate, Vance Stafford (Junior, Physical Education/History). "He'll just be lying there, and you can do whatever you want to him and he won't wake up."

McIlhenney reports that during his two days aboard the Levyathan, *he has personally harpooned two whales. "Of course I'd never shot a harpoon gun in my life, where the hell would I have shot a harpoon gun?" the marksman told the* School Paper. *But for the* Levyathan, *which had struggled in its whaling efforts before McIlhenney showed up on board, a hot hand with the harpoon can be the difference that separates the Ahabs from the A-hab nots.*

It's a story that seems straight out of Hollywood. You're probably reminded of the hit movie Free Willy. *But sadly, many parts of Cormac's journey do not resemble the storybook ending of* Free Willy, *but rather the sad parts of* Free Willy, *the parts before the storybook ending. Or perhaps one of the poorly received sequels,* Free Willy 2: The Adventure Home, *or* Free Willy 3: The Rescue. *Both were widely considered not as good as the original film, and that is more along the lines of what Cormac McIlhenney's experience has been like.*

The dean moved the lit end of his cigar closer to the paper.

Yesterday, in the midst of a storm that threatened to sink the boat, McIlhenney lost the pinky finger on his left hand when a harpoon rope wrapped around it and severed it. McIlhenney was quite inebriated at the time, but has managed to piece together that the captain cauterized the wound with a red-hot poker while several whalers held him down. The injury has already had ramifications back in the modern day: unable to play the guitar without the finger, McIlhenney has been given the boot from his band, Uncle Jemima.

McIlhenney is unsure why he started going back in time. "It just started happening," he says. "I didn't get hit on the head by a flowerpot and I wasn't cursed by any gypsies that I'm aware of. I can only hope that because it started randomly, it will end the same way."

In addition to losing the finger, McIlhenney says that his class attendance has suffered since he started spending 50 percent of his days aboard the ship. He hopes his professors will understand, and plans on contacting them soon to explain why he's been absent.

Fortunately for McIlhenney, his roommate Vance is there for him. "It's been tough for Mac, sure. It's been tough for all of us. I had to build most of the stadium seating couches by myself since he was on the boat that day. But I'm going to be there for him. I'm gonna make sure he's OK when he's lying there, and if that means missing classes on those days, then dammit, sometimes friendship just has to prevail. Put in that I got choked up there," the roommate said, getting choked up during the sentence before the last one.

Speaking off the record, McIlhenney admitted that he's been near tears several times during his ordeal and almost peed his pants when the captain of the Levyathan tried to make him walk the plank. Continuing to speak off the record, he confided to the School Paper when Vance was in the bathroom that he thought the stadium seating couches were "one of the stupidest ideas anyone has ever had" and that he "might accidentally knock them over the first time he was alone with them." He also indicated that he regretted giving Vance his monogrammed towel, a fact that seemed unrelated to the story, but I'll include it here for the sake of journalistic thoroughness.

Nevertheless, McIlhenney lets a ray of optimism shine through, acknowledging that the past few days have been a unique experience. "Sure, I've gotten to do something that nobody else alive ever has— because people stopped whaling because it was stupid and dangerous and pointless. And if they did still do it, they'd have real guns and they wouldn't eat hardtack!"

Suffice to say, after making the journey from dorm life and mid-term fails to horn pipes and big sperm whales, this is one Harrington Student who won't mind if you call him Ishmael. Buckler out.

It was the worst written article that Frampton Q. Bickerstaff had ever read in all his years as Harrington dean. It was also exactly the sort of story that might just save his job. The dean was dressed and out the door in three minutes.

As he drove his Lincoln Town Car down the hill toward the campus, the dean thought that if there was any truth to the incoherent drivel he had just choked down, it would be one of the more sensational things he'd ever encountered. The first person to ever actually travel back in time just happened to be a Harrington student. The school's name would be on the front page of every paper and website across the country. A media blitz would descend upon the Harrington campus and when it arrived, the face of the school would be there, cigar in mouth, to welcome the press with open arms.

By the time the dean turned onto Craymore Street, it was clearly going to be a beautiful day. The idiots he'd read about in the paper obviously weren't the type of students who got up before noon on the weekends, but Bickerstaff was not in the habit of operating on other people's schedules. He parked outside of the house that the university registrar indicated Cormac McIlhenney resided in. Based on the dismal exterior, the dean could already envision the horrors that awaited him inside. Rental-white walls, bong-water-stained carpets, rolls of paper towels next to empty toilet paper holders . . . But he'd have to grit his teeth and endure the squalor of these degenerates' daily lives if he wanted keep his job.

Frampton got out of the Lincoln and waddled up to the front door, careful to avoid the broken beer bottles that littered the front yard. He rapped on the door with his shillelagh and waited. No answer. He banged louder.

Eventually, there were some muffled sounds from inside. Footsteps gradually got closer to the door, but were interrupted by a loud bang. The person inside let out a cry of pain and then a frustrated "What the hell is the DVD player doing there!" Finally, the dean heard the deadbolt slide and the knob began to turn. He straightened up to his full five feet and tried to look official.

The person who answered the door was wearing only a towel.

"Is Cormac McIlhenney in?" asked Dean Bickerstaff.

"Yes. Actually, no. Well, kind of. He's . . . sleeping," said Vance.

"You must be Vance," said Frampton. Vance squinted and nodded warily. "Vance, I'm Dean Bickerstaff. Would you mind if I came in and asked you a few questions? Don't worry, you're not in any trouble."

Vance noticeably relaxed upon hearing this. "Of course not," he said. "Come on in."

Vance opened the door wider and gestured toward the living room. "Say," he said, sounding impressed. "That is one fine looking shillelagh."

Dean Bickerstaff grinned and stepped inside.

* * *

Before he opened his eyes, Cormac felt the gentle rocking of the ocean and knew he was back on the *Levyathan*.

He was disappointed, but it was a different kind of disappointed. Sure, he'd have *preferred* that the situation be different, but he really didn't *expect* that it would be. He'd felt this way before, when he bought a lottery ticket that didn't win the three hundred million dollar jackpot. Also, the time he and Vance had dressed up two stray cats like those fat twins in the *Guinness Book of World Records* and unsuccessfully tried to teach them to ride big wheels.

That seemed like a simpler time, Cormac thought as he rolled out of bed on the whaling ship, roughly 120 years before he was born.

The bunks surrounding him were full of snoring whalers, and it dawned on Cormac that this meant the *Levyathan* must have survived the storm. Things had seemed pretty grim by the time he passed out, but for all Cormac knew, being a whaler might mean dealing with storms like that once a week. The sleeping men were all certainly tougher than him, Cormac had no doubts about that. But he must have a leg up on them somewhere . . . What was the infant mortality rate in 1867? A heck of a lot lower than in 2013, that was for sure. He'd bring that up if anyone ever questioned his toughness. "You may be burly and know your knots, but most of you probably lost a child to a horrible disease before they turned two!" he'd tell them. "That kind of thing doesn't fly where I'm from! I bet very few of you can read either!"

Feeling rather smug, Cormac opened the door to the whalers' quarters and stepped outside. It was a beautiful morning: a touch brisk, but with a clear sky, a pleasant wind, and a calm sea. Toward the bow, a familiar figure stood with his back to Cormac, slowly swabbing a mop back and forth.

"Mornin', Ziro!" Cormac shouted. The former slave turned to face him as Cormac waved and walked over to one of the storage bins. "Think I'll hit the buffet!" he yelled over his shoulder to Ziro as he lifted the lid and observed the offerings inside. No surprises there, just salt pork and hardtack. Cormac hated to admit it, but there was a great chance that everything in his refrigerator back home was *less* edible than these two nautical staples that had been engineered to maximize shelf life and portability at the expense of all flavor and nutrition. He took one serving of each, and slipped an extra hardtack into his pocket for later.

Ziro was still staring at him when Cormac joined him at the bow.

"This stuff's pretty gross," said Cormac through a mouthful of hardtack. "Think I could get them to make it over easy some day?"

"All our hardtack is surplus from the war," said Ziro. "I believe it was made over five years ago in a factory in Ohio and the captain bought it in bulk on the black market from an unscrupulous railroad attendant who was later hanged. I don't think there's much room for customization."

Now it was Cormac's turn to stare. "I was kidding, Ziro," he said incredulously.

"Oh," said Ziro. They both looked out to sea, and Cormac took another bite of his breakfast.

"Looks like the *Levyathan* weathered the storm," Cormac remarked.

"She did," said Ziro. "That was one of the worst storms I've ever seen. And we wouldn't have survived it without you."

Cormac choked on his breakfast.

"Surprised?" asked Ziro. "Don't be, I'm not just blowing smoke. Without you we'd be writing our names in Davy Jones's ledger right now. First, you discovered the leak in the rum storage area. And then on top of that—"

At this point Ziro realized that Cormac hadn't just been taken aback by his compliment; he actually was choking on a piece of salt pork.

"Oh, for the love of God, Cormac," he said. He stepped behind Cormac and gave him three sharp smacks on his upper back. The chunk of salt pork shot out of Cormac's mouth and arched across the sky before it fell into the sea, where a whale quickly gobbled it up.

"You've got to be more careful! This is the third time you've nearly died!" lectured Ziro.

"Well, that was ridiculous!" Cormac said, still gasping for breath. "You call that a bite-size piece of salt pork?"

"Nobody ever said it was a bite-size piece of salt pork! You're supposed to slowly nibble it!"

"It's just so salty," said Cormac, sticking out his tongue and wiping it off with his fingers.

"What the hell does 'bite-size' even mean?" yelled Ziro.

"Gentlemen, gentlemen!" came a booming voice from behind them. "Let's not start arguing so early on such a beautiful morning!"

Cormac and Ziro turned to see Captain Anson striding toward them with a broad grin on his face. When he was ten feet away, the captain stopped and raised a hand to shield his eyes from the sun. He squinted, pretending not to be able to tell who was standing there. He pulled out his spyglass and peered through it.

"Is that . . . Could it be?" said the captain in mock surprise as he adjusted the spyglass focus back and forth. "Old nine-finger Cormac, hero of the *Levyathan*? Is he gracing us with his presence again? Do my eyes deceive me?"

"The lens cap is on your spyglass" said Ziro.

"Dammit, Ziro!" bellowed the captain. He quickly put the spyglass away and walked up to Cormac with his palm outstretched for a handshake. Cormac cautiously offered him his hand, and the captain pumped it furiously.

"You really saved our hides, Cormac," said the captain. "Without you we'd be writing our names in Davy Jones's ledger right now."

"I just told him that," protested Ziro.

"Well dammit, Ziro, you don't have a monopoly on hero thanking. I can thank a hero, too"

"No, I mean, I just told him exactly that. 'Without you we'd be writing our names in Davy Jones's ledger right now.' Those were my words. You copied me."

"I hardly think that's true. The phrase just popped into my head," said the captain.

"Well it is, and it didn't," replied Ziro.

"I've never heard you say that before," said the captain.

"*Everyone* heard me say it!" said Ziro. "You were going to dump Cormac's unconscious body overboard during the storm, and nobody else wanted to, so you made us take a vote, and we all outvoted you, and you still were going to do it so I slapped you and grabbed you by the collar and said 'For God's sake, captain, without him we'd be writing our names in Davy Jones's ledger right now!'"

"Well, I really don't think that Davy Jones is even known for keeping a ledger, so your phrase is stupid," said Captain Anson, ending the discussion.

"Excuse me," chimed in Cormac. "Why does everyone keep saying I'm a hero? I got drunk, nearly got killed, and then passed out."

"Well, I was trying to explain to you before," said Ziro, shooting Captain Anson a look. "But maybe I should just show you."

Ziro picked his mop back up and marched off toward the center of the boat. The captain gestured for Cormac to follow, and brought up the rear behind him. Ziro led the way to the rum storage area and stopped outside of the closed door. He turned to Cormac and started to explain.

"By the time you harpooned your whale, the leak you discovered was out of control and only getting worse. I think it could have caused irreversible damage if it had gone on for another half hour. It's a testament to the corners that were cut in the *Levyathan*'s construction and a major red flag that without severe improvements, we're essentially sailing around in a death trap that's eventually going to—"

Captain Anson cut Ziro off. "It turned out that your finger plugged the hole perfectly. You may not have meant to, but you saved the day, son." He thrust the door open. The rum storage area smelled mustier than usual, but it appeared to be completely dry. Toward the back corner, sticking out of the floor, was the unmistakable shape of Cormac's severed pinky finger.

Cormac took a step or two into the room, then turned to face the captain and Ziro.

"You just left it there?" he shrieked.

The captain and Ziro looked at each other.

"Well . . . yes?" said the captain.

"There's nothing else on the ship that could plug this up? I mean, in the heat of the moment, I can understand not being able to find something just the right size. But once the storm died down, you didn't bother to find a more permanent solution?"

"More permanent solution? I don't understand what you mean." Captain Anson was confused. "The salt water will preserve it. Kind of like a pickle. It'll last for years."

"You're going to keep that there for years. My finger. Sticking out of the rum storage area floor." Cormac thought that hearing this out loud would convince Anson and Ziro how stupid their idea sounded, but they just stared right back at him.

"What if a rat nibbles on it? What if it the heat causes it to shrivel up? What if lightning strikes it and it pops itself out and starts crawling around the ship, jamming itself up the nose of those who wronged it?"

"Well, over the years, none of those things have proved to be an issue," said the captain. "Knock on wood, of course."

A chill went down Cormac's spine. The captain didn't really mean what Cormac thought he meant, did he?

"Are you telling me that this is not the first time you've plugged a leak with a body part?"

Captain Anson slung an arm around Cormac's shoulders. "Cormac, when you're at sea, sometimes you just have to make do with what you've got," he said with a friendly tone. "In my time as captain of the *Levyathan*, I've washed my clothes in salt water. I've brushed my teeth with salt water . . . And yes, I've plugged a couple of leaks with severed body parts and left them that way for years."

"So your compromises either involve substituting salt water for regular water in minor hygienic tasks or *plugging holes with body parts*? Where are all these body parts coming from? Are there . . ." Cormac stopped short as another chill ran down his spine. "Are there any in the bunk room? Where I sleep, are there body parts stuck in the floor there?"

The captain chuckled and gave Ziro a 'can you believe this guy?' look. "Cormac, I'm not sure what kind of opulent palace you live in in the future. But the truth is, whaling is messy, dangerous work. Nobody *wants* to get swept overboard. Nobody *wants* to lose a limb. But the important thing is that all these men have signed waivers acknowledging that I am not responsible for any harm suffered due to anyone's negligence, especially mine."

"I never signed one of those," chimed in Ziro.

"I forged your signature while we were dragging your unconscious body aboard," said Captain Anson. He turned to Cormac and flashed him a grin.

Cormac involuntarily looked down at the missing finger on his left hand. "Which of those jugs are the breakfast rum?" he asked.

"Cormac, my boy," said Captain Anson, ignoring him. "What do you say we go and take a look at what's left of those whales you killed?"

Dean Frampton Q. Bickerstaff stared at the student who stood in front of him, trying to figure out why he was wearing a towel and desperately wishing he hadn't let him touch his shillelagh. After Vance had let Frampton into the house, all he wanted to talk about was the dean's shillelagh. He studied the knots with great interest, and kept talking about how he'd been thinking about getting one for a long time. The shillelagh typically drew worried looks from adults and made children cry, so the dean was happy that someone was showing it the respect that he knew it deserved. But he was also careful to subtly dissuade Vance from pursuing this particular affectation. Dean Bickerstaff loved being *The* Guy With the Shillelagh. He had no desire to be *One of Those* Guys With a Shillelagh.

Vance was so focused on the shillelagh that he seemed to have forgotten that the dean was even there. Frampton was happy to humor the degenerate for a while, but he eventually had to get down to business. Vance was acting out some strange role-playing that involved hobbling around the living room, hunched over with one eye squeezed shut, using the shillelagh to whack away invisible goats. After a few minutes of watching this, the dean cleared his throat.

"Er, Vance? Is it true that you are the man who put this structure together?" Vance snapped out of his fantasy as Dean Bickerstaff gestured toward the couches with his shillelagh.

"That's correct, sir," said Vance, reluctantly handing the shillelagh back over to its owner. "Stadium seating couches. Been sort of a lifelong goal of mine."

It was one of the stupidest things the dean had ever seen. "Very impressive," he intoned while sizing up the furniture. "Looks comfortable." It looked like a death trap. "I can really see the advantages of a system like this." The board must never learn that Harrington students were spending their free time on projects like this. "I may have to get you to do one in my living room." Surely this marked a low point for mankind.

"Yeah, it's pretty bitchin,'" Vance said proudly. "You wanna test her out? I downloaded bootlegs of some movies that are still in theaters. You can hear Russian people talking in the background, but you start to tune it out after a while."

Vance started to pull himself up onto the elevated couch but the dean interrupted his ascent.

"Vance, would you mind if I took a look at your roommate? The faculty at Harrington is very concerned that one of our students is in this odd situation."

Vance shrugged and led him down the hallway to Cormac's bedroom. Frampton stepped around beer bottles, junk food wrappers, and other assorted debris as he followed. When they arrived at Cormac's bedroom door, Vance turned the knob and pushed it open. He gestured for Frampton to enter, and the dean did as he was directed.

As Vance walked into the room behind him, Dean Bickerstaff peered down at Cormac's comatose body. Vance turned on a desk lamp, then walked over to the window to move aside the bedsheet that functioned as a curtain in order to let more light in.

"So that's pretty much Mac," said Vance, as he tried to get the sheet curtain to stay open. "Every other day at least. He'll just lie there. It's like he's asleep, but he just won't wake up no matter what."

Vance was right. If Dean Bickerstaff didn't know any better, he would have just assumed that the young man in front of him was asleep. His eyes were shut and he lay perfectly still except for the deep, slow breaths he drew regularly. Unable to control his curiosity, the dean raised his shillelagh and gave Cormac's midsection a few quick pokes with it.

Having secured the sheet, Vance turned around just in time to see the dean quickly pull the shillelagh away and act like he hadn't been doing anything.

"No, don't worry," Vance assured the dean. "He doesn't feel a thing. Trust me, I've tried a ton of stuff. You can poke him, blow hot air in his face, nothing. Even loud noises." Vance walked over to Cormac's desk and tapped a few keys on his computer. The opening notes of Chris De Burgh's "Lady In Red" started to play from the speakers and Vance turned the volume up as loud as it would go.

"I CRANKED IT UP TO THE POINT WHERE IT WAS RATTLING THE WINDOWS," Vance shouted to the dean. "MADE IT ALL THE WAY THROUGH THE SONG AND HE DIDN'T EVEN STIR."

"YOU SAT ALONE IN A ROOM WATCHING YOUR ROOMMATE SLEEP WHILE YOU LISTENED TO 'LADY IN RED'?" Dean Bickerstaff shouted back.

Vance quickly shut off the song.

"Look, Deano," he said. "The point is that I don't think he's making this kind of thing up. I've seen Mac sleep until six in the evening when he's been really hungover. But even then he'd wake up to puke or just kind of lie there and groan."

Dean Bickerstaff turned his attention back to Cormac's body. He gave it a few more pokes with his shillelagh just to satisfy his curiosity. The situation in the squalid little house on Craymore Street was even better than he had hoped. Short of an outright fraud, which the unconscious, fingerless student did not appear to be, the only thing that could have stood in the way of his plans was the roommate.

A caring and compassionate cohabitator would have made things very difficult for Dean Bickerstaff. In order to exploit this victim for the maximum possible gain, he was going to require unquestioning obedience and he'd need to lie quite a bit to the people providing him with it. Fortunately, in Vance he had found someone who was not only devious and insensitive to the needs of others, but also obviously weak willed, who the dean could manipulate like a puppet master.

Frampton dug his index finger into his ear to clean out some wax that had come loose while "Lady In Red" blared. "So you think he'll wake up tomorrow?" he asked Vance.

Vance yawned. "I guess so. That's the way it's happened so far."

"And what do you think the explanation is for this condition?" the dean asked. "What has Cormac's doctor said?"

"Doctor?" asked Vance.

"Yes, his doctor. When your roommate regularly started spending entire days in a vegetative state in which he'd be transported to a whaling ship over a hundred years ago, what did the doctor you called in to examine him say?"

Vance looked confused.

"When he got one of his fingers severed, what theories did the trained medical professional who treated his mutilated hand put forth about why this might be happening?"

Vance shrugged and scratched himself under the towel.

"He hasn't seen a doctor?" the dean asked, bewildered.

"Look, Deano, doctors are expensive and waiting rooms are disgusting. Also, there was a booth during orientation that would give you a free t-shirt if you signed away your health insurance rights, so Cormac and I both did that."

Frampton shook his head in disgust. "It was an outrage that that guy's booth was allowed to operate as long as it did." The shadowy man, whom the dean presumed was some sort of exiled war criminal, had provided Frampton a healthy kickback to allow the booth on campus.

"So neither of you have health insurance?" Dean Bickerstaff asked. Vance gave a big thumbs down. Outside, the dean tried to look sympathetic. Inside, he was twirling his shillelagh with glee. No insurance, no plans, no money. Exploiting these two desperate idiots was going to be even easier than he'd thought!

"Vance," said Dean Frampton Q. Bickerstaff. "I think I know someone who can help."

* * *

The cold storage area of the *Levyathan* was larger than Cormac could have imagined. It seemed like it must take up the entire below-deck area of the ship. Cormac didn't think he'd be able to throw a tennis ball from one end to another. In fact, *walking* from one end to another seemed like a bit more effort than he wanted to expend at the moment.

The cavernous storage area seemed even bigger at the moment because of how little was actually being stored there. What Cormac assumed were the remains of his two whales were way off in a distant corner. The room appeared to have been optimistically designed to hold over a hundred whales, but aside from the two he'd already harpooned, the blocks of ice that kept the room cool, and a few jugs of surplus rum, it was empty.

"Hello!" shouted Captain Anson, who grinned as his voice echoed off the far walls of the storage area. "I love that sound," he chuckled.

"It sounds like a hollow reminder of our collective failure," said Ziro.

"Dammit, Ziro!"

"It *is* pretty depressing," agreed Cormac. "I kind of wish you hadn't brought me down here."

"Shut up, both of you," snapped the captain. "It's not hollow, it's full of promise! It's a blank canvas that we have a chance to paint every morning! Why must we fill the cold storage room with the hacked-up carcasses of whales? Because it's there, dammit!"

Captain Anson's emphatic last words echoed throughout the chamber. Cormac took a second look at the giant room and tried to imagine it full. For a split second, he was able to lose himself in the possibility of chunks of valuable, glistening whale blubber, as far as the eye could see. It was awe inspiring.

In the distance, an object rolled by and snapped him back to the reality of the dismal, empty room.

"Is that a tumbleweed?" asked Cormac.

"Dammit!" shouted the captain. "How do those keep getting down here?" He ran after the tumbleweed as it rolled across the empty storage area.

"Weren't you going to show Cormac the whales he caught?" Ziro yelled after him.

Captain Anson caught up to the tumbleweed and gave it a kick. It sailed twenty feet in the air, then rolled off again once it hit the ground. The captain turned, breathing slightly heavier, and motioned for Cormac and Ziro to follow him over to the remains of the two whales.

The two gigantic mammals had been rendered unrecognizable by the saws and knives of the *Levyathan*'s crew. The slices of blubber were stacked three times Cormac's height. Piles of bones that hadn't yet been claimed for scrimshaw were neatly arranged next to them. The two titanic rib cages were still intact, and placed end to end they formed an eerie tunnel. Cormac walked beneath it and looked up at the ribs of the animals he'd shot.

"Pretty spectacular, huh?" asked Ziro as he joined Cormac beneath the rib cage. Cormac nodded.

Captain Anson pointed out the baleen, which the whales used to strain for krill. "Filthy stuff," he said. "Krill and shrimp get stuck in it—it's all bristly and gross. I don't know why we just don't throw it overboard as soon as we cut it out."

"It's used for bows, parasols, and corsets," said Ziro. "Pound for pound, it's one of the most valuable parts of the whale."

Captain Anson moved on, seemingly not having heard the former slave. "This pile is various organs. We'll grind those up and use them for chum. This is blubber, this is meat . . ." Ziro tapped Cormac on the shoulder and silently mouthed "meat" and pointed to the stack that the captain had identified as blubber, then "blubber" and pointed to what the captain had said was meat.

"Blubber from one whale can keep an entire town's oil lamps lit for a year," the captain continued. "Every time the sun goes down and the lamps start to light up, it's a reminder of man's triumph over nature's abominations. Goddammit, it's beautiful."

Cormac found himself agreeing with the captain. He ran the remaining fingers on his left hand along one of the overhead ribs as they walked. It kind of smelled down here and the whale meat looked revolting, but he was proud of the fact that none of it would be here without him. Cormac had gone his entire life without triumphing over a final exam, let alone over nature's abominations. It felt pretty good.

"I think the skulls are over here if you want to stare into the lifeless void of their hollow eye sockets," the captain was saying. The butchered whales had gotten Captain Anson slightly worked up over the course of the tour. It sounded intriguing, but something else had caught Cormac's attention. Off in the corner, apart from the rest of the tidily arranged whale parts, a handwritten sign was nailed to the wall. It said "discard," and beneath it were two long, thick cuts of whale.

"What's in the discard pile?" asked Cormac. "I thought you whalers would be like Indians. You know, using every part of the buffalo."

"Oh God, don't get him started on the buffalo," muttered Ziro.

Fortunately, the captain had wandered over to the skulls and hadn't heard him. Pride took over and Cormac reached down and picked up one of the pieces. He hated to see anything from his catches go to waste. The piece of whale was about eight feet long, and quite heavy, so Cormac lifted it in the middle and let it droop down on either side.

"I don't understand why you're just going to get rid of this," he yelled after the captain. "I mean, it looks tastier than that gross pile of meat over there." Cormac ran his hand along the underside of the whale piece. "Leaner, less fatty . . . I mean, cut this into steaks, sear 'em on either side, and eat them medium-rare. I think the whalers would enjoy that. Certainly beats the hell out of more hardtack. I mean, seriously, what's the rationale behind throwing away a perfectly good piece of—"

"That's the whale's penis," interrupted Ziro.

Cormac shouted in disgust as he dropped the gigantic penis onto the ground. It flopped onto his feet. He kicked his foot to shove it off, and the penis rolled onto the ground in front of him.

"How come you waited so long to tell me?" demanded Cormac.

"Why did you tell him at all?" shouted Captain Anson. "He would have eaten it!"

"God, that's disgusting!" Cormac shuddered as he glanced down at the whale penis. It lay on the floor, still gently quivering. "That thing is huge!"

"Actually," said Ziro, walking over and giving it a nudge with his foot. "This guy must have either been young or pretty unpopular with the female whales. This is the smallest one I've ever seen. We sometimes cut off ones that are three times this size."

"You still think we should save them, *admiral*?" asked the captain in a mocking tone. "Maybe tie them from the mast to show us which way the wind's blowing?" The captain chortled at this mental image. "By the look of that whale penis, it's coming in from the southeast at twelve knots! Ha!"

Cormac stared down at his hands, which were covered with a strange filmy substance. He shook his hands to try to flick it off, to no avail. Ziro noticed and dug a rag out of his pocket and handed it to Cormac. It was filthy, but whatever Cormac's hands were coated in, he didn't want it on his clothes. He took the rag from Ziro and wiped his hands on it.

"You're lucky nobody else saw you," said Ziro, waving off the rag when Cormac tried to return it. "Touching the discard pile is a good way to get thrown overboard. There was a rumor that one of the whalers used to sneak down here in the middle of the night and . . . do stuff with them . . . He got tossed overboard with the biggest whale penis I've ever seen tied around his neck like a noose."

"That has to be the worst way to die I've ever heard of," said Cormac.

"It was during Junior Whaler Week, so his two sons were on board and saw it happen," said Ziro.

"Yep, that was not one of my best ideas," said the captain, striding over between them. "Those kids did not leave with the best impression of the whaling industry. Or with a father . . ."

Captain Anson slung an arm around Cormac and the other around Ziro. "Gentlemen," he said with a grin. "These whales look lonely. What do you say we get them some company?"

The captain slapped them both on the back with a hearty laugh and strode off toward the cold storage area's exit. He was loudly humming "Treasures o' the Sea" until he caught himself and shouted, "Dammit, Ziro!"

Cormac looked at Ziro, who shrugged at him and turned to follow the captain. Cormac tossed the slimy rag into a corner, then hurried after Ziro toward the *Levyathan*'s main deck. The whale penis quivered slightly with each footstep.

* * *

Dean Frampton Q. Bickerstaff dangled his feet off the edge of the airborne couch and silently cursed the *College Review* and their X-Factor. The dean didn't care much for heights as a general rule; because of his short stature it always seemed like he had farther to fall. So even if the airborne couch had been constructed soundly, which it most certainly had not been, the dean would not have been thrilled about sitting on it. The fact that he was now wearing only a towel added to his uneasiness considerably.

Vance had been not-so-subtly nudging the dean toward the towel ever since it became apparent they'd be spending the afternoon together. As a powerful grown man, the dean had of course politely laughed off the initial suggestions. But Vance's demeanor had cooled noticeably as Dean Bickerstaff rebuffed his offers. Frampton had thought he might be able to ingratiate himself by agreeing to scale the stadium seating couches, but Vance seemed offended that the dean would even consider sitting on the couches without a towel on.

The dean couldn't risk losing Vance's trust at this point. He would prefer to exploit Cormac McIlhenney fully clothed, but if that wasn't going to be possible, then dammit, he'd have to go with the flow.

So, still not really certain why it was necessary, he'd agreed to change into a towel, and Vance perked up immediately. He'd darted off to the hall closet and retrieved a towel with a graphic of two kittens at the beach on it. Vance had cautioned the dean that the towel belonged to his roommate, and that Cormac wouldn't be happy if he found out someone else was wearing it while he was unconscious. The dean liked this. The shared deception meant he had earned a bit of Vance's trust. He had looked Vance in the eye and solemnly promised never to breathe a word of it to another human being. Then he went into the bathroom in the middle of the day and took off all his clothes.

When the dean emerged from the bathroom in the towel, Vance had glanced at him and immediately said, "You've got to take off your underwear, too." Dean Bickerstaff looked down. You couldn't see a trace of his underwear through the towel and nothing was sticking up around the waist. He'd decided he didn't want to know how Vance could tell. When he came back out holding a pile of his clothes that now included his boxer shorts, Vance gave him a smile and said, "There, isn't that better?"

From there, they'd gone to work getting the dean up onto the airborne couch. Frampton had tried to politely defer the superior couch to his host, but Vance wouldn't hear of it.

"House policy, Deano. First time visitors have to check out the view from the airborne couch."

Five minutes, a lot of huffing and puffing, and several cases of indecent exposure via towel flap later, the dean was on top of the couch. He looked around. He had to admit, the discarded pizza boxes that littered the floor did look slightly less depressing from up here. Vance flopped himself on the lower couch and grinned up at the dean.

"Kick back and relax, Deano! We lead the good life here."

Dean Bickerstaff gritted his teeth and attempted to kick back. He carefully swung his legs up onto the couch and slowly lowered himself into a prone position. Careful not to disturb the curtain of decency that was his towel, he carefully raised his hands and put them behind his head. He attempted to let out a sigh that he hoped would indicate to Vance how "chill" he found this situation, but it came out as more of a wheezing death rattle. Vance looked concerned, so the dean attempted to cover it up by pretending that it had been a mild cough, but because of his awkward stance on the couch, it triggered an actual coughing fit and he found himself gasping for air.

He sat bolt upright and gave himself a few whacks on the chest while signaling to Vance with the other hand that it wasn't anything serious. Once the coughing had subsided, Dean Bickerstaff, now red faced and sweating, looked down at Vance and gave him the A-OK sign. At this point, he noticed that his arm had broken out in a rash, which was definitely some sort of reaction to whatever microscopic substances were lurking in the couch upholstery.

"Yep," said Vance with a contented look. "The good life."

The dean sat and watched Vance lie there with a far-off expression for about five minutes before he realized that this was it. This was Vance's plan for their Sunday afternoon. The dean was all for immersing himself in Cormac and Vance's lifestyle, but in order to be here he had blown off a meeting to discuss evil deeds that had negative environmental consequences with a state representative, so he would have preferred his afternoon be a bit more ambitious. Eventually he broke the silence.

"Sure is nice up here, Vance," he said.

"You're telling me, Deano," Vance said.

This "Deano" business had crept up so suddenly that the dean hadn't had time to put a stop to it. He feared it was too late now. The dean loathed the trappings of familiarity, none more so than the casual nickname. He'd once struck a man in the kneecap with his shillelagh because he referred to him as "Ol' Hoss" when serving him a drink in an airport bar. He would have done the same to Vance if he didn't need his cooperation. He'd have to figure out a way to nip it in the bud while still seeming "chill," but for now, Frampton bit his lip and soldiered on.

"You know what would really make this perfect, Vance?" the dean asked. It could be a colossal blunder serving up a blank slate to Vance like this. The dean feared his response. Visions of TBS action movies and delivery chicken wings flitted through his mind. But he was already sitting in nothing but a towel on a couch five feet off the ground, and he wondered if his Sunday could really get any more dismal.

Vance's face brightened immediately. "You read my mind, Deano! Couch beers it is!"

It was only 11:15, but Frampton had to admit that this was probably the best outcome he could have hoped for.

Vance stood from the couch and stretched. Towel-clad movements like this still made the dean very uneasy, but obviously Vance had much more experience in this wardrobe, and the towel appeared not to be going anywhere. Vance started to head for the kitchen, but had an idea and stopped after a couple of steps.

"You think your friend wants a beer, Deano?"

The friend Vance was referring to was Dr. Moira Franklin. She wasn't a friend of Dean Bickerstaff's, he was blackmailing her. And she had now been examining Cormac for the better part of an hour.

"I don't think so," the dean said, not sure if Vance was joking or not.

Vance looked confused. It was as if the dean had told him that Dr. Franklin didn't want a hundred dollar bill.

"She's not here for fun, Vance," Frampton explained. "She's a doctor, and she's examining a patient."

Blank stare.

"Your roommate!" the dean shouted. "Dr. Franklin is examining your roommate, who is lying in bed unconscious due to an extremely serious medical condition!"

Vance nodded his head, pretending to understand why any of this would prevent Dr. Franklin from having a pre-noon beer.

"So . . . you think I should ask her before I open one?"

"Just get two damn beers!" Dean Bickerstaff yelled. As Vance scurried out of the room the dean furiously itched his arm.

Once Vance had revealed that his lack of health insurance prevented Cormac from seeking medical attention, the dean had quickly formulated a plan. Dr. Franklin had been in his pocket ever since he had caught her falsifying her transcript when applying to medical schools as a Harrington undergrad. She had been falsifying her transcript using a transcript-falsifying service that the dean had started over a decade ago. The dean had been looking to step up his bribe receiving and Harrington students were being turned down from graduate programs at an all-time-high rate. It was a win/win for everybody in the equation who was named Frampton Q. Bickerstaff.

For a modest fee, a Harrington student could bump up their GPA to a level that graduate, law, and medical school admissions would find more appealing. For a substantially higher fee, they could do this without owing Dean Bickerstaff a lifetime of servitude if they didn't want their scandalous secret revealed. Most students opted not to purchase this second tier of pricing, because it was not advertised. The dean preferred the first tier anyway. It never hurt to have a future doctor or lawyer owe their entire career to you.

Dr. Franklin was one of his earliest success stories. After med school, she'd gone on to a mediocre career as a general practitioner. Her ascension to the top of the medical profession had been somewhat hampered by the fact that Dean Bickerstaff expected her to drop whatever she was doing any time he needed the services of a doctor. At best, this meant an interrupted dinner or a few less hours of sleep. At worst, it meant that patients waiting to find out how long they had to live sat alone in a waiting room for hours while Dr. Franklin dashed off to help the dean after he'd accidentally ingested shampoo.

The dean had called her in today to examine Cormac. He didn't really care what the diagnosis was, but he thought that the gesture of free medical attention would endear him to both the unconscious student and his roommate. Vance had seemed skeptical of the idea of a doctor examining Cormac without his consent, but once Dean Bickerstaff suggested that Dr. Franklin might prove exceedingly generous with her prescription pad, Vance was on board. The dean opposed free medical care for anyone with every fiber of his being, but like most of his principles, it was one he was always willing to compromise for the most minor of personal gains.

Obviously, it wasn't a routine examination, but the dean had still hoped it wouldn't take too long. Dr. Franklin had indicated very quickly, however, that she was going to need to spend a solid block of time with Cormac. She'd made a phone call to her office, told the receptionist to inform the patient she'd abandoned that the tumor was indeed malignant, and shut herself in Cormac's bedroom. That was about the time when Vance started to apply some serious pressure regarding the towel.

Vance returned with two open bottles of beer and passed one up to the dean.

"To towels, and the men who wear them," he said. The dean raised his bottle in agreement and went to take a sip, but Vance wasn't done.

"To stadium seating couches, and the men who sit on them. To cases of beer, and the convenience store clerks who get distracted when you let a stray dog into their store, allowing you to shoplift them."

The dean realized Vance had no intention of stopping his toast and so he chimed in. "How about," he said, elevating his pandering to the next level. "To new friends, and to helping old ones."

Vance reacted as if the dean had just raised his glass to toast the ovens at Dachau.

"To towels, and the men who wear them," the dean muttered sheepishly. They clinked bottles, and the dean took a sip of beer.

The afternoon continued in an uneventful fashion. Dr. Franklin continued to work behind a closed door, providing no updates on any progress or discovery. Vance retrieved beers from the kitchen every time they needed new ones. As the empty bottles stacked up, the conversation shifted from Vance's plan to someday build a third tier of couches to his band's search for a new guitarist. The dean still felt like an idiot wearing just a towel, and the rash on his arm had grown itchier, but after about four beers he realized he was kind of enjoying himself.

In the middle of a particularly animated discussion about why the dean had never whacked a goat with his shillelagh, Dean Bickerstaff realized he needed to use the bathroom. He lowered himself off the airborne couch, noticeably more unsteady than when he'd ascended it, and Vance went to the kitchen to retrieve two more beers.

The conditions in Cormac and Vance's bathroom were abysmal. It would not have surprised the dean to see perverts, having mistaken it for a highway rest stop, lurking outside of it seeking anonymous sex. Disgusting, thought the dean, as he untied the towel from around his waist with his rash-stricken right arm and began to urinate into the toilet while completely naked.

Dean Bickerstaff knew he had to be careful. Earning Vance's trust with some strategic afternoon relaxation was one thing, but he was undertaking a multi-faceted plan and couldn't afford to lose too much mental acuity. The rest of his day was going to depend on Dr. Franklin's diagnosis. If it worked out the way he hoped, Cormac's condition could easily be treated with a simple drug. The dean would of course then suppress this information and dole out the drug based on whether Cormac was willing to do his bidding.

At the other end of the spectrum was the possibility that Dr. Franklin came back with bad news. Maybe Cormac had a horrible, life-threatening condition and the doctor would only give him forty-eight hours to live. To have a time-travelling wonder appear within his grasp only to be snatched away so quickly would be, in the dean's mind, the greatest tragedy of his life. Vance would probably hit him up for Cormac's share of the rent, too. The dean couldn't let it come to that.

As Frampton carefully flushed the toilet with one fingertip and re-tied the towel around his waist, he realized that it had been at least three hours since he'd had a cigar. He couldn't remember the last time he'd gone that long without a stogie, aside from being asleep. Vance would be cool with it. Vance was a cool guy in general, thought the dean.

He left the bathroom and peered down the hall. The door to Cormac's room was still closed. Dean Bickerstaff considered busting in and putting the screws to Dr. Franklin, pressuring her for a speedy diagnosis. He'd done this once before, making the argument that there were no wrong diagnoses. But it turned out the saying was actually *questions* that there were no wrong ones of. There were many, many wrong diagnoses. Fortunately, several prosecutors and judges in Harrington's jurisdiction had also falsified their transcripts through his service and he was able to help Dr. Franklin avoid losing her license.

But even with a well-paid-off judicial system in his back pocket, Frampton preferred to cut as few corners as possible with Cormac's diagnosis. Knowledge was power, and in many cases, *accurate* knowledge was even greater power. And the dean was a man who subsisted off power, who craved power more than anything. On that note, he made sure his kitty cat towel was secure and went to go find his pants.

Vance emerged from the kitchen with two beers just as the dean was rummaging through his pants pockets looking for his cigars.

"You're not putting those on?" asked Vance, warily.

"Of course not," said Dean Bickerstaff, as if resuming wearing pants on a Sunday afternoon was the stupidest idea he'd ever heard.

"Good," said Vance, as he pressed the side of one of the bottles up against the small of the dean's back. The bottle was frosty cold and the dean straightened up with an involuntary shriek. He instinctively swung his shillelagh hand at Vance's kneecap before he realized that the staff was leaning against the wall next to his clothes.

Vance just laughed. "You just got BeerBacked, Deano! Little game I just invented. Me one, you nothing. Seriously, what are you looking for?"

Dean Bickerstaff restrained his anger at being BeerBacked and calmly held up two cigars.

Vance's eyes lit up. "Alright! I didn't know if you were down or not! I've been sneaking hits in the kitchen every time I've grabbed beers."

Vance somehow produced a bag of what the dean could only assume was marijuana from the inside of his towel. "Personal blunts may be a tall order though, Deano," he said, looking concerned. "It's been pretty stressful around here since the whole whaling deal started—I may have been going through the stash a bit faster than normal."

The thought of the idiot in a towel gutting one of his smuggled *Romeo y Julietas* to make a blunt made the dean feel ill. "Vance," he asked, "have you ever smoked a fine cigar?" Vance shook his head no. "A truly fine cigar is an experience greater than any drug," the dean continued. Vance looked unbelievably skeptical.

"Oh sure, you may not see visions, or get the munchos, or think you're in The Three Dog Night." The dean had never done drugs before. "But only a cigar can one moment provide the subtle aroma of fine Spanish leather, only to shift gears into a lush peppery taste, redolent of the *terroir* of Thomas Jefferson's Monticello plantation."

Dean Bickerstaff held up the cigars to admire them. "Yes," he continued, "to behold the velvety smoke and that perfect half-inch of ash . . . Vance, it's as if you're smoking a work of art. You can truly see why Rudyard Kipling once said, 'A woman is only a woman, but a good cigar is a—' GAAAAAAAHDammit, Vance!"

Vance pulled the glistening beer bottle off of the dean's lower back. "Two to zero," he said, and took a sip.

The dean lifted the back of his towel an inch or two to wipe off the moisture. With the hand that still held the cigars, he furiously gestured at Vance.

"Look, you idiot," Frampton sputtered. "This is one of the finest cigars Cuba has to offer. We're not just going to carve it up and fill it with marijuana some hippie grew in his toolshed. These are rare, they're expensive, they're illegal, and I don't even know if my—"

"Illegal?" Vance interrupted. He plucked a cigar out of the dean's hand.

"It's a Cuban cigar, of course it's illegal!" snapped the dean. Vance observed the cigar with newfound interest. The prospect of smoking one of the world's finest cigars hadn't intrigued him one bit, but now that it was forbidden by the government, Vance appeared to be fully committed to experiencing it. Dean Bickerstaff changed his tone.

"But if we smoke these, Vance," the dean said, lowering his voice to a conspiratorial tone. "You've got to keep it quiet. I can't risk anyone finding out and turning the heat up on my connection."

Vance nodded knowingly, undoubtedly picturing the connection as a Cuban gangster in a white suit, gold medallion nestled comfortably in a thicket of chest hair. The dean had no intention of correcting this misconception. It would divert suspicion from Norma, the sixty-eight year-old substitute customs agent who had tearfully agreed to let the cigars slip through the port authority after the dean threatened one of her many cats.

The dean bent down and rummaged through his pants pockets again. He eventually produced a glistening white cigar cutter and a butane lighter. "Now what you've got to do is cut off the end of it, just like so," Dean Bickerstaff demonstrated. He passed the cigar cutter to Vance. "Be careful now, that cutter's real ivory."

Vance tentatively fit the cutter around the end of the cigar and snapped it shut. The trimmed end fell to the floor. He looked very proud of himself.

"Now when I light this end for you, you puff the other end and rotate the cigar so it burns evenly." Vance gave him a thumbs up and chomped down on the cigar. The dean effortlessly lit his own cigar and took a few satisfying puffs before extending the lighter to Vance.

"Now don't inhale this, just puff on it," he said as bursts of cigar smoke started to emerge from Vance's mouth. After a few seconds, the lit end of Vance's cigar was glowing orange, and Dean Bickerstaff pulled back the lighter. "And that's all there is to it!" he exclaimed. "Just relax and let the robust flavor overtake you. You taste that Vance? That's what being a man tastes like."

"I taste it," Vance said through a cloud of smoke. "It tastes like . . . Spanish leather. A bit of Thomas Jefferson. Very redolent."

The dean smiled as Vance repeated his words back to him. Just pull the strings and make him dance, Frampton, he thought to himself. "The finest cigars change as you smoke them," he said in between puffs. "So right now you may get that real earthy taste, but halfway through it may switch to a more pure tobacco flavor. And then at the end, you may even detect hints of BEERBACK!"

Dean Bickerstaff reached around Vance's waist and pressed the beer bottle against his skin. Vance gasped at the bottle's coldness, which caused him to inhale a gigantic cloud of cigar smoke. He instantly began to coughing violently and fell to his knees.

"Two to one, you son of a bitch!" the dean shouted over Vance's hacking. The BeerBack revenge had felt even sweeter than he had imagined, and he wasn't done yet.

"Two to two!" he yelled as he pressed the bottle into Vance's back again. Vance fell to all fours, and was heaving as he coughed and wheezed.

"Three to two! Four to two!" Dean Bickerstaff cackled as Vance appeared to be unable to draw a breath. The fifth BeerBack caused Vance to vomit onto the floor, and after the sixth his elbows began to buckle. Frampton puffed on his cigar as he walked in a half-circle around his fallen victim.

"Who's the BeerBack champion, Vance?" he demanded. "Who's the BeerBack champion? Seven to two!" he shouted when Vance was only able to wheeze. Dean Bickerstaff bent down to apply the bottle to Vance's glistening back. This seventh BeerBack was the sweetest one of all, and he really shoved the bottle down, good and hard. Frampton clamped his cigar between his teeth and roared with laughter as Vance lay at his knees, quivering slightly in a pool of his own barf. It was good to be king.

"Dear God, Frampton!" Dean Bickerstaff instantly stopped laughing at the sound of a woman's voice behind him. He turned to see Dr. Franklin, her mouth agape, standing next to the stadium seating couches. She was clutching her medical bag and looked to be on the verge of fleeing the house.

"Dr. Franklin!" said the dean, trying to sound casual. Dean Bickerstaff realized that he was breathing heavily and sweating after the exertion of seven consecutive BeerBacks. He set his beer down next to Vance and straightened up. He attempted to take a first step toward the horrified doctor, but Vance still had enough strength to reach up and grab onto a corner of the dean's towel. His grip was enough to cause the towel to fall to the ground when the dean took his next step.

Dr. Franklin let out a shriek as Harrington Dean Frampton Q. Bickerstaff strode toward her, naked and smoking a cigar.

The dean, who had felt close to naked in the towel anyway, didn't notice right away. He finally sensed something was amiss when he was about five feet from Dr. Franklin. When he realized he was fully nude, he turned and scrambled back toward the heap of towels and human flesh that was Vance. Nearly slipping on the spilled beer and vomit, he snatched his kitty cat towel away from Vance, re-attached it around his waist, and spun around to face Dr. Franklin once again.

"So," he said with a grin that indicated he found nothing unusual about the circumstances Dr. Franklin had discovered him in. "How's our patient doing?"

"Jesus Christ, Frampton," said Dr. Franklin. "What the hell is wrong with you? I come over here at the drop of a hat to attend to a seriously ill student of yours, and while I examine him for two hours, you're out here drinking, wrapped in a towel, fighting another student half your age!"

It was at times like this that Dean Bickerstaff was glad he lived a completely unethical life. Apologies and explanations were so much more difficult than blackmail and hush money. The dean reached out and plucked his shillelagh from where it leaned against the wall. He gave it a few jaunty twirls while he puffed on his cigar.

"Dr. Franklin," the dean said calmly. "I could get into a long explanation about the harmless fun we're having here today."

Behind him, Vance dry heaved loudly for a few seconds, then groaned.

"But perhaps we all have some explaining to do," the dean continued, undeterred. "Two hours? Really? You needed that long to examine a sleeping student?"

"I ran an extensive battery of expensive tests to determine exactly what affliction this young man is suffering from," replied Dr. Franklin.

"Well," chuckled Dean Bickerstaff. "That may be the case. I just hope there wasn't anything else going on in there."

"Frampton, what the hell are you implying?"

"Did you touch his wiener?" the dean asked. Behind him, an intrigued Vance managed to roll over and prop his head up on a pizza box. He resumed smoking his still-lit cigar and watched the developing scene closely.

"Did I touch his . . . Frampton, I went in there at your request and gave him a thorough medical checkup!" Dr. Franklin was growing flustered. "You told me to make sure I examined every possibility!"

"Well, sweetheart," the dean said, sinking fully into his finest oily condescension. "I'm glad you considered my authority in the matter. But the unfortunate truth is, a college dean doesn't really have any authority to send a stranger into a student's room to touch his wiener. That's not a typical item you find in a school charter."

Dr. Franklin's shoulders slumped and the dean grinned around his cigar. Checkmate.

"To be honest, I think Mac would've been cool with it," Vance chimed in. "Doc, if I ever wake up on a whaling boat, you can come in and touch my wiener all you need to."

"Regardless of what his loyal roommate thinks," Dean Bickerstaff said, shooting Vance a look. "I think it would be best if all of us kept quiet about what happened here today."

Dr. Franklin nodded her resigned agreement.

"Grand," said the dean, exhaling a large puff of cigar smoke. "So tell us, did you find out what's wrong with our friend Cormac?"

Dr. Franklin took a deep breath, as if she were trying to put the past three minutes out of her memory. She took a seat on the arm of the lower couch.

"Yes, and no," she said. The dean and Vance looked at each other. "There doesn't appear to be a reasonable medical cause for his trips to the whaling boat."

"So he's faking it?" asked Vance.

"No, not at all. I have every reason to believe that Cormac is actually travelling to the nineteenth century and sailing around catching whales."

"And how do you know that?" asked the dean.

"Because," said Dr. Franklin. "When you look into his ear, you can see everything he's doing aboard the boat."

It was Dean Bickerstaff's turn to be confused. "What the hell are you talking about, Franklin?"

"I'm not really sure how to explain it," Dr. Franklin said. "But the very first thing I did was a routine ear, nose, and throat exam. And when you peer into Cormac's ear, it's like you're looking into the world that he's in."

Neither the dean nor Vance could respond while they tried to wrap their heads around this, so Dr. Franklin continued. "It was quite fascinating. The captain was showing him where they keep the whales they've killed; there were these bones that were just huge! I really got caught up in it. To be honest, I didn't have time to actually run any tests, but I'm not gonna find anything. This kid is pretty much fucked from a medical standpoint."

The dean and Vance tried to figure out if this was bad news.

"Oh, he's not going to die or anything. But I sure as hell can't cure him. But come on, you've got to check this out! Looking into his ear is really, really cool."

Dr. Franklin gestured for Dean Bickerstaff and Vance to follow her back to Cormac's bedroom. The dean wasn't certain, but if he understood the doctor correctly, it sounded to him like Cormac's situation had grown exponentially more exploitable. He tried to suppress the wide grin that was threatening to spread across his face as he puffed his cigar and waddled after the doctor.

Vance followed after them, his stomach sticky with both regular beer and thrown-up beer. He gave the dean a knowing little jab in the ribs with his elbow. Frampton took it to mean that the towel pull made them even for all the BeerBacking. Dean Bickerstaff had gone toe-to-toe with devious and powerful adversaries before, but Vance had an air of unpredictability about him that made the dean nervous. Just a few hours with Vance had left Frampton buzzed on cheap beer and naked on a Sunday afternoon. He was worried about the depths of debasement that an extended partnership might require him to descend to.

"Do you have any more beers?" asked Dr. Franklin when they got to the door of Cormac's bedroom. Vance nodded and walked off to the kitchen. Dean Bickerstaff walked over to the side of Cormac's bed. Still feeling kind of stupid, he set his cigar down on the bedside table and rested the shillelagh on the ground. He knelt down beside the unconscious student, careful to make sure the towel still covered his butt. Exposing himself to Dr. Franklin was the exact type of leverage-shifting move he needed to avoid. He couldn't afford to let it happen a second time.

"Is there anything I need to know here?" asked the dean, his voice betraying his skepticism. "I'm not going to get sucked into there and be trapped in his head forever, am I?"

Dr. Franklin shook her head. "All you need to do is put your eye up to his ear, like you're looking into a microscope. Trust me, you've never seen anything like this."

Vance returned, awkwardly gripping three beers and a roll of paper towels. He handed two of the beers to Dr. Franklin, then used some of the paper towels to wipe off his chest. Dr. Franklin popped the tops off both the beers and handed one to Dean Bickerstaff. Still kneeling, the dean took a sip, then raised his bottle to the other two people in the room.

"To one hell of a strange Sunday," he said.

"To towels, and the men who wear them," Vance responded.

"I'm here against my will," said Dr. Franklin.

They all drank.

After a hearty pull from the bottle, Dean Bickerstaff closed his right eye and slowly lowered his left toward Cormac's ear. He saw nothing but darkness in the cavity until his eye was directly pressed up against the ear hole. For a moment, he thought that Dr. Franklin has been messing with him. He was instinctively reaching for his shillelagh to deliver a blow to her kneecaps when all of a sudden it happened.

At once, a brilliant vision was all the dean could see. It was a huge panoramic view that became his entire world. It was as if he'd been transported onto the deck of the *Levyathan*. Above him, the dean saw crisp white sails against a bright blue sky. To his left, a wide section of wooden boat deck was all that separated him from the rolling ocean, and to the right, tough-looking whalers drank rum and coiled lengths of rope. Straight ahead, a fellow was strumming an instrument with a mop across his lap. It felt like he was looking straight at the dean as he demonstrated something on the instrument.

Frampton forced himself to lean back, overwhelmed. The vision disappeared, and he was back in Cormac's bedroom. "That's incredible!" he gasped.

"Pretty cool, huh?" said Dr. Franklin, finishing her beer. "You're seeing everything Cormac sees. It's like you're looking out of his eyes." Not sure where to set her empty bottle, Dr. Franklin tried to hand it to Vance, who looked at her like she was an idiot until she shrugged and tossed it over her shoulder into the hallway.

"It looked like he was watching someone play some kind of musical instrument," said the dean.

"Ah yes, I watched them fashion that thing," said the doctor. "A crude little stringed one, right? Seemed like kind of a pussy guitar to me, but what the hell do I care."

"Mac could shred before he lost his finger," said Vance nostalgically. "But Doc, I've got a question."

"What is it, Vance?" Dr. Franklin asked.

"If you were just looking into Cormac's ear the whole time you were in here, when did the wiener touching come into play?" Vance asked.

Dr. Franklin looked uncomfortable. Vance took this to mean she hadn't understood his question.

"When did you touch Cormac's unconscious wiener?" he clarified.

Dr. Franklin sighed and pulled out her prescription pad. "You don't seem well, Vance," she said pointedly. "Take two of anything you want and call me in the morning." She tore off a dozen or so blank, signed prescription forms and pressed them into Vance's palm. Vance stared at them for a few seconds before he realized what he'd been given and began to smile.

The dean loved to see business being done his way. Maybe Dr. Franklin had gotten a real education at Harrington after all. He grinned and tightened his towel around his waist. Then Dean Frampton Q. Bickerstaff turned his back to both of them and once again lowered his eye to Cormac McIlhenney's ear.

* * *

Spirits were high on the deck of the *Levyathan* after the most successful day of whaling anyone on board could remember. The whalers performed their tasks with rarely seen enthusiasm, singing and laughing while they coiled ropes and dragged the record haul down to the cold storage area. Copious amounts of rum were being consumed, of course, but this time it was in a celebratory manner. Nobody was silently weeping while they drank, and only one jug got smashed, but it appeared to be an accident and none of the whalers tried to stab the other whalers with the shards.

Captain Anson strode about the deck, barking the occasional order but mainly complementing the men on a job well done. Cormac noticed that the captain didn't seem as entirely lost in the moment as he expected. A ship full of dead whales represented the fulfillment of the captain's ultimate dream, but it also posed a unique problem. Every single one of those whales represented a pile of money, and between his wife, her lawyer, and all his disgruntled employees, lots of different people wanted Captain Anson's money. When there were no whales, there was no money, and everyone who had their hand out could go to hell. But it was going to be a lot harder to put off a payday now that they had landed a record catch.

However, when the whales were just beginning to stack up on the deck of the *Levyathan*, the captain had been ecstatic. He had waved his spyglass, shouted toward the heavens, and bounded from sail to sail making potentially harmful adjustments.

"Swine of the deep!" the captain had bellowed. "Prostrate thyself before me! Alexander wept when he had nothing more to conquer but when the final whale becomes a corpse at my feet I shall laugh and laugh heartily! The laughter of a conquering god! Oh, Ziro, there you are, could you put your finger on this rope? It's so much easier for me to tie a knot when someone puts their finger on the rope."

Cormac slowly sipped a tin cup full of rum and smiled at the memory. It was a good problem for the captain to have, he figured. After all, he certainly hadn't asked Cormac to stop hauling in the whales at any point.

Cormac's first day as a full-fledged whaler had gone better than he ever could have expected. His previous success, though it was impressive and certainly something he was willing to take credit for, bore the stench of dumb luck, drunkenness, and attempted murder. When he first picked up a harpoon gun that morning, Cormac had gotten the sense that until he landed a whale while reasonably sober, none of the whalers were going to take him seriously. Earning the respect of the surly drunks who were abject failures at their menial jobs instantly became Cormac's main goal in life.

Fortunately, a harpoon gun was still easily operated by someone with only nine fingers. Cormac had remarked that this was fortunate, before he took a glance around the ship and realized that this was obviously by design. It seemed like about half of the whalers on the *Levyathan* were missing at least a finger. Ziro had pointed out that harpoon gun manufacturers clearly understood the risk of digit loss on whaling ships and adapted their products to be compatible with potential handicaps. Unfortunately, making a harpoon gun functional for a whaler with nine or fewer fingers meant introducing compromises in design that made it exceedingly dangerous for a man with all ten fingers to operate. When Cormac had tried to determine if that made sense or not, his head started to hurt, so he decided to stop thinking and just shoot a damn whale.

His first harpoon had sailed in a beautiful arch and hit a large adult whale right in the middle of its side. The startled whale let out a low moan and began to thrash in the water. Cormac handed the harpoon gun to Ziro, who quickly tied it off while Cormac picked up a freshly loaded gun. The few whalers who had been working nearby stopped what they were doing to watch. Cormac observed the panicked whale for several more seconds, then pulled the trigger and let the second harpoon fly.

The whalers let out scornful chuckles and resumed what they had been doing as the harpoon sailed high. Ziro pulled the rope connected to the first harpoon tight and walked over to Cormac.

"Well, they can't all hit their mark," Ziro said, patting Cormac on the shoulder. "Still, you've got nothing to be—" Before Ziro could finish his sentence, the wounded whale, in a desperate attempt to rid himself of first harpoon, leapt out of the sea. At the peak of his jump, Cormac's second harpoon connected, sinking deep into a spot a foot above his eye. The whale immediately ceased its flailing and fell back to the ocean, dead.

Cormac handed the second harpoon gun off to Ziro and immediately picked up a new one. "You better keep 'em loaded," he told the former slave. To punctuate his quip, he attempted to cock the harpoon gun as if it were a shotgun. Harpoon guns were not designed this way of course, and after several seconds of Cormac attempting to force non-moving parts into making a sweet action-hero sound, there was a loud crack. Now sweating, Cormac handed the broken gun to Ziro and remarked that the harpoon looked like it needed sharpening. Then he picked up a new gun and got to work.

Cormac scored six straight hits and three more kills before his first miss. By the time it came, all the whalers aboard the *Levyathan* had made their way to his side of the boat and were gambling on his performance. Lacking steady paychecks and thus any currency, they preferred to bet with erotic scrimshaw. Depraved scenes were carved into each of the wagered whale bones, with larger bones sometimes containing entire narratives. From the glimpses that Cormac caught, he had trouble imagining how the erotic scrimshaw possibly helped accomplish the sole purpose it existed for. The carvings were technically crude, and many of them depicted the whaler who had carved it as a main participant. Cormac assumed, then hoped, that the whalers were being generous with their self-portraits. Starting at the wrong end of a carving, he had mistaken several of them for whales.

The roar of the rowdy gamblers behind him made Cormac feel like he was rolling dice at a craps table every time he pulled the trigger. An expectant hush fell over the crowd each time a harpoon launched out of his gun, the silence occasionally broken by cries of "get in the blowhole!" or "double or nothing for that dolphin-on-mermaid piece!" When the harpoon landed, loud roars went up from the winners and even louder roars went up from the losers. As someone who would be returning home to the perverted embrace of the internet, Cormac may have scoffed at the erotic scrimshaw, but it was not a commodity the whalers parted with lightly.

When the first harpoon sailed high over a breaching whale and landed with a distant splash, Cormac felt his stomach drop. Five days ago he had never even seen a harpoon gun; now he felt devastated to have ruined his flawless hit percentage. The fact that he'd arrogantly tried a behind-the-back trick shot did nothing to make him feel any better. In fact, the whalers who had lost their erotic scrimshaw because of his screwing around looked pretty pissed. Cormac chuckled nervously and muttered something about the wind, then walked over three feet to his left to where the harpoon had embedded itself in the deck of the boat and pried it free. He was lucky it hadn't gone through his foot. He looked down at his missing finger and vowed to stop messing around.

Taking it more seriously after that—aside from the occasional quip and constant intake of rum—Cormac landed nine consecutive hits and five more dead whales. The number of whalers who were willing to bet against him quickly dwindled, despite some very attractive odds being on the table. Desperate for action, one whaler offered up a piece of scrimshaw that was so powerfully erotic he kept all but six inches of it concealed by burlap. Cormac found it very difficult to concentrate with such a mysterious object behind him, and was glad when the whaler found no takers and had to drag it back to the sleeping quarters.

Eventually, even the most degenerate of the gamblers decided that betting against Cormac was a losing proposition. There was plenty of work to do anyway. The sun was still high in the sky, but it would probably take them the rest of the day to butcher and drag nine dead whales down to the cold storage area. Cormac was reluctant to put away the harpoon so early in the day. He was enjoying himself, but it seemed to go beyond enjoyment. For the first time that he could ever remember, he felt a deep sense of satisfaction in a job well done. Plus butchering a bunch of gigantic whales looked a hell of a lot more difficult and gross than just shooting them.

Unfortunately, the whales had finally come to their senses and put some distance between their pod and the *Levyathan*. Their occasional spray was barely visible on the horizon. Cormac had stood ready with the harpoon gun, steadfastly sizing up the distant spray as if any minute he might fire again. He managed to keep up this ruse for half an hour before Captain Anson barked at him to get to work or he'd shove a piece of erotic scrimshaw up his ass. Ordinarily, Cormac might have assumed this was a colorful but hollow threat. However, several of the erotic scrimshaw pieces that had been wagered that afternoon depicted other, less fortunate pieces of erotic scrimshaw being used in exactly this manner. Cormac grabbed a knife and started in on the nearest whale.

Nearly six hours later, here he was. Only busy work remained, and while the whalers somehow seemed to shift into another gear once the finish line was in sight, Cormac was exhausted. He'd tried his best to contribute until the end, but fatigue and dehydration caught up with him. Eventually Ziro discovered him trying to cut a slice of blubber off an anchor and insisted that he sit down and relax before he collapsed.

The clear evening sky was beginning to turn a beautiful color. Cormac looked over at Captain Anson, who was arguing with a group of whalers about how they'd stacked some blubber down in the cold storage area. Cormac figured that the captain was looking for minor infractions that he could use to dock the sailors' theoretical pay. He'd already seen the captain confront other whalers about the length of their hair, their use of the lord's name in vain, and a whale penis that someone had placed in a fire lane. None of it seemed to matter though. The whalers just laughed off the fines with the knowledge that as soon as they docked, there would be more than enough money to go around.

Cormac sipped his rum and wondered how Vance had spent his Sunday. In terms of raw tonnage of dead animals, it was hard to imagine a scenario where Vance could have him beat. Even in the extremely unlikely scenario that Vance had opted to ignore his precious couches and instead fill in as a day laborer at a commercial slaughterhouse, Cormac estimated that the amount of cows he'd personally be able to kill in a single afternoon still would be outweighed by the whale haul.

Cormac was chuckling at the thought of Vance stunning a cow while wearing only his Seahawks towel when he saw Ziro coming toward him. Ziro had assisted in almost every facet of the whaling process and somehow managed to find enough time to swab the entire deck. Cormac's entire body ached and his clothes were stiff with dried sweat, but Ziro appeared none the worse for wear. He carried a small sack slung over his shoulder and offered Cormac a piece of salt pork as he approached.

"Eat some of this," Ziro said. "But maybe not so fast this time."

Cormac took the salt pork and gnawed off a piece. It was tough and salty and disgusting, and Cormac finished the entire chunk before Ziro could even sit down.

"I thought you'd be hungry," said Ziro, as he handed Cormac another piece. "You've got to remember to eat when you're here. Whaling's hard work—you're never going to make it if you just drink rum all day."

"The rest of the crew seems to get along fine just drinking rum all day," said Cormac.

"The average life expectancy for a whaler is thirty-four years," countered Ziro. It was a fairly compelling argument for making sure to eat some salt pork while whaling.

Cormac polished off the second piece and washed it down with some rum. He was already looking forward to gorging himself when he got home in the morning. He had it planned out in his head: he'd drink about a gallon of Gatorade in the shower, then eat an entire pizza in bed. It would not be the first time he'd done this, but it *would* be the first time he honestly felt like he'd earned it.

"I hope you realize that what you did today was incredible," said Ziro, as he chewed on his own hunk of salt pork. "I've never seen anyone that accurate with a harpoon gun."

"It probably doesn't help my 'I'm not a witch' cause very much, does it?" asked Cormac, half joking.

"Not at all," said Ziro. "But I don't think anybody is going to care as long as you keep it up. Nobody on the ship really minds occult, satanic stuff as long as they're benefitting from it. Captain Anson even tried to cut a deal with the devil once. He sold him a bunch of the crew's souls, but it turned out he wasn't the devil, he was just a guy with a cane."

"The devil isn't really known for carrying a cane . . ." said Cormac

"The captain tends not to use his best judgment when an opportunity to screw the crew over presents itself. Look, the point is, it's fine if you're a witch or a wizard or a . . . I don't know, an enchanted pixie princess!"

"I'm definitely not that last one," Cormac said loudly, noticing that some of the whalers had moved within earshot. "Not a pixie princess!" he shouted to them, shaking his head and pointing to Ziro with a 'can you believe this guy' expression on his face. The annoyed whalers grunted and moved on.

"Look," said Ziro, trying to remain patient. "I just want to know how you're able to do what you do."

"I've been thinking about this," said Cormac, by which he meant "drinking rum for hours." "And I think I've got it figured out. For every skill that's out there, there's got to be someone in the world who's the best at it, right? Like Michael Jordan was the best basketball player and Jimi Hendrix was the best . . ."

Ziro stared straight ahead with no reaction to the unfamiliar names.

"Bad examples," said Cormac. "How about, who's the best blacksmith in the world? Or the best guy at pushing one of those hoops with a stick?"

"Well, everyone knows that the best blacksmith is Elmer Greyson of Boston," said Ziro. "The best hoop roller is a different story. Personally I think it's Abner Lowell, but you could get killed if you go saying that south of the Mason-Dixon Line."

Cormac had no idea the world of competitive hoop rolling was so bloodthirsty, but couldn't allow that to distract him when he was so close to making a point.

"So what I'm saying is," he continued, "what if Elmer Greyson had never gone into blacksmithing? Would that talent still be hidden somewhere inside him? What if Abner Lowell had never picked up a hoop?"

"Picking up the hoop is actually a disqualifiable infraction," said Ziro.

"I think I'm the world's greatest harpooner," Cormac proclaimed in moment of rum-soaked pride. "I just never had been given a chance to realize it."

Ziro had no response.

After a few seconds, Cormac broke the silence. "Or maybe I'm just a pixie princess," he laughed.

Two whalers carrying a chunk of blubber stopped in their tracks and glared at him menacingly.

"Not a pixie princess! Not a pixie princess!" Cormac assured them.

Ziro realized he wasn't going to get an explanation that made any more sense than this. He waited for the whalers to move on, then opened his sack and pulled out a newly fashioned ukulele.

"Do you mind if I play?" he asked Cormac.

Cormac eyed the tiny instrument warily, wondering if it could do anything but fuel the pixie princess rumors that were undoubtedly now swirling in the whalers' quarters. Before he could articulate his uneasiness, Ziro gave it a strum and began to tune the instrument.

"The other men on board don't like the ukulele, but I think it has its appeal," he said as he tightened the strings. "I don't think there's a better instrument for playing sea shanties. Maybe the accordion, but I'm not trying to get thrown overboard."

"What do you tune it to?" asked Cormac. "C?"

"Yeah, C's a good shanty key," said Ziro. Surprised, he looked up at Cormac. "Do you play?"

"Guitar," replied Cormac. "Or, that is to say, I played." He held up his mangled left hand and looked at it with a glum expression. "Kind of hard when you're missing a finger."

Ziro brightened. "That's great!" Cormac glared at him and he backtracked slightly. "Not that you're missing a finger, that's not what I meant. Even though it did save all our lives . . ."

Cormac glared and took a swig of rum and Ziro feared he was headed down a surly path.

"Listen," Ziro continued, "the ukulele has only four strings! The chords are really simple. If you had any talent on the guitar at all, you'll be able to play it, even missing a finger!"

The former slave enthusiastically thrust the tiny instrument toward Cormac, who looked at it suspiciously. Strumming a ukulele was the most damaging thing to one's credibility as a guitar player that Cormac could imagine. Even worse than losing a finger and being physically unable to play the guitar. It seemed like if he was going to play the ukulele he should gain two hundred pounds or wear a propeller beanie or probably both. You didn't shred on a ukulele as much as you gently strummed it until you got punched in the face.

"You want me to take that?" Cormac asked.

"Don't worry, I usually make a couple at a time," said Ziro. "They tend not to last very long on this boat." Still holding the first ukulele, Ziro pulled another, nearly identical instrument out of his sack. "On the plus side, I've gotten good at constructing them out of just about anything."

Cormac reluctantly reached out and took the ukulele. He gave it a tentative strum.

"For example, this one's strung with tendons from one of those whale penises you saw earlier," said Ziro.

Cormac dropped the ukulele like it had just come out of an oven.

"Dammit, Ziro!" he shouted. He frantically looked around for something to wipe his hands on.

Ziro laughed and strummed a jaunty chord on his uke. "I'm just kidding," he chuckled. "Those are baleen fibers. Come on, pick it up."

Slowly, Cormac reached out and picked up the ukulele again. He was drunk enough to think that Ziro's little joke was one of the greatest pranks he had ever witnessed. His head spun as he excitedly tried to think of how he himself might pull it on an unsuspecting victim. Unfortunately, he was just barely sober enough to realize that the "that ukulele you're holding is made out of a whale penis" gag might be the least-applicable practical joke in history. Any of the whalers would heave him overboard instantly, and anyone back home, upon being informed by a stranger that their ukulele was made of a whale's genitals, would probably just think the prankster was having a stroke.

Disappointed, Cormac sighed and fingered the ukulele's strings. The instrument was much lighter than his guitar—it felt like he was holding a toy. Instinctively he wanted to launch into Black Sabbath's "Paranoid" but was reluctant to do such a sweet riff the injustice of being played on a homemade ukulele.

"So you play sea shanties with this thing, huh?" he asked Ziro. "Which shanty gets the ladies back on shore the most excited? 'Born to Swab the Deck'? 'The Rope Coiler's Anthem'? 'Amos Reeks of Fish Guts'?"

"I know you're making fun of me, but 'Amos Reeks of Fish Guts' is actually pretty popular with the women," said Ziro. "Look, Cormac, don't let the tiny instrument fool you: sea shanties aren't kiddie songs. You'd get arrested if you just stood in a town square and yelled at people about sex or gross fish or sex with gross fish. But if you're playing a ukulele while you're doing it, then it becomes a sea shanty. People don't necessarily want to hear those either, but in many states they're not technically a crime."

Cormac instinctively fingered the strings of the ukulele. The opportunity to upset and offend people with music was outweighing any reservations he had about playing a ridiculous-looking instrument. Besides, it was either this or try to get in on what the whalers were doing, which appeared to be a game that involved trying to knock rum jugs off each other's heads by hurling other rum jugs at them. Nobody seemed to be winning, and nobody seemed to care.

"Alright," said Cormac. "Let's do it."

"Great!" Ziro was clearly excited to have someone he could play in front of without fear of physical violence, let alone a full-fledged student.

"I'll teach you a song I wrote," Ziro said. "It starts with G, so you're going to want to lay your index finger down here and put your ring finger on the third string, third fret." He demonstrated the chord on his own ukulele.

Cormac gave it a strum. It didn't sound terrible.

"Good!" said Ziro. "After that comes C, which only needs one finger on the third fret on the last string."

Cormac transitioned from G to C effortlessly. Even without a pinky finger, the chords were easy, and as far as he could tell, playing the ukulele had not yet caused his testicles to retract inside his body.

"And then for D, you just lay your finger across the first three strings like this," said Ziro. Cormac imitated him and played the D chord.

"Sounds pretty good," said Ziro. Cormac sipped some rum in agreement. "Not just follow me on the changes, I'll sing you a verse."

Ziro started to strum his ukulele and Cormac quickly picked up on the simple pattern. It didn't necessarily wail, but it was still music and it felt good to play it. Ziro began to sing "Treasures o' the Sea":

On her birthday I gave my wife a woven tapestry,
"Hang it on the wall" I said, "for all your friends to see."
She rolled it out upon the floor, her face it did turn red,
"That's not a tapestry, it's just a lobster and it's dead."

I'd let her down and made a mess of her special occasion
"I'll get my money back for this misleading ol' crustacean."
Turned out the lobster wasn't dead, and it reacted quick,
You'll forget about your refund when a lobster grabs your—

OHHHHHH
You can keep your diamonds, and you can keep your gold . . .

Cormac was won over even before the lobster pinched the narrator's genitals. The shanty was jaunty and fun to play, and the dirtiness was a huge bonus. After strumming through a few verses, he was able to add some flourishes into the chord progression, which Ziro acknowledged with a respectful nod of his head. The duo tore through seventeen verses of "Treasures o' the Sea," blowing the previous record for "verses completed before a whaler destroys the ukulele" out of the water. The previous record had been one.

Cormac and Ziro were unaware that sixty feet away, Captain Anson was watching them. He had been peering through his spyglass out one of his cabin's portholes for the past five minutes.

The captain watched his former slave laughing it up with the mysterious stranger from the future and worried that control of the *Levyathan* was slipping away from him. Overseeing a crew of desperate losers was easy. Once those losers started to have a glimmer of hope, they'd grow confident and unmanageable. They'd start thinking for themselves and questioning his authority. The only thing Captain Anson feared more than his wife's lawyer was a mutiny. At least the lawyer would leave him with half. A mutiny would cost him everything.

The port at St. John's was a week away if the weather cooperated. Captain Anson knew he had some big problems to solve before they dropped anchor.

DAY SEVEN

Cissy woke up to a loud pounding on her front door. Someone must be dead, she thought to herself. Why else would she have a visitor in the middle of the night?

She closed her eyes and figured whoever it was wasn't getting any deader. She could deal with the distraught person at the door, presumably a close family member or a representative of one, in the morning.

The banging didn't stop. Cissy's eyes snapped open and she fumbled with her right hand for her phone. She hit the unlock button and looked at the time: 1:13 a.m. She was definitely still drunk. She hoped whoever died had suffered.

Cissy tossed her phone onto the floor and laid back down, hoping to get just a few more minutes of rest to steady herself. Then something occurred to her: she shouldn't be able to hear her front door from her bed.

Her eyes still closed, Cissy reached her right hand out again and tried to feel out her surroundings. She waved it around in the air for a while, then gradually lowered it to tap what she assumed was her bed. All she felt was hard wood and Cissy realized she was sleeping on her living room floor.

Slowly, Cissy sat up. With her eyes still half-closed, she peered around the room. She was lying on the floor where her couch had been before Vance and Cormac came to take it off her hands. She was wearing a tank top and bra, but no pants. Cissy was confused by this until she realized that while asleep, she had taken her pants off and put one of her bare arms through each of the pant legs in order to keep them warm. Evidently the bath towel that she'd been using as a blanket wasn't doing an adequate job.

Cissy rubbed her neck and wondered what the hell had happened. The last thing she could remember was drinking all Sunday long.

She looked down at the floor behind her and saw that she'd been using a Lucky Charms box as a pillow. That would explain the stiff neck. Cissy picked up the box and fumbled around inside it until she located a few marshmallows. She popped them in her mouth as the banging on her front door continued.

Cissy pulled back her jeans to expose her hands, then rested them on her coffee table to steady herself as she slowly got to her feet. She decided that she would size up through the peephole whether or not the person at the door was representing anyone who may have left her anything worthwhile in their will. The decision to open it and talk to them would be made accordingly. Swaying back and forth, Cissy rolled her pants off her arms and with great effort, managed to pull them onto her legs.

She buttoned her pants and slipped her phone into her pocket out of habit. Then, sticking her arms out in front of her in a sort of Frankenstein-y fashion to make sure she didn't bump into anything, Cissy made her way to the door.

The knocking continued loudly and constantly. When Cissy got to the door, she paused for a second, just to make sure she wasn't going to throw up on whoever was at the door to deliver the bad news. She hoped that it wasn't her Great Uncle Frank who had died. She'd always been fascinated by his lustrous ear hair. She took a deep breath and the feeling fortunately passed.

Cissy put her eye up to the peephole on her front door. There was nobody there. She leaned back from the door, confused, but also aware that she was still drunk. She stuck her thumb in her mouth to get it wet, then rubbed it on the lens of the peephole to try to clean it off, just in case that had been the problem. She looked through it again. Still nothing.

The knocking continued.

A very small part of Cissy's brain was convinced that it was the actual angel of death at her door. That was why she couldn't see him. She figured this wasn't likely, but it was still a possibility. However, if it was anybody else at the door, they couldn't do her much more harm than the grim reaper himself, so throwing caution to the wind, she unlocked her front door and pulled it open.

A short little man was standing on her stoop. His head did not enter the visible range of her door's peephole. He was gripping a gnarled sort of cane that he had evidently been using to rap on the front door. A lit cigar hung out of his mouth. He was only wearing a towel.

"I have a taser," Cissy lied.

"Cissy," the man said. "Frampton Q. Bickerstaff, Harrington dean. I need you to come with me."

Cissy stuck out her hand to steady herself on the doorframe. She looked down at the little man in front of her. He was a hideous, unimportant little man who clearly could never have risen to the rank of Harrington Dean. But deep down, she vaguely remembered something from a meeting in the sub-basement where the *School Paper* had its headquarters. What was it . . . Oh yes, it was a controversial editorial written nearly two years ago that opined, "The dean is a hideous, unimportant little man who clearly should have never risen to the rank of Harrington dean."

"What is it?" Cissy asked.

"You're needed at the *School Paper* office," the dean said.

Cissy swayed and squinted at the dean. "The paper?" she asked as she tried to figure out what ethical infraction she might have been busted on. "Look, I can't drive. I need to sleep this off. Tell Brixon to go to hell."

She feebly groped for the door handle to slam it shut but the dean smacked her hand away with his staff.

"I'm sorry to use my shillelagh on you, but you've got to listen, Cissy," the dean said as he reached into the towel around his waist and somehow produced a flask from inside it. He unscrewed the top, took a slug from it, and passed it to Cissy. He obviously wasn't going to continue until she did the same so Cissy tilted the flask back and emptied the contents into her mouth. The cognac burned her throat and made her cough, but it also had the effect the dean was hoping for and snapped her out of her half-asleep state.

"I need your help," the dean continued. "I'm here with Vance. He says you two have . . . How do I put this, a bit of history?" The dean raised his eyebrows suggestively.

"Vance? The guy who lives with Cormac?" Cissy was bewildered. "He drunkenly propositioned me a day or two ago."

"Well, he's waiting in the van," said the dean, fidgeting and looking over his shoulder.

"Why are you wearing a towel?" asked Cissy.

"Look, I'll explain it on the way," said the dean. Before Cissy could ask another question, he'd reached his weird little walking stick around her and pulled her door shut with its knotted end. As it clicked shut, he turned and walked across her lawn toward the road.

"What the hell, dean?" Cissy yelled after him, but he just kept walking. Cissy didn't have her keys on her. It was either sleep on her porch until morning when she could call her landlord or a locksmith, or follow the dean and see what he wanted. Against her better judgment, she found herself leaving her house to follow the half-naked stranger who wanted her to get in his van.

She quickly caught up to the dean, who was waddling toward the road in the moonlight. "Alright, I'm coming with you," Cissy said. "I may need some more of that booze though. Hair of the dog and all."

Without breaking stride, the dean just said "Don't worry. It's in the van."

"Where is this van you keep talking about?" asked Cissy.

And then she saw it.

Idling menacingly across the street about fifty feet from her house was a white Chevy Astro van. Other than on the driver and passenger doors, it had no windows. Those two windows and the windshield were both tinted far darker than the legal allowable limit. Portions of the van's paint had flaked off, revealing a dull grey coat of primer underneath.

"Oh . . . Oh, hell no," said Cissy, stopping in her tracks.

Whoever was in the van, presumably Vance, must have seen them coming, because the headlights flashed on and off three times.

"Come on! It's just a van!" said the dean, continuing to shuffle toward the vehicle.

"No way," said Cissy, refusing to move. "That is a stone-cold pervert mobile."

"This?" asked the towel-clad man smoking a cigar in the street at one thirty in the morning. "Hogwash!" The dean rapped on the passenger window with his shillelagh. "Vance!" he shouted. "Open up!"

The window gradually lowered, with a herky-jerky motion that indicated it was physically being rolled down. Vance peered out of it through a pair of binoculars.

"Cistress!" he shouted, not lowering the binoculars. "Looking good, babe! Climb aboard the party van!"

Cissy inched a bit closer. She could see that Vance was shirtless as well. She assumed, then hoped, that he was also wearing a towel.

"Vance?" she hissed at him. "What are you guys doing? You look like a child molester!"

Vance lowered the binoculars. "What are you talking about, Cissy? We're here on important school business. Psh! Child molester . . ." He snorted in contempt.

"Well, you're sitting in a windowless van in the middle of the night with no pants on, looking through a pair of binoculars," countered Cissy. "And your friend here just lured a woman into leaving her house with him by giving her booze."

"Come to think of it, some dogs *were* barking at us when we drove by," said Vance.

"Cissy," the dean said bluntly. "We don't have much time. Get in the van."

"Alright, alright," said Cissy. She reached out to the passenger side door handle and gave it a tug. The door was locked. Vance chuckled.

"Whoa, whoa. I don't think so, sweetie," he said. "There's only two seats up front. I'm afraid you've got to ride in back."

The van's rear doors emitted a horrible rusty creak as the dean swung them open.

Cissy's mouth dropped open in horror as Dean Bickerstaff turned and grinned. "Hop in," he said, pointing with his shillelagh.

Cissy inched over to where the dean was standing and stared into the back of the van. Inky black darkness was all that she could see.

"Where did this van come from?" she asked the dean, her voice belying her confident/drunk exterior.

"We got it from the police impound lot," Frampton said. "I've got a guy on the inside who gave us a great deal."

"The police impound lot?" yelled Cissy. "Dean Bickerstaff, this was definitely some pervert's van!"

"You're making assumptions," said the dean. "This van could have been sitting in the impound lot for any number of reasons." The dean puffed on his cigar as he tried to think what these reasons might have been. "Maybe the owner had some unpaid speeding tickets, or maybe they had to tow it when he left it parked in a school zone."

"He left it parked in a school zone because he was looking at the kids through the binoculars!" yelled Cissy.

A light switched on in the closest house to the van. The blinds parted as the person inside tried to figure out what was going on outside.

"You're waking people up," the dean warned her.

Cissy lowered her voice. "Why do you two even need an Astro van?"

"Cissy, I drive a Lincoln Town Car," Dean Bickerstaff said with a haughty, knowing tone. He paused to let this fact sink in. Cissy stared right back at him.

"Do you . . . do you not know what a Lincoln Town Car is, or do you know and you're just not impressed by that?" the dean eventually asked her with a bit less confidence.

"I don't give a shit about your Lincoln Town Car," she whisper-yelled back at him. "What the hell does it have to do with this monstrosity?"

"Look. Vance and I have a plan. And in order to pull it off, I'm going to need to spend a lot of time over at Vance's house. The thing is, Cormac can't know that I'm there. And when you park a car outside someone's house, like a top-of-its-class, J.D. Power–rated 2011 Lincoln Town Car, that's going to attract attention."

"So *this* won't attract attention?" Cissy snapped. "Your huge, windowless van is going to let you come and go inconspicuously?"

"Of course," said the dean. "Why else would they be so popular in the pervert community?"

"This thing is an Amber Alert on wheels! Any parent, any good citizen, is going to call the cops as soon as they see it parked in their neighborhood!"

"Look, we don't have time to mess around. I don't care who has done or not done various things in the back of this van. Just get in and I'll explain everything on the way." He took a large puff on his cigar and exhaled the smoke with a grin. "Trust me."

Not sure if she was ever going to return to her house, Cissy climbed into the back of the van. Still unable to see into the blackness, she turned to ask the dean where she should sit.

"Are there any seat belts back he—" she started, but the rusty back doors were already slamming shut.

Cissy found herself in total darkness, and again had to resort to sticking her hands out in front of her to feel out her surroundings. Eventually she was able to find the side of the van. She gradually felt along the inside wall until she had walked a foot or two into the vehicle. Trying to find a safe place to sit, Cissy gradually knelt and felt down the walls until she could locate the spot where the floor met the wall. When her hands reached the floor, Cissy instantly recoiled. It was covered with a thick shag carpet. Even as drunk as she was, Cissy was sketched out about her surroundings. Why the hell did a van need shag carpeting? She turned her back to the wall and slowly slid down until she was sitting on the carpet.

She heard the dean's footsteps outside the van as he walked to the door, opened it, and climbed into the driver's seat. He turned the key in the ignition and after a few seconds of the engine attempting to turn over, the van lurched to life. Cissy heard the parking brake release, and then the van was off.

It only took about ten minutes to get to the *School Paper*'s office from her house. Cissy figured that if she was stuck back here for longer than that, she could always call the police on her phone. She pulled it out to take a look at the clock. 1:27 a.m.

The glow from her phone's screen acted as a dim sort of flashlight, illuminating a couple feet in front of her hand. Cissy stuck it out in front of her and tried to get her bearings. Before she had a chance to find out if there was anything weirder back here than wall-to-wall shag carpeting, she heard a static-y crackle as an intercom system clicked on.

"Cissy," said a deep, distorted voice out of a speaker in the van's ceiling. "How is everything back there?" It sounded like the type of distortion TV shows use to disguise a witness's voice: low, robotic, inhuman.

"What?" Cissy asked. "Who are you?"

"This is Dean Bickerstaff," replied the intercom, in a voice that sounded nothing like the dean's. "The van came with an intercom system to communicate with people in the back."

"It's making you sound like the killer in the *Saw* movies, Dean," yelled Cissy. "This van definitely belonged to some sick fuck!"

"Let's not lose focus of our goal here," said the dean's horrible distorted voice through the intercom. "Here's what we need you to do, Cissy. The *School Paper* goes to press in just about an hour. We need you to write an article about how any interested Harrington students can come by Vance's house on Craymore Street tomorrow and peer into Cormac's ear to get a glimpse at nineteenth-century whaling life."

Cissy sat in the back of the van in silence.

"What?" she finally said.

"Look Cistress," said a new voice. It still had the garbled, sinister tone that the intercom imposed upon every voice that it projected, but it was noticeably different than the one that had just been speaking to her. "We just discovered this afternoon that if you look into Cormac's ear while he's on the whaling boat, you can see everything he's doing there. It's really sweet, trust me. You need to let everybody know that on Tuesday, they can come by our place and pay five bucks to look into his ear for ten minutes."

"Vance?" asked Cissy as the van continued to speed along toward what she hoped was the *School Paper*'s office.

"Yes, that was Vance," the dean chimed in. "Listen, Cissy, honey. We just need you to write the article and convince the paper to run it tomorrow. I don't think I have to tell you how important this story is. We both know that Cormac is your best chance at winning the Buckler Award."

The ungodly intercom voice had finally stopped making Cissy's skin crawl. Right now she just wanted to do whatever it was the two idiots in towels wanted her to do so she could go back home and sleep for eighteen hours. And dammit, they were right. Cormac was her ticket to journalistic acclaim. If getting a scoop about his situation meant climbing into windowless Astro vans in the middle of the night, it was her responsibility as a journalist to do so.

"Listen," Cissy said. "I don't know what the hell you're talking about and I don't understand why you couldn't have explained this to me before you threw me in the back of your van. But I'm down for anything that's related to the Cormac story."

"Good," said the dean. "Vance, she'll need the laptop."

The intercom cut off, but Cissy could hear Vance shuffling around. All of a sudden, with the sound of rusty metal sliding, a thin slot opened toward the front of the van. The dim inner lights of the van's cabin shone through and Cissy heard what she thought was Chris de Burgh's "Lady In Red" playing softly. Vance's hand pushed a small laptop through the slot. It just barely fit. Cissy unsteadily crawled to the front of the van and took it. As soon as she had it in her hands, Vance quickly closed the slot again.

The intercom clicked back on. "You can use that to write the article," said the dean.

"That slot was definitely used to pass things to victims!" yelled Cissy. "He'd keep people back here and pass them individual slices of bread through the slot!"

"That seems like quite a leap to make," said the dean. "Frankly, I think it says more about you that you're projecting such things onto a perfectly normal van. Now get writing."

Cissy turned on the laptop. The glow from the screen finally let her see a bit of her surroundings. She turned the screen around and slowly moved it from side to side, casting a dim light onto the contents of the back of the van.

"There's a clown suit back here," she informed the dean and Vance. "And a big bag of candy. I think this was a Tickle Me Elmo, but it's missing its eyes."

The ghastly voice from the front was silent for a second. Finally it croaked out, "Just write the article, Cissy." The intercom clicked off.

Cissy reached into the bag of candy, pulled out a fun size Snickers, and got to work.

When the van's doors eventually swung open, Cissy reacted like a gun had just gone off. She'd been so engrossed in what she was writing that she hadn't even noticed they had stopped.

The dean peered into the rear of van and puffed his cigar. "Are you done?" he asked.

"Just going through to make sure I didn't misspell anything," Cissy said, scrolling through her document.

"No time," barked the dean. "Get out." When Cissy continued to scroll, he poked his shillelagh into the back of the van and rattled it around, trying to shoo her out.

"OK, OK, I'm coming—OW! That hurt!" The shillelagh had connected with her right ankle. "Why do you even carry that stupid cane?"

The intercom clicked on. "It's not a cane, Cistress," said Vance from the front. "It's a shillelagh."

"That's damn right," said the dean. He sounded rushed and irritated. "And if you don't get that article in before the deadline, I'm going to show you how unpleasant it feels when these knots get shoved somewhere you don't want them to be!"

"I wish I could believe this is the first time that someone in the back of this van has been threatened with forcible sodomy," said Cissy as she closed the laptop and scooted toward the exit.

"How's your breath?" Dean Bickerstaff asked. "Will they be able to tell you've been drinking?"

"I don't think so," said Cissy. "I pretty much went through the entire candy stash. Not sure who that guy thought he was going to lure with Lemonheads and brown Tootsie Pops."

"Don't forget the fake article!" yelled Vance from the passenger seat.

"Of course, the fake article, I almost forgot." The dean reached inside the waistband of his towel and pulled out a small USB drive.

"What is that?" Cissy asked as the dean handed it to her. "What fake article?"

"The only wrinkle in our plan," said the dean, "Is that we've got to tell as many people as possible about the miracle of looking into Cormac's ear without Cormac finding out about it."

"Why don't you want him to know?" asked Cissy. "Seems like a bunch of weirdos coming over and paying money to stare into his ear is something he'd probably want to weigh in on."

"Vance didn't think it was a good idea and frankly, neither do I. He's been moody ever since he started waking up on that whaling boat, and we don't want him depriving the world of this gift just because he feels like his privacy is being grossly invaded."

"So you want me to turn in one article, and feed a dummy one to Cormac to keep him in the dark."

"Exactly," said the dean.

"I want a split of all the dough you two rake in."

"Sounds like things are going south back there, Deano!" shouted Vance.

"It's my name on the byline, and it's my career I'm risking," said Cissy.

"We'll certainly be willing to discuss a minority partnership at some point in time," lied the dean as he puffed on his cigar.

"OK," said Cissy. "So, one copy of the fake article on the laptop and then have them actually print the one on the USB drive."

"No," said Dean Bickerstaff. He waved away his cloud of smoke and stepped through it. He gestured at the computer with his shillelagh. "It's the exact opposite. Look, don't screw this up."

"It's just that I'm kind of drunk," said Cissy pointedly. "I hope I don't get confused."

"Give her what she wants, Deano!" yelled Vance, who had quickly reconsidered his position from the front seat. "She's in too deep, man!"

Dean Bickerstaff glowered at Cissy, trying to look as angry as a squat man in a towel could at one thirty in the morning. He took a last puff on his cigar, then leaned over and extinguished it on the van's bumper. Cissy imagined that if the van were personified as a disgusting Pixar car, it probably would have enjoyed that.

"Fine," muttered the dean. "You're in for a third, as long as you act as our mouthpiece. Manipulating the press is going to be vital to the success of this operation, and we can't have any mistakes." Dean Bickerstaff stuck out his hand.

Cissy reached out and shook it. "I look forward to working with you." She paused and smiled before adding, "partner."

The dean's towel fell to the ground.

As he sputtered curses and apologies while picking it up off the parking lot asphalt, Cissy made a hurried beeline for sub-basement C.

* * *

Cormac opened his eyes and glanced up at his bedroom ceiling. As far as he could tell, he wasn't hungover. Good. He had some stuff he wanted to accomplish today.

He threw off the covers and darted over to the computer. As soon as he moved the cursor, unread email alerts started to pop up in the lower right corner of his screen. They were mostly from outraged TAs or the occasional outraged professor, and the subject lines contained phrases like "last chance," "imminent failure," and "respond immediately." He figured they could wait. Cormac opened up a web browser and pointed it to eBay. When the page loaded, he quickly typed "ukulele" into the search bar and hit enter.

His eBay search returned thousands of listings. There were twenty-dollar ukuleles that somehow looked even crappier than Ziro's homemade ones, and there were vintage ukuleles that cost over seven thousand dollars. Cormac assumed those were some kind of sick joke.

By the time Cormac had gone to bed on the *Levyathan*, he realized that he had ukulele fever. Ziro had been concerned— evidently there had been an epidemic of ukulele fever after the ship had docked next to a Hawaiian vessel two years prior. It was actually transmitted through rat feces, but everyone on the *Levyathan* was quick to blame the Hawaiians' strange instruments. Cormac had explained to Ziro that he had just used it as an expression, and there was no reason to burn the ukuleles.

He'd picked up the instrument quickly, and his missing pinky finger hadn't proven to be a liability. By the time they'd played through the sixth verse of "Treasures o' the Sea," Cormac had been able to break from the strumming pattern and add in a few improvised flourishes. By verse ten he was confident enough to attempt a solo. By verse fourteen he was legitimately concerned that the shanty might never end. After three more verses he had to excuse himself to take a leak off the side of the *Levyathan*. But by that time, he was hooked on the ukulele.

Cormac heard the toilet flush and the shuffling of feet in the hall. He quickly minimized his browser window. Selling Vance on the concept of having a ukulele in the house was going to require some effort. Springing it on him while he was half-asleep and hungover wasn't the way to go.

"Morning, Vance!" he yelled into the hallway. The grunt he got in return was indeed surly and hungover, but in a much higher pitch than what he expected from Vance.

Cormac pushed off from his desk and wheeled his desk chair back toward the door. He looked through and was able to see a disheveled female walking down the hallway.

"Cissy?" he asked, somewhat bewildered. Without turning, Cissy shot up a middle finger over her shoulder and continued trudging toward the living room.

Cormac got up out of his chair and followed her down the hall. When he got to the living room, Cissy was attempting to climb onto the airborne couch. Balancing precariously on the anvil, she swayed as she fumbled with the extension cord. She was only wearing one shoe and reeked of booze.

"Cissy, do you need a hand?" Cormac asked. Cissy tried to hoist her right leg onto the couch, but her left leg buckled. Cormac walked toward her, offering an outstretched hand.

"Here, let me help you," he said in gentle voice. "Do you want to sleep on the lower couch? Let's just lay down on the lower couch, it'll be much easier." Cissy turned and glared at him.

"Cissy, there is another couch three feet to your right! One that requires no agility whatsoever to lie down on!" Cormac was debating just grabbing her around the waist and transporting her to the couch like a sack of potatoes when he heard a voice from the other end of the hall.

"Mac! What the hell are you doing looking at ukuleles?"

Cormac turned and stared down the hall. He'd forgotten to close his web browser. A critical error. What was Vance even doing awake this early? Did it have something to do with Cissy's unexplained presence in their house?

He turned to explain to Cissy that he'd be back to help her as soon as he got Vance out of his room, but was surprised to see that she was already snoring on the airborne couch. Evidently she'd pulled off some acrobatic heroics while his back was turned. He left the snoring reporter and hustled back to his bedroom.

Vance spun around in the desk chair as Cormac entered his bedroom. He was in his boxers and a ratty grey Seahawks shirt.

"Well, well, well," Vance smirked. "Ukuleles, huh? I thought you were on a whaling ship, Mac, not a gayling ship."

"Very funny," said Cormac.

"Seriously, buddy, what was it that got cut off the other day? I thought it was your pinky finger, but you're sure it wasn't your dick?"

"Vance, what are you doing in here?" Cormac snapped. "Why are you awake? Why is Cissy passed out on our couch?"

"The Cistress locked herself out of her house," said Vance. "So she came to a trusted place to spend the night. And much like the noble innkeeper who opened his doors to Mary and Joseph, I offered her the best spot in the house."

"That innkeeper made Mary and Joseph sleep in his stable," said Cormac.

"Exactly," said Vance enviously. "All that hay everywhere."

"She seems pretty hungover," said Cormac.

"Well I wouldn't be much of an innkeeper if I didn't provide my weary travellers with booze when they arrived would I, Mac?"

"You're not an innkeeper. Get out of my chair," said Cormac. "I don't care what you think, I'm getting a ukulele. I learned to play it yesterday."

"I'll believe it when I see it," said Vance. "But hey, maybe keep it under wraps while the Cistress is here? I'm trying to work out a plan to hit that and I don't want her to be overwhelmed by your new instrument's raw sexual energy."

"Go to hell," said Cormac.

Vance grinned and got up out of the chair. Cormac sat back down and absentmindedly scrolled through the ukuleles, waiting for Vance to leave. He had hoped to have a relaxing Monday of skipping class and perhaps buying a ukulele. But now there was a hungover girl on his couch and Vance was onto his plans. He was already spending half his days on a whaling ship in the 1800s, was it too much to ask for his time at home to not be weird?

Vance wasn't leaving. Cormac turned around in his chair. Vance was typing something into his phone, but quickly shoved it into his pocket as Cormac turned around.

"Who are you texting?" asked Cormac. He had wanted to be able to tightly control any flow of information about his ukulele, but this plan had gone off the rails almost immediately. Who knew what sort of exaggerated rumors Vance was now spreading.

"Nobody," said Vance. "Don't worry about it. You want some breakfast, buddy?"

Cormac narrowed his eyes and tried to figure out what Vance was up to. He had never made breakfast for himself, let alone for Cormac. Obviously this was a shallow attempt to appear gentlemanly to the woman sleeping on the filthy airborne couch. Accepting the breakfast would be a subservient gesture that thrust Vance into a position of dominance. But then again, he hadn't eaten anything but salt pork and hardtack in over twenty-four hours.

"That sounds great," said Cormac cautiously. "The food on the boat is really terrible." Just then he remembered that he had stashed a piece of hardtack in his pocket to eat later. He patted both his pockets, imagining how nice it would be to watch Vance try to choke down the Civil War–era ration. But his pockets were empty. Transporting objects between the two eras must not be possible. Whatever, Cormac thought to himself. Makes about as much sense as any of this.

"Alright!" said Vance. "Breakfast coming right up!"

Vance leaned out the door and yelled down the hallway. "Cistress! Breakfast time, baby!"

A loud thump, followed by a groan indicated that Cissy had most likely just rolled off of the airborne couch and landed on the ground. Vance grinned and shook his head.

"That chick can party," he said. "I think I'm in love."

Cissy loudly dry heaved from the living room.

Vance turned and smiled at Cormac. "It's good to have you back, Mac," he said.

It was the closest thing to genuine warmth Cormac had ever seen Vance display, and it terrified him. Cormac felt the hairs on the back of his neck stand up as Vance left his bedroom, heading for the kitchen.

* * *

Somewhere in the darkness, Dean Bickerstaff's phone was buzzing. The dean stuck his hand out and tried to feel around for it. He ran his hand over his pants, his towel, his shillelagh, and the eyeless Elmo doll.

Deciding to spend the night in the back of the Astro van had made a lot more sense at 3:30 a.m. The celebration of Cissy emerging triumphantly from sub-basement C with a fake copy of Monday's edition of the *School Paper* had been muted only by her constant complaints about how creepy the van was. As they continued to down late-night shots of cognac in the parking lot, the dean had grown tired of her negative attitude. Despite the mounting pile of evidence that the van had indeed been owned by a pervert of the highest degree, he felt obliged to defend his purchase.

At some point, Frampton had made the bold claim that the van was so non-creepy that he was willing to forego his luxurious bed and spend the night in it. He figured that embracing the van like this would put an end to Cissy's griping, but unfortunately his declaration was poorly timed. As soon as he'd arrogantly informed Cissy and Vance of his decision, Cissy discovered that a large box in the corner of the van was in fact an economy-sized package of adult diapers. It was a small consolation for the dean that a couple of piled up diapers served as a decent makeshift pillow.

Frampton felt his way to the back of the van and pushed the rear door open to let in some light. He'd left it unlatched since there was no way to open the van from the inside once the doors were closed. He squinted as daylight poured into the van. He was hungover, but considering how early he'd started drinking yesterday, he didn't feel as bad as he should have. The comfortable, almost womb-like atmosphere provided by the van probably deserved some credit for this, thought the dean. He'd be sure to mention it to Cissy the next time he saw her.

The dean crawled back into the van and started to look for his phone. He eventually found it inside one of the giant floppy shoes that had been part of the clown costume. Not a scratch on it, he thought to himself. Another point for the van!

Dean Bickerstaff pulled his pants on as he checked the messages on his phone. There were several emails from board members that he ignored for now. The dean didn't intend on meeting with the board until he was confident the X-Factor numbers were going to be enough to let him keep his job. If exhibiting Cormac to the public got as much attention as he hoped it would, it shouldn't take much time at all.

Next, Frampton checked his text messages. The one that had woken him up came from Vance. It read: "The rooster (Mac) has crowed (is awake) -Farmer Tim (Vance)."

The dean would have to talk with Vance about making his coded messages a bit more difficult to crack. But for now, it was showtime. The dean's suit was a bit more wrinkled than he'd have liked, and sleeping on a pile of adult diapers had generated considerable static electricity, leaving what was left of his hair an unruly mess. But he wasn't addressing the board, he was just here to schmooze an unsuspecting student.

Frampton picked up the fake copy of the *School Paper* from underneath the diaper box. He'd carefully stashed it there last night to keep it looking brand new. In the right hand corner, below the fold, there was a follow-up article one Cissy Buckler had written about Cormac McIlhenney.

"NO CHANGES FOR CORMAC," read the headline. The article went on to describe how absolutely nothing had changed for Cormac, and how no new discoveries had been made, and that there was no reason to suspect there was anything else going on. The dean and Vance had cooked it up to lure Cormac into a false sense of security. The real article, which Cissy had suddenly "remembered" after the *School Paper*'s night editor had run off the copy of the paper that Dean Bickerstaff now held in his hands, would serve to inform the rest of the school about the exciting new twists that Cormac's case had actually taken.

The dean planned to keep Cormac in the dark with fake editions of the paper as long as it took to exploit his situation for maximum X-Factor gain. Vance was positive that if Cormac knew they were charging strangers money to peer into his ear while he lay in bed unconscious, he'd do something selfish and unreasonable, like asking them to stop. But as long as they could maintain control of the media, there would be nothing to arouse Cormac's suspicions.

Of course, they'd have to keep Cormac far away from any of the real *School Paper*s, and that was what the dean intended to set in motion right now.

* * *

Cormac heard a knock at the front door. He was never going to be able to find a ukulele with all these distractions. He looked out into the hallway. Vance was still busy preparing god-knows-what in the kitchen. Maybe Cissy would answer it. Cissy groaned in agony.

Frustrated, Cormac got up and walked toward the front door. As he walked back into the living room, he saw that Cissy was indeed no longer on the airborne couch. She was curled up in the fetal position underneath it. Her head rested on the base of the anvil. The slightest jostle to the highly precarious structure would bring the entire couch crashing down on top of her. She'd be killed instantly.

Cormac went to answer the door.

He swung it open and stared down at the squat little man standing on his doorstep. From the fake smile to the wrinkled suit down to the gnarled walking stick, everything about him screamed "I am here to tell you about an extremely unpopular religion."

"We don't want any," said Cormac. He slammed the door shut. Dean Bickerstaff was just barely alert enough to stick his shillelagh into the door frame and prevent the door from closing. It slammed into the shillelagh, and the dean gave it a little push to open it enough to look Cormac in the eye.

"Is Cormac McIlhenney in?" Dean Bickerstaff asked with a grin, determined not to let the rude greeting visibly bother him.

"No," lied Cormac without missing a beat. "I think he's at class."

Before Cormac could start to close the door again, the dean spoke up. "Would that be Professor Kerr's Psych 201 class?" he asked in his oiliest possible voice. "The one that started twenty-five minutes ago and that Cormac hasn't been to in three and a half weeks?"

While Cormac stood there in surprised silence, Dean Bickerstaff took the opportunity to light a cigar. A stranger showing up at his door with insider knowledge like this had undoubtedly freaked Cormac out. One of the dean's favorite strategies was to terrify a mark, then befriend them once they were vulnerable. At this point in time, Cormac probably thought he was about to be hauled off to jail, so helping the dean out with a little favor would seem like a wonderful alternative.

"Don't worry, Cormac," said the dean with a wink and a friendly puff. "I'm not a cop."

"I didn't think you were," said Cormac.

"You didn't?" The dean was momentarily taken aback. He hoped he hadn't revealed his disappointment.

"Not for a second," said Cormac.

"But who else besides a cop would be here, at your door, asking questions? Who else would know your schedule?" asked the dean.

"I'm not sure," said Cormac. "But a cop? You? Really?"

The dean was furious. Imitating law enforcement personnel was one of his favorite forms of intimidation.

"I could be a cop!" he insisted.

"A mall cop, maybe," said Cormac, who was beginning to enjoy himself. "If the other mall cops were on strike."

"A substitute mall cop?" sputtered the dean. He waved his shillelagh around agitatedly. "This is an outrage!"

"It probably wouldn't be at the good mall either," said Cormac, who had just as quickly grown tired of the game. "It would be at the *other* mall in town."

"The *other* mall?" Dean Bickerstaff shouted. "The one where those stray dogs bit a guy in the Foot Locker and the only place to get your parking validated is the Sbarro bathroom?"

"Yep, that's you," said Cormac, not really paying attention. "Validating stray dogs' parking at the other mall's Sbarro." Where the hell was Vance with breakfast?

"Both of you shut up!" yelled Cissy from underneath the airborne couch.

The sound of Cissy's voice snapped the dean back into the moment. He was here on a mission. Cormac's insults had sidetracked him almost instantly, but he had to right the ship. Failure was not an option today. He lowered his shillelagh and took a calming puff from his cigar.

"Cormac," he said. "My name is Frampton Q. Bickerstaff. I'm the dean at Harrington."

Cormac's face dropped momentarily, but enough for the dean to notice. Advantage: dean, he thought to himself.

"I just need to talk to you about your . . . situation," Frampton said. "May I come in?"

Cormac nodded and stepped back to allow the dean to enter the house. This couldn't be good. A visit from the dean was not something you earned by succeeding, or making the university a better place. No, when the dean descended down from whatever opulent mansion he surely lived in, it had to be for the sole purpose of making problems go away. Cormac quickly came to the grim realization that he must be the problem.

"Look, Dean Bickerstaff," he said in a much less confident tone than he'd used when the dean was still on the doorstep. "I'm sorry about all that substitute mall cop talk. It's just that we get a lot of religious freaks coming by here, and we sometimes try to mess with them when they won't leave us alone."

Dean Bickerstaff dismissed Cormac's concerns through gritted, cigar-chomping teeth. "Don't worry about it, son. I know how it is with the door-to-door crazies. The nice thing about a shillelagh," he said, twirling his shillelagh, "is that you can beat religious people with it."

Cormac had been expecting a quip that was a bit more clever, or subtle, or both. He didn't really have a response prepared. Fortunately, the dean had already moved on.

"This is quite a structure," Frampton said, pointing at the couches with his shillelagh.

"Yeah," said Cormac. "My roommate built those. Stadium seating couches. You gotta do something with your spare time I guess."

"Is it safe for her to be under there?" asked the dean.

"I think so," said Cormac.

Just then Cissy received a text message and her phone vibrated twice in her pocket, causing the airborne couch to almost collapse.

"We should probably talk quieter," Cormac said, lowering his voice. The dean nodded in agreement.

"Who's ready for breakfast?" Vance yelled from the kitchen. The couch emitted a loud creak.

"Let's go to my room," Cormac whispered. He gestured for the dean to follow him down the hall to his bedroom. Cormac had no reason to suspect that the dean already knew the way.

When they got to his bedroom, Cormac offered the dean his desk chair, then sat down on the corner of his bed. Vance appeared at the door carrying three Bloody Marys.

"I thought I heard a visitor!" Vance said with a smile. "Will you be joining us for breakfast?"

"I don't think so," said Dean Bickerstaff. "I wouldn't want to impose."

"Nonsense!" said Vance. "Any friend of Cormac's is a friend of mine." He offered the first Bloody Mary to Cormac, then handed off the second one to the dean.

"I'm Vance," he said, sticking out his free hand.

Maintaining the ruse they'd agreed upon last night, the dean shook it in return. "Frampton Q. Bickerstaff," he said.

"Vance, this is the dean of all of Harrington," Cormac said glumly.

"The dean?" said Vance as he downed half of his Bloody Mary. "Uh-oh! What'd you do now, buddy?" He turned to Frampton. "You guys finally find out about his counterfeit textbook operation?"

"He's kidding," said Cormac, a little too quickly. "I mean, that was just an idea, and I talked about it *once*. I was drunk." He shot Vance a glare.

"Cormac, Cormac," said the dean. He rested his shillelagh between his legs, holding his cigar in one hand and the Bloody Mary in the other. He looked right at home. "You're not in any trouble! I just read about your predicament in the *School Paper* and wanted to personally visit to see if there was anything that Harrington could do to make your situation any easier."

Cormac was naturally wary of the Harrington faculty, especially the man who was in charge of them all. He'd never seen the dean before, but had heard whispers around the campus about the power he wielded. Now that he finally had a chance to meet the man face-to-face, part of him wondered what the big deal was. The dean didn't look like a leader; he looked like the type of guy that had received at least one lifetime ban from a bowling alley. But Cormac knew that appearances could be deceiving. After all, Frampton had been dean at Harrington for almost as long as Cormac had been alive. Unimpressive physical stature aside, evidently the man knew what he was doing.

But Cormac couldn't figure out why he'd taken an interest in him. "I'm not really sure what you can do to help me, Dean. Can that shillelagh cast a spell to make me stop going back in time?"

The dean laughed and took another sip of his drink. "No, I'm afraid the only thing this shillelagh is good for is convincing professors that they don't want tenure anymore."

"Hell yeah, Dean," said Vance. "Show those whiners who's the boss!" Why was Vance still part of this conversation? Cormac noticed that his roommate had already finished his Bloody Mary.

"These drinks are all you're making for breakfast, right?" Cormac realized out loud.

"That is correct," said Vance, wiping his mouth with his wrist. "And you're gonna wanna take those kinda slow. There's four shots of vodka in each."

Dean Bickerstaff quickly glared at Vance before turning his attention back to Cormac.

"I can't offer you any help back on the ship, Cormac," the dean said. "But from what I hear, these trips of yours are making it difficult for you to attend classes." Cormac nodded. "Well I hardly think it's fair that your academic record should be penalized because of this remarkable experience you're having! It's unreasonable for these snooty academics to hold you to the same standard as all the other students who aren't spending half their days in the 1800s." The mere mention of Harrington professors made the dean snort with contempt.

"It *is* hard to get to class when I'm stuck on the *Levyathan*, sir," said Cormac. He hoped the conversation was going in the direction he thought it was.

"Please," said Dean Bickerstaff. "Sir, is what people call me when it's already far too late to avoid a shillelagh beating. Dean Bickerstaff will do just fine."

"How about Deano?" asked Vance. Cormac noticed that he'd slipped out and refilled his Bloody Mary. The dean issued Vance a more pronounced glare this time. Vance flashed him a tipsy smile and raised his glass in response.

"I'll cut to the chase, Cormac," said the dean. "I'm prepared to offer you a free pass to help ease the burden of this unique problem of yours. Straight A's, in all your classes, for the rest of your time at

Harrington. No questions asked. Just say the word and it'll kick in retroactively back to the start of the semester."

Cormac's heart jumped. He thought back to all the D's and F's he'd already received this semester. Free straight A's would wipe all of them out and let him cruise all the way to graduation! It was like he'd applied a video game cheat code to his academics, as opposed to the rampant level of traditional cheating he usually employed.

"That would be great," Cormac said slowly. He was still waiting for the other shoe to drop. He took a cautious sip of his drink. When the dean didn't immediately offer a catch, Cormac felt obliged to inquire. "What's the catch?" he asked.

Dean Bickerstaff grinned, puffed his cigar, and swigged his Bloody Mary. "There's no catch! I just want our students to know that in a case of extenuating circumstances like yours, the Harrington faculty stands behind them. I'd only ask that you grant the *School Paper* exclusive access to any stories about your progress. Let them break the news of adventures you might be having back in the 1800s. It'll give Harrington journalists a chance to get some solid scoops. Fortunately, I believe you're already familiar with one of the paper's best and brightest reporters?"

From the living room, they could barely make out Cissy croaking the words "Please . . . kill . . . me . . ."

Cormac had never heard of a college dean showing up at your doorstep to offer you straight A's. But in a week where more strange things had happened than in the rest of his life combined, he was inclined to just go with the flow. The thought briefly entered Cormac's head that without this offer falling out of the sky, he definitely would have failed all his classes, been placed on academic probation, eventually kicked out of school, been unable to find a job, and dead within six months. The vision was startlingly clear. Vance delivered his eulogy in a towel to a hastily assembled audience of debt collectors and enemies. Cormac quickly pushed it out of his mind.

"So, as long as I don't talk about the *Levyathan* to anyone but the *School Paper*, I get straight A's?" he asked

Frampton nodded. "You didn't really want to talk to the *Roustabout*, did you?" The *Roustabout* was the other paper on the Harrington campus, a snarky alternative weekly. Despite never having interacted with any of their writers, Cormac assumed that everybody on the staff thought they were cooler than him. They were the kind of people who drank at Mickey's ironically, instead of being thankful for the great values and friendly but limping dogs. Cormac imagined having to stare at a *Roustabout* reporter's waxed mustache while being interviewed. He thought he might prefer losing his other pinky.

"Absolutely not," said Cormac. "This all sounds good to me. A deal's a deal!" He stuck out his Bloody Mary, and Dean Bickerstaff clinked his glass against it.

"I'll have my people take care of all the paperwork today," the dean said. "If you have any problems with your professors, you just let me know and I'll handle them personally." He twirled his shillelagh.

Cormac assumed their business was finished. Without classes to worry about, he could focus on relaxing and mastering the ukulele. A guy could get pretty good if he didn't have to worry about schoolwork. By graduation, he'd pretty much be a pro. Cormac imagined wearing his cap and gown as he delivered a eulogy at Vance's funeral to a crowd of naked women. The women were there to sleep with him immediately afterwards, not to mourn Vance.

His roommate's voice quickly pushed this vision out of his mind as well.

"What about me?" asked Vance. Cormac turned to look at him. Vance was grinning at the dean and swirling the last third of his Bloody Mary in his glass.

"What *about* you?" hissed the dean through his cigar. He had been on the verge of leaving with everything going according to plan. Whatever Vance was doing, it wasn't something they'd discussed. A plan this deviously unethical couldn't have unexpected developments popping up. Vance was a wildcard that would need to be contained.

"I'm going to be looking out for my roommate," said Vance. "Every other day. Someone's got to make sure he's OK. Mac's unconscious half the time. Vulnerable. I'll have to make sure nobody takes advantage of him." Vance downed the rest of his Bloody Mary, never breaking eye contact with the Dean. He wiped his mouth with his wrist. "I'd think Harrington would be happy to offer me a similar deal," he finished.

Dean Bickerstaff was furious. Vance had trapped him. He'd have to give him what he wanted or else risk him poisoning the operation from the inside. Cormac was furious. Vance also getting straight A's would only dilute the value of his Harrington degree and severely reduce the chance of post-eulogy group sex happening anytime soon. Both of them silently seethed. Vance looked very pleased with himself.

"Of course," said the dean in a flat voice. He slowly removed his cigar from his mouth and extinguished it in his Bloody Mary. "We'd be happy to help anyone who's looking out for Cormac's best interests." He stared daggers at Vance and silently plotted a shillelagh-based revenge.

"In fact, Mac," Vance continued. "You might consider signing over power of attorney to me."

"Why would I do that!?" shouted Cormac at the exact same time the dean was shouting "Why would he do that!?"

"It was just a thought," chuckled Vance. "Hey, don't look so put out, buddy! We both just made the honor roll!"

It wasn't ideal, but Cormac had to admit he was pleased. At this point, he just wanted to get the papers signed before Vance could screw anything up further.

Thankfully, Dean Bickerstaff felt the same way. "It's been an honor meeting you both. Keep an eye out for the paperwork. And Cormac, if you need anything, anything at all, you give me a call." He handed Cormac his business card. The thick stock had an embossed picture of a shillelagh on the left side, and the dean's phone number on the right. Above the phone number, "I'm Dean, Bitch" was printed in large, bold letters.

"Did you rip this off from Facebook founder Mark Zuckerberg?" Cormac asked.

"Who?" asked the dean, with a dismissive air.

"Mark Zuckerberg," said Cormac. "He famously had business cards printed that said 'I'm CEO, Bitch' like, seven years ago."

"Not familiar with him," said the dean. "He probably ripped me off, whoever he is."

"You're claiming that not only did you not rip off his business cards, but that you have never even heard of one of the richest, most famous men in the country?" Cormac asked incredulously.

"This card makes it look like your name is Dean Bitch," remarked Vance.

"Alright, give me that!" yelled the dean as he snatched his card back.

"How am I going to get in touch with you if I don't have your business card?" asked Cormac.

The dean reluctantly handed the card back to Cormac and made a mental note to burn the remainder of the lifetime supply of cards he'd ordered after watching *The Social Network* two weeks earlier.

"I believe we're done here," Dean Bickerstaff said testily. "Cormac, I don't want to take any more of your time. Have a great rest of your day. Vance, could you show me to the door?"

Vance nodded as he tilted his glass back, trying to coax the last few drops of Bloody Mary out of it. He rattled the ice cubes around for a second or two and, once he was satisfied, sat the glass down on Cormac's desk and waved for the dean to follow him out the door.

Cormac waited for the two of them to leave, then sat back down in his desk chair. He looked at the card in his hand again, just to make sure what had just happened was real. In a week full of unlikely scenarios, scoring straight A's may have been the unlikeliest yet.

Cormac set the card down next to his keyboard and hoped he wouldn't have to call the phone number on it. Everything about the dean oozed untrustworthiness. But as long as he delivered on his simple promise, Cormac didn't care about what his real motives might be. Then Cormac tried to think what his real motives might be. But the mental image of the dean sitting in a tall-backed chair and laughing as he concocted a vile scheme to take advantage of him was quickly replaced in his mind by an alternate one: gigantic, sexy letter A's fanning him with palm fronds as he somehow funneled a beer while lying in a hammock.

Chuckling one more time at the "I'm Dean, Bitch" inscription on the business card, Cormac tapped the space bar to wake up his laptop. After the screen powered back on, he clicked over to his browser and once again began to browse the ukulele selection on eBay.

* * *

"What the hell was that?" hissed Dean Bickerstaff as he and Vance got to the door. He was confident that Cormac couldn't hear them from his bedroom, and from underneath the airborne couch, Cissy did not appear to be conscious.

"That's called seizing an opportunity, Deano," said Vance, giving Frampton a smug nod.

"That's called unpredictability, you jackass!" He raised the shillelagh up in the air and brought the knotted end down on Vance's head. Vance let out a sharp yelp, but appeared too startled and drunk to do anything about it.

Dean Bickerstaff looked around to make sure nobody had heard Vance. The shillelagh blow had been over the line, but he also did not appreciate Vance putting him on the spot. "Look, Vance," he said calmly. "This plan isn't going to work if we don't stick to the script. We've got to contain all the unpredictable elements, and that means ourselves too. Can I trust you not to surprise me anymore?"

"Hey, it's a two-way street, pal," said Vance, grimacing while he rubbed the top of his head. "Do I look like a goat to you? You're gonna just whack me over the head with that shillelagh like I'm a goat? Keep that thing to yourself!"

Eventually, Dean Bickerstaff would have to straighten Vance out regarding his insistence that shillelaghs were primarily used for whacking goats, or at least discover where this bizarre belief originated from. But that would have to wait. Tomorrow was a big day and he couldn't risk leaving on bad terms. If Vance started to carry a grudge, there was no telling how he might sabotage their venture once the public started showing up. He was a maniac one-on-one; with an audience he might find a frightening new gear.

Reluctantly, the dean stuck out his hand. "I'm sorry, Vance," he apologized. After a moment of hesitation, Vance shook his hand. Their uneasy truce could continue for another day.

"I'll be back with the paperwork—for both of you—in about an hour." The words tasted bitter in Dean Bickerstaff's mouth. "We probably won't be able to talk then, so why don't you give me a call when the coast is clear, and we can iron out some details for tomorrow." Vance nodded. The dean took one last look at the couches and the young woman who probably needed medical attention lying on the floor, then walked out the door.

The dean was about halfway to the van when Vance called after him.

"Oh, speaking of unpredictable elements, Deano . . . I know how you hate them, but there's one more you should probably know about." The dean stopped in his tracks and braced himself for whatever Vance was about to spring on him.

"He's looking into buying a ukulele," said Vance. Dean Bickerstaff whirled around immediately. Evidently Vance could see the shock in his eyes, because he smirked and said, "Yeah. I thought you'd like that."

Dean Bickerstaff hurriedly waddled back to the porch and stepped into the house. "He's looking to buy a what?" he demanded.

"A ukulele," said a gleeful Vance. "You know, doot doo dee doo doo dee doo doo dee doo doo . . ." As he hummed, Vance pantomimed a ukulele performance that would not have been allowed to be broadcast on network television.

"Alright, alright," said the dean after he'd seen enough. "So he liked playing the ukulele on the ship, did he . . ." The gears were turning. Ideally, the dean wanted Cormac holed up in the Craymore Street house, far away from any copies of the *School Paper* that might tip him off to what was really going on. Dean Bickerstaff had assumed that with no classes to attend, the familiar comforts of booze, drugs, and TV would be enough to keep Cormac entertained. But if he had a new toy to keep him busy, that was even better. It might ensure that Craymore Street's toxic atmosphere of unambitious filth remained bearable long enough for the dean to raise Harrington's X-Factor ranking.

"I think there was a ukulele in the back of the van!" the dean whispered excitedly.

"You're kidding," asked Vance.

"No, no," the dean reassured him. "I woke up spooning it in the middle of the night. Lord knows what it was doing back there."

From under the couch, Cissy spoke up for the first time in a while. "It looks like a toy, so kids can relate to it. The creep who owned that van played it and they followed him into the back of the van where he did god-knows-what to them. He was like the Pied Piper!"

"I hardly think that's how that tale went," said the dean.

"No, the Pied Piper was much more uplifting! He just drowned the kids next to a bunch of rats!" It sounded like Cissy was getting a bit of feistiness back. The dean wanted to leave before she emerged.

"Listen, Vance," Dean Bickerstaff said, keeping an eye on the pile of reporter beneath the airborne couch. "I'm giving Cormac that ukulele."

"A ukulele?" Vance protested. "In my house? No way man, I won't—"

The dean cut him off with a raised shillelagh. "We've got to keep your roommate happy," he said. "And right now that means he's getting a ukulele, whether you like it or not."

Vance's face fell and for a moment, the dean felt like he had regained the upper hand. Quickly, before Vance could say anything, he left the house and shuffled out to the van. He threw open the back doors and rooted through the objects that littered the floor until he found the ukulele. Then, proudly holding it aloft like the head of a conquered rival, he waddled back toward Vance.

Vance looked crestfallen. Dean Bickerstaff pushed the ukulele into his chest and held it there until Vance reluctantly took ahold of it. Vance held it between two fingers, the way you might a dirty diaper, and the dean could tell that holding the tiny instrument went against every musical principle he held. Excellent.

Dean Bickerstaff prepared to exit once again, this time on a high note. He gave the shillelagh a jaunty twirl, pulled a cigar out of his lapel pocket, then turned his back on Vance and walked out the door.

"Where do you want me to tell him this came from?" Vance asked in a defeated voice.

The dean stopped and thought about this for a second. He took the time to pull out a match and light his cigar. He puffed on it a few times to heighten the drama.

"You tell Cormac," the dean said, not bothering to turn and look at Vance. "That it's just a little gift from the ukulele fairy."

As soon as the dean said it, he regretted it.

"The ukulele fairy?" asked Vance.

The dean's remark had sounded much less ridiculous in his head.

"You're calling yourself the ukulele fairy?" The dean refused to turn around and look at him but he could tell by Vance's voice that he was starting to smile again.

"I bet there's already a fairy costume somewhere in the back of that van," shrieked Cissy from under the couch.

Having both gained and relinquished the upper hand in what had to be world-record time, Dean Frampton Q. Bickerstaff glumly puffed his cigar and took the first step toward his van.

* * *

Cormac's mouse cursor hovered over the "buy" button as he tried to justify buying a ukulele with an etching of a cobra down its neck. By his own hasty mental math, the added cost of the sweet snake would mean three weeks of eating only one meal on the days he was not on the *Levyathan*. He figured he could make up for the loss of vital nutrients by eating approximately twenty times as much hardtack when he was on the ship.

Before he had a chance to mortgage his health for a novelty musical instrument, Vance tapped on his door. Cormac minimized the window, even though he knew it was too late. He spun around in his chair and prepared himself for Vance's insults.

To his surprise, his roommate was standing in the doorway gingerly holding a ukulele.

"Here you go," said Vance. He tossed the ukulele onto Cormac's bed and turned to leave, looking down at his hands as if he'd just changed his car's oil.

Cormac sprung up from his desk chair and darted over to his bed. He picked up the ukulele and turned it over in his hands. It felt solid, but then again, anything would feel more legitimate than Ziro's makeshift instruments. The lack of a venomous animal anywhere on it was disappointing, but in retrospect, maybe it made sense to get the more expensive ukulele after he had played the instrument more than once.

"Vance," Cormac shouted after his roommate. Vance continued toward the kitchen. Cormac leaned out into the hallway and yelled after him. "Where did this come from?"

Vance rinsed his hands in the kitchen sink, then dried them on his pants and began to fix another Bloody Mary. "The dean left it for you," he said. "Said he wanted you to have it."

"He just had a ukulele on him?" Cormac was confused.

"Look, Deano . . . I mean, the dean is a powerful man, Mac," said Vance. "If he wants a ukulele, he knows people who can get him a ukulele. You're lucky he likes you. A man who can get a ukulele that fast can make you disappear just as quickly if you piss him off."

Cormac didn't really see a connection between rapid ukulele procurement and disappearing one's enemies, but he didn't want to argue with Vance any more today.

"I'll be sure to thank him the next time I see him," said Cormac. Vance nodded curtly. Cormac looked down at the ukulele in his hands. He was itching to give it a try, but he wondered if he was obligated to take a moment to celebrate with Vance. After all, they'd just had the greatest moment of their collective academic careers.

"What do you think about making me another one of those, too, buddy?" asked Cormac. Vance pointed at his Bloody Mary. "Yes indeed," Cormac replied. "Looks like I already aced that quiz I'm supposed to be taking right now, and something tells me you're going to do the same tomorrow. Not bad for a Monday morning if I do say so myself."

"Alright, alright," said Vance, warming up to the idea. He retrieved another bottle of vodka from the pantry and cracked it open for the first time. Cormac suspected that the first bottle had been new as of this morning, but didn't say anything. Vance poured vodka into a pint glass of ice until it was about halfway full. Then he went to the fridge to get the Bloody Mary mix.

"So, another day at sea, huh Mac?" Vance said. "Now don't tell me the only thing you did yesterday was learn to play the ukulele. There's got to be more going on than that."

Cormac chuckled. "No, it was a pretty packed day. Killed a bunch of whales. Went down to the room where they store them all. At the rate I'm going, it's going to be full pretty soon."

Vance walked over and handed Cormac the drink. Cormac thanked him, and they clinked glasses. Cormac took a sip and nearly choked. It was incredibly strong and the vodka tasted like paint thinner. But the only reason he was even drinking it was to offer an olive branch to Vance, so he smiled, and choked down another sip.

Cormac went on to tell Vance a bit more about how the whales got broken down and stored in the cold storage area, and before he knew it, he'd polished off a third of his drink. They hadn't even left the kitchen. Cormac wasn't sure if it was the brute strength of the drink or just a desire for some camaraderie, but he suddenly thought it was very important to tell Vance something.

"I touched a whale dick," he said.

Vance played it cool. "Oh did you? And how did that go?"

"It was repulsive!" Cormac broke out laughing and Vance was unable to resist following suit. "Holy shit, Vance! It was slimy and quivering and, my God, the size of those things! You could use them to divide the lanes at a swimming pool!"

"Oh God, I know, man. I spent almost an entire day last summer looking at pics of them online." Vance chuckled at this fond memory. "Crazy how valuable they are, though."

Vance laughed a bit more and downed the last third of his drink. He went to fix a new one.

"Valuable?" asked Cormac. He also wanted to know what had provoked Vance to look up whale penises online and then keep looking at them once he'd seen one of them. But this was a more intriguing topic at the moment.

"Yeah, man," Vance said as he poured vodka into his glass. "Pound for pound, they're like, by far the most valuable part of any sea creature."

"Are you sure about that?" asked Cormac. "On the *Levyathan*, they're the only part they throw away."

"They throw them away!?" shouted Vance, almost spilling the vodka, which he was still pouring. "That's idiotic! The Chinese will pay an arm and a leg for them!"

"The Chinese?" asked Cormac.

"Hell yeah, the Chinese," said Vance. "They think that whale dicks are like, an aphrodisiac. They're like rhino horns or shark fins. Your guys are just tossing them overboard?"

"Well, yeah," said Cormac. "I mean, they probably sort of push or prod them overboard with a long stick. Nobody wants to touch them." Vance's claim sounded ridiculous, but he didn't put it past Captain Anson and the rest of the crew to have missed this very important detail. After all, the crew had pretty much been doing everything else wrong before he arrived there. It actually wouldn't surprise him at all if they were discarding the most valuable part of their catch because having it around creeped people out.

"Well, you gotta tell them to cut that out, Mac," said Vance. He was starting to slur his words. Cormac wondered if it was even ten thirty yet.

"I'll try to talk some sense into them," said Cormac as he started to make his way back to his bedroom.

"Hey, hey, Mac, Mac." Vance waved Cormac back over to where he was leaning against the counter. "You wanna know what?" he asked conspiratorially. Without waiting for Cormac to reply, he continued. "I got some. In the medicine cabinet."

"What?" Cormac asked. "What are you talking about?" He was already regretting being friendly. Now he just wanted to play some ukulele in peace. Then all of a sudden he realized what Vance meant and his eyes widened.

"Whale dicks? You've got whale dicks in this house, Vance? Where the hell did you get them? How on earth are you storing them?"

"Ssh, ssh . . ." Vance waved his hand to try and get Cormac to bring down the volume a bit. If ukuleles didn't figure into his plan to woo Cissy, aphrodisiacs made of whale dicks certainly wouldn't either. Vance swung his arm around Cormac's shoulders and whispered into his ear. "They grind up the whale dicks and make pills out of them. I got some in Chinatown a few months ago."

"There's no Chinatown near Harrington," said Cormac. "Do you mean China Tom? There's a delivery guy at the Chinese place named Tom. Did he sell you these pills? If he did, throw them away now. That guy has definitely been to jail."

Vance just sort of grinned a drunk grin at Cormac. Cormac looked disgusted. "Vance!" He grabbed Vance by the shoulders. "Where are these pills!?"

Vance sort of swayed back and forth for a while before muttering "Advil bottle."

"They're in the Advil bottle?" The Advil bottle was the only thing in their medicine cabinet. Cormac took Advil nearly every time he was even slightly hungover. "Why did you put them in the Advil bottle!?"

"Because I'm hiding them, Mac, and they look just like Advil!" slurred Vance. "If I put them in a Tums bottle, everyone could see them because they don't look anything like Tums."

"So . . . just to make sure I understand this," said Cormac. "Somehow you learned that the Chinese delivery guy, Tom, was selling pills made of ground-up whale dicks. At what point did you learn this? Was it while you were asking him for a few extra soy sauce packets or . . ." Cormac was exceedingly curious about the finer points of this transaction but had to stay focused, lest he lose his entire Monday to unraveling the mystery.

"So you buy these pills," he continued "and you decide to just blend them in with the Advil so that nobody will find them, the side effect of this being that the next time one of us has a minor muscle ache, neither you or I will be able to tell if we're taking over-the-counter pain relief or an illegal pill made from whale dongs."

"You leave Tom out of this!" Vance said defensively before starting to hiccup.

Cormac had had enough. He set his glass down in the sink and gave Vance a friendly pat on the back as he walked past him. Vance gave him a happy thumbs up, their conversation of ten seconds ago completely forgotten.

Cormac walked into his bedroom and sat down on the corner of his bed. He picked up his new ukulele and gave it a test strum. It resonated well and sounded like it was well tuned. Cormac fingered the chords to "Treasures o' the Sea" while he mouthed the words to himself. When he thought he was ready to give it a run-through, he stood up to close his door.

From the living room, there was a loud coughing noise, then a bang, and a cry of pain from Cissy. It sounded like she'd hit her head on something.

"Stupid goddamn couch!" she yelled in anger.

"Morning, Cissy," Cormac yelled down the hall. "Don't take any of the Advil in the medicine cabinet! Trust me!"

Cissy replied with a surly groan. Cormac closed the bedroom door and sat down to play the ukulele.

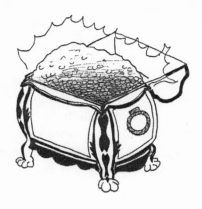

DAY EIGHT

Captain Anson paced in his chambers. He had spent most of the night tossing and turning, worrying about what was going to happen when they arrived in St. John's. Once he paid the crew the substantial amount of money they were owed, would they still remain subservient? Would they demand he spend his own cut of the windfall improving the ship, ridding it of death traps and plugging holes with something other than severed appendages? And worst of all, what if that greedy harpy Eleanor was tipped off that the *Levyathan* was there, offloading their biggest catch of all time?

Captain Anson tried to focus on the positive: his crew had killed a lot of whales, broken them down into their various parts, and seemed poised to kill even more. And just as he was starting to see the glass as half full, Captain Anson got some more good news.

When he opened his cabin door after a few hours of pacing, there was a dead carrier gull at his feet. There was a rolled-up paper tied to one of its legs. Carrier gulls had it rough. They were the most reliable way of sending messages from ship to ship, able to travel great distances in harsh conditions. Sadly, their rate of survival after delivering their messages was approximately 0 percent. This lack of reusability, combined with the many, many man hours it took to raise and train them, meant they were an increasingly scarce resource.

The *Levyathan* had burned through their supply of carrier gulls their first afternoon at sea. Captain Anson had sent carrier gulls to all the boats he could think of to deliver vulgar stick-figure drawings of their captains, or sometimes parchments that just said the word "balls." He and the other whalers thought this was a riot, but Ziro pointed out that their budget did not allow for new carrier gull purchases for another decade, and they were now without means of communication in an emergency. They also had a decade worth of gull food in storage, which wharf rats claimed as their own almost instantly.

The captain braced himself for bad news as he unrolled the paper and was surprised when it was actually *good* news. Unfortunately, this made him feel even worse.

The gull had been sent by the captain of the *Sea Spirit*, another Nantucket boat that the *Levyathan* had occasionally encountered over the years. The *Sea Spirit* captain had always been a pleasant fellow, offering assistance with equipment repairs or tips on emerging weather patterns. Anson loathed the man, and was pleased that his message indicated he was probably going to be dead by the time anyone received it.

The message read:

Dear Captain Anson,

I hope this gull finds you well. I pray that the recent storm did not damage the water pump I assisted you in repairing last spring. I will never forget the happy look on your face when your slave and I got it working.

The Sea Spirit *unfortunately took major damage during the storm. In an attempt to outrun the torrential rains, we were forced to dump our whaling haul, which had been substantial. Sadly, even this drastic measure, one I undertook even though it tore at my soul, was not enough to save us. Our ship has been devastated. I am sending gulls to all known ships in the area. If you receive this and are able, please send help. Our situation is dire. Soon we will be clinging to driftwood. Many men have considered . . .*

Captain Anson skipped ahead.

Word from shore is that many other ships have suffered the same fate. In fact, rumors of a devastated whaling industry abound. Those who were able to escape the storm with their lives were either forced to jettison their catch or lose it to spoilage. My contact indicates major shifts in the market have occurred as a result. Buyers along the coast from Newfoundland to Charleston are said to be offering three to five times the normal market price. I tell you this in the hopes that in exchange for tipping you off to this lucrative opportunity, you will aid us in turn, as again, clinging to driftwood is a fate that grows more imminent with . . .

Captain Anson crumpled the paper in his hand. So their already-substantial catch was now worth even more. It seemed as if the universe was mocking him, dumping good fortune all over him in an attempt to make him miserable. In his frustration, he reared back and gave the dead carrier gull a hard kick. He hoped it would gracefully sail overboard, but it was less aerodynamic than he'd guessed. A spray of feathers shot up into his face, and the bird skidded about three feet away before coming to a halt. Brushing the feathers out of his face, Captain Anson left the bird for Ziro to swab up later.

The captain began to trudge the length of the deck of the ship. It was another beautiful day. Yippee. From the prevailing winds, they were probably making great time toward the port of St. John's. Hooray. When they arrived, they'd offload their cargo for one of the biggest paydays in whaling history. Whoop-de-doo. And then his men would leave him, his wife would repossess his boat, and he'd be arrested for fraud, theft, and kidnapping. Or even worse, he'd have to go back to working at the bank.

Captain Anson sighed. Perhaps berating Ziro would cheer him up. It usually did. The captain remembered the time some of the whalers had discovered him berating Ziro in his sleep. He'd been standing outside the slave's quarters in his pajamas, yelling epithets while Ziro tried to sleep. The captain hadn't remembered it at all when they told him about it the next morning. He started to smile just thinking about it.

He stopped smiling when he rounded the corner and saw Cormac and Ziro. The two of them were yukking it up and singing "Treasures o' the Sea" as they sharpened harpoons and coiled ropes.

"Dammit, Ziro!" Captain Anson barked. "The captain of the *Sea Spirit* is clinging to a piece of driftwood as we speak! Show a little respect!"

Ziro looked confused. "The captain of the *Sea Spirit*? You hate that guy. How do you know he's in trouble?"

"Never mind that," said Captain Anson. "What are you two doing?"

"Just getting ready for another big haul," said Ziro enthusiastically. "Cormac's harpooned two whales already!"

Ziro pointed to a nearby cleat that had two taut harpoon lines attached to it. The captain followed them out to the sea where two tired whales were futilely trying to shake themselves free.

"I know the crew won't be up for a few more hours," said Cormac sheepishly. "But the whales were just floating there and it was hard to resist. I figured if they get away, no big deal, and if not, they'll be tired by the time the men are ready to haul them in."

Captain Anson had never felt more conflicted. More whales meant more money, which would only complicate things further once he got to shore. But looking at the two whales struggle as they tried to keep afloat awakened a primal part of him that refused to be discouraged. He gripped his spyglass in an attempt to calm himself, but it was useless.

Rushing to the edge of the boat, Anson brandished the spyglass and began to scream at the whales.

"Wicked brutes, born of a noxious womb! Quake as your world crumbles! The tips of these spears that have pieced your rugged hides are but the first and meekest pain you shall feel as you descend into the inferno that awaits you in eternal whale hell!"

The whales thrashed feebly, and the captain turned around, exhausted. Panting slightly, he walked over to Cormac and Ziro. In the face of all his financial concerns and worries about his wife, he'd forgotten how much he enjoyed doing that.

"Keep up the good work, Cormac," Captain Anson said, wiping beads of sweat from his brow.

Cormac was very intrigued by the metaphysics of whale hell, but just nodded at the captain. He'd ask Ziro about it later.

"Ziro, there's a dead carrier gull in front of my quarters," continued the captain. "I trust you'll deal with it post haste. It must have slammed into my door as it landed, it's quite a mess."

"You have a gull feather stuck to your forehead," said Ziro, reaching out to try to pluck it off of the captain.

Captain Anson knocked Ziro's hand aside and pawed at his forehead until the feather came loose. "I'm not sure how that got there," he lied. "Anyways, welcome back Cormac. Things are certainly quieter when you're not here."

He turned to leave, intending to go decompress in his quarters over some hardtack, but Ziro called out to him before he could get away.

"Sir," the former slave said. "Cormac actually had an idea."

Captain Anson turned and eyed the unlikely duo. What were these two up to? Palling around out here so early, all buddy-buddy. He didn't like it. He didn't like it one bit.

"Initiative. I like that, Cormac," he lied again. The captain decided that his initiative going forward would be "crush initiative."

Cormac looked over at Ziro, then spoke up. "Sir, this may sound a little crazy to you but . . ." Cormac paused, realizing he might be thrown overboard within five seconds of finishing his sentence. "I think I may have discovered a way to make a ton of money off our, our . . . well our discard pile, sir."

Captain Anson narrowed his eyes and walked forward until he was nose-to-nose with Cormac. He leaned forward and whispered into his ear. "Choose your next words carefully, my boy."

Over the years, there had always been a whaler who came up with some scheme to make a fast buck off the whale penises. Usually the plan revealed inner perversions so horrible that the crew had no choice but to toss him overboard and pretend he'd never shared the plan in the first place. This still didn't prevent someone else from chiming in six months down the line with some new scheme that they thought was a sure thing, until they too were sailing over the edge of the *Levyathan*.

"Well, when I was at home, I did some research," Cormac said tentatively. "And I'm pretty sure that if we could find any Chinese sailors, they'd pay top dollar for . . . well, for the whale dicks, sir."

"Dammit! The Chinese!" The Chinese were among Captain Anson's least favorite people to deal with. With most of the other whalers, you could hammer out a business deal over a few jugs of rum, but the Chinese were always more complicated. The captain found their eccentricities exhausting. Every time he dealt with them he was out of commission for the next twenty-four hours. Of course, this was a substantially shorter amount of time than the rum swigging sessions with the other whalers put him out of commission for, but he never seemed to realize this.

"Do we have to deal with the Chinese?" he pleaded. "They're so strange."

"Well, we don't *have* to do anything," said Ziro.

"But the more whales we catch, the larger that discard pile will get," added Cormac. "We wouldn't want anybody to think we were hoarding those things down there. In a big, sticky pile, quivering—"

"Alright!" yelled Captain Anson. "We'll sell them to the Chinese. And you're sure they'll buy them?"

"Absolutely," said Cormac. "Whale penises have long been thought to have sexually enhancing properties in their culture."

"Of course they have," muttered the captain. "Creepy little weirdos . . ." He closed his eyes and shuddered. Eventually he snapped them back open.

"We'll need all hands on deck. But we're not touching the discard pile. The Chinese can haul them out on their own."

"Aye aye, captain!" said Ziro.

Captain Anson turned and walked to the edge of the ship. He looked past the two trapped whales and contemplated the horizon. His encounters with the Chinese had been few, and he was reluctant to add another to the list. But he had noticed that the discard pile was larger than it had ever been before, and he couldn't risk it getting to the point where someone on the crew decided to push him into it as a practical joke. That would be a fate worse than mutiny. If the Chinese were willing to take them off his hands, then so be it.

"Ziro," the captain said as he stared out to sea. "It's time to do business with the Chinese. Please go and fetch me my flute."

* * *

Dean Bickerstaff peered in the door to Cormac's bedroom one more time, just to be sure. Like the previous five times, Cormac was lying there in his typical *Levyathan* state. So far the dean had poked him with the shillelagh, clapped his hands really loud, and even blared "Lady In Red" all the way through. Cormac didn't stir. The dean had no reason to believe that today was going to be any different, but he was nervous just the same. Today was for all the marbles.

As of 9:00 a.m., the house on Craymore Street was officially open for business. Per the articles that Cissy had written for today's and yesterday's issues of the *School Paper*, anyone who was interested was welcome to drop in during normal business hours and peer into Cormac's ear for five bucks.

Vance was in the kitchen preparing their cash box. This involved eating all the pretzels that were left in a plastic tub, then filling it up with change. He had already prepared a round of Bloody Marys, and to the dean's dismay, was wearing his Seahawks towel. Vance claimed the towel was part of "the complete Mac experience," which also included free access to the stadium seating couches before and after looking into Cormac's ear.

Cissy was currently taking full advantage of this access. Vance had informed the dean that Cissy's hangover yesterday proved too debilitating for her to make it home, and she'd spent the day recovering on Craymore Street. Eventually she realized that she wasn't going to be able to write Tuesday's article in the state she was in, so she started drinking again with Vance.

Around four in the afternoon, she received a call from an angry man who was wondering when she might be home to sign for the couch he was attempting to deliver. Cissy had forgotten all about the couch, panicked, and handed the phone over to Vance. After some bitter negotiations and lots of profanity, Vance had convinced the delivery man to bring the couch to the Craymore Street house so Cissy could sign for it there.

While the delivery men were hauling the couch out of the truck, Vance convinced them to come inside and take a look at the stadium seating setup. He assumed that, as people "in the industry," they would take a special interest in the revolutionary stuff he had going on in the living room. They were in a hurry and didn't seem to care, and more profanity was exchanged.

Cissy was currently hungover on the filthy airborne couch while the five-piece, Italian leather sectional that her brother had sent her sat on the porch.

Vance had relayed all this information to Dean Bickerstaff when the dean arrived that morning. Petty couch-related squabbles were the last thing the dean wanted to hear about. His morning had started with an email from a board member, sarcastically inquiring how his quest to raise Harrington's X-Factor rating was going. It included a link to a CNN report about a fundraising initiative some students at the University of Wisconsin had started that had gone viral and raised hundreds of thousands of dollars for a local women's shelter.

That university was being hailed as a hotbed of crowd-sourced activism. The board member had taken the opportunity to include a link to the only recent news story she'd been able to find about Harrington. It was about a rabid dog that had bit someone in an alley behind the humanities building. The person had been in the alley to buy drugs. The dog belonged to a tenured professor who was in the habit of leaving him chained to his car's bumper while he was inside teaching. The car had been illegally parked in a handicapped space. The dog had also bit the handicapped person who the space was reserved for. He had been there to sell the first person the drugs.

The dean didn't have time to deal with what the board member referred to as "potentially the scandal of the decade." He had a business to run. He checked his phone. 9:07 a.m.

Where the hell were the massive throngs of people, pushing through the door to experience this miracle?

"Vance!" the dean yelled into the kitchen. "How's that cashbox coming?"

"Lookin' pretty sweet, Deano," came the reply. "Did you know that Alaska put a giant bear on their state quarter? How awesome is that! Bear quarters have got to be worth at least double, I bet."

The dean left Vance to finish assembling the cashbox and walked into the living room. He took a quick look out the window to make sure their sign was still there. In a moment of panic, he'd realized that morning that there was no way for potential customers to identify the house as the one they were supposed to go into. Scrounging through Vance and Cormac's house for materials for a sign, he'd ended up scrawling the words "LOOK IN GUY'S EAR – $5" on the inside of an old pizza box and nailed it to one of the trees in the front yard. There was currently a crow pulling at some cheese that was caked onto the box, but it would be hard to miss from the street.

The dean turned his attention to Cissy. The window was behind the airborne couch, and a man of the dean's height could not see over the back of the couch to where Cissy was laying. Rather than walk around to the front of the couch, Dean Bickerstaff simply cleared his throat.

"Ahem . . . Cissy. Cissy! CISSY!" he yelled.

"What!" Cissy shouted as she quickly sat upright. The dean could only see her head over the back of the couch, but she was obviously confused and terrified. She jerked her head back and forth, trying to get her bearings and as she did, the anvil and the computer that were each propping up a leg of the couch began to wobble.

"Cissy, be careful! My God!" the dean shouted, fearing the worst. A mangled body in the living room would be very bad for business. Unfortunately, Frampton's shouting only made Cissy more panicked and she started to scream as the couch's foundation shook violently. Dean Bickerstaff stood rooted, helpless to stop the inevitable collapse, and eventually realized he was screaming as well. The dean locked terrified eyes with Cissy as they both unintelligibly yelled at the top of their lungs.

The couch stopped wobbling about five seconds before either of them noticed. The dean paused to take a deep breath and noticed that the couch had somehow steadied itself while they were yelling. Cissy, who had not yet noticed, continued to shriek in abject terror. The dean attempted to get her attention.

"Cissy! You're OK! Cissy! The couch stopped moving!" Dean Bickerstaff waved his shillelagh over his head since Cissy probably couldn't hear him over her own voice. Eventually she noticed that he appeared to no longer be concerned about the airborne couch's impending structural collapse, and her yelling petered out.

A few seconds after they'd gone silent, Vance yelled from the kitchen.

"What the hell's going on out there?"

"Everything's fine!" replied the dean.

"I think I'm gonna barf!" yelled Cissy.

"What did Cissy just say?" asked Vance.

Dean Bickerstaff ignored Vance and walked around to the front of the couch. He gave the anvil a whack with his shillelagh. The staff vibrated like a tuning fork, but the couch remained steady. Evidently Vance's "bend but don't break" construction was more stable than Frampton gave him credit for. He didn't want to think about what code-violating techniques Vance had employed to stabilize the airborne couch, or which corrupt contractor had taught them to him. Right now he had a hungover reporter to whip into gear.

"Cissy," the dean said. "Are you ready to do this? There could be someone at the door any minute."

Cissy looked pale and the dean was pretty sure her eyes weren't focusing on him.

"Look, Cissy, all I need you to do is get something in the *School Paper* that shows people how amazing it is to look into Cormac's ear. And I know it would be really easy to just fabricate some quotes or plagiarize something from the *New York Times*..." Cissy nodded. "But we can't do that today," the dean continued. Cissy's face fell. "This story is too important. Other people are going to read this, not just people at Harrington. It needs to hold up to scrutiny."

Dean Bickerstaff sized up Cissy's ability to write something gripping enough to raise Harrington's X-Factor, let alone something coherent. He didn't see it happening. Cissy needed a fire lit under her.

"That's a really nice sectional couch out there on the porch," Frampton said. "Your brother who gave it to you won the Buckler Award and is much more successful than you." Dammit! That hadn't come out as subtle as the dean meant it to.

But his words appeared to have their intended effect. Cissy's eyes narrowed and appeared to focus, and she straightened up. The need to barf appeared to have passed.

"Let's do this," she said in a low voice.

There was a knock at the door. The sudden noise broke Cissy's concentration and evidently the need to barf returned very quickly. Her eyes went wide, and she clumsily half stepped, half rolled off of the airborne couch. She hit the ground running and the bathroom door slammed shut before the dean could even get a word out.

His ace reporter was throwing up in the bathroom and his partner was counting change in nothing but a towel. But waiting outside was someone who was about to have their mind blown, and in turn, save Frampton's job. Clutching his shillelagh, Dean Bickerstaff went to answer the door.

The cloud of marijuana smoke that hit the dean as he threw the door open was so strong that it physically knocked him back a step. Standing outside were two lanky men in their early twenties. Their hair was shaggy and their eyes were red. One of them held the last bit of a lit joint, and they giggled at nothing in particular.

Eventually, the one who wasn't holding the joint registered that the door was open and the dean was standing there. He smacked his buddy on the shoulder, and pointed to the dean. The friend's eyes went wide, and he quickly tossed the joint over his shoulder. Evidently they weren't expecting to be greeted by an adult.

"Hello uh, sir," the first stoner said. The other one stifled a laugh while his friend continued. "My colleague and I are here to . . ." As soon as his friend unexpectedly identified him as his "colleague," the second stoner began to guffaw uncontrollably. The laughter proved infectious and the first stoner started laughing hard enough that he was unable to finish his sentence.

Dean Bickerstaff stood there in disappointed silence while the two degenerates yukked it up on the porch. So this was who they'd attracted. Funyun-munching potheads. The dregs of society. Two buffoons without any future plans besides running their model trains or tying fishing lures. Or maybe stringing garlands of popcorn and cranberries.

The dean didn't really have the firmest grasp on stoner culture, but he knew he didn't care for it. He glared at the two idiots who were still laughing at the "colleague" comment. It had been going on for so long that he started to suspect they were somehow mocking him. He instinctively flexed his grip on his shillelagh. Customers or not, it was going to feel good to break them out of their merriment with some quick blows to the shins.

"G-Dimes? Mako? Holy crap, why didn't you tell me you two were coming over!" The dean turned and looked behind him. Vance was standing there in his towel, a broad smile on his face.

"G! G, look," said the stoner who was evidently Mako. "It's Vance!"

G-Dimes was still laughing so hard that all he could do was gasp as he attempted to get ahold of himself, but he managed to raise his hand to acknowledge Vance. Vance walked past the dean and engaged in an elaborate handshake routine with Mako. Steps of it involved dribbling invisible basketballs, shooting finger guns at each other, and pretending to hit imaginary joints. It lasted about thirty seconds, and by the time they were done, G-Dimes had finally calmed down.

"Man, it's been so long since I've seen you guys!" said Vance.

"Yeah, we've been laying low ever since Turnip got busted," said Mako.

"How's Turnip holding up?" asked Vance. The dean wondered how worthless a degenerate Turnip must have been if these lowlifes were allowed to walk the street while he rotted in prison.

"He got stabbed in the showers on day one. He's dead," said Mako. The dean was silently glad he hadn't vocalized his last thought.

"Bummer. Well, are you here to see Mac?" Vance asked.

"Hell yeah!" said Mako as G-Dimes nodded vigorously. "This sounds like a trip. By the way, man, I'm diggin' the towel."

Vance smiled and gestured for the two of them to come inside. The dean stood his ground, sizing them up, and Vance eventually had to elbow him to get him to move out of the way.

Mako and G-Dimes were very impressed with the stadium seating couches. Mako claimed he had been thinking about doing something similar for a long time, which did not surprise the dean in the slightest. By the time Cissy emerged from the bathroom, Vance and Mako were attempting to hoist a terrified G-Dimes up onto the airborne couch. The dean cleared his throat.

Cissy stood next to the dean and shot him a look. The dean misinterpreted her desire to lay back down on the couch as a shared contempt for the stoned idiots. Everyone else seemed to have forgotten why they were gathered in the living room in the first place, so Frampton took it upon himself to speak up. "You gentlemen are interested in peering into the world of the nineteenth century, right?" he asked.

"Oh right," Vance said, as he strained to support G-Dimes's right foot. "Yeah, you guys should check it out now before there's a line. You can take in the view from up there when you're done."

Mako and Vance lowered G-Dimes to the ground. Cissy sullenly approached them and before Vance could introduce her, she grabbed onto the extension cord and swung up onto the airborne couch, where she promptly lay down and fell asleep. Mako and G-Dimes looked disappointed, but Vance beamed.

"She's gotten damn good at that," he said proudly.

Dean Bickerstaff wanted to move things along before they wasted any more time. "What do you two say we go and blow your minds?" he asked, rubbing his hands together enthusiastically.

Mako looked enthusiastic, G-Dimes slightly more terrified. Vance urged both of them closer to the dean. "We're just going to need five dollars from each of you," he said. "That'll get you ten minutes of ear time."

Mako pulled out the thickest wad of bills that Dean Bickerstaff had ever seen. The dean nearly did a double take. Mako would be considered unemployable by even the lowest quality pizza delivery chain; he was obviously selling massive amounts of drugs. Frampton wondered if perhaps he had sold out his friend Turnip in order to move in on his turf. But instantly he worried that his face might betray his suspicion and he forced the thought out of his mind.

"Do you have change for a hundred?" Mako asked. The dean's eyes bugged as he realized that the entire roll was actually hundred dollar bills. Mako was an even bigger player in the drug game than he had thought.

"I'm afraid we don't," the dean said, patting his pockets in a lame attempt to make it look like it was at least a possibility. What the hell were the campus police doing as this mafioso ran the school's drug trade unchecked?

"You know what," said Mako. "If this is anywhere near as sweet as you guys said it was, we're gonna want to spend a lot of time in there. Especially if we can . . ." He looked at Vance and made a hopeful smoking gesture. Vance gave him a thumbs up.

"Yeah," said Mako excitedly. "We'll just pay for time in advance." He handed Dean Bickerstaff the hundred dollar bill.

Dean Bickerstaff looked down at the drug money. A hundred dollars was a hundred dollars he figured. Mako had just booked the next three and a half hours of ear time.

"Do you normally carry around all of your money like this, Mako?" the dean asked as he walked over to deposit the bill in the pretzel tub that Vance had set in the corner.

"*My* money?" Mako asked incredulously. "No way man, this is G-Dimes's money. I just sort of . . . manage it for him."

Dean Bickerstaff looked over at G-Dimes, who was staring intently at the pattern of the airborne couch fabric from about three inches away. Amazing. The dean figured that if the roll was just his walking-around money, G-Dimes had to be one of the three richest people on campus. He could be a powerful ally, if he was ever able to pry himself away from staring at *Match Game* reruns on cable.

But business alliances with drug dealers could wait. Today was all about the X-Factor, and they had to make sure their first customers were satisfied with the experience.

"Who wants to go first?" the dean asked. Mako deferred to G-Dimes, but the kingpin now appeared to be silently crying at whatever message the couch had revealed to him.

"I guess I'll go," Mako said.

"OK! Let me show you to the bedroom," the dean said gesturing toward the hallway. But before he could take a step in Cormac's direction, Vance swooped in.

"I've got this one, dean," Vance said with a knowing look. Another unexpected development. Dean Bickerstaff gritted his teeth. He thought he had made his stance on surprises very clear.

"Mako," the dean said, attempting to mask the rage welling up inside him. "Why don't you make your way down to Cormac's room. I'll join you there in a second."

Mako nodded. Before he left, he reached his arm out to Vance, and the two of them reprised their intricate handshake ritual. This time around, it involved even more steps, including each of them pantomiming pulling a quarter from the other's ear. When it eventually ended, Mako nodded to the dean and walked down the hall.

The dean looked over at G-Dimes and quickly decided that they could talk freely in front of him.

"What the hell are you doing?" he hissed at Vance. "I thought we had a plan? You work the door, I supervise Cormac's room."

"I called an audible, Deano," Vance said in a serious tone. "I'm pulling patrol duty. We can't have guys whackin' it in there."

The dean was caught off guard. Whackin' it? Did Vance mean what he thought he meant? "Whackin' it?" he asked, knowing deep down that he'd already lost the battle.

"Let's face it, Deano," Vance said with a slightly condescending air of wisdom. "This little shop of ours is going to attract some weirdos. And once they start peering into Mac's ear, some of them are going to want to whack it in there. Per the roommate's code, I can't let that happen."

Dean Bickerstaff was flabbergasted. Vance had never voiced a single concern about any of their customers being compelled to masturbate by the experience of peering into Cormac's ear. But evidently it had been his primary concern all along.

"Weirdos?" Frampton demanded. "Weirdos?! That guy down there, Mako, it seems like he's your best friend!"

"Best friend?" asked Vance, sounding confused. "No way, I've only met Mako once."

"You've met him *once*?" Dean Bickerstaff's astonishment continued. "What the hell was this all about then?" The dean did an exaggerated, full body, one-man impression of Vance and Mako's handshake from a moment ago, ending it with two middle fingers pointed at his business partner.

"Well yeah, we only met once. But we spent most of that time working on our handshake." Vance said this like it was the most obvious thing in the world.

Frampton was about to protest that he'd be able to prevent people from whacking it in Cormac's room just as well as Vance could, but he decided that this definitely wasn't a battle worth fighting. He actually wasn't sure if it was true and he wasn't even sure he wanted it to be.

"OK, go!" the dean yelled, waving his shillelagh toward Cormac's bedroom. "Just go! I'll stay here and . . ." Dean Bickerstaff glanced over at Cissy and G-Dimes. Neither seemed to necessitate any attention at the moment. In fact, they both appeared to be drooling. "I'll work the door," he declared.

Vance smiled and gave the dean a little salute. Then he hurried on down the hall after Mako. Dean Bickerstaff picked up the pretzel tub and gave the change in it a little shake. Mako's hundred dollar bill sat on top of the quarters and dimes, looking wildly out of place.

Oh well, thought the dean. At least someone showed up. He walked over to the grounded couch and sat down. Down the hall, Cormac's door slammed shut. Dean Frampton Q. Bickerstaff sighed, pulled out his phone, and set the timer on it for ten minutes.

* * *

Cormac tried to ignore his pinky sticking out of the floor. He'd gone into the rum storage area to retrieve a couple of jugs. It was the first time he'd been there since the accident. Even though his pinky was apparently serving a valuable purpose, Cormac wasn't thrilled about being in the same room as his severed digit. He kept his distance from it as he retrieved two jugs, but never let it out of his sight on the off chance that it might pop out of the floor and slowly start to inch its way toward him, upon which point he would have to throw himself over the side of the boat, screaming.

That wouldn't do today. He had video stats to check on when he got back home.

Yesterday, after a long afternoon of practicing the ukulele, Cormac had felt confident enough to attempt a complete run through of "Treasures o' the Sea." On a whim, he flipped his laptop's webcam on and recorded himself playing the song. His performance was by no means flawless, but he thought it captured the ramshackle energy of the song pretty well. During the seventh verse, if you listened carefully you could faintly hear Cissy dry heaving in the background, and during the tenth you could hear Vance exclaim "goddammit that hurts!" when he stubbed his toe on the couch anvil. But his remark actually came at an appropriate moment in the song, when the narrator was describing a frankly quite-avoidable accident involving an electric eel that had proved unwilling to perform its duties as suspenders.

Cormac debated uploading the video for the rest of the day, and finally pulled the trigger right before he went to bed. He figured it wasn't like Uncle Jemima could kick him out of the band again. Plus, Ziro's song was really catchy. Cormac could easily picture drunken frat party attendees shouting along with the more vulgar and degrading lines. It deserved to be heard, and if it gained an audience, he deserved to be the person who everyone assumed wrote it, since the real author had been dead for a century. Now all he could do was hope that somebody would watch it.

Having retrieved the jugs, he quickly backed out of the rum storage area. Before he made his way back to the main deck, he set one jug down and uncorked the other. He tilted it back and took a long, satisfying swig of rum. When he was done, he wiped his mouth with the back of his mangled hand. Then he looked down at the silk robe with a dragon printed on it that Captain Anson had insisted he wear, and tilted the jug back a second time.

Cormac had hoped that he might have a somewhat normal day aboard the *Levyathan*. Maybe catch a few whales, help the crew hack them up, then spend the rest of the afternoon talking shop with Ziro about the ukulele. Little did he know that his brilliant suggestion that they sell whale penises to the Chinese would have so severely altered the course of the day.

In retrospect, Cormac figured he should have known the plan was no good the moment it left Vance's lips. Nothing his roommate said was ever as easy or free of complications as he made it out to be, least of all his get-rich-quick schemes. A plan to sell an enormous pile of enormous genitals for an enormous profit should have immediately raised a red flag.

But Cormac had once again been bewitched by the idea of casually saving the day on the *Levyathan*. Not only would he be the man responsible for harpooning the whales, but he'd also increase profits by finding a market for their dicks. Like Icarus, his hubris had proved to be his undoing, only instead of falling to his death he was wearing a robe that looked kind of stupid.

As soon as Captain Anson had decided to sell to the Chinese, normal operations on the boat ceased. Cormac found this surprising. As far as he could tell, they were still days from their destination. If they were headed to port, Cormac figured they may as well maximize their haul so they could take advantage of the seller's market when they docked. But the captain seemed to not even consider the idea. He just demanded that Cormac put on the robe and fetch some rum.

At least he wasn't the only one wearing a robe. Captain Anson and Ziro had also donned the ridiculous garments. The captain had pulled them out of a dusty trunk in his chambers. There was a red one, a green one, and a teal one, which Cormac had been forced into by virtue of picking last. Each robe had scenes of dragons and mountains and lanterns embroidered onto it, and small bells were attached to the sleeves that jingled every time they moved.

Cormac walked with the two jugs to the bow of the ship, where Captain Anson and Ziro were standing. He didn't see much of a difference between the long, flowing robe and a dress. He also hoped that Vance never learned of this particular fashion. He didn't think he could deal with someone wearing it around the house. Sure, it covered more bare skin than a towel, but the sound of swishing silk and bells that jingled with every step you took would not make the tradeoff worthwhile.

Captain Anson didn't see Cormac coming. For some reason, in addition to his robe, he'd also donned a conical straw hat, like a rice farmer might wear. It was wide enough around that it obscured his peripheral vision. Ever since he'd put it on, he'd relied on Ziro to point him in the right direction. He didn't even realize Cormac had returned with the rum until Ziro tapped him on the shoulder and spun him ninety degrees to his left.

Cormac held up both of the jugs of rum. "Here you go," he said. Captain Anson reached out and snatched one of the jugs away. "Are you OK, Captain?" Cormac asked. "You seem kind of on edge."

The captain ignored him and fumbled with the jug's cork. Once he got it off, he tried to tilt it back and take a sip but the brim of his hat kept getting in the way. He couldn't lean back far enough because the back of the brim hit his neck. When he tried leaning forward, the front of the brim slipped down and hit the jug. Next, he tried to hold the hat in place with one hand and pour the rum into his mouth with the other, but the jug was too heavy to manipulate properly and he started spilling rum all over his face. Ziro took this time to whisper an explanation to Cormac.

"He always gets this way," the former slave said. "He doesn't like dealing with the Chinese."

"It got in my eyes!" yelped Captain Anson.

Cormac and Ziro took a step or two away from the captain. "But why is he dragging us into this with him?" he asked Ziro. "We're not due to dock for several more days. We should be catching whales. There's a ton of them off the port side and nobody's shot at them in hours! I think they're getting cocky."

As Cormac said this, two whales simultaneously breached off the port side of the *Levyathan*. One shot a burst of water out of its blowhole and the other one angled itself in midair so that the stream of water arched directly into its own blowhole. They crashed back into the sea, and in the distance, other whales in the pod shot water out of their own blowholes in appreciation.

"Was that just a sex thing?" asked Cormac.

"I'm not sure what that was," said Ziro.

"It really stings!" yelled Captain Anson, who was by now down on his hands and knees, trying to keep his hat out of his face so he could rub his eyes with his sleeve.

"Well why the hell aren't the rest of the whalers at least trying to harpoon something?" demanded Cormac. "I haven't seen them all day."

"Cormac, just trust me," Ziro reassured him. "This is all going to make sense shortly. Just follow my lead when the Chinese show up."

"When the Chinese show up?" Cormac asked. He was confused. The Chinese had no way of knowing that they'd decided to sell them whale dicks today, and the *Levyathan* had no knowledge of where the Chinese boats might currently be sailing.

"Yes, when the Chinese show up," said the captain as he slowly got to his feet. Rum still dripped off his chin and he sputtered as he tried to regain his composure. His hat hung forward and his breaths were labored. "Seems like Mr. Superstar Whaler still has a bit to learn about the ways of the sea!"

"We're over here, sir," said Ziro as the captain smugly lectured in the opposite direction.

Captain Anson lifted the brim of his hat up so it no longer obscured his vision. Seeing nobody in front of him, he wheeled around to face Cormac and Ziro. Once he had located the two of them, he tore his hat off and threw it to the ground. He gave it a kick and it sailed into the air, where a stiff gust of wind picked it up and blew it over the port side of the *Levyathan*. A whale surfaced beneath it, and with a quick blast of the blow hole, sent it sailing back up onto the ship, where it came to rest at the captain's feet.

"Son of a bitch," he muttered. He picked up the soaking hat and shook some of the water off of it.

Ziro piped up. "Sir, there's really no reason to delay this any longer."

The captain put the still-dripping hat back on and sighed. "You're right, Ziro. I suppose we should get it over with. Let's have the flute."

Ziro produced a long, silver instrument from the folds of his robe. The captain looked at it skeptically for a second, then reluctantly took it from Ziro. He gingerly held it in his palms as if he expected it to start moving on its own. When the sun glinted off it, Cormac thought it shone unlike anything he'd ever seen.

Captain Anson took a deep breath and raised the flute to his lips. He blew a short progression of minor key notes, paused for a breath, then repeated it. The shrill music resonated off into the distance, and it could have just been a coincidence, but Cormac felt like the wind suddenly died down as the captain was playing.

When he was done, Captain Anson held out the flute until Ziro took it from him. Then they waited.

After about thirty seconds of waiting, Cormac broke the silence. "This is ridiculous," he said. "I'm going to go kill some whales."

He turned to leave, but Captain Anson spoke before he had a chance.

"Whales? And where, pray tell, are you planning on finding these whales?"

Cormac looked over at him. Captain Anson was still looking in the direction he'd been facing when he played the flute. Cormac couldn't tell if he was talking to him this way for dramatic effect or if the captain actually thought he was looking at him and didn't realize he wasn't because of the hat. Cormac decided it didn't really matter.

"I'm going portside," said Cormac. "I'll have a dozen kills before lunch." But even as he said the words, Cormac sensed that something was off. Moments ago the ocean had been busy with the sound of whale songs and splashes and blowhole spouts. But it had gone eerily quiet. Cormac turned to look, and was stunned by what he saw.

The port side of the boat, sunny and bustling just minutes ago, had gone silent and still. There was not a trace of a whale to be seen. The sun had suddenly retreated behind clouds and a mysterious mist now hung over the water. Cormac had been sizing up whales that were three hundred feet off the side of the boat, but now a thick wall of fog prevented him from even seeing past fifty. Cormac turned to ask the captain what the hell was going on when he realized he was shivering.

Captain Anson saw the look of bewilderment on Cormac's face and smirked. "Just remember," he said. "You wanted this."

The captain smoothed out his dragon robe and straightened his hat, then walked over to the port side of the boat. Ziro shared a sympathetic look with Cormac, then shook his head and walked after the captain. Cormac flexed his mangled left hand and wished he was carrying a harpoon gun. Eventually he wandered over to the side of the boat and stood next to them.

"Just to make sure," Cormac said, "we are selling the whale dicks to the Chinese right? That's still our plan? I just wanted to make sure that we were on the same page and that you guys didn't come up with some other scheme and that's actually what we're doing now. Because all I wanted to do was hand the Chinese whalers the dicks when we got to port, then they give us a lot of money, end of story. I didn't ask for any of this weird stuff." Cormac gestured to his dragon robe and mimicked a little flute playing.

Captain Anson stared out into the fog. "I'm afraid that's not how the Chinese work, my boy," he said.

Before Cormac could ask him what the hell he exactly meant by this, the titanic crash of a gong echoed from somewhere in the distance. Cormac jumped about a foot in the air and raised his hands to cover his ears. Captain Anson and Ziro looked at each other, then turned their attention back toward the fog that the sound had emanated from.

There was another ear-splitting gong sound. Even though he was covering his ears, this one seemed louder than the last, as if the source had moved closer. As it resonated, Cormac watched in awe as the fog parted and something began to emerge.

It was another ship. It slowly pulled out of the cover of fog and glided toward the *Levyathan*. It was silent except for the occasional blare of the gong. The ship was a good deal smaller than the *Levyathan*, and the sails were rigged in a completely different style. It was a much older ship than the *Levyathan*, too, though it was obvious that it was better maintained. As the gong rang out and the ship came even closer, Cormac saw that the boat's name was written in Chinese characters.

Cormac whispered out of the side of his mouth at Captain Anson. "You summoned this boat? You played that flute and it showed up out of nowhere?" But Anson didn't respond. Cormac looked over at the captain. Both he and Ziro were bent over at the waist, bowing theatrically with their hands folded at their chests. They both slowly rose and the captain hissed at Cormac. "Just do what I do, you idiot, or you'll screw everything up!"

Anson and Ziro both took another deep bow as the boat approached. Feeling like an idiot, Cormac tentatively leaned forward as well. Out of the corner of his eye, he kept a watch on his two shipmates for an indication of when it was OK to stop bowing.

The captain and Ziro simultaneously straightened after five to ten seconds of bowing, and Cormac followed their lead. By now the bow of the Chinese ship was only about ten feet from where the trio was standing. The mysterious fog that it had emerged from had dissipated and the sun was rapidly beginning to peek out from behind the clouds. As the boat's movements slowed, two shadowy figures raised a long plank up into the air, then rotated it until it touched the side of the *Levyathan*. The gong rang out its loudest blast yet.

Ziro walked up to where the plank had touched the *Levyathan* and quickly tied it to the railing. The two figures on the Chinese boat who had raised it signaled to another person at the stern, who pushed a large anchor into the water with a splash. The gong sounded yet again and for the first time, Cormac was able to pick out where it was coming from. The gigantic metal instrument, at least as big around as a tractor wheel, was mounted on a small platform on the stern. A shirtless, barrel-chested Chinese man stood next to it. He held an enormous gong mallet that required both hands to swing. He looked like he had definitely killed a guy with it before.

Cormac really regretted suggesting the whale penis clearance sale.

A figure appeared at the other end of the gangplank, and the gong sounded as it gracefully began to walk the narrow path toward the *Levyathan*. As he came closer, Cormac could see that it was a short Chinese man, wearing a red dragon robe that looked like a much more expensive version of the one Captain Anson was wearing. The man had a long black ponytail, wore a pair of sandals, and carried a small box with both hands.

When the Chinese sailor effortlessly stepped off the gangplank and onto the deck of the *Levyathan*, the gong sounded. Captain Anson and Ziro bowed at the man, and Cormac followed suit. After they were finished, the Chinese sailor bowed in turn, still holding the box. When he straightened, he turned back toward his own ship, and another figure stepped into view as the gong sounded yet again.

Cormac really wanted to take in the gong player's technique, but the scene playing out in front of him was too fascinating to turn away from. Plus he was terrified of making eye contact with the gong player, who now appeared to be gnawing on a gigantic haunch of something in between gongs.

The new Chinese sailor coming down the plank was very tall. His dragon robe was even more adorned and expensive looking. He had a long, thin Fu Manchu moustache and his glide down the plank was so effortless it almost looked like he was floating. Cormac could tell by the way he carried himself that back on his own boat, this guy was obviously in charge.

When the sailor with the Fu Manchu, presumably the captain, stepped onto the *Levyathan*, the other Chinese sailor, Captain Anson, and Ziro all bowed in unison. Cormac was already tired of this ritual, and bowed about as half far as he had the last time. The gong sounded an unprecedented three consecutive times. The Chinese captain remained standing straight. He did not seem interested in returning the gesture.

Without breaking the silence that settled in between gongs, the Chinese captain looked at his cohort and nodded once. The sailor instantly took a step toward Captain Anson, bowed, and while he was still bent over, stuck his arms out and offered the captain the box as the gong rang out once more.

Captain Anson took the box and immediately lifted the lid and took a peek inside. Once he'd had a chance to size up the contents, he handed the box off to Ziro and bowed to the Chinese sailors. Gong.

Anson straightened back up and turned to Ziro. Cormac leaned in to hear what the captain's instructions were.

"It's tea," Captain Anson said. "It's a gesture that means they come in peace to do business with us. We just have to scatter it to the four winds in order to reciprocate."

"How do I go about scattering something to the four winds?" Ziro asked. "There's barely even a breeze right now, let alone four winds!" Captain Anson laughed nervously and glanced at the two Chinese sailors, who were standing there silently with stern expressions. The captain quickly turned back to Ziro.

"Just toss some off the bow, stern, and each side of the ship," he whispered. "And do it quickly, you're making us look like amateurs!"

Ziro opted not to argue and hustled to the bow of the *Levyathan*. Cormac watched as the former slave shook some tea into his hand and then unceremoniously tossed it over the side.

"Ziro!" Captain Anson hissed. Ziro turned to look at him and the captain made an exaggerated gesture, as if he were a magician releasing a dove. Ziro's shoulders heaved as he sighed. He poured some more tea into his hand, turned back to the ocean, and with an exaggerated motion flung the tea high into the air off the bow of the *Levyathan*. This must have been more to the Chinese sailors' liking, as a loud bang of the gong rang out as the tea was dispersed. Ziro shot the captain a look as he scurried off with the box toward the starboard side of the boat.

"It's important to show them respect, even if it seems like a bunch of horseshit," Captain Anson said to Cormac in a conspiratorial tone, all the while smiling and nodding at the Chinese captain and the sailor. Two more gongs rang out, presumably as Ziro cast the tea into the second and third winds, and he eventually came into sight after making a complete lap of the boat. Ziro walked up to the four of them, poured the remainder of the tea into his hand, bowed deeply to the Chinese sailors, and then cast the tea off the port side of the boat. Four gongs symbolized the completion of the ritual.

Cormac was still intimidated by the gigantic man playing the gong, but was starting to come around to the instrument in general. He figured that convincing Vance to do chores or pay him the money he owed him would be a lot easier if he could punctuate all of his arguments with a loud gong. He'd have to look into a more practical sized one when he got home. A gong and a ukulele could be a powerful combination.

Once Ziro reassumed his position at Captain Anson's side, the *Levyathan*'s captain produced a collapsible fan from a fold in his robe. With a flick of his wrist, he opened the fan, which was printed with a beautiful scene of a temple surrounded by cherry blossom trees. Anson handed the fan to Ziro, then pointed to the sailor who had presented them with the tea. Ziro walked over and stood face-to-face with the man. Then Captain Anson gestured for Cormac to do the same.

Cormac reluctantly did what he was told. He walked over and stood next to Ziro, keeping one eye on the gong player the whole time. Cormac wished he could remain an observer in this whole affair, but he also figured whatever weird, humiliating thing he had to do to welcome the Chinese aboard the ship, he was capable of doing it.

Then Ziro dropped to his knees and Cormac very quickly reconsidered.

If Ziro had taken another two seconds to remove the Chinese sailor's right sandal, Cormac probably would have been sailing overboard of his own free will. Fortunately, Ziro had a quick hand with a sandal strap, and Cormac was relieved to see that he was just helping the other sailor out of his shoe. He knelt down next to Ziro, hoping his shaky hands didn't reveal that he had believed Ziro was on the verge of performing a welcoming sex act. Cormac undid the buckle on the sailor's left shoe and helped the man step out of it.

Ziro pulled out a small bottle of some sort of liquid. He uncapped it and turned it over three times, each time dropping a small drop of some sort of scented oil onto the sailor's right foot. He handed the bottle to Cormac and gave him a nod to indicate that he should follow suit in anointing their visitor's feet.

Cormac tried to release a drop of oil, but evidently there was a trick to this particular kind of bottle and a gushing stream of oil instantly poured out onto the sailor's left foot. It ran down between his toes and pooled up on the sides of the deck.

Cormac quickly tilted the bottle upright and looked up at the sailor, who was trying very hard to pretend that it wasn't an incredibly unpleasant feeling to have perfumed oil in between his toes.

"Sorry," Cormac nervously chuckled. "The bottle kind of pours all at once if you don't know what you're doing." Midway through the sentence, Cormac realized that the sailor didn't understand a word he was saying. He decided to just barrel ahead with the ritual.

The second time he tipped the bottle over, about twice as much oil poured out onto the sailor's foot. Ziro snatched the bottle away before Cormac could perform the ceremonial third pour.

"Why didn't you tell me it came out so fast?" he snapped at Ziro.

"It's not that difficult! This is the first time I've done it, too!" Ziro hissed back.

"Well, you probably loosened it up then," said Cormac. "Like a bottle of Heinz!"

"I don't know what that is!" said Ziro as the sailor wiggled his toes, hoping that the disgusting sensation, which felt like he had just stepped into a bucket full of oil, would quickly cease. Ziro glared at Cormac and set the bottle down. He picked up the fan and began to wave it at the sailor's right foot. After a few flicks up and down, the drops of oil began to shrink, and after a few more seconds of fanning, they had evaporated entirely.

Ziro handed the fan to Cormac, stood up, and bowed to the sailor. The gong sounded from the Chinese ship.

"Your turn," said Ziro. He left Cormac and walked back to stand next to Captain Anson.

Cormac looked up at the sailor and smiled. The sailor stared straight ahead, as if he were attempting to not make eye contact while using a urinal in a public restroom. Cormac started to fan his left foot.

And then he kept fanning. In this quantity, the evaporating properties of the oil seemed to slow considerably, if not vanish entirely. In fact, the breeze from the fan seemed to just sort of cause some ripples in the oil, as it sloshed around on the sailor's foot. Cormac tried to fan faster, but this proved futile. Eventually, his right wrist started to hurt and he switched the fan to his left. It was awkward at first, but he quickly got the hang of it. Unfortunately, the sailor's foot remained covered in oil.

After a few minutes of this, Cormac looked over his shoulder at the captain and Ziro. The captain looked furious, Ziro simply shrugged. Cormac turned back to the foot and started to fan even faster. The oil was not responding to the fanning, but its odor was. Initially, it had emitted a pleasant, lavender perfume smell, but it was quickly starting to more closely resemble rotten cabbage. And it was getting worse. Cormac somehow found another gear, and fanned even faster. The sailor began to whimper; evidently the oil was starting to sting, or burn, or very likely both.

About seven minutes in, Cormac's wrist felt like it was about to fall off when he heard a voice say "about how much longer is this going to take?" He looked over his shoulder, ready to tell the captain and Ziro to go to hell, but neither of them appeared to have spoken up. Exactly the opposite, in fact: both of their eyes were wide as they stared at the Chinese captain.

Cormac stopped his fanning. Still crouching in front of the sailor, he looked over at the Chinese captain. He held a pocket watch by its chain and waved it at Captain Anson. He looked irritated.

"We haven't got all day," the Chinese captain said, in accent-free English. The sailor whimpered as the oil on his foot began to emit faint wisps of smoke.

Captain Anson sprang into action. "Er, of course! We're here to do business" he said. The captain walked over to Cormac and pulled him away from the Chinese sailor by the back of his shirt. Cormac backed away on his hands and knees until Anson let go, then he raised himself to his feet. Ziro took the fan from him, folded it up, and slipped it into his pocket.

The Chinese captain walked over to his sailor and knelt to examine his foot for a few seconds. He stood up and pointed to the gangplank. "Lotus root," he said. "In the medicine chest." The sailor nodded and hobbled back across the plank to the Chinese ship. The Chinese captain turned and shook his head.

"I'm sorry, er . . ." Captain Anson paused as he realized he did not know the Chinese captain's name.

"Lao. Captain Lao," he responded.

"I'm sorry, Captain Lao," Anson stammered. "I didn't know you could speak English."

"What the hell is all this?" Lao demanded. "What is all this oil and fanning shit? It's bad enough every time to sit through it when you get it right, but then you make us stand here for ten minutes and it starts to burn my guy's foot? What is even in that bottle?"

"I'm very sorry, sir, er, Lao, er, Captain Lao." Captain Anson was obviously not prepared for a berating from the Chinese. "We were told that this was an ancient custom for welcoming the Chinese aboard your ship."

"Who the hell told you that?" demanded Captain Lao.

Captain Anson paused, embarrassed. Ziro chimed in. "Captain Anson bought it off a guy in a bar one night." The captain nodded sheepishly. "I told him not to but he bought it when I went to the bathroom." Ziro continued. The captain jabbed Ziro in the ribs with his elbow.

"Unbelievable," sighed Captain Lao.

"Well, if I may ask *you* a question," said Captain Anson, back on the offensive. "Why the hell didn't you say anything before?"

"We thought it was *your* custom!" shouted Lao. "Every time we'd see you guys you'd start taking our shoes off and oiling up our feet. We just wanted to get the hell away from you as soon as we could without seeming rude!" Captain Lao paused as if he'd just had a realization. "You don't normally wear dragon robes, do you?" The gong sounded from the Chinese boat.

Captain Anson snorted derisively. "Of course we wear these! You thought we just put these on in order to impress you guys when you showed up?" He looked at Ziro and Cormac and pointed with his thumb at Captain Lao. "How arrogant is this guy?" Anson asked in an exaggerated tone. "Thinks we all dress differently just because he shows up."

Just as the captain said that, two whalers rounded the corner wearing traditional whaler garb. The stopped when they noticed the discussion taking place, but it was too late. Lao observed their filthy whaling outfits, still stained with whale drippings from at least four days earlier. He looked back at Captain Anson with his eyebrows raised.

"Their dragon robes are being cleaned," Captain Anson lied.

"And why the hell do you always throw our tea off the side of your boat?" demanded Lao.

"We thought we were supposed to scatter it to the four winds," said Ziro, shooting Captain Anson a look.

"Scatter it? You're supposed to drink it, you idiots. That's good tea! It's not the *best* tea, but it's pretty good! And we only have a limited amount at sea! I mean, we still have a quite a bit of it, but you hate to waste it. Jeez . . ." Captain Lao rubbed his forehead and temples. There was an awkward silence.

"You were interested in the whale dicks?" Captain Anson finally asked.

"Yes, yes, we're here about the dicks," Captain Lao said, still massaging the sides of his head.

"Do you have a headache?" Anson asked.

"It comes and goes," replied Lao.

Cormac chimed in. "Is that what the whale dicks are for?" Lao stopped rubbing his head and looked at Cormac like he was an idiot. Cormac soldiered on, undeterred. "The dicks? You grind the dicks up and then like, the powder has medicinal properties? Relieves headaches and stuff?"

"You know what's really good for a headache? A hot cup of tea!" snapped Lao.

Ziro intervened before the discussion grew any more contentious. "To be fair," he said, "you weren't really doing much to play down your mysteriousness. After all, we do summon you with a flute."

"If you guys could afford carrier gulls you wouldn't have to!" retorted Lao.

"You do accent just about every single action that you take with that gong," continued Ziro.

"We may be overdoing it with the gong, now that you mention it," said Lao. The gong rang out as he finished his sentence. Captain Lao turned and waved his hand at his throat to get the gong player to knock it off.

Captain Anson walked over to Captain Lao and slung his arm around him before Cormac or Ziro had any further chances to scuttle the deal. "What do you say we take a look at this merchandise, captain?" Captain Lao threw up his hands to indicate that it was about time they got down to business. "Right this way," said Anson. He walked off to lead the way to the cold storage area. Captain Lao turned and nodded to his boat to indicate he would return soon, then followed after Anson. Cormac and Ziro waited a second or two to give the captains some distance, then followed after them.

"Who swabs your deck?" he overheard Captain Lao ask Captain Anson. "It looks incredible."

"It's a team effort," Anson replied without missing a beat. Ziro sighed.

When they got down to the cold storage area, Cormac was happy to see that Lao seemed impressed at the size of their recent haul. The storage area was much fuller than it had been the first time Cormac had visited. Huge stacks of whale parts now took up nearly a quarter of the available space. Captain Lao nodded his head in approval as they walked down an aisle that separated stacks of blubber from a giant pile of bones that would someday be used for scrimshaw.

When they got to the discard pile, Cormac was slightly appalled by how large it had grown. Even beneath the giant length of burlap that covered the penises, he could still make out the seemingly perpetual jiggling.

Captain Anson gave Ziro the "go ahead" nod and Ziro pulled the burlap cover off the pile. Careful not to let any part of it touch him, Ziro let it fall to the ground and quickly stepped around it. Cormac imagined they would burn it as soon as Lao and his crew were gone. The risk of keeping it around and accidentally using it as a bandage or Thanksgiving tablecloth was too great.

The three of them were silent as Captain Lao took a walk around the pile to inspect it. Cormac was quietly appalled by how long this took due to the size of the pile. Once he had made a complete lap, Lao stood in place where he had started, still sizing up the haul. He began to rub his right temple while he concentrated, but quickly stopped when he saw Cormac looking back and forth between his pained face and the pile.

"That wouldn't help!" Lao said.

"You never know," Cormac replied.

Lao did some final mental calculations, then announced, "I'll give you four thousand dollars per penis."

Ziro let out a gasp. He quickly tried to pretend like he had just been stifling a sneeze, but Cormac knew that the figure must be enormous in 1867 dollars. Captain Anson didn't look satisfied, though.

"I don't know, Lao," the captain said, walking up to the merchandise he had planned to throw in the garbage as soon as they docked. "You've got a great deal of variance in the sizes here. Girth . . . length . . ."

"Trust me," said Lao. "I've taken that all into consideration. That's an average rate, I figured it would be easier for you to process."

"You've sized all these things up mentally?" Captain Anson asked, not trying to mask his skepticism.

"I've been doing this for a long time," said Captain Lao. "It starts to become second nature. But if you insist, I can show you the math behind it."

"I think that would be best," said Captain Anson.

"Can you fetch the abacus that we gave you as a goodwill present the first time we met?" Lao suggested. "I can show you all the calculations on that."

Captain Anson had shattered the abacus less than an hour after the Chinese had given it to him when he hurled it at Ziro's head but missed and hit a wall.

"You know what, four thousand per penis sounds good to me," Anson quickly backtracked. "No need to get bogged down in the numbers."

Lao stuck out his hand. Captain Anson hesitated, unable to remember whether Lao had touched any of the whale penises while he inspected them. He folded both his hands on his chest and tentatively leaned forward to see if he could seal the deal with a bow instead. Captain Lao kept his hand outstretched, even as Captain Anson inched forward bit by bit. Eventually Lao won the battle of wills and Captain Anson straightened up and shot his hand out. He gave the Chinese captain's hand a quick pump, then quickly pulled his hand away to inspect it for residue.

Finding none, Anson asked Captain Lao, "How do we want to haul this onto your boat?"

"You just leave that to us," said Lao. Out on the surface, the gong sounded. Cormac looked toward the cold storage area entrance, expecting to see some Chinese workers appear dramatically, but he was disappointed that it was empty. He was then very surprised when he turned back toward the discard pile and found it already swarming with Chinese sailors who had stealthily entered and were already hauling the whale penises toward their boat.

The Chinese workers moved rapidly, and the path they took brought them very close to Captain Anson. He was forced to flatten himself up against the wall as the Chinese sailors, two to a dick, carried the cargo past him.

"Ziro," Anson said, trying not to breathe too deeply. "Let's bring Captain Lao up to the deck to finalize the details." Ziro gestured for Captain Lao to follow him, and Cormac walked behind the two of them. Captain Anson waited for a gap in the procession of Chinese sailors and whale genitals, then dashed through, then up and out of the cold storage area.

Once the final pair of Chinese sailors had transported their cargo off the *Levyathan*, four more sailors hauled a large treasure chest down the gangplank. They left it at Lao's feet, and then hurried back to their own boat. Captain Lao lifted the hinged top, revealing a shiny pile of gold doubloons and pieces of eight. The gong rang out from the Chinese boat.

"I think you'll find it all there," Captain Lao said. "But I understand if you'd like to count it."

"I think I had better," said Captain Anson.

"Why don't you grab that abacus we gave you, I'll show you a real neat technique for quickly counting things. It'll save you—"

"You know what, it looks like it's all here," Captain Anson said, cutting the other captain off. Anson quickly shut the lid of the chest. "I guess we're done here!" he said with a smile.

"I guess so," said Captain Lao. "Gentlemen, it was a pleasure doing business with you. If you keep catching them at this rate, I hope you'll keep us in mind. You know how to get in touch." Lao winked and turned to walk up the gangplank.

Cormac still couldn't believe that the Chinese had just parted with such a large sum of money for some phony aphrodisiac. He'd bit his tongue the entire time the Chinese had been on board, but now that the deal was complete, he felt compelled to ask what the hell they were thinking.

"Sir? Captain Lao?" he called out. Captain Lao turned and took a few steps back in Cormac's direction. "You really think that these whale dicks are going to make you super virile? Because, long story, but I come from the future, and nobody is going around eating whale dicks to make them get boners." Cormac willfully neglected to add the phrase "except for my roommate" to the end of his sentence.

Captain Lao looked at Cormac as if he had misheard him. "You're asking if I think that? Me? Personally?"

"Well, yeah," said Cormac, slightly confused. "I thought that Chinese people thought these things had special powers."

Captain Lao shook his head. "You guys think that Chinese people are just one big group of weirdos, don't you? Bowing, sprinkling tea to the four winds, eating whale dicks to get boners . . ." Captain Anson nodded vigorously before he realized this was the wrong answer.

"Do you have any idea how big China is?" Lao asked. "It's a gigantic country. Think about how many idiots there are in America. We have many, many more idiots by several orders of magnitude. Of course there are people who think they should eat whale dicks if they can't get it up."

"I guess that makes sense," Cormac admitted.

"So you're from the future?" Captain Lao asked. "How do things work out for China?"

Cormac stared at Captain Lao while his mind raced trying to think of a single fact he knew about China. "Well . . . there's this boxer named Mike Tyson and he has a tattoo of a Chinese guy named Mao on his arm. I think he was your president."

"Was he a good leader?" Lao asked.

"I haven't ever really looked into that," Cormac said, hoping Lao would drop the subject. He didn't.

"Is Mike Tyson Chinese?" the captain asked. Cormac shook his head no. "Then why does he have this Mao man's face tattooed on him?"

"Look, I've probably said too much already," Cormac said, as he felt his face flush. "If I tell you any more I could risk altering your entire country's history." Cormac made a mental note to find out a fact or two about said history when he got home. Not knowing a single thing about the biggest country in the world was kind of embarrassing, even if the person confronting him about it had just finished loading thousands of pounds of giant penises onto his ship.

"Maybe you already have," replied Captain Lao. "Maybe this Mao guy's father will be unable to get it up one night and he'll eat one of these penises you just sold us and the placebo effect will kick in and that's how his son will be conceived."

Cormac felt really dizzy all of a sudden. "Could that really happen?" he asked.

"Nah, eating one of these things is probably going to leave you unable to reproduce," Captain Lao said. The gong rang out from the Chinese ship. "I think they're getting impatient," Lao said. "I'll see you all later."

Cormac waved goodbye, and Captain Lao glided back up the gangplank. Ziro waited until the Chinese captain had stepped onto his own ship, then untied the knots that secured the plank to the *Levyathan*. Once he stepped back from the side of the ship, two Chinese sailors pulled the plank back onto their ship. The gong rang out three times and Cormac, Ziro, and Captain Anson watched the ship sail away. Cormac hadn't noticed, but a curtain of fog had rolled in sometime in the last five minutes. The temperature was a good fifteen degrees cooler than it had been while the Chinese were loading their ship.

The boat sailed toward the fog, and was quickly swallowed up. As the stern disappeared from view, the gong rang out one last time.

"Weirdos," muttered Captain Anson. "Ziro! Help me push this trunk into my cabin."

"Are you going to distribute any of this to the crew?" Ziro asked.

"Of course," Captain Anson said. "Eventually. Once I make sure there's no mysterious Chinese curse on it that makes you age eighty years in one night. I won't have that happening to my men, Ziro! If I age eighty years in one night due to a sinister curse, then so be it! But I won't let that happen to my men!"

"That's very noble of you, sir," Ziro said.

"Also, I've never seen this much gold before, so I'm going to get naked and spend the next hour lying in a pile of it," the captain said.

Ziro nodded his head and started to push the heavy chest.

"Cormac!" Captain Anson said, leaning in to push as well. Cormac looked at him, expecting a thanks or some sort of congratulations for making the whole deal possible. "If you get a single drop of whale blood on that dragon robe, next time I'll sell *your* dick to the Chinese!" the captain barked. "Take it off and leave it outside my door!"

The captain and the former slave slowly pushed the trunk away. In between grunts, the captain instructed Ziro to lock up the food crates for the rest of the day. He felt that the whalers he was so determined to protect from cursed gold were going through the hardtack supply too fast.

Cormac watched them struggle with the trunk for a few more seconds but quickly lost interest. The fog had lifted and the sun was out again. The day was still young.

Cormac walked to the rum storage area, where he'd left his normal clothes sitting in a pile, and slipped off the dragon robe. He dressed, uncorked a jug of rum, and had a long, satisfying swig. He picked the dragon robe up off the floor and started to fold it, but halfway through he stopped and wondered what he was doing. He looked at the robe, rolled his eyes and tossed it into a corner. If the captain was so damn concerned about it he could retrieve it himself.

Cormac took another swig of rum and re-corked the jug. He set it down and in exchange picked up the harpoon gun that he'd left next to his clothes. He loaded a freshly sharpened harpoon and stepped out of the rum storage area. Finally, it was time to go to work.

* * *

Dean Bickerstaff swung his shillelagh back and forth in front of him like a blind guy in an effort to clear a path down the hallway. Vance had spent the morning being fairly liberal with his clock watching, doling out a free minute here and a free minute there. This was no longer a nicety that they could afford.

The hallway was acting as an overflow area for people waiting to peer into Cormac's ear. The dean assumed that about half of them were on drugs. The other half he had personally witnessed *doing* drugs in the living room, so no assumptions were necessary.

Earlier in the day, when Mako emerged from Cormac's room for the first time, the dean could tell they had something special going on. Mako whipped out his phone the second he sat down on the grounded couch, texting friends and tweeting about what he had just experienced. When Dean Bickerstaff had tried to ask whether he had enjoyed himself, Mako could only respond with giddy laughter and the occasional "whoa" or "oh my God." He actually appeared to be *so* moved by the experience that the dean wondered if perhaps Vance had been right to sit in as an anti-whacking sentry.

Mako's friends started to show up not long afterward. They shuffled in and Mako greeted each of them with another intricate, personalized handshake. Some of them bought drugs from him almost instantly, while others appeared to be waiting to do business with the dean first. Frampton later realized that they just wanted change so they could buy drugs from Mako.

Mako's friends did not paint the brightest picture of student life at Harrington, but Dean Bickerstaff tried to look on the bright side. Their clothes were ill-fitting and ironic, but hey, at least none of them wore towels. Most of them appeared not to have showered that morning, but hey, he hadn't either yesterday and he'd managed to have a productive day! And while none of the students seemed to recognize the powerful man who ran the school they attended, Frampton did notice several respectful glances toward his shillelagh.

Besides, these were the students who had been able to drop what they were doing the moment Mako texted them. He didn't expect that the more respectable students at Harrington would be so quick to ditch class on a weekday afternoon. That is, if a population of respectable students at Harrington actually existed.

As more and more people started to trickle into the house on Craymore Street, the dean found himself in a bit of a bind. People were coming into the house, but nobody was coming out of Cormac's bedroom. They were only about ninety minutes into the three and a half hours that Mako and G-Dimes had prepaid for. He sincerely doubted any of these people had any place else to be, but he wasn't about to ask them to wait two hours for their turn. Some of them appeared to be on the verge of passing out as it was.

Eventually there were about two dozen people meandering about inside the house. The dean realized they could be charging much more for a shorter window of time. Sure, they'd lured everybody there with the promise of ten minutes for five bucks, but basic supply and demand dictated that those rates were, in retrospect, idiotic. Dean Bickerstaff was actually kind of excited about an opportunity to pull the ol' bait and switch. It had been one of his favorite scams during his formative years, but he'd quickly graduated to more advanced grifts. It would be like reuniting with an old friend, Dean Bickerstaff thought as he pushed his way down the hall to Cormac's bedroom.

He waved away two girls who were sharing a joint in front of Cormac's door. They looked at each other and giggled, then stepped aside to let the dean through. Glaring over his shoulder at them, Frampton banged on Cormac's door with his shillelagh. After a few seconds he heard it unlock from the inside. Vance cracked the door open and peered through.

"What the hell, Deano?" he whispered. "It's not time yet!"

"We've got two dozen stoners out here with money to burn, Vance," Dean Bickerstaff whispered back. "We've got to get them in here before they get bored and go home!"

Vance opened the door a bit more and peered out into the hallway. He smiled as he saw the gathered crowd. One of the two girls that the dean had just shoved aside smiled and waved at him. "Hey, Vance!" she said in an alluring voice.

"Hey, baby," Vance said. "You save some of that for me you hear?" Vance hit an imaginary joint and blew her a kiss. For someone who appeared to never leave his house, the dean thought, Vance appeared to be a beloved fixture of the Harrington social scene. Vance opened the door wider and the dean waddled into Cormac's room.

G-Dimes knelt motionless at Cormac's bedside, his eye pressed into Cormac's ear. "He's locked in, Deano. I went over there fifteen minutes ago to make sure he was still breathing." Dean Bickerstaff stared over at G-Dimes then looked back at Vance. "He *is* still breathing," Vance said, noticing the dean's concern.

"Vance, we've got to do something," Dean Bickerstaff said. "These people aren't going to wait over two hours for a turn."

"Alright, alright," Vance said, placing a reassuring hand on the dean's shoulder. "We'll just ask Mako if they'll accept a refund. I'm sure he'll be understanding—he's a businessman himself. He knows how these things work."

"Good," the dean said. "Come on, we should probably sort this out now."

"Oh, I won't be asking him," Vance said, removing his hand from Frampton's shoulder. He walked over to Cormac's desk chair and sat down in it. "I'm not crazy. But come on, Deano, you've faced down bigger opponents than this guy!" It was true, Dean Bickerstaff thought. But usually *he* was the one willing to sink the lowest in terms of morality and legality. The looming threat of a shillelagh beating might not intimidate Mako and G-Dimes the same way it did a donor or librarian.

"Alright, I'll talk to him," the dean said. "But another thing: we're charging too little, Vance. Five dollars is not nearly enough and ten minutes is way too long. We need to get people in and out to get some real word of mouth going!"

"The ol' bait and switch! I like it!" Vance said. "Alright, so why don't we charge twenty bucks and knock it down to two minutes."

"Two minutes?" Dean Bickerstaff asked. "Is that going to be enough time?"

"Of course," Vance said. "It's more than enough. In fact, it may be dangerous to do it this long." They both looked over at G-Dimes. "And if they catch Mac while he's taking a piss or something, they'll just get back in line and pay us again." Vance grinned.

Dean Bickerstaff did some mental math. Two minute shifts meant they could cycle thirty people through in an hour, and at twenty bucks a head, that would clear them a cool six hundred dollars. Not bad for an operation that required no overhead. And he was sure Mako would understand that they needed to give other people a chance. After all, they were his friends—he'd invited them over.

"Hey, G! G-Dimes!" Vance yelled. G-Dimes showed no signs of moving from Cormac's ear. "We're going to have to pull him off, Deano," Vance said as he stood up. The dean tried to avert his gaze as Vance secured his towel, and then walked over with him to stand behind G-Dimes. They each put a hand on his shoulder, which he didn't seem to notice.

"On three," Vance said. "One, two, THREE!" They pulled G-Dimes away from Cormac's head and the drug dealer let out a loud gasp as he fell backwards. G-Dimes looked panicked, and his unfocused eyes darted about the room as he tried to figure out where he was. Maybe it was the psychological stress of being so rudely yanked out of another world, or maybe it was a state that G-Dimes found himself in multiple times a day. The dean didn't have time to worry about which scenario it was.

"Sorry to pull you away from there, G," the dean said, "But Mako wanted to take his turn." G-Dimes blinked his bloodshot eyes a couple of times and then looked longingly back at Cormac's ear. "Don't worry," Dean Bickerstaff said reassuringly. "You'll get to come back soon."

Slowly, unsteadily, G-Dimes got to his feet. "I wonder what he saw," Vance said.

"Who cares," said Dean Bickerstaff. "Cormac could have been watching someone mend a tarp and this guy would have been entranced." The dean waved his hands in front of G-Dimes's face, but the drug dealer never stopped staring at Cormac.

"Alright," the dean said. "I'll send in the next person in a minute. Are you ready? The pace is really going to pick up."

Vance nodded and gave the dean a thumbs up. The dean tried to indicate to G-Dimes that it was time to leave the room, but he wasn't picking up on any signals. The dean tried a subtle nudge with his elbow, but G-Dimes just stood there staring at Cormac, slightly swaying back and forth. Eventually the dean gave the back of G-Dimes's knee a poke with his shillelagh. G-Dimes took a startled step forward. Not seeing another way to get the burnout out of Cormac's room, the dean gave him another poke, and G-Dimes took another step toward the door.

"Just like herding goats?" Vance asked with a sly smile. Dean Bickerstaff shot Vance a look as he led G-Dimes out of the room with his shillelagh.

Once they were outside G-Dimes seemed to get his bearings and he was able to move without the dean herding him. He wandered back to the living room, where he sort of wobbled back and forth for a while until he located Mako. G-Dimes walked over to his friend and the dean followed suit.

Mako was holding court on the airborne couch, talking loudly about how awesome it had been to look inside Cormac's ear. Cissy sat next to him. She had powered up her laptop and apparently convinced one of the more functional stoners to fix her a Bloody Mary. Cissy sipped the drink and occasionally, after Mako said something that got a big laugh from the crowd, she would tap out a note on her laptop keyboard.

"I'm glad you're up and at 'em, Cissy," the dean said as Cissy tried not to look him in the eye. "Working on tomorrow's story?" Cissy turned her laptop around so the dean could see it. It was a dirty picture of the Noid and Marge Simpson.

"Regardless," the dean said, making an effort to sound disgusted as Cissy turned her attention back to her computer. "It looks like the story that ran today really got the job done. Congratulations. This is an impressive turnout."

When the first group of Mako's friends had arrived at the door, the dean asked them if they had come because of the article in the *School Paper*. "The Cissy Buckler story?" one of them asked incredulously. "Of course not. I assumed every word of it was either a lie or wildly inaccurate." It turned out they had waited for Mako—the pillar of integrity and honesty—to tweet about it before they considered making the journey. Cissy had sat bolt upright on the couch and glared at the guy who had slandered her. The dean decided to stop asking people if they read the *School Paper*.

"Cissy, you're going to want to get this in the article," the dean said. "We're adjusting our rates. Effective immediately, twenty dollars will get you two minutes."

"Sounds good," Cissy said as she downed the last of her Bloody Mary.

"Are you going to jot that down?" Dean Bickerstaff asked. Cissy clinked the ice cubes around loudly until someone came along and took the glass. The dean figured he could always remind her later.

He turned his attention to Mako, or more accurately, to Mako's shoes, which dangled near the top of Frampton's head. "Mako, how are you?" the dean called out.

"Hey, little man!" Mako said boisterously, just noticing the dean. "Looks like G-Dimes had a ball in there! You ready for me again?" He started to lower himself down from the couch but Dean Bickerstaff interrupted him.

"Mako, I'm afraid we're going to have to ask you to accept a refund of your remaining time. See, we've got all these people here, and we can't keep Cormac's ear tied up for the next two hours. We're sorry about the inconvenience. We'll be happy to cycle you back in after everyone else has had a chance."

"Oh, that's no problem, that's no problem," said Mako, grinning broadly. "Sure, we've got to let all these other people check it out. Man, there's a lot of people here . . . You said you were going to start charging twenty dollars for two minutes?"

"That's right," said the dean. "Supply and demand. I'm sure you know how it works!" The dean laughed, trying to cover up how nervous he felt talking to the drug dealer.

"I sure do. I sure do," Mako said. Suddenly his grin disappeared. "We'll take our refund at the current rate."

"Excuse me?" Frampton said apprehensively. Mako's happiness level appeared to be rapidly decreasing. Drug dealer mood swings were generally something the dean tried to avoid.

"You heard me. We've got two hours of ear time remaining. One hundred twenty minutes. Sixty two-minute sessions at twenty dollars a piece. That comes out to . . ." Mako paused to figure out the math. G-Dimes tapped him on the foot and Mako bent down so his boss could whisper in his ear.

"G says it's twelve hundred dollars," Mako said as he straightened back up. "Cash."

The dean gulped. "You better do what he says," said Cissy, not looking up from her laptop. "When we were talking off the record just now, he told me all about some of the crazy stuff that he's done."

Mako suddenly looked worried. "Yo, I thought off the record meant, you know, hush hush."

Cissy rolled her eyes. "Why do people always fall for that?" she asked to no one in particular.

The dean didn't want any trouble, and every minute spent negotiating was a minute that someone wasn't peering into Cormac's ear.

"No problem, Mako," he said. "Again, I'm sorry for the inconvenience. You'll get your money by the end of the day."

Mako seemed content, but G-Dimes tapped him on the foot again. Mako bent down and G-Dimes whispered in his ear one more time. Mako listened intently, then sat back up. "We're gonna need exclusive rights."

The dean was confused. "To sell our product," Mako clarified. "Inside the house, the porch, and all sidewalks in a five-hundred-foot radius. This is all our turf."

The dean was confused and terrified. "Are you worried about other people trying to . . . claim this turf?" he asked.

"Turf is turf!" shouted Mako, loud enough to make Cissy flinch. The sudden outburst was startling enough that the rest of the people in the living room instantly stopped talking and looked in their direction. Mako's ambiguous statement still left things up in the air as far as the dean was concerned, but he had to reassure his customer base.

"Calm down everyone," he said, trying to appear at ease. "Nobody's going to be fighting a gang war over drug dealing turf with this house at its epicenter. Please, as you were."

Everyone looked slightly more confused than normal for a moment, but quickly forgot what the dean had been talking about and went back to waiting around for a turn to look in Cormac's ear.

"OK!" said the dean, turning back to Mako. "This is all your turf!" He wondered if he should run it by Vance before he turned his house over to the drug dealers, but opted not to. This situation called for an executive decision.

Mako leaned back on the couch, looking happy and satisfied. He produced a gigantic blunt from behind his ear, lit it, and passed it to G-Dimes as a gesture of respect. Dean Bickerstaff wiped some sweat off of his brow. Finally, he could start sending people into Cormac's room.

"OK, everybody," he said. Everybody just kept talking. Addressing the crowd was not as easy when they hadn't been intimidated into silence by a dangerous outlaw, but the dean soldiered on. "I have good news! G-Dimes and Mako have generously agreed to give up the rest of their time, so we can start sending you in now!"

One excited guy in the corner yelled out "Yeah!" When nobody else said anything, he hung his head and tried to pretend it hadn't been him.

"Disregarding that," Dean Bickerstaff continued. "If we could all just form a line starting in the hallway outside the bedroom door. Careful now. Yes, single file—DEAR GOD! Whatever you do, don't bump into the airborne couch!"

The gathered crowd, impatient and eager, pushed and jostled their way into some semblance of a line. Cissy and Mako watched from the airborne couch. G-Dimes had settled lengthwise into the grounded couch and was puffing on a blunt that had moments earlier been substantially longer.

The dean sized up the motley crowd gathered in front of him and picked up the pretzel tub. It had not been an easy morning. But he was Harrington Dean Frampton Q. Bickerstaff, and most of these people had probably waited for instant ramen to go on sale before stocking up. Dean Bickerstaff gripped the knotty end of his shillelagh. The time had come. Harrington's X-Factor ranking wasn't going to raise itself.

"Ladies and gentlemen," Frampton shouted, waving his shillelagh above his head as he walked to the front of the line. "There has been a slight change in plans!" He stopped in front of the first person in line, a slovenly young man in sweatpants and a backwards baseball cap. Frampton whirled to face him.

"Twenty dollars for two minutes. Take it or leave it," he snarled.

"Yeah man, whatever," the guy said, handing the dean a twenty. "I just wanna check it out."

Dean Bickerstaff snatched the twenty out of the guy's hand. He dropped it into the pretzel tub. The dean didn't care that this payment and many subsequent ones would go straight to Mako. What he did care about was what he saw as he looked down the line. Nobody was leaving, nobody was going home. Instead, people were on their phones, texting, telling their friends to get down here, they're finally letting people in.

Word was travelling.

The dean smiled, opened the door to Cormac's room and pointed the first customer in with his shillelagh. Sweatpants guy shuffled through the door and the dean leaned in to talk to Vance.

"Two minutes," the dean said. "Set your timer."

"No problem, Deano," Vance said. "Hey, could you freshen me up here? W-Patrol is thirsty work." Vance clinked the half-melted ice cubes in his Bloody Mary glass. The dean walked in and took it from him.

"Yeah, you can just kneel down next to him there," Vance was telling sweatpants guy. "You close one eye and look into his ear like a microscope. No! Look into his ear with the eye you *don't* close!"

The dean looked down at Cormac lying there. He wondered what he might be doing in the 1800s at that moment. While his comatose body lay in bed, Cormac was having an adventure on an entirely different plane of existence. He had been given an opportunity that nobody else on earth would ever experience. The dean suddenly felt very small. While some people *lived* life, here he was simply exploiting it. Maybe he had been doing things wrong. Maybe his entire life was . . .

"I bet this guy whacks it," Vance whispered.

Startled and unsure if he'd heard him correctly, the dean leaned his head in next to Vance's. "I bet he goes for it right away," Vance continued. "He's got that look in his eye."

Dean Bickerstaff stared at sweatpants guy, eager to see if Vance was right. He tried his hardest to remember what his train of thought had been before Vance derailed it, but he was unable to. It was lost. Ah well, he thought, it was probably unimportant.

Despite Vance's intuition, sweatpants guy's hands stayed where they were, gripping the side of Cormac's bed for support. When the timer on Vance's phone hit the two-minute mark, an alarm sounded, but the customer showed no signs of moving. Vance grumbled, realizing that pulling people out of the world of Cormac's ear might require a physical effort every time. He stood up from the chair, walked over the bed and pulled sweatpants guy back by his shoulder.

"Time's up," Vance said.

Sweatpants guy immediately wanted more time, but the dean told him he had to get back in line, which he quickly did.

Dean Bickerstaff shrugged and looked at Vance. "That seemed to go smoothly," he said.

"Time is money, Deano," Vance replied, as if he'd expected no other outcome. "Let's get this baby moving!" Vance snapped his fingers as he slumped back in Cormac's chair.

Frampton walked out of Cormac's room and sized up the line. It stretched down the hallway and into the living room, where it nearly reached the front door. The people bringing up the rear were grilling sweatpants guy about what he'd seen, but he was having trouble articulating it. He just stood there grinning from ear to ear and shaking his head in amazement. Frampton was pleased to see him occasionally tapping out messages on his phone.

"You next?" the dean asked the girl at the front of the line. The girl took a final hit from the joint she held, passed it to the person behind her in line, and nodded at the dean. "Twenty dollars," he said. She passed the money over and Dean Bickerstaff waved her into the bedroom.

From that moment forward, the Cormac-exploiting operation ran like a well-oiled machine. Every two minutes, the door to Cormac's bedroom would swing open and a dazed but happy-looking person would stagger out. Dean Bickerstaff would take twenty dollars from the eager person at the head of the line, let them enter the bedroom, and it would start all over again.

The people who had already looked into Cormac's ear began to talk amongst themselves, piecing together what they had seen. People put forth their theories about what was going on and who the other people on the boat were. The dean gathered that there wasn't any whaling happening at the moment, but people still seemed overwhelmingly pleased. Even the girl whose session consisted of watching Cormac scratch himself as he walked to the rum storage area seemed delighted with the experience.

The line was the biggest indicator of the venture's success: it just kept growing. Almost everyone who left the bedroom got right back into line as soon as they were done, and new people were constantly arriving. And while the initial crowd had been mostly cut from the same bongwater-stained cloth, the people showing up now looked moderately more employable, at least by the dean's standards.

This didn't stop Mako and G-Dimes from plying their trade. Word circulated quickly to the new arrivals that if they needed any weed, they could find it on the stadium seating couches. Mako gregariously sold the illegal product with the charm of a veteran baseball stadium beer vendor, chatting people up and laughing uproariously. So far the threat of rivals encroaching on their turf had not materialized, or perhaps it had and G-Dimes had already silently eliminated it.

Cissy occupied a permanent spot next to Mako on the airborne couch, typing away on her laptop. Mako had paid someone to see to it that her Bloody Mary was never empty. The dean was having trouble breaking away from his position outside Cormac's door, and when Cissy walked by on her way to the bathroom, he took the opportunity to inquire about the chatter in the living room.

"What's going on out there, Cissy?" he asked as Cissy walked by. Cissy reluctantly stopped in her tracks and rolled her eyes. She had hoped to make it to the bathroom without talking to the dean.

"Mako ordered some kegs," she said, without turning to face Frampton.

"Kegs?" Dean Bickerstaff asked. "It's not even one thirty in the afternoon."

"Dean, the party never stops when Mako's in the hizzy," Cissy said with a snort of contempt.

All the way back in the living room, Mako shouted, "The party never stops when Mako's in the hizzy!" which was met by appreciative cheers from the people gathered around him. Great, thought the dean. A drug dealer with a catchphrase.

"Well, is the word spreading?" Dean Bickerstaff asked. "Are people . . . you know . . ." The dean imitated someone typing on a cell phone.

Cissy gave him a full body eye roll as if the dean's lameness was physically paining her.

"Yes, people are posting about it," Cissy said. She pulled out her phone and tapped on the screen a few times. "#CormacsEar is the fourth most popular Twitter trend at Harrington." She showed the dean the screen. Sure enough, fourth on the list was #CormacsEar, right behind #exams, #summerplans, and #HoesBeBangin.

"Really?" the dean asked. "We provide a portal to another time and place and we're one behind 'Hoes Be Bangin'"?"

"Hoes Be Bangin' dropped to number three?" Cissy said in utter disbelief. She snatched her phone back and gave it a few taps to confirm. "Wow," she said after confirming the drop. "That had been the top trending topic at Harrington for the past two months."

No wonder our X-Factor ranking is so dismal, thought the dean.

"Are those kegs going to be free?" asked a guy in a knit cap who was standing in line and had just finished processing Cissy's statement from two minutes ago. The dean and Cissy both ignored him, and in a few seconds he appeared to forget that he'd even asked.

"What can we do to bump our trend up even further?" asked the dean.

"I don't know," said Cissy, obviously frustrated. "Have Vance take pictures for people to post on Facebook or something? Can I please go to the bathroom?"

Dean Bickerstaff waved her away and Cissy stormed off to the bathroom. The door to Cormac's bedroom opened and someone staggered out. The dean took twenty dollars from the girl at the front of the line and stuck his head through the doorway after she walked inside.

"Hey Vance. Maybe this lady here would like you to take a picture of her and Cormac. To share with her friends who aren't here?"

"Ooh, that sounds fun!" said the girl. She handed Vance her phone and walked over to Cormac. She knelt down at the side of the bed, thrust both her hands toward Cormac in exaggerated pointing gestures, and scrunched up her lips into a hideous face. Vance snapped a picture and handed her the phone back.

"Thanks!" she squealed.

"Now you're going to share that online, right?" asked the dean.

"Of course," the girl said, already tapping on her phone's screen. "#Hoes be—"

The dean winced and cut her off. "Actually," he said, "we've got our own topic going under #CormacsEar." The girl looked confused. "That guy is named Cormac," the dean told her. The girl started to look panicked, as if she had just realized that she was alone in a stranger's bedroom having her photo taken by another stranger after paying a third, older stranger who carried an intimidating wooden staff.

"Your next time though is free if you post it under #CormacsEar," said Vance. Instantly the girl's face brightened, and with a few taps, she posted her photo. Disaster averted, the dean left Vance to manage her and ducked out of the bedroom. Cissy was just emerging from the bathroom.

"Cissy, I meant to ask earlier," Dean Bickerstaff said. "How's your article coming?"

"Great," said Cissy, who did not stop walking.

"I look forward to reading it!" said the dean. He hoped he could count on Cissy. There would be no better advertisement for the next session than a well-written, attention-grabbing news story detailing how much fun people had on the first day. And since that wasn't possible, having Cissy write something up would hopefully be the next best thing.

A loud cheer erupted from the living room. The dean assumed this marked the arrival of the beer kegs. He pulled out a cigar, lit it, and prepared for things to get a lot more intense.

As people filed in and out of Cormac's room, the crowd grew more and more eager to see Cormac harpoon a whale. The interaction with the Chinese sailors was exciting for the spectators, and speculation ran rampant about what sort of deal the *Levyathan*'s crew was making with them. But seeing something as gigantic and awe inspiring as a whale getting killed was undoubtedly what everyone was waiting for.

As the beer started to flow, enthusiasm to see Cormac harpoon something grew even stronger. Eager to stay at the center of attention, Mako made an announcement that he and G-Dimes would issue a cash prize of three hundred dollars to whoever witnessed the first whale harpooning. Dean Bickerstaff did not appreciate that the living room had slipped out of his control. Working the door to Cormac's bedroom left him very few chances to venture back there, and when he did, the mood seemed to be edging further from "crowd gathered in squalid hovel" and closer to "Dionysian orgy." People were chugging beers, loud rap music was playing, and in one corner a crude wall of pizza boxes had been erected that Frampton was pretty sure two people were having sex behind.

Once Mako's offer was on the table, waiting for people to emerge from Cormac's room became an event in itself. The bedroom door would open, and everyone near the front of the line would hold their breath until the person shook their head or gave a thumbs down. A cheer usually went up once it was confirmed that the prize was still up for grabs.

Eventually, one customer claimed to have witnessed the kill. This was quickly rebutted by the next person, who reported that Cormac was not reeling in a whale or standing triumphantly over his kill, but instead peeing off the side of the boat. This was also confirmed by the person who came in after that. Cormac had evidently thrown back quite a bit of rum.

Mako, who had started counting out the reward from the airborne couch, quickly pocketed the money again. He did not look happy. A few moments later, two men burst through the door and carried out the student who had tried to pull a fast one. They were in the house for less than ten seconds, and they wore bandanas over their mouths, but the dean recognized them as people he had hired before. They were thorough, but they were not cheap. He respected that Mako chose to work with the best.

After that, there were no more false alarms and eventually, there was a legitimate winner. The first person to be staring into Cormac's ear while he harpooned a whale was a skinny sophomore named Brock. When he emerged from Cormac's room, the dean could tell right away what he had seen. In addition to the blissful, contented look most people wore after their session, Brock had a strange, fidgety energy about him. The person after him confirmed that the crew of the *Levyathan* was indeed hauling a dead whale aboard, and the house erupted.

The Craymore Street house had a new celebrity. Brock told the story over and over again to a rapt audience, who were definitely more interested than they would have been if they had not been intoxicated. Mako counted out three hundred dollars, but Brock barely seemed interested in the prize. Instead, he kept describing what had happened: how Cormac had tested the wind with his finger, then shot a harpoon that looked to be way off target until the whale jumped at the last moment, thrusting itself directly into the harpoon's path and falling back into the water, already dead.

Every time the dean ducked back into the living room, he heard Brock telling a slightly different version of the story. Cormac had purposely been looking back at the rest of the whalers when he pulled the trigger. Another whale had shot water out of its blowhole that diverted the harpoon into just the right spot. Cormac had whispered Brock's name right before Brock leaned into his ear.

The dean didn't think Brock was well. He was very disappointed when the sophomore quickly used half his winnings to bribe his way back to the front of the line. Frampton wished there was a way to outlaw that sort of thing, but the student at the front of the line really seemed to need the money. He was wearing a "Buffalo Bills Super Bowl Champion" t-shirt that the dean was pretty sure you could only get if you lived in some third-world country where they sent all the losing team's Super Bowl shirts to. It was inside out. His dinner appeared to be a packet of Parmesan cheese that he had found in a pizza box, possibly one that had been part of the sex wall. Frampton watched him take the money from Brock, walk directly to Mako, and buy an enormous bag of marijuana.

Frampton made it a point to blow cigar smoke in Brock's face while he waited in line, but the kid seemed not to notice. He just fidgeted with his twenty dollar bill until the bedroom door opened. Then he thrust the money in Dean Bickerstaff's general direction and rushed into Cormac's bedroom before the last person even had a chance to leave.

Dean Bickerstaff pulled the most recent customer aside as they left Cormac's bedroom.

"What did you see in there?" he asked the person, a petite girl with a pierced nose.

"It was incredible," she responded. "All he did was carefully load a new harpoon into his gun, start to aim it at a whale and rest his finger on the trigger waiting for just the right moment, but it was like . . . I could *feel* that I was there."

An ecstatic yelp came through the bedroom door. It was not the sort of sound that Vance was in the habit of making.

"Dammit," muttered the dean. He puffed his cigar and waited for two minutes to be up. When Brock opened the door, he had a far off look in his eye.

"He got another one," Brock muttered.

"Yep, he tends to do that," said Dean Bickerstaff, taking twenty dollars from the next person in line and waving them into the bedroom. "He's on a whaling boat, they kill whales."

"I think it means something," Brock continued. "I think I was chosen to see him shoot those whales."

"It's a coincidence, Brock," said Frampton. "Don't go telling people you're a chosen one, you'll just bum them out." Down the hall in the living room, the dean could see a large dog wearing a sombrero and sunglasses drinking from the beer tap as a crowd of people cheered. Flickers of light indicated that a few small fires were now burning indoors. Perhaps this group could actually use some bumming out, he thought.

"Could I have your spot in line for a hundred and fifty dollars?" Brock asked the next person in line. The person shrugged, took the cash, and went to go cheer on the dog.

"Kind of rude of you to keep monopolizing all the ear time, don't you think, Brock?" Dean Bickerstaff asked.

"It's what Cormac would want," said Brock.

Dean Bickerstaff puffed his cigar furiously, a few inches from Brock's face, but he seemed not to care. When the door opened, Brock tossed a twenty in Frampton's general direction and rushed into the bedroom.

"Did he shoot anything?" Dean Bickerstaff asked the guy who had just left the bedroom.

"He missed," the guy said with a shake of his head.

The dean chomped down on his cigar. He didn't expect that Cormac would miss twice in a row, and thirty seconds later, he heard the same excited cry from Brock. This time, however, a much different noise followed a few seconds later. It was unmistakably Vance, and he did not sound happy.

The bedroom door burst open. Vance held his towel around his waist with one hand and pushed Brock into the hall with the other. Brock stumbled, partly because of Vance shoving him, partly because his sagging, unbuckled pants were making forward progress difficult.

"You still think I was being overly cautious?" Vance demanded.

"What the hell happened?" Dean Bickerstaff yelled back.

"Cormac shot another whale," Brock said. He was breathing heavily.

"He started whacking it!" Vance yelled.

"I couldn't help it," Brock explained. "I just felt so honored."

"Why the hell do you keep sending this guy in, Deano?" Vance sputtered.

"It just feels so overwhelming to have been chosen to witness this," Brock said, his distant voice nearly a whisper.

Dean Bickerstaff knew he had to take quick action. Word of the attempted masturbation was rapidly spreading down the line and into the living room. When Frampton heard a loud "oh shit!" he knew that word had reached Mako. If this situation wasn't addressed quickly and decisively, it could gross out potential customers, or even worse, inspire copycats.

The dean straightened up and gripped his shillelagh tightly. "Brock," he said, "you haven't been chosen by anyone. You've just had a lucky streak of timing. Brock! Brock, listen to me, dammit!" Brock was attempting to peer around the dean back into the bedroom. Dean Bickerstaff turned and gestured for Vance to close the door.

"Brock, you're banned from this house," continued the dean. "Buckle up your pants, get the hell out of here, and don't come back."

"I don't think that's what Cormac would want," said Brock, as he reluctantly zipped up his fly and rebuckled his belt.

"Listen, buddy," said Vance as he pushed past the dean. "Me and Mac may not see eye to eye all the time, but I'll tell you this." He poked Brock in the chest with his finger as he delivered his point.

"If there's one thing my roommate would not want, it's for pervs like you to be sitting next to his bed, whacking it while staring into his ear while he's unconscious."

Dean Bickerstaff had never heard a friendship described in such touching terms.

Brock stood there for a second, appearing as if he were still processing his ban. Then, without warning, he pushed Vance aside and made a break for the bedroom. Instinctively, the dean lunged forward and smacked him on the knee with his shillelagh. Brock crumpled to the ground and Dean Bickerstaff flipped the shillelagh around and jabbed him in the ribs with the thick, knotted end. Brock groaned.

"Get this pile of garbage out of here," the dean said, feeling very much like a movie action hero. He looked down the hall to the living room, where most of the crowd was gawking in his direction. Standing apart from them, G-Dimes wobbled slowly back and forth as he gave the dean a silent, respectful nod of approval.

Incredibly psyched to have earned the violent criminal's approval, Dean Bickerstaff poked Brock in the side a couple of times to try and get him to roll over onto his back. Brock wasn't budging. "Vance," the dean said. Gearing up for another devastatingly cool quip, he paused long enough that Brock was able to slowly roll over. The quip died in Frampton's throat as it became evident to everyone looking that Brock was still very much aroused from his time spent next to Cormac.

"Yes?" Vance asked.

"Er . . . Help Brock . . ." Frampton found it very hard to focus. Brock's erection was like a car wreck that you couldn't help but gawk at. "Help Brock to the door," he finally managed to get out.

"No way, man," said Vance, horrified. "This is above and beyond the call of duty."

"Cormac . . ." groaned Brock, in what the dean hoped was pain.

"Jesus . . ." muttered the dean.

From the living room there was a loud, shrill whistle. In a matter of seconds, the two men in bandanas were back in the house and making their way down the hall. The dean inadvertently made eye contact with one of them, and was fairly certain he detected a glimmer of recognition before he looked away. Without saying a word, the bandana men roughly lifted Brock up off the ground by his arms. The suddenly silent crowd parted to let them through. Once they disappeared from view, the dean heard the sound of the front door opening and then a loud thump as Brock was tossed out onto the porch.

"Nobody messes with my roommate!" proclaimed Vance, who sounded proud of his role in dispatching Brock. "Now, who's next? The clock's ticking, Deano." Vance walked back into the bedroom and sat back down in his usual chair. "Someone bring me beer!" he shouted to nobody in particular.

"That'll be twenty dollars," said the dean. The next person in line passed the money over eagerly and walked into the bedroom. "Probably best if you don't whack it," the dean added, hoping the warning was no longer necessary. The music kicked back on from the living room, the smell of fresh joints and relit blunts filled the air, and the door to Cormac's bedroom slammed shut.

* * *

Cissy sat on the airborne couch putting the finishing touches on her article. The remaining people in the Craymore Street house buzzed around her feet, tidying up. As messy and dirty as the house had already been, the first day of operating the Cormac-exploiting business had rendered it nearly uninhabitable. Spilled beer covered the floor, way more garbage than usual had piled up, and a dog was either dead or passed out in the corner.

Cissy heard an irritated voice rapidly speaking in Spanish and looked down at her feet. A tiny woman was there, furiously pointing her mop handle at Cissy's feet. When it had become apparent that cleaning the house up was a far bigger task than Vance and the dean could handle, Mako and G-Dimes sprung for a crew of three cleaning ladies. They had worked very efficiently, almost as if they feared deportation or physical harm if they did not, and the house had quickly come to resemble its old self.

Cissy raised her feet so the woman could walk underneath her. The cleaning lady quickly mopped back and forth under Cissy's legs, then disappeared under the airborne couch. The woman was several inches shorter than the dean, and could stand under the couch without ducking. Earlier, someone probably would have objected to her endangering her life by wandering under the couch, but now the attitude seemed to be that since it had stayed standing throughout the chaos of the day, there wasn't going to be much that could bring it down at this point.

Cissy lowered her legs again and banged out another sentence. The dean had really been holding her nose to the grindstone for the past hour. He and Vance had decided to shut down the operation at around 10:30. It had just been getting good as far as Cissy was concerned. Mako was treating her like royalty. Once the crowd started to spill out onto the porch, he posted bandana men outside to make sure nobody messed with her new couch. He had an underling or someone who owed him money bringing her a drink every time her glass got low. Plus, he'd told her about a website that only posted pictures of cats having sex, which was hilarious.

But then the dean had got all nervous and sent everyone home. Cissy thought he was being overly cautious. It wasn't like as soon as Cormac went to bed on the *Levyathan* he was going to wake up here. Cissy had no way of knowing whether this was true or not, but now her drink was empty and nobody was refilling it and she was upset.

Dean Bickerstaff popped his head into the living room from the hallway. "How's the article coming, Cissy?" he asked. Cissy rolled her eyes. "We're almost done here," the dean said, "then I'll drive you down to the office, OK?" Cissy gave him a half-hearted thumbs up and the dean went to try to wake up the dog.

She didn't know why the dean was being so fussy about her article. She personally thought it was the greatest thing she'd ever written. If Dean Bickerstaff was worried that she'd missed any details, well guess what? She'd been there all day, and he could go to hell. He wasn't a big shot. Or Vance. Who cares. Cissy was drunk.

Ignoring the red underlines that the spellchecker put under every instance of *Levyathan* and whackin', Cissy decided to give her article a final read through.

Students Experience Whaling, Partying Thanks to Other Student's Ear

By Cissy Buckler

The whale that swallowed Pinocchio was named Monstro, but you're much more likely to find a Monstrobe light on Craymore Street. The hottest party in town isn't on fraternity row but rather on a boat that would have to row, row, row (if its sails were to be somehow rendered inoperable.)

Cissy shuddered ever so slightly. Good journalism always gave her chills.

Today (yesterday when you're reading this), hundreds of students gathered at Cormac McIlhenney's (Junior, Undeclared) home for a chance to pay twenty dollars to look into his ear for two minutes. No, they weren't looking for earwax! They were joining their fellow student aboard the mighty whaling ship, the Levyathan.

The turnout exceeded the expectations of the organizer, Vance Stafford (Junior, Physical Education/History). "We had no idea word of mouth would travel so quickly," said Stafford while wearing just a towel. "It was overwhelming at first because you've got to keep a sharp eye on people or else they might whack it while they're looking in Mac's ear."

Vance managed to intercept the first student who attempted to whack it, and wanted make it clear to School Paper readers that he had cut him off before the act was completed. "I stopped him in his tracks," Stafford assured us. "His D didn't come anywhere near Mac's ear. I didn't touch the D either, if any ladies were concerned. My point is, you can peer into Mac's ear with confidence that Brock's junk was not inserted into where you're sticking your eye. Though I'm sure he probably thought about doing that when he got home and finished up."

Brock (Sophomore, Finance) is the student who Vance caught attempting to masturbate. He was given a lifetime ban from the

Craymore Street house. His whereabouts are currently unknown. Speaking to the School Paper *after he became the first student to witness McIlhenney kill a whale, he said, "I'm not going to be able to resist whackin' it if I see him kill two more whales. Alright, I'm going to go get back in line."*

Harrington Dean Frampton Q. Bickerstaff attempted to downplay the whackin' incident. "Don't put that in," he said, speaking off the record. "It was just one sicko. Look, at least don't start off the article with that story, and certainly don't focus on it for too long," the dean said, again referring to the incident where a Harrington student attempted to masturbate while peering into another unconscious student's ear.

After reading this article over my shoulder, Dean Bickerstaff also wished it to be made clear that, like Vance, he did not touch Brock's D either. The School Paper *was unable to verify this claim.*

The experience of some students varied. Some witnessed a tense encounter with Asian sailors, while others saw McIlhenney do his best Tashtego impression (literary reference). Others simply witnessed the quiet, early moments of the day, and enjoyed the out-of-body experience. "Me and my top dog G-Dimes have been here all day," said Mako (PhD program, Comp Sci). "Time flies when you're looking into a stranger's ear."

Though the main attraction drew long lines, many were in high spirits as they waited. Literally! That is to say that many students were smoking marijuana while they waited, and there were drug dealers selling it in case you didn't bring any. One of the dealers, speaking under condition of anonymity, said, "Me and G-Dimes are gonna be here every day, so come get your puff on!"

Kegs and music were also provided as a courtesy.

Since McIlhenney will not be on the boat tomorrow (today when you're reading this), Dean Bickerstaff wanted to make it very clear that nobody should come by the house tomorrow (today). Everyone should come by in two days (tomorrow). If you come by tomorrow (today), you could ruin the whole thing because Cormac will figure out that Harrington's dean and his roommate are charging people to look into his ear. So come in two days (tomorrow). Not tomorrow (today).

So if you missed out today (yesterday), make sure you take the opportunity to come say "holla" to Harrington's own Fedallah! (literary reference). Doors will open at 9:00 a.m. Masturbating is strongly discouraged and will result in a lifetime ban with no refunds. Buckler out.

Cissy imagined that this was how Jayson Blair felt. But when he had written one of his good articles, not one of the ones where he made stuff up. She triple checked that it had been saved, then quickly banged out a fake version for the paper that only Cormac would see.

Student Doing Fine
By Cissy Buckler

Though interest has understandably waned in his mundane saga, we're obliged to inform you that Cormac McIlhenney (Junior, Undeclared) is doing fine. There's pretty much nothing to report. He's still waking up on a whaling boat every other day in the nineteenth century, but since nobody else can really experience this, it's of very little interest. Were it possible for this to somehow impact other students, we would probably write more about it, but obviously that's not the case.

Cormac spent yesterday alone in his bed. His roommate Vance Stafford (Junior, Physical Education/History) was going to keep an eye out in case anyone tried to break in and mess with him, but then he realized that nobody would do that since it's so uninteresting. Stafford instead just made sure the stadium seating couches were secure. He thought that he might also do a little bit of cleaning, so if the house looks a bit different, perhaps overly clean in an effort to eliminate traces of something or someone or a party, it's because Vance cleaned. "It wouldn't hurt Cormac to pitch in on the days he is awake," Stafford complained. "You don't need all ten fingers to push a mop."

Stafford is right. At least two members of the Harrington janitorial staff are missing at least one finger. When asked how the missing digit affected his mopping, one of the janitors named Ol' Marty responded "I thought this closet was locked! Don't touch that pesticide, that's Ol' Marty's pesticide!"

This reporter was unable to observe Ol' Marty's mopping, but his pesticide consumption did not appear to be affected by his missing finger. Buckler out.

Stumbling upon Ol' Marty's secret closet was finally paying off, Cissy thought to herself. She hit save on the fake article and moved both documents over to a thumb drive. The media always made journalism seem like an endless slog, pursuing leads and pounding the pavement. Well she just wrote two entire articles without even leaving the couch. They might as well get it over with and rename the Buckler Award after her right now. Or at least on their website they could clarify that it was now named after her instead of her grandfather, since the name technically wouldn't be changing.

"Hey, Dean Bickerstaff," Cissy yelled without looking up from her laptop. "Article's done!"

Dean Bickerstaff gave up trying to revive the dog and tossed it out of a window that faced the side yard. The startled dog woke up when it hit the ground and attempted to leap back in through the window, but the dean slammed it shut just in time. The dog, apparently still a bit drunk, opted to lick the window for a few minutes, then ran off into the night.

"Did you take out all that stuff about today and yesterday and two days from now at the end?" the dean asked as he walked over to Cissy. Cissy shook her head.

"It just strikes me as very confusing," Frampton pleaded. "Unnecessarily so. I'm sure the paper has standards regarding which tense you are supposed to use."

"And I'm sure Rosario here would be honored to take this thumb drive with my articles home with her," replied Cissy. The tiny cleaning lady emerged from under the couch and stared at the thumb drive eagerly.

"OK, OK," said Dean Bickerstaff. "The article stands as written. After all, you're the one with journalism in your blood." Cissy nodded.

"Vance!" called Dean Bickerstaff. "Have you got this under control?

"No problem, Deano!" Vance leaned out of Cormac's bedroom holding a garbage bag in one hand and a two liter soda bottle filled with keg beer in the other. "A job well done! See you in two days!"

Cissy looked back and forth between her two unlikely business partners. Amongst all the chaos, she had forgotten that she earned a tidy sum of money today. Just another added perk, she figured as she gripped the extension cord and unsteadily lowered herself to the ground.

"Are you going to take your laptop?" Dean Bickerstaff asked as Cissy headed toward the door.

Cissy waved him off disdainfully. One of these days she was going to have to figure out how to get back into her house. Until then, she figured her stuff was safe here as long as she wasn't gone long.

Cissy walked outside and looked over at her new couch. There were a few leaves and a pizza box resting on it, but otherwise it had survived the night on the porch intact. It was amazing how effective armed felons with nothing to lose could be.

The dean followed her outside. Cissy made sure to keep a few steps in front of him and it wasn't until she'd walked halfway from the porch to the street that she remembered what she was walking toward.

She stopped dead in her tracks and looked up at the van.

"Oh goddammit," Cissy muttered.

"Nothing like a ride in the old van, huh?" Dean Bickerstaff asked with a smile as he walked past her. The dean walked to the passenger side and unlocked the door. It opened with a rusty creak. Cissy stood her ground.

"Don't want to ride up front?" Dean Bickerstaff asked. "Well, suit yourself. The back has its own appeal I guess." The dean waddled over to the back doors and threw them open. Cissy took a step backwards.

"Oh, before I forget, let me give you your share of the money from today." Dean Bickerstaff pulled a thick wad of bills out of his pocket and started to thumb through them. "We had to pay off Mako and G-Dimes . . . Divide by three . . . Here you go." The dean peeled off several bills and offered them to Cissy. She shook her head.

"Come on," said the dean. "Take the money and get in!" He thrust the bills at Cissy with one hand and gestured toward the blackness of the rear of the van with his other. Cissy could only shake her head more vigorously. Dean Bickerstaff took a step toward her and Cissy heard a shriek from behind her.

She turned and saw Rosario and the other two cleaning ladies standing there. They were on their way to their own car, but had stopped to stare in horror at the scene in front of them. None of the ladies spoke any English, but they knew that a gringo luring women into the back of his Astro van with wads of cash was not a scene they wanted any part of.

Rosario pointed at the dean and yelled something rapidly in Spanish. Frampton looked around, not realizing at first that they were talking about him. Once it clicked into place, his eyes widened in terror and he began to stammer.

"No, no, no! This is not what you think it is! We work together! We are business partners! Tell them, Cissy!"

Still waving the cash, Dean Bickerstaff started to shuffle toward the cleaning ladies, but they shrieked again and scattered to their car. Two of them hopped in the backseat and Rosario took the wheel. She floored the ignition as soon as she could get the car started and the cleaning mobile peeled off. In their haste to flee the dean, they left a perfectly good mop bucket sitting in the gutter.

Cissy turned and grinned at the dean. "See?" she said. "They know their vans." She walked up to the dean and plucked the wad of bills from his hand. That little scene had been worth it, Cissy figured. As the dean stood there, still trying to process what had just happened, Cissy shoved the bills into her pocket and hopped into the back of the van.

DAY NINE

Captain Anson had forgotten to carry the two. He balled up a piece of paper and threw it over his shoulder. Calculating his expected earnings from the past week was proving more difficult than he had hoped. He really wished he hadn't broken that abacus.

Anson grabbed a fresh sheet of paper and started to jot down numbers again. Unable to sleep, he'd been working all night long, but his math was rusty. Every time, his figures came out way too high to be accurate. At least that's what he told himself. Factoring in all the whales Cormac had killed, plus the inflation in prices caused by the storm, combined with the trunk of money the Chinese had given him resulted in a sum that made his head spin. If he received even half that much once he arrived in St. John's, he'd be set for life.

After a few minutes, Anson had arrived at another sum. It was so high that he yelped in terror and tore the paper to shreds. The captain took a few deep breaths and tried to imagine life with that kind of money.

In his fantasy, a completely overhauled *Levyathan* soared past other ships with her sails billowing. No longer a rotting eyesore, the ship was outfitted with gleaming steel, polished ivory, and fine oak. Harness systems held scores of whales in place in a spotless cold storage area. The rum storage area was completely devoid of wharf rats. No! It was *swarming* with wharf rats, but they were all neatly groomed and sported jaunty bandanas around their neck. And the sea wenches . . . Oh the sea wenches . . .

The fantasy *Levyathan* crested a wave and the spray tickled Captain Anson's nose. He laughed heartily and gestured with his spyglass for the *Levyathan* String Quartet to play something classy. One sea wench poured him rum while another dumped a trunk of hardtack overboard to make room for the abundance of steak and pheasant the crew now enjoyed three times a day. A bandana-clad rat sat on his shoulder clutching its own miniature spyglass like a hunk of cheese.

The fantasy *Levyathan* was cresting yet another wave when suddenly a dark cloud covered the sun. The quartet launched into a screechy version of "Treasures o' the Sea" while the sea wench dropped the jug of rum and Anson's shoulder rat fled for safety. A horrible roar echoed from below the surface of the suddenly frothy water, and seconds later a gruesome beast burst up into the air. It had a long, scaly green body, huge flippers, and the snarling face of his wife Eleanor.

Captain Anson fell out of his chair. In a panic, it took him a few seconds to realize that a sea monster with his wife's head was not actually attacking his boat. His heart pounding, he pulled himself back up to his desk chair and took a seat. The rude interruption of his daydream only underscored the dark side of his potential riches: Eleanor stood to take him to the cleaners.

The captain had come around to the idea of paying his men, mostly because it would barely put a dent in his haul. He'd even gotten used to the idea that Ziro was deserving of some form of compensation for his years of unpaid service. But that harpy Eleanor trying to suckle even a single piece of eight from him, let alone the 50 percent she probably thought she was entitled to . . . He'd rather a beloved member of his crew like Ziro or Cormac take a harpoon through the gut than let that happen.

Adorable little rat-sized spyglasses now a distant memory, Captain Anson put his quill and paper away. He still had a few days before they arrived in St. John's. There must be some way to offload the cargo and escape with the riches without Eleanor or her lawyer tracking him down.

But his brain was fuzzy with fatigue, and no sparks of insight were to be had. The captain decided that a nap would do him some good, so he folded his arms on his desk and lay his head down on them. He yawned once and muttered, "just fifteen minutes" before drifting back into his dream world of busty sea wenches and rat bandanas.

Captain Anson did not wake up until four and a half hours later when a cannonball shattered the door to his cabin.

* * *

As soon as he opened his eyes, Cormac could tell that something was amiss. Propping himself up on his elbows, he blinked his eyes and looked around the room. His door was closed. His bed was intact. Vance had not shattered his ukulele in a fit of rage while he slept. But he felt something nagging that he couldn't put his finger on.

He reached over and grabbed his phone to see what time it was, but when he hit the unlock button, nothing happened. Still half asleep, Cormac looked down at his bedside table. The phone's power cable hung down off the side of it. That must be what was bothering him: he had forgotten to plug his phone in.

Well, that was easily fixed! Cormac plugged the phone in to recharge and hopped out of bed. He darted over to his desk and booted his laptop, half expecting to hear a gong when the screen came on. After a morning of brokering genital megadeals with the Chinese and his most fruitful afternoon of whaling to date, Cormac was surprised how eager he was to do something as mundane as checking how many views his ukulele video had received. But as night fell yesterday, he'd been unable to think about anything else.

YouTube loaded and Cormac braced himself. He was prepared for disappointment, but hoped he'd have at least one comment to pass along to Ziro tomorrow. Then he saw a video called "Pug humps potbellied pig" in the "Recommended for you" section of the homepage and immediately forgot about his video.

Cormac watched the pug hump the pig three times in a row, then clicked through to four more humping animal videos before he remembered what he had sat down to do. Reluctantly he paused a video of a St. Bernard humping an unfortunate nun and clicked on the "My Channel" link. Once the page loaded, Cormac was amazed by what he saw.

"Treasures o' the Sea (ORIGINAL)" had been viewed 4,632 times since he uploaded it! Cormac clicked on the video, eager to read what the twelve comments said.

"hahaha haahaha wat a dipshit," read the first one. That was certainly discouraging. Cormac looked at the user name of his new enemy: BigVance69. Cormac sighed and rolled his eyes. Fortunately, the other eleven people who had weighed in all seemed to be quite a bit more positive.

"Listening for a third time! :)" said one. "Dirty, but sooooooo funny LOL," said another. "Love it, I'm posting this to my sea shanty blog," read a third, presumably written by the loneliest man on earth.

Cormac typed out a few responses, thanking the people who had left compliments. He wasn't sure how they had discovered the video. It seemed unlikely that thousands of people were searching for videos of ukulele sea shanties performed by unknown college students on any given weekday. But Cormac didn't really care. It was way more views than he'd hoped for, and he was sure that Ziro would be very impressed, if he only knew what videos, computers, and recorded sounds were.

Humming the chorus of "Treasures," Cormac jauntily shimmied out of his bedroom into the hall. It felt good to get Ziro's unappreciated masterpiece some recognition, but it would feel even better to rub Vance's face in his overnight success. His roommate's door was open, so, figuring he was awake, Cormac headed down the hall to the living room.

The deafening snores emanating from the living room instantly proved Cormac wrong. As he got closer, Cormac realized that they were actually coming at him in stereo. Covering his ears with his hands, he stepped into the living room and observed a body on each of the couches.

Cissy lay sprawled on the airborne couch. A stream of drool hung off her slack jaw and was slowly descending toward the grounded couch, where Vance lay in his Seahawks towel, which fortunately covered everywhere that mattered. If the drool stream maintained its structural integrity, in another two feet it would drop directly into Vance's mouth. Cormac had never seen a total eclipse of the sun, but imagined this was even rarer and more spectacular. But after only a few more seconds of Vance and Cissy's combined snoring, Cormac couldn't take it anymore.

Still holding his mangled left hand against one ear, he walked over to Vance and shook him by his bare shoulder. Vance seemed unresponsive and in fact seemed to snore louder, so Cormac grabbed him by both shoulders and shook him as hard as he could without disturbing the towel's delicate placement.

Eventually Vance's eyes snapped open. He looked confused, and Cormac hovered over him until his world came into focus. Eventually Vance shook the cobwebs out of his head and locked eyes with Cormac. He immediately sat bolt upright, slamming his forehead into Cissy's drool string, which snapped its tether from her mouth and sprung toward Vance's head like a broken rubber band. The volume of drool was substantial enough that when the end of the string finally hit the puddle that was accumulating on Vance's forehead, there was a noticeable splash sound. Cormac realized with only the slightest tinge of regret that this was probably going to end up being the greatest moment of his life.

Vance, however, appeared undeterred. He rapidly glanced back and forth around the living room. Cormac wasn't sure what he was looking for, but eventually Vance appeared satisfied. He sighed and relaxed his posture, and only then did he wipe the drool away from his forehead. It took him several passes with the back of his hand before he got it all. "Dammit, Cissy," Vance muttered. Cissy snored.

"What are you doing out here, Vance?" Cormac asked. "Did something happen to your bed?"

Vance ran his fingers through his hair and shook his head. "Things just got a little wild last night Mac. Must not have made it to the bedroom."

"You guys partied?" Cormac asked. "It looks pretty clean in here."

"Well, as you can see, I had some help cleaning up." Vance smirked and pointed at Cissy with his thumb. "Quite *a bit* of help," he added lasciviously.

"Vance, are you implying that you banged Cissy?" Cormac asked.

"He absolutely did not," croaked Cissy, not even opening her eyes. Vance looked disappointed and made the "this close" gesture for Cormac with his thumb and forefinger.

"Are you ever going home, Cissy?" Cormac asked, but a snore was all he got in reply. "Look, never mind about all that," he continued. "I put a video of me playing ukulele on YouTube, guess how many views it got!"

Vance snorted. "That sea shanty thing? Maybe one, if someone's voice search really screwed up when they said 'I want to see panties.'"

"Almost five thousand!" Cormac said triumphantly.

Vance raised his eyebrows. "That's a lot of people," he said, very impressed.

Cormac smiled and nodded. "Come check it out," he said. Giving his head a few final shakes to finalize the transition from asleep to still drunk from the night before, Vance slowly rose from the couch. He tightened his towel and followed Cormac down the hallway.

"I've gotta say, buddy, you may want to be careful about this," said Vance as they entered Cormac's bedroom. "You go posting these weird little videos of yourself all over the internet, you could get a reputation. Things are finally starting to look good for Uncle Jemima—the last thing we need is word getting around that Lil' Miss Sea Shanty used to jam with us."

"The video got twenty-five hundred views in the past two minutes!" Cormac exclaimed as he refreshed the page. "It's over seven thousand now!"

"Frankly, Mac, it's pretty selfish of you not to mention your former band anywhere on this page. A little shout-out to the group where you got your start could really mean a lot, and man, we are struggling right now."

Cormac read a new comment. "'You're on the front page of GeekySquid. Get ready for the views to pour in.' What the hell is GeekySquid?" Cormac quickly googled the phrase while Vance continued to talk in the background.

"Joey swallowed a janitor mustache at our last practice. He really hasn't been well in a while."

"'GeekySquid – A compendium of nerd culture and fantastic finds.' Vance, I think this page is really popular. Hey, there I am!"

"I spilled my beer Heimliching him," Vance continued, not listening.

Cormac scrolled through the GeekySquid homepage. "Did you have any idea that ukuleles and old timey crap were so big on the internet? We should have been performing sea shanties all this time!" He clicked back to the tab with the video in it and refreshed it. Four hundred more views in the past minute. Cormac was quickly self-conscious of how messy his hair looked and the poor quality of the webcam video. He'd also been unable to suppress a laugh during an especially dirty line in the fourth verse about sperm whales and now he realized it made him sound like a dork. But all that was out of his control now. Instead he spied the top rated comment, which was somebody requesting an MP3 version of "Treasures." He figured he needed to strike while the iron was hot.

"That's great, Vance," Cormac said. "Glad Joey's doing OK. Look, I'm going to try to get an MP3 version of this recorded, can you try to get Cissy to stop snoring, or maybe muffle her with a rag of some sort? I don't want you guys showing up in the background of the recording."

Cormac turned and looked at his roommate. The expression on Vance's face made it clear to Cormac that he had said the wrong thing. It was a mix of bewilderment, anger, and scanning the room for the ukulele so he could smash it over his knee. Cormac couldn't allow this to happen. Losing the ukulele would be bad enough, but the act of raising a knee to smash it would almost certainly cause objectionable parts of Vance to become exposed. The ukulele was replaceable; what remained of Cormac's innocence sadly was not.

Fortunately, a loud knock on the door delayed any potential showdown. For a moment, Vance looked the way he did anytime there was someone at the door: hopeful that if he did nothing, Cormac would answer it. But then, as if there had been a startling noise that only Vance could hear, his eyes widened and he snapped to attention.

"I'll get it!" Vance said, and he darted out the door and down the hall.

Vance had been acting a bit more high-strung than usual, Cormac thought. Maybe something actually had happened between him and Cissy. Or, much more likely, maybe there was something far more immoral and illegal going on that his roommate wasn't telling him about. Reluctantly, Cormac refreshed his video again, saw that it had gained another three hundred views, then followed Vance down the hall.

As Cormac entered the living room he could see that Vance was already in a heated discussion with whoever was at the door.

"I thought we told you to stay the hell away from here!" Vance hissed. He held the door with one hand and the frame with the other, blocking the entrance with his body.

"If I could just come inside, I'm sure he'd want to see me," said the person at the door.

"Hell no!" said Vance. Cormac tried to peer around Vance's body to see who was there. He was able to make out a skinny guy who looked slightly younger than him and Vance. He was rubbing his hands together and looked nervous and fidgety. Evidently the skinny guy saw him too. His expression grew excited and he weaved his head back and forth trying to make eye contact with Cormac despite Vance's interference.

"Cormac!" the guy at the door exclaimed. Vance turned around and grumbled when he saw Cormac.

"What's going on, Vance?" Cormac asked. "Who is that?"

"It's me! Brock!" came the excited voice from the doorway. Still facing Cormac, Vance slammed the door shut behind him, right in Brock's face.

"What the hell?" Cormac asked.

"Mac, you've got to trust me on this," Vance tried to reassure him. "You do not want to talk to that guy. I had a class with Brock once and he is one weird dude. This one time he told the TA that he considered *Measure for Measure* Shakespeare's greatest comedy."

Cormac stared back at Vance. "What is so weird about that?" he asked.

"Disregarding how utterly ridiculous a claim that is, and the fact that *Measure's* comedic ending seems tacked on for the sake of fitting the genre, it also happened in economics class! And, you may be interested to know, he was wearing sweatpants that day and had a huge boner throughout that entire class. I shit you not, an hour and a half, Mac. Straight up and down."

"You might have led with that last point," said Cormac. Vance gestured with his hand to illustrate the already crystal clear point he was trying to make. "Yes, I got it," said Cormac, lowering his head to avoid looking at Vance's reenactment.

"Look, buddy, I'll handle this," Vance said as he walked toward Cormac. "You go back to your room and lay down that MP3. You've got fans now! You've got to give them what they want."

Cormac looked back up at Vance, who was smiling and nodding. In a friendly gesture, Vance reached his arm out and patted Cormac on the shoulder.

"Vance," Cormac said abruptly. "You've never sat through an hour and a half of econ *total* in your entire time at Harrington. And if there ever *was* a guy sitting next to you with a perma-boner, you definitely would have let me know about it. Probably while it was happening!"

Cormac shook off his roommate's affectionate outstretched arm and pushed past him to answer the door. Caught in his boldfaced lie, Vance looked blindsided.

The door swung open. Brock was still standing on the doorstep. He gasped in surprise when he saw it was Cormac this time.

Brock instantly made Cormac feel uneasy. He was staring at him in quiet awe, the way a child might look at Santa Claus. He constantly shifted his weight back and forth from foot to foot. He had scruffy stubble on his gaunt face, his clothing was torn in several places, and the twigs and leaves in his hair suggested that he had spent the night sleeping in the woods.

"Hi Cormac," Brock said in a flat voice. Cormac instinctively glanced at his guest's hands for a gun or knife. He had no desire to get Hinckley'd if Brock was dead set on impressing some Hollywood starlet.

"I just wanted to tell you that I am . . . just *so* honored that you chose me as a conduit for your message," Brock continued.

"Message?" Cormac was confused. "I'm sorry, have we met?"

"We were of one body before there was even time," Brock solemnly intoned.

Cormac looked around outside for some clue as to what the hell this guy was talking about. Instantly he spotted a creepy windowless van parked across the street. Obviously Brock was driving that thing around town, probably pantsless, perving on whatever his sick little mind desired.

Cormac started to close the door. "Sorry man," he told Brock. "I've got stuff I need to do."

Brock stuck his foot in front of the door. Cormac tried to push it shut, but for a skinny guy, Brock held his ground well.

"I saw you kill those whales," Brock said. He was looking Cormac in the eye but his gaze seemed fixed about ten feet behind him. "I was with you then and I'm with you now. You've been chosen, Cormac, and you in turn chose me. You served as my portal, and now I'm here to serve you. Give me a mission and I will do your bidding."

Cormac was more creeped out than he had ever been in his life. He was finding it all too easy to imagine Brock in an orange prison jumpsuit, staring ahead blankly as the family members of his victims tearfully took the witness stand, one after another. On the other hand, his Volvo really could use a good wash.

"How do you feel about washing my car?" Cormac asked.

"It is my privilege to serve you, Cormac," Brock said, bowing his head.

"And then maybe pick up some pizzas." Cormac looked back at Vance and smugly nodded. Yet another thing his roommate had been wrong about. If Vance had his way, they'd be turning away every potential servant who showed up at their door just because they seemed like they might one day wear his skin. A hit viral video and now his own personal disciple. Things were really starting to go in his—

"Boner! Boner!" yelled Vance, pointing at the doorway. Cormac spun around and saw that indeed, Brock was staring at him with renewed vigor and a noticeable erection. Cormac summoned a new level of strength and pushed the door hard enough that Brock's foot was forced out of the way. It latched closed and Cormac locked the handle and the deadbolt in rapid succession.

"Holy crap!" he exclaimed after he had a chance to catch his breath. Vance seemed just as shaken. Cissy snored.

"What the hell was that?" Cormac asked, not really expecting an answer. "Some guy I've never seen before shows up at the doorstep, telling me I've been chosen? He says he saw me kill whales? What hole did this guy crawl out of?"

"I warned you, buddy," Vance said with a shrug. "You start posting videos of you playing that ukulele for the whole world to see and you're going to attract some weirdos."

Vance patted Cormac on the shoulder again and started to walk toward the hallway. "Who wants a Bloody Mary?" he asked the room.

"Me," Cissy grunted without sitting up.

"Mac?" Vance asked. Cormac nodded, still not really sure what had just happened. He was almost certain he didn't have the whole story, but he wasn't sure how to figure out what the missing pieces were. What had Brock meant when he said Cormac was his portal? Why had Vance been so keen on not letting him talk to Brock face-to-face?

Cormac had lots of questions, but getting a straight answer from Vance was obviously not going to happen. Cissy wouldn't be much help—Cormac wasn't sure how much of the past few days she had even been conscious for. And talking to Brock again wasn't an option, even though he had already thought of several more menial tasks he wouldn't mind someone else doing for him.

Cormac sighed. Days back home were supposed to be less stressful than the days he was hauling titanic beasts out of the sea. But what could he do? After double checking that the deadbolt was secured, Cormac walked over to the grounded couch and flopped down on it. He picked up a copy of the latest *School Paper* that Vance had left on the floor next to the couch and absentmindedly scanned the front page. As his towel-clad roommate walked down the hallway toward the kitchen, Cormac could hear him whistling "Treasures o' the Sea."

* * *

Ziro spotted the pirate ship just seconds before they opened fire. With Cormac on an off day, he had been enjoying a lazy morning. He didn't expect that they'd have much whale hauling to do, so he'd been alternating between swabbing the deck and composing a new song. He'd swab a length of the deck while thinking of a chord progression, then take a little break to see what it sounded like strummed out on the ukulele.

Ziro was an accomplished instrument maker and held his own when it came to actually playing. His songwriting career had stalled after "Treasures o' the Sea," but the enthusiasm that Cormac had shown for his tune had reignited his spark, and he was determined to craft a worthy follow-up.

He thought he might have a breakthrough when he realized that the bridge should begin with a D# instead of a D, but as he triumphantly raised his head in anticipation of strumming the chord, he saw it. A large ship, barreling across the water at top speed toward the *Levyathan*. It flew a skull and crossbones flag, and before Ziro even had a chance to react, he heard two explosions. The first came from a cannon on the approaching pirate ship. The other came just a few seconds later, when the cannonball struck the door to Captain Anson's quarters.

As soon as the projectile struck the ship, Ziro dropped his ukulele. He couldn't believe that a pirate ship had just snuck up on them like that. Ziro cursed his own negligence under his breath. He should have noticed. Manning the crow's nest was technically not his job; the whalers were supposed to take shifts up there. But crow's nest duty had long been neglected in favor of sleeping in and drinking. Ziro glanced up at the lookout tower. Not only was nobody manning it, but one of the whalers had actually gone to the trouble of hanging a large, canvas bullseye target off of it. That seemed aggressively irresponsible.

But there was no time to worry about that. They still might be able to ward off the attackers if the crew acted quickly. Ziro took off running toward the captain's quarters.

When he rounded the corner, he immediately skidded to a halt when he saw the splinters of what used to be Captain Anson's door. The cannonball was a direct hit, and pieces of wood and metal were now scattered all the way to the edge of the ship. Ziro silently hoped that the pirates would choose a different target for their second volley, and after a deep breath, sprinted toward the doorway.

Ziro darted inside and flattened himself up against the wall. The captain's quarters were in disarray. He quickly scanned the room for scattered pieces of Captain Anson. Not detecting any, Ziro concluded that he must have survived the attack, or possibly been pulverized into a fine mist by one of those new-model cannonballs he'd heard rumors of.

While he was squinting in an attempt to detect any sort of airborne particle cloud, Ziro heard a noise from the back of the quarters. There was a rustling coming from behind the captain's overturned desk. Ziro took a step toward it, already envisioning the sight of the dying captain pinned beneath a pile of rubble.

The moment Ziro's foot hit the ground, a wooden dowel shot up in the air from behind the overturned desk. There was a soiled white rag attached to the end of it, which, upon closer inspection, Ziro determined was an undershirt. The dowel waved back and forth a couple of times before a terrified voice spoke up.

"I surrender!" Captain Anson said. "Take everything! The ship is yours! There's a former slave on board named Ziro who's great at swabbing decks! He's only been free for a few days, so you could probably easily convince him that he should still be a slave! Please, just let me live!"

"Captain?" Ziro asked cautiously. "It's me, Ziro."

Captain Anson's eyes and nose popped up over the edge of the desk. "Ziro!" he shouted when he realized it wasn't a pirate. "Thank God!"

For the time being, Ziro decided to ignore the captain's bafflingly immediate attempt to sell him out. "Get up, Captain," he yelled. "We've still got a few minutes before the pirates try to board us. We've got to act quickly!"

Captain Anson popped the rest of his head up. "They haven't boarded yet? Well then there's still a chance, dammit!" Anson dropped the makeshift surrender flag and sprung to his feet. He thrust his chest out and stood tall. Gone was the cowering wretch of a captain from a moment earlier. For the first time that he could remember, Ziro felt like he was in the presence of a true leader of men.

"There's a secret emergency lifeboat. Screw the other men. Scoop as much of the Chinese gold as you can into my pants while I look for my spyglass."

"Scoop what into where?"

"The gold that the Chinese guys gave us!" Captain Anson said, pointing at the treasure chest. "The chest is too heavy to bring it all and my pockets won't hold enough, so I'll tuck my pants into my boots and you just pour it into the pants. Where the hell is that spyglass?"

Captain Anson got down on his hands and knees and started sifting through the scattered objects and debris on the floor. Ziro glanced at the doorway. He didn't approve of the captain's plan, but at this point in time, there wasn't much that he could do. The pirates would be on board before he could rouse the whalers, and if there was actually a secret lifeboat, it seemed foolish not to take it.

"I don't feel any gold in my pants!" yelled Captain Anson.

Ziro ran over to the chest and scooped out a handful of coins and jewels. He ran over to the captain, who was scrounging around underneath his overturned desk. His lower half was sticking out and Ziro, after a sizeable pause, lifted the waistband of Captain Anson's pants and dropped the treasure in.

"Poseidon's trident!" the captain bellowed. "Those coins got cold overnight! Ziro, warm them up with your hands next time!"

Ziro ran back and forth between the treasure chest and wherever Captain Anson was currently crawling, rubbing the Chinese treasure to heat it up, then depositing it in the captain's pants. Eventually the captain discovered that his spyglass had been clipped to his belt the entire time and he stood up. His pants bulged noticeably from his knees down to his ankles, and now that he was dragging along dozens of pounds of treasure with each step, his mobility was greatly reduced.

"Move that circular rug out of the way," he told Ziro, pointing at a hideous rug in the corner of his quarters. "There's a trap door underneath that leads to the life boat. I'll be there in a minute—it's not so easy to move with all this gold." The captain took a few labored, bowlegged steps toward the general area of the rug.

Walking unburdened, Ziro reached the rug in a few seconds, and pulled it aside. There was indeed a trap door beneath it. Ziro was impressed that even after five years aboard her, there were still things he didn't know about the *Levyathan*.

"I wonder why they haven't fired any more cannonballs at us," the captain asked. He was only halfway to the trapdoor and his pants emitted a loud jingle with every step he took.

"Well, there was absolutely no response after their first one," said Ziro. "Nobody fired back, or changed course, or even woke up. They probably figure they're in for the easiest plunder of their careers and don't need to waste any more ammo."

"Well, they didn't count on one thing," said Captain Anson as he lurched closer. "Me filling my pants with Chinese treasure and escaping in a lifeboat."

"No," Ziro sighed. "They almost certainly did not."

As soon as the captain finished speaking, the weight of the treasure tore through the right leg of his pants at mid-calf level. Gold poured onto the floor in a steady stream until the right leg was empty. The captain cursed and took a cautious step forward with his left leg, which also tore the moment his foot hit the ground, spilling more treasure everywhere.

His pants now devoid of gold, Captain Anson was once again able to move at normal speed. With torn fabric flapping, he jogged over to the trapdoor ladder.

"It was slowing me down anyways," he mumbled to Ziro, before stepping onto the ladder and beginning his descent.

As the captain lowered himself down, Ziro took a moment to look back over his shoulder. He gazed through the doorframe of the captain's quarters. He assumed that this would be his final glimpse of the ship that had been his home for the past five years.

As soon as he descended the ladder and saw the state of the lifeboat, Ziro realized that would not be the case.

The lifeboat was undoubtedly the most dilapidated part of the entire *Levyathan*. Being kept a secret for so long meant that it had not even been subjected to the minimal maintenance the rest of the boat so rarely received. The wood was rotting, there were several holes in the sides that were big enough to stick your hand through, and a particularly feisty looking wharf rat was guarding her nest in the center of the boat.

Ziro knew right away he would rather take his chances with the pirates. At least with the pirates he might just be taken as a slave again. Venturing out onto the open sea in this lifeboat would mean certain, possibly instant, death.

It would prove difficult to convince Captain Anson of this, for at the moment he was attempting to force the wharf rat out of the lifeboat with the only oar that remained. The rat hissed and clawed the air in a frenzied attempt to defend her nest, but the captain was eventually able to stun it with a lucky blow to the head. He picked it up with the flat side of the oar and flung it off into a corner of the secret lifeboat chamber where it hit the wall with a thud and slid to the floor.

"Ziro!" yelled Captain Anson. "Help me get rid of these rat eggs!"

"Rat eggs?" asked Ziro. He peered into the boat. Indeed, there were four blue-green eggs inside it. Each one was about twice the size of a chicken egg.

"Sir, rats don't lay eggs," Ziro said. "These must be some sort of reptile egg that she was attempting to hatch and raise as her ungodly offspring."

"Snake-rats, eh?" said the captain. "Yes, I've heard whispers of such things. Clearly they're an abomination, but apparently it's unlucky to destroy their eggs. Ziro! Gather them up. You'll have to raise them as your own."

One of the eggs wobbled a little bit. Clearly whatever was inside would be hatching soon. Ziro decided it was time to say goodbye.

"Sir, I'm sorry. I'm not going with you," he informed the captain.

"Well of course, you're not," Captain Anson replied. He stared at Ziro with a puzzled expression for a few seconds before he came to a realization. "Ohhhhhhh! Oh, oh, oh, you thought I wanted you to join me in the lifeboat!" The captain chuckled, quietly at first but quickly a bit heartier. "No, I just needed your help launching this thing! There clearly aren't enough emergency rations in here for both of us."

"I don't think there are any emergency rations, sir," said Ziro as he eyed some crumbs near the nest. "I think the rat ate them all. Besides, this boat is a death trap! It's going to sink as soon as you launch it!"

"Yeah, well, that's what my wife said about the *Levyathan*," said the captain. He had stopped laughing and his rigid stare made Ziro realize that changing the captain's mind was now going to be impossible. Ziro flinched as some muffled yells and thumps came from somewhere on the boat above them. The pirates must have finally boarded.

The captain heard them, too. "There's a secret panel that slides open," Captain Anson said, pointing toward the wall past the bow of the lifeboat. "We're actually right at water level right now, so if you push it aside, I can shove off and I'll be on my way." The captain lowered himself unsteadily into the lifeboat, trying to keep as far away from the rat's nest as possible, Ziro noted.

Ziro walked over to the wall that the captain had pointed at. He felt around in front of him and eventually grasped a metal handle. He turned around and looked at the captain. Anson huddled in the stern of the boat, holding the oar. Ziro couldn't have predicted it in a million years, but the moment had him feeling more than a little emotional.

"Sir," he said, a lump forming in his throat. "I just wanted to say that the past five years have been—"

"Oh God, it's chipping its way out!" Captain Anson shrieked. "One of the eggs is hatching! Dammit, Ziro, open the door!"

Ziro pulled as hard as he could and with a series of creaks, the wall slowly began to slide open. Sunlight lit up the previously dark secret chamber. Ziro turned his head and the captain shielded his eyes. When the door was finally all the way open, Ziro ran around to the back of the boat and leaned into it, attempting to shove it out toward the open sea. Captain Anson tried to help by pushing off the floor with his oar, but the boat was heavy and hadn't been moved in years, so the going was slow.

After a few seconds of pushing, Ziro noticed that the captain had stopped contributing even his token effort. "Captain, I could really use some help here," he said, straining as hard as he could to move the lifeboat.

"That won't be necessary!" came a nasty-sounding voice from somewhere nearby. Ziro looked up for the first time since he'd started pushing. Floating just outside the *Levyathan*'s secret door was a small dinghy carrying three men.

They were burly and rough looking, and obviously were scouts from the main pirate ship. They each wore a striped shirt and two of them had thick, bushy beards. The one who did not wear a beard wore a red bandana tied around his head, and he was the one who addressed Ziro and the captain.

"Greetings, gentlemen!" he said in a snide tone that indicated the formality was very much in jest. "I'm afraid I'm not going to be able to let you launch that lifeboat." Ziro stopped pushing and straightened up. He sized up the three pirates, paying close attention to the long cutlasses the two bearded ones wore strapped to their belts.

"You see," continued the pirate in the red bandana, "My name is Pete, and my friends and I are pirates of the most feared ship on the seven seas: the *HMS Mongrel*. Though in our case, the M stands for Marauding." The other two pirates laughed warmly at what was surely a familiar joke.

"What do the H and S stand for?" asked Captain Anson.

"Never mind that," snapped Pete, already looking slightly disgusted. "The point is, we've just taken your boat, with quite minimal resistance I might add. And now, I'm afraid that per the terms of the Pirate Code, I have to offer you two choices. Two choices that, though they may seem unfair, are merely an extension of the ocean's own fickle hand. For our fates ebb and flow, just like her majestic tides, and I'm afraid that at this point, your own fate—"

"The first one," blurted Captain Anson. "We'll take the first one! I don't care, just . . . Oh, Jesus, that thing is almost out of the egg!" The captain dove out of the lifeboat and onto the floor of the secret chamber. He flailed his legs until he found his footing, then hurriedly crawled over to Ziro and hid behind his legs.

Pete slouched, disappointed that his big speech had been cut off. But he also appeared very curious about what had made the captain flee. "What's in there?" he asked, peering into the secret chamber.

"Snake-rats!" said Captain Anson, peering out from behind Ziro. "Get us the hell out of here!"

"Snake-rats! Here? And you sat in a boat with them? Good God, man, get over here right now!" Pete rapidly gestured for them to get into the dinghy. Captain Anson wasted no time, jumping up and dashing over to the pirates. Ziro sighed and slowly followed after him. As he passed by the lifeboat, he glanced into the nest. A baby alligator was sitting in a pile of broken egg shells. That was still pretty weird, thought Ziro, but not as weird as a snake-rat would have been.

He heard a high-pitched wheeze from a corner of the room and saw the wharf rat getting to her feet. Ziro figured if she had already cared for the eggs for this long, she could certainly handle whatever came next. Or she'd be quickly be devoured by the newborn alligators. Ziro didn't care. He had far more pressing concerns at the moment.

With his oar, one of the bearded pirates navigated the dinghy toward the side of the *Levyathan* and Captain Anson gingerly stepped in. Still shaking from his terrifying encounter with the hatching egg, he took a seat next to the bearded pirate who wasn't holding an oar. Pete offered Ziro a weathered hand to help him into the boat.

"How'd you know we were down here?" Ziro asked him.

"Oh, the whalers," the pirate said. "Yeah, they said they'd known about this place forever. Every time we tied a man up, he'd tell us that we could find the captain down in the secret room, even if he'd just heard the man in front of him say the exact same thing. It was like they were unable to help themselves from selling you out."

Ziro couldn't really blame them. He took the pirate's hand and stepped into the boat. Widening his stance for balance, the pirate pulled the door to the evidently not-so-secret chamber closed. Once it was shut, he sat down and took up the other oar.

Ziro took a seat as the two buccaneers began to row around the *Levyathan*, back to wherever they had launched the dinghy. The men sat in silence until Ziro was compelled to speak up.

"What was option two?"

"Oh, don't worry, you picked the right one," said Pete. "Though it would have been polite to let me finish my speech."

Another silence descended upon the dinghy. The only sound came from the two oars simultaneously cutting in and out of the water. Eventually Captain Anson chimed in.

"Hell, what is option one?" asked the captain. "What exactly did I sign us up for here, huh?" He shot Ziro a grin that was not returned.

"That," said Pete. "Is something you'll find out soon enough." He shot his fellow pirates a hideous grin. It was most definitely returned.

* * *

By noon, Cormac had amassed over thirty-four thousand YouTube views and three of Vance's Bloody Marys. So when he got an email that Channel 9, the local NBC affiliate, wanted to interview him, he thought it was a spectacular idea.

The "Treasures o' the Sea" video had spent the morning going viral. Visitors to GeekySquid had discovered it, then posted it to their own sites and social networks. There were already several cover versions, as well as a parody, "Treasures Make Me Pee," that Cormac felt somewhat cheapened the whole endeavor.

The hundreds of comments it received were almost universally positive. There were a few calling him a loser or telling him he should die in a fire, but they were few and far between, and often had "fire" misspelled. An even smaller number of comments appeared to be just plain nonsensical. Cormac figured stuff like "Isn't this that guy where you can look in his ear?" was just some sort of elaborate Russian spambot.

Once Cissy woke up for good, the house was quiet enough for Cormac to record an MP3, which he uploaded and posted a link to in the YouTube description. The commenters were appreciative. At least one indicated a desire to have sex with Cormac while the song played. Cormac was trying to talk himself out of emailing her when the email from Channel 9 arrived.

After he'd read it twice to make sure it was real, Cormac strutted out to the living room. He'd heard the stories about how fame could change people, make them forget their roots and abandon their values. He totally understood how that could happen. It would be the most satisfying thing he could imagine to forget all the little people who had helped him get where he was right now.

Vance and Cissy both had not moved from the stadium seating couches since they woke up. Cissy was sitting up and typing on her laptop, a lit joint hanging from her lip like a cigarette. She held a Bloody Mary between her knees. Vance was flattened out on the grounded couch. He was explaining to Cissy why auto manufacturers should install U-turn signals in every car. Cormac instantly knew that Vance had shared some of the joint. It was an argument he had heard many times.

"Who doesn't benefit from this? That's my question," Vance was saying. "It's all about processing information, man."

Cormac tried to stand around until they noticed him, but they were both locked into their own little worlds. Eventually he wandered over to the window and peered out of it.

"That van is still parked there," he said, addressing the room. "Kinda creepy how that Brock guy is just hanging out in there, huh?"

Vance stopped talking and looked at Cissy. Cissy put the joint out on one of the arms of the airborne couch.

"Yeah, totally, buddy," Vance said. "Get that perv outta here, that's what I say." He attempted to stifle stoned laughter, and was managing to do a decent job of it until Cissy snorted. All hell broke loose after that. Cissy and Vance were rendered speechless by uncontrollable giggles.

Once they had subsided, Cormac folded both his hands behind his back and walked over to stand in front of the stadium seating couches. "Well, you'll be interested to know," he said with a haughty tone, "that I just got contacted by Channel 9. They want to interview me."

Vance stopped laughing and sat up on the couch. "What did you tell them?" he asked. He sounded concerned.

"Well, I haven't written them back yet, but obviously I'm going to say yes," said Cormac. He was confused. He expected Vance to be jealous, not panicked.

"Look, Mac," Vance said as he got up from the couch. "You gotta be careful here. You can't just go spouting off to the media. If I'm not mistaken, our agreement with the dean was contingent on Cissy having exclusive press access."

Cormac was blindsided. His mental picture of accepting a major award and forgetting to thank a bunch of people quickly vanished. Sure, he'd agreed to talk only to Cissy, but he hadn't thought that opportunities like *this* would come along!

"But . . . I don't . . ." Cormac stammered as Vance stared, waiting for him to make a point. "Sure, I agreed not to talk about the *Levyathan*, but . . ."

"And what do you think Channel 9 wants to interview you about?" Vance asked. "Your little video? You wake up in the nineteenth century every other day, Mac! Which of those sounds more newsworthy to you!?"

"I just thought that since it had gotten so many hits," Cormac said, not bothering to conceal his disappointment.

"That's not news," Cissy informed him. "I know news. Buckler out." Cissy lay back down on the couch and quickly fell asleep.

Cormac was deflated. Waking up on the *Levyathan* was like catching the flu. It was just something that happened to you. Or more specifically, to him. The point was, it was beyond his control. But having a hit video was something that had actually required effort. He was willing to accept media attention for the stuff that had fallen into his lap, but he wasn't nearly as excited about it.

"Look, Mac," Vance said in a reassuring tone that made Cormac feel the exact opposite of reassured. "Maybe you're right. Maybe the Channel 9 News Team: Your News When It Matters, Number One in the Metropolitan Area Four Years Running, decided it was important to report on a guy playing his ukulele. But you ought to double check the agreement you signed with the dean. Both of our GPAs depend on it."

Vance walked over to the living room window. "Seems like there's too much light coming in here," he said as he pulled the cord that closed the blinds. "No wait, that's too dark." He opened the blinds again. "Which do you guys prefer? Closed? Open? Closed? Open?" Vance pulled the cord back and forth over and over, opening and closing the blinds a few times in rapid succession. Before Cormac could respond, he opened them one last time and dropped the cord.

"You know what? I think it was fine the way it was. Anyways, just take a second look at the agreement you signed, Mac. You never know what kind of stuff is in the fine print." Vance spoke with the treacherous voice of someone who knew exactly what was in the fine print. "I know I could really use straight A's. When was the last time *you* went to class?"

Cormac had trouble even remembering which classes he was enrolled in. He *had* enrolled at the beginning of this semester, hadn't he?

Sensing that his argument had worked, Vance smiled. "I'm not trying to tell you what to do, Mac. All I'm saying is, just talk to Deano. Er, talk to the dean. Oh, I'm sure he'll be willing to listen." Vance chuckled nervously and fiddled with the waistband of his towel.

Cormac wasn't sure what to do next and Vance seemed determined to keep fiddling until he went away, which he was just about to do when there was a knock at the door.

"Oh look. Here he comes now," said an apparently now-awake Cissy in the flattest tone she could muster. Cormac and Vance both leaned to look out the window, and indeed, there was Dean Bickerstaff, waddling toward the door.

Cormac didn't want to talk to the dean. The dean made Cormac feel exceedingly uncomfortable. He had never bought a used car before, but everything that Hollywood had told him about the experience led him to believe that talking with the dean was not unlike talking to a particularly repellent used car salesman.

Reluctantly he walked over to the door and swung it open before the dean had a chance to knock. Dean Bickerstaff was in the process of lighting a cigar. He held his shillelagh awkwardly between his knees. It looked like he had to pee. He was also evidently having trouble with his lighter. He flicked it eight times before it finally lit, sporadically making fleeting eye contact with Cormac. Clearly it was not the impressive entrance the dean had planned.

Eventually he got the cigar lit and he removed the shillelagh from between his legs with his left hand. "Good morning, Cormac!" he said with all the genuine warmth of an undertaker who was about to inform you that, when it you really thought about it, everyone's ashes were pretty much the same.

"Morning, Dean Bickerstaff!" Vance yelled from the grounded couch. Cissy grunted. Cormac stared back at the dean. He had an increasingly less vague feeling that he was being taken advantage of. He couldn't prove a damn thing, but there was something strange happening on Craymore Street. Aside from him waking up on a whaling ship in the nineteenth century every other day, of course.

"Hello, Dean Bickerstaff," Cormac finally said. "Would you like to come in?"

"No, no, that won't be necessary," the dean said with a friendly puff of his cigar. "I just wanted to swing by and see how things were going!"

Before Cormac had a chance to respond, Vance piped up from the couch. "Channel 9 wants to interview him. Mac's probably too modest to bring it up, but they really want to talk to him."

Dean Bickerstaff raised his eyebrows and smiled. "Channel 9, eh? They've been Number One in the Metropolitan Area . . . What is it, four years running I believe? That certainly is exciting news!"

Cormac glumly shrugged. He still held out the smallest hope that the agreement the dean had made him sign was just a formality and that he'd laugh it off and let him do the interview.

"Of course, we agreed that Cissy had exclusive media access," the dean said, no longer smiling. "Sorry to rain on your parade, Cormac, but a deal is a deal. Speaking of that, I have a few graded exams for each of you." The dean cupped his hand over his mouth conspiratorially and said in a knowing voice, "Hope you did OK . . ." He produced a stack of papers from the inside of his jacket. Cormac saw that the first one had his name on it and a large A+ written in red sharpie.

The dean handed the stack to Cormac and blew a smoke ring into the air. "Anyways, I just wanted to stop by and drop those off. Sorry to have to bring the hammer down about the interview, Cormac, but hey! You read the great piece Cissy wrote in the *School Paper* today, right? Boy is she talented!"

"I want straight A's too," said Cissy, not looking up from her laptop.

"I don't think that's something we need to discuss at the moment, Cissy," said the dean, not bothering to disguise the irritation in his voice. "I'm happy to talk it over with you during my office hours."

"You know, maybe Cormac should do the interview," Cissy countered. "It's a pretty big opportunity."

The dean folded instantly. "OK! You've got straight A's!" He furiously puffed on his cigar and glared at the back of the airborne couch.

Cormac had had enough. Now that two people were benefitting from his unusual circumstances, he felt even more powerless to challenge the dean. Who knew how many more would come to depend on him? An image popped into his head of a stadium seating couch that stretched up dozens of levels into the sky, each couch populated by another deadbeat sponging off of him. He couldn't see all the way to the top, but the last person he could make out was definitely wearing a towel.

Cormac decided to put his foot down before the situation got any more out of control. Straight A's weren't worth his freedom. He cleared his throat and looked the dean in the eye. "I'm sorry, Dean Bickerstaff," he said. "I'm afraid I'm going to have to go back on our . . ."

Cormac trailed off as he noticed someone walking up the lawn toward his house. At first he was worried that Brock might be back, but he quickly realized this was fortunately not the case. Still, Cormac didn't recognize whoever it was. The stranger was better dressed than the people he and Vance knew. His shirt had a collar.

Once he realized Cormac had seen him, the guy raised his hand and waved hello. Dean Bickerstaff turned to see what Cormac was looking at. The dean sized up the situation, calmly took a final puff of his cigar, and flicked what was left of it over the side of the porch.

"Hello!" the stranger said in a friendly tone. "I'm here for the ear guy? Did I beat the crowds or—"

Before the stranger could finish his sentence, Dean Bickerstaff lunged forward and cracked the knotted end of the shillelagh across his head. The stranger crumpled to the ground with a thud. With surprising agility, the dean leapt forward, clutching the shillelagh with both hands. As he landed, he drove the end of the staff into the fallen student's stomach, eliciting a loud grunt as he knocked the wind out of him.

"Holy balls!" Cormac said. He ducked back inside. "The dean's beating the shit out of some guy!" he yelled in the general vicinity of the couches.

Vance stood up and stretched. He appeared unconcerned. "Well yeah, Mac," he said. "You don't carry around a badass shillelagh like that unless you're prepared to use it. I know I certainly don't plan on crossing or defying the dean any time soon. Bloody Mary?"

Cormac could only stare at Vance with an open mouth.

"Cistress?" Vance asked.

Cissy grunted in the affirmative and Vance took off for the kitchen. Cormac looked back outside. As Dean Bickerstaff stood over his fallen, unmoving foe, two men emerged from the bushes that lined the property. They wore bandanas over their mouths and looked very intimidating.

"Where the hell were you guys?" the dean demanded. "This guy almost got to the door!"

The two mysterious thugs nodded their heads contritely, then picked up the collared shirt guy by his arms and legs. They hauled the limp body back into the bushes and disappeared from sight. The body, and hopefully not the corpse, Cormac thought as he stared in horror.

Dean Bickerstaff turned and looked at Cormac. Noting Cormac's terrified expression, he chuckled. "He was late on his tuition payment."

Fearing the answer, Cormac managed to croak, "Is he dead?"

"No, but his credit rating certainly will be," the dean said while he lit another cigar.

"Who were those masked men?"

"Those gentlemen were from the registrar's office," the dean said. The tone of his voice indicated that he knew full well that Cormac knew he was lying and he did not care in the slightest. Cormac took this as a sign that he should stop asking questions.

"Anyways," Dean Bickerstaff said. "What were you saying, Cormac? You were going to go back on something?" The dean gave his shillelagh a jaunty twirl. The motion caused a drop of liquid to fling off the knotty end. It arched through the air and landed on Cormac's shoe. It was blood.

Cormac looked down at it, then at the dean, then back at the blood. He swallowed deeply. "Nothing," he said. "Don't worry about it."

"Excellent!" Dean Bickerstaff chomped down on his cigar and smiled broadly. "Well, Cormac, I must be going. Lots of dean stuff to do today. You remember that if you need anything at all, you can always call me. That's not an empty promise, Cormac. I'm here for you."

There was a rustling from the bushes. The dean whipped his head around and stared. Cormac noticed him clutch the shillelagh tighter. But the disturbance ended as quickly as it began and the dean relaxed. Turning back to Cormac, he laughed heartily and patted him twice on the shoulder.

"Have a great day, Cormac," he said. The dean turned and waddled across the lawn toward the sidewalk. Cormac watched him go, simultaneously noting that the pervy van was still parked on the street. Normally, this was the sort of thing he'd call the cops about, but he got the feeling that the last thing he needed at the moment was police poking around his house. The dean might not be too happy about that.

When the dean reached the sidewalk, he turned and saw that Cormac was still watching him. He laughed a fake-sounding laugh and yelled back to Cormac. "Forgot where I parked!" he yelled. Cormac kept watching as the dean exaggeratedly looked up and down the street for his car. "Oh, there it is!" he eventually yelled. "Over there! Bye!"

Cormac watched as the dean waddled off down the sidewalk. Once he was out of sight, Cormac stepped back inside and closed the door. He walked back into the living room, where Vance and Cissy were sipping their Bloody Marys. Vance raised his eyebrows as if he was waiting for Cormac to speak up, but Cormac had nothing to say. Vance turned his attention back to his drink.

Some motion from the window caught Cormac's eye. He looked out and saw that the dean was walking back down the sidewalk, retracing his earlier steps. Cormac quickly looked away. He didn't want any more interaction with that man today. Clearly, the dean had methods in place for dealing with people who displeased him. If getting on his bad side was as easy as the unfortunate person who'd appeared on their lawn had made it look, it seemed like outright avoidance was the best way to steer clear of the dean's wrath.

Cormac left the living room and walked down the hall toward his room. As he walked, he tried to remember what the collared shirt guy had said before the dean whacked him with his stick. Something about how he hoped he had beat the crowds for the "ear guy." Cormac had no idea what that meant, and he didn't imagine he was going to get a straight answer any time soon.

Something was going on back home while he was on the *Levyathan*, Cormac was sure of that. At the moment, his suspicion was only outweighed by his abject terror. He wanted to know what the dean and Vance were up to, but his motivation was greatly lessened by his even deeper desire to not incur any further lasting bodily harm.

With a heavy sigh, Cormac sat down at his computer and reluctantly shot off a quick email to Channel 9, politely declining their interview request. After he hit send, he clicked over to YouTube and reloaded his video. 77,329 views. Yippee.

* * *

Climbing up the side of the *Levyathan* via rope ladder gave Captain Anson a chance to appreciate a view of his ship he'd never seen before. Of course, it was hard to truly appreciate it since he was making the climb at gunpoint. Also, the flaking paint and rotted wood wasn't really a good view to begin with. Climbing up the side of the *Levyathan* via rope ladder was actually a pretty crappy experience.

The captain paused for a moment and took a deep breath. Climbing the ladder had been easy at first, but as he went higher, the rungs seemed farther and farther apart. One of the bearded pirates had been the first to scale it, and he had done so very quickly for such a large man. The pirates had tied the dinghy off to the side of the *Levyathan* and some of the pirates who were already on board dropped the rope ladder down from the main deck. The bearded pirate scampered right up it, then gave the all clear to the two pirates who remained on the dinghy, who produced pistols and encouraged the captain and Ziro to get moving.

"Why are you stopping?" asked Ziro from a rung or two below the captain. "Keep going!"

"Dammit, Ziro! I'm going as fast as I can," said Captain Anson. He scowled at Ziro, but this involved looking down, and the captain quickly realized this was a very bad idea. They hadn't been climbing long, but they were already higher than he cared to be. "Just give me another second."

"What's the hold up?" Pete yelled from the dinghy.

"Nothing!" Captain Anson replied. "Just taking in the view!"

"You probably don't want to stand too long on any particular rung!" the pirate informed them. "They're liable to snap if they bear weight for more than a few seconds!"

"Well then, Pete, perhaps you guys should consider getting a new rope ladder!" Captain Anson said. Pete fired his pistol into the air with a loud bang. "I'll climb faster!" the captain reassured him. He took a deep breath and continued to pull himself up, rung by rung.

Eventually, Anson reached the railing that the ladder was attached to. He flung both of his arms around it and threw his legs over one by one. When he was free of the ladder, he rolled off the railing and flopped onto the deck of the *Levyathan*. Ziro followed moments later.

While he lay on the deck catching his breath, Captain Anson looked around and attempted to size up how dire the situation was. There were maybe a dozen pirates milling about the deck of the ship. They were a rough-looking group. They had already helped themselves to the *Levyathan*'s rum supply and were passing jugs back and forth while laughing heartily. Their ship was anchored about fifteen feet from the *Levyathan*, and the gangplank they had used to board was still stretched between the two ships.

Most of the pirates wore the same style striped shirt as the pirates on the dinghy. About half of them had thick beards and they all sported a weapon of some sort attached to their belt. There were bandanas and shabby tri-corner hats and gold hoop earrings. Anson made a note to investigate the gold hoop earring look if he made it out of here alive. He thought he might be able to pull it off if he really embraced it, just acted like it wasn't even a big deal.

One pirate was standing apart from the others, observing their carousing with an air of detached authority. His adornments were much more ostentatious than the other pirates. The velvet of his admiral's hat looked brand new and there was a skull and crossbones embroidered in the center of it. An identical skull and crossbones was also embroidered on the black eye patch he wore over his right eye. A bright green parrot sat on his shoulder and the man periodically fed it bits of hardtack. He always fed it with his right hand because in place of his left hand he sported a gleaming silver hook. He wore a thick ruffled coat with shiny brass buttons, his gold earring gleamed the brightest of all them all, and he stood with a slight limp because his right leg was a wooden peg. Obviously, this was a pirate who did not mess around.

Eventually Ziro piped up. "Captain," he whispered. "Do you see that?"

"Yeah," replied Captain Anson. "He must be like, the king of all pirates!" The captain was very impressed.

"I'm not talking about the pirate! Over there, it's the rest of the crew!"

Reluctantly, the captain tore his gaze away from the über-pirate and looked in the direction Ziro was pointing. Next to the *Levyathan*'s main mast, the whalers were grouped together in a circle. Each whaler faced inward, and two pirates stood close by, keeping an eye on them. Looking closer, Captain Anson could see that the pirates' hands were bound behind their backs, and each whaler was tied to the next by a rope that connected their legs. The whalers default mood on any given day was surly, but even from a distance the captain could tell that they looked especially displeased with their current predicament.

"Captain," Ziro asked, trying to take advantage of the last moments before the other two pirates climbed aboard. "What's our plan?"

"Well, I'm certainly not going anywhere near those guys," Captain Anson said, gesturing at the crew. "They look cranky."

"You may not have a choice," said Ziro. He crawled forward until he was next to Captain Anson. "Sir, I think our best chance for getting out of this alive is for you to strike a deal with their captain." Anson and Ziro both looked over at the pirate with the parrot. While the other pirates were loudly singing drunken songs and dancing, he had produced a pipe and was smoking it while he observed from a distance.

"Him?" asked the Captain. "I dunno, do you really think he'd talk to me?"

"Sir, this is no time to be starstruck!" Ziro looked over his shoulder. The second bearded pirate was climbing over the railing and Pete was right on his heels. They'd almost certainly bind them with the rest of the crew as soon as they were settled. Ziro and the captain didn't have much time to act.

"The pirate captain probably just wants our treasure. But if you tell him about how the price for whales has skyrocketed, he won't want to leave that money on the table."

"Won't he just take the cargo and sell it himself?" the captain asked.

"Pirates can't just show up at a mainland market with dozens of whale corpses," Ziro said. "They'd be hanged! But if we tell them that we'll conduct the deal ourselves and then give them the money, we may be able to escape with our lives."

"I don't know," said Captain Anson. "It sounds complicated."

"It's actually incredibly straightforward," Ziro replied. "And it's the best shot we have at escaping."

Anson looked at his former slave with something that was approaching admiration. He had to give Ziro credit, he had a knack for keeping his cool in stressful situations. Slowly nodding, Captain Anson pulled himself to his feet.

"You're a good man to have on board, Ziro," the captain said. "You've really thought this through and I'm grateful for your advice." Ziro started to wish the captain good luck, but Anson wasn't done talking. "But I'm gonna go with my gut on this one," the captain informed him. Anson took a look over his shoulder at the two pirates who had just climbed the rope ladder. Then before Ziro could protest, he took off running toward the peg-legged pirate.

Ziro sighed and slowly rose to his knees. At least he had tried.

As Captain Anson ran toward the pirate he shouted "Captain! Captain! Captain, I have a proposal for you!" at the top of his lungs. Anson waved his hands in the air in an effort to demonstrate that he was unarmed, but this only had the effect of making him look like a flailing lunatic. Every pirate on board drew their weapon as they watched him approach. By the time Captain Anson slowed down a few feet from the pirate captain, there were cutlasses, rapiers, and pistols all pointed at various parts of his body.

"Don't shoot, don't shoot," Captain Anson said, hoping that the pirates would be bound to hear him out by the Pirate Code. "I'm the captain of this ship, and I, in turn, wish to speak with your captain!"

"Should I slash him?" asked an ugly pirate who resembled an evil little goblin. A few pirates murmured their assent and began to close in on Captain Anson.

"No! Don't do that!" The goblin pirate slashed the air with his cutlass and cackled, and Captain Anson decided to try a risky gamble. "I demand an audience with your captain per the terms of the Pirate Code!" he shouted.

"The Pirate Code?" screeched the goblin pirate. He didn't look convinced, but he had stopped advancing.

"Er, yes. Yes! The Pirate Code!" Captain Anson was relieved to at least have bought himself some time.

"Pirate Code! Pirate Code!" squawked the parrot on the pirate captain's shoulder.

"There's no such provision in the Pirate Code!" said the goblin pirate.

"There's not?" Captain Anson was out of ideas if this failed.

"Well, that depends," said another pirate. This one was fat and wore two braids that hung down on either side of his head. "The Code was revised in 1846, but not ratified by all members of the

Pirate Caucus. Some consider the matters that were resolved at the caucus that year to be canon, while others treat them simply as a formality, while still another subset rejects that caucus as illegitimate due to the fact that Ol' Chairman Sharky was accused of taking bribes from the West Indies."

"I'm familiar with the dispute about the '46 Caucus," the goblin pirate sighed, as if debating the legitimacy of this particular caucus was something he'd done dozens of times before. "Fine, you can speak with the captain. And Ol' Chairman Sharky was innocent! Of the bribes, that is. As a pirate, he kidnapped and murdered many people."

The goblin pirate sheathed his cutlass and stepped back into the circle of pirates that had formed around Captain Anson. The fat pirate looked satisfied and gave Anson a nod. Anson took a few steps toward the pirate captain, the only man who had not drawn a weapon when he approached him.

The pirate captain stared at Captain Anson, and Anson could feel him sizing him up. He was trying not to let his intimidation show, but the pirate captain was very imposing. The mere sight of him commanded respect. Staring him down was impossible because of the eye patch, and his fine clothes made the captain feel underdressed and shabby. His peg leg was slightly longer than it needed to be, which let him tower even higher above anyone who addressed him. Then of course there was the razor-sharp hook hand. At least there was nothing worrisome about his parrot.

"I'll peck your crotch! Peck your crotch!" chirped the parrot, ruffling his wings.

Captain Anson took a step back. The pirate captain raised his hook hand to the parrot to silence it. The parrot looked irritated. It puffed up its feathers and turned its back on Captain Anson.

"Sir," Captain Anson spoke. "I am Captain Anson of the proud ship *Levyathan*."

The pirate captain did not move or offer any sort of formal greeting. Eventually the little goblin pirate shuffled up to Captain Anson and hissed at him. "That's the Black Barnacle, that is." He then retreated back to the rest of the gathered pirates.

Captain Anson continued. "I know that only you, as captain of the *Mongrel*, can relate to where I am coming from. Only a fellow captain can understand that this boat is as much a part of me as my own hand . . ." Captain Anson glanced at the Black Barnacle's hook hand. "Er, I mean as my own leg . . ." He peered down at the peg leg. "Er, how about as my genitals? Are those . . .?"

The Black Barnacle nodded that his genitals were indeed intact. Captain Anson continued. "The boat is as much a part of me as my genitals. And so, from one captain to another, I make you this proposal—"

"Wait, wait, wait just one damn second," came a voice from the circle of pirates. The captain looked around for the pirate who had interrupted him. He hoped there wasn't going to be any more debate about the Pirate Caucus of '46. The fifteen seconds of it earlier had nearly bored him to death.

Pete was walking toward Captain Anson with his arms spread wide in disbelief. "What the hell?" Pete demanded. "Why do you assume he's the captain?"

Captain Anson was confused. He looked at the Black Barnacle, then back at Pete. "Well, it's just . . . I mean . . . He pretty much . . . Is he not the captain?"

"*I'm* the captain!" shouted Pete. He looked hurt.

"You?" Captain Anson asked in disbelief. "Really?"

"Yes really!"

"*Pete* is the captain of this pirate ship and not the Black Barnacle? Pete?"

"Oh for God's sake . . ." Pete hung his head, shaking it in dismay.

Captain Anson looked back at the Black Barnacle one more time. "Not this guy?" he asked, just to make sure.

"I've been the captain of the *Mongrel* for seventeen years!" Pete was very upset. Clearly this was something that had happened before. These were obviously frustrations that were just now boiling over.

"How come people never think I'm the captain? I run a damn good ship! Damn good!" The other pirates vigorously nodded their assent. Captain Anson thought it was pretty obvious that they were overcompensating to try to soothe his hurt feelings. "But it's always 'We thought it was the Black Barnacle' and 'You're sure the Black Barnacle isn't the captain?' I'm getting pretty tired of it!"

"Jeez, OK, settle down. It was just a simple misunderstanding," Captain Anson reassured him. "It's just that, well, the Black Barnacle looks really captain-like. He's got the peg leg and the eye patch. The hook hand . . ."

"How the hell can you captain a boat with a peg leg?" Pete demanded. "He can barely walk the length of the deck when the seas are calm, let alone during a storm. Show him!" Pete gestured for the Black Barnacle to take a few steps, which he tentatively did, wobbling the whole way and nearly toppling over twice.

"And an eye patch? On a captain?" continued Pete in disbelief. "He'd navigate us in circles!" Captain Anson watched as the Black Barnacle tried to steady himself by leaning on one of the other pirates. His lack of depth perception caused him to try to grasp a shoulder that was actually six inches to the left and he nearly fell over again.

"And that hook hand means he's useless! The only thing he can do with it is break up blocks of hardtack."

Captain Anson looked back at the Black Barnacle. "Well, the parrot seems very authoritative?" he offered.

"That parrot's the reason he has the hook hand!" said Pete. "It bit his hand and it got infected, and it vowed to bite him again if he ever made it leave his shoulder!" Anson looked at the Black Barnacle. A single tear rolled out of the pirate's good eye. The parrot chirped out a sinister laugh. The captain felt a bit of sympathy, but even stronger feelings of relief that the bird had not pecked his crotch.

"His clothes though," Captain Anson said feebly.

"The Black Barnacle does dress well, we'll give him that," Pete said. "Spends more money than most of us consider prudent, but then again, he's in the minority in that he doesn't have a family to support."

"Ah, see! He's a lone wolf! A mysterious stranger who strikes fear into the heart of any unfortunate who crosses his path!" Captain Anson was grasping at straws.

"A lone wolf? Fear? Hey Barney, introduce yourself to the captain."

"Barney?" Captain Anson asked.

The Black Barnacle spoke up in a horribly nasal, childish voice. "Hi, I'm the Black Barnacle, but to be honest, I prefer Barney." Captain Anson recoiled in horror. The Black Barnacle sneezed.

"You see?" Pete asked, sounding rather satisfied.

"Barney's almost as bad a captain's name as Pete," Captain Anson said.

Pete glared at him. "It's his decision! We told him it sucks, too!"

"I want food!" the parrot demanded. Startled, the Black Barnacle nearly toppled over. He nervously excused himself to chop up some hardtack for the parrot.

"You should probably introduce yourself as the captain," Captain Anson told Pete. "That might solve your problem right there."

"I shouldn't have to!" Pete countered. "People should assume it from the way I carry myself."

"Maybe start by not doing the menial tasks? Why should a pirate captain take a dinghy to retrieve the runaway captain of the boat he's capturing?"

"Captains always do that!" Pete yelled. "It's in the Pirate Code!"

"Technically, that's disputed," the fat pirate with braids offered. Pete and Captain Anson ignored him.

"Well anyways, Pete, I wanted to talk to you, captain to captain." This had all been an interesting diversion, but now it was time for Captain Anson to save his ship.

"I'm listening," Pete said.

Captain Anson paused, trying to pick the right words to say. As he pondered how best to sum up his point, he noticed that Ziro had crept to the outskirts of the circle of pirates. Ziro caught his eye and mouthed instructions to him. "Whales! Mention the whales!"

Ziro mimed a giant whale blowing water out of its blowhole, then breaching, and then someone throwing a harpoon.

Captain Anson nodded and smiled at Ziro, who was now clasping his hands together in a silent begging gesture. The captain turned back to Pete.

"Pete, this entire ship is cursed. We're all dead already, and before that we were witches. It's a hellish existence, Pete, I'm not gonna lie. You don't want any part of this. So why don't you take off before we have to go and curse you too."

Anson shot Ziro a sly thumbs up and winked. Ziro buried his head in his hands.

Pete stared at Captain Anson and nervously took a step back. He looked to the pirates on either side of him. None of them knew what to say. Somewhere else on the ship they heard Barney's parrot squawk, "Cut smaller pieces! I'll choke on that!" Barney apologized in his whiney voice.

Captain Anson looked over in Barney's general direction. Turning back to Pete he warmly chuckled, "I can't believe I thought that guy was the cap—"

Anson's words were cut off by two pirates grabbing him from behind. Each one took an arm and pinned it behind his back, holding him in place. Pete appeared to have gotten over the insult. Now he just looked angry. He walked up to Captain Anson and looked him dead in the eye.

"I'm the captain of the *Mongrel*. And as soon as we throw you overboard, I reckon I'll be captain of your ship, too." Captain Anson's face fell and the pirate captain grinned as he watched it happen. "I want you to die cursing the name of Captain Pete."

"I just don't understand why if he doesn't even *like* the name the Black Barnacle, that *you* don't start going by it," Captain Anson asked. "It would be a win/win, man!"

Pete wordlessly gestured toward the side of the boat and the pirates pushed him forward. Captain Anson heard some hoots and cheers from the area where his men were tied up. He chose to ignore them. It felt good to take the high road. Not as good as it had felt when he attempted to abandon them and flee at the first sign of danger, but still pretty good.

The two pirates were half pushing, half lifting the captain and carrying him forward when Ziro called out, "Stop!" The pirates stopped pushing and looked at Pete. Pete was trying to figure out who had spoken up and he gave his men a signal to hold on. Eventually Ziro stepped forward and addressed the pirate captain.

"Listen to me! Whale prices are at an all-time high, and we've got a cold storage area stocked with dozens of them! You'd be fools to just plunder our ship for treasure and leave us all for dead. You'd be throwing away a small fortune."

"You've got whale parts?" Pete asked.

Ziro nodded vigorously.

"Why the hell didn't you say so earlier?" Incredulous, Pete looked over at Captain Anson.

"I decided to go with my gut," Captain Anson sheepishly replied.

"You're going to need us to conduct the sale for you. They'll hang you if you show up in a market," Ziro told Pete.

"Who the hell are you anyways?" Pete asked the former slave.

"That's Ziro," Captain Anson butted in. "He swabs the decks."

"Is there anyone else on this ship who's not tied up that we don't know about?" Pete demanded.

"No," said Captain Anson. "Well, except for Cormac. He shows up every other day and . . ." Captain Anson trailed off as he noticed Ziro furiously shaking his head no. He quickly corrected himself. "Nope! Nobody else!" Captain Anson chuckled nervously.

"Alright," said Pete, suspicious but satisfied. He gestured for two pirates to attend to Ziro. They grabbed him and hauled him over to where Captain Anson was standing.

"We'll take your treasure," Pete said to the two of them in a menacing voice. "And we'll take your whales. And when it's all done, we'll take your boat. Don't like it? We'll throw you overboard. Or make you walk the plank. It depends what kind of mood the crew is in at that moment."

"Sounds fair to me," said Captain Anson.

"Oh, I wasn't talking to you," Pete sneered. "I was talking to Ziro here. So you're handy with a mop eh? I think you better keep up your swabbing." Recognizing the importance of a well-swabbed deck was the trait that Anson considered most important in a captain. He and Pete probably would have been friends under different circumstances.

The goblin pirate had retrieved Ziro's mop from the spot on the deck where he had dropped it when the pirates attacked. He flung it at Ziro, who awkwardly caught the handle. After shooting Captain Anson a "what other choice do I have?" expression, he started to swab.

"As for you," Pete said, now addressing Captain Anson. "As I'm sure you know, there's a provision in the Pirate Code for how you deal with the captain of a captured ship. Whether this is canon is disputed, *of course*," Pete said with a roll of his eyes. "But what we do is . . . at daybreak, we let your own crew decide your fate."

Captain Anson's eyes widened in horror and Pete smiled. The two pirates who had been standing behind Anson grabbed his wrists and quickly bound them.

"I'm sure you have nothing to worry about," Pete smirked. "You were taking that dinghy to go find help, right?" Anson was speechless. Pete waved his hand dismissively and the two pirates seized Captain Anson. They hauled him over to the area where the whalers were all bound together and tossed him into the center of the circle they formed.

As Captain Anson wriggled his way to a sitting position, he could feel the eyes of all the whalers staring at him. There was no doubt in Anson's mind that they'd pick the most unpleasant option the pirates presented them with. He had less than a day to curry their favor. Captain Anson cleared his throat. "Why doesn't everybody take the rest of the day off?" he suggested.

Nobody laughed.

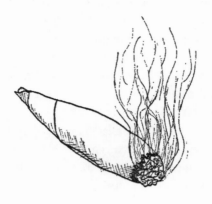

DAY TEN

Dean Frampton Q. Bickerstaff cracked open the rear doors of the van and peered out into the street. The first rays of daylight were just beginning to shine over the horizon. A mother pushing a stroller, noticing movement from the van, nervously crossed to the other side of the street. Dean Bickerstaff opened the door slightly wider, leaned out, and waved to reassure the mother that he was on the up and up. The baby began to cry.

"Oh come on," the dean said, louder than he'd planned. "Like that baby could even see me from forty feet away."

Leaving the door ajar to let some light in, Frampton retreated back into the van. He rubbed a hand across his stubbly cheeks as he tried to figure out where he'd left his pants. Frampton had slept in the van again last night. The events of the day before had further cemented his belief that he needed to be nearby at all times, just in case there were any issues that Vance couldn't deal with alone. In other words, in case there were any issues.

Plus, they were getting an early start today. Frampton expected a much bigger crowd than last time, and in order to maximize profits and exposure they needed to start funneling people through as soon as possible. So he hadn't had time to shave. Big deal. He felt like a little five o'clock shadow added a hint of ruggedness to his image, a little bit of danger.

Of course some people freaked out at the merest hint that someone else was living life on the edge, not bowing down to society's rules. Like, for instance, the person who had left a note on the van's windshield at some point in time yesterday.

"This is a good neighborhood with decent people," it read. "Please blight another area with your presence you horrible (I presume) man." The note had only deepened Dean Bickerstaff's resolve to stay put. Diversity was what this country was built on, what made it great. If you wanted a home without rootless transients parking their creepy vans a few feet from your lawn, you may as well go live with the rest of the lobotomized automatons in one of those Disney planned communities.

Yesterday, once he'd made the decision to keep a close watch on the Craymore Street house, the dean needed to pick up a few essentials. He drove the van to the grocery store, where he picked up some granola bars, a jar of peanut butter, and a bottle of cognac. Then he swung by his office to check his mail and make sure the board hadn't staged a coup and changed the locks since he'd last been there.

Of course, just popping in and out of the office had been impossible. Frampton had run into one of the board members as soon as he'd arrived. He'd been leafing through the mail that had stacked up on his desk when he heard a voice behind him.

"Frampton? Is that you?" The dean turned and saw the feeble little man, George, the one whose daughter's wedding he had weaseled out of. He turned his back on him and continued to sort through his mail.

"Is everything alright, Frampton?" George asked. "You haven't returned any of our phone calls and you look kind of . . . tired?"

"Everything's fine, Gerson," Dean Bickerstaff said without turning to face his accuser.

"Now come on, you know my name is not Gerson," George said.

The dean turned around, hoping that his irritation would be evident and that George would leave him alone. "I'm sorry, Gary," he said. "Do you need something? I'm very busy at the moment."

"Well yes, I'm sorry to bother you, dean, but there's actually quite a bit to sort out. The budget needs to be approved in the next forty-eight hours and you haven't even commented on the proposals we submitted."

"Well, Gerald, you can't expect me to get back to you before I even open my mail, can you?" Dean Bickerstaff gestured at the pile of documents on his desk. "Besides, I believe I've got a mandate from the board that raising Harrington's X-Factor is priority number one across the board."

"We submitted that budget to you three months ago," George said testily. "And raising the X-Factor is not an across-the-board priority and you don't have a mandate. It's *your* priority because you think it's the only way you're going to get to keep your job."

"And when Frampton Q. Bickerstaff gets a mandate, he gets results," Frampton said, not really listening. "You may have noticed that Harrington has been getting quite a bit of attention on Twitter lately?"

"Yes," George said. "It appears that you've determined the only way to raise the school's online reputation is by exploiting an unknowing student for personal financial gain. Frampton, this has all the makings of a gigantic scandal, and the board has unanimously voted to censure you for your involvement in it."

"Another censure?" Frampton laughed. "How many does that make?"

"You are one away from a dozen. It has been eighty-three years and seven deans since the last dean was censured."

"I could have sworn it was at least at fourteen," Frampton said with a hint of disappointment.

"Regardless of how you perceive what should be a great professional shame, it's all going to be irrelevant if you don't approve that budget," George continued. "Massive faculty strikes are inevitable if we don't renew department funding."

"Really? The faculty is going to strike at a time like this? When all signs point to us overtaking #HoesBeBangin at some point in time this afternoon?" Frampton scoffed. "Listen, Geronimo, I hear your concern. Please let the board know that I'm working on a solution as we speak."

"What is in that shopping bag?" George asked.

"My lunch," Frampton replied.

"Peanut butter and cognac? Are you sure everything's OK, Frampton? Does this have anything to do with that awful van that's parked in your spot?"

"Glinda, I would love to let you a test drive the van, but I really must be going." Frampton deposited the entirety of his stack of mail in the garbage can and picked up his shillelagh. "But please, send that budget to me and I'll get to it as soon as I can." George silently fumed and a broad grin broke out across Dean Bickerstaff's face.

The dean had informed the board member that he was looking forward to his daughter's upcoming wedding, then waddled out of his office. He'd driven straight back to Craymore Street, where he parked the van and spent the rest of the day keeping an eye out for anyone who might approach Cormac's house and blow their cover.

Frampton fished a granola bar out of the plastic bag. After he tore the wrapper off, he dipped it into the already half-empty jar of peanut butter, then ate the whole thing in three bites. Dean Bickerstaff had always been a driven man, and his constant striving for gain and the ruin of others had never allowed for the type of existence he was currently enjoying, the type of existence that Vance and Cormac wallowed in every day. Emulating Vance in order not to be bested by him was primarily a strategic decision, but Frampton would be lying if he said he wasn't enjoying the burnout lifestyle just a little bit.

While he was licking peanut butter off of his fingers, the dean of Harrington University spotted his pants. They were crumpled in a corner next to the cognac bottle. He grabbed both items, each vital to the day's success, shuffled into the pants, and in a few moments was standing outside the van.

The morning air was brisk and there wasn't a cloud in the sky. It was going to be a beautiful day, and Frampton was in high spirits already. But even in his good mood, he wasn't ready for the sight that greeted him when he slammed the van doors shut and started to walk toward Cormac's house.

There were already dozens of people gathered on the front lawn. Students were draped in blankets and several held mugs of coffee. There was clearly some sort of makeshift line system established; these students had been here for a while. The dean quickly scanned the crowd. He was pleased that Brock did not appear to be anywhere nearby. Two beatings in as many days was not a pattern that Frampton wished to continue. He didn't mind doling them out, but paying customers tended to stop showing up at places where they might be savagely beaten and hauled away by masked men. Frampton's main legacy as dean of the Commerce School was that every student was taught that lesson on day one.

Heads began to turn in the crowd as the dean waddled up to the house. The students whispered to each other and Frampton strained to make out what they were saying. "Dean," "in charge," and "watch out" were each muttered a couple times, but so were "what's with the stick," "under a bridge," and "I heard that guy ate the three billy goats gruff."

The last phrase was so oddly specific that the dean was certain Vance had seeded that idea in the crowd. Frampton was not pleased about this betrayal, but he did his best to suppress his irritation. He forced a tight grin onto his face and nodded and waved as the crowd parted to let him through.

When he made it to the front porch, Dean Bickerstaff turned and addressed the crowd. "Looks like we've got some early birds today!" He was trying his hardest to sound excited, despite actually being furious that these idiots had flagrantly violated the protocol that Cissy had clearly outlined in her article. Showing up just a few hours early could easily spiral into more intrusions like the one yesterday. Nevertheless, the dean kept grinning and continued on.

"Who's ready to take a trip back in time?" he asked the crowd. There were tepid cheers from a few people. Most of the crowd hadn't planned on being enthusiastic this early in the morning. "I said," the dean repeated, trying to ramp up the energy. "Who's ready to take a—"

His sentence was cut off as a man standing near the front of the crowd collapsed onto the ground unconscious.

"Oh, Jesus Christ," Dean Bickerstaff muttered.

The student who had been standing with the collapsed man knelt down next to him and shook him by the shoulders in an effort to revive him. "Sorry," the friend told the dean apologetically. "He took a lot of mushrooms." He slapped his unconscious friend's face gently in an effort to revive him. The dean waited, hoping he wasn't going to have to call an ambulance.

The pressure of the moment proved too much for another person in the crowd to bear. A girl in a woolen cap stood twitching for a few moments as she stared at the unconscious man, but she eventually snapped and ran screaming from the yard, never to return.

"What the hell was her problem?" the dean asked.

"Mushrooms!" answered a voice from the crowd.

"How many of you are on mushrooms?" the dean asked. Well over half the crowd raised their hands. "How about illegal drugs in general?" Nine or ten additional people raised their hands.

"Do mushrooms count?" asked a guy near the back who was obviously on mushrooms.

"Of course they count!" the dean snapped. The guy who had collapsed opened his eyes and started giggling. Frampton took a deep breath. He should have expected that the people who gathered here before the sun had even come up would be the hardcore substance abusers. Half of them would probably forget what they were here for as soon as they got inside.

317

Smiling again, he addressed the crowd. "I'm just going to go inside and make sure everything is ready. In just a few minutes, we'll let you all in!" Several more people raised their hands to indicate that they were on mushrooms.

Dean Bickerstaff turned his back on the drug-addled crowd and opened the door to Cormac's house. As he stepped through the doorway, jackhammer-volume snores nearly pushed him back outside. When the horrible noise momentarily subsided, Dean Bickerstaff dashed inside, rounded the stadium seating couches as quickly as he could, and jabbed the end of his shillelagh into Vance's ribs. As Vance woke up with an unappealing series of snorts, the dean leaned over the grounded couch and fully extended the shillelagh to poke Cissy awake, too.

Vance groggily sat up and rubbed his eyes. "Deano? What time is it?"

"It's time to open for business," the dean replied. He handed Vance the bottle of cognac. "Take a swig of this, it'll get you moving." Vance did what he was told and tilted the bottle back.

"Cissy, how are you doing?" the dean asked. "When was the last time you got off that couch? You should be careful or you're going to end up getting bedsores." Cissy made a grabbing gesture toward Vance and he passed up the bottle of cognac. Cissy took a pull, then tossed it at the dean, who barely reacted quickly enough to catch the bottle before it hit the floor.

As Vance and Cissy yawned and scratched themselves, the dean took a look around the living room. Nothing appeared out of the ordinary. "How did everything go after I popped in yesterday?" he asked.

"Fine," Vance said as he smoothed out the wrinkles on his towel. "Mac mostly stayed in his room playing the ukulele. Me and the Cistress ordered pizza and watched . . ." Vance stopped as the memory of what had been on the TV just a few hours earlier eluded him.

"I'm sure it was a fine evening," the dean said when it was apparent that the information was not forthcoming. "Listen, there's already a bunch of people out there. I know it's earlier than we'd planned but I think we've got to start moving them through. Otherwise there's already going to be a backlog when the on-time people start showing up."

"Does his other ear work?" asked Cissy.

The dean instinctively ignored Cissy. "Now Vance, a lot of the people out there are on mushrooms right now, so we're going to have to be extra careful not to freak them out."

Vance was on top of it. "I'll throw on the *Koyaanisqatsi* soundtrack and put *A Clockwork Orange* on DVD. Then they can see if they synch up."

Dean Bickerstaff was completely sober and the idea of that experience still made him nervous. "No, that sounds like exactly what we *don't* need to—" The dean stopped in the middle of his sentence. He looked up at the airborne couch.

"Cissy, what did you just say?"

"I said does his other ear work. If you can stare into Cormac's other ear, you can send twice as many people through. You really haven't tried looking in his other ear? I never mentioned it until now because I thought it seemed too obvious." Cissy rolled her eyes and grabbed for the cognac bottle again. Dean Bickerstaff passed it over and pointed with his chin for Vance to investigate her situation.

Vance peeled himself off the couch and hustled down the hall to Cormac's bedroom. After a few seconds he called out, "Roger on the second ear!" Vance emerged from the hallway beaming. "Looks like this operation just doubled its profits!" he shouted and broke into a little dance.

The dean was pleased by this news, not as much by the dance. Sudden movements greatly increased the chance of towel exposure. "Vance, please," he cautioned. "Let's keep it professional here."

"Professional?" Vance laughed and continued to dance. "Fuck that! Deano, we're gonna clean up today! I'm gonna go see if anyone wants to trade some 'shrooms for the first ear time of the day!"

Dean Bickerstaff stuck his shillelagh out to block Vance's path as he attempted to shimmy past. Vance stopped and looked at the dean with a puzzled expression.

"Now, Vance," the dean said. "I'm going to need you to keep your wits about you. We've already had two incidents where we needed . . . external assistance. Twice as many people circulating through Cormac's room, that's twice as many potential whackers, right?" Vance's face fell. "Today's an important day," the dean said. "After all, we're on the verge of surpassing #HoesBeBangin."

Vance nodded solemnly. "I understand," he said. "We've got to be professional." For a split second, Dean Bickerstaff was relieved to have averted a crisis. But as soon as Vance said, "Speaking of professionalism, Deano . . ." he realized that he had made a terrible mistake.

"I've been thinking," Vance continued. "There's going to be so many people in here today, way more than two days ago. Lots of strangers, lots of unsavory characters. It's going to be important for people to know who's in charge. You know, just so if anyone has any issues, they can look around the room and identify who can help them right away."

The dean couldn't put his finger on it, but when Vance finished his sentence, something strange happened. Only later would he come to realize that at that exact moment, the birds had stopped chirping outside. He stared at Vance, fearing what he was about to say, but knowing all too well what it was going to be.

"I want you to wear the towel," Vance said in a low, cold-blooded tone. He reached underneath his own towel and pulled out the towel with the two kittens on it.

Dean Bickerstaff stared Vance square in the eye. The moment had come to decide who was the alpha. But in his heart, the dean already knew he had lost. "What else have you got under that towel, Vance?" he asked, hoping the entire time that his voice wouldn't crack.

"Whatever it takes," Vance responded. The coolness of Vance's response sealed it. Cissy stifled a giggle from the couch. It was time for a final desperate act.

"I'm not going to wear that," Dean Bickerstaff said. "That's final."

"Cissy," Vance said, not breaking eye contact with the dean. "How are those social networks looking this morning?"

The dean heard Cissy bang out a few keystrokes on her laptop. "Oooh, it looks like there was some serious Bangin' going on in the Ho community last night. Number one overall trending topic at Harrington. Followed by #HoesWantTheD, #HoesOnMyJock, and #EconTermPaper."

Vance smirked ever so slightly. "Where might #CormacsEar be on that list?"

Cissy took a moment to scan the list of trends. "It's behind a #HoesBeBaangin where bangin' is accidentally spelled with two A's."

The dean flinched as he heard the bad news. They couldn't afford to lose the momentum they'd gained two days ago. Vance was being completely unreasonable, but now that he'd gotten it in his head that they should both be wearing towels, he wasn't going to relent. Reluctantly, trying to mask the defeat in his voice, Dean Bickerstaff spoke up.

"Alright. Give me the towel."

"You're already holding it," Vance said with a smile. The dean looked down. Vance was right, the towel was in his right hand. Frampton tried not to think about what the towel had just been pressed up against and silently prayed that Vance would never focus his energies on true evil.

"Just think, Deano," Vance said, suddenly friendly again. "Someone has a problem, they just scan the room for a guy in a towel. Need change for a fifty? Find a man in a towel. Guy in line behind you is pre-whackin' it? Find a friendly towel-clad gentleman. Someone starts telling ladies that he can get them to the front of the line in exchange for hideous sexual favors? They'll know not to do it . . . unless the guy is wearing a towel!"

Frampton had to admit that Vance had a point. The chaos of the last Cormac-exploiting session had been barely controlled. If they were going to attempt to funnel twice as many people through his bedroom, it would be helpful to be identifiable. The dean just wished he had thought of a way to do so that would let him keep his pants on.

Noting to himself that the birds outside had resumed their chirping, Frampton marched down to the bathroom and quickly changed out of his clothes and into the towel. The dean took the moment to size himself up in the mirror. If you observed him from the right angle, he sort of nailed the classic "important Hollywood producer making a business deal in the sauna" look. But from virtually every other angle, the look was much more "schlub sitting in the exam room while the doctor explains that evidently paunch cancer is a thing, and you have three of them."

Dean Bickerstaff checked the towel one last time to make sure it was tightly secured, then left the bathroom. Vance grinned as he saw him coming out.

"Alright, Deano! Check it out, Cistress! Are we two dudes who are large and in charge or what?" Vance slung an arm around the dean's shoulders, and Frampton instinctively shrank from the flesh-on-flesh sensation.

"We could have earned a hundred and twenty dollars while he was changing," Cissy said while typing.

"She's got a point, Deano," Vance said. "Come on, let's open our doors."

The morning had already been packed with bullshit, but Dean Bickerstaff was still eager to get to work. He gave his shillelagh a quick twirl and nodded at Vance. Then Frampton walked over to the front door, and after a quick pause, threw it open.

The gathered crowd quickly went silent as everyone turned to look at him. The dean paused to let the anticipation build. Eventually he raised both his hands in a welcoming gesture, at which point yet another idiot on mushrooms freaked out and ran screaming from the front yard. Dean Bickerstaff decided to abandon any grand gestures, and instead just muttered, "Twenty dollars. Cash only."

The students started to file into the house, where Vance barked orders at them. "If any of you have a problem, you talk to a guy in a towel! Now form a line people! Hey! Don't pass out there!"

Dean Bickerstaff watched for a second as the queue formed, then turned around to see how many more people were left outside.

He nearly suffered his own freak-out when he saw that Mako and G-Dimes were now standing directly in front of him.

"Hey, Dean B!" Mako said with a big smile. "You weren't going to start without us now, were you?"

"Jesus Christ, Mako," Frampton said, trying not to let the drug dealer see how startled he had been. "Don't just appear out of nowhere like that!"

Mako laughed while G-Dimes sort of swayed back and forth. "Relax, Dean!" Mako chuckled. "We're all good! Though you look a little chilly in that towel! But seriously, we heard it's been an eventful twenty-four hours in this neck of the woods."

"Yes," Frampton said, wishing more than anything that he was wearing his suit. Wearing a suit always made it easier to look upon drug dealers with scorn. "Your thugs let their guard down and nearly compromised our entire operation. You need to tell those guys that they can't—" Mako raised his hand to indicate that Frampton should stop talking.

"First of all, Dean, those two are not thugs. Those two are very far from thugs. Those two are altar boys compared to our thugs. If you ever deal with our thugs, you will know it." G-Dimes giggled. "And second," Mako continued, "if Cormac finds out about all this, it's not going to be from people showing up at the door. It's going to be from people online."

"Online? What do you mean?" Dean Bickerstaff asked.

"Your boy's going viral, Dean," Mako informed him. "A guy who racks up a quarter million views in just a few days is a man who people want to know more about. Magazine profiles, interview requests, marriage proposals . . ."

"You can get interview requests and marriage proposals just for making a stupid video?" Frampton asked. Cormac's video success had been exactly the sort of wildcard that the dean had hoped to avoid. He felt foolish for giving Cormac the gift that had set it into motion.

"That pug that humped the pig got two marriage proposals *while* he was being interviewed," Mako replied. Evidently, just hearing a mention of that infamous video brought G-Dimes great joy and he began to silently convulse with uncontrollable laughter.

"You're lucky though, Dean B," Mako said. "G and I can help you out. We prepared some custom filtering software. You let us install it on Cormac's computer, and any comments, emails, or tweets that mention keywords like 'whales' or 'ear' get caught before Cormac can see them. Then G and I can approve or edit them from our phones."

Dean Bickerstaff stared at Mako. "Filtering software?" he asked. "You created custom filtering software for Cormac's computer?"

"Well of course not," said Mako. "We tweaked one of our existing products. It's a bit light on features compared to what a Fortune 500 company would need, but we figure unless Cormac's situation changes dramatically, it won't become an issue."

The dean was flabbergasted. "You're telling me that you have a software company, and you sell your products to Fortune 500 companies?"

Mako chuckled. "We're trying to keep a slightly lower profile, at least until we graduate. Of course, that got kind of hard after our company, MakoG, was on the cover of the Harrington alumni magazine two months ago." Dean Bickerstaff shook his head. He had never bothered to read the alumni magazine. In fact, he'd recently spent twenty-five minutes on hold trying to reach someone who would cancel his subscription.

Mako tried again. "Well, I'm sure you heard that they are renaming the Comp Sci building the MakoG Computer Science building. We made a generous donation in honor of G-Dimes's grandfather, may he rest in peace." G-Dimes started to cross himself, but forgot how the gesture was supposed to go after he touched his navel.

"Mako, if you two are already successful software developers, what the hell are you doing here?" Frampton gestured wildly with his shillelagh at the assembled drug abusers.

"G-Dimes made a promise to his grandfather," Mako solemnly informed the dean.

"Ah, I understand. He promised him on his deathbed that he would stay in school to finish his PhD."

"No, he promised him we'd spend a year dealing drugs," Mako said, starting to sound impatient. "Grandpa G thought it would toughen us up for the cutthroat Silicon Valley culture that we'll have to deal with once we earn our degrees. Dean B, maybe you'll find a PowerPoint presentation a bit easier to understand."

A PowerPoint was the last thing Dean Bickerstaff wanted to see from the drug dealers/doctoral candidates/evidently wildly successful entrepreneurs. But before he could tell them to piss off and get to work, G-Dimes produced a laptop from a bag that the dean had assumed contained only drugs. Without a word, he flipped it open and after a few taps on the keyboard, the PowerPoint logo splashed on the screen. When the presentation opened, a sleek, minimalist MakoG Software logo was displayed on the first slide.

"Hey, I recognize that logo!" Dean Bickerstaff looked behind him. Vance had sidled up to them at the end of their conversation. He was clutching the pretzel tub full of money and smiling. "Yeah, MakoG. I've got bootlegged versions of some of their programs on my computer."

The dean noticed Mako briefly narrow his eyes in response to Vance's remarks. Without saying a word, the drug dealer raised his right index finger in the air. Frampton tried to glance over Mako's shoulder without being noticed. Outside, the dean saw one of the bandana men emerge from the bushes and begin to stride toward the house.

"I would uninstall that software, Vance," he muttered out of the side of his mouth.

"Uninstall it?" Vance was incredulous. "Hell no, I stole it fair and square!"

"I think you should uninstall it!" The dean said, louder this time. To emphasize his point, he jabbed Vance in the ribs with his shillelagh.

"Ouch! Alright, I'll uninstall it, you dick! Jeez!" Vance rubbed his side. Frampton quickly glanced at Mako. The dealer was still glaring at Vance, but appeared to relax. He then held up two fingers, made a fist, then a slashing gesture. The bandana man outside immediately stopped advancing. He repeated Mako's gesture in acknowledgment, then retreated to the cover of the bushes.

Dean Bickerstaff turned to Vance and offered him a "remind me to tell you later how I just saved your life" look. Turning back to Mako and G-Dimes, he smiled and said, "Gentlemen, I greatly appreciate your willingness to help us. How much are you asking for this service?"

"One thousand dollars," Mako said. Dean Bickerstaff was shaking his head before Mako even finished the word "thousand."

"I'm afraid that's outside our price range at the moment, but we'll certainly keep it under consideration." He had been prepared to offer that response no matter what the first quote was. He'd given most of his earnings from the first day of Cormac-exploiting to these two and wasn't prepared to do it again. He smiled condescendingly at the two of them and gestured that they should get to peddling, or scoring, or talking smack, or whatever it was they did.

"Out of our price range?" Vance chimed in. "A thousand dollars? Deano, we've got two ears running today, our profits just doubled! What exactly is it that costs a thousand dollars? I missed that part of the conversation, but whatever it is, we sure as hell can afford it."

The dean closed his eyes and imagined smoking a cigar as his own personal bandana men rained down shillelagh blows upon Vance's already unconscious body. When he reopened them, Vance was shaking hands with Mako, apparently sealing their thousand-dollar deal.

"Relax, Deano!" Vance told him. "We can more than afford it! We're going to pack 'em in today! You know why?" Vance grinned a huge grin and grabbed the dean by his bare shoulders as he leaned in closer. "We've got pirates!" he said excitedly.

For the second day in a row, Cormac woke up feeling that something was off. At first he thought it might be that he'd had trouble falling asleep. Last night, his eyes kept flying open at the slightest noise from the living room or sound from outside, as he imagined the sounds coming from someone who was about to receive another beating from the dean. But he quickly realized the feeling didn't have anything to do with being tired.

The whalers' quarters was quieter than it ever had been. There wasn't a single whaler snoring or cursing Captain Anson's name in their sleep. Bracing for the worst, Cormac took a tentative sniff of the air. The distinctive odor of hardtack-and-salt-pork flatulence was present, but muted. Nobody had farted in here for hours. Cormac raised his head and looked at the bunk across the quarters. The bed was empty.

"Maybe I slept in," Cormac muttered as he swung his legs over to the side of the bed. But that seemed unlikely. The whalers generally didn't stumble out of their quarters until almost lunch time. Perhaps they'd been lured out of bed by a mermaid sighting, or the debut of a particularly erotic piece of erotic scrimshaw. Or maybe this was the day they'd decided to begin the mutiny that Cormac had figured was inevitable the entire time he'd been waking up on board the *Levyathan*.

Cormac pondered all these possibilities, but as he stood up and stretched, he mostly wondered if hardtack-and-salt-pork was a widespread enough varietal of flatulence to base a sea shanty around. He was already thinking about recording a follow-up video.

Yawning deeply, Cormac pushed open the door to the whalers' quarters and stepped outside. As soon as his feet touched the deck, his sense that something was amiss was greatly amplified. Cormac was by no means a knowledgeable sailor, but he felt like he had spent enough time on the *Levyathan* to start to recognize her rhythms and mannerisms. Today, it felt like she was cruising along faster, her tacking was tighter. In fact her whole operation just seemed more competent and efficient.

This couldn't be good.

Cormac quietly closed the door to the quarters and pressed himself up against the wall. He strained to hear any of the typical noises that would indicate it was business as usual on board. Whaler grunts, Ziro-berating, rum chugging. But other than the sounds of the ocean and the flapping sails, there was nothing to hear.

Maybe the reverse of his situation had happened to everyone on board, Cormac thought. Maybe Captain Anson, Ziro, and the whalers had all woken up one hundred and fifty years in *their* past. That would be around the 1720s and they would have to deal with . . . Actually, what the hell happened in the 1720s? Cormac had no idea. It must be one of those lost eras of history, just like the '50s, he thought.

Cormac hoped the rest of the crew wasn't somewhere else in time. If they were, he'd surely be blamed for it. After his mysterious arrival and the interest he'd shown in the whale dicks, sending everybody else hurling around to the time of Magellan or Picasso or whenever the hell they ended up would certainly result in him being thrown overboard.

From where he was, Cormac could only get a view of the entrance to the rum storage area. There was no activity, which confirmed his suspicions that something was seriously wrong. Quietly and slowly, Cormac inched his way toward the end of the wall in order to get a better look at the rest of the deck. Then, very slowly, he leaned his head around the corner.

The shocking sight that greeted him was worse than he had feared. All of the whalers on the *Levyathan* were tied up in a circle. In the middle sat Captain Anson, with his wrists bound behind his back. Standing all around the crew were men that Cormac had never seen before, but who he instantly feared were pirates. They laughed evilly. They wore bandanas. They carried long, shiny swords. What else could they be but pirates? Also there was a gigantic fucking pirate ship tethered just a few feet off the side of the *Levyathan*.

His heart pounding, Cormac snapped back around to the other side of the wall. What the hell was he going to do? He quickly ruled out his first idea: immediately defecting to the pirates. If that were possible, most of the whalers would have already done it. His second idea was to go back to bed, hopefully fall asleep, and see if the problem had worked itself out by the time he came back in two days.

Cormac was not impressed with his less-than-heroic instincts. He was glad there were no women and children aboard to use as bartering chips or human shields. He hoped that involving them would have at least been the fourth or fifth thing he tried, but he couldn't guarantee anything. Dammit! If only Ziro were here, he'd know what to do.

Wait a second, Cormac thought. Ziro! He hadn't seen Ziro tied up with the rest of the men. Carefully, he leaned forward and stole another glance at the tied-up crew. Captain Anson was feebly dancing a hornpipe at gunpoint, which even the captive whalers seemed to be enjoying. But Ziro was nowhere to be seen.

Cormac watched the captain dance around like the Platonic ideal of a white uncle at a wedding, then quickly scanned the rest of the deck for any signs of the former slave. They wouldn't have thrown Ziro overboard, he told himself. He's the only one who knows what the hell is going on here. But if he wasn't sitting on the deck with the rest of the men . . .

The deck! Cormac looked down at his feet. The deck looked clean enough to eat off of. That is to say, if a piece of hardtack were dropped on the deck, it would not make the hardtack that much more unpalatable. Of course, it was widely accepted as fact on the *Levyathan* that wharf rats were going out of their way to urinate on the hardtack supply, so the deck would have to be pretty damn filthy in order to reduce any dropped hardtack to inedible status. But the deck wasn't filthy at all! In fact, it appeared to have been swabbed within the past half hour. Ziro must still be alive! And if he wasn't tied up or in the process of swabbing the deck, he must be back in the slave's quarters, refilling his bucket or wringing out his mop.

Ziro's efficiency made his trips to the slave's quarters brief affairs, so Cormac had to act fast. The only problem was that the slave's quarters were across the ship. In order to get to it, he'd have to abandon his current cover and make a dash across the wide open deck. There was no way he could make it without being spotted, unless there was some way to distract the pirates.

Cormac looked around and tried to size up the situation. Standing where he was, his best option seemed to be throwing his voice. Since this was not a skill that Cormac actually possessed, he was forced to consider other plans. Trying to move as quietly as possible, he hustled back down to the whalers' quarters and popped his head inside.

The whalers' quarters had two main features: stained mattresses and objectionable odors. Unfortunately, Cormac didn't see how those two things could combine to cause a diversion. His heart pounding, he closed the door again and looked around. The only other place he could access without leaving his cover was the rum storage area. But there was nothing in there except for hundreds of jugs of rum.

Oh well, Cormac thought. At least he'd be able to wait out the death of everyone else on board while drunk. He glumly shuffled down to the rum storage area and opened the door. Unable to help himself, he instantly glanced at the pickled pinky finger sticking out of the floor. Hoping with all his might that it did not shoot out of its hole and into one of his orifices, Cormac picked up the nearest jug of rum, uncorked it, and took a huge swig. When he was done, he recorked the jug and decided to toast his doomed crewmates.

"It's been real, fellas," Cormac said out loud. "At least you didn't die with a whale dick tied around your neck." Cormac extended the jug to cheers one of the other jugs in the storage area. The glass jugs made a faint clink as Cormac touched them together. Not wanting to be rude, Cormac uncorked his jug and took another sip. Looking around the room, he wondered how many of the jugs he could finish before the pirates threw the whole crew overboard.

Wait a second . . . Cormac realized he was on the verge of having an idea. In order to help it along, he decided to retrace his steps. He glanced nervously at the finger, took a third swig of rum, then toasted his doomed compatriots again. Sadly, he couldn't remember the exact words he'd said fifteen seconds earlier, but Cormac knew he could approximate them. "Real whale dicks, fellas. Neck. Die." That was close enough. He stuck out the jug he was drinking from and clinked it against another one.

That was it! All around him were shelves full of extremely breakable jugs of rum! Cormac reached out and pressed down on the nearest shelf. Like most of the wood on the *Levyathan*, it was rotting and warped. In fact it was a miracle it was supporting anything at all. The slightest disturbance would result in dozens of rum jugs falling to the ground and shattering. The cacophony would certainly draw the attention of the pirates, and the fact that it was coming from the direction of the precious rum supply would make it an all-hands-on-deck, code red situation.

Cormac looked back out the door. When they heard the crash, the pirates would come running from the bow. He would have to book it in the opposite direction, and make a dash for the slave's quarters once the pirates were out of sight. If it worked, he'd have just enough time to make it to Ziro. If it didn't, well he'd just have to hope that these pirates weren't the sex-slave-taking type.

Cormac tilted the jug back and guzzled one last swig of rum. Then he recorked the bottle and tried to size up which point of impact would result in the loudest noise. He scanned back and forth, but nothing stood out immediately. Cormac started to panic. What the hell should he aim at?

And then, out of the corner of his eye, he saw it. Sticking out of the hole it had plugged, his pinky finger began to rotate. Cormac watched in horror as it spun a one eighty so that he could see its fingernail. He braced himself for the possibility that in the next few seconds it might shoot out of the floor toward him. Cormac quickly ranked his holes in terms of which was least desirable for his own severed finger to penetrate. After a clear winner, there was a five way tie for second place.

But the finger showed no signs of advancing toward Cormac. Instead, it slowly bent forward until it was sticking out of the floor at a forty-five-degree angle. Cormac stared at it in terror for a few seconds before it dawned on him that the finger was pointing at something.

Cormac traced the path through the air and saw that his severed finger was pointed at a particularly dilapidated top shelf. It sagged in the middle and the wood was splintered around the bolts that were holding it to the wall. If he hurled the jug he was currently holding directly at the middle of that shelf, dozens more jugs would crash down onto the shelf below it, and hopefully start a noisy domino effect of destruction.

Cormac looked back at his finger, but it was sticking straight up again, the way it had been when he entered the room. "Thanks, ol' buddy," he told it, but the finger remained motionless. Perhaps severed appendages got a bad rap, Cormac thought. You never really considered their potential helpfulness, only the fact that they might crawl into your bed during the night and try to kill you.

But eliminating the stigma against ungodly sentient body parts was a social campaign for another time. Right now, it was time to cause a ruckus. Cormac positioned himself in the doorway and took a deep breath. Then, staring straight at the shelf that the finger had identified, he raised the rum jug over his head with both hands and flung it forward, like an overhead pass in basketball.

It sailed straight and true, and connected with the shelf almost exactly where the finger had pointed. The jug exploded on impact, and the wooden shelf splintered. Cormac really wished he could stay and watch the mayhem, preferably in slow motion while a choral version of "Ode to Joy" blared at top volume, but he had to get going. As jugs of rum started to fall from the shelf and shatter, he turned and bolted out of the rum storage area at top speed.

The noise of dozens of rum jugs falling and shattering was even louder than Vance and Cissy snoring. As he ran toward the stern of the *Levyathan* it only seemed to get louder. Evidently the shelving system in the rum storage area had been a very balanced ecosystem that had quickly collapsed as soon as a strong outside force acted upon it. If he was able to successfully defeat the pirates, Cormac hoped that at least one jug would survive so that everyone he rescued could toast him with it.

When he reached the stern of the boat, Cormac slowed down and cautiously turned the corner. The rum storage area and the whalers' quarters were connected to each other, and his cover ran out where this structure ended. Cormac tiptoed along the wall, and when he reached the corner, he was able to peer out onto the main deck of the ship.

Right away, he saw that his disturbance was working. Every pirate on board was in the process of making their way from the front of the boat toward the source of the sound. The pirates looked confused and angry. Cormac hoped that the destruction of many jugs of rum that they'd hoped to plunder was not the thing that pushed them over the edge from normal, non-sex-slave pirates into pirates who were more than happy to just take a whole bunch of sex slaves willy-nilly.

Cormac waited for the pirates to disappear behind the side of the whalers' quarters, then took off running toward the slave's quarters. The entire time, he braced himself for a gunshot or an angry pirate yelling at him, but nothing of the sort happened. He made it to the slave's quarters in less than ten seconds, but the journey felt like it took minutes. Cormac dove through the doorway onto the floor of Ziro's tiny cabin and quickly kicked the door closed behind him.

"Cormac!" Ziro exclaimed. "How did you get over here?" Cormac looked up from the ground at Ziro. He had never been in Ziro's quarters before, and he was instantly amazed that Ziro had spent the past five years sleeping in here. There was maybe enough room to lie down if you crumpled into the fetal position, but that was only if you found someplace else to put the bottles of cleaning supplies, spare mop heads, and raw materials for ukuleles.

"Severed finger . . . diversion . . . rum jugs . . . kablooey . . ." Cormac stammered as he tried to catch his breath.

"Slow down, slow down," Ziro said. "Did you see the pirates?" Cormac nodded. "They captured the ship yesterday," Ziro continued. "It looks pretty grim. They're going to decide Captain Anson's fate any minute now."

"Oh God, they're going to make him a sex slave, aren't they!?" Cormac wailed.

"What? A sex slave? The captain?" Ziro was very confused. "I would say there is an absolute zero chance of that happening. I don't think that pirates taking male sex slaves is or ever has been a thing. Why is that something that concerns you?"

"Never mind," Cormac said, hoping to change the subject. The sprint across the boat's deck had left him winded. That was to be expected. But he was also suddenly feeling light-headed. Cormac figured he must be more out of shape than he realized. He took several deep breaths as he tried to remember what he had wanted to say to Ziro.

"Are you OK, Cormac?" Ziro asked.

"Am I shaking my head to indicate no or is this room turning on an axis?" Cormac asked.

"Nothing's moving that I can see," replied Ziro.

Cormac looked over at a collection of jugs holding cleaning supplies. Several of them were bubbling and emitting wisps of multicolored smoke. The air above them shimmered and fluttered and it looked like you could grab it with your hands. Cormac suddenly realized that he could hear the smell of ammonia.

"Is it safe to be breathing near this cleaning stuff?" he asked Ziro right before he collapsed to the ground, unconscious.

* * *

"I think he's dead," a girl said to Dean Bickerstaff as she walked out of Cormac's room. The dean choked on cigar smoke, then dashed into Cormac's bedroom.

Vance casually sat in his chair, staring up at the ceiling and swirling his Bloody Mary as if nothing was the matter. G-Dimes was at Cormac's desk, furiously working to put the finishing touches on the filtering system he'd spent the past forty-five minutes setting up.

"He's dead?" Frampton bellowed.

"Who's dead, Deano?" Vance asked, unconcerned.

"The chick who just walked out of here said that Cormac was dead!"

"Well that's ridiculous," Vance said condescendingly. "If Mac were dead, would that guy still be glued to his ear?"

Vance pointed toward the customer who was currently supposed to be looking into Cormac's left ear. He was a bleary-eyed waste of space whose dreadlocks protruded from a ratty knit cap. He sat with his thumb sticking in Cormac's ear as he stared slack-jawed at Cormac's bedside table.

"No, dammit!" Vance sighed. "Terry, you've got to *look* into his ear, not stick your thumb in it. I thought we'd been over this!" Vance looked at his phone. "You know what, your time's up anyways. Get the hell out of here." Terry reluctantly removed his thumb from Cormac's ear and shuffled out of the bedroom. He still appeared to have enjoyed himself.

"So maybe that guy would not have actually noticed if Mac died," Vance conceded. "Bad example. But check it out, he's still breathing, right?" Dean Bickerstaff took a few steps closer and was relieved to see that indeed, Cormac's chest was still rising and falling regularly.

"I wonder what she was talking about," Frampton said. "I've gotta take a look."

"Well, let someone else in on the other ear while you do," Vance demanded. "This is prime time, man, we gotta keep the line moving." Vance sipped his Bloody Mary to indicate that as far as he was concerned, the discussion was over.

Dean Bickerstaff walked back to the doorway and gestured for the next person in line to come on in. A guy with red hair marched over to Cormac's left ear. Frampton took a look at the line to make sure nobody was on the verge of pulling a Brock, then shut the door behind him and joined the red-haired student at Cormac's other ear.

Frampton felt kind of strange peering into Cormac's ear at the same time as someone else. It was a very intimate space to share with a stranger. It had been a much more comfortable, private experience to just stare into an unconscious man's ear alone. But the red-haired guy didn't seem to care, or even notice, that the dean was hovering just inches from his head. He simply peered into Cormac's ear and shut out the rest of the world.

"Get a move on, Deano!" Vance yelled from across the room. Dean Bickerstaff shrugged, placed his still-lit cigar on the bedside table, and leaned into Cormac's ear.

Instantly, the world of the *Levyathan* whooshed into view. The dean had trouble getting his bearings at first, but quickly realized that he was looking up at a ceiling from the floor. A man stood above Cormac, shouting and occasionally dumping liquid onto his face. Dean Bickerstaff figured that Cormac must have passed out and this guy was trying to revive him. Eventually the man reached down and started to shake Cormac by the shoulders, stopping to deliver the occasional slap across the face.

After a few seconds of this activity, the man who had been trying to revive Cormac appeared to relax, then ceased his efforts and sat down on the floor. He started talking and laughing, and the dean took this to mean that Cormac had been revived. Reluctantly, he pulled himself away from the eye and gave Vance a thumbs up.

"He's not dead," Frampton said as he picked up his cigar and puffed it to get it going again. "He was just passed out or unconscious or something."

"Good to know. Was it something the pirates did to him?"

"I don't think so," Frampton said.

"Did you see any pirates?" Vance asked.

"No. Vance, what if passing out had the same effect as going to sleep? What if he'd woken up in the middle of all of this?" The Dean waited for a response but eventually realized that Vance had tuned him out once he admitted he hadn't seen a pirate.

G-Dimes emphatically hit the enter key and closed Cormac's laptop. Wordlessly, the most powerful, most dangerous man on the Harrington campus swiveled around in his chair, stood up, and promptly walked into a wall in his attempt to leave the room. Eventually, after a few more bumps along the way, G-Dimes got his bearings, was able to locate the doorknob, pulled the door open, and shuffled through the doorway.

"Do you really think he was able to get the filters set up?" Frampton asked Vance.

"You are more than welcome to question his competence to his face," Vance said. "But personally, I would prefer not to find out what those bandana men do to you when they get you to the bushes. Hey!" he yelled at the red-haired guy looking into Cormac's right ear. "Time's up, buddy, take a hike! Dammit, he's going to need some help, Deano."

Dean Bickerstaff walked around the bed and pulled the student off by his shoulders. The red-haired guy looked around nervously, as if he were worried he'd done something wrong. Dean Bickerstaff just pointed to the door and said "Time's up." Looking relieved, the red-haired guy stood up, smoothed the front of his shirt, and left the room. Dean Bickerstaff followed after him.

Outside the door, Frampton took a ticket from the next person in line and gestured them into the room. Even though there were two ears open, the next person would have to wait. Staggering the two ears a minute apart allowed for a more constant flow of customers. It meant there was never any down time when Cormac was not being exploited.

The idea had been Mako's. It was one of several tweaks to their business model he'd suggested. There was also the new ticketing system. Once word got out that pirates were now part of the picture, the house was flooded with people who wanted to see Cormac conquer them or get captured by them. "Or get taken as a sex slave," Vance pointed out. "I think Mac himself told me that used to happen all the time."

But there was not enough room to accommodate a permanent line of hundreds of people. And besides, nobody really wanted to spend their day standing in a line. So Mako had suggested that people pay in advance for a numbered ticket. That way they could secure their place in line, but also enjoy the non-stop party atmosphere that Mako and G-Dimes were providing in the living room, on the front porch, and, increasingly, on the lawn. Every ten minutes, Mako would call out a range of numbers from the airborne couch, and twenty people would form a line outside Cormac's door. Everyone else would continue drinking, getting high, and eating breakfast.

The dean had been skeptical of the change in policy. He had enjoyed the rigidity and sense of subservience that came with waiting in a line. But Mako had pointed out that if people pre-paid, it wouldn't matter if they got too drunk to take their place in line or were having too much fun partying on the porch or got beaten unconscious and carried into the bushes by the bandana men. They'd already have handed over their money.

Mako had also suggested a 50-percent rate increase. A two-minute session now cost thirty dollars. Abolishing the lines had made this easier for people to swallow, as had the fact that Mako had figured out how to accept University Arts Dollars. At Harrington, through the generosity of donors and external grants, every student was given one hundred Arts Dollars at the beginning of the school year. By swiping their student ID, they could gain admittance to school plays, art galleries, and dance recitals.

Ninety-nine percent of Arts Dollars were never used. Harrington students were not the type to attend school plays, art galleries, or dance recitals. There had been one exception, when word got out that a school play had a brief scene of rear nudity. It had been a disaster. Fire hoses were needed to disperse the rowdy crowd and the unfortunate actress fled the country that night and retreated to a small convent in Southern Peru. "Butt's All Folks!" read the headline of Cissy Buckler's article in the *School Paper* about the incident.

However, by classifying Cormac's ear as a performance art installation, Mako had obtained approval to accept Arts Dollars. With a swipe of their Harrington IDs, students could now gain admittance using funds that would have evaporated at the end of the school year. The students got in free as far as they were concerned, and the rapidly expanding Cormac-exploiting operation raked in the dough.

The dean begrudgingly conceded that Mako's ideas had been for the better. Vance's idea to wear a towel, however, he was still very skeptical of. The basic thought behind it—that the dean would stand out in the crowd—was certainly working. But with the operation running smoother than ever, very few students had a legitimate need to seek Frampton's assistance. The vast majority of the students who approached him only seemed to be doing so on a dare, and the only questions they ever asked were about the towel.

Still, Dean Bickerstaff could not complain about the direction the day had taken. The kegs started flowing early, the beautiful day encouraged students to linger once their ear time was up, and, of course, there were the pirates.

The first person to spy the pirates had quite possibly been the biggest degenerate that Frampton had ever seen. He had been part of the early mushroom crowd, but didn't have enough money to buy any ear time. It actually turned out that he had been wandering around on mushrooms before the sun came up, saw a crowd, and decided to stand near it in case any of the people in it had more mushrooms. It was only after Mako revealed the new Arts Dollars policy that he was able to gain admittance. The burnout carried a garbage bag that occasionally rustled, was wearing several grease-stained aprons of varying lengths, and, over the course of the morning, forgot he had hands several times.

Vance informed the dean that this gentleman was named Joey, played bass in his band, and was one of his closest friends at Harrington.

When Joey had surfaced from Cormac's ear muttering about pirates, it set off an excited series of whispers all the way down the hall. Excitement was somewhat muted until the next person confirmed the pirates, because even for these people . . . you know, it was *Joey*. But once it appeared that Cormac was indeed hiding from a group of pirates who had captured the rest of the crew, people started jostling for the chance to hand over their money.

Dean Bickerstaff had no idea that pirates were so popular, but he quickly realized that the misfortune of the *Levyathan*'s crew was the best thing that could have happened to their operation. People had been content to observe Cormac doing just about any old thing. But now that there was an actual dramatic situation developing with honest-to-god pirates involved, excitement levels were off the charts. #CormacsEar had soared to the top of the trending topics as soon as people started tweeting about pirates, and the ranking was holding fast. The shadowy figures behind #HoesBeBangin attempted a counterstrike, incorporating a series of Pirate Ho themed puns, but most of them centered on the word "booty" and the hashtag quickly plummeted from its once-lofty perch.

Frampton checked that his towel was still secured around his waist and waddled over to the couches. Cissy and Mako were still sitting on the airborne couch, but Cissy was now reclining from one end to the other with her feet extended over Mako's lap. Mako had evidently arranged for someone who was in particularly desperate need of drugs to stand next to Cissy and hand-feed her from a platter of fruit and nuts. This sad bastard looked enviously toward the clouds of marijuana smoke that enveloped most of the living room, threatening to merge with each other and become a THC superstorm.

Dean Bickerstaff raised his shillelagh in a friendly greeting. "Mako, Cissy, how are you? We just had a close one there. Thought we had lost Cormac for a minute. Mind if I have some of those almonds?" Dean Bickerstaff had not eaten anything except for the peanut-butter-dipped granola bars back in the van and he was quickly getting hungry. He'd also been nipping back cognac whenever the excuse presented itself, and didn't want to drink too much more on an empty stomach.

Presuming his inquiry merely to be a polite formality, Frampton reached out toward the plate. But Cissy evidently did not want to share. She attempted to tell the dean to stay away from her food, but her mouth was full and she was unable to form distinct words. As Frampton's hand moved closer and closer to her platter, Cissy grew more agitated and began to spit the contents of her mouth, which turned out to be mostly grapes, into her hands.

Frampton looked in wonder as Cissy spit out nearly a dozen grapes. He wasn't sure where she had been storing them or why it was necessary to eat so many grapes at once when there was someone directly next to her who was being paid by a violent crime lord to dote on her hand and foot. But there was no time to wonder about that because in her attempt to expel so many grapes so quickly while lying on her back, one of them accidentally got stuck in her throat and Cissy began to choke.

The *School Paper* reporter hacked and wheezed in a panic, and eventually managed to sit upright. "Are you OK, Cissy?" Frampton asked. Cissy clutched her throat and shook her head no. The unfortunate guy holding the platter looked like he wanted to disappear and Mako looked more stoned than confident. Cissy started to turn blue.

Dean Bickerstaff tried to remember what he had done in situations like this before. Usually if he was with someone who was choking, it was because he was trying to get them to sign a contract. His typical response was to push an even more unfavorable contract toward the panicked victim and offer them a pen. Nobody had turned it down yet.

As for the next part, the whole "saving them" thing, this duty usually fell to a pre-determined underling or kindhearted but meddling member of the restaurant wait staff. Not knowing what to do for a choking he had not personally arranged, Frampton resumed reaching for the almonds. Still struggling to draw a breath, Cissy reached her leg out and kicked his hand away. For someone who had spent the better part of a week on a couch elevated five feet off the ground, Cissy could be awfully strong-willed when she wanted to be.

As the seconds ticked by, Dean Bickerstaff began to strongly consider making a break for the van and telling everyone on the board that his evil twin had assumed his identity earlier in the week. But just when things looked their grimmest, the dean noticed the crowd part behind the airborne couch. He couldn't tell who was coming through, but nobody seemed to want any part of him.

Then, Frampton watched in wonder as one of the bandana men vaulted over the back of the airborne couch. The dean braced himself for the entire structure to come crashing down, but the bandana man was as graceful as he was sinister. With catlike agility, he sat on the back of the couch so that his legs straddled Cissy from behind. Then, raising his right hand in the air, he delivered one quick karate-chop-style motion to Cissy's back.

The grape shot out of Cissy's mouth and hit Frampton right in the forehead. It fell to the ground and the dean watched it roll away. When it eventually went behind the TV, he looked back at the couches. The bandana man was already gone. Cissy was wheezing, but the color was returning to her face. Mako was lighting a brand new joint.

"You assholes," Cissy gasped. "You just stood there while I was choking!" She lay back down in a huff and gestured for more grapes. The platter bearer reluctantly plucked one from a bunch and handed it to Cissy, who popped it in her mouth.

"Relax, Cissy!" Mako said, taking a puff. "I knew he would come through. Those guys take a one-for-one oath. He just saved your life, so now he feels that he's justified to take out somebody else."

"Which particular philosophy do they subscribe to?" Dean Bickerstaff asked, genuinely curious if there were legitimate legal loopholes these guys had figured out.

Mako shook his head. "They don't appreciate people asking questions about their philosophy."

"Dammit, Dean, stay away from my almonds!" Cissy shrieked. Frampton pulled his hand back. He had hoped that the philosophy question would have caused more of a distraction.

"Well, I'm glad you're OK, Cissy," Frampton told her, trying to sound hurt that she wouldn't share. He looked at the guy who was holding the tray, but he refused to make eye contact. Mako had taught him well. The dean began to scan the room just in case there were any other servants holding snack trays who appeared to be weaker willed.

"What if he actually dies? Grape me!" said Cissy, who had apparently made a full recovery. The servant handed her another grape.

"I beg your pardon?" Frampton asked.

"Cormac! He's not dead now, but he is on a boat, vastly outnumbered by a bunch of pirates. So he's probably going to die, right?" Cissy gestured for another grape. "So does that mean he dies back here, too? His finger got cut off there and it was cut off here, too. So what are we gonna do if he dies?"

"Damn, Cissy!" said Mako. "Someone needs a little puff and a little drink!" Mako snapped his fingers and someone appeared with a mimosa. Mako took it and handed it off to Cissy, who, having apparently learned nothing, started to guzzle it while still on her back. Mako passed her the joint next and she calmly hit it mid-mimosa, then passed it back and finished the rest of her drink.

Dean Bickerstaff watched in a combination of amazement and horror while he thought about what Cissy had just said. Cormac's not being dead had been such a relief that Dean Bickerstaff hadn't even bothered to wonder what might happen to him over the course of the rest of the day. Cormac was in an extremely perilous situation and there was no telling when someone might pop up from one of his ears and inform everyone that the last thing they'd seen was a pirate's cutlass slashing Cormac's neck.

My evil twin is named Zachary, Dean Bickerstaff decided. He kidnapped me nine days ago, and everything that has happened at the Craymore Street house was part of his diabolical revenge for a bet we made on a polo match back in 1997.

As Mako passed the joint around to the various other people who were gathered around the couches, the unpleasantness of the choking incident seemed quickly forgotten. The line outside Cormac's door dwindled and eventually Mako looked at his watch and yelled out, "Two-sixty-one through two-eighty! Form a line!" The dean watched as people checked their tickets and filed toward the bedroom if their turn was up. But for the first time that Frampton could remember, Mako's announcement was followed by a series of boos from outside.

Mako and Cissy both looked as confused as the dean felt. Cissy sat up and tried to crane her neck to look out the window. Were people growing tired of waiting? Had one of the kegs kicked? Frampton looked at the line, which appeared orderly and devoid of people who might lose consciousness in the immediate future, and decided he had time to investigate. He grabbed his bottle of cognac off the floor and headed for the porch.

As he stepped outside, Frampton was amazed by the scene that had developed on the front lawn of the Craymore Street house. There were hundreds of people milling about, most of them with a red cup of beer in hand, which had either come from one of the two kegs in the living room or the four currently tapped on one side of the porch. On the other side was Cissy's brand new couch, which remained untouched and unsoiled due to the invisible threat of the bandana men. Some drunk idiots kicked a hacky sack nearby it, and Dean Bickerstaff wondered if they'd be acting so cavalier if they knew that one of the bandana men had just tipped the balance back in his favor by saving a life inside.

Loud music blared from a DJ booth near the front porch and a food truck was hawking hot dogs and soft pretzels to appreciative buyers. It was like the crowd at a summer music festival, but they were all here to peer into someone's ear for two minutes. And much to the dean's excitement, half the students appeared to be on their phone, posting pictures to show how much fun they were having or letting their friends know how stoned they were gonna be when they looked in that guy's ear. For the most part, Frampton was delighted. He also was slightly concerned by how public posts like these would affect everyone's employability, and thus Harrington's job placement rate, once they graduated, but he pushed that thought aside. After all, he himself had a prestigious, high-paying job and here he was wearing only a towel.

Frampton graciously allowed three drunk chicks in bikini tops to pose for a picture with him, but only after he'd lit a cigar. He was pretty sure the girls' picture request had solely been made in order to mock him, but he was also pretty confident that it was harder to take a cooler picture of yourself than one of you smoking a cigar, shirtless, holding a shillelagh in one hand and a bottle of cognac in the other, with three bikini babes, as a party raged on in the background. He hoped the two kittens on the beach towel were cropped out in the photo.

Another round of boos went up from the part of the yard closest to the sidewalk and Frampton waddled toward the disturbance. At least it was happening on the outskirts of the party, he thought to himself. No need to bring down the awesome vibe they had going here. Frampton looked down at the cognac bottle, which turned out to be a little under half empty. Perhaps in his efforts to allay his anxiety about marching around the house in just a towel, he'd indulged in a little too much liquid courage. Ah well, he could always take a nap in the back of the van if he needed to.

As he approached the sidewalk, the dean saw that the angry students who were booing were in fact facing away from the party, toward the street. They appeared to be quite worked up, and were yelling at someone on the other side of Craymore Street who Frampton couldn't see yet. The dean stuck out his shillelagh and cleared a path so he could get a look. When he got to the edge of the yard and could finally see what everyone was yelling at, his face fell.

Brock was on the other side of the street, leading a group of five or six other people. They marched back and forth, holding signs and wearing sandwich boards like workers on strike outside of a factory. The dean leaned forward and squinted to try and make out what the signs said. "CORMAC 3:16," "FIVE LOAVES AND TWO WHALES," and "KEEP YOUR LAWS OFF MY ERECTION" were the ones he could make out. Brock appeared not to have shaved or bathed since the last time Frampton saw him.

The positive vibes he'd built up on the walk across the lawn quickly forgotten, Dean Bickerstaff frowned and angrily puffed his cigar. "What the hell is this clown doing?" he asked one of the onlookers.

"He thinks that Cormac is a god or something," the student said while sipping a beer. "And he claims Cormac named him the chosen one to communicate his message to all of us. The rest of them are people he's recruited to be his followers."

"He's formed a cult?" The dean was astonished. Who could have predicted that one rogue boner might have such ramifications?

"Yeah, I guess so. He keeps trying to come over here and tell us that Cormac wouldn't approve of our sinful ways. Screw that, man! One time I was at an Uncle Jemima show where Cormac was so wasted he took off his pants onstage and puked in them before his band had ever played a note! He would have loved this party!"

"You paid to see that . . . performance?" Frampton asked.

"Hell yeah, man! It was the best show I've ever been to! Oh check it out, here he comes!"

Brock had started to cross the street toward Cormac's house, holding a sign with the mathematical equation "CORMAC > GOD" scrawled on it. The dean admired the conciseness of the blasphemy, but everything else about the situation enraged him. The gathered students felt the same way, and started to boo and jeer Brock as he approached. One particularly worked-up guy threw a full beer at him, but he was then booed and jeered for wasting beer, and he quickly retreated to the porch for a refill.

Brock attempted to speak over the din as he crossed the street. "My fellow students," he intoned in a gentle monotone. "Reject Brock if you must, for I am merely a husk. But open your hearts to what I say, for this husk serves as a vessel for the teachings of Cormac."

"You suck!" yelled someone in the crowd. "Quit trying to ruin our party!" shouted someone else. "Brock, is our game theory problem set due on Tuesday or Wednesday?" called out a third.

Brock continued on undeterred. "Cormac clearly has unique powers that span the ages. Join me, and together we shall spread his message. Abandon this debaucherous lifestyle and embrace the teachings of the whaling one."

"What are his teachings?" yelled someone from the crowd.

"When I peered into his ear, Cormac instructed me that I should assemble his disciples to spread his teachings," Brock informed them.

The crowd was silent, waiting for Brock to continue.

"So, that's what they've been so far," Brock eventually continued. "That I should spread his teachings. Look, I haven't been allowed back in his bedroom since then!"

Holy crap, Dean Bickerstaff thought. He's recruited a half dozen idiots already with that flimsy snake oil. Who knew how large this enterprise could get if this charlatan were allowed to continue unchecked?

"I did receive a vision last night during meditation," Brock added. "Clearly it was communication from Cormac. He instructed me to create a graven image of the moment he anointed me his apostle."

One of Brock's disciples now approached the crowd holding a stack of t-shirts folded over one of his arms. With his other hand he held up one of the shirts for display. They had Michelangelo's *The Creation of Adam* from the Sistine Chapel ceiling printed on them, but the dean noticed a few details had been changed. Cormac's face had been superimposed onto God's body and Brock's face was on Adam's. The dean noted that, unfortunately, while God was still reaching out to touch Adam, the extended part of Adam's body was no longer his hand. The caption "Harpoon This!" was written under the image in Comic Sans.

"Twenty dollars, cash only," the disciple said.

The crowd was still not sure about Brock's message, but the t-shirt was too hilarious to pass up. Several students walked into the road to buy one.

Dean Bickerstaff had seen enough. He retreated from the sidewalk and hastily waddled back toward the house. These unpredictable elements just had a way of springing up without warning. If only there was some way to anticipate them! Clearly, Brock was a problem that must be dealt with before he could spread his message any further. Fortunately, there were people in this house that could make problems go away. And come to think of it, probably make them die. Frampton realized that he was fairly certain that the people who the bandana men were dragging off wound up dead. He paused to ponder the ethical ramifications of this, but then decided to get a hot dog instead.

After devouring the hot dog in four bites, Frampton threw open the door to the house and pushed his way past a group of dancing idiots. He waddled over to the couches and waved his shillelagh to get Mako's attention. Mako was bobbing his head to the blaring music and rolling a gravity-defying blunt. He smiled when he saw the dean.

"Dean B!" Mako said. "What's the good word?" He gestured for Dean Bickerstaff to hand him the cognac bottle.

"I'm afraid there is no good word, Mako," Frampton said as he raised the bottle up to Mako's level. Unconcerned, Mako uncapped it and tilted the bottle until he was able to dip the end of the blunt in it. Then he took a swig and handed it back to the dean.

"We've got a situation out there. The student who we had to forcibly remove during the last session, Brock?"

"Oh yeah!" Mako laughed at the memory. "Freaky little bastard, right?"

"He started a cult. He thinks that just because Cormac transcends time and space every other day in a manner unlike anyone who's ever lived, he's a god." Frampton made a mental note not to be so specific about Cormac's godlike bona fides in the future. He'd almost convinced himself just there.

Mako nodded. "I see, I see. This sounds like something that needs addressing. Yo, G!" He called out for G-Dimes, who tore himself away from a particularly interesting DVD player screensaver on the TV and shuffled over to the airborne couch.

Mako leaned over and whispered into G-Dimes's ear. G-Dimes waited for several seconds after Mako had stopped whispering, then straightened up and nodded to himself. Then he shuffled over to the window and stared out at the street.

While Frampton waited for the drug dealer to assess the situation, he decided to attempt some small talk with Mako.

"So . . . drug dealing, huh?" Mako smiled a tight, polite smile and nodded without saying anything, like you would to a stranger who remarked about the weather in an elevator. G-Dimes remained motionless by the window, so Frampton barreled ahead. "I heard on the news the other day about these guys who kidnapped a drug dealer and hooked a car battery up to his scrotum." Mako's face fell, as if that stranger in the elevator had then pressed every floor button and started to pee his pants.

"I'm completely naked under this towel," Frampton said, in a desperate and ultimately failed attempt to make the situation less awkward. "Oh my God," muttered Cissy in utter disgust. Fortunately, G-Dimes shuffled back over to the couches before Frampton had a chance to embarrass himself further. Mako leaned down and G-Dimes whispered into his ear. After a few seconds, Mako nodded and sat back up.

"Dean B, that cult out there is a problem. It could be bad for business and attract unwanted attention. Their leader needs to get got." Frampton nodded in agreement. He craned his neck toward the window, expecting any second to hear the brief but horrible sound of Brock being dealt with by the bandana men.

"Unfortunately, we're of the opinion that Brock and his followers are exercising their constitutionally protected rights of assembly and religious freedom. As long as he doesn't cross over onto Cormac and Vance's property, they're cool with us." Mako sat back on the couch and took a gigantic puff from his blunt to signify that there would be no discussion on the matter.

Dean Bickerstaff grimaced and clutched his shillelagh. He enjoyed nothing more than being selectively ethical when the situation favored him, but it frustrated him to no end when others displayed the same inconsistency. Now his hands were tied. Going behind the drug dealers' backs and trying to work out his own side deal with the bandana men was not something he wanted to do so soon after implanting the idea of testicle shocking in Mako's head. The dean would just have to hope that Brock would do something horrible that would embroil his new religion in scandal, causing his followers to abandon him as quickly as they signed on.

"Two-eighty-one through three hundred!" yelled Mako. A new group of people abandoned the bacchanal and started to move toward the bedroom. Dean Bickerstaff figured he should probably make sure this new group got lined up properly. He hoped that Vance hadn't been overwhelmed while he ventured outside. Frampton twirled his shillelagh once and started down the hall to Cormac's bedroom.

The tipsy crew of degenerates who were lining up in the hallway hooted and cheered as the dean walked by in his towel. Frampton responded by holding his bottle of cognac up in the air, which provoked louder cheers, then tipping it back for a large swig, which caused the crowd to completely lose their minds. The dean smiled. There was no denying that at the moment, Craymore Street was the epicenter of the Harrington Campus, if not the known Party Universe. Brock and his cult could go to hell, Frampton thought. If that was the only distraction they had to worry about today, they'd be sitting pretty.

At that exact moment, Vance threw open the door to Cormac's bedroom. He was holding a panicked-looking man by his collar. He quickly scanned the hallway until he spotted the dean. Vance looked furious. "Dammit, Deano!" Vance shouted. "Where the hell have you been?" Frampton tried to inconspicuously hide the cognac bottle behind his back.

"Put that bottle down and come help me!" Vance commanded. "We've got ourselves a goddamn spy!"

Cormac felt a sharp pain in his cheek and his eyes popped open. Ziro stood above him. He looked worried.

"Are you awake?" Ziro asked. Before Cormac could respond, Ziro picked a bucket up off the floor and poured its contents on Cormac's head.

Now dizzy and soaking wet, Cormac sat up and shouted at the former slave. "Yes, I'm awake, dammit! What the hell was that for?" Cormac wiped the liquid out of his eyes and silently gave thanks that it was apparently just salt water.

"I was just trying to revive you," Ziro said. "You passed out."

"I know I passed out!" Cormac hissed at him. "It was the toxic fumes from your cleaning supplies! How the hell do you sleep in this enclosed area, Ziro? The air must be 90 percent chemicals!"

"I guess you just kind of get used to it," Ziro said sheepishly. "Don't worry, I pried one of the boards off the wall to let some air in."

"I don't think I can see the color red anymore!" Cormac said, the panic in his voice rising.

"Oh yeah, that'll happen," Ziro told him. "Don't worry, it'll come back once you get outside and take a few deep breaths. I guess I never really put two and two together on that one."

Cormac tried to calm down. His nostrils still stung from the foul air of the slave's quarters, but at least his head had stopped spinning. "Ziro, what the hell are those pirates going to do?"

"Well, we're still headed toward St. John's. But instead of us selling all the whales and making a ton of money when we get there, the pirates are going to sell them, take the money, probably take the ship, and abandon whoever they haven't already killed. Oh, and assuming the crew hasn't had a monumental change of heart, they're probably just a few minutes away from throwing Captain Anson overboard."

"Those bastards," muttered Cormac. "How could they? It's not fair!"

"Yeah, he could be unreasonable, but you hate to see your Captain go like that," Ziro agreed.

"*I* killed those whales, and they're going to sell the parts and keep the money themselves? Who do they think they are? What's that about Captain Anson?"

"They're going to throw him overboard," Ziro reminded Cormac.

"Well I suppose if we can also prevent that, we might as well," Cormac said in the same tone he might use to agree to add a slice of tomato to a sandwich, as long as it didn't cost anything extra. "But dammit, Ziro, I worked hard to catch those whales! That cold storage area full of assorted organs and hacked-up chunks of blubber is the greatest thing I've ever accomplished in my life!"

Cormac paused for a second. "That sounds a lot better if you can actually see the room. Like really take in the enormity of it, you know?"

Ziro nodded. "You don't have to convince me. You're the greatest harpooner I've ever seen Cormac. You've really turned things around on the *Levyathan*."

"Well I'm not going to let these damn pirates just take everything that we've worked for," Cormac said. "We've got to stop them! How do we go about doing that?"

"I've been trying to figure that out," said Ziro. "Here's what I think. The pirates think that they've got everyone on board tied up, except for me. They don't know you exist, so you've got the element of surprise working for you."

"Yes, the element of surprise." Cormac stroked his chin. He'd never hatched a plan of any actual consequence before, and the action felt surprisingly natural. "This may sound crazy, Ziro . . ."

"I'm all ears," the former slave responded.

"What if I hid somewhere where they couldn't see me, and shot the pirates with a harpoon gun?"

"That doesn't sound crazy at all," Ziro informed Cormac. "It sounds alarmingly straightforward and coldblooded, especially since it's the first idea you thought of. Do you really think you could do it?"

"Of course I think I could!" Cormac tried to sound incredulous. "After all, you just said that I'm the greatest harpooner you've ever seen!"

"I didn't mean whether you are skilled enough to do it," Ziro said in a somber tone. "I meant whether you'd be capable of taking another person's life, let alone a dozen lives. It's not something to enter into lightly, Cormac. It's a burden you'll forever carry with you once it's done. You should think long and hard about whether that's the kind of person you're willing to be. Or . . . if it's the kind of person you already are . . ."

"What if right before I pull the trigger I say, 'What's the best way to kill a pirate,' and then say 'With an *Arrr*-poon'?" Cormac asked as he rummaged through Ziro's belongings looking for a harpoon gun.

"There's one underneath that cigar box," Ziro sighed. Cormac crawled over to the pile of junk that Ziro was pointing at and moved aside a cigar box. A beat-up old harpoon gun was lying underneath it. "I don't get it why you would say that. Are pirates known for not pronouncing the 'h' in the word 'harpoon'?"

Cormac picked up the harpoon gun and blew some dust off of it. It had definitely seen better days, but it wasn't like the other equipment he'd been using was top-of-the-line stuff either. "It's a joke, Ziro. 'Arrr,' you know? Pirates say 'Arrr.'"

"I've never heard these pirates utter anything like that," Ziro informed Cormac.

"That's like the number-one thing they're known for."

"Well, I've spent the past twenty-four hours getting captured, threatened, and held at gunpoint by pirates," Ziro said. "I think if they were in the habit of saying 'Arrr,' they probably would have let one or two slip by now."

"They probably say it when they're talking to each other, when there aren't any outsiders around," Cormac said, trying not to get flustered as he peered down the shaft of the harpoon gun, sizing up the sight.

"Then how would it become so widely known as to be the number-one thing they're known for?"

"Look, it's a great line!" shouted Cormac, before remembering that he was still technically hiding out from murderous pirates. He lowered his voice. "It's a great line! And I bet I can think of others! I'm using the 'Arrr' joke, Ziro!"

"I just see it confusing people," Ziro explained.

"I'm not going to argue with you!"

"See?" Ziro said. "Not funny."

"That wasn't an 'Arrr' joke!" Cormac fumed. "I didn't draw out the 'Arrr' in 'argue'!"

"I still don't think it would have been funny," said Ziro.

"Well we'll never know now, will we?"

"Will that harpoon gun work?" Ziro asked, trying to change the subject. "I just brought it in here to use for ukulele parts."

Cormac took a deep breath and tried to relax. "Yeah, I think it'll be OK. If I'm firing into a group of them, it won't matter if the sight isn't 100-percent accurate."

"That brings me back to my earlier point," Ziro said. "You're sure you're going to be OK with this? I know that some of the whalers still wake up screaming about *accidental* deaths they were involved in."

"Look, the only screaming I'm going to do is if those pirates sell off my whales and keep all the dough. That, and maybe some screaming if they capture and torture me. Probably a lot of screaming in that situation. But seriously, Ziro, don't worry. It'll be just like a video game." Cormac paused and rolled his eyes. "Sorry. Forgot that you don't know what those are."

"Sad," muttered Ziro.

"That wasn't an 'Arrr' joke either! Dammit! Where are the harpoons?"

Ziro walked over to a chest that was covered by a filthy tarp. He pulled the tarp away and opened the lid. Inside were harpoons, ropes, winches, and canvas patches, all in various stages of disrepair. Cormac dug through the junk for a while until he'd found a half dozen harpoons that he felt were suitable.

"Where do you think I'll have the best shot from?" Cormac asked Ziro.

"Well, the slave's quarters actually have a pretty good vantage point. If we could pry off a few of these wall boards, I bet you could line up a shot without having to find new cover."

Cormac loaded a harpoon into the gun with a satisfying click. "Well," he asked Ziro. "What are we waiting for—*dammit,* that wasn't a joke!"

* * *

On the deck of the *Levyathan,* Pete was futilely trying to put Captain Anson's fate to a vote. The crew of the *Levyathan* seemed committed to the idea of throwing him overboard, but Anson had so far managed to delay this via a series of devious, underhanded tactics.

Mainly this involved trying to make it seem like one of the whalers had yelled "Nay" whenever Pete asked if anyone wanted to vote against throwing him overboard. Pirate Code required the entire crew to vote before a captain could be disposed of. It also ordered that anyone who cast a dissenting vote to be given the floor to voice their concerns. So when the captain mumbled "Nay" out of the corner of his mouth, Pete had to stop the vote and try to figure out who had said it so they would be allowed to speak. When nobody came forward, the vote was declared invalid and the process started over again.

After three consecutive interruptions, Pete caught on to what the captain was doing and ordered him to be gagged. Unfortunately for the pirates, by this time the Black Barnacle's parrot had decided that saying "nay" was a fun game, and it began to vote against the measure as well. Pete ordered the Black Barnacle to shut his parrot up, but the Black Barnacle was so terrified of the bird that he refused. Pete evidently wanted no part of it either, so the bird was allowed to continue to vote nay, then given the floor to explain his reasoning, which consisted mostly of threatening to peck the Black Barnacle's crotch.

Captain Anson silently watched the evil little bird with admiration. He knew that the parrot would eventually lose interest, so he was trying to figure out another plan with the time it had bought him. But as hard as he thought, it was difficult to imagine a scenario with a happy ending. After years of mistreatment, his crew finally had their chance for revenge, and they were going to seize it, even if it took all day.

From his seat on the deck of the *Levyathan*, Anson looked up at Pete. The sun was already bright in the sky and the pirate captain was starting to sweat. Pete wiped his brow and began the process of starting a new vote.

"OK, for an eighth time," said Pete. "Who is in favor of throwing Captain Anson overboard?" An unenthusiastic, tired sounding "Yea" went up from the whalers, who were still sitting tied together in a circle around Captain Anson.

"Alright, and who is opposed to throwing him overboard?" Pete glared at the Black Barnacle, who trembled in fear of the parrot on his shoulder. The parrot remained quiet this time, and Pete cautiously began to smile. Captain Anson saw this and tried to grunt out a "Nay," but the gag was effective and he was unable to vocalize anything coherent.

"Well," Pete said. "It appears that we have a unanimous—" He was cut off by a whaler shouting out "Nay." Captain Anson's heart rose briefly. The whaler was sitting behind him and he couldn't turn to see him, but perhaps this signaled a sea change.

"Dammit!" Pete yelled. "What the hell are you voting 'Nay' for all of a sudden? Don't you want to throw him overboard?"

"I was just wondering," the whaler asked. "Is throwing him overboard and making him walk the plank the same thing? Because I had been voting under the assumption that we'd be making him walk the plank, but then I started to worry that the specific language of 'throw him overboard' would make a difference."

"Well, that depends." said the pirate who looked like a goblin. "What is your opinion regarding the legitimacy of the definition of 'plank' as laid out by the Executive Pirate Council that met in the off-caucus year of '43?"

"He doesn't get to have an opinion about the EPC," yelled Pete. "He's not a pirate!"

"Hey, I'm just doing my due diligence," muttered the goblin pirate. "You know, the *Mongrel*'s gone three years without an EPC audit. That's a sizable fine if anyone asks to see our paperwork."

"We can throw him overboard or make him walk the plank, whatever you want," pleaded Pete. "Heck, we can throw him overboard, fish him out, *then* make him walk the plank. Just please, let's finish this vote so we can get on with our damn day!"

For the moment, the whaler appeared satisfied. Pete took a deep breath and started the process one more time. "Who is in favor of throwing the captain overboard or making him walk the plank?" A bored sounding "Yea" went up from the circle of whalers.

"And who is *against* disposing of the captain in this manner?" Captain Anson held his breath. He looked over at the parrot. It was busy whispering something in the Black Barnacle's ear that, based on the Black Barnacle's facial expression, must have been a terrifying threat. The captain's eyes flicked around, sizing up all the whalers he could see for any sign of sympathy. Nothing. After a few more seconds, Pete, now noticeably giddy, exclaimed "We have a unanimous vote! Seize him!"

Two pirates stepped over the whalers into the circle and lifted Captain Anson to his feet. They roughly pulled him out of the circle and held him up next to Pete so the pirate captain could sneer at his victim.

"How does it feel, captain?" Pete asked. "How does it feel to know that your own men wanted you dead?"

"I think he's going to have trouble answering you with that gag on," the goblin pirate pointed out.

Pete grimaced, but quickly produced a knife. He leaned forward, then cut one end of the gag and pulled it out of Captain Anson's mouth.

"Nay! Nay!" yelled Captain Anson as soon as it was removed.

"I'm afraid it's too late for that," Pete chuckled.

"It was worth a shot," said Captain Anson.

"So, I'll ask you again. How does it feel, captain? Your men voted unanimously. Every single one of them wanted to throw you overboard." Anticipating an outburst, Pete quickly added, "Or have you walk the plank, we certainly aren't ruling that out!" The whaler who had recently voted "Nay" nodded smugly.

Captain Anson looked at Pete, then back at the whalers, then back at Pete. To hell with these guys, Anson thought. If they couldn't take a little light swindling, forced labor, and deceit, they weren't cut out for the seafaring life. Captain Anson puffed out his chest and prepared to die with his pride intact.

"To tell you the truth, Pete," he said. "I'd have done the same thing to all of them. Every single one. Especially Ziro . . ." Wait a second! Ziro! Captain Anson spun back around and quickly surveyed the assembled whalers. Ziro was nowhere to be seen! He must be off swabbing the decks or changing out his mop!

"Ziro's not here!" he called out giddily. "Everyone didn't vote! Pirate Code—you can't throw me over until Ziro's part of the vote!"

Pete's face fell. "Dammit!" he cursed. "Damn this code and damn the Pirate Caucus and damn the EPC! Being a pirate used to be cool!"

"Maybe if the rest of you followed the example of . . . You know who. . ." Captain Anson nodded his head toward the Black Barnacle, who was trying to get his parrot to stop tugging on his hoop earring with its beak.

"We're not going to be like Barney!" snapped Pete. "Barney sucks!" Barney let out a hurt groan, followed by a shriek of pain as the parrot resumed tugging on his earring.

"You two!" Pete pointed at the two closest pirates. "Go and round up the deck swabber. We'll vote one last time once he's here." The pirates set off toward the slave's quarters. Pete watched them go, then stepped toward Captain Anson. He poked his finger into the captain's chest, and with his hands bound, there was nothing Anson could do about it.

"You *will* go overboard. Or you will walk the plank," Pete said, punctuating every sentence with another poke of his finger. "But you are going to drown, captain. And it's going to happen soon."

Cormac peered out through a jagged hole in the wall of the slave's quarters. He was careful not to put his face too close to the splintery edges and exposed nails that surrounded the hole. Ziro had initially managed to neatly pry off a small panel of wood, but Cormac had quickly grown impatient and ended up smashing the hole bigger with the butt of the harpoon gun. Ziro would have preferred to be able to easily patch the hole back up once it was no longer needed, but this was now impossible.

On the other hand, there was now a hole in the slave's quarters wall big enough to shoot a harpoon gun through. And it appeared that taking the quick and dirty way had been a good decision, because they were now able to see two pirates heading their way. Captain Anson had just been yelling Ziro's name, so Cormac figured the pirates were on their way to retrieve the former slave. Whatever the plan was going to be, they only had a few seconds left to finalize it.

"I'll try to get the whalers untied once the murdering starts," Ziro said as he fumbled with his mop. "Er, the confusion! Once the *confusion* starts. You just keep shooting, Cormac. If you can take out the captain as early as possible, that will cause a lot of chaos and really help us out."

"Got it," said Cormac. "Shouldn't be a problem. I could hit a whale's blowhole at twice this distance. Want to bet on whether I can get two pirates with one harpoon?"

Ziro shook his head. The footsteps from outside were getting nearer. Cormac ducked down from the hole in the wall and put his finger to his lips to shush Ziro.

"Good luck," mouthed Ziro. "We'll be catching whales by lunchtime," mouthed Cormac in return. "What?" mouthed Ziro, confused by the unexpectedly complex utterance Cormac evidently intended him to lip-read. "Never mind," replied Cormac. He waved Ziro away with a smile. Ziro tucked his mop under his arm, picked up a bucket, and stepped out of the slave's quarters. Cormac heard the pirates approaching as Ziro swung the door shut behind him.

"There you are," hissed one of the pirates. "You're holding everything up. Come on, we don't have all day." Cormac listened as they led Ziro away from the door, and once the footsteps faded, he raised himself up until he could peer out of the hole in the wall again.

The pirates flanked Ziro as they led him toward the rest of the crew. Cormac gripped the harpoon gun and watched them until they came to a halt. They shoved Ziro down next to the circle of whalers, then laughed as they went to rejoin the rest of the pirates. Everyone was too far away for Cormac to hear them unless they were shouting, but he figured that it didn't really matter what they were saying. Nothing was going to change what had to be done, and there didn't really seem to be any reason to delay it any longer.

Cormac raised the harpoon gun until the shaft rested on the rim of the hole in the wall. The pointed tip of the harpoon stuck out two or three inches from the slave's quarters as Cormac slid it side to side, trying to find his first target per Ziro's instructions: the captain.

Almost immediately, he spotted a man with a peg leg, a hook hand, and a parrot on his shoulder. Bingo, thought Cormac as he trained the harpoon on the guy who was obviously the pirate captain. Cormac waited until he thought the wind felt right, then pulled the trigger on the harpoon gun.

The harpoon whizzed across the deck of the *Levyathan*, obliterated the parrot into a puff of feathers, and struck the peg-legged pirate directly in the throat. A jet of blood spurted out as the pirate dropped to his knees. Well, I can definitely see red again, Cormac thought. Ziro must have been right about the fresh air.

Cormac saw Ziro flinch as the body dropped, but the death had happened so quickly that nobody else appeared to notice. Cormac quickly loaded a second harpoon into the gun and set a third down within arm's reach. He fixed his aim on a pirate who had his back to him and pulled the trigger. Before he even had a chance to see if it connected, he loaded the next harpoon and shot it into the same general area as the first. When Cormac took a moment to look out the hole, there were three dead pirates lying on the ground. Now people were starting to notice.

The *Levyathan*'s deck was utter chaos. Captain Anson had hit the deck, the whalers were doubled over to try to avoid the projectiles, and the pirates were looking around in panic. Nobody was sure where the harpoons were coming from so nobody knew where to hide. Everyone was yelling. One pirate made a break for the gangplank that attached the *Levyathan* to the pirate ship. Cormac loaded a harpoon as he watched him. He pulled the trigger when the pirate was just a few steps from his own boat, and just a second later the dead body plummeted off the plank and into the water.

Four down. Eight to go.

Cormac saw Ziro hunched over between two whalers. Hopefully he was trying to get them untied. Cormac figured he would try and buy him some time. He ducked down so his face wasn't visible and yelled out of the hole in the wall.

"Hello pirates! I've just killed your captain and his parrot!"

"Dammit!" yelled a voice from out on the deck. "Every single time!"

"Ha! Suck it, Pete!" cackled Captain Anson.

"I've killed three others too!" Cormac continued. "But I'm willing to spare anybody who wants to surrender! Set down your weapons and put your hands up!"

Slowly, Cormac raised his head and peeked out of the hole in the wall. Three pirates were nervously looking around with their hands in the air. This is too easy, Cormac thought as he locked another harpoon into place and pointed it out the window.

* * *

"What the hell do you mean by a spy, Vance?" Dean Bickerstaff had assumed that a jilted pervert establishing a cult across the street was the strangest thing he'd have to deal with all day. But now here was Vance holding a thirty-something year-old man by his collar. The man looked startled, and a false mustache hung down off the side of his mouth.

"Don't you recognize this punk, Deano? Dennis Stark, human interest reporter for the Channel 9 News Team: Your News When It Matters!

"Number One in the Metropolitan Area Four Years Running," the dean continued, starting to catch on.

"That's right!" Vance was livid. "He was trying to bug Cormac's room to get footage for the evening news!"

"Let me go," Dennis said. "You've got no right to keep me here."

"Shut up!" Vance demanded. "I thought he looked familiar, Deano, but I figured we must have just had a class together at one point in time. But then I recognized this!" Vance plucked the mustache off of Dennis's face, and the reporter yelped in pain. "That's my brand of janitor mustaches! I'd recognize them anywhere!"

"You son of a bitch," the dean muttered as he leaned in toward the reporter, trying to sound intimidating. "Trying to rake up some muck after Cormac denied your interview request? I believe that constitutes trespassing, and it's well within my right to jab the knotted end of this shillelagh up your—"

"Excuse me." A petite blonde girl timidly tapped the dean on his shoulder. "Is it my turn now?"

The dean spun and faced her with a smile. "Oh, I'm so sorry. Go right in, dearie, just kneel at the open ear and enjoy."

"You're not a spy are you? If you're a reporter we're going to find out!" Vance shrieked at her. The girl shook her head no, looking slightly more uncertain about venturing into the bedroom than she had been fifteen seconds ago.

"We've got to do something about this, Deano," Vance said. "There could be dozens more spies. Channel 8: Action News. Channel 4: Eyewitness News. Even those bottom-feeding scumbags at Channel 7: ActionWitness News with Jenna McMilf the Bikini Weather Girl could send one of their sleaze peddlers out here."

The dean was impressed that someone Vance's age had such detailed knowledge of the local news scene. But then again, the lad did spend a lot of time watching TV. But regardless of which news team had tried to smuggle in a camera, this was not the sort of thing they could allow. Stoners and drunks tweeting from the scene of the party was one thing; their allegiance could be bought with free beer and cheap drugs. But an independent media would want to do things their way: asking questions, uncovering secrets, righting social injustices.

So long as Cissy remained the only source who was actually connected to Cormac, the dean could control the narrative. Anything the mainstream media reported could be swiftly and unequivocally denied. But if this Channel 9 idiot had actually managed to plant a camera in Cormac's room, the power of exclusivity would be lost. The unpredictable elements his own partners brought to the table had proven difficult enough to manage. Dean Bickerstaff wasn't prepared to let the local news throw their own into the mix.

The bedroom door opened and the customer who had been in before the blonde girl shuffled out in a daze. The guy at the front of the line started to walk through the door but Dean Bickerstaff stuck his shillelagh out to block the way.

"Not so fast," Frampton said. "How do we know you're not a reporter?" The guy at the front of the line giggled nervously. He could not have looked less like a reporter, let alone an employable individual. He was going to town on a bag of gummy worms and wore a t-shirt that said "Got Weed?" His belt appeared to be made out of a rolled-up newspaper.

"Make him take a hit," Vance said. Dean Bickerstaff turned to look at him, still blocking the entrance with his shillelagh. Vance held onto Dennis's collar with one hand, but his other was offering Dean Bickerstaff a tightly rolled joint.

"Make everyone who wants to look into Mac's ear take a puff of that before they go in," Vance said. "Reporters won't be allowed to do drugs while they're on the clock. If anyone refuses to smoke, they don't get to go in. It's as simple as that."

The dean eyed the joint skeptically. "You think that will really work?" he asked Vance. Vance pulled back on Dennis's collar and shoved the joint in the reporter's face.

"Want a hit, Stark?" Vance demanded as Dennis tried to wave the joint away.

"Get that thing away from me," Dennis said. "Are you trying to get me fired? I'm a professional. You guys are crazy. Let me go!"

Vance looked at Frampton with an "I told you so" expression. The dean reached out and took the joint. Turning back around to the line, he offered the joint to the gummy-worm eater who was waiting for his turn.

"Nobody enters unless they take a hit of this," Dean Bickerstaff informed him. The fellow at the head of the line tried to size up whether he was being tricked. As he gradually realized that the dean meant to force him to smoke free marijuana, a dopey grin crept onto his face. He reached out, took the joint from the dean, and pulled a lighter out of his pocket. He lit the joint, took a gigantic puff, and exhaled proudly. He handed it back to the dean. Now satisfied, Frampton waved him into the bedroom with the shillelagh.

"Tell Mako we're going to need enough drugs for everyone who comes through to take a hit," Frampton instructed Vance. "He better get to rolling joints."

Vance nodded. "What do you want to do with this guy?" he asked, giving Dennis a little shove.

"I don't care," the dean replied. "Tie him up somewhere."

"What?" sputtered a terrified Dennis.

"Really? Tie him up?" Vance sounded surprised and uncertain. "Are we allowed to do that?"

"Or just make him go outside and don't let him back in! Just get rid of him!" Dean Bickerstaff was already mentally trying to crunch the numbers to figure out how much weed they were going to need and how that would affect the bottom line. It seemed like every step they took to maximize profits resulted in new costs and complications. Hopefully, when it came time to quote dollar figures, Mako would ignore the fact that he was the only supplier of a good they now desperately needed a lot of.

Vance looked satisfied with the second option and shoved Dennis toward the living room. "And don't come back!" he yelled as the terrified reporter scampered away.

Channel 9 would probably still run some less-than-flattering report filed from across the street, Frampton figured. It would almost certainly condemn his actions and ask if he were truly suited to run an institute of higher learning. They'd probably run that same damn photo they always used of him kicking a dog, which the paparazzi had snapped totally out of context. But without any footage of what was actually going on inside Cormac's house, the story would be toothless. The dean wasn't concerned.

The two men in towels looked at each other. A problem had arisen and they had dealt with it like professionals: by forcing strangers to ingest illegal drugs. Perhaps this was where their operation turned the corner, Dean Bickerstaff thought. He gave Vance a begrudging nod of respect. After a moment's consideration, his partner returned the gesture. And then a terrified female voice screamed out, "Oh my God, he killed him!" from Cormac's bedroom.

Vance's eyes went wide and Frampton felt his do the same. A hush fell over the hall outside Cormac's room as everyone within earshot quickly stopped talking and tried to hear what the girl said next.

"Holy crap . . ." the dean muttered under his breath.

"No kidding," Vance replied. "I totally lost track—that girl's gone way over the time she paid for."

"That's not what I meant, you idiot!" Dean Bickerstaff turned and bolted into the bedroom, with Vance right on his heels. Inside, the blonde girl who had cried out was still kneeling and peering into Cormac's right ear, while the Got Weed? guy was glued to his left.

"Hey!" barked Vance. "Time's up, freeloaders!" He started to approach the girl, but Dean Bickerstaff waved him away with his shillelagh. Vance veered to the other side of the bed and started to pull the Got Weed? guy away from Cormac's ear.

The dean knelt down next to the girl and gently placed his hand on her shoulder. Frampton was afraid to look too closely at Cormac on the off chance that the telltale breathing had finally ceased.

"Sweetie?" Frampton said, trying to remain calm. "Is everything OK?"

"He killed him . . ." she muttered, not looking up.

The dean gripped her shoulder tighter. "Who killed someone?" he asked her.

"This guy, the guy in the coma," she said, her eye still glued to the ear. "He harpooned a pirate!"

The dean ignored her misdiagnosis of Cormac's condition and breathed a sigh of relief. Cormac had not died on his watch. However, if the harpoons were flying, it was clear he wasn't out of the woods yet. Cormac was fighting for his life in a thrilling battle against bloodthirsty villains. This was serious business. This was a potential PR nightmare. This was an ideal opportunity to raise prices again.

The dean whacked the girl on her hip with the shillelagh. She yelped in surprise and popped her head up from the ear. "Take a hike, sweetheart," he told her. The girl frowned at the dean, then looked longingly back at the ear. The dean took the opportunity to give her a further shove with the shillelagh.

Reluctantly, she got to her feet and scooted out of the room before the dean could hit her again. Vance assisted Got Weed? to the door and gave him a shove to maintain his momentum out into the hallway. The assembled people in line were all quiet, and the dean could feel them all staring at him, waiting for an update.

Pausing a moment or two to maximize the anticipation, Frampton eventually raised his shillelagh in the air. "Don't worry folks! Cormac's not dead!" the dean exclaimed. There were more audible groans of disappointment and utterances of "goddammit" than the dean would have expected. People began exchanging money; evidently several wagers had been made with Cormac's death being the favored outcome.

There is an appalling lack of humanity lurking in some corners of this house, the dean mused to himself. Disgusting, just disgusting. Then he pushed the thought out of his head and informed the crowd that the cost to peer into an unconscious student's ear would double while said student was killing pirates.

The student at the front of the line looked uncertain about ponying up more dough, but the people behind him vocally indicated that they would be more than happy to take his place. Dean Bickerstaff had no patience for indecision at a critical moment like this. He refunded the student's money in the form of several wadded bills thrown in his face and menaced him with the shillelagh until he fled the scene sobbing.

Frampton waved the next two customers toward him, took their money, and passed them the joint. "Got to make sure you're not a spy," he said. The students did not ask for any further clarification. Frampton imagined he could just as well have said, "This is not marijuana. It is deadly ricin laced with industrial drain cleaner. Do not smoke it." These two weren't the types to turn down free things they could smoke.

The level of enthusiasm of the people waiting in line had greatly increased since the dean announced that Cormac had killed and might kill again. Additional onlookers had started to crowd the hallway. If there was pirate murdering going on, they wanted to be nearby when it happened. The dean got a sense that the crowd's collective intoxication level had risen rapidly in the past hour. He gripped his shillelagh tighter. Sadly, he realized that if an event of this size got out of control, dropping his towel to the floor might be the best crowd-control measure he had at his disposal.

The student who had taken the first hit was ready to go. He blew a smoke ring into the air as he passed the joint to the guy in line behind him, which got a huge reaction from the appreciative crowd. A few of the onlookers began to clap and chant "Pi-rates! Pi-rates!" The rest of the crowd was quick to join in, and the student whose turn it was reveled in the attention. He started to do a little dance toward the bedroom door, and the crowd went wild. When he reached the doorway, the student took a deep bow to thunderous applause. It then became apparent that he believed he had accomplished whatever his forgotten goal was, because he started to walk back down the hallway toward the living room.

Vance grabbed him and turned him around as the dean watched in disgust. Vance followed the stoned student into the bedroom and resumed his standard position in Cormac's desk chair. He shot the dean a thumbs up and barked a few instructions at the student. Frampton turned back toward the next student and instructed him to pass the joint back down the line in order to make sure everyone was clear. The next student had barely had a chance to smoke when an excited voice shouted "He got another one!" from the bedroom.

The gathered crowd erupted, and the next student looked upset that he had missed it. The dean waved him into the bedroom and pretended to monitor the crowd while actually keeping a keen ear on the activity in the bedroom. Just seconds after the other student took his place at Cormac's free ear, there were simultaneous yelps of excitement from the room. The crowd went nuts again in anticipation of whatever news the two students might have when their ear time was up.

When Vance escorted the first student out of the bedroom, the crowd held its breath. For a moment the kid looked terrified, as if he wasn't sure what he was supposed to do. Taking a wild stab at what he imagined the crowd wanted to see, he halfheartedly reprised his dance from minutes ago. The crowd responded with impatient silence. Even the music from outside went quiet. Dean Bickerstaff rolled his eyes and indicated to the next person in line that they should go ahead and enter, but the student waved him off. He wanted to hear what the last guy had seen.

Eventually a voice from the far end of the hallway yelled out, "What happened?"

The student who had just exited the bedroom thought about it for another second, then responded. "He got 'em. He shot two pirates." Outside, one of the DJs chose that moment to drop an absolutely massive beat. Pandemonium.

People were dancing and kissing each other like they were in the streets of New York on VJ Day. The next student in line threw his hands in the air and emitted a primal yell of victory, then charged into the bedroom at top speed. Several of the other students in line slung their arms around each other and started singing "Auld Lang Syne."

Typically, Frampton would have complained that the off-key New Year's tune contrasted horribly with the hip-hop blaring from the rest of the party. But even he had to admit that the moment was pretty great. He silently hoped someone had held up their cellphone to get a video of the announcement. Frampton lit a fresh cigar, took a swig of cognac, and passed the bottle to the closest person, expecting to never see it again. Scanning the room, he was even more delighted to see that everyone was on their cell phones, posting that everyone should drop whatever the hell they're doing and get their ass over here because Cormac is killing some goddamn pirates.

Dean Bickerstaff looked over at Vance. His partner was spraying a champagne bottle on a pair of girls who did not appear to have requested that specific act be performed. Vance briefly locked eyes with the dean. He had a huge grin on his face. For the time being, customers whacking it bedside seemed like the furthest thing from his mind. Which seemed like a healthy attitude, as far as the dean was concerned.

Frampton puffed his cigar and tried to detach himself from the euphoria. Taking some time to celebrate with everyone else was fine. It would help the students think of him as just one of the gang, make him seem more relatable, thought the wealthy, middle-aged man wearing just a towel and holding a shillelagh. But it was going to be up to him to keep this machine running smoothly. Cormac not dying at the hands of nineteenth century pirates also played a role, of course, but the dean would do all he could on this end of the space-time continuum.

At present, this meant forcing students to smoke illegal drugs to prove that they weren't muckraking journalists. The dean scanned the line of students, trying to determine who had hit the joint last. As he tried to locate it, the kid who had just seen Cormac kill the pirates shuffled past him toward the living room. To nobody in particular, the student muttered "I think that was the greatest moment of my life." Frampton would never admit it to anyone, but he had been thinking the exact same thing.

* * *

Cormac looked through the hole in the slave's quarters at the three pirates who were standing up with their hands in the air. They had sheepish, nervous looks on their faces. From what Cormac gathered, surrendering was never really looked favorably upon, and he imagined that pirates held it in a special kind of contempt. It didn't really fit with the swashbuckling lifestyle. Still, he couldn't blame them for trying.

"That's good," Cormac yelled through the hole. "Now drop your weapons and kick them away!" He watched as the pirates dropped their swords and pistols to the ground, then pushed them away with their feet. They glided smoothly across the well-swabbed deck of the *Levyathan*. Cormac stole a glance at Ziro and hoped the former slave was sizing up the quickest path to the weapons.

"Excellent," Cormac continued. "Now, you're free to go back to your boat, as soon as you answer me one question." The pirates fidgeted with their hands in the air, sensing that their freedom, shameful as it may be, was soon at hand.

"What's the best way to kill a pirate?" Cormac bellowed. The pirates looked confused

"Cholera claimed the lives of seventeen buccaneers on the *Mangy Cur* two years ago," one pirate stammered out. He was obviously still shaken by the memory.

"The best way to kill a pirate," Cormac continued, "is with an *Arrr*-poon!" He pulled the trigger on the harpoon gun and in a split second, the projectile spear shot through the air and struck the pirate who had just spoken in the chest. He toppled backwards, instantly dead.

"Eh? An *Arrrrr*-poon!" Cormac reiterated, feeling rather satisfied.

"My God!" yelled one of the other pirates who had attempted to surrender. "He had a wife and children!"

"Why aren't you pronouncing the 'h' in 'harpoon'?" the other surrendering pirate wailed.

"He was just trying to get home to them!" the first pirate continued.

Dammit, thought Cormac. From his English classes, he knew that a lot of what was considered "humor" back in the olden days hadn't actually been funny, but he assumed that killer material like "Arrr" jokes would transcend the boundaries of time. These idiots were probably too busy not laughing at *Poor Richard's Almanac* or Will Rogers to understand it. Oh well, it was their loss. He loaded another harpoon and considered tossing out the joke a third time just in case it needed one more repetition to really hit home.

"Arrr? Like the well-known pirate saying?" Cormac yell-asked.

"You've been grossly misinformed about pirate culture and blood has been shed as a result!" the first surrendering pirate cried.

"He told me just last night he was going to abandon pirating and join the clergy!" sobbed the second.

These guys were bumming everyone out, thought Cormac. No wonder his pirate jokes were going over so poorly. You couldn't be expected to deliver the laughs when two guys were lamenting how the guy you'd just killed had a family. Perhaps after he killed two more people, people might be more receptive to a few chuckles.

Cormac aimed the harpoon gun out the window and shifted it back and forth between the remaining two surrendering pirates. The other pirates were still lying on the ground, and the whalers were sitting in the same position they had been in initially. Cormac noted that Ziro's position had shifted among the whalers; he hoped that meant that by now, most of them were untied.

It was hard to be sure from this distance, but it appeared to Cormac that the pirate who had been so upset about his dead colleague's family was now crying. At least that made Cormac's decision easier. He pulled the trigger on the harpoon gun and the crybaby slumped to the ground a split second later.

That made it six dead pirates and six alive ones. The halfway mark was as good a time as any to take a moment to evaluate the situation, Cormac figured. He set down the harpoon gun, leaned back against the wall of the slave's quarters and flexed his mangled hand. Not a bad performance, Cormac thought to himself. Six direct hits, and on substantially smaller targets than he was used to. Of course, the last two hadn't even been moving. In fact, their hands raised straight up in the air as gesture of surrender actually straightened their posture, thus increasing their harpoonable surface area. But still, Cormac was pleased with his accomplishment.

Of course, he didn't want to get a big head about it. It's not like those dead pirates had anywhere near the same cash value as a whale. Now, if Ziro informed him that there existed a similar shady retail channel for pirate corpses as there had been for whale dicks, that would change everything. It would transform a morning of *pro bono* heroism into one of shrewd capitalistic endeavors. Cormac didn't want to admit that attaching a sizeable number of dollar signs to a murder spree would make the act much more attractive. He'd prefer it to remain about the sheer joy of killing. But he knew deep down that this was sadly not the case.

But before he had a chance to muse about the relationship between money and intrinsic enjoyment, a bullet burst through the wall two feet to the right of his head.

Cormac instinctively slid to the floor and looked up at the bullet hole. One of the remaining pirates must be attempting a desperate last-ditch bid for freedom. Hopefully, this would get Ziro and the rest of the crew moving. Cormac heard some distant, faint shouting from outside, but nothing that indicated that the whalers were overtaking the pirates. He waited a few more seconds to make sure that no more shots were being fired, then reached for the harpoon gun and gradually raised back up to peek out the hole.

Just as his eyes reached the level where they'd be able to see out onto the deck, a second bullet ripped through the wall of the slave's quarters. This time it was less than a foot above his head. Cormac fell back onto the ground and tried to lay as flat as possible. Obviously, one of the remaining pirates had him pinned down. Firing out of the hole wasn't something he was going to be able to do anymore. He'd have to leave the slave's quarters to get this job done.

Bursting out of the shelter and charging toward the pirates would obviously be suicide. He'd need some sort of distraction to buy him some time. Ideally it would be the sort of thing that would allow Ziro to give the whalers a signal to throw off their bindings and help subdue the pirates. But what the hell could he do to distract the pirates from this distance?

His head swimming, Cormac looked around the shed. It was hard to think clearly with this level of excitement, and the chemical-laced air of the slave's quarters wasn't making it any easier. While he'd been shooting out of the hole in the wall, it'd been much easier to get breaths of fresh air. Now that he was down on the same level as the cans and buckets of chemicals, Cormac was finding it harder and harder to breathe.

Wait a second . . . The chemicals! Cormac looked over at the collection of various cleaning supplies that Ziro had accumulated over the years. Some of this stuff had to be flammable. If he could dip a harpoon and then somehow light the end of it, he could have a flaming dead pirate as a distraction.

Cormac grabbed the nearest harpoon and crawled over to the collection of cleaning supplies. He lifted the neck of his shirt up over his mouth and nose as a makeshift breathing mask. The corroded buckets and cans of cleaning supplies bubbled and oozed liquids of diversely unnatural colors. Gripping the harpoon as far back on the shaft as he could, Cormac dipped the pointed end in one bucket, then the next, then four more down the line.

The chemicals hissed every time he dipped the harpoon, more and more as the combination of toxic oozes built up and interacted with each other. After he dipped it in the last bucket, Cormac took a look at the point of the harpoon, careful not to get it too close to his face. The smoke it emitted stung his eyes and the chemicals appeared to already be eating away at the steel harpoon tip.

Careful to not let it drip on Ziro's bedding or underwear, Cormac set the toxic harpoon down on the floor of the slave's quarters, where it bubbled and smoked and even started to turn a neon shade of green. Realizing that he had to act quickly, Cormac grabbed two more harpoons. All he had to do was rub the sharp metal points together to create a spark, ignite the chemicals on the tip of the third harpoon, then load it into the harpoon gun and shoot it out of the hole and into a pirate.

At this point Cormac realized that the fumes were definitely affecting his judgment. There was absolutely no way he was going to be able to start a fire with two pieces of metal. He had trouble starting a fire when he was working with a Duralog and a butane lighter. In fact, the pilot light had gone out on his stove four months ago and he'd been unable to figure out how to get even that relit. But still, he was a different man now, self-sufficient and wise in the ways of pre–Industrial Revolution America.

He rubbed the two harpoon points together furiously. No sparks. He kept rubbing. The noise they made was horribly unpleasant, but there was no sign of them ever producing something capable of igniting liquid chemicals on fire. Oh well, thought Cormac as he gave up on the futile task. At least there haven't been any more gunshots in a while. Maybe whoever was shooting thought one of the bullets had connected. Still careful not to breathe too deeply, he loaded the harpoon he'd dipped in the cleaning chemicals into the harpoon gun. Trying his hardest not to let the liquid drip on him, he grabbed the other two harpoons and crawled to the door of the slave's quarters.

Slowly, Cormac pushed the door open and waited for any sign of an ambush. After a few seconds passed without incident, Cormac continued to crawl out onto the open deck of the *Levyathan*. He turned to his left and ever so gradually peered out at the central area of the deck.

The surrendering pirate was still standing, but now there were three other pirates on their feet as well. These ones did not have their hands above their head, and two of them were brandishing guns. Cormac looked over at Ziro, Captain Anson, and the whalers. What the hell was Ziro doing letting these pirates get to their feet and start shooting at him? The whalers outnumbered the living pirates now, they should have rushed them while they were still lying on the deck!

He would hash that out with Ziro later. Hopefully, Ziro would have the good sense to take action after this next dead pirate.

Cormac gripped the harpoon gun with both hands and pointed it at the pirates. He sighted each of the four standing pirates one by one, but eventually settled on the pirate who was still attempting to surrender. Cormac was still fairly bitter about that guy's efforts to sabotage his "Arrr" joke. He was hoping that he'd be able to get some mileage out of it later with the whalers, and killing the people who had actively disparaged it might ensure that they were more receptive to it.

Cormac caressed the trigger until the wind felt right, then pulled it with a satisfying click.

The harpoon sailed through the air and landed in the pirate's outstretched right arm. The pirate cried out in pain, while his non-surrendering colleagues hurriedly looked around to try and pinpoint where the projectile had come from.

Cormac frowned. He hadn't been aiming for the arm, he had been hoping for a direct hit in the heart. A shot in the arm wasn't going to kill the pirate, which meant he'd just wasted one of his remaining harpoons. The pirate continued to scream, but it was of little satisfaction to Cormac. In fact, the guy seemed to be overdoing it. It was just a harpoon through the arm, and this guy was a hardened career pirate. Why the hell was he still shrieking at the top of his lungs?

But as Cormac watched, it quickly became apparent why the pirate was reacting the way he was. Before his fellow pirates even had a chance to help him pull the harpoon out, the flesh on his arm around the entry point began to emit green wisps of smoke. The other pirates watched in horror as the smoke grew thicker, and the unfortunate pirate's skin began to bubble and sizzle. Obviously, the combination of chemicals that Cormac had dipped the harpoon in was not something you wanted coming into contact with your skin.

The other pirates backed away from their screaming friend as the smoke thickened and the area of melting flesh began to expand. Nobody really seemed to know what to do. Throwing a bucket of water on him seemed like an obvious first thing to try, Cormac thought, but nobody appeared to be on the verge of moving.

Cormac couldn't blame them. This quite honestly seemed like the sort of thing most of them would be telling the grandkids about in thirty years. It would be irresponsible to look away. Plus, at the rate the guy's skin was dissolving, you'd be lucky if there was any more than a foot left to douse by the time you retrieved a bucket.

The harpoon fell away as the flesh that had been holding it went up in smoke. The clothes, skin, and muscle on the pirate's arm dissolved entirely, leaving behind only white bones. Everyone took a precautionary additional step back as the harpoon clanked to the deck. The melting pirate looked around helplessly as the path of dissolving skin crept over his shoulder and onto his torso.

The pirate stopped wailing for a moment to try and halt the spread of the caustic chemicals by blowing on the flesh they were currently dissolving, a gesture so naïve and obviously futile that Cormac found it sort of adorable. The blowing only served to increase the rate at which it spread, and soon his entire upper body had melted away, leaving behind a bright white ribcage. As the pirate gave one last anguished scream, Cormac couldn't help but wonder if his skeleton might be claimed for erotic scrimshaw purposes.

His most vital of organs now rendered into a bubbling ooze, the pirate collapsed to the deck, dead. Fearing splashback, the other pirates took two additional steps away as the body continued to melt. Cormac feared that the toxic stuff might spread to the deck of the *Levyathan*, but exposure to the chemicals through Ziro's regular swabbing routine must have built up some sort of protective layer, and the melting was contained to what was left of the former pirate.

As the final bits of clothing and skin dissolved away, the remaining five pirates could only stand there, dumbfounded, staring at the skeleton of their former crewmate. Ziro chose this moment to finally give his signal. The swift action of the whalers even caught Cormac off guard; the pirates were totally blindsided. Before any of them even realized that the captives had been untied, there were two brawny whalers behind each pirate, grabbing them by their arms and forcing them to the deck. The pirate skeleton continued to sizzle.

Cormac stood rooted to the wooden deck. For the first time all morning, he was aware of how fast his heart was pumping. Now that the risk had passed, the true enormity of what he'd just done descended upon him. Seven pirates. He'd killed seven pirates, three of whom were attempting to surrender. The agonized screams of the final pirate as his body melted away still echoed in his ears. My God, Cormac thought. The coolest thing I've ever done and video cameras won't be invented for a century.

Cormac picked up the two remaining harpoons from the deck and loaded one into the gun, just in case. Slowly he began to walk toward the chaotic scene unfolding in front of him. Ziro darted around from one fallen pirate to the next, instructing the whalers how to properly tie their hands behind their backs. To the side of the action, Captain Anson raised himself out of a hiding space behind a hardtack barrel. The captain scanned the deck to make sure all pirate threats had been eliminated, then proudly strode forth to taunt the helpless prisoners.

Captain Anson made a beeline for a particularly angry-looking pirate, and Cormac headed in that direction. When he got within earshot he could hear the captain loudly mocking the fallen pirate. The captive was lying on his stomach, his mouth gagged with a bandana while one whaler knelt on his back and another bound his wrists.

"How about that, Pete?" Captain Anson was shouting gleefully. "Looks like you idiots fell for the oldest trick in the book! The ol' 'crew pretends like they're going to throw their beloved captain overboard' ruse! Pirates fall for it every time!"

The two whalers who were tying Pete up shot each other a look. It was a look that Cormac interpreted as "I am moderately relieved to be free of the pirates" mixed with a heavy dose of "what a colossal dick, huh?" Nevertheless, Anson continued to gloat. Cormac watched as the captain began to dance a jig around the captive pirate.

"Ooh, I'm Pete," Captain Anson said in a mocking voice. "I'm the big bad pirate captain and I'm going to take all your whales and throw you overboard!"

"Captain?" Cormac said in disbelief.

"Dammit," muttered Pete through the bandana gag.

Captain Anson appeared not to have heard the interruption and continued his mockery. "Oh no, what's this? Harpoons? Eek, I surrender!" Here Captain Anson threw up his hands in an exaggerated surrender gesture, then screamed as he acted out getting hit by a harpoon. Pete winced at the recent memory of the death of the man who presumably had been his friend.

Captain Anson laughed, then knelt down next to Pete. The whalers decided that their work was done and went off in search of the nearest rum jug. They looked noticeably startled once they realized Cormac was standing there, and gave him a wide berth as they walked past. Cormac was puzzled by their reaction but then looked down at the harpoon gun in his hand. He *had* just killed seven people. He supposed that was the sort of thing that could cause people to look at you differently. Cormac figured that this newfound fear/respect would probably come in handy when the whalers discovered the severely reduced inventory in the rum storage area.

On the deck of the *Levyathan*, Captain Anson continued to taunt Pete. "That's right, Pete," Anson said, getting an inch or two from his foe's face. "You're not getting our ship. You're not getting our whales. You're not getting any of the gold the Chinese gave us for the giant pile of whale dicks we sold them."

"Pile of what now?" Pete mumbled through the gag.

Cormac decided that Captain Anson appeared to be occupied for the time being. He took a final disbelieving look at the man who was evidently the pirate captain and walked over to Ziro. The former slave was supervising two whalers as they finished tying up a pirate. Ziro noticed Cormac approaching and gave the whalers a final knot-tying tip before turning away from them and taking a few steps in his direction.

Ziro held his hands out in a "what the hell?" gesture that indicated he wanted an explanation. Cormac smiled and nodded knowingly. "Pretty great, huh?" he asked. Ziro just stood there with his mouth agape, shaking his head as if he didn't know what to say.

"Seven pirates dead, five captured," Cormac bragged. "I assume we kill those guys too, right? Maybe let some of our men use them for target practice? Sort of as a goodwill gesture for the rum I destroyed?"

The whalers exchanged alarmed glances. "Relax," Cormac told them. "You can re-up in St. Johns in four days." The whalers' looks shifted from alarmed to irritated, so Cormac hoisted the harpoon gun into a more prominent position. The whalers quickly decided that perhaps a few days of lessened rum consumption might do their health some good, and hauled the pirate away to join the rest of the captives.

"How ungrateful is that!?" Cormac asked Ziro, not noticing that his companion had yet to speak since he had rejoined him. "You kill seven pirates, they think why didn't you kill eight. Some people, huh? You want any hardtack? I haven't eaten all morning."

"You're insane!" Ziro blurted out.

Cormac raised his eyebrows. "Insane-ly talented with a harpoon gun?" he said in an optimistic attempt to complete Ziro's sentence.

"Those men were surrendering!" Ziro yelled.

"That's a common pirate tactic," Cormac replied. "Pretend to surrender, then the next thing you know they're making you their sex slave."

Ziro threw up his hands and changed the subject. "You know what? Let's just overlook wherever you are getting these wildly inaccurate ideas about pirates and focus on that last guy."

Cormac nodded and smiled. "How about that, huh?"

Ziro was flabbergasted by Cormac's nonchalant attitude. "How about that? You melted a person in fifteen seconds! That's outrageous! Does that happen all the time where you're from?"

"Hey, relax," Cormac said. He was getting kind of peeved that the words "thank you" had yet to be uttered by anyone since his killing spree ended. "I just dipped the harpoon in your cleaning supplies. By the way, I would strongly reconsider sleeping next to that stuff. The ship hits a big wave, the wrong combination of stuff spills on you, and you get dissolved in your sleep."

"My God," Ziro muttered in horror.

"So what's next?" Cormac asked. "Do we throw these guys overboard? What the hell do we do with their ship?"

Realizing that these practical questions actually needed to be addressed forced Ziro to stop dwelling on the memory of the melting pirate. He looked over at the *Mongrel*. The pirate ship floated off the side of the *Levyathan*, connected by the gangplank.

"We'll tow the ship to St. John's," Ziro said. "They have a pretty active shipyard, I'm sure we'll be able to sell it there. There's almost certainly a reward posted for the captain as well, so we'll probably keep him around until then. As far as the rest of his crew, that will probably be up to Captain Anson."

Cormac and Ziro looked over at the captain. He was still bouncing around, gleefully yelling insults at Pete. As Cormac watched, Captain Anson emphatically gestured at the pile of bones that had been the unlucky pirate. They were too far away to hear what he was saying, but he seemed to be instructing Pete to watch him.

Once he had the pirate captain's attention, as well as everyone else's, Captain Anson paused dramatically. Then he took off running toward the skeleton. As he approached it, the captain drew his right foot back and delivered a running kick to the pile of bones as if it were a football on a tee. The pirate's skull flew into the air and soared in a glorious arch over the side of the *Levyathan*, until it eventually landed in the ocean with a small splash.

Captain Anson turned to face Pete again with a wide smile on his face. Evidently he had made whatever point he had set out to make. Anson began to walk back toward the captives, but after just a few steps he stopped in his tracks. He looked confused, a look that quickly turned to terror once he peered down at his feet. The boot he had kicked with was emitting faint wisps of smoke. There must have been residual chemicals on the bones, which were now eating away at his shoe.

The captain shrieked at the top of his lungs and started to run in panicked circles. As the smoke started to rise faster, he stopped running and began to shake his foot back and forth in an effort to work the boot off. Unfortunately, balancing on one foot while violently flinging the other one around proved difficult, and after a few seconds the captain toppled backwards. He landed on the deck with a thud, and, still shrieking, continued to flail his foot in a kicking motion. The well-secured boot unfortunately did not appear to be going anywhere.

Still lying on his back, and still screaming his head off, Captain Anson pulled his knee toward his chest and gingerly plucked at the laces of the boot. His first two or three tentative stabs were not successful, but eventually he was able to grasp the end of the lace long enough to untie the knot. Now that the shoe was somewhat loosened, the captain pushed himself up off the ground and hobbled over to the side of the boat, where he grasped the railing and resumed swinging his foot back and forth. The dissolving boot started to slip off his foot and soon, with one final sweeping kick, it sailed off his foot, over the railing, and into the sea.

Huffing and puffing, Captain Anson looked down to make sure the chemicals had not spread onto his foot. Once he was satisfied that the menace had passed, he turned and limped his way back toward the center of the deck, taking great care to avoid the now-headless skeleton. He ignored Pete and the rest of the captives. Whatever point he had been trying to make had surely been overshadowed by the absurdity of his recent brush with death. Instead the captain headed for Cormac and Ziro.

"I'm going to need to borrow your right boot," Captain Anson informed Ziro as he approached them. "I'm not sure if you noticed, but mine appears to have gone missing."

"Absolutely not," said Ziro.

"We'll discuss it when you're prepared to be civil," Captain Anson replied. Cormac cleared his throat and finally the captain appeared to notice him.

"Cormac, my boy!" the captain said, slinging a weary arm around Cormac's shoulders. "That was quite a display you put on out there. You really saved our hides, I can't thank you enough."

"I appreciate that," said Cormac. "It was my pleasure."

"Can you talk to Ziro about lending me his boot?" the captain asked in a conspiratorial tone. "I think he might listen to you."

"I am right here!" Ziro shot back indignantly. "Sir, why do you even want my shoe? You have several extra pairs of boots in your closet! I've seen them with my own eyes!"

"Yeah, but they're all the way over there," the captain whined. Ziro stared at him. Sensing he was not going to receive any sympathy, Captain Anson sighed. "Fine, you can keep your stupid boot. But clean up those bones, some idiot could get himself killed with those things just sitting there."

"What are you going to do with the pirates?" Cormac asked.

"Whale bait," the captain said as if it were a stupid question. "Toss them overboard and those filthy scavengers will swoop in to scarf them down their vile gullets. They grow fat off of refuse and mock those of us who work for our keep!" He was quickly getting worked up. "To mock man! To taunt man! This is what the whale lives for! And yet, if man were to be driven off this mortal coil by the incessant hectoring of his mighty foe, the whale would weep, for there would be no more purpose left to its foul existence!" The captain shook his spyglass at the sky as Cormac tried to figure out what the hell he was talking about.

When the captain was finished cursing and lamenting, he turned his attention back to Cormac and Ziro. "So yeah, toss the pirates overboard and harpoon the whales when they come to eat them," he instructed.

"I think you may be thinking of sharks," Cormac said.

"The kindly shark?" the captain sputtered. "Man's best friend? How dare you impugn their good name on my ship!"

Ziro butted in before the captain had a chance to get physical. "Sir, a captured pirate captain usually brings in a hefty reward. Might I suggest we at least hang on to Pete and see what kind of a price he might fetch in St. John's?"

"Sure, sure," the Captain said, "As much as I'd like to see him torn asunder by the jaws of those behemoths, it will be even more satisfying to hand him over to someone in exchange for a lot of money. And speaking of money, we're not made of it! I want you two to pull those harpoons out of those dead pirates and reuse them when the whales come!" Having issued this command, and thus in his mind restored a semblance of order on his ship, Captain Anson limped off to his quarters to retrieve a new shoe.

Cormac wasn't thrilled at the assigned duty, but he was eager to add a few dead whales to the day's haul, so he walked off toward the pirate corpses. Ziro was already ahead of him, carrying out the grim task he'd been assigned. Cormac watched Ziro's technique for prying the harpoon out, which involved pinning the corpse down with his foot and jimmying the harpoon back and forth a few times before pulling it straight out in one motion. Cormac gave it a shot on the nearest pirate and found that the harpoon came free surprisingly easily.

Cormac wrested a second harpoon free before he came to the corpse of the Black Barnacle. After taking a moment to try to come to grips with the fact that this guy had not been the pirate captain, Cormac placed his foot on the dead man's chest. He gripped the harpoon and was ready to try and pull it out when he stopped. He looked down at the corpse for a few seconds, then called for Ziro to come over.

"What is it?" Ziro asked as he walked up, three harpoons tucked under his arm.

"Look at this guy," Cormac said, pointing down at the Black Barnacle. "I could have sworn he was wearing an eye patch when I shot him."

Ziro looked down at the corpse. the Black Barnacle's eye patch was definitely missing. It had been covering an empty, withered eye socket that now stared back at Cormac and Ziro.

"He had an earring, too," Ziro remarked. Their puzzlement did not last long, because Captain Anson loudly shoved his way in between the two of them a moment later. The captain had retrieved a new boot from his quarters and was now walking normally again. His boisterous demeanor was one of a man who had forgotten that his own idiocy nearly caused him to be eaten alive by caustic chemicals just minutes before.

"There we go! Look at those harpoons, that's what I like to see!" The captain pounded Cormac on the back enthusiastically. "Let's start hauling in a catch, huh boys?"

"Where did you get that earring?" Ziro asked Captain Anson. Cormac hadn't noticed, but the captain was now sporting a gold hoop earring that he couldn't recall ever seeing him wear before.

"Oh this?" Captain Anson said, attempting to sound nonchalant. "Yeah, it's not even a big deal. It's pretty cool though, huh?" The captain tilted his head in a very unnatural way, clearly so that Cormac and Ziro would have no choice but to take a closer look at it.

"How soon after he died did you take that off the Black Barnacle's body?" Ziro asked.

"What? Don't be ridiculous, Ziro." The captain did his best to sound offended. "I didn't steal jewelry off a dead guy!"

"It must have been almost instantaneous," Ziro continued. "You must have run over to loot his corpse as soon as I set everyone free, when all the other men were running to subdue the pirates who were going to throw you overboard."

Captain Anson rocked back on his heels and stalled for time. He had obviously not thought his lie through.

"Did you take his eye patch, too?" Cormac broke the silence.

"His eye patch? Of course not!" the captain stammered. "I don't even need an eye patch!"

"So if you turned out your pockets right now, they wouldn't have the eye patch in them?" Ziro inquired knowingly.

"Look, that eye patch kicks ass!" Captain Anson admitted. "It's got a skull and crossbones on it! As captain, I'm entitled to loot all corpses on my ship before the crew gets a crack at looting!"

"That's definitely not a rule," Ziro informed him.

"You sterilized that earring before you shoved it through your ear, right?" Cormac asked.

"Did what?" Captain Anson replied.

"You've got to pour some rum on that earring," Cormac said.

"On your ear, too. I'm sure that pirate hadn't showered in months and you just shoved all of his germs into an open wound."

"It does feel like my ear has been set on fire," Captain Anson admitted. "I assumed that was something that all those earring guys were just dealing with all the time."

"Also, I might have destroyed the rum storage area and all the rum." Cormac figured this was as good a time as any to inform the captain of this. Captain Anson looked surprisingly nonplussed about the news.

"All of the rum?" He said coyly. "Oh, I think you'd have trouble destroying *all* of the rum on board this ship."

"You keep a secret stash of rum hidden from all the men?" Ziro interpreted. "How long have you been doing that? They'd be furious if they found out!"

"Dammit, Ziro!" barked the captain. "You weren't supposed to figure that out!"

"You hint was pretty obvious," Cormac told the captain. "Why did you even mention it? Why didn't you just excuse yourself and go sterilize the earring without telling us what you were doing?"

"That's not what an earring guy would do!" the captain protested. "They say confident stuff and then wink so you know they meant something else!"

"You forgot to wink," Ziro informed him.

"Dammit, Ziro! Look, I'm going to go and tend to my ear. You two get those pirates tossed overboard and start hauling in some whales. Oh, and Cormac." The captain looked at Cormac and jutted his chin toward his shoulder, awkwardly emphasizing his new earring. "Shoot the first one of those bastards with this."

Captain Anson grabbed the harpoon that was still sticking out of the Black Barnacle's neck. He gave it a hefty tug, but was unable to remove the well-entrenched projectile. After adjusting his grip on the shaft of the harpoon, Anson pulled once more, but it did not budge. The captain's shoulders slumped and without saying a word, he turned and rapidly marched off toward his quarters. His earring glistened in the afternoon sun.

* * *

Dean Bickerstaff gulped the last swig of water from a red plastic cup and immediately refilled it from the kitchen tap. He downed about half of this new water, refilled the cup to the brim, and headed back toward the hallway. He needed to pace himself. There was still work to be done.

The dean wasn't in the habit of getting drunk, sobering back up, then getting drunk again in the span of a single afternoon. But then again, drinking usually meant expensive spirits and toasting the memories of the foes he'd crushed that day. Today's drinking, for the sole purpose of getting drunk and seeing what would happen, was an outlier. But Frampton would be damned if it wasn't a lot of fun.

Out in the hallway, Dean Bickerstaff was relieved to see that the mood remained relatively subdued. Of course at this party, "subdued" just meant that the dean could spot no more than four dogs wearing sunglasses. Back when Cormac was in the middle of killing all those pirates, Frampton could have sworn he'd seen at least seven dogs wearing sunglasses roaming the hallway and living room. He didn't know where they had come from, but they were the coolest dogs he'd ever seen.

Cormac's heroics on the *Levyathan* had continued to whip everyone into a frenzy. The partygoers had really embraced their role as Cormac's cheering section. It was as if they were the audience at a great action movie or an exciting sporting event—just one that only two of them could watch at a time. Whenever a customer exited Cormac's room, a hush fell over the crowd. You could even hear people outside telling people to quiet down so the people inside the packed house could relay them a message.

When someone reported that Cormac had harpooned a pirate, there were cheers. When they reported that Cormac was dodging bullets, the crowd gasped. When one guy reported that Cormac did not kill anyone because he was dipping one harpoon in some buckets and rubbing two other harpoons together, the crowd booed, and a small but frenzied mob chased the guy who had delivered that report from the party. The dean had never seen anything like it.

The only time that people seemed on the verge of losing their enthusiasm was when a terrified-looking young lady emerged from the bedroom and started sobbing about how Cormac had melted a pirate with a magic harpoon. A few people in the crowd thought this was the greatest news of the evening and promptly lit off some fireworks indoors. But the girl seemed really shaken up by the vision and the rest of the crowd wasn't sure how to respond. She kept crying about how she could smell the dissolving flesh, a claim that the dean sincerely doubted. Eventually the small but frenzied mob returned and the dean slipped them forty dollars to chase off the terrified girl as well.

When people started reporting that the pirates had been captured and Cormac was no longer actively killing people, it felt like the room collectively exhaled for the first time in a while. The dean announced that the cost of admittance would be reduced back to where it had been at the start of the day. Everyone who was in line already stayed there. After all, the reports were that it looked like the crew was getting ready to do some whaling. But most of the crowd that had gathered outside Cormac's bedroom retreated back to the living room and the front yard.

As far as Dean Bickerstaff was concerned, this lull was just fine. Cormac killing the pirates had been a "where were you when" flashbulb moment that nobody in the room would ever forget. For some people, the answer to that question was "on the front lawn mooning the cult." For others, it was "trying to buy the awesome sunglasses off of the guy behind you in line who turned out to be a dog." And for one unfortunate guy, the answer was "being carried off by the bandana men after nearly spilling a beer on Cissy's porch couch."

The best part was, for every person who had been at the Craymore Street house that afternoon, there would be at least ten more people who got texts or read about it online who would claim they were there as well. These liars' stories were just as viral in the impartial eyes of the X-Factor ranking. Chronicled under the

#CormacsEar hashtag, Cormac's accomplishments were spreading across the internet like a new, often misspelled type of folklore.

There were some whispers in the crowd, mostly by people who didn't seem to be drinking enough and who the dean pegged for churchgoing types, that Cormac's pirate killing was not the sort of thing that should be celebrated. In fact, some people were calling it "multiple counts of felony murder." Frampton wasn't too worried about this. He figured that the only effect this would have would be to make these people keep their distance from Cormac on the alternate days when he was conscious.

The dean of course had no objection to Cormac defending himself. His only concern was that all the recent focus on murder might cause some people to apply undue scrutiny to the heavy-handed techniques employed by the bandana men. So far none of the people who Mako's goons had dragged away had actually turned up dead, and the dean was pretty sure that without a body, you technically didn't have a murder case. All that aside, the dean had to admit he would not be able to confidently state whether more people had died this week on the *Levyathan* or in the vicinity of the Craymore Street house.

Dean Bickerstaff pushed these negative thoughts from his mind and reminded himself that he was at a party. He finished off the water in his cup, tossed it over his shoulder, and lit up a cigar. The smoke from his *Romeo y Julieta* mingled with the stench of marijuana, spilled beer, and wet cool dog that wafted through the living room. Frampton spied Cissy in her usual place on the airborne couch and raised his shillelagh to her. Cissy pretended to fall asleep to avoid acknowledging him, but unfortunately she had attempted her deception in the middle of a swig of Bloody Mary and most of her drink spilled down the front of her shirt. Sitting next to her, Mako snapped his fingers twice and in the corner of the room one of his minions sprang into action.

As the dean watched, the servant offered the most attractive girl within his immediate vicinity fifty dollars for her shirt. Tipsy and determined to let the good times roll, the girl complied, stripping down to just her bra as the appreciative crowd applauded and encouraged each other to drink to celebrate the occasion. The minion silently presented the shirt to Mako, who nodded in approval and instructed him to hand it over to Cissy. Cissy looked skeptical of the garment, but eventually she decided she was probably due for a wardrobe change one of these days and departed the couch to change in the bathroom.

Dean Bickerstaff looked over at the woman who had given her shirt up. She was now posing for pictures with two of the coolest looking sunglasses dogs. The dean admired Mako's skill at crisis management. The drug dealer had solved a problem while at the same time elevating the party to new heights of fun that bordered on "beer commercial" level. But as much as he wanted to appreciate the good times, Frampton couldn't stop thinking about the murmurs of the concerned people who were worried that Cormac, the unconscious man at the heart of their celebration, was technically a vicious murderer. The dean feared the crowd might turn on their comatose portal to the nineteenth century. And God forbid anybody tried to get the present-day authorities involved. The dean knew that possibility was remote, but it was far too easy for him to imagine the sound of police sirens.

The dean cocked his head to one side and tried to concentrate. He *was* imagining the sound of police sirens, wasn't he? But as Dean Bickerstaff listened, the sound grew louder and louder. As other students turned their attention toward the source of the sound, Frampton realized there were sirens approaching the Craymore Street house. The sirens got louder and louder for a few seconds, until they abruptly came to a stop outside.

Frampton hoped that the police were just there to deal with the disturbance that Brock and his followers were causing. Or perhaps one of the food vendors did not have their permits in order. He peered out one of the windows and saw that sadly, this was not the case. Two uniformed policemen were making their way toward the front door. Outside, the party continued at essentially the same pace. A few of the more sober attendees stood off to the side and watched the police approach, plotting their getaway in the extremely likely event that tear gas was deployed. But most people's judgment was impaired enough that they were beyond the point of caring. In fact the DJ's music seemed to escalate in volume to celebrate the arrival of the new guests, one of the food vendors announced a temporary two-for-one special on churros while police were on the premises, and one of the cool sunglasses dogs was so unconcerned that he started licking his butt in the middle of the living room floor. People cheered.

Slightly puzzled by this attitude, the dean made his way to the door. He knew that the police would be willing to look the other way once they realized that their beloved benefactor Dean Frampton Q. Bickerstaff was one of the hosts of the party. Frampton would wager that nobody else at the party had made the systematic bribing and blackmail of the Harrington Police Force a priority for the past twenty years. The dean hoped that this interaction with the police would go smoothly. At least if it didn't, he had the numbers on his side.

In preparation for schmoozing the boys in blue, Dean Bickerstaff reached down to straighten his tie and grasped only a tuft of chest hair. He looked down and remembered that he had only been wearing a towel since early that morning. Frampton silently cursed Vance's name and tried to remember if he had ever addressed the police in such a state before. Avoiding interactions with police while shirtless had been a key point in a Harrington commencement speech he'd given over a decade ago, and here he was, about to disobey his own advice. And yet, in that same speech, Frampton had strongly reiterated the value of paying people in positions of power so they would compromise the ideals of the public in favor of your own. Reporting on the speech, the *School Paper* had called it "a disgrace" and "we cancelled the UN Secretary General for this?" But clearly, the wisdom Frampton imparted had been valuable and timeless.

The dean took a deep breath and told himself this was true as he thrust the door open and greeted the two policemen, wearing just a towel.

Frampton immediately relaxed upon opening the door. Two irritated-looking cops stood outside, but their faces were familiar to the dean. The officer on the left sported a mustache and a crew cut, and the dean immediately recognized him as someone who had inquired several years ago about the possibility of doctoring his Harrington transcript to increase his chances of being accepted to the police academy. Dean Bickerstaff had quoted him an outrageous rate, then informed the unfortunate prospective officer that he would be informing the police department about his attempted fraud the next day, disqualifying him from any potential jobs on the force. Unless of course, he was willing to keep the dean in mind during his tenure as a police officer, in which case Frampton was perfectly willing to knock a few zeroes off the price of a transcript.

The second guy was someone who the dean had naked pictures of. Not as elegant a scam, but it had the same end result.

Dean Bickerstaff smiled broadly, neglecting to remove his cigar from his mouth. He casually swung his shillelagh back and forth, anticipating a quick encounter.

"Hello gentlemen," the dean smirked. "Is there a problem?" He looked for a hint of recognition or, preferably, trembling fear from either of the men. Instead, the two policemen just peered around him, trying to get a look at the party inside.

"We've had some complaints about the noise," said the officer with the mustache. "Well, the noise and the trespassing, cars parked in front of driveways, sidewalk urination, arson, public nudity, firearms being discharged, widespread intoxication, gang beatings, and unlicensed pony rides."

"Those sons of bitches told me they had a valid license!" Frampton roared, before taking a moment to calm himself. "That is to say, there must be some mistake," the dean said, trying to sound far less crazy than a man in just a towel typically would.

"Sir, are you a resident here?" the second cop asked. It was as if they didn't recognize him at all!

"Of course I'm not a resident here," Dean Bickerstaff responded. "I don't live in this dump, I'm Dea—"

The first policeman cut the dean off and gestured with his billy club that he should step out of the doorway. "I'm sorry, sir. I'm sure you're having a great time here, but we don't have time for any nonsense. We've got to talk to the person who lives here about shutting this party down."

Dean Bickerstaff refused to budge. He glared back and forth at the two policemen, waiting for the telltale moment where one of them would realize the terrible mistake they were making. But neither one of them showed any signs of recognition, and eventually the mustache cop stepped through the doorway and pushed the dean out of the way.

"You son of a bitch!" Frampton yelled. "Do you have any idea who I am?" As soon as the words left his mouth, Dean Bickerstaff regretted them. He had heard people yell those words before. Feeble people, right as they had realized that he was about to crush them. If you were somebody important, it was one of the last things you ever wanted to resort to saying, other than "I'd like to make a reservation for one at this Denny's."

The second cop stopped in his tracks and looked back at the dean. He pointed his club at the dean's face. "Watch it, towel boy," he said with a stern expression on his face. "We've had numerous complaints about this party and we're here to shut it down. Now step aside and let us do our job."

Numerous complaints? How was that possible! Who would complain? The entire campus must have trickled through the house at some point in time over the past few days. This had to be the work of the board! It all made sense, the dean thought to himself. Unable to control the incredible viral success of the #CormacsEar campaign, the board was resorting to a last-ditch Hail Mary to stop Harrington's X-Factor rating from soaring any higher than it undoubtedly already had. The dean scoffed audibly at this sad little attempt as the cops wandered into the living room. This party was far too awesome for two cops to shut down on their own.

And yet, as the cops strode into the living room, the dean saw that they were already having a noticeable effect. People who had been smoking joints freely hid them behind their backs. The girl who had relinquished her shirt to Cissy crossed her arms over her chest and retreated behind the stack of empty kegs. Even several of the dogs appeared to have removed their sunglasses in an attempt to appear as normal, uncool dogs. More than anything so far, this made the dean feel utterly betrayed.

"Smells like marijuana in here," the mustache cop said to his partner. The partner nodded and looked around, trying to identify a source. For the first time, the dean realized that if these two policemen actually intended on arresting people who were breaking the law, the results could be disastrous. Virtually every person here had consumed massive quantities of illegal substances. And many of them had done so at the insistence of two men who they could easily identify: the only two guys wearing towels.

Dean Bickerstaff rushed up behind the two cops, determined to appear more contrite this time around. "Excuse me officers. I'm sorry," he said as he fell into step behind the two cops. "I'm not sure if you recognized me under the circumstances, but I'm Frampton Q. Bickerstaff. *Harrington Dean* Frampton Q. Bickerstaff."

The two police officers stopped in their tracks and turned around. They looked at the dean with another expression that he recognized all too well. It was the expression of a man who was swallowing a bitter pill and choosing between the lesser of two evils. But for the first time that the dean could remember, betraying him—and the horrible consequences that would invite—was the lesser evil.

The cops pursed their lips and glumly shook their heads at the dean. Frampton thought he detected a vague hint of "at least hold off on publishing those naked pictures until my elderly grandmother kicks the bucket in a few months" in the second cop, but Frampton was unwilling to entertain such a compromise. If the cop didn't want people snapping his photo, he shouldn't have passed out naked on a Little League field.

Guests and dogs were starting to inch their way toward the front door to avoid confrontation with the cops. The policemen themselves were now rounding the stadium seating couches, a structure they eyed with a mixture of awe and disgust. The mustache cop shook his head and muttered something about how many drugs must have been involved in the construction of the couches. Dean Bickerstaff imagined it was an all too accurate assessment of the situation.

As the officers rounded the couches and turned down the hallway, Frampton rapidly sized up his options. The powerless sensation he was feeling was not one that he cared for, and he was on the verge of lapsing into several panic-induced shillelagh beatings when he heard a voice boom out from across the living room.

"Who the hell let these pigs into my party?" The cigar fell out of Dean Bickerstaff's mouth as his jaw dropped in surprise. The expensive smuggled cigar fell to the ground and the dean put it out with the end of his shillelagh while he and the police officers scanned the room trying to determine who had spoken. The dean located the source before the officers: Mako. Sitting on the side of the airborne couch with a wide grin on his face, he was staring directly at the two cops.

The dean braced himself as the two officers furiously tried to figure out who had uttered the slur. Their expressions were not ones of men who were amused. They were more like ones of men who had just found the tear-gassing excuse they had been looking for. Frampton wondered how far the bandana men's loyalty extended. Dragging off mostly innocent civilians was one thing, but disappearing armed officers of the law had to constitute an entirely different pay grade.

The cops did not pinpoint Mako as their heckler until the drug dealer grew impatient and blew a large cloud of marijuana smoke toward them. As they waved the smoke away from their faces, the two cops finally realized who their man was. The dean noticed them instinctively grip their billy clubs as they took the first step toward Mako.

And then they both stopped! The dean couldn't believe it. The two men were staring straight ahead, frozen in their tracks. A few feet behind them, Frampton realized that without being aware of it, he had raised his shillelagh up over his head, ready to crack one of the officers on the back of the neck the moment the situation warranted it. Trying to remain casual, he lowered the blunt object and looked around to make sure that nobody had seen him prepare to assault the policemen. But everyone who still remained in the immediate vicinity was transfixed by the scene playing out in front of them.

Eventually the mustache cop spoke up. "Milo?" He said, sounding unsure. "This is one of *your* parties?"

Mako looked over his shoulder and chuckled nervously. "Milo?" he asked the cop. "No, there aren't any Milos here." He waved his hand at his throat in an irritated cut-it-out gesture that the dean took to mean "ix-nay on the ilo-may." Frampton moved in closer to get a better look at the interaction.

The mustache cop stammered in a panic to correct himself. "Sorry, Mako," he said, putting extra emphasis on the drug dealer's evident nickname. "Mako! This gentleman's name is Mako!" he announced to the crowd before continuing. "We didn't know you guys were here, we don't want any trouble."

Mako smiled, the Milo-calling incident evidently forgotten, at least for the time being. At Mako's side on the couch, Cissy flipped open her laptop and began to jot down a note. Without turning around, Mako reached out to his side and closed the laptop again. Cissy looked put out for a second, then leaned back and quickly fell asleep.

"Look, we should have just kept driving," the second cop was saying apologetically. "We had no idea that you were running things here."

"Excuse me, gentlemen," Dean Bickerstaff said, stepping into the area between the policemen and the airborne couch. "But I happen to be the one running things here, and if I'm not mistaken, both of you are on my payroll as well. So it really should be the corruption that *I've* blackmailed you into that is causing you to leave us alone."

The two policemen looked at each other. The mustache cop shook his head at the dean. "Sorry, Dean Bickerstaff," he said. "You know that I'm forever in your debt. But Mako and G-Dimes are shaking down the police on an entirely different level. Really advanced, sinister stuff that they've got us neck deep in. If we have to choose which of you we're more beholden to because of bribes and corruption . . . Well forgive me, sir, it's going to be Mi—I mean, Mako."

"Hands down," the second cop added, before whispering, "But please don't print those pictures. I beg of you."

"But I've been blackmailing you for years!" Dean Bickerstaff said, ignoring the plea while trying to mask the hurt in his voice. "I've got the blackmail precedent established!"

"Sorry, sir," the mustache cop said sadly. "But length of blackmail tenure is just one of many factors to consider when you're establishing a blackmail hierarchy."

"Dammit!" Frampton sputtered. He pulled a new cigar out from the waistband of his towel and bit the end of it off. The dean lit the stogie and puffed it until a gigantic cloud of smoke enveloped him. How long had he been the second most powerful person blackmailing the Harrington Police Force? More importantly, how many other people were out there subverting his corruption efforts by offering more efficient and devastating blackmail? The thought of it made Dean Bickerstaff furious.

Mako seemed amused though, and calmly puffed his blunt and nodded as the two policemen stammered through a drawn-out apology. When his cloud of cigar smoke subsided, the dean looked around the living room. The tension seemed to have evaporated, and partygoers were back to drinking, smoking, and grinding on each other. And that was just the dogs.

Eventually, the policemen expressed enough contrition that Mako seemed satisfied. He passed them each a blunt, which the officers tucked into their pockets before walking off to one of the kegs in the corner to fill up a beer. The dean glared at them as they walked by.

"I trust we'll see you at the annual Police Benevolent Society Gala, Dean Bickerstaff?" the mustache cop said. "I believe there might be an opening for the role of charity auctioneer this year."

Dean Bickerstaff's ears perked up. Being the auctioneer at the Benevolent Society gala was one of his favorite things to do. He loved pounding the gavel and intimidating people into spending money they didn't have on stuff they didn't need. Unfortunately, in recent years the police wives had complained that his conduct was unbecoming of a charity auctioneer. Foul language and gaveling things that were not intended to be gaveled were the two main complaints, though the incident where he mistakenly identified the commissioner's wife as the item up for auction instead of the bracelet she was modeling was the final straw. The dean had made a series of lewd comments to entice bidders, then presided over a frenzied betting war before outbidding everyone himself and thrusting himself upon the poor woman.

The offer to reprise the duty was merely an olive branch, and clearly there would have to be further steps taken to atone for the slight the dean had just suffered. But for now it would do. He shook the mustache cop's hand, then nodded respectfully at the second cop. "Please no pictures," the cop whispered. "I'm just starting to turn things around with my kids."

Dean Bickerstaff pretended not to hear him. "I'll see you two at the gala," he said with a thin smile. The dean puffed on his cigar as he watched the two officers fill up red cups with beer, then turned to address his friends on the airborne couch.

"So," the dean said. "Milo?"

Mako waved away some blunt smoke dismissively. "Cops, huh?" the drug dealer said. "You can't believe a word out of their mouths." The dean looked unconvinced and Mako realized that he wasn't going to forget about the slipup so quickly.

"How's that weed supply holding up down at the bedroom, Dean B?" Mako asked. "Testing everyone who walks in that door to make sure they're not a reporter? You must be running through it pretty quickly." Dean Bickerstaff nodded. This new requirement had put a noticeable dent in their bottom line. Even with the bulk discount Mako had offered them, they were still spending more money than he'd hoped on drugs, and Frampton wasn't sure their customer base would tolerate yet another rate hike to offset the cost.

"Tell you what," Mako said. "Why don't we cover your supply for the rest of the day?"

"I'm not sure, Milo," Frampton said, making sure it was loud enough for Cissy to hear. "I'd sleep better if I knew we were well stocked for the next session, too."

Mako puffed his blunt and nodded his head as he sized up the dean's request. Before Mako could respond, Dean Bickerstaff felt a bare hand on his shoulder. He turned around and saw that G-Dimes had silently sidled up behind him. He was holding a plastic bag that was big enough to brine a Thanksgiving turkey, filled to the bursting point with marijuana. Wordlessly, he thrust it toward the dean.

Dean Bickerstaff took the bag, and was surprised by how heavy it was. He could feel eyes all around the living room staring at him. It was obviously the most marijuana anyone in the room had ever seen. Mustache cop looked particularly impressed.

"Thank you, G-Dimes," the dean said. G-Dimes unsteadily swayed back and forth in response. Frampton turned back to the couch.

"Thank you . . . *Mako*," he said pointedly. Mako flashed a smile that was all business and nodded. The thrill of a successful negotiation still filled the dean with excitement and he stood up straight as his bare chest swelled with satisfaction. His head barely reached the soles of Mako's shoes.

Dean Frampton Q. Bickerstaff clutched his enormous bag of weed tightly as he turned and walked down the hall toward Cormac's bedroom. Loud music blared from outside and the dean noticed the two cops refilling their beers. Behind him Mako called out, "Numbers four hundred and twenty through four hundred and forty, grab a beer and get in line!" A cheer went up from the lucky few whose turn had arrived. The dean gave his shillelagh a twirl and smiled.

* * *

Cormac leaned over the railing of the *Levyathan* and observed the four pirates thrashing about as they tried to stay afloat. For men who had spent most of their lives on the water, they looked surprisingly uncomfortable actually being immersed in it. Cormac noted that this appeared to be much more related to the fact that their hands were bound behind their backs rather than a fear that any minute, bloodthirsty whales were going to arrive and devour them.

Captain Anson stood to Cormac's right, also watching the pirates attempt to tread water. The captain's earring ear was red and swollen. He had doused it in rum, a process which, judging from the scream that echoed across the deck, had been extremely painful. Some of the rum had evidently poured into his ear canal as well, and every so often the captain would turn his head at a ninety-degree angle and jump up and down in an attempt to dislodge the liquid. For the most part, the stubborn rum stayed put. But every time a few ounces of it were dislodged, it stung the wound again and the captain shrieked in pain. For an item of jewelry he had tried to pretend wasn't that big of a deal, it would have been impossible for him to call more attention to it.

"I don't think they're going to attract any whales," Cormac informed the captain.

"You just wait," Captain Anson said as he pushed the palm of his hand against his ear over and over, like he was plunging a toilet. "Those filthy jackals will be here any minute to scarf down their unfortunate prey. You got those harpoons ready?"

Cormac held up the loaded harpoon gun and clutched the trigger with his index finger. Captain Anson's head was tilted so that it was parallel to the ground, so he approximated the closest thing he could to a nod of approval. The awkward nod evidently loosened a few drops of rum, and the Captain yelped in pain as it stung his open wound.

Cormac tried to avoid laughing at the captain's predicament and was relieved to see a welcome distraction approaching in the form of Ziro. The former slave had been tasked with seeing that Pete was secured in the cold storage area. Pete hadn't been thrilled about the arrangement, but nobody was really concerned with providing the pirate captain luxurious accommodations. Captain Anson had indicated that if Pete continued to complain, there still appeared to be a thick layer of sticky residue where the discard pile had sat, and they'd be perfectly happy to tie him up over there. Pete toned down the vehemence of his protest once that was on the table.

"Any whales take the bait yet?" Ziro asked with a smile. Captain Anson glared at him, his neck still tilted at a ninety degree angle.

"They're on their way," he sneered. "How'd it go with Pete?"

"Well, he's not very happy," Ziro sighed.

This news made the captain quite pleased. He smiled and tilted his head back to a normal angle. "I bet he isn't!" Anson cackled. "How come, did you shove some blubber down his pants?"

"What? No, I didn't do that. Did you want me to do that?" Ziro said, sounding confused. Anson's face fell as Ziro continued. "He's not happy because we captured his ship, killed all his men, and are going to sell him to someone on the mainland who's almost assuredly going to hang him."

"We haven't technically killed *all* his men yet," Cormac reminded them. The three of them looked over the railing at the pirates. Their strength was beginning to sap and it seemed that it was getting harder and harder for them to stay afloat.

"You down there!" Captain Anson yelled. "Are there any whales swimming around beneath you?"

"Go to hell!" one of the pirates shouted. Opening his mouth to speak caused him to take in several gulps of seawater and he sputtered and choked as he tried keep his head above the surface.

Captain Anson ignored the insult. "If you're lucky, they'll just gulp you down in one bite!" he replied. "But most of them tend to nibble. They start with the toes and work their way up!"

"How long have you captained a whaling ship, you idiot?" gasped another pirate. "Whales don't eat people!"

Captain Anson looked over at Cormac and Ziro. "Denial," he informed them. "Fairly typical when you're staring death in the face."

"Gahhhhh!" screamed one of the pirates from down below.

"What was that? Was it a whale?" Captain Anson asked excitedly as he leaned back over the railing.

"No, some seaweed brushed against my leg!" the pirate who had screamed responded. "It was gross!" The pirate bobbed up and down as he pumped his legs below the surface, trying to push the seaweed away.

"Don't kick it over here!" one of the other pirates shouted at him. "I hate touching that stuff!"

"Dammit," muttered Captain Anson. "I don't have time for this. I'm going to go shove some blubber down Pete's pants. Cormac, when the whales show up, go ahead and harpoon them without me. I'd love to watch it personally, but duty calls."

The captain walked off toward the cold storage area. Cormac watched him go, feeling slightly frustrated. After all the excitement of that morning, the afternoon was turning out to be a letdown. The pirates, rather than luring whales closer as Captain Anson insisted they would, appeared to be actively repelling them. There hadn't been a whale sighting all day. Cormac hadn't seen sea this quiet in all his time on the *Levyathan*.

"This is ridiculous," Cormac told Ziro. "Where the hell are the whales?"

Ziro shook his head. "I don't know. Maybe it's just a slow day. Although I suppose it's possible that the pod has learned to fear our ship. You've certainly given them reason to over the past week.

"Well I've gotta harpoon something," Cormac said. "I'm getting antsy." He lifted the harpoon gun to his shoulder and peered down the shaft at the floating pirates.

"Yeah, about that," Ziro said as he reached out and pushed the end of the harpoon gun down toward the deck. "You've got to stop killing people so cavalierly. The whalers are willing to look the other way if you kill someone in order to save their life. But if you start murdering just because you're bored, they're not going to want you on their ship."

"Well excuse me!" Cormac said, trying his best to sound offended. "I didn't realize I was on a whaling ship with a bunch of uptight puritans!"

"It's hardly an unreasonable request," Ziro responded.

"But they're going to die anyway!" Cormac protested. "A whale's going to come along and devour them!"

"You know that's not true," Ziro sighed.

"Well, they're definitely going to drown!"

"And that's between them and the sea." Ziro reached out and placed a calming hand on Cormac's shoulder. "The whales will come, Cormac. Just give it some time." Ziro gave Cormac's shoulder two quick pats, then walked over to where his mop was leaning against the railing. He picked it up and whistled a few bars of "Treasures o' the Sea" as he began to swab the deck. Under different circumstances, Cormac would have found Ziro's actions a touch condescending. But there really was a lot of pirate blood and innards scattered around the deck, and the swabbing was quite warranted.

Cormac took one more look at the floating pirates and decided he didn't really want to watch the men drown. It lacked the rapid-fire excitement of death by harpooning. If methods of dying were sports, drowning would definitely be soccer. A couple of the whalers were currently searching the *Mongrel* for plunder. Perhaps he'd head over there and see if there was anything worth salvaging. At the very least, it would be interesting to see what another ship was like. Cormac realized that he hadn't stepped off of the *Levyathan* on any of the days he'd been back in time.

Cormac set the harpoon gun down and turned his back on the floating pirates. He'd walked halfway to the gangplank when he heard the scream. Cormac stopped in his tracks and spun around. Ziro had heard it too. They looked at each other, and Ziro dropped his mop as they both rushed to the railing. Cormac and Ziro peered over and tried to figure out which of the whalers had screamed.

"What happened?" Cormac yelled at them.

"More seaweed!" one of the pirates replied. "Gross!"

Cormac rolled his eyes and looked back and forth between Ziro and the harpoon gun. Ziro shook his head no, and walked back over to his mop. Cormac waited until Ziro turned his back on him, then picked up the harpoon gun. A little warning shot might cause the pirates to think twice the next time they wanted to make a big fuss about seaweed brushing up against them. Cormac closed one eye and raised the harpoon gun to his shoulder. He looked down the barrel and tried to size up which pirate was the biggest troublemaker.

He was about to pull the trigger when he saw it. Off toward the horizon, a small but telltale spray of water shot up into the air. Cormac opened his eye to make sure he wasn't seeing things. Sure enough, in a few seconds there was another spray, then another one after it, and then another. Whales. A small pod was quickly approaching the *Levyathan*.

"Ziro!" Cormac called. "I think you're going to want to see this!"

Ziro was next to him in a few seconds, raising his hand to shield his eyes from the sun as he peered off into the distance.

"Well, I'll be," Ziro said. "You don't think they're coming to . . ."

"I don't know!" Cormac said. "Is there a chance the captain was right?"

Ziro changed the subject. "What were you doing with that harpoon gun?" he asked Cormac.

"Well . . . The whales! Got to shoot the whales, right?"

"So after you saw these whales about a half a mile away, you picked up the harpoon gun and pointed it in what looks to be the general direction of the pirates, despite the fact that the whales won't be here for probably another three or four minutes?" Ziro did not attempt to hide his skepticism.

"Look, just let me shoot one of them!" Cormac pleaded.

Ziro ignored Cormac and looked out at the rapidly approaching whales. Eventually Cormac relented, deciding that if the whales were actually going to devour the pirates, it might be a sight worth delaying his gratification. He lowered the harpoon gun and observed the approaching pod. Judging by the visible spray, there appeared to be three whales cruising toward the *Levyathan*. Regardless of whether or not they feasted on the pirates, Cormac thought that at least he'd finally have something that nobody could object to him shooting.

As the whales neared the ship, their path appeared to be taking them straight toward the area where the pirates floated in the water. Ziro looked at Cormac with an excited expression on his face. "Is this really happening?" Ziro asked. Cormac just shrugged. He figured they would find out soon enough.

Down below, the pirates sensed that something was amiss. "What's going on?" one of the pirates shouted up at the *Levyathan*. Even for a man who'd been thrown overboard and left to drown, he sounded rather worried. "How come it got so quiet up there?"

"Looks like our captain may have known what he was talking about," Cormac yelled back. He pointed at the horizon and shouted, "Look to the west!"

All four pirates nervously turned their heads to try and figure out what Cormac was talking about. The whales chose that moment to cease their spraying. The surface of the ocean remained flat and calm, with no perceptible marine life activity.

"Why are you mocking us?" one of the pirates wailed. "Why can't you let us drown in peace?"

"Or better yet, haul us out of here and not let us drown at all!" another of the pirates optimistically suggested.

"Shut up!" Cormac responded. "The whales are coming, and they're going to eat you up!"

The pirates laughed at him, and Cormac seethed as he rapidly scanned the ocean surface for a sign of the whales' current location. There was no spraying and no breaching. It was as if they'd disappeared. Down below, the pirates began to sing a bawdy sea shanty. For men who were actively in the process of drowning, they certainly were smug. Cormac was wondering if a well-placed harpoon might change their tune when Ziro tapped him on the shoulder.

"Look at that," Ziro said. He traced the air in a triangle around the pirates. Cormac squinted and tried to make out what he was supposed to be looking at. The pirates were alternately singing and choking on the sea water that the singing caused them to swallow; there was nothing new there. But as Cormac stared, the sea darkened in three spots on the sides of the pirates. Cormac watched in amazement as the dark spots grew larger and darker as the three whales gradually approached the surface.

"The captain's probably going to want to know about this," Ziro said quietly. Cormac nodded. Neither of them wanted to miss whatever was about to happen. From their position in the water, none of the pirates knew how close the whales were. They continued to sing, every so often one of them dipping below the water when their strength failed, only to resurface with an adrenaline fueled gasp a second or two later.

The whales had nearly reached the surface, and Cormac and Ziro could now see just how big they were compared to the men who floated nearby. Their long, menacing shapes shimmered just beneath the water surface, their heads only ten feet away from the unaware pirates. The tension was unbearable, and Cormac nearly jumped out of his shoes when Ziro broke the silence by shouting "CAPTAIN ANSON!" at the top of his lungs.

"What the hell, man?" Cormac asked. "You trying to make me go deaf?"

"Sorry," Ziro replied. "I don't want to miss this any more than you do."

Cormac glared at Ziro and rubbed his ear with the index finger of his mangled hand. He wasn't able to stay resentful for very long, though, because in a matter of seconds, Captain Anson skidded to a halt behind them, breathing heavily.

"What's going on?" he panted. "Did I miss anything?" Without a word, Cormac just pointed toward the three whales that floated ominously around the oblivious pirates. "Holy crap," Captain Anson muttered when he realized what was about to happen.

"I'll admit I was skeptical, Captain Anson," Cormac said as he turned to face the captain. "But I'm a big enough man to admit that I was wrong. Those whales are going to devour those pirates and I'm looking forward to watching it. I hope you'll forgive me."

"What the hell are you holding?" Ziro asked the captain.

"Oh this?" Captain Anson said, holding up his right hand, which grasped a large, rubbery, dripping blob. "This is blubber."

"And that?" Cormac pointed to his left hand.

"Well, that's a belt," the captain said as if it were obvious. "I was trying to shove the blubber down Pete's pants."

"Sir, I'm pretty sure that is your own belt," Ziro said with a touch of concern in his voice.

"What, this?" Captain Anson scoffed as he hitched up us sagging pants with the hand with no blubber in it. "Hogwash. Why would I take off my own belt? You're crazy, Ziro!"

"Sir, your pants are falling down as we speak," Ziro said, as the captain's pants rapidly descended again.

"Look, it was confusing down there!" Anson said. The captain dropped the blubber to the deck before pulling his pants up and quickly tying the belt around them. "Shoving blubber down someone's pants sounds easy, but it gets confusing in the heat of the moment!"

"I don't see how it could be so confusing that you remove your own belt," Ziro pointed out.

"Oh, listen to Mr. Perfect over here," Captain Anson said snidely. "I suppose you've never screwed up when you were shoving blubber down someone's pants?"

"I have never tried shoving blubber down someone's pants," Ziro replied calmly. "It's not a very widely practiced torture method. In fact, I had never even heard someone suggest it until you did fifteen minutes ago."

"That's right!" Captain Anson said with a touch of pride. "I invented it. And I can do it any damn way I please."

"And the way you choose is to shove blubber down your own pants?" Ziro asked.

"Unfortunately I never got that far, because a couple of idiots interrupted me!" the captain yelled.

"Unfortunately?"

Hoping to head off blubber being shoved down anyone's pants, Cormac interrupted the argument. "Will both of you shut up? Something's about to happen."

Ziro turned his attention back to the sea. After wiping the hand that had held the blubber off on his now-secured pants, Captain Anson joined them at the railing. The pirates were still singing, but the whales had gone still. Their massive forms seemed almost unreal as they floated so close to the tiny men. For a split second, Cormac felt the natural human instinct to call out a warning to the pirates. But he quickly suppressed it, the desire to see three gigantic whales tear some guys apart easily overwhelming his desire to help his fellow man.

All of a sudden, the pirates stopped singing. It was as if they'd all got the feeling that they were being watched at the same time. They looked at each other, and the ones who were able to kicked their legs so they slowly rotated in the water to look behind them. Not seeing anything, the pirates shrugged and prepared to launch back into their song. The whales chose that moment to simultaneously blow large streams of water out of their blowholes.

"Holy crap!" yelled Cormac. He covered his head, as droplets from the nearest whale's blowhole landed on the deck of the ship. Down below, the pirates were in a panic. All of them had seen at least one of the geysers of water, but none of them knew what to do. They had been floating in the water for nearly an hour, so they were all tired, not that any of them could have swum very far with their hands tied. Even if they had been Olympic-caliber swimmers, there wasn't any land for hundreds of miles. They were at the mercy of whatever the whales had planned for them.

"How do you like that?" yelled Captain Anson. "Oh, you doubted that these briny sea devils would come forth to devour you, but now you see what these unholy behemoths are truly capable of! I'm going to enjoy watching this!"

"You're sick!" yelled one of the pirates.

"Haul us out of here!" shouted another.

"Gahhhh! Seaweed!" yelled a third.

The pirates screamed in terror for a bit longer, but eventually they got tired and had to stop. From the deck of the *Levyathan*, Cormac noted that the whales were no longer visible. They must have taken a dive after they sprayed; there was no sign of them.

"They're toying with them," Captain Anson assured Cormac and Ziro. "They're sadistic bastards." Cormac resisted the urge to point out that the captain was the one who had ordered the men thrown overboard, and from the look on his face, Ziro was trying his hardest not to bring it up as well.

The pirates in the water and the men on the boat all held their breath as they waited to see what would happen next.

Ziro heard it first. "What was that?" the former slave asked, cocking his head toward the ocean. Cormac couldn't hear anything at first, but when he listened closely he picked up on a faint rushing sound that was quickly growing louder, like a fast-approaching train. The captain heard it, too.

"You might not want to be leaning over the railing," he told Cormac and Ziro. The two of them looked at the captain, who had already taken several steps back, then followed his lead. The sound continued to grow.

Seconds later, one of the whales burst through the surface of the water in the exact same spot where the pirates were treading water. It emerged headfirst and soared straight up into the air until only its tail was left in the water. It looked as if a child just below the surface was holding a whale balloon by a string attached to the tail. Water rushed off of the whale's body, and it opened its mouth wide to emit a strange, haunting whale song.

As the whale reached the peak of its jump, it shut its mouth and stopped making the noise. Everything was silent as it hung there for what seemed like a second longer than should have been possible. But then gravity kicked in and the whale fell back to the surface with a gigantic splash that rolled the *Levyathan* backwards, nearly knocking Cormac and the other two off their feet. The three men steadied themselves, but quickly rushed back over to the railing to observe the aftermath of the whale's jump.

The sea was frothy and angry where the whale had emerged and fallen back. White-capped waves rolled toward and away from the *Levyathan*, and the boiling water was now an unsettling mix of light green and dark, almost black, blue. The pirates had been dispersed by the impact, so they were no longer all clumped together. They were confused and gasping for air as the whale's wake rolled over their heads. Most importantly, Cormac could only see three of them.

"He did it," the captain said as he wiped sea water off of his face. He sounded stunned. "The bastard really ate him!"

Cormac had a lot of questions about what he'd just seen, but he didn't have time to ask any of them because he heard another noise. Just like the last one, it was quiet at first, but rapidly getting louder as it got closer. But this time something was different. At first Cormac thought it might just be muted by all the activity in the ocean, but he eventually realized that wasn't it at all. The sound was higher pitched, and it wasn't coming from below them. It was coming from the sky.

The screaming pirate fell onto the deck of the *Levyathan* with a loud thud about fifteen feet from where Cormac was standing. The impact knocked the wind out of him, interrupting the screaming for the first time since his descent started. He lay there, sucking wind until he was able to draw a full breath. As soon as he was able to do so, he resumed screaming.

Captain Anson rushed over to the fallen pirate with Cormac and Ziro on his heels. After a solid ten seconds of listening to the pirate's screaming, Captain Anson reared back and kicked him in the ribs. The pirate yelped in pain, but the kick jolted him out of whatever fugue state he'd been in since he'd fallen from the sky. He looked up at the three men who stood over him.

"What the hell just happened?" Captain Anson demanded. "We thought that whale ate you!"

"It did!" The pirate gasped. "It swallowed me whole! But then it spit me back out, like a watermelon seed!"

From behind them came the sound of another gigantic pair of splashes a couple of seconds apart, followed by the distant hum of a screaming pirate. It quickly grew louder until another pirate fell to the deck fifteen feet away from where they were standing.

"Those curs are trying to save you!" Captain Anson bellowed. "They're doing it to mock me!"

"It was really slimy in there," whimpered the first pirate who had fallen to the deck.

"Cormac! Ziro! Seize those pirates and throw them overboard! Again!" Captain Anson commanded. Cormac and Ziro shrugged at each other, then each walked over to a pirate and hauled him up off the *Levyathan* deck.

"Ouch!" yelped the second pirate as Cormac lifted him. "I think I cracked a rib when I landed! That thing must have shot me higher than the mast."

"You know, I was pretty sure that whales didn't eat people," Cormac told the pirate.

"Of course they don't eat people! What giant buffoon told you they did?" the incredulous pirate yelled back at him. Captain Anson heard this, and glared at the pirate.

"Him first," the captain said, pointing his spyglass at Cormac's pirate. Cormac figured he had no choice and shoved the pirate up against the railing. They both looked down at the water. The remaining two pirates were still floating there, and they were pretty much losing their minds. The two whales that had already surfaced were swimming back and forth along the side of the *Levyathan*, and the third was evidently still submerged.

"Salty! Scurvy!" yelled the pirate at the railing. "I'm alright! The whales are our friends! They're trying to save us!"

"Your buddies are named Salty and Scurvy, but your captain is named Pete?" Cormac asked the pirate.

"I know, right?" the pirate said. "What's weird is that it didn't seem strange when I was living it every day, but now that I've got some distance from it, it's—" Cormac rolled his eyes, already regretting his inquiry. He saw nothing to gain from an extended discussion about pirate names and how they affected your career path, so he shoved the pirate up and over the railing. He fell head over heels and landed with a splash. Ziro shoved his pirate over next, and he fell into the sea not far from where his buddy had landed.

The concerned whales swam over to the area where the two pirates had splashed down. The pirates futilely attempted to swim back to where their friends were still floating, but the whales were eager to save them and were having none of it. One whale submerged beneath one of the pirates, who groaned in dismay. The other whale turned its back on the second pirate and swam forward until its broad tail was floating just underneath the man. With a mighty whooshing noise, the whale flicked its tail up out of the water, catapulting the pirate into the air, where he soared in an arc, screaming, until he landed back on the deck of the *Levyathan* with a painful-sounding thud.

"This is so much worse than just drowning," the soaking pirate moaned.

"Throw him back!" shouted Captain Anson. From the ocean, there was another gigantic splash as a whale leapt in the air, launching another of the pirates onto the deck. A few seconds later, it happened again. Both of the two new pirates groaned in pain when they landed. The whales, though well-intentioned, were failing to take into account that the men they were rescuing were plummeting from a great height at a rapid speed onto a solid wooden deck. Frankly, it was stunning that it had happened four times and none of the pirates had died upon impact.

Cormac picked his pirate up yet again and walked him over to the railing. Despite the beating he'd taken and the exhaustion caused by an hour of treading water, the pirate was resisting much more than the first two times Cormac had thrown him overboard.

"Don't do it, man," the pirate pleaded as he attempted to dig his heels in. "I can't take any more of the whales' help. Just toss me back in once they're gone!"

"Just try and drown quicker," Cormac offered as he lifted the pirate by his collar and the seat of his pants and heaved him over the railing. The pirate fell toward the water, but just before he hit the surface, a helpful whale that had been monitoring the situation quickly swam under his body and blew a jet of water out of its blowhole.

The whale must have been intending for the stream to gracefully push the pirate back up through the air toward the safety of the boat. But it had clearly miscalculated the strength of the water and the load it was capable of supporting. Rather than gently balancing the pirate and slowly raising him back up in the air, it was as if the whale had turned a fire hose on a rag doll. The concentrated force of the water blasted the pirate in the legs, causing his limp body to careen wildly as it fell.

The concerned whale swam forward a foot or two to compensate for blowing the pirate off course and tried again. This time the jet of water hit the pirate in the side, halting his forward movement by spinning him in a barrel roll like a rotisserie chicken. The whale shimmied ever so slightly backwards in the water to line up his aim for another shot, then unleashed a third spout of water. This time it finally had the desired effect. It caught the pirate right in the small of the back, halting his fall. Then slowly, majestically, the powerful pillar of water from the whale's blowhole juggled the pirate's body back up into the air.

Unfortunately, the previous attempts at catching the pirate had rapidly depleted the whale's water reserves, and the stream of water sputtered out after raising the pirate just a few feet. Gravity kicked in and the pirate resumed his descent. But this time, instead of landing in the water, he fell onto the back of the whale that had been trying to help him. There was a sticky sounding crunch as he hit the back of the giant mammal.

"Fucking whales," the pirate moaned, as he lay there, unable to move. The whale flicked its tail happily, delighted that it had been able to help a human in need.

Back on the ship, Ziro was dealing with one of other victims of whale assistance. "Captain Anson!" the former slave called out. "I think this one has a concussion! He's having trouble standing up!"

"He's faking," Captain Anson assured Ziro. "Classic pirate trick. But if he really does have a concussion, I guess he won't be able to object if I shove some blubber down his pants?" Captain Anson picked up the chunk of blubber he'd attempted to torture Pete with and walked over to Ziro and the pirate. The captain started to untie his belt, and only stopped when Ziro coughed and pointed toward the pirate's waist. Anson quickly retied his own belt, then pulled the pirate's belt off and shoved the chunk of blubber inside the waistband. The pirate swayed back and forth as his eyes struggled to focus.

"Overboard!" bellowed the captain, right before the unfortunate pirate who Cormac had just thrown overboard dropped out the sky for a third time.

"Is this really effective, sir?" Ziro asked. "I don't think those whales are going to let these pirates drown."

"Dammit," muttered the captain, pretending not to hear the whimpering pirate who had landed just a few feet away. "I suppose you're right. As godless abominations themselves, they refuse to let the natural order of things just take its course!"

"The natural order of pirates drowning because we threw them overboard against their will?" Ziro asked.

"Shut it, Ziro! Cormac!" The captain scanned the deck looking for Cormac.

"Way ahead of you, captain," Cormac said, already peering down the shaft of the harpoon gun. Before the captain could even give the order, he pulled the trigger and sent a shiny harpoon soaring through the air.

Looking Into Cormac's Ear: Our Generation's Woodstock? (Yes)
By Cissy Buckler

Many people consider the Woodstock Music & Art Fair, (commonly known as Woodstock '69 to differentiate it from Woodstock '94 and Woodstock '99) to be the defining event of a generation. Musicians such as Jimi Hendrix, Janis Joplin, and some guys called the Keef Hartley Band played before a crowd of half a million people, spreading a message of peace and love that still has cultural resonance today.

This reporter feels it is safe to say that coming over to the Craymore Street house and looking into Cormac McIlhenney's (Junior, Undeclared) ear is undoubtedly shaping up to be the Woodstock '69 of our generation. In fact, many people are claiming that it is already a better event, and not just because at Cormac's house there are no performances by the Keef Hartley Band, whoever they are. For one thing: wherein you had to pay for drugs at Woodstock '69, on Craymore Street you get free weed with your purchase of ear time. (This is a measure implemented to keep out spies; I will address it later in the article if time allows.)

Woodstock '69 famously issued a warning about brown acid. Well, the pirates in the nineteenth century would have been wise to issue a warning about Cormac! (This is because Cormac killed several pirates today, as will be explained in the next sentence.) Lucky Harrington students were treated to a thrilling sight as Cormac rescued the crew of the Levyathan from the pirates who had taken over the boat. Earwitnesses report that Cormac harpooned seven of the pirates, several of whom were foolishly attempting to surrender. The closest thing that Woodstock '69 had to a pirate was probably someone who was pretending to be a pirate, or possibly someone who had taken enough brown acid that they thought they were a pirate. These were not real pirates; thus this is another reason that looking into Cormac's ear is better than Woodstock '69.

Once the harpoons were done flying, many thought that the show was over. This was not the case, just as those who thought that the show was over at Woodstock '69 after the first day of music were proven wrong when there was also music the next day. (And the day after. Three Days of Peace and Music was the Woodstock '69 motto.) The surviving pirates were thrown overboard to drown, but three whales showed up and tried to save them. Customers who had missed Cormac shooting pirates were able to watch the whales flinging the pirates around and trying to balance them with their blowhole water. The whale's heroics proved futile though, as Cormac quickly harpooned all three of them and the pirates drowned soon afterward.

Cormac harpooned several other whales this afternoon, giving the customers who paid to look into his ear a good show. This was good because rates to look in his ear have risen rapidly. This is not all bad news, though, because Arts Dollars are now being accepted. You were going to waste these one way or another, either by not using them or by seeing a play, so you may as well come down to Craymore Street and use them to look into an unconscious guy's ear. Needless to say, as it was not an event sponsored by Harrington, Arts Dollars were not accepted at Woodstock '69. Advantage, Craymore Street.

There were only two negative things that happened all day. One was that Dennis Stark, human interest reporter for Channel 9 News: Your News When It Matters, Number One in the Metropolitan Area Four Years Running, attempted to smuggle a camera into Cormac's bedroom. Clearly, Stark was not aware that Cormac had agreed to an exclusivity agreement with the School Paper. *Stark was escorted from the premises and attempted to report from outside the house. Obviously, Stark and the rest of the Channel 9 News team do not care about the quality of their reporting. As you can see from this report, the only way to do a good report is for the reporter to be in the house, reporting, not out on the street, talking to the men who are out there. Whoever heard of a TV news reporter talking to a man on the street?*

Speaking of men on the street, there are many men gathered across the street from the Craymore Street house. This brings us to our second negative: the men gathered across the street from the

Craymore Street house. *They are a newly formed cult led by Brock (Sophomore, Finance), who was last seen being banned for life for masturbating (just like Channel 9 reporter Dennis Stark, at least the lifetime ban part). The cult believes that Cormac has been chosen by God and they are his faithful disciples, at least they would be if they were allowed near him, but they are not, because of their leader's lifetime ban for masturbating and the fear that his followers would also masturbate. Still, one might argue that at Woodstock '69, they let the potential guys who would masturbate while looking in your ear stay in the concert, because they were hippies and thought everyone was great. At Craymore Street, we know that is clearly not the case and the masturbating cult is not allowed in. Suck it, Woodstock '69.*

Also, there were a bunch of cool dogs wearing sunglasses at the house today.

Some people might cite a third negative: that Cormac killed several people. In this reporter's opinion, these people are just a bunch of whiners who probably are upset that Cormac was just standing around during their ear time. Listen, gang: if Cormac starts killing people back in our modern time, we'll gather at that point to discuss whether that is right or wrong. But everyone he killed would already be dead anyways by this point in time, so who cares?

In addition to cool dogs, there were DJs, food trucks, beer kegs, and to re-emphasize, no Keef Hartley Band.

It's been a whale of a day for Harrington's resident super-ear-o and those who gathered to look into his ear. If you're one of the few dorks who hasn't dropped by yet, don't let the fact that Cormac killed a bunch of people without a second thought deter you: come on down to Craymore Street and experience the event that the School Paper *is calling "the Woodstock '69 of our generation." Buckler out.*

The dean was speechless. He looked up at the airborne couch. Cissy sat there looking very satisfied with herself. The dean passed the laptop he'd been reading on back to Cissy.

"You wrote this?" The dean asked. "You personally came up with the ideas and typed them down? You didn't dictate it into voice recognition software that horribly malfunctioned? You didn't then translate it into Russian, then Japanese, then Swahili, then Esperanto, then back into English?"

"Pretty impressive, huh?" Cissy said with a smile. "I think it's my finest work yet. And I don't think I'd have been legally allowed to drive since like, before noon. That is some JUI: journalism under the influence." Cissy folded her laptop closed and swung her legs around to lie down on the couch. "I would not want to be Woodstock '69 when that thing hits newsstands tomorrow," she chuckled.

Dean Bickerstaff sighed. He couldn't tell if he was drunk, or hungover, or a combination of both. He just knew he was tired and happy to be back in his suit and out of the towel. Now all he wanted to do was get a finished article to the *School Paper* so he could go to sleep in the back of the van.

Frampton looked around the living room. The crew of cleaning ladies were finishing vacuuming and mopping. On the grounded couch, Vance snored from the position he'd been in for the last two hours. Mako and G-Dimes huddled together in the corner, counting the large stack of cash they'd earned that day. Outside, Frampton could make out the faint flicker of the candles that Brock and his followers were keeping lit as part of their twisted little vigil.

The dean felt a tap on his shoulder and turned around. Rosario stood there holding a pair of sunglasses in her outstretched hand. One of the cool dogs must have left them behind, the dean figured as he reached out and picked them up. Turning them over to inspect them, he spotted a familiar logo: Louis Vuitton. Jesus Christ, Dean Bickerstaff thought to himself. Those dogs were wearing six-hundred-dollar sunglasses.

Sighing even deeper, he handed the sunglasses back to Rosario. "Keep 'em," Dean Bickerstaff instructed the cleaning lady, who smiled excitedly and nodded her thanks. If a dog was cool enough to wear Louis Vuitton sunglasses, Frampton guessed it wouldn't be super uptight about donating them to a needy cleaning lady. Hell, it probably had a drawer full of them.

Turning back to Cissy, Dean Bickerstaff decided that the abysmal quality of her article was not a point worth losing any sleep over. "And you've got the fake article too?" he asked Cissy.

Cissy nodded and flicked a thumb drive at Dean Bickerstaff, who caught it and slipped it into his pocket. "I don't suppose you want to keep me company on the drive to sub-basement C?" Frampton asked. He got a loud snore in response.

Pushing everything from his mind but how high Harrington's X-Factor numbers must be soaring, Dean Bickerstaff gave his shillelagh a twirl and walked out the front door, heading toward the van. It had been a very long day.

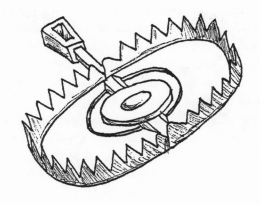

DAY ELEVEN

Cormac woke up and instantly checked how many views his ukulele video had accumulated. He silently thought to himself that today was off to a much less bad-ass start than yesterday.

This didn't prevent him from being delighted that the video now had nearly half a million views. The first few comments led Cormac to believe that most of the newfound popularity was due to the fact that a late-night talk show had parodied the song the night before. Cormac clicked over to the related video link, and sure enough, there was the host performing "Treasures o' the Sea" while doing an impression of the singer from the Spin Doctors. That was unfortunate, Cormac thought as he closed the tab after less than three seconds. But still, he'd take the views.

A couple of other commenters had posted links to articles that they claimed were about Cormac, but none of them seemed to work. Links to MSNBC, CNN, even the original GeekySquid article all gave error pages after timing out. There must be some sort of widespread internet problem, Cormac figured. He was incredibly frustrated by his inability to instantly access information from all over the world for free, despite the fact that yesterday he'd been in a time when most homes were powered by mules turning mill wheels. At least Cormac assumed that's how things worked back then. He made a note to ask Ziro if his vision in any way resembled the day-to-day reality of the 1860s.

The clock on the computer said that it was 10:37. Cormac was surprised that he had slept this late. He'd actually gone to bed fairly early last night. This was partially due to the fact that the only rum on board was being jealously hoarded in the captain's quarters. With getting hammered no longer an option, and ukulele playing severely frowned upon, there wasn't much to do on the *Levyathan* after the sun went down. But after a morning of daring rescues and an afternoon that saw him haul in a total of nine whales, Cormac was downright exhausted. He'd been the first one to retreat to the whalers' quarters, and fell asleep the moment his head hit the filthy folds of burlap, which was the closest thing on the ship to a pillow.

Of course, Cormac usually did not consider waking up at 10:30 "sleeping in." He had a feeling that, if left to his own devices, Vance wouldn't be up for a few more hours. Cissy too, in the extremely likely event that she had not peeled herself off the airborne couch and slumped home. Cormac weighed how he should spend his morning. He definitely wanted to record a new ukulele video. The success of his first YouTube upload had quickly changed Cormac's thinking about the instrument. What had at first seemed like a pleasant enough diversion was now the closest thing he'd ever had to a potential career path. Cormac figured he would be an idiot not to try and take advantage of all the attention he was getting. He needed to keep the hits coming.

But playing the ukulele was noisy, and it would almost undoubtedly cause Vance or Cissy to wake up angry. This would negate the possibility of doing the other thing Cormac wanted to achieve this morning: figuring out what the hell was going on in his house while he was on the *Levyathan*.

The ukulele would have to wait. Cormac quietly crept over to his bedroom door, slowly pushed it open, and peered out into the hallway. Both the door to Vance's bedroom and the bathroom were open, and there was no sign of activity from the living room. Seconds later, a gigantic snore followed by a slightly more feminine-sounding gigantic snore came booming from the living room. Wishing he had some gun-range-quality ear protection, Cormac covered his ears and tiptoed into the hallway.

He quietly walked toward the living room, but right away, he could tell that something was amiss. He eventually realized that his ability to actually walk quietly was the tip-off. The floor of the Craymore Street house had always been covered with a fine layer of crunchy filth and sticky slime that made each step a symphony of gross sound effects. But now here he was, padding along quietly like a cat. Cormac stopped walking and raised one of his feet to look at the sole. He had gone at least ten steps and his foot was not black yet. Something was definitely not right. Someone had cleaned the floors.

Could it have been Vance? Cormac had to lower one of his hands to his mouth to stifle what would have otherwise been uproarious laughter. If Vance was scrubbing floors, whatever was happening was much more serious than Cormac had even imagined. "Money owed to Russian politician" serious. Surely it hadn't come to that, Cormac thought to himself, though he noticed that the desire to laugh had suddenly passed.

Another deafening tandem snore greeted Cormac as he entered the living room. During band rehearsals and performances, he'd always been rather blasé about the loud music's effects on his hearing. Ear plugs were something for deaf old men to wear. But this noise might provide a severe obstacle to his reconnaissance mission. You couldn't be expected to conquer the ukulele world with busted ear drums. He'd have to gather whatever information he could quickly.

Scanning the living room, Cormac noted that it, too, was tidier than it had any business being. Thinking back to two days ago, Cormac realized this had been the case then, too. He'd been so excited about his video taking off that he hadn't taken enough time to be properly suspicious. But clearly, many subtle improvements had been made that were not the type of thing Vance was in the habit of doing. The windowsills had been dusted. The carpet had been vacuumed. The pile of money in the corner was neatly stacked and tightly bound with rubber bands.

Pile of money in the corner?! Cormac did a full-body double take that would have been extremely comical if the sight of thousands of dollars that hadn't been there two days ago wasn't so deeply unsettling. Cormac cautiously inched toward the money, as if the violent criminal it most assuredly belonged to was going to materialize and shoot him if he made any sudden movements. When he got close enough, Cormac was able to see that there were three separate bundles of cash, each of them about an inch thick

After looking over his shoulder to make sure Vance and Cissy were still asleep, Cormac reached out and picked up one of the stacks. The bill on top was a twenty, and flipping through the edges, it appeared that so were the rest of the bills the stack. He was probably holding well over two thousand dollars. There was a decent chance that the pile of cash was worth more than the Craymore Street house itself. What the hell was Vance doing to get this money? More specifically, what was he dealing to get this money? This money was dirty as hell. Cormac could almost smell the drugs.

Actually, there was no "almost" about it. He really could smell drugs. Cormac hadn't realized it initially, but the living room was thick with the stench of marijuana. And not just marijuana smoke, but the smell of fresh weed. Cormac set the stack of bills back down and sniffed the air, trying to pinpoint the source of the smell like a cartoon dog seeking out a grill full of sausages.

The smell grew stronger as Cormac approached the couches. Of course, Cormac thought. That would explain Vance's idiotic obsession with the couches lately. He must be dealing weed and stashing the excess product inside the cushions. Cissy must be in on the racket, maintaining a constant presence on the airborne couch to guard the valuable contraband inside.

Cormac leaned over the grounded couch to see if he could pinpoint a secret opening in the cushions of the airborne couch. This was actually a fairly sophisticated scheme, he thought to himself. It must have taken an initial spark of ingenuity, then the drive to implement it, the willpower to keep it a secret, and the business savvy to recruit Cissy as a partner. Every time Cormac underestimated him, Vance found a way to remind Cormac how foolish and potentially lethal it was to do so. A vague feeling of pride in his roommate was starting to form inside Cormac when Cissy shifted in her sleep and he saw that underneath her head was a giant Ziploc bag of marijuana.

There was no sophisticated scheme. There was just a pillow of drugs.

Even worse, Cormac felt like this still didn't explain his strange feeling. Normally, if you had the sense that something odd was going on in your home, uncovering a drug ring operating out of your living room would seem like the answer you were looking for. And perhaps this did go a long way toward accounting for the creepy van outside and the strangers showing up on the doorstep. But how did the cleanliness figure into it all? Maybe Vance had discovered a way to fill a gap in the marketplace. Drug dens were typically filthy places; perhaps he was delivering a cleaner, more refined drug purchasing environment?

But this still didn't make any sense, mainly because there was no reason to keep Cormac in the dark about Vance's felony activity. Cormac had always been down for some light law breaking, and even though dealing amounts of drugs that seemed more appropriate for cartel members who had severed a head or two was not an activity he would have engaged in personally, he wouldn't have minded reaping some of the benefits of Vance doing it. Especially if it was bringing in the level of cash it apparently was.

No, there was definitely another layer beyond what he'd just discovered. Cormac was certain of it. Unfortunately, he didn't have time to poke around any further because Vance emitted a snore so loud that he woke himself up. Still leaning over the grounded couch, Cormac instinctively froze, hoping that Vance's consciousness, as so often was the case, was only temporary.

This time it unfortunately was not. Vance lazily blinked his eyes and smacked his lips. Then, to Cormac's dismay, he stuck his hand underneath the waist of the towel and began to aimlessly scratch his crotch. Fearing that if he backed away, he'd wake Vance up for sure, Cormac stood there hovering over him, as still as a statue. Looking straight ahead meant staring directly at Vance's increasingly vigorous crotch exploration, so Cormac rolled his eyes upwards as much as he could. He tried to pretend he couldn't see anything in his peripheral vision as he stared at the tattered fabric on the front of the airborne couch.

Vance had obviously never been much of a morning person, but Cormac had never been this close to him during his waking-up routine. In addition to the genital scratching and occasional grunting, morning breath also turned out to be a major player in the process. With every breath Vance took, he blew a stream of musty, damp air toward Cormac's face that made it even harder to stand still. Dear God, Cormac thought. It smelled like Vance had slept with a dirty wrestling singlet in his mouth. Vance appeared to be passing out on the couch most nights. Putting in the minimal effort to walk down the hall and brush his teeth certainly seemed like something he might not have considered worthwhile for the past several days.

The awkward posture required to avoid looking at Vance's towel and smelling Vance's breath was getting to be too much to bear. Cormac felt beads of sweat starting to form on his forehead. From beneath him, he heard Vance belch. Cormac knew he had to act quickly; if the stench of Vance's clammy mouth was bad now, after a burp it was going to be potentially fatal. He took a huge gasp of air and held his breath. Moments later, his eyes began to water as the stinging, befouled air reached him. Cormac knew he must have dodged a particularly rank bullet.

But he also knew he couldn't hold his breath forever. As the seconds ticked by, Cormac started to fear the burp might not have enough time to properly dilute in the living room air before he needed to breathe again. He would go as long as possible, but then he'd have to take another breath, even if it meant exposing himself to what was left of the smell.

Cormac felt his face beginning to quiver. He started to feel light-headed. He told himself to just count to five to better his chance of breathing non-toxic air. He made it all the way to four. And then Vance burped again.

This burp made the last burp sound polite and dainty. It was akin to the roar of some prehistoric beast. Cormac's eyes went wide in horror. Somewhere in the distance, a baby started to cry. The smell of Vance's burp couldn't be powerful enough have caused that, could it? Cormac had no choice. He could either pass out for the second time in twenty-four hours or find out.

Cormac's mouth popped open and he noisily gasped for air. At the sound of Cormac sucking wind, Vance's eyes snapped open and he spied his roommate standing over him. Vance pulled his hand out from under the towel as his face went white in terror. At the same time, Cormac realized that the burp air he had just inhaled a deep breath of tasted like runoff from a hog farm. He hacked and retched while Vance leapt to his feet and retreated behind the other side of the grounded couch. Cissy snored.

"Don't kill me! Oh God, please don't kill me!" Vance pleaded. Cormac looked at his cowering roommate in wonder as he alternately gasped deep breaths and tried not to throw up from the horrible taste of the deep breaths.

"Kill you?" Cormac wheezed. "Vance, it's me! I'm not going to kill you!"

"I'm not a pirate!" Vance wailed, throwing up his hands to cover his face, a gesture that left his towel perilously close to coming untucked.

"Jesus, we're getting you a bottle of Listerine," Cormac said, wiping away tears from his still-stinging eyes. "Of course you're not a pirate, you idiot. Are you still drunk? How much weed did you smoke?" Cormac stuck his tongue out and scraped at it with his fingernails. "Ugh, I may need a bottle of Listerine myself."

Vance lowered his hands and eyed Cormac suspiciously. "If you aren't here to kill me, then why were you standing there?"

"Why was I standing here? Oh, I'm sorry, Vance, but last time I checked, I still pay half the rent for this living room and I'm free to wander into it whenever I want!" Cormac's lungs still burned, but the breaths were coming slightly more naturally now. He looked over at the snoring houseguest on the airborne couch. "Even if you two have worked out some kind of weird little arrangement where she lives here now, this is still at least one-third of my living room, dammit!"

"Oh, don't get all high and mighty on me, man," Vance countered as he thankfully tightened the tuck on his towel. "You were the one hovering over me watching me scratch myself!"

"Well . . . You're scratching yourself in the middle of the living room!" Cormac stammered. He had thought he had Vance on the ropes, but clearly his roommate wasn't done swinging.

"Just how long had you been standing there?" Vance asked, sensing the momentum shift.

Cormac panicked. Sensing a chance to go in for the kill, Vance narrowed his eyes. "I don't think I ever caught you watching me scratch myself before that ukulele came into our house," he said in a sinister tone.

Vance's eyes flicked toward the hallway and Cormac prepared himself for a physical encounter before remembering that he had an ace up his sleeve. As Vance got off the couch and began to walk toward Cormac's bedroom, Cormac yelled out "How long have you been dealing drugs?"

Vance stopped after just two steps. He looked at Cormac, once again uncertain. "Drugs? The hell are you talking about Mac?"

Cormac had seen Vance lie thousands of times. Sometimes it was for a practical reason, such as to the person at the go-kart rental counter who asked if they'd been drinking. Sometimes the reason was baffling, like when he pretended to be a compatible bone marrow donor for a soon-to-be very disappointed and very dead old woman. But once you pinpointed a few key tells in Vance's demeanor, you could easily identify when he was lying. The strange thing was, this bewilderment right here seemed genuine. Nevertheless, Cormac pointed toward the stacks of money. Vance looked over at the stacks, then cursed under his breath. He looked back at Cormac. "Where did those come from?" he inquired feebly.

"Very funny," Cormac said. "I saw Cissy's pillow, too." Vance turned and looked at Cissy. The left side of her face was firmly embedded in the bag of marijuana. She snored deeply, an act that had to cause at least a mild degree of intoxication being that close to so much marijuana. Vance turned back to face his roommate.

"I'll admit this looks bad," he said matter of factly. Cormac nodded emphatically. "But you've got to trust me, Mac," Vance continued. "Despite the presence of both drugs and thousands of unaccounted-for dollars in our house, I am not dealing drugs. Now I'm not saying that drug dealers haven't been here, or that those drug dealers have not sold drugs while they were here. But the fact of the matter is, I hit it pretty hard yesterday, and from about 2:00 p.m. on is pretty much a blur. I can honestly say I have no idea why that stuff is here."

Vance looked about as earnest as a guy who had worn a towel for the past week possibly could. Cormac couldn't believe it, but it sounded like Vance had told him the truth twice in the span of a minute. Well, to be more accurate, Vance had not lied to him. The differences between telling the truth and not lying were subtle, but the impact could be vast. Cormac considered this as he weighed what to say next.

"Why did you say 'I'm not a pirate?'" he asked Vance. Vance shook his head, trying to indicate that he didn't understand the question, but his hands betrayed him. Cormac noticed them tense into fists ever so briefly. Regaining a bit of confidence, he pushed on. "Vance, when you leapt off the couch, you were shouting 'I'm not a pirate, don't kill me.' Why?"

"Whoa! I really said that?" Vance chuckled. "I must still be high or something. I don't know where that came from, man. I guess I must have been dreaming. A pirate, you're serious? I dunno . . . Maybe you were hearing things, Mac." Vance stopped chuckling. "You got pirates on the brain, buddy?"

"Pirates?" There went the confidence. Cormac repeated the word, trying to buy some time. "Pirates? Of course not, why would I be thinking about pirates?"

"I don't know," Vance said in a calm tone that Cormac found incredibly unsettling. "Are pirates even a big problem back where you go? You've never mentioned encountering them."

"No," Cormac said. "I guess we've been lucky." He wasn't sure why he was lying to Vance about yesterday's encounter. But if Vance was keeping secrets from him, he saw no reason to be upfront about the multiple homicides he'd committed in return.

"You've never seen a pirate?" Vance repeated, more accusing than questioning. He stared right at Cormac. The only response Cormac could muster was shaking his head. Vance eventually appeared satisfied. "Weird," he said. "Maybe they're just another Hollywood invention."

Vance walked around the grounded couch, keeping his distance from Cormac as he made his way toward the hallway. The two roommates eyed each other, each trying to figure out what the other one was hiding. Cormac was having trouble keeping all the threads of deception separate in his head. Whatever was behind the drugs and money was still a mystery, and now he was lying to Vance about the pirate encounter, which was strange, because it seemed like Vance had brought it up in the first place. But there was no way for Vance to know about that. Was there?

One thing was for sure: he wasn't going to get an answer out of Vance under these circumstances. Which is why twenty minutes later, when Vance knocked on his door and suggested they hit up Mickey's for a few early afternoon pitchers, Cormac quickly agreed. After a few drinks, maybe his roommate might let his guard down and tell him what he wanted to hear. Little did he suspect that Vance was thinking the exact same thing.

* * *

"This is a good call, Vance," Cormac said as they walked toward the front door. "I don't think it would be possible to have a conversation with Cissy snoring like that." He looked over at Cissy, who was emitting jackhammer-volume snores and showed no signs of waking up any time soon. When Cormac looked back at Vance to see what was taking him so long, he saw his roommate shoving one of the stacks of money into the pocket of the pants he'd reluctantly changed into.

"Jesus, Vance, what the hell are you doing?" Cormac asked, suddenly very nervous.

"Don't worry about it, Mac," Vance said with a nonchalant wink. "I think this ought to cover at least a few of our pitchers, don't you think?"

"I don't think you should spend money that just turned up in the house while you were blacked out, Vance. At least wait to see if Cissy knows where it came from. It almost definitely belongs to a dangerous drug dealer."

"Oh sweet, naive Mac," Vance said, gently shaking his head. "A drug dealer is quite possibly the least dangerous person to steal money from. Look, if you take a drug dealer's money, they can just deal more drugs to replace it! Now if you took *my* money, you better watch out! Because I'd be furious since I have no way of getting more money." Vance looked at Cormac who stood in awe of the scope of Vance's ignorance.

"Don't take my money," Vance added, in case Cormac had missed his point, which he in fact had. His pocket now bulging with thousands of dollars in cash, Vance walked with Cormac to the front door. When Cormac opened it, he was surprised to see a fresh copy of the *School Paper* sitting on the porch.

"When did we start having the *School Paper* delivered?" Cormac asked as he bent down to pick the paper up.

"Must be a perk of having an ace reporter crashing on your couch, huh?" Vance said. "Anything about you in there?"

"Yeah, looks like it." Cormac flipped to page B2 and read Cissy's story out loud. "'There is no news to report. Everything is totally fine with Mac. His video sure is great. Everyone should watch it. He plays the ukulele in it.' She doesn't get paid for these does she? This sounds like a dumb first grader's book report."

"I'm not gonna stand here and pretend to be a media critic, Mac," Vance said. "Leave that to the Hubert Pulitzers of the world."

"I don't think Pulitzer's first name was Hubert," Cormac said, not entirely sure if he was correct.

"Oh shit," Vance replied, no longer paying attention. Cormac looked up from the paper. Across the street he saw a couple of shabby looking tents. Two strangers standing outside of the tents had noticed Cormac and Vance on the porch and were pointing in their direction. As Cormac watched, another person popped his head out of a tent, then ducked back in to alert whoever else lurked inside.

"We should get in the car," Vance said, waving Cormac toward the Volvo.

"Vance, who the hell are those people?" Cormac asked. The overarching philosophy for virtually every facet of his life was to do the opposite of whatever Vance instructed him to do, yet he found himself instinctively following Vance toward the Volvo.

Vance jiggled the passenger side handle as he waited for Cormac to unlock it. "You remember that guy two days ago? The one with the boner?" Vance asked.

Cormac nodded and wondered how his life had hit the point where his panicked best friend was asking him if he could recall "the guy with the boner." He supposed that it could be worse: there could have been multiple guys with boners, leaving Cormac unable to differentiate which guy with the boner Vance was talking about.

"Well, that's his cult," Vance said as Cormac opened the driver side door and hit the unlock button. Vance swung the passenger door open and jumped into the car. Cormac stood there in disbelief as Vance slammed the door shut and quickly locked it behind him. Cormac looked back over at the ramshackle camp that the cult had established. There were now a few more people stirring, and all of them were looking in his direction. One of them held a sign above his head that said "IN CORMAC WE TRUST."

"Jesus," Cormac muttered, before sitting down in the driver's seat and closing the door. After he'd placed the keys in the ignition, Cormac turned to Vance. "You're sure this is a bad thing? I know cult leaders get a bad rap, but what if you were just someone who gave the cult tasks and told them what to do without being an official member? Sort of like a cult advisor?" Cormac glanced longingly at the Volvo's filthy windshield

"Did you not see that guy Brock's boner, Mac?" Vance asked, flabbergasted that Cormac was even considering engaging with the cult. "That was just from him introducing himself to you. Do you have any idea what's going to happen if you let him and his creeps wash your car? Are you actually willing to eat pizza that they picked up for you? You're really considering letting one of those guys stand in for you at jury duty? One errant boner, and BAM! You're getting held in contempt of court!"

The last scenario had not really occurred to Cormac. But he had to admit that Vance had a point. If cult members were normal people who other normal people wanted to be around, they wouldn't have joined a cult. Cormac looked in the rearview mirror and saw that a dozen or so cult members had slowly started shuffling toward the driveway. He turned the keys in the ignition and put the Volvo in reverse.

"The gas cap is on, right?" Vance asked.

Cormac looked over at Vance as the car began to roll backwards. "Of course it is. Why do you ask?"

"I wouldn't put it past one of these guys, Mac. Being in your presence causes a boner, they're unable to control themselves, they see the gas tank hole . . . You do the math, buddy."

"Vance, nobody is going to try to bang my gas tank," Cormac said, not sure at all whether that was true.

"I'd lock your door, too," Vance said, slumping down in his seat like a celebrity trying to avoid the paparazzi. Cormac took his advice, and hoped he wasn't making a huge mistake trying to drive his car past these lunatics. At least they had stopped advancing. Most of the cult stood in the middle of the street with a few hanging back on the opposite sidewalk.

As he slowly backed the Volvo down the driveway, Cormac hoped that none of the fanatics were intending to throw themselves under his wheels in a maniacal act of martyrdom. He wished that he knew more particulars about the cult's dogma. As far as he could piece together, it involved wanting to molest him or possibly just whack it in his presence while he was unconscious. For a split second, the most horrifying image he could imagine flashed through his mind, of Vance gleefully stacking the money that these creeps paid him as they filed into his bedroom one by one. But that was too far-fetched, even for Vance. Wasn't it?

The Volvo rolled out of the driveway and Cormac steered the wheel so the car started to turn in the direction of Mickey's. He noted with dismay that the creepy white van was still parked nearby. It didn't appear to have moved in days; perhaps he could call and have it towed. That was a problem for later, though. Now he had to deal with the throng of admirers who were slowly approaching his car.

Brock's followers stood in the street in front of the Volvo, and as it inched forward, they parted to flank it on either side. Forced to drive at a snail's pace to avoid running them over, Cormac was able to observe his worshippers up close. They were a tad scruffy after a night spent camping, but for the most part, they looked like normal college kids. However, being so close to Cormac's exalted presence was causing some of them to weep and they all wore matching Sistine Chapel t-shirts. Cormac made a mental note to steal the great "Harpoon This!" line when he was back on the *Levyathan*.

The cult stood so close to the car that Cormac could hear them speaking as the car crawled past. "It's closed everyone! Gas cap is closed!" announced the first person in line on the driver's side. Cormac looked over at Vance, who appeared too nervous to say I told you so. Other cult members muttered his name, or thrust babies forward hoping that Cormac would kiss them. Cormac wasn't sure whether kissing the babies would make the cult more or less likely to return them to wherever they'd obviously been stolen from. He decided that kissing them would be taken as a sign of approval, possibly even as a step toward initiation as a full-fledged cult member. He kept the car rolling.

Eventually the last few people in the crowd parted to the side, and only Brock was left standing in the path of the Volvo. The cult leader smiled warmly at Cormac and spread his arms wide to welcome him. He did not appear to be in any hurry to move. Reluctantly, Cormac lightly applied the brakes and the Volvo came to halt.

"Dearly beloved, the sacred harpooner graces us with his presence," Brock intoned to his congregation.

"May the shafts of his spears travel long and true." The reply came in unison from the cult members on all sides of the car.

Brock now addressed Cormac. "Holy art thou, oh prophet. We are here to receive your word and do your bidding."

"Let's get out of here, Mac," Vance muttered through clenched teeth as he slunk down even lower in his seat.

Cormac rolled his window down a half inch so Brock could hear him. "Why are all of you here?" Cormac shouted. "I don't have any answers for you! I don't even know what's happening myself!"

"There is light in your darkness, Cormac. Knowledge in your mystery. We do not seek answers, but have faith that we will find them if we follow your path."

"Ask him how the boners figure into everything," Vance suggested. Cormac ignored him.

"You've given us a gift, Cormac," Brock continued. "A chance to experience a higher plane. But when the dark ones defy us, they in turn defy you, and this cannot be allowed." At the mention of the dark ones, the rest of the cult began to murmur nervously, but Brock silenced them with a raised right hand.

"I'm afraid I don't entirely understand what you mean by experiencing a higher plane," Cormac said. "And who are the dark ones?"

"The troll is one," Brock intoned. "And the other sits by your side. They betray you, Cormac. Their insolence towards us, your loyal followers, is the reason for your shipmates' brush with death yesterday."

Cormac felt a chill go down his spine. For the second time that morning, somebody appeared to know what had happened to him yesterday. When Vance had brought up pirates, it had seemed odd. But the idea that these creeps somehow knew what was happening on the *Levyathan* was petrifying.

"How do you know what happened on the boat yesterday?" Cormac asked, fearing the answer.

"You radiate wisdom, oh leader," Brock replied. "We bask in your illumination. In you we shall find transcendence."

"Hey, there's no lock! The gas tank just flips open, you guys!" yelled a voice from the side of the Volvo.

Brock sized up this news and issued a new proclamation. "We shall commune with your vessel until you turn over the dark one. Give him to us so we can serve you without impediment." Cormac looked over at Vance. His roommate looked uncharacteristically anxious.

Brock motioned for the members on the driver's side of the car to line up behind the gas tank. Then he pointed first at Vance, then at two of the larger cult members, who walked over to Vance's door and began pulling on the handle.

"Holy crap!" Vance yelled. "What are you doing, Mac? They're trying to drag me out of here! Drive!"

"I can't do anything!" Cormac yelled back, not sure whether the idea of Vance being kidnapped by a cult or his "vessel" being "communed" with was causing him more panic. "He's blocking the road, I can't run him over!"

"We exist to serve you, Lord," Brock said, raising his voice and extending his fists toward the sky. "But you must not allow these dark ones to tempt you! Only once they have been removed can we truly instill our vision of—"

The cult leader was interrupted by the loud honk of a car horn. Cormac looked in his rearview mirror and saw a red pickup truck on the road behind them. The driver was a stocky guy wearing a tattered old baseball cap, and he looked pissed off as he rolled down his window.

"Hey, assholes!" the driver yelled as he leaned his head out the window. "Quit blocking the fucking road! I'm trying to drive here!"

"Sorry, Coach Newberry!" Brock said as he waved apologetically. He scurried out of the path of the Volvo and gestured for the rest of the cult to follow. They retreated back to the sidewalk, leaving Cormac's path clear. Frank Newberry, head coach of the Harrington football team, impatiently floored it into the oncoming traffic lane to pass the Volvo, making sure to give Cormac and Vance the finger as he sped past.

"That sorted itself out quickly," Cormac said.

"Just get the hell out of here," Vance pleaded. Cormac didn't have to be told twice. He stepped on the gas, and the Volvo lurched away from the disappointed cult.

"That was a close one!" Cormac said. "Those guys are creepy as hell! What do you think they would have done to you?"

"Let's hope we never find out," Vance said, clearly not wanting to dwell on the subject. "Hey do me a favor, Mac, stop the car for just a second."

"Stop here?" Cormac protested. "We've only gone twenty feet! The cult will catch up to us and bang my car!"

"It'll just take a second. Look, stop the damn car!" Vance commanded.

Cormac hit the brakes and the car skidded to a halt. Cormac looked to his left and saw that they had stopped right in front of the creepy windowless van. Before he could ask what they were doing, Vance leaned over in front of Cormac and hit the car horn three times.

Before Cormac could even wonder what the hell was going on, Vance leaned ever further over and flicked the Volvo's lights on and off three times as well. Then he hit the horn three more times and retreated back to his own seat.

"What in God's name was that?" Cormac asked.

"I thought it might scare off the pervert who keeps it parked there," Vance said. "Guess it didn't do the trick. Ah well . . . What do you say, Mickey's time?" Cormac was so flustered by Vance's weird little routine that he didn't notice the van flash its headlights once in response to Vance's coded sequence.

"Yeah, let's hit Mickey's," Cormac said. He let out a sigh as he stepped on the gas and started to drive toward the bar for a third time. He felt like the past ten minutes had earned him at least a half dozen pitchers. The entire encounter with the cult had gone by like a blur, but now that it had ended without incident, he had time to think about what Brock had said. Who was the troll? The brush with death on the *Levyathan* yesterday, that had to refer to the pirates, right? Or was it all just the ravings of someone who was obviously unwell?

Cormac stared straight ahead as he contemplated these new complications. But if he had glanced in the rearview mirror at that moment, he would have seen the Astro van rumble to life and slowly pull onto the road behind them.

* * *

Dean Frampton Q. Bickerstaff floored the gas pedal and blew through a red light. Actually, "blew through" was a fairly relative term. The maximum speed of the creaky van topped out at around twenty-seven miles per hour. The driver of an oncoming SUV that technically had the right of way slammed on his brakes when he saw that the approaching white van had no intention of obeying basic traffic regulations. The SUV then sat halfway through the intersection as the van slowly chugged across. By the time the dean's car was halfway across, the light had changed again, and the irritated SUV driver put his car in reverse and backed up to wait for his turn to come a second time.

Looking in his driver's side mirror, Dean Bickerstaff saw that the SUV driver was directing a few choice gestures his way. It was not the first time he'd irritated a fellow motorist during his tear across town, and it would not be the last. The pissed-off drivers were inconsequential, as far as Frampton was concerned, as was the flash of the traffic light camera that had registered several times as the van inched across the intersection. The van was not registered, or maybe it was registered to a dead woman. Or maybe she was just old. The dean had not really been paying attention to that part of the transaction.

What he did know was that there were only two things that could stand in his way of beating Cormac and Vance to Mickey's: traffic regulations and the cops who were paid to enforce them. Any of the latter who attempted to pull him over for violating the former could easily be bribed, if they hadn't been already. But the minutes it would cost the dean could prove the difference between pulling off his mission successfully and not.

So far his journey had involved running a red light and two stop signs, travelling for half a mile down a one-way street, and cutting across a playground. This last action had been the only one that had given Frampton pause before deciding to go for it. It would knock at least two minutes off of the trip, but the odds seemed relatively high that the van would make some type of contact with at least one child in the process. High risk, high reward, Dean Bickerstaff had thought as he turned right at the monkey bars.

But to his surprise, he did not run down any children. In fact, the alert parents supervising the children had seen the van when it was still rumbling toward the outskirts of the playground and used some sort of emergency signal to gather the children into tightly knit groups. It must have been a drill that the children had practiced, because they responded quickly and methodically, though at times several of them were sobbing hysterically in fear. It was disgusting how bigoted people were at the sight of a perfectly normal van, the dean thought as a curly slide came out of nowhere to clip off the passenger-side mirror. Aside from being wildly driven on a stretch of public land never intended for vehicle traffic, the van posed no threat to the children. If there were time, the dean would have stopped to give the parents a piece of his mind, but they might have had trouble hearing him over those damned whistles they started blowing as soon as the van appeared.

Dean Bickerstaff hastily rounded a corner and breathed a sigh of relief as the sign for Mickey's came into view. Still slightly hungover from yesterday's day-long drunk, spending several hours in a sleazy dive bar was the last thing that Frampton wanted to do. But Vance's coded instructions could not have been clearer. He and Cormac were headed to Mickey's and the dean needed to make sure there wasn't going to be any trouble with loudmouths who might spill the beans about their scam. The day after Frampton bought the van, Vance had provided him with a lengthy list of code signals, which the dean had largely ignored. But a few had struck Frampton as worth committing to memory, and "get to the bar as soon as possible" seemed like one that Vance would probably have a reason to use one day, and if he didn't have a reason, he'd probably find one.

The dean rolled over the curb and into the Mickey's parking lot. This was where having an inconspicuous vehicle really paid off. If he'd been driving his own car, he would have to park at least a couple blocks away to ensure Cormac wouldn't spot it. But with the van, he could pretty much park next to the front door and it would fit right in with the other decrepit junkers that Mickey's customers drove under the influence to and from the watering hole. Well, for the most part, they were all decrepit junkers. Frampton noted that there was, shockingly enough, a black Lincoln Town Car parked right near the door.

No doubt it belonged to a player from the Harrington basketball team. Fancy cars were just one of the many under-the-table benefits that boosters used to lure top recruits to the school. The dean had long approved of the illegal activities, and used his connection at the Lincoln dealership to provide rides for the players that were only slightly less luxurious than his own. Frampton hit the brakes and maneuvered the van into the empty parking spot next to the Town Car. Perfect, he thought. With this ostentatious, top-of-the-line automobile parked next to it, the Astro van may as well be invisible.

The dean creaked the van door open and hopped out. Even though time was of the essence, he allowed himself a moment to admire the sleek exterior of the Town Car. Then he slammed the van door shut, lit up a cigar, gave his shillelagh a twirl, and walked into Mickey's.

Mickey's was exactly the type of bar that the dean imagined Vance spending his rare hours off the couch in. The lowlifes who filled the place winced as the gust of fresh air raced in when the dean opened the door, then relaxed as the dean's putrid cigar smoke quickly cancelled it out. Every customer looked like they were no more than an hour removed or away from doing something stupid or illegal. The dean was slightly alarmed to see that there appeared to be a severed human leg sitting on one of the barstools, but it turned out that it was just a prosthetic. Its former owner had lost it in a billiards bet and now sat in a booth trying to figure out how he was going to be able to get to the bar for another beer. The man who had won the leg was not wearing a shirt at the moment. The dean thought it best to avoid any man who considered fake legs a more desirable thing to wager than say, who has to buy the next pitcher.

Fortunately, Frampton's business was not with the customers but rather the bartender. He grinned as he approached the rough-looking man who stood behind the bar. The dean knew the importance of always maintaining a confident exterior, but right now that was made difficult by the fact that the bartender was wiping a sticky substance off of a rusty steel bear trap that sat on the counter. Nevertheless, he confidently waddled toward the bar, lifted himself onto the barstool, and cleared his throat.

"Doing some bear hunting later?" Frampton asked the bartender.

"Nope," the bartender said, not looking up from the bear trap.

"Well, sir, I have an unusual proposition for you," Frampton continued, undeterred and more than a little terrified. "I'd like to buy out the entire bar for as long as I'm here."

This got the bartender's attention. He stopped wiping and looked up at Frampton.

"Whatever any of these gentlemen want, it's on me," Frampton said as he reached into his pocket to pull out some cash. This was an old trick that he had heard Sinatra's posse used to pull. Walk into a bar ahead of the Chairman of the Board and tell everyone their drinks were taken care of as long as they left Frank alone. And shillelagh beatings for anyone who disobeyed. Dean Bickerstaff had never actually seen a picture of Sinatra in the presence of a shillelagh, but he figured that Ol' Blue Eyes would have insisted his goons use only the finest blunt objects to deliver their beatings, and obviously a shillelagh would have been in the rotation, if not at the top of it.

The bartender appeared not to have heard of this particular strategy before. He stared at the dean with his one good eye for a few seconds, not saying anything. Then, without warning, he lifted his eye patch, revealing a hollow, withered eye socket that was without a doubt one of the worst things Frampton had ever seen in his life.

"What kind of a bar do you think this is?" the bartender asked angrily. The dean could only stammer as he tried to avoid looking into the revolting pit of ocular horror. The bartender repeated himself. "What kind of a bar do you think this is? Look me in the eye socket and tell me what kind of a bar you think this is."

Frampton forced himself to look the bartender in what used to be his eye. His eye socket looked like the mouth of the devil. "It's a dive bar," Frampton eventually stammered.

"That's right," the bartender said. "It's a dive bar for people to get drunk without any funny business."

"I certainly don't mean to cause any funny business," Frampton said. He tried to look away from the socket, but now it seemed to have locked his gaze to its horrible void.

"You walk in and tell me you want to buy every man in my bar a drink. That sounds like funny business to me." The bartender did something with his eye that Frampton later realized must have been the hollow-eye-socket equivalent of a wink. It caused the knotted, gnarled folds of the eye socket to expand and contract. The dean was terrified that any moment something was going to emerge from the eye socket and latch onto his face.

"Ah, no, see that's an old technique that Frank Sinatra used to use," Frampton tried to explain.

"Are you insinuating that Frank Sinatra used to buy men drinks?" the bartender said in a voice that suggested that a line had been crossed. Frampton finally managed to tear his gaze away from the eye socket. He looked up from the bartender's face, hoping to gain a moment's respite from the withering gaze, only to immediately spot a framed picture of Frank Sinatra. It was centered in a place of honor above the bar, and personally signed "To Mickey" from Sinatra himself.

"Listen, Mickey," Frampton said, attempting to right the ship. "You are Mickey, right?"

"Nobody but The Voice himself is allowed to call me Mickey," Mickey said.

This caught Frampton off guard. "Really? You made the name of your bar something you don't want anyone to call you?"

Without a word, Mickey leaned over the bar and grabbed Frampton's shillelagh. As he pulled it back to his side of the bar, Frampton lunged for it, missed, and fell off the barstool. When he pulled himself back up, what he saw made his jaw drop. Mickey was holding the shillelagh inside the open jaws of the bear trap. If he pressed it onto the trigger, the trap would snap shut and splinter the shillelagh like a toothpick.

"I didn't like the looks of you from the minute you walked in the door," Mickey growled. "We serve hard drinks in here for men who want to get drunk fast, and we don't need any characters around to give the joint atmosphere. I'm gonna break your little stick, and then if you're still around when I'm done I'm gonna pick you up and stick your leg in here too."

The rest of the bar patrons, apparently used to this type of thing, ignored the ruckus taking place at the bar. One man was waiting patiently for Mickey to finish up with the dean so he could get change for the jukebox. The dean was more scared than he could ever remember being, but he couldn't help but satisfy his curiosity.

"*It's a Wonderful Life*?" Frampton stammered.

"Is that so?" Mickey said. "I guess we'll see about that. He slowly lowered the shillelagh into the trap an inch or two.

"What you just said," the dean sputtered. "About serving hard drinks for men who like to get drunk fast, and you don't need any characters. It's from the movie *It's a Wonderful Life*. The bartender says it to Clarence the angel!"

Mickey looked at the dean, then looked around the bar to see if anyone else had heard him. Without a word, he pulled the shillelagh out of the mouth of the trap and handed it back to the dean. Frampton wanted to exhale in relief, but was still waiting for the other shoe to drop.

"I've been saying that line for twenty-three years hoping somebody would recognize it," Mickey said in a hushed tone.

"It's a great movie," Dean Bickerstaff said, carefully climbing back onto the barstool.

"Crushed a lot of bones in this bear trap waiting for someone to get that reference," Mickey said wistfully, with a distant tinge of regret in his voice.

"I'm pretty sure that was avoidable," the dean said, making sure he kept a firm grip on his shillelagh.

"I just get frustrated with people not remembering the classics," Mickey said. He gave his head one last shake, then pulled the eye patch down over his eye again. He picked up a bar rag and gave the area in front of Frampton a quick wipe down. "Now what was it you were asking about again?" the bartender inquired.

"Look, I just have a big shot coming in here," the dean explained, making a mental note to be sure to exploit any future disfigurements he might suffer for intimidation purposes. "And it's very important that your customers leave him alone. I'm willing to pay their bar tab in advance to make sure they get the message."

"Ah, the old Sinatra ploy," Mickey said with a chuckle. "One of my all-time favorites."

Dean Bickerstaff didn't even bother. Instead he once again reached into his pocket. He pulled out the thick wad of cash that he'd earned yesterday and started to thumb off hundred-dollar bills.

Mickey was doing some quick mental math. "So you guys'll be here a couple hours, we got a dozen or so people in here already. Make it fifty bucks."

"Fifty bucks?" Frampton was surprised and dismayed. Any slob could buy out a place for fifty bucks!

"I pride myself on my reasonable prices," Mickey said. "Helps build customer loyalty."

Frampton rolled his eyes and stuffed the wad of hundreds back into his pocket. He rooted around some more and found a few crumpled-up twenties. He tossed three of them onto the bar, noting that at least one of them was wrapped around old chewing gum. "Keep the change," he instructed Mickey.

Mickey nodded appreciatively and walked over to the cash register to ring up the sale. Then he reached up and grabbed a cord attached to a bell that was mounted on the wall. He rang the bell sharply three times, and a hush fell over the bar. The dean thought everyone looked kind of nervous all of a sudden; evidently this bell was not typically used to announce news that would benefit them.

"Listen up, people!" Mickey barked in a voice that was very much his pre–*It's A Wonderful Life* identification voice. Mickey pointed at Frampton. "This guy right here is with me! You give him and his friends their space, hear me?" Frampton nodded smugly. "Anyone who bothers them, we hold you down and stick your dick in the bear trap!"

Frampton flinched so hard he nearly dropped his shillelagh. "That really won't be necessary," he tried to assure Mickey. "Just tell them that we'll buy them drinks if they leave us—"

"Now you all saw how much that hurt the first guy today," Mickey reminded his customers, barreling right over the dean's pleas. "And lord knows I don't want to clean the trap twice in one afternoon!"

"You already cut some guy's dick off with that thing today?" Dean Bickerstaff said in disbelief. "What happened to him? Is he still here drinking?" For a guy who was so concerned about building customer loyalty, Mickey certainly issued a lot of bear-trap-based threats.

443

Mickey gave him a wave of the hand that said "Don't worry about it." He then finished addressing the crowd. "Now this man has been nice enough to buy you all a few rounds of drinks."

"Whoa, look at Sinatra here!" one of the more coherent barflies blurted out. Mickey immediately pointed at the bear trap and the barfly shut up. The rest of the customers mumbled their appreciation and slowly started to shuffle toward the bar. Frampton took a deep breath and slowly exhaled. It had not gone as smoothly as he hoped, but he had accomplished his mission. And not a moment too soon, for just then the dean heard a familiar voice call out from behind him.

"Hey! What's a couple of guys got to do to get a pitcher around here?"

Dean Bickerstaff turned and saw that Vance and Cormac had just entered the bar. Vance was the one demanding the immediate service. He and Cormac were walking toward the bar, but neither of them had spotted the dean yet.

"Let's go! It's almost noon here!" Vance yelled. "Whatever's cheap, two pitchers!" When he got to the bar he banged on it with both hands. Cormac stood behind him looking slightly chagrined. Mickey glared at both of them before walking over to the tap handles and filling up two pitchers with beer.

"Hey Mac, check it out, they've got the bear trap out!" Vance said, excitedly pointing at the trap. "If you can pull your drink out of the trap before it goes off, you get the next one half price! Hey!" he yelled to Mickey. "We wanna do the trap game!"

Mickey set the pitchers down in front of Vance and shook his head. "Won't be necessary today, fellas. These are already taken care of."

"Would a third one also be taken care of?" Vance asked quickly.

Cormac pushed past him and grabbed the pitchers. "These will be fine for now," he said before Vance could order any more.

"How many glasses do you need?" Mickey asked, eager to move on to the next customers.

"Well, it's just going to be us," Vance informed him. "So why don't you just give us . . ." Vance paused mid-sentence as he pretended to notice Dean Bickerstaff sitting a few stools away. "Wait a second. Dean? Dean Bickerstaff?"

"Oh goddammit," Cormac muttered as he saw the dean smiling from his barstool. Cormac set one of the pitchers back down on the bar and grabbed a straw from a box of bar supplies. He tore the top of the paper wrapper off with his teeth, blew the rest of it off, then plopped the straw into the pitcher and walked off to find a booth.

"We'll take three glasses," Vance told Mickey as the dean hopped off his barstool and walked over to join his partner in crime. "Looks like you took care of business, Deano!" Vance said.

"You owe me one for this," Dean Bickerstaff hissed. "What the hell kind of place is this? Didn't you have enough to drink yesterday? What are we doing here?"

"Relax, Deano," Vance said, picking up the second pitcher. "I'm just a guy who wants to spend some quality time with his roommate. And use information I obtained while he was unconscious to catch him in a web of lies so I can hold it over his head and get him to do stuff for me. Grab those glasses, would ya?"

Vance walked off to join Cormac in the booth, leaving Dean Bickerstaff to pick up the three pint glasses that Mickey had set down. The dean grabbed them and followed after Vance. He was happy to see that his confrontation with the bartender had not been in vain. Cormac sat alone in the booth, sipping on a pitcher that was surprisingly low for how recently it had been ordered. The dean noticed several of the barflies glancing in Cormac's direction, perhaps recognizing him from the photo that accompanied Cissy's article in that day's *School Paper*. But nobody approached him to discuss his whaling exploits due to the fear of their genitals being forced into the bear trap. Frampton had to admit that it served as an effective deterrent.

"Hey, there he is!" the dean beamed as he slid into the booth next to Vance. "What's the good word, Cormac?"

Cormac took a long pull from his straw and burped. "What are you doing here, Dean Bickerstaff?" he asked. "This doesn't really seem like your kind of place."

"Nonsense!" Frampton said as he attempted to pour a beer from the second pitcher. Pouring beers was not a skill that the dean had ever bothered to learn and the first few drops of liquid immediately foamed up to the brim of the glass and over onto the table. The dean forced himself to laugh and pushed the glass aside. "There's plenty of guys like me who love coming down to a blue-collar joint like this to relax. I know there's at least one guy here who's doing OK for himself. I'm sure you spotted his Town Car in the parking lot?"

Cormac shook his head. "The only thing I saw in the parking lot was another one of those pervert vans. Is there a convention in town or something? It's like they're everywhere now."

The dean pursed his lips in frustration. "You must mean that van that was parked next to the Town Car? Can't say I paid much attention to it. Too busy admiring the craftsmanship of the luxurious Lincoln Town Car."

"Didn't notice it," Cormac said, reaching across the table and deftly pouring Vance a beer using only one hand. "In fact, I don't think I'd even notice a Town Car if I passed by a parking lot full of them."

"Oh, I think you'd notice a Town Car," the dean said. He did not appreciate his favorite brand of luxury automobile being disrespected and was trying not to let his frustration boil over. "They cut a very striking presence on the road."

"I don't even have an association with them," Cormac said. "Actually, I think you're the only person I've ever heard mention them. Wait a second . . . You know what, I think maybe I did see it. Was the Town Car that bright purple convertible?"

"Go fuck yours—" Vance jabbed the dean in the ribs to cut him off before he said something he couldn't take back. Frampton corrected himself. "'Go fuck yourself' is what all the other drivers on the road will enviously be thinking when you cruise by in a luxurious Town Car. Take a look on the way out, Cormac, I don't think you'll regret it."

"No dice," Cormac informed him. "I'm going out the side door to avoid the pervert van."

The dean started to reply but Vance chimed in before he could speak up. Frampton had no choice but to sit there and stew.

"Hey, I just want to say cheers to hanging out on a Friday with old friends and new." Vance said as he refilled his already-empty beer glass. "And hey, free drinks never hurt either, right?"

"Why were they free again?" Cormac asked as he half-heartedly clinked his pitcher against Vance's glass.

"Don't look a gift horse in the mouth, Cormac!" Dean Bickerstaff said as he tapped his glass of foam against the other two. He attempted to tilt the glass back and sip whatever beer there was at the bottom of the glass, but the foam went up his nose and he half-choked, half-sneezed, spraying more foam all over the table.

"Let me help you with that, Dean Bickerstaff," Vance said. He reached over and dumped the contents of the dean's glass onto the floor underneath their booth. Then Vance filled up the pint glass with beer and handed it to the dean with a smile.

Cormac rolled his eyes in embarrassment at the dean's amateurish beer drinking habits and sucked at his straw until it was pulling nothing but air. "Well, looks like I need another one," he informed the rest of the table. "How are you holding up, Vance?"

"Right behind you, buddy," Vance said. "Get two, I'll be done by the time you get back." Vance looked at the dean, who was sniffing in an attempt to make his nose stop tingling from beer bubbles. "Why don't you get the dean something that's a bit more to his liking, huh? What'll it be Dean, cognac?"

The dean pressed one of his nostrils closed with his finger and blew out through the other one while nodding that he would very much prefer a cognac. Cormac got up from the table and carried his empty pitcher over to the bar. He was hoping that all of the high-proof rum he'd been drinking on the *Levyathan* had increased his tolerance for watery light beer. Vance was always willing to get drunk enough to say something he'd regret; Cormac just had to stay a few steps behind him so he didn't do the same thing. Cormac figured that the presence of the dean, while unexplained and off-putting, could only help his cause. Vance would be trying to impress him, and that meant he wouldn't be turning down any drinks he was offered, lest the dean perceive it as a sign of weakness.

Cormac set his pitcher down on the bar and waited for the bartender's attention. Glancing to his right, Cormac observed that the gentleman sitting on the nearest barstool was carving something into the bar with a medium sized boot knife. The knife's handle was a creamy white color that Cormac thought he recognized.

"That's a nice piece of scrimshaw," Cormac said to the stranger. Normally, talking to knife-wielding strangers was not high on his list of desirable activities to engage in, but he'd just guzzled an entire pitcher of beer and was feeling kind of friendly.

The man with the knife unfortunately was not feeling anything close to friendly. He had a greasy, grey ponytail, narrow, cruel eyes, and apparently was the kind of guy who did not appreciate having his knife complimented. He jammed the knife straight down into the surface of the bar and intertwined his fingers, flexing them outward to crack his knuckles. "What did you say about my blade?" he muttered, as he turned to look at Cormac.

Fearing he'd made a critical error in addressing this man, Cormac instinctively looked around for a harpoon gun within reaching distance. In most places in the twenty-first century, this was a pointless act, but if any establishment was going to have one lying around, Mickey's would be it. But seizing a deadly weapon proved to be entirely unnecessary. When the man with the knife turned and saw who he was talking to, his eyes went wide. He looked at Cormac, then over at Vance and the dean, then at the bear trap that sat at the other end of the bar.

"I didn't mean it," the man stammered. "I mean . . . You can . . . Crap!" The man turned and fled out the front door, leaving his knife still quivering in the wooden surface of the bar. Cormac watched him go, then turned around, just to make sure there wasn't an even more dangerous character with an even bigger knife standing behind him. The only thing he saw was a sick-looking dog gnawing on what appeared to be a prosthetic leg. As cool as that was, Cormac doubted it had caused the ponytailed man to turn and flee like that.

Cormac shrugged and turned his attention back to the bar, where the bartender was attempting to work the knife free. "He'll be back," the bartender assured Cormac. "Nobody ever leaves a good piece of steel behind for long." He wobbled the knife back and forth a few more times, then managed to pull it free. The bartender reached under the bar and grabbed a cardboard box. He placed it on the bar and Cormac saw that it bore the handwritten label "Lost & Found – Knives." The bartender dropped the knife into the box, which Cormac couldn't help but notice had at least a dozen knives already in it.

"I thought you said nobody ever leaves a good piece of steel behind?" Cormac said.

"These are all just from today," the bartender assured him, sliding the box back under the bar. "What'll it be?"

Cormac requested two more pitchers and a cognac. While the bartender was fetching them, he looked back over at Vance and the dean. Vance had finished his pitcher and was telling a story to the dean with the emphatic hand gestures that Cormac knew were a sign that he was on his way to drunkenness. Still, it couldn't hurt to speed things along.

"Can I also get three shots of vodka?" Cormac asked when the bartender set the pitchers down.

"No problem," he responded. "Looks like you'll have your hands full, you want me to just bring them over to the table?"

"No thanks," Cormac said. "Right here will be fine."

The bartender shrugged, then produced a bottle of cheap vodka from the bar rail and poured out three shots. "No charge, of course," he said, and walked away before Cormac could inquire as to what the reason was for this unprecedented generosity. Cormac picked up another straw and placed it in one of the pitchers, then, after making sure Vance wasn't watching him, quickly dumped all three of the vodka shots into the other one. Vance was going to be a few steps ahead of him, whether he knew it or not.

Cormac picked the glass of cognac up with his mangled hand and grabbed both pitcher handles with his other. He brought them over to the table, where Vance stopped the story he was telling to cheer the arrival of more beer. Noting the straw, Cormac was careful to make sure Vance grabbed the pitcher with the extra vodka in it. He sat down, waited for Vance to pour himself a glass of vodka beer, then extended his pitcher to his two drinking buddies.

"Cheers," Cormac said.

* * *

The afternoon passed slowly at first, but eventually the pitchers and drinks seemed to come quicker and quicker. Cormac was determined to keep track of how many rounds they were putting away in order to pace himself, but eventually even he lost track of whether they were on their sixth or seventh pitcher. All he could do was continue to supplement Vance's beers with vodka and hope his roommate would eventually slip up and reveal something about what was going on while he was unconscious.

So far, Vance's performance would have rivaled even the most tightlipped witness in a mafia trial. Every time that Cormac tried to steer the conversation toward how he was spending his days while Cormac was on the *Levyathan*, Vance managed to find a way to change the subject. Cormac marveled at how deftly Vance was able to deflect inquiries about what he had done yesterday, though he started to wonder if techniques like "pretending he couldn't understand what Cormac was saying" and "falling asleep on the table" were really strategic maneuvers or just the result of all the booze they were drinking.

Still, Cormac kept charging ahead, knowing that at some point in time, Vance would have to slip up. He still thought his roommate was acting weird in general. Vance kept asking him leading questions about the previous day on the *Levyathan*, whether he'd seen anything cool, or done anything immoral, or evaded any specific marauding dangers. A couple of times when he'd nodded off, he'd been frightened to see Cormac when he woke up.

He also kept calling the dean "Deano," which Cormac felt was kind of inappropriate and risky. Sure, Dean Bickerstaff evidently had enough free time that he could spend Friday afternoon binge drinking with two students he barely knew, but he was still a powerful man who could easily affect their future. You didn't want to piss him off. He'd already tricked Cormac into his media exclusivity clause; who knew what other things he had embedded in the fine print of their contract that could allow him to renege on the straight A's bargain.

The dean didn't appear to appreciate Vance's casual demeanor, and frequently glared at him in between gulps of the double cognacs he was now ordering. Cormac found the dean's distaste for Vance slightly endearing, and he had begun to warm to the strange little man over the course of the afternoon. Again, this probably had a great deal to do with the large amount of alcohol he'd consumed on an empty stomach. But when Cormac went down his mental list of people who were most likely to beat Vance over the head with a knotted stick of some sort, the dean was by far the top contender, and that made him OK in Cormac's eyes.

The dean was currently telling a story about a time he had blackmailed a Harrington admissions officer into accepting a student who turned out to be a horse. It had belonged to a very wealthy, yet very unstable alumnus. Cormac was enjoying the dean's tales of corruption and graft, and he was disappointed when this one came to an abrupt end. One moment the dean was doing a hilarious impression of the unfortunate admissions officer trying to feed the new student a sugar cube, the next he and Vance were staring at Cormac with their mouths open.

"What's the matter?" Cormac asked them.

"Is something wrong with your ear, Mac?" Vance asked. Cormac was briefly taken aback, but then realized that he was absentmindedly fiddling with his left earlobe with his mangled hand. He quickly pulled his hand away from his ear like an ashamed dog who'd been caught drinking out of an unflushed toilet.

"No, nothing's wrong." Cormac said. "Please, Dean Bickerstaff, finish the story."

"You've been rubbing it for like the past five minutes," Vance said warily. The dean nodded to confirm that this was true.

Without being conscious of what he was doing, Cormac reached back up and started to rub his ear again. He caught himself after a second or two and instantly stopped. "Sorry," he said. Across the table, Vance and the dean shared a concerned glance.

"It doesn't hurt, does it?" Dean Bickerstaff asked.

"It doesn't feel like you may have caught some weird disease from having a bunch of strange stuff or people come into contact with it?" Vance added as a follow-up.

"No," Cormac said. He wasn't sure why he'd been rubbing his ear. It did feel a little raw, but maybe he'd been rubbing it as a nervous tic and just hadn't noticed. "It's nothing like that. You know what? I think I must have just been remembering about Captain Anson on the *Levyathan.*" Cormac chuckled at the memory of the previous day. "The idiot found an earring and just shoved it through his own ear without sanitizing it or anything. It flared up right away, I bet it's gonna get infected."

The dean winced and involuntarily raised his hand to his own ear, but drunkenly missed by a few inches and whacked it against the back of the booth. "See!" Cormac said. "It's not a very pleasant thing to think about!" He laughed again and took a sip from his pitcher.

"He just found an earring on the ship while you guys were at sea?" Vance sounded skeptical. "Where was it, like stuck in between one of the floorboards or on a dead body or something?"

Cormac instantly regretted mentioning the Black Barnacle's earring. He had no desire to discuss the events that lead to scavenged earrings being readily available on the *Levyathan.* Instead of answering Vance, he stood up and gestured to the bar. "Another round?" he asked.

Vance nodded emphatically. Dean Bickerstaff pulled his sleeve back to check a watch that wasn't there, then shrugged his approval. He pulled a cigar out of his pocket and set to figuring out which end was supposed to go in his mouth as Cormac headed toward the bar. Evidently Mickey had seen him coming, because by the time Cormac reached the bar, two pitchers of beer, a double cognac, and three shots of vodka were already laid out for him.

Cormac took a deep breath and glanced back at the booth as he dumped the three shots of vodka into Vance's pitcher. Vance's guard was down and his judgment was even worse than normal. It was now or never. If Cormac waited any longer to try and get information from him, he ran the risk of Vance losing the ability to form coherent sentences or succumbing to the alcohol poisoning he'd been so gallantly defying the odds against for the past three years.

Cormac was also somehow still cognizant enough to realize that his own descent into abject drunkenness was not that far behind. In fact, as he analyzed the situation with a more critical eye, it now appeared that he had poured two of the vodka shots onto the crotch of his pants instead of into the pitcher. Wait, that *was* vodka, wasn't it? Cormac bent over, attempting to lower his nose close enough to the crotch of his pants so that he could sniff out whether it was vodka or urine, which turned out to be a very uncomfortable position. After a few deep, incredibly awkward inhales, he straightened back up, around 80 percent confident that it was vodka. Yes, taking care of business soon was definitely imperative.

Cormac picked up the drinks and wobbled back over to the booth. Vance and the dean had their arms around each other and were singing along to the jukebox. Neither of them was singing the song that was actually playing on the jukebox, or the same song as each other for that matter. But their enthusiasm could not be denied. His roommate's judgment was shot, his filter was non-existent. All Cormac had to do was deftly time the start of his interrogation and he'd have the answers he needed.

"I guess I had that bartender wrong all along," Cormac said as he handed them their drinks. "Turns out he's a pretty friendly guy. Had our drinks all ready to go. Say, Vance, what was going on with that bag of—"

Cormac was interrupted by Dean Bickerstaff spitting his sip of brandy out onto the table in surprise. Frampton stared at Cormac in disbelief, too shocked to mop up his mess. "Friendly?" The dean yelled. "That guy? He's insane! Before you guys got here he took off his eye patch and made me stare into the hollow void where his eye used to be!"

"Why did he do that?" Vance asked, taking a break from belting out the wrong lyrics to another song that was not playing.

"Never mind that," Dean Bickerstaff grumbled. "It was awful."

"Why did you obey him?" Vance needled back.

"I don't want to talk about it!" The dean snapped, wishing he'd kept his mouth shut.

"I saw underneath a guy's eye patch yesterday." Cormac chimed in. "It's not a pretty sight, is it?" An opportunity to have a conversation that Vance could not participate in pushed whatever Cormac had been about to say from his mind. A feeble voice somewhere in his head cried out that even vaguely alluding to the pirates might be a bad idea. Hogwash, the rest of his brain slurred. This was his best chance to spite Vance in recent memory. He'd just gracefully tiptoe around the subject of pirates, *if* it happened to come up.

"Was the guy with the eye patch a pirate?" Vance asked.

Cormac was screwed. He felt his face flush. He had no idea how to tiptoe around the subject. To stall for time, Cormac lifted his pitcher and gulped down half its contents. Midway through the chug, a plan came to him. Cormac sat the pitcher down and wiped his mouth with his wrist. It was definitely outside the box, but if he really sold the delivery, it just might work.

"No," he said.

Unfortunately, with the skill of a ruthless prosecution attorney, Vance pressed the issue. "Are you sure it wasn't a pirate?" he asked.

"Alright! It was a pirate!" Cormac blurted out, unable to keep up the ruse any longer. "I killed a bunch of pirates yesterday! I've lied to you every time you asked me about it!" Dammit. That had gone about as poorly as humanly possible.

"Jeez, Mac," Vance said. "Multiple homicides don't strike me as very 'you.'"

"Look, it's hard to describe." Cormac's mind raced as he realized this was true. "It just doesn't feel the same there as it does here. It doesn't feel like real life. Killing those pirates was like shooting people in a video game, where you have a free pass to do whatever you want. Then you wake up and let other people deal with the consequences."

"I dunno, Mac," Vance said with a shake of his head. "A video game? I mean, you're here just as often as you are there."

Cormac slumped back in the booth as this realization descended on him. He had never thought about his situation from this perspective. He had been waking up on the *Levyathan* for two weeks, but he still considered *this* the real world. Cormac realized that he'd been operating under the unspoken assumption that at some point his travels back in time would eventually end. If this turned out not to be the case, recklessly killing people might be something he should think about scaling back.

Vance put on his best concerned face and looked at the dean, who had nodded off. "I'm not sure if I feel comfortable going to sleep at night knowing that there's an admitted murderer in the next room." He turned back to Cormac. "Maybe you should be paying a larger share of rent?"

"Why is there a giant bag of weed and stacks of cash in our house?" Cormac demanded, unable to control himself. This was far from the masterful interrogation he had envisioned when they left the house several hours ago.

"Whoa, man." Vance threw up his hands. "That hardly seems relevant in light of the bomb you just dropped, Mac. Even if it were, I'm way too drunk to talk about that. I might say something I'd regret!" Vance laughed at the thought while Cormac balled up his fists and bit his lip in frustration.

"It's probably time to get out of here," Vance continued. "Hell, I haven't even had breakfast yet. Deano! Hey, Deano!" He elbowed Dean Bickerstaff in the ribs and the dean snorted as he woke up.

"It's time to go, Deano," Vance informed him. "We're calling a cab, do you need one?"

"We don't need a cab," Cormac said, feeling rather defiant. "I can drive."

"You? Come on now, Mac!" Vance laughed. "I didn't want to say anything before, but we all saw that you peed your pants. Too bad killing pirates doesn't help you hold your liquor!"

Cormac thought about protesting that he hadn't peed his pants, but he had no desire to have any more of his recent duplicity exposed. Letting Vance, who probably would have peed his own pants several times that week if he hadn't switched to a towel-based wardrobe, believe that he had wet himself was better than risking him finding out he'd been spiking his beer with vodka all morning.

"You guys go ahead," Dean Bickerstaff said. "I'll call for a Town Car."

"A what?" Cormac asked. Vance may have bested him at the information-extraction game, but he could still needle the dean. Frampton fumed, a state of mind not improved in the slightest by the fact that Vance was attempting to get out of the booth by crawling over him.

"Was that a light beer or something, Mac?" Vance asked as he awkwardly straddled the furious dean's face. "I feel like I shouldn't even be able to walk after all those pitchers." Immediately after finishing his sentence, Vance swung his leg over the dean, climbed out of the booth, then promptly buckled at the knees and passed out on the filthy floor of Mickey's.

"Can you make that two Town Cars?" Cormac asked the dean. The size of the puff of cigar smoke blown directly into his face led him to believe that he should probably just call a taxi.

* * *

The one advantage to getting so drunk that you have to take a cab home, Cormac realized, is that any cults camped out in front of your house won't recognize your car coming and you can get to your front door before they harass you. He didn't imagine that this was the sort of sage advice you could build a TED Talk around, but he was still glad to get inside without dealing with Brock and his crazies.

Not that Vance didn't make it interesting. The total sum of the day's alcohol consumption seemed to have descended upon him all at once as they were leaving Mickey's. The only indication Vance gave that he was alive on the way home was a brief insistence that the cabbie take them to a Mexican joint so they could get burritos. The driver, who was surprised that anyone could be this drunk before 3:00 p.m. on a weekday afternoon without technically being dead, took some convincing. Vance provided it in the form of a hundred dollars that he peeled off his stack of cash. After this, the driver would have taken them anywhere, which was something Cormac sincerely hoped Vance did not ask him to do.

At the Mexican place, Vance had peeled off another hundred bucks and tossed it into the drive-thru window. "Give us that much burritos," he slurred, before passing out again. The confused drive-thru attendant confirmed that the three men in the taxi, one of them potentially newly dead, really wanted the approximately thirty-one burritos that this would buy. Cormac thought it was easiest to just nod yes.

The burritos came out in a garbage bag with a speed that made Cormac question just how edible something prepared that quickly could possibly be, but he was pretty drunk himself and managed to polish off three on the way home. The cab cruised past the cult without any trouble, but the members began to stir once it pulled into Cormac's driveway. Cormac slapped Vance awake and told him to pay the cabbie. Vance peeled off another hundred dollars from his roll and tossed it into the front seat. This would have been more than enough to cover the twenty-three dollar fare, but Vance also insisted that the confused driver accept two burritos as a tip.

Brock's cult hung out in the street, the members appearing to keep their distance, but Cormac didn't want to risk it. He jumped out of the cab and ran over to the other side, where he opened the door and pulled Vance out by the back of his shirt. Vance thrust the two tip burritos toward the driver, and just managed to grab the garbage bag full of the rest of them before Cormac slammed the cab door. The taxi pulled out of the driveway and Cormac shepherded

Vance and his enormous bag of Mexican food toward the front door.

The cult began to chant something ominous sounding while Cormac fumbled with his keys. Actually, to an impartial observer, the melody and intonation of the chant would have been fairly pleasant sounding, upbeat even. But it turns out that if a cult starts chanting because of your presence, it's going to sound ominous no matter what. Cormac looked over his shoulder and noticed that some cult members had flagged down the taxi and were climbing into the now-hallowed backseat that their savior had sat in. Vance had paid the cabbie well, but Cormac couldn't imagine that two hundred dollars was worth whatever the cult was planning to do back there. He finally got the front door open, pushed Vance inside, then slammed and locked the door behind him.

Vance shuffled into the living room, dragging the bag of burritos as Cormac leaned back against the front door. Evading the cult had gotten his adrenaline pumping and he was breathing heavily. This was made very difficult by the thick cloud of marijuana smoke that drifted up from an unseen source on the airborne couch. Cormac coughed and shook his head and followed Vance around to the front of the couches.

He was relieved when he rounded the couch and saw that Cissy was sitting alone, puffing on a thick blunt and watching a muted nature program on TV. He was not relieved at all when his last step landed on a large Ziploc freezer bag that was empty aside from a few bits of weed shake. Cormac looked back up from the bag at Cissy. She had the look of someone who was not sure if she was high, or dreaming, or if it was yesterday.

"Cissy! Hey, Cissy!" Cormac snapped his fingers to try and get her attention. Eventually Cissy turned her head to look at him. She giggled when saw him standing there. Evidently she hadn't noticed their arrival until now. "Cissy, this is important. Did you smoke all the weed that was in this bag?"

"Yes," Cissy replied, unable to suppress a snort of laughter.

"Good God, that must have been five pounds of weed!" Cormac's terror unfortunately outweighed how impressed he was.

"We've got to get you to a doctor! The smoke inhalation alone has to be almost deadly!"

"You wanna burrito?" Vance asked.

"No," Cissy replied. Vance handed her a burrito. Cissy tore the wrapper off of it and devoured half of it in about two bites. Cormac watched, trying to piece together what the hell was going on. He was drunk enough that very little was making sense in general, but he'd also spent enough time with Vance to understand the twisted logic of a serious stoner.

"Cissy, are you so high that you answered our questions in the reverse order, even though when you answered me Vance hadn't asked his question yet?" Cormac asked. Now it was Cissy's turn to be terrified. Her eyes went wide and she shrank back into the couch at the sight of whatever lay behind the terrifying new mental doors Cormac's deep question had opened.

"Sorry, relax. Let's try this," Cormac said. He thought he knew what was going on but he had to tread carefully. "Cissy: do you want another burrito?" Cissy shook her head no and looked like she might be about to cry. Cormac pressed on. "And did you smoke all the weed in this bag?" Cissy nodded, and Vance handed her a burrito. She promptly tore the wrapper off and took a huge bite. Due to the fact that she was now holding a burrito in each hand, Cissy was forced to smoke her blunt by pressing the burritos together to pick it up, but she instantly appeared more relaxed.

Having played the role of the most depressing Santa Claus in existence, Vance appeared to consider his work done. He lurched out of the living room and down the hall, dragging the garbage bag behind him. Cormac watched him go. The Mexican order had seemed ridiculous at first, but Cormac had forgotten how much better a burrito was than hardtack, and he was already drunkenly scheming to raid the fridge later. But Vance appeared to have other plans. He hauled the bag all the way to his bedroom door. Here he stopped and wobbled for a few seconds before heaving the garbage bag into the room. It landed with a squishy thump, and Vance stepped inside and slammed the door shut.

Cormac wondered what grim fate might possibly be in store for those burritos, but didn't have time to think about it for long. Something struck him in the back of the neck, and he turned and looked back at Cissy. She giggled at him from her perch on the couch, still holding half-eaten burritos in each hand. Cormac looked down at the ground and saw a long, fat blunt at his feet. He bent down to pick it up, wondering how Cissy had managed to toss it at him when another one struck him in the head.

Cissy evidently found this hilarious. When Cormac picked up the second blunt and looked up at the couch, her head was thrown back and her body was shaking with silent, overpowering laughter.

"Cissy, where are these blunts coming from?" Cormac asked. Cissy gripped her own blunt between the two burritos and raised it to her mouth. Then, puffing furiously, she set the burritos down and pushed aside the couch cushion that was sitting next to her. Cormac's jaw dropped when he saw what it had been concealing.

There was a gigantic pile of blunts on the couch next to Cissy. No, calling it a pile implied a certain amount of disorganization. What Cissy had constructed was more of a structure. It looked like a tiny cabin made out of weed-filled Lincoln Logs. There must have been at least one hundred blunts total, all tightly rolled to the point of near bursting. While they had been boozing it up at Mickey's, Cissy had had one hell of a productive afternoon.

"Jesus, Cissy, you rolled up the entire bag of weed?" Cormac asked. "That must have taken hours!"

"Yeah. It's like a sweatshop in here, man," Cissy snickered. "We need an exposé on these conditions." She was laughing harder now, and it was making it harder for her to get the words out. "Where's a reporter when you need one?" she managed to wheeze, before tears started rolling down her face and she was overwhelmed by laughter once again. Clearly, Cissy was on another plane of consciousness at the moment. If he wanted her presence to be even slightly tolerable, Cormac was going to have to join her.

"Can I get a light for one of these?" he asked, waving the blunts at Cissy. She tapped the couch next to her, much to Cormac's dismay. Scaling the airborne couch was tricky enough sober. He walked over to the electric cord and gave it a gentle tug. A crack instantly formed in the wall plaster at one of the points where the cord was stapled, and quickly spread across the ceiling, all the way across the living room and down the hall. There was a muffled thump, and then Vance yelped in pain as whatever the crack had knocked loose from the ceiling fell on his head.

Not surprisingly, Cissy found this hilarious and started to laugh uncontrollably. It might have been the gallons of beer he'd put away, but Cormac had never noticed until right now that Cissy had a fairly sexy stoned laugh. Vance's snores indicated that whatever injury he'd suffered had only been temporary, and Cormac decided that getting next to Cissy was worth risking one himself. He hoisted himself into the air with the extension cord, and after flailing his legs around for a few seconds, he swung one over the arm of the couch and awkwardly flopped forward across Cissy's lap.

Cissy paid the intrusion no mind. Her focus was entirely on the burritos, which she reflexively raised over her head like a pair of power-walking weights in order to keep Cormac from smooshing them. After a moment, Cormac tentatively crawled off of Cissy's lap and manipulated his body into a standard sitting position, careful to avoid crushing Cissy's delicate rolling handiwork as he moved. He then placed one of the blunts she'd tossed at him back onto the structure, chomped the other one between his teeth, and turned to face Cissy. She had a lighter ready and looked him in the eye as she lit his blunt. The whole gesture was actually kind of romantic, if you ignored the entirety of the extremely awkward minute that led up to it. Cormac was touched that Cissy had set down one of the burritos to light his blunt, but when he was unable to determine where it was, he quickly realized that she had actually just devoured it while he was facedown on the couch.

He inhaled deeply, and instantly felt the smoke go to his head. Man, why didn't they have weed on the *Levyathan?* Cormac wondered as he shut his eyes. Everyone would be so much chiller. You could just watch the sun go down every night, listen to the waves, try not to think about how terrifying octopuses were with all those tentacles and they can change color and what if one of the whalers had put an octopus in your bed and it was there when you went to sleep? Oh God, what if that happened? What if Vance was putting one in his bed right now!?

Cormac snapped his eyes open and looked around to see if Cissy had seen him freaking out. She was lighting a new blunt and appeared not to have noticed. He took a deep breath, then another puff, and tried to relax. Maybe it was for the best that they didn't have any weed at sea. Getting the munchies when your only options were hardtack and salt pork certainly wasn't a very attractive prospect.

The effect of the marijuana smoke was multiplied by his drunkenness, and Cormac already felt his eyes narrowing to small slits as he looked over at Cissy. His intent had been to put the moves on her, but when he saw that she was already staring at him, he lost his nerve and looked back at the TV. He wouldn't mind getting busy, but the weed was quickly eroding whatever confidence the alcohol had built up.

"Cormac?" He warily turned back to look at Cissy. She leaned in close to his face and whispered "I wanna look in your ear."

Cormac instantly began preparing his excuse for why he had to leave as soon as they were done having sex.

"Uh, sure! You can look in my ear," he said, trying to sound cool with the request. Either Cissy had a really different idea of what to do when you were stoned or this was a new thing that the Harrington ladies were into that he hadn't heard about yet. Regardless, this would be the first intimate contact he was going to have with a woman in months. If it started off a little weird, that was OK with him. Just as long as no octopi were involved . . . Dammit! Why did he even let himself think that?

Cissy set her blunt down on the back of the couch and pulled her hair back behind her shoulders. Then she cupped her hands over Cormac's left ear and gradually lowered her eye closer to his head.

"Ear goes nothing," Cormac joked, feeling pretty certain it was the cleverest thing he'd ever said. Cissy recoiled as if a wasp had emerged from Cormac's ear and stung her in the face, and he began to vigorously apologize. Once Cissy felt like she could trust him that it would not happen again, she leaned back in and pressed her eye up against his ear.

Maybe it was because he was drunk, maybe it was because he was stoned, but Cormac could definitely see the appeal of this ear-gazing thing Cissy was into. It was subtle, yet extremely intimate. He really felt closer to her and he was about to tell her how good it felt when Cissy pulled back from his ear. "Didn't work," she said as she picked her blunt up with a sigh of disappointment.

"Didn't work? What didn't work?" Cormac asked, but Cissy slumped back into the couch; there was no further information forthcoming. "Well, maybe I should take a turn looking in your ear?" Cormac suggested with a knowing nod. "You know, return the favor?"

"What?" Cissy snapped. She shot him a stoned yet withering glare. "Why would you look in *my* ear? Gross! Just watch the TV!"

Cissy's sudden mood swing was dismaying, but Cormac was not ready to give up just yet. He reached his left hand over to Cissy and placed it halfway up her thigh. She promptly smacked it away, then quickly rearranged the blunt pile so it formed a high enough barrier between their two bodies to prevent future hand-to-thigh contact. A Berlin Wall of ganja, Cormac thought. Man, what if instead of building that wall, the Germans had just sat down with each other and smoked some weed? He quickly pushed the idea from his mind as his imagination conjured up a crowd of Germans fleeing a gigantic octopus through the streets of Berlin.

Cormac was confused by Cissy's behavior, but as he puffed at the final nub of what used to be a six-inch blunt, he figured this was to be expected. His visions of suavely making himself scarce post-sex now shifted to figuring out how he was ever going to get down from this couch. But even that was rapidly being forgotten in favor of the absolutely mind-blowing stuff these cheetahs were doing on this nature program Cissy had been watching.

"Hey Cissy, what do you . . . Shouldn't we . . . Do you think we should turn the volume on?" Cormac eventually managed to ask.

Cissy slowly picked up the remote control, and after a great deal of effort located the volume button. She pointed the remote at the TV and clicked the volume up a few dozen times until Cormac could make out what the narrator was saying.

"That's better," Cormac said, focusing intently on the majestic cheetah that filled the TV screen. They both sat there in silence, passing what was left of Cissy's blunt back and forth, unable to do anything but stare straight ahead at the vivid nature images.

Forty-five minutes later, Cormac realized that Cissy had actually just turned up the contrast.

DAY TWELVE

Cormac woke up pretty sure he was still high. This didn't really surprise him. The rest of the afternoon and the brief portion of the evening that he was awake for had involved smoking weed at a prodigious rate. They'd gone through blunt after blunt, and didn't appear to have even put a dent in Cissy's pile. It was a unique experience having that much pot around. Cormac and Vance had never bought weed in bulk before, they just purchased an eighth at a time. This was in part because of funds limitations, but also because of something Vance referred to as the Choco Taco Theorem.

The way Vance described his theory was: Choco Tacos were delicious, and a great thing to buy individually from 7-11. Sure, you could save some dough by buying them in bulk. But the temptation of having all those easily accessible Choco Tacos in the house would be irresistible, and you'd end up negating any cost benefits by consuming them at a greatly increased rate. Probably because of the munchies brought on by all the weed you'd be smoking if you ever bought more than an eighth at a time. Cormac didn't understand the Choco Taco Theorem, even after Vance had drawn him a diagram, and it certainly wasn't making any more sense now.

A Choco Taco would sure as hell be better for breakfast than hardtack, Cormac thought as he swung his legs out of the bunk and tried to stop feeling like he was floating. He definitely should have stopped smoking weed after the cheetah program ended, or at the very least after the orangutan program that followed it. But he had been holding out hope that sparks still might fly, which seemed hopelessly naive in retrospect. After her peculiar ear-gazing session and his brief attempt at touching her leg, there had been no further physical contact between him and Cissy. They'd spent the evening sitting on the airborne couch in stoned silence until a promo ran for an upcoming show called "Mysteries of the Octopus" and Cormac had hurriedly excused himself to his bedroom before he started weeping in terror.

Last night's fear of octopi was all but forgotten now, despite the fact that his odds of encountering one were substantially higher on the *Levyathan* than in his living room. Nevertheless, Cormac breathed a sigh of relief when he stepped out of the whalers' quarters and saw that nobody was in the midst of warding off a horrible sea monster. No whalers were being dragged underwater by a giant tentacle, or having their crotches pecked by a fearsome octopus's beak. What the hell was an octopus doing with a beak anyways? Cormac was more than happy to stick to killing whales. At least whales made sense.

Cormac yawned and made a beeline for the food storage. What he wouldn't give right now for another burrito. Sadly, whatever desirability those burritos possessed as potential nourishment disappeared as soon as the door to Vance's bedroom closed. Congealing as they sat out all night was the most appetizing fate Cormac could envision for them, and all the other options that came to mind made his imagined octopus-crotch attack seem like a pleasant encounter with an old friend.

Cormac silently cursed his roommate's name and wondered how he had been bested by him yet again. He should have sprung his trap earlier, or maybe he should have been pouring five shots of vodka into each pitcher. Maybe he should have just driven to a sporting goods store, bought a baseball bat, and beat Vance with it until he told him what was going on. That's certainly how the dean would have handled it, if the dean wasn't so obviously in on whatever scam Vance was running. Why else would a guy who drove a . . . What was it again, some kind of Mustang? Why else would a guy with an indeterminate fancy car randomly be drinking at Mickey's unless he was a co-conspirator?

Tomorrow, there would be no more screwing around. No more convoluted plans, no more dancing around the issue, no more drinking. Well, make that no more drinking *to excess*. No need to reinvent the wheel here, Cormac thought. Just wake up, have a few drinks, beat the truth out of Vance, celebrate with some drinks, eat breakfast, then record the "Treasures o' the Sea" follow up the internet was so lustfully demanding.

Cormac smiled as he mentally laid out the promising next day. And as he glanced around the *Levyathan*, he noticed that many of the other men seemed in good spirits as well. Whalers whistled as they coiled their rope and smiled at each other as they ran the sails up the mast. A particularly erotic piece of erotic scrimshaw was being circulated, and every time it changed hands a boisterous cheer went up from the whalers who were waiting their turn. It was then thoroughly scrubbed by the whaler who had received it before he retreated to whatever nether region of the *Levyathan* he chose to do his dirty work in.

But the point was, people seemed genuinely happy. Cormac only saw two whalers get punched during his walk to the hardtack bins, and both those guys really seemed to have pushed the suggested maximum time spent alone with the erotic scrimshaw far beyond its limit. Even the rats he encountered seemed more laid back. In fact, a few of them seemed to be bobbing their heads to the funky Caribbean rhythms that were suddenly floating through the sea air. At this point, Cormac realized that he was definitely still a little bit stoned. When he arrived at the food storage bins at the bow of the ship he saw Ziro swabbing the deck, so he grabbed a fistful of hardtack and headed in his direction.

"Morning, Ziro!" Cormac called. Ziro paused his swabbing just long enough to nod in acknowledgment. Cormac shoved one of the hardtack biscuits in his mouth and chomped down. The hardtack instantly absorbed all the saliva in his mouth and turned into a thick, paste-like substance. It took all of Cormac's concentration to choke it down. He could still feel the lumpy clod slowly making its way down his throat when he found himself going in for another bite. Yep, he was definitely still high.

"What's with the crew?" Cormac managed to ask in between kneading the glob in his mouth. "I don't think I've ever seen them so chipper."

"We dock in two days," Ziro informed him. "As soon as we unload our cargo, they get shore leave. If you think they're excited now, wait until tomorrow. They're going to be bouncing off the walls."

Men as burly and weather-beaten as the *Levyathan*'s crew didn't do "giddy," but the way the whalers were behaving was probably as close to it as they were capable. Cormac noticed one particularly brutish-looking whaler actually come skipping around a corner. When the whaler realized that Cormac had seen him, he tried to pretend like his skipping had really been him stumbling. This hastily conceived ruse caused him to actually stumble, then trip, then plummet forward and land facedown on the deck. He slid forward several feet on the freshly swabbed surface. When he eventually skidded to a halt, he lay unmoving on his stomach for a few seconds. Eventually he got to his feet, grabbed the nearest coil of rope and quickly realized it needed to be somewhere on the stern of the boat immediately.

"It couldn't be timed better," Ziro continued. "If you'd destroyed all the rum when we were still a few weeks away from docking, it could have gotten really ugly."

Still about 30 percent positive that violent retribution might be forthcoming from the whaler he'd caught skipping, Cormac preferred not to think about that possibility. "Yep, everyone certainly seems eager to head ashore," he mused instead.

"Well, not exactly everyone," Ziro said. He pointed his mop toward the port side of the boat. Cormac looked and saw Captain Anson pacing and wringing his hands. "He's convinced that his wife is going to track him down and her lawyer will take the *Levyathan*. It's even worse now that we've got the pirate ship to sell and the captain to ransom. I honestly think he'd rather set it all on fire than let her get a dime of it."

Fear of success had never been much of an issue for the residents of the Craymore Street house. For Cormac and Vance, worrying about succeeding was about as practical as developing a fear of polar bears. So Anson's simpering attitude earned him no sympathy from Cormac, who narrowed his eyes as he stared at the captain with contempt.

"It sounds like somebody could use a pep talk," Cormac muttered.

"I don't know if you want to approach him right now, Cormac," Ziro cautioned. "I don't think he's had much sleep." But it was too late. Cormac was already off, striding with purpose toward Captain Anson. In his head he replayed classic movie scenes of locker room speeches and generals addressing their troops before battle. He considered dozens of motivational poster quotes and t-shirt slogans, trying to decide which might be the most effective in pumping the captain up. As he approached Captain Anson from behind, Cormac envisioned taking the podium on the steps of the Lincoln Memorial, ready to make a speech that would inspire the nation.

Cormac cleared his throat and the captain turned around, looking tired and nervous. "You may ask yourself," Cormac solemnly intoned. "Why do we . . ." Cormac froze as his mind went blank, his inspiring words instantly forgotten. Captain Anson stared at him as he tried to regain his train of thought.

"Some look at the world . . . Um, here I stand . . . Er, if you can't run with the big dogs . . ." Cormac stammered as the captain tried to figure out what the hell he was talking about. Eventually, in a panic, Cormac reached out and slapped the captain across the face. In his vision, the masses were now pelting the steps of the Lincoln Memorial with the rotten fruit and vegetables they'd brought, evidently anticipating his immense potential for failure.

"Ow!" Captain Anson yelped. He raised his hand to his stinging cheek and glared at Cormac. "What the hell was that?"

"You shape up do good," Cormac tried to say. But before he could even get through all five words of his barely coherent motivational speech, Captain Anson reached out and slapped him right back.

"What's gotten into you, you idiot?" Captain Anson asked. "That really hurt!"

"No kidding!" Cormac said, now rubbing his own cheek. "You hit me about as twice as hard as I hit you!"

"I think you knocked my earring out," the captain said. "Help me find it." Anson knelt down and started feeling around for his pilfered earring. Cormac watched him crawl around for a few seconds until the stinging in his cheek subsided. Then he crouched down next to the captain and scanned the surface of the deck for the earring that had belonged to the Black Barnacle only forty-eight hours ago.

"I'm sorry that went so poorly, sir," Cormac half-heartedly apologized. Captain Anson indicated his disdain with a snort. "Did you see which direction it rolled in?" Cormac asked, hoping they could change the subject.

"Who knows with these slick surfaces," the captain muttered. "They're too clean if you ask me. Who knows how much money we could save on replacement mop heads if that idiot wasn't swabbing the deck all the time."

Captain Anson shot Ziro a glare. As he turned his head toward the former slave, the captain's ear shimmered in the morning sun.

"Captain, I think the earring is still in your ear, sir." Cormac pointed at the captain's left ear, which he only now noticed was incredibly puffy and swollen.

"In my ear? Hogwash!" Captain Anson pawed at the general area of his left ear. "I can't feel a thing."

"That's because your earlobe has swollen to twice its normal size and is starting to envelop the earring in its folds."

"No, I really can't feel any part of my ear," the captain said, sounding a touch panicked.

"It's definitely infected, sir," Cormac said. "You need to take that earring out immediately."

"Am I touching it now?" Captain Anson asked.

"No, sir, you're sticking your finger into your ear," Cormac replied.

"How about now?" Anson asked as he repositioned his finger.

"Even further into your ear, actually," Cormac informed him. The captain moved his finger once more. "How are you able to fit it that far in there?" Cormac was astonished. "No, don't push it in farther! Sir, you should pull your finger out of your ear right now before you do any more serious damage!"

Captain Anson cursed as he pulled his finger out of his ear. "This is the last thing I need right now," he lamented as he wiped an alarming amount of sticky substance off his finger and onto his pants.

"Well that's what I wanted to talk to you about," Cormac said. "You've got to snap out of this funk, sir. You've got a great situation here. There are dozens of whales to unload, a new ship to sell, all the Chinese gold. You can't let your wife haunt you like this. It's not a healthy way to live."

"My wife?" The captain looked puzzled. "What the hell are you talking about? I'm not upset because of my wife!" Captain Anson took a look over each of his shoulders to see if anyone else was listening. After confirming that the coast was clear, he leaned in close to Cormac.

"It's Pete!" the captain whispered. "I think I may have killed him!"

"I think you should move the van, Deano," Vance said as he peered through the blinds. "One of the DJs was talking about setting up a limbo bar there today."

From the fetal position on the grounded couch, Harrington Dean Frampton Q. Bickerstaff groaned.

The blinds snapped shut as Vance pulled his hand back and turned to face the dean. "Do you need any more coffee?" he asked. "It'll make you feel better." Dean Bickerstaff shuddered at the memory of the "coffee" that still lingered on his tongue. Vance had pulled a dusty old can of instant coffee out of an unused kitchen cupboard. The dean had not been aware that Idaho was known for its coffee-growing climate, but the can advertised itself as being the finest the state had to offer. The coffee brand was endorsed by former Detroit Tigers manager Jim Leyland. A picture of the skipper lighting a cigarette was prominently featured on the front of the can. A testimonial quote, "It'll do," was printed in block letters next to his photo. Vance said the can had been propping open the back door when they moved in.

Desperate for relief from his hangover, Frampton had accepted Vance's offer to make some of the coffee. The grounds ate away at the spoon that Vance tried to scoop them out with, so he poured them directly into a mug. Once they were mixed with hot water, the drink began to bubble, which was not a behavior the dean usually associated with coffee. It also emitted a faint yellow gas. The dean had nevertheless tried to choke it down.

On the plus side, each can promised to include an authentic, game-used Jim Leyland cigarette butt. Vance eagerly dug through the remaining coffee grounds trying to find it, but nothing had turned up. He was in the midst of composing a scathing letter to the surely long-defunct Boise Coffee Roasting & Industrial Rodent Abatement Company accusing them of false advertising until the dean took sip of coffee and nearly choked on the soggy butt. Vance had fished it out of the mug with glee as the dean waddled to the bathroom to vomit.

Frampton feebly shook his head to indicate that no further coffee was necessary. "Alright, but don't say I didn't offer," Vance cautioned him. "I'm surprised you took such a shine to Mickey's, Deano. How long did you stay there after we left?"

Dean Bickerstaff tried to remember. He had intended to stick around just long enough for Cormac and Vance to catch a cab so he could hop into the van unnoticed. But then Mickey had asked if he wanted to do a tequila shot, and said that he'd cut the dean's dick off with the bear trap if he refused. This was a new type of social interaction for the dean and he couldn't tell if Mickey was joking or not, so he did the shot and the rest of the day was sort of a blur after that.

The dean could distinctly remember three events. The first was leading a sing-along when "Piano Man" by Billy Joel came on the jukebox. The dean did not care for Billy Joel and could not recall if he had ever listened to that song all the way through before yesterday. But this had not stopped tears from welling up in his eyes at the failed dreams of the song's blue-collar subjects and vowing to anyone who would listen that he was going to start taking piano lessons. In the spirit of the song, he'd attempted to place an order for a "tonic and gin" instead of a gin and tonic, but Mickey made it very clear (bear trap) that this type of behavior would not be tolerated in his establishment.

Second was an argument with a guy who claimed that his worthless Harrington degree had rendered him unemployable, that the financial aid office had ruined his credit, that his wife had left him for someone with a real education, and that Frampton was personally responsible for all of this. This took the dean by surprise. He thought it seemed like Mickey was doing pretty OK for himself. He did another tequila shot with him to ensure that it was all water under the bridge.

The third and final memory was fleeing the premises. This was necessary because of a foolish billiards wager the dean had made. At some point in time he'd found himself holding a pool cue, and against all odds had been putting together a rather impressive streak of victories, when a barfly approached him and suggested that they bet something on the next game, oh, the title to their car perhaps. Frampton agreed, and arrogantly asserted that he could win even if he used his shillelagh as the cue. He immediately scratched on the break, losing the game before it could even get started. The twisted, knotted shillelagh made a very poor pool cue.

His hasty exit from Mickey's was a blurry jumble of shillelagh blows, angry drunks, and broken glass. The dean was in no shape to drive, but he was in no shape to have the tar beaten out of him either, so he made a beeline for the van and floored it out of the parking lot. There were a few jolts on the way that he hoped were speed bumps or curbs. The next thing Frampton knew, he was lying on Cissy's porch couch, Vance was standing over him in a towel, the sun was up, and the van was parked in the middle of the lawn.

"You're lucky those cult freaks didn't do anything to you last night, Deano," Vance said as he opened the front door and waved in two bandana men who were carrying a keg. "Me and you are evidently the devil in their religion. I'm surprised nobody tried to sacrifice you while you were passed out. Or at least drew a dick on your face with a Sharpie." Vance pointed to a corner, and the bandana men set the keg down and went back outside to retrieve another. The dean groaned. From the airborne couch, he heard the sound of Cissy snoring.

"You know what the trick to avoiding this kind of hangover is?" Vance asked, circling back in front of the couches. "A full stomach. You should have stopped for some burritos on the way home like me and Mac did. They soak the booze right up! Oh man, we were so drunk we ordered a whole garbage bag full!" Vance shook his head and smiled, fondly recalling the memory of what appeared to be one of the top five days of his life.

The thought of a big, greasy burrito made the dean feel ill again, but he knew Vance was right. This feeling was not going to go away on its own. Moving as slowly as he could, Frampton rolled over onto his back. He took a few deep breaths while he tried to find the strength to speak. Eventually he managed to croak out, "Can . . . I . . . have . . . one?"

Vance laughed. "Oh no, I'm afraid those burritos are long gone, my friend. Evidently I polished off the whole bag in bed. Judging by the wrapper count I nearly broke my personal record!"

The dean gasped and slumped back into the fetal position, exhausted by the effort of requesting a leftover burrito. There was no way he was going to be able to run the Cormac-exploiting operation today. He needed to get home and sleep in a good old fashioned king-size brass four-poster bed. No more of this couch or van nonsense. Then after that, maybe a few hours in the hot tub and sauna to sweat out some of the accumulated filth from the past week. Of course, right now Frampton didn't think he'd be able to walk to the van, let alone drive it home.

But as he had this thought, a familiar scent wafted past the dean's nose. A complex, woody scent, with notes of the lush soil and bold lifestyle of an expensive Cuban hacienda. The dean patted his breast pocket. Evidently a cigar had managed to survive the night intact. As he pulled the cigar out of his pocket, he caught another whiff of rich, Vuelta Abajo tobacco and felt a tingle go down his spine.

Dean Bickerstaff sat up for the first time all morning and motioned for a lighter. Vance pulled one out of the waistband of his towel and tossed it to the dean, who caught it without taking his eyes off the cigar. It had him entranced, and he could feel his strength returning just looking at it. The dean bit off the end and felt another surge of energy run through him. His headache was receding, his eyes began to focus. The solution to his hangover had been right there in his pocket the entire time! As the dean lit the cigar and filled his mouth with the first puff of smoke, he felt a renewed vigor, like Popeye downing a can of spinach, or Barry Bonds injecting a variety of illegal, untested substances into his ass. Frampton leapt off the couch and raised his shillelagh in the air, confident and ready to conquer the day.

That feeling passed almost instantly and was replaced by a new, much stronger wave of nausea. The dean dropped the cigar on the floor and ran to the bathroom to vomit again, coughing all the way.

Vance watched him go, then turned to the bandana men who were patiently waiting at the door despite holding a very heavy keg.

"He'll be fine," Vance informed them. "He's just got to get it all out of his system." The bandana men gave no indication that they were concerned in the slightest. "I think we're good with kegs for now," Vance told them after they set the keg down next to the first one. Vance peered out the door. A substantial crowd was already waiting to be admitted, but none of the food vendors had shown up yet. "Why don't you two run out and get us some burritos," Vance suggested. The bandana men nodded and turned for the door.

"Hey!" Vance yelled after them. They turned and looked at him, awaiting further orders. Vance pulled a wad of money out from under his towel and peeled off one hundred dollars in twenties. "I want you to buy them. Don't rob the place." The bandana men nodded their disappointed assent and walked out the door.

When Dean Bickerstaff emerged from the bathroom, he was pale and sweating, but the latest purge seemed to have done him good. Vance noticed the change, too.

"You feeling better, Deano? Get some of that residual booze out of your system? How about some water?"

Dean Bickerstaff nodded. He was still breathing heavily, but he at least felt like he'd be able to keep down some liquids.

Vance walked off to the kitchen and came back with a large plastic cup full of water and two Bloody Mary's. "For when you feel up for it," he told the dean with a wink. The dean pushed the booze aside and took a long, satisfying gulp of water.

"Give me your hand," Vance said. "Take a couple of these." The dean stuck his palm out and Vance shook five Advil into his hand. "Just a head's up, Deano: some of those may be whale dick pills."

The dean stared at Vance and tried to imagine how he would have reacted two weeks ago if someone had burst into his office and told him that before the month was over, he'd be boozing it up with lowlifes in a dive bar, drunk driving a second-hand van, waking up on a porch couch, vomiting his brains out, then accepting five pills potentially derived from whale dicks from a business partner clad only in a towel. It was too far-fetched a scenario to even warrant a shillelagh beating for the person who predicted it. Frampton could only shake his head and wearily ask, "Whale dick pills?"

"It's a long story," Vance said. "Look, how much worse can they make you feel? The Chinese know their medicine. And besides, the Advil I mixed them with are expired anyways, so you may actually be better off with the whale pills. Now swallow them down, we've got a big crowd out there already."

Dean Bickerstaff knew that he had no chance of making it through another session of Cormac-exploiting without medication. Reluctantly, he popped the pills in his mouth, took a big swig of water, tilted his head back and swallowed.

"That's more like it!" Vance said with a smile. "Let me know if you feel anything funny going on anywhere in particular." To Frampton's horror, Vance pointed knowingly at his crotch. "I still think I may have gotten ripped off."

Dean Bickerstaff finished off his glass of water and hoped with all his might he did not feel any stirrings below the belt. He walked over to the window and peered through the blinds. There were dozens of people crowded on the lawn and more were approaching from both sides of the sidewalk.

"Why are there so many people outside already?" the dean asked. "What time is it?"

"Oh, it's not even eight yet," Vance said. "I passed out pretty early yesterday, so I've been up for a while. You can thank Cissy for the turnout. She did a great PR job for us today."

The dean felt a sudden chill. Anything that Vance approved of had to come with a tremendous downside. Vance walked over to the airborne couch and lifted Cissy's feet up. They had been resting on a copy of the *School Paper*, which Vance pulled out and handed to the dean. Frampton snatched the paper from Vance. He sat down on the grounded couch, picked up his still-smoldering cigar, and puffed on it furiously as he snapped open the *School Paper*.

"Cissy's article is on page A-4," Vance said, but the dean held up his hand to indicate he wasn't interested. Before he could read whatever libelous drivel Cissy had scratched out in the name of yellow journalism, he had to make sure there weren't any headlines reporting hit-and-runs involving a certain Astro van. Dean Bickerstaff flipped through the first dozen pages of the paper, rapidly scanning the headlines for any mention of an unsolved automobile fatality. With every page he turned, he began to rest easier. Surely if there had been an unsolved accident last night, it would not be confined to one of these back pages.

This theory was quickly proven wrong. An elderly faculty member had been struck by a car last night and was in the hospital in grave condition. The driver had not been found. The story was on page B-19, where a picture of the man's grieving family at his bedside was printed next to a story explaining that the WonderMuttz—the halftime act at the next Harrington basketball game—would be short one Frisbee-catching dog due to illness. The dean read until he determined that the professor had been struck by a motorcycle, not a van, then quickly lost interest in the story. Before flipping to Cissy's story, he finished the article about the sick Frisbee dog and made a mental note to send the WonderMuttz trainer some rawhide chews as a get well soon present.

Then it was on to Cissy's story. The dean turned to page A-4 and was greeted by the headline "Pirates Guarrranteed At Cormac's House Today!"

"Goddammit," Frampton muttered. He looked back to glare at the comatose reporter on the airborne couch. Cissy emitted a snore that contained no trace of remorse. Frampton turned his attention back to the paper and read the first paragraph of the article.

Just a reminder that you'd be a scurvy dog to miss the festivities at Cormac's house today! After all the excitement and drama involving pirates two days ago, who knows what the high seas have in store for Harrington's resident landlubber today? Obviously, nobody can know for sure, but speaking off the record, this reporter absolutely guarantees that there will be even more pirates today, so get there bright and early! If I'm wrong, you get your money back.

"Jesus Christ!" the dean yelped. "You can't quote yourself off the record in your own article! That defies every journalistic convention and probably a few laws of physics! How stoned was Cissy when she wrote this?"

"I'm guessing a 'high as balls' out of ten," Vance speculated. "The Cistress kept pretty busy while we were at Mickey's. Check it out." Vance slid a shoebox out from underneath the grounded couch and opened it for the dean. "She spent all afternoon rolling the bag of weed Mako gave us into blunts. Guessing she happened to indulge in quite a few during the process. Can't say I blame her either, rolling that many blunts can really take it out of you."

"Holy shit!" Dean Bickerstaff exclaimed, only half hearing Vance. "Listen to this! '*As a special exclusive to the* School Paper, *yours truly did a little research yesterday and can confirm that you cannot see into the* Levyathan's *world while Cormac is awake. This involved a lengthy process of convincing him that I was really high, which required getting really high, in case any future employers want to know why I failed a drug test. Cormac got high, too (off the record of course).*' What the hell is she doing looking in his ear? She's going to blow our whole cover!"

"I saw that, Deano," Vance said. "It's especially bad timing since Mac was suspicious already from finding the money and weed lying around the apartment."

"He found what?" Dean Bickerstaff screeched.

"Yeah, I know. I may have tipped him off that we knew about pirates, too. But hey, I caught him lying to me, so he definitely owes me. I'd say at least a couple of pitchers."

Dean Bickerstaff's headache had returned. He puffed his cigar as he reached for the Bloody Mary Vance had brought him.

"But I'm with you, Deano," Vance continued. "I think we need to have a little talk with the Cistress about journalistic integrity. But obviously it can wait until she wakes up. For now, how about you give me the keys so I can move the van?"

The dean was fuming. Cissy was supposed to be their handpicked mouthpiece, and she had betrayed them twice in the same article. Promising customers pirates was irresponsible; offering a money-back guarantee was ludicrous. And then taking matters into her own hands and looking into Cormac's ear while he was awake! Not to mention Vance's carelessness that he had oh-so-casually revealed. The whole operation seemed to be hanging by a string and his two closest partners were drunkenly snipping the air with garden shears.

But still, they had a business to run today. Cissy's guarantees could be easily explained away with legalese, or possibly the threat of shillelagh beatings. At least, Frampton hoped they could be. If #CormacsEar continued the trajectory it had been on, today was destined to be the biggest day yet, and if the crowd of early birds was any indication, possibly by an order of magnitude. Reminding himself that this was all for the sake of keeping his job, the dean reached into his pocket and tossed the van keys to Vance.

"Alright," Vance said as he caught them. "I've been looking for an excuse to drive this bad boy." Frampton didn't doubt for a second that this was true.

"There's a lot of people out there, Vance, so don't go cruising around the neighborhood in that thing," the dean said. The van attracted enough attention when a respectable pillar of the Harrington community like himself was driving it. Putting Vance behind the wheel could only have negative consequences. "Just park it on the street and get right back in here so we can open up shop."

Vance's face briefly fell, but he quickly recovered and flashed the dean a smile. "No problem, Deano!" Vance headed for the door, and when he paused before stepping outside, Frampton knew what was coming before his partner even said it.

"Your towel's hanging up in the bathroom!" Vance crowed as he let the front door slam behind him.

* * *

Captain Anson and Cormac stood over Pete's body.

"I think we should get Ziro," Cormac told Captain Anson, not taking his eyes off the pirate captain.

"I hardly think that's necessary," Captain Anson snapped.

"Well it definitely looks like he's dead," Cormac said. "What the hell did you do to him?"

"Nothing!" Captain Anson insisted.

"His face looks green and he's not wearing any pants."

"Ok, so we were drinking a little bit," Captain Anson admitted. "And they prefer the term pantaloons." Cormac did not appear satisfied with this explanation. "Look, I had trouble falling asleep, and I wanted somebody to drink with. Obviously I couldn't tell any of the men that I'd been hoarding rum, they'd heave me overboard. And I'm not going to drink with Ziro. So I dragged Pete up here and we opened a few bottles. He's actually a pretty fun guy when he isn't trying to kill you, or in the process of dying himself. He told this joke about a whaler from West Nantucket that everyone thinks is from East Nantucket, and so he has to—"

"What the hell did you give him to drink?" Cormac demanded, even though he was curious how the joke went.

"Just some stuff from my secret stash." Captain Anson walked over to a small trunk in a corner of his office. On the side of it, hand painted letters read "Maps – Contains NO Erotic Scrimshaw."

"To keep the men out," Anson explained. He lifted the lid of the trunk and pulled out a bottle. "I haven't had to break into this supply for a long time since we usually have such a well-stocked rum storage area." He glared back at Cormac, who ignored the look. "So I made Pete taste all of it first just in case it had gone bad."

"Well, it's incredibly common for liquor to age for at many years," Cormac replied. "I'm sure that wasn't the problem."

"We had some of this. Two Palms rum from Puerto Rico." He passed the bottle to Cormac and pulled another out of the trunk. Cormac pulled the cork out of the Two Palms and took a sniff. It smelled like normal rum to him.

"Then we moved on to this añejo tequila from the Jalisco Lowlands. *El Burro y La Cebra.* Serious stuff." The captain admired the ornate, skull-shaped bottle, which was painted with black and white zebra stripes.

"Was there a worm in there?" Cormac wondered, nervously glancing back at Pete. "Maybe that's what did him in."

"It's a misconception that the worm comes in tequila bottles," the captain said with a snooty air. "You'll really only find it in bottles of mezcal, and even then it's only for tourists."

"I was just asking," Cormac said rather defensively. The time that Vance had brought a bottle of Wormy Paco brand tequila home with him from spring break that advertised "a worm in every shot!" made a bit more sense now. At the time, Cormac had been suspicious that Vance had just been sold a relabeled worm trap. Now he was certain of it.

"There *was* a worm in this bottle of vintage Château La Bete Bordeaux," Captain Anson said, holding up an empty wine bottle. "That should not have been the case."

"It seems like you certainly have amassed a fine collection of booze, sir," Cormac said, trying to hurry the process along.

"Now this one I did not sample last night," the captain said as he held up a large, dusty bottle. "Turpenntinney from the Transvaal Republic."

"I don't think that's still a country back in my time," Cormac said. "What the hell is Turpenntinney? I've never heard of it."

"It did not smell like something I wanted to drink. Judging from Pete's reaction, I made the right decision!" The captain paused to laugh at the memory of last night's drunken antics. "He was so hammered that I kept pouring him more of this stuff and telling him it was something else and he'd totally drink it! He would almost puke drinking it, then I'd hand him another glass and tell him it was fine scotch and he'd slug it right back!"

"Let me see that bottle," Cormac said. Captain Anson held it out behind him with his right hand as he continued to rummage through the liquor chest with his left. As soon as Cormac glanced at the label he knew what had done Pete in.

"Sir, this is a bottle of turpentine," Cormac informed the captain. "It's not pronounced turpenntinney, it's turpentine. It's an industrial paint thinner, you use it to varnish wood!"

Captain Anson looked up from the liquor chest. "You sure? It says 'Pure Gum Spirit' on the bottle. I assumed it was a Transvaal pronunciation."

From behind them, there was a wheezing noise that sounded like a balloon slowly deflating. Cormac turned to see what had made it and was surprised to see that Pete had rolled over onto his side. His right leg was twitching.

"Well I'll be damned," Captain Anson muttered under his breath.

Cormac stared for a second at the now apparently alive pirate captain, then wheeled back around to face Captain Anson. He shook the bottle of solvent in his face. "How much turpentine did Pete drink last night?" Cormac demanded.

"I don't know, like five or six glasses!"

"Jesus . . . I'm getting Ziro." Captain Anson could only muster a half-hearted protest as Cormac dropped the bottle and headed for the door.

By the time Cormac was able to track Ziro down and drag him back to the captain's quarters, Pete's condition had either taken a turn for the better or worsened immensely. Now both his legs were twitching occasionally and he was ever so slightly foaming at the mouth.

Captain Anson held up a bottle from his liquor chest as Cormac and Ziro entered his quarters. "I think I found the culprit," he announced. "Canadian whiskey. Dear God, this stuff is terrible." Cormac ignored him and led Ziro over to the bottle of turpentine. He picked it up and handed it to the former slave.

"So that's what happened to my turpentine," Ziro said. "This disappeared from my supply closet three months ago."

"One of the men must have been desperate for booze," Captain Anson suggested. "They broke into your supply closet, willing to suck down any liquid they could find to satisfy their cravings."

"And then they snuck into the captain's quarters and stashed it inside your secret alcohol chest that nobody on the boat even knew was here until you slipped up and revealed its existence to Cormac two days ago?" Ziro did not sound convinced.

"Are you going to help him or not?" Captain Anson snapped. Ziro set the bottle down on the floor and scurried over to Pete. He knelt down next to the pirate captain and placed his hand on his forehead.

"It's definitely turpentine poisoning," Ziro informed them.

"Ah, you recognize the symptoms. A common affliction, I'm sure." Captain Anson elbowed Cormac in the ribs, proud that he wasn't the only one who had ever made this mistake.

"No, I've never seen anyone mistake turpentine for a drinkable substance," Ziro said. "A lot of times the rats will get into my supplies and drink stuff they shouldn't. But they never touch the turpentine. I think even they know to stay away from it. I can just tell by his complexion that this is something other than alcohol poisoning. We need some water, really quickly. And grab a wet rag for his forehead."

Captain Anson pointed to a decanter of water that sat on his desk. Cormac hustled over and grabbed it, then carried it back to the liquor chest, where Captain Anson was shaking the last few drops out of one of the cups they'd been drinking out of the night before. He held out the cup and Cormac tilted the decanter to pour the water, but at the last minute he reconsidered and righted it.

"What was the last thing you were drinking out of that cup?" Cormac asked suspiciously.

"Nothing," Captain Anson replied. After Cormac stared at him for a moment or two he clarified. "*I* wasn't drinking anything out of it. Pete was drinking turpentine."

"Will you get a new cup that didn't at any point contain the poisonous substance that put him in this position in the first place?" Cormac yelled.

"Jeez, OK!" Captain Anson said as he set the cup down and grabbed a fresh one off a shelf. "Thought I'd just save having to wash a dish or two, but whatever." Cormac poured some water into the cup and passed it to Ziro, who had already ripped a section of fabric from the waist of his shirt. Ziro doused the fabric with water and pressed it onto Pete's head. The pirate captain emitted a wheeze of relief as the cool cloth touched his head.

"We need to dilute the turpentine that's left in his system," Ziro informed them. "That means we're essentially going to have to continuously force water down his throat since he's in no condition to drink it himself."

"By the way, he took his pantaloons off totally on his own," Captain Anson interjected. "I think the turpentine made him think his legs were on fire. Just in case you were wonder—"

"Will you shut up and pay attention?" Ziro shouted. Captain Anson looked appropriately chagrined, but Cormac had to admit that he had been wondering about the pantaloons the whole time. He had another question, too.

"Why are we so concerned about saving this guy?" he asked as he knelt down next to Ziro. Ziro passed him the cup and Cormac refilled it with water. "I mean, we killed a dozen pirates two days ago without a second thought. How come you seem so shaken up about this one, sir?"

Captain Anson took a deep breath followed by a long exhale as he pondered the question. "I guess . . ." He paused as he tried to find the right words. "I guess it's just different when you stop thinking of someone as a pirate, and start thinking of them as a person. I was talking to Pete last night and it occurred to me: we could have been friends. We could have been brothers if the universe had played out differently. And then when he started to get sick . . . He just looked so helpless!" A single tear began to roll down the captain's cheek. "It doesn't matter what flag you fly on your mast, or what your boat is called. We owe it to each other to honor and acknowledge what we share. After all, it's our humanity . . . that truly makes us human."

"He wants to save him because the reward for an alive pirate captain is about ten times bigger than the reward for a dead pirate captain," Ziro said matter-of-factly.

"Dammit, Ziro!" Captain Anson quickly wiped the tear off his cheek and flicked the residue off of his hand. "It can be a combination of both!"

Cormac watched Ziro carefully pour a few drops of water into Pete's mouth and then rub his throat to get him to swallow them, as if the pirate captain was a dog who wouldn't take a pill. Obviously, if Pete was going to recover, it was going to be a long, tedious process. Ziro was essentially providing him with a low-tech IV, and Cormac felt like he had seen enough.

"Well, I'm glad we got to the bottom of that," he said as he stood up and headed for the door. "I'll just leave the pitcher here, Ziro. I'll bring you some hardtack in a few hours, OK?"

Captain Anson took a step to the side to block Cormac's path. "Where do you think you're going?" he asked in a far more condescending tone than Cormac had expected.

"I'm going to go harpoon some whales," Cormac said, unsure if it was a trick question.

"Ziro," the captain called out, looking over Cormac's shoulder toward the former slave. "How many people is it going to take to keep Pete alive?"

"An assistant would definitely improve his chances for survival," Ziro said.

"Well, I think that settles it!" Captain Anson smiled a big fake smile. "Cormac, you stay here and play nurse with Ziro. It would set my conscience at ease to know that we're doing everything we can to help him."

"But this is the last day I have to add to the haul before we dock in St. John's!" Cormac protested. "I can't waste an entire day just sitting here pouring water into a cup!"

"You'll be periodically rubbing his throat too," Ziro called out from the back of the room.

"See?" Captain Anson grinned. "Your nursing duties just got even more exciting!"

"Stop calling me a nurse!" Cormac demanded. "I don't understand, why don't you want me out there with a harpoon?"

"Cormac, my boy, you've done a great job reeling in those whales. And I'm sure if you spent all day on the deck, you'd haul in five, ten, maybe a dozen more whales. But right now I'm all about asset diversification." Captain Anson spoke with the air of someone who was only about 60 percent sure they knew what they were talking about, which for the captain, probably meant that the figure was actually closer to 20 percent.

"When we dock at St. John's, if Eleanor happens to be there with her lawyer, what's the first thing they're going to try and seize? What's our most visible, easiest-to-liquidate asset?"

The captain waited for Cormac to answer, and eventually he spoke up. "The whales?"

"Yes, the whales! Good job, son!" Captain Anson patted Cormac's shoulder in a hollow imitation of a proud gesture. "We're a whaling boat. They know we've got whales, and they won't have any trouble selling them in a port town. She could serve me with divorce papers, unload them for some lowball offer to spite me, and then get the hell out of town. If we spend all day today hauling in whales, that's a lot of work that could end up being all for naught. But if you help Ziro nurse Pete back to health . . ." The captain paused ever so slightly to appreciate Cormac's grimace, then continued. "You're working to preserve a very valuable asset that's easy to keep hidden from Eleanor and her vulture of a lawyer. Ziro, what's a pirate captain worth in terms of whales?"

"I'd say anywhere from three to five whales," Ziro estimated. "Depending on the degree and amount of atrocities they've committed. The pirate, not the whales."

"Five whales!" Captain Anson whistled to indicate how impressive he found this, even though Cormac was pretty sure he'd already known the answer. "So if you start harpooning, you'll have to catch at least six whales to make it a worthwhile tradeoff, and even then there's still a chance that my harpy of a wife seizes the entire haul in forty-eight hours! Obviously you can see how it's worth it to keep Pete alive just so we have a secret asset to start over with. You know, if the worst case scenario happens . . ."

Cormac had to admit that for someone who had been unable to read the word "turpentine," the captain had a good point. Essentially they were arriving at port with several very visible assets: the haul of whales, the *Levyathan* itself, and the captured pirate ship *Mongrel*. The captain also had the Chinese gold squirrelled away, but it seemed like they might have difficulty keeping an overflowing treasure chest inconspicuous from a lawyer's prying eyes. Pete, on the other hand, they could slap a disguise on, trot him into town, and allow any potential scenario involving Eleanor to play itself out. Once she'd taken the captain to the cleaners and left town, he could turn Pete in for the reward money and use it to fund a fresh start.

Reluctantly, Cormac nodded his head. "I understand," he told the captain. Whaling would be a hell of a lot more fun than spoon-feeding a pirate captain back to health, but on the bright side, the captain's quarters might be the best spot on the ship for him and Ziro to play the ukulele without anyone bothering them. Perhaps today they'd finally have a chance to work on a follow-up song. Being in such close proximity to the captain's private stash of fine booze wouldn't be such a bad thing either.

"Just one condition," Cormac said.

"Anything you want, my boy!" The captain said with a smile. Cormac savored the happy look on his face, knowing how quickly it would disappear after what he said next.

"Go and fetch a couple of ukuleles from Ziro's room. So we can practice while we *nurse*." Captain Anson's face fell as Cormac emphasized the last word and it was even better than Cormac had hoped it would be.

"Alright," he muttered "I'll get you your ukuleles. Just don't let him die."

Captain Anson quickly shuffled out of his quarters and disappeared onto the deck of the *Levyathan*. Cormac knelt back down next to Ziro and picked up the water jug. "I figured this might be a good chance to get in some ukulele time," he said as he poured more water into the cup.

"That's a good idea," Ziro replied. "Finally we'll get to play in peace."

"I have a question about transitioning from E to G minor," Cormac said. "I'm finding tricky to reposition my—"

"Cormac," Ziro interrupted. "If you're going to talk I need you to massage his throat at the same time."

"Right, sorry," Cormac said. He reached out with his mangled hand and gripped Pete's Adam's apple between his thumb and index finger. He slowly rubbed it up and down while Ziro dripped water onto the pirate captain's lips.

"Now what were you asking?" Ziro continued.

"It can wait," Cormac said. It turned out it was incredibly difficult to form a coherent sentence while you were rubbing an unconscious man's throat.

* * *

"This is bullshit!"

Dean Bickerstaff groaned. He had made it nearly five minutes without a complaint. The dean fished a new blunt out of the waistband of his towel and handed it to a customer at the back of the line. Then he waddled back down the hall toward Cormac's bedroom.

A young woman stood outside the open bedroom door. She had both her hands on her hips and somehow looked both very stoned and very angry. Frampton braced himself for yet another confrontation.

"What the shit was that?" the woman demanded. "Is this some kind of joke?"

Dean Bickerstaff sighed. "What seems to be the problem, miss?" he asked, already knowing what the answer would be.

"I skip class to come down here and wait in line for hours," the angry woman explained. "I pay you good money. You force me to use illegal drugs. And then when I look in that guy's ear, what do I see? Two minutes of him sitting there, rubbing a dead guy's neck!"

Dean lowered his eyes and nodded apologetically. "I'm sorry if Cormac's seafaring adventures have been a tad mundane today."

"Mundane?" the woman screeched. "It looks like he's jacking his throat off! Where the fuck are the pirates we were promised?"

A murmur began to spread down line of waiting customers. Dean Bickerstaff turned and addressed them with a broad grin. "Now, now, everyone. Nobody's jacking anyone's throat off in there!"

The dean turned back to the rabble-rouser. "I'm sorry if you weren't happy with your experience. Unfortunately, some members of the media took it upon themselves to make unauthorized guarantees that we are in no position to honor."

"So what the hell are you saying?" the woman said. She folded her arms across her chest and moved to the side to block the bedroom doorway.

"I'm saying no refunds, honey!" The dean raised the shillelagh over his head with both hands like he was wielding a broadsword. "Now get the hell out of here before I ram this so far down your throat you'll need to use a measuring tape to jack it off!"

The terrified woman fled toward the living room, and everybody else who was waiting in line was too scared to point out that the dean's quip had made absolutely no sense. The dean forced a smile back onto his face as he lowered his shillelagh. Stepping toward the front of the line, he warmly gestured for the next customer in line to enter the bedroom, which she only did because she was too high to remember how to run away herself.

"What's going on out there, Deano?" Vance asked from Cormac's desk chair.

"Just another whiner," Dean Bickerstaff said dismissively. "Listen, Vance, I'm taking a break to check out the scene in the living room. Remember our policy: absolutely no refunds." Vance shot back the A-OK sign. As long as any jacking, whacking, or whatever you wanted to call it stayed firmly back in the 1860s with Cormac, Vance was a happy camper. The dean stepped into the hall, closed the door behind him, and headed for the living room.

The past few hours had been full of encounters like this last one. Cissy's promise of pirates had lured record crowds to the house. Not only had these people been unable to observe a single buccaneer, but based on their reports, Cormac was not even attempting to catch any whales. Instead, customer after furious customer had informed Dean Bickerstaff that Cormac had spent their two minutes pouring glasses of water or sitting on the floor fondling an unconscious man's throat. Needless to say, this was not the swashbuckling drama they had been expecting.

A few of the dumber and higher customers still seemed to enjoy the experience. But there was an overall tone of grumbling dissatisfaction that the dean did not care for. Not that this had done anything to diminish the revelry taking place on the rest of the property. Dean Bickerstaff had to push past dancers, drinkers, and fornicators just to get to the couches. Apparently, a portal across the borders of known time and space could only impress college students for so long. Their love of free beer and drugs, however, appeared to be inexhaustible.

Dean Bickerstaff had yet to speak to Cissy about her article. Until this point, he had only glared at her from across the room. Cissy hadn't woken up until the house was already overrun with customers, and by then Frampton had no time to express his displeasure with her rogue actions. That was about to change though. Frampton navigated through the crowd until he was finally standing in front of the stadium seating couches. Cissy reclined on the airborne couch, holding an iPad that the dean had never seen her use before. She held a blunt between her teeth that she occasionally removed and attempted to use as a stylus on the touchscreen.

"I hope you're happy!" Dean Bickerstaff sneered at her. "Because of you, I'm getting chewed out by half the people who walk out of that bedroom."

Cissy rolled her eyes. "What the hell do you care?" she asked Frampton. "They already paid you."

"I care, Cissy, because we've spent the past week building up buzz about our operation," the dean explained. "If our customers think we intentionally deceived them, they'll get pissed off and stop posting about us!" A chilling thought occurred to the dean. "Have those bastards at #HoesBeBangin gotten to you, Cissy? Whatever they're paying you, I'll double it!"

"Right," Cissy said as she rolled her eyes again. "Because angry customers *never* go online to post about the companies that piss them off."

"What? What are people saying?"

Cissy lowered the iPad down to the dean's eye level. He still had to stand on his tiptoes to see it. Cissy had Twitter open and was monitoring a feed of search results for #CormacsEar. The dean swiped through the stream of tweets. It wasn't until he scrolled through a few dozen that he noticed that everything he'd just read had been posted in the past three minutes.

"Bullshit! I want a refund! Hey @CNN, since the @SchoolPaper has been bought off, how about some coverage of the #CormacsEar scandal?"

"lol, didnt see ne pirate #lame but tha clok just struck #420 and it's off the hook @ #cormacsear"

"smh at these lines for the food trucks at #cormacsear. smdh :)"

"Look at these these freaks hanging out across the street from #CormacsEar. Does the guy on the right have a boner? instagram. com/p/ZB9gHPnz/"

"Line was too long at #CormacsEar so me and @GDimesPHD are gonna break into this nasty van that's parked outside and do it"

The dean found the last tweet troubling, but overall there were way more posts today than any previous day. Evidently negative stories went viral much more quickly than positive ones. And now that he thought back on it, Frampton couldn't recall the board saying anything about the X-Factor discriminating between positive and negative online buzz, just as long as Harrington's name was getting out there.

The dean had serious doubts that Cissy had intended any of this when she oozed out the THC and booze that eventually congealed and formed her most recent article, but he had to admit that from a keeping-his-job perspective, it might end up accidentally working out for the best. As long as people stayed for the admittedly off-the-hook party, their complaints didn't seem to be able to hurt him.

"I guess the old saying is true," Dean Bickerstaff said with a shake of his head. "Any press is good press."

"I've never heard that expression," Cissy said.

"How is that possible?" the dean asked, dumbfounded. "You work in the press. Your entire family works in the press!"

Cissy shrugged.

Frampton stared at her in disbelief for a solid ten seconds. "Where'd you get the iPad?" he eventually asked with a sigh.

"It was a gift from Mako. Hey, speaking of, can you tell him to have someone bring me a Bloody Mary?" Cissy asked him as she held her blunt over the back of the airborne couch. Within a few seconds, a bandana man silently popped up and lit it for her. Cissy dismissed him with a wave of her hand, then took a long, deep puff.

The dean took this to mean that Cissy had exhausted her allotted verbal communication with him for the afternoon. So be it. He had little to gain by arguing with someone whose feet had barely touched the ground over the course of the past week. Besides, according to the last tweet, the defiling of his van was imminent. Vance must not have locked up after he moved it off the lawn.

Whatever had happened in the van before he owned it was water under the bridge as far as Dean Bickerstaff was concerned. Plus, odds were, everything the previous owner did in there had been on the up and up. Innocent until proven guilty, you know. But a lowlife like G-Dimes getting busy in the van was not something the dean felt like he'd be able to mentally get past. Especially if he was going to keep the van around after Cormac's situation necessitated using it. Which, Frampton just realized, he was now leaning toward doing. He'd grown kind of attached to the thing.

The dean left the couches and had taken only three or four steps toward the front door when Mako emerged from a throng of dancing partygoers and stepped directly in front of him.

"What's shakin', Dean B?" the notorious drug dealer asked with a smile on his face.

"Not too much, Mako." Frampton kept his eyes on the door. "Have you seen your associate?"

Mako's grin grew even wider. "I don't think you want to go looking for G right now. He met up with one of his exes."

"I know that," Dean Bickerstaff said curtly. "That's what I'm afraid of. I'm sorry, I'm in a bit of a rush, Mako."

The dean started to walk past Mako toward the door, but the drug dealer followed him. "Whoa, whoa! Slow down! I shouldn't be talking up G's love life anyways. Listen, I just thought I should let you know that those loonies across the street seem awfully riled up."

"Brock's cult?" Dean Bickerstaff stopped and pivoted to face Mako. The cult had been so quiet all morning that Frampton had forgotten about them. What the hell could they be doing now? If Mako—who valued their freedom of assembly so much—was concerned, it wasn't a good sign.

"Look, this is just what I heard but . . ." Mako looked around the room, then leaned in close to Dean Bickerstaff and lowered his voice to a whisper. "Evidently they got word that Cormac was jacking some guy off back on the boat." He straightened back up and scanned the room again to make sure nobody had heard. "Look, Dean B, I'm not judging a damn thing. I'm just telling you what they think is going on. But they seem pretty upset. The leader's going on and on about how this is a betrayal of the true believers."

The metaphysics of Brock's religion seemed to be based around the two pillars of Cormac and whacking it, so Frampton had no doubt that he was upset that these things were supposedly coinciding without him. And who knows how much more distorted the message had grown as it travelled out to the yard and across the street.

"I'll go and speak to him," Dean Bickerstaff assured Mako. "Will you see to it that everyone in line has plenty of marijuana? Nobody goes in . . ."

"Unless they hit the blunt. I got it, man!" Mako said with a smile. He gave the dean's shoulder a light tap with his fist. "Good luck with those freaky little bastards out there!"

"Oh, and Cissy needs a Bloody Mary!" Frampton yelled back at Mako as he turned back toward the door. "So does Vance!" came a faint cry from down the hall.

Frampton hoped those precious seconds wouldn't be the difference between a perfectly usable van and a horribly defiled van that he'd have to leave burning under an overpass. He figured that if Vance had parked it close enough to the house, he would be able to see if it was, as they say, a-rockin'. And if so, he figured that Mako, or at the very least his bandana men, could help provide fuel and accelerant to burn it with, or at least recommend a suitable overpass.

Unsure of what horrors the back of his van might hold, Dean Frampton Q. Bickerstaff stood up straight, gripped his shillelagh tightly, and took the first step toward a sure to be unpleasant series of confrontations. Then he immediately froze.

Standing in the doorway was George, the board member who had only two days ago informed Frampton of his most recent censure. Wearing a cheap suit and holding a briefcase, George looked quite uncomfortable as all the depravity swirled around him. Dean Bickerstaff was torn between trying to hide and getting him the hell off the property as fast as possible, lest George's lameness bring the party down to a place it would be impossible to recover from. On one hand, a board member seeing him like this could cause irreparable harm to his career and his legacy. On the other, what if one of the sunglasses dogs saw this uptight square at the party? Frampton thought he might die of embarrassment if that were to happen.

However, it seemed like the decision was no longer in Frampton's hands, because the horrified expression on George's face indicated that he had spotted the Harrington dean. Frampton took a quick breath to steel his nerves, then forced a grin onto his face and waddled toward his adversary with open arms.

"John!" he bellowed as if he were greeting a lifelong friend. "What the hell brings you down here?"

"Dear God, Frampton! Look at yourself!" George was staring at the dean as if he had just wandered into a church without any pants on. Frampton knew he wasn't in church, but just to be safe on the other point, he glanced down to make sure that his towel was still secured. The telltale lack of any recent screams made him fairly confident this was the case, but it helped to be certain. And yes, the familiar sight of the kittens enjoying their day on the beach greeted him when he looked down.

Frampton gave his towel a pat and chuckled at George. "Well, Paul, I think you'll find that, unlike the Harrington boardroom, people are free to be themselves here. Nobody's going to hassle you for being proud of who you are. It's a very accepting environment, which I wouldn't expect you to understand. Thanks for stopping by, ladies!" the dean called out as two attractive young women walked out the door.

"Don't come near us you gross little troll!" one of them hissed back at him.

Frampton gritted his teeth and swallowed his anger. He turned his attention back to George. "What can I do for you?" he asked the uneasy board member.

"Well, since this event you're sponsoring is the talk of the school, I thought I'd pop in and see some of the pirates that the *School Paper* guaranteed would be on display," George said as he suspiciously sniffed the air. "But clearly there are bigger issues to deal with here. Frampton, you're an ambassador for Harrington! It's inappropriate for you to be parading around a drug den in a towel!"

Frampton decided to ignore the second part of George's remarks. "Yes, the pirates have proven to be a popular attraction. Unfortunately, we do have a process in place to determine the order of our customers and I'm afraid we can't make an exception, even for someone of your stature. First, you pay the entrance fee, then you're assigned a number. When Mako calls your number, you form . . . Look, I'll be happy to attend to you in a minute but you'll have to excuse me. I have to go make sure G-Dimes isn't having sex in my van, then tell the cult across the street that Cormac isn't jacking anybody off back in the 1860s."

Dean Bickerstaff started to walk past George but the board member sidestepped into his path. "As much as those issues may require your expertise," George said snidely, "I have to talk to you. Whatever this is you've got going here is really starting to make some waves, Frampton. Viral tweets, news reports . . . There are people out there who drove five hundred miles just so their friend could take a picture of them chugging a beer on Cormac's lawn!"

"Did you notice any dogs in sunglasses?" Frampton asked. He now realized that he hadn't seen any of the cool dogs all day, and was getting pretty concerned.

"I don't think you're taking this seriously!" George said sharply. "The board is not happy, Frampton! We fear that you may be doing permanent damage to Harrington's reputation! You're clearly prioritizing your own twisted self-interest over the school's!"

"Kind of seems like that's something you guys should have considered before you tasked me with improving our X-Factor, eh Ringo?"

"Darn it, Frampton! You have called me every single one of the Beatles except for the one actually shares my name!" George stomped his feet and shook his briefcase. "You are so disrespectful and so inconsiderate to me and all the other board members!"

"Now that's ridiculous," Frampton said calmly. "I honestly intended no offense. After all, I'm so looking forward to your daughter's wedding."

George's face turned bright red and he started to emit a high-pitched whine from his pursed lips. Frampton was strongly considering delivering the final blow, which would be an actual shillelagh blow to George's knee, when he heard a voice behind him.

"Oh my God, you two are hilarious. Do your grandkids know you're here?"

Frampton looked behind him and saw three babes standing there in bikini tops and cutoff shorts. They each held red cups of beer and swayed uneasily on absurdly high heels.

"Do you think we can get a photo?" one of them asked, drunkenly brandishing her phone.

Dean Bickerstaff was inclined to tell them to go to hell. The girls were clearly mocking him, and he had no desire to willingly play into their little game. But when he glanced back at George, he saw that the board member was even more uneasy than he was. And if George was against it, it probably meant that it was going to do the dean's cause some good. Any press is good press, Frampton thought, recalling his earlier conversation with Cissy. Besides, the internet had to be fairly burned out on pictures of absurdly attractive college girls in bikinis by this point in time. Most likely this wouldn't attract any attention at all.

"Sounds good to me!" Frampton said. "Gather round, ladies!" Frampton walked over to George and turned to face the camera. But George wasn't having any of it.

"I'm leaving, Frampton. For heaven's sake, these girls are younger than my daughter. Believe me, the rest of the board is going to hear about this. You should really be ashamed of yourself." George walked out the front door and promptly had a beer spilled all over him by a shirtless guy who was trying to catch a thrown hot dog in his mouth.

"Too bad," one of the girls said as they each struck a pose on either side of Frampton. "That suit was so lame it was almost hot."

"Yeah, and how about that briefcase?" Frampton chuckled.

"Don't address or touch me," the babe said coldly. Her mouth briefly fell to a sneer before her friend announced that she was ready to take the picture. Her bright white smile quickly returned and the phone's flash went off.

"Fucking hilarious," said the girl who had taken the picture. She tapped on her phone for a few seconds, captioning the image with something Frampton was sure he wouldn't want to see. She walked to her friends, who spun away from the dean as if he'd been a cardboard cutout in a photo booth and headed for the door

"I heard they hired that guy to scare off rats!" the babe with the camera said.

"Someone told me it lives under the house and eats worms," her friend chimed in.

Any press is good press, Dean Frampton Q. Bickerstaff reminded himself as he walked outside to make sure a drug dealer wasn't having sex in his van.

★ ★ ★

The orange glow of the setting sun flickered through a porthole in the captain's quarters and Cormac suddenly realized how late it was. An entire day had slipped past while he sat on the floor looking after a poisoned pirate. Previous sunsets on the *Levyathan* would have found him aiming his harpoon at the last whale of the day, or proudly helping to butcher another record haul. Today, on the other hand, his current state could best be described as "hoping he fell asleep and went forward in time before Pete had to use the bathroom because of all the water they'd been giving him."

It hadn't been an entirely wasted afternoon, though. Ziro had shown Cormac the start of a catchy new ukulele ditty he'd been working on. While it might not have the staying power and mass appeal of "Treasures o' the Sea," the new song, "Briny Bonin'" made up for it in its sheer volume of filth. He'd also tasted a variety of fine liquors and wines from the captain's personal stash and was feeling pretty damn good. Oh, and the human being they'd been tasked with keeping alive had not died. Somehow that seemed like a minor triumph compared to the couplet he suggested for "Briny Bonin'" that managed to rhyme "love gravy runs thick" with "shoved Davy Jones's dick."

Ziro sat next to Pete's head, attempting to work out the chord changes for an instrumental segment that would follow the seventh verse. Every so often, he'd stop strumming to help Pete take a sip of water. The pirate captain was swallowing on his own by this point in time, so Cormac did not have to rub his throat any longer, which came as a huge relief. There were times when, despite being on death's door, Pete seemed to be enjoying that part just a little too much. Now Cormac was content to mimic Ziro's fingering on his own ukulele, and take frequent swigs from a bottle of Danish akvavit that had tasted like fire the first time he sipped it, but was going down pretty smooth now that nearly half the bottle was gone.

Ziro's latest chord transition caught Cormac's ear and he was about to ask him to play it back for him when Captain Anson appeared in the doorway.

"How's Pete doing?" he demanded.

"It looks like he's going to make it," Ziro said. "He's drinking more water and he's progressed from incoherent gurgling to moans of despair."

"Excellent!" Captain Anson said. Now that all opportunities for leadership and heroism had passed, he stepped into his quarters for the first time in hours. "I knew you two could do it!" The captain gave Cormac a thumbs up as he walked past, then greedily rubbed his hands together as he approached his trunk of booze. "So, what are we drinking?" he asked.

Cormac held his current bottle out toward the captain. "Akvavit?" Anson grimaced. "Why the hell did you open that? Ziro uses this to clean the floors!"

"I only did that once, and it was because you had stolen my turpentine!" Ziro shot back. Not seeing any other immediate options, Captain Anson shrugged and grabbed the bottle. After a moment of hesitation, he took a deep breath, then raised the bottle and tilted it back. After a mighty swig, he let out a loud whoop.

"Woo!" The captain emitted a series of coughs and wheezes as he handed the bottle back to Cormac. "Dear God! I have a hard time believing that anything Pete drank yesterday could have been worse than that." Lying on the floor, Pete raised his trembling hand about a half inch off the floor and made a noise like a dying toad.

"What the hell was that?" The captain asked, cautiously taking a step or two away from the pirate captain.

"I'm guessing that was him telling you to go to hell, then attempting to throttle you," Ziro said. "It's the best he's looked all day."

"Well, seems like he's in the clear," Captain Anson replied. "Cormac, my boy, it looks like that weird little throat thing you were doing is no longer needed. Why don't you take a walk with me?" Cormac was slightly worried that the captain had a sinister ulterior motive for requesting his presence, but he was also drunk enough not to care. He carefully got to his feet.

"Can I come too?" Ziro asked. "I've barely eaten today and this is the longest I've gone without swabbing the decks in five years."

"Of course not, Ziro!" Captain Anson chuckled as he poured the remaining akvavit into a large tankard. "This man is on death's door!"

"You just said he was in the clear," Ziro reminded him, but his plea fell on deaf ears. The captain rummaged through his liquor chest until he found a bottle of non-Canadian whiskey. He pulled the cork out and took another long swig.

"Oh yeah," the captain said. "That's the good stuff." He poured half the bottle into another tankard, then handed the akvavit to Cormac and kept the whiskey for himself. "Let's go, Cormac. Ziro, I'll bring you some hardtack if I remember."

Cormac shot Ziro a "what are you gonna do?" look and followed the captain onto the deck of the boat. He stayed a step or two behind so that he could make a hasty getaway if Anson started hitting on him, or worse, started crying. Eventually they wandered to the *Levyathan*'s bow, where the captain stopped and leaned forward onto the railing, looking out at the setting sun. He sipped his tankard of whiskey and stared straight forward. Not sure what he was supposed to do, Cormac stood next to him and gulped down the akvavit.

Eventually, Captain Anson spoke up. "I know you're disappointed you didn't get to harpoon any of those foul beasts today, Cormac. Believe me, nothing would have given me more pleasure than to see their dirty flesh pierced with the tip of your mighty harpoon."

"Can you maybe not talk about me doing that in those terms?" Cormac asked. He'd spent the whole day writing vulgar sea shanties, but hearing the captain describe his own exploits in such a manner made him kind of uneasy.

"There's no need to be humble, my boy," the captain said, not taking his gaze away from the horizon. He was talking to Cormac, but he seemed alone with his thoughts. "I just wanted to say that having you on board these past few days has really been a great experience. You've made a big difference for everyone on board. And that includes me. Whatever happens when we dock in St. John's, I just wanted you to know that."

"Thank you, sir," Cormac said. He shifted his gaze to the horizon as well. It really was quite a sight. Oranges, purples, and blues filled the sky as the last sliver of the sun slowly disappeared from sight. A few seconds after it vanished, there was a brilliant green burst of light from the point on the horizon where the sun had been moments earlier. It was one of the most beautiful things Cormac had ever seen. He looked over at the captain, not sure what they had just witnessed.

"The green flash," Captain Anson whispered. "All these years at sea I thought it was just a myth." He fell silent again, as they both let the sight of what they'd seen sink in.

After a minute or two that felt like an eternity, Cormac tentatively broke the silence. "Why do you hate them so much? The whales, I mean."

Captain Anson took several long gulps of whiskey. Cormac hadn't really been counting, but now that he thought about it, the captain had put away a sizeable volume of booze since he'd reappeared in his quarters. Now that Cormac was looking for it, he could definitely tell that the captain was more than a little drunk.

The captain breathed a heavy sigh and began to tell his tale. "It was a long time ago. I was a young lad, not much older than you. One week Eleanor's parents came to stay with us. We never really got along, if you can believe that. Really horrible people. The first time I met them I should have taken it as a warning sign about Eleanor. Whatever I did was never good enough for them. You're the vice president at the bank, they want you to be president. Your home has three bedrooms, why not four? You marry one of their daughters, they criticize you for not marrying both of them."

"That last one is pretty weird," Cormac said.

"Like I said, they were horrible," Captain Anson acknowledged. "So I would stay at the bank as long as I could while they were in town just to keep out of the house. One night after I closed up, I just couldn't bear to return home to their nagging, so I stopped to have a pint at the tavern. It ended up turning into a couple pints, and then a couple pints more. By the time I left for home, it was already late at night."

"I still remember the flicker of the oil lamps in the windows as I stumbled home. I knew that I'd catch hell for staying out so long when the in-laws were in town, but I was also drunk enough not to care. But I wasn't prepared at all for what awaited me when I walked in the door."

"I saw my mother-in-law first. She was crumpled at the bottom of the staircase. She'd been shot directly in the forehead and then tumbled down the stairs. My father-in-law had put up a bit more of a fight. He took a few shots in his leg, and had some slashes on his hands, knife wounds. One of the bullets must have nicked an artery; he bled out on the kitchen floor. Eleanor survived by hiding in a closet upstairs, listening to every moment of her parents' deaths."

Captain Anson looked at Cormac with wild eyes. He clenched his fist and spoke his next words slowly. "I vowed that night to get revenge on the whales that killed my in-laws. But that wasn't enough, no sir. I swore an oath that I would not stop until every whale on the face of the earth was wiped out, until their entire species paid for what they had done!"

Cormac stared at the captain. It really felt like there was a piece missing from his story, but he appeared to be done talking. Eventually Cormac asked for clarification. "Is that it?"

The captain nodded solemnly. "It was a dark chapter."

Cormac was still uncertain that he had heard all the particulars of the story correctly. "OK," he said, choosing his words carefully. Clearly this was an incident that still affected the captain deeply. "So you came home one night. You found your in-laws murdered in your house, shot and stabbed. And your instant reaction was to assume it was whales and swear a brutal vengeance on their species as a whole?"

"That night altered the course of my life," Anson said.

"That is ridiculous! Why did you assume that whales had done it?"

"I wasn't thinking clearly!" the captain protested. "It was a very traumatic moment. Plus I was really drunk! Oh, and some guy at the tavern had told a dirty joke about a killer whale and I guess it was still on my mind. It was really funny, it was something like 'What's the difference between a killer whale and a nun with diarrhea? With the nun, at least you can—'"

"I don't care about the stupid joke!" Cormac lied. "So the next day, once you realized that whales were not able to properly grip muskets or knives, not to mention fit through the front door of your house, let alone crawl out of the sea to kill humans, why did you still feel it was necessary to exterminate them from the face of the earth?"

"I made a vow," the captain said, all of a sudden deadly serious again. "I'm not sure what that means to you, Cormac, but to me, keeping your word is just about the most important thing a man can do."

"But your vow was based on a horribly flawed assumption! I mean, thank God you didn't suspect Indians or the Irish and vow to wipe them out instead!"

"I guess some of us just choose to live by a code," the captain said defensively. "Plus, a lot of people don't know this, but it's actually pretty damn fun trying to wipe an entire species off the face of the earth."

Cormac was still trying to wrap his head around all of this. "OK, OK . . . So your hatred of whales stems from a few hours when you drunkenly thought that whales had killed your in-laws. But who actually killed your in-laws?"

"Some hit men I hired," the captain said matter-of-factly.

Cormac threw his hands up in the air, unable to believe how this story was unfolding. "Hit men? You hired hit men to kill your in-laws? Forgive me for asking, sir, but why did you not stop to think that maybe the hit men that you had personally hired were the people who murdered your wife's parents?"

"They came a day early," Anson shrugged. "I wasn't expecting them until the next night. I took them for professionals. I didn't think they'd screw up a detail as big as the day they were supposed to kill Eleanor's parents. I mean, come on! What if I had needed her dad to help me move something heavy that night?"

"So your in-laws were killed by unseen assailants less than twenty-four hours before the unseen assailants who you personally hired were scheduled to kill them. Your gut reaction: it must have been whales."

"Can we change the subject please?" Captain Anson asked as he downed a sizeable gulp of whiskey. "This is all very painful stuff you're dredging up here." The captain stared back out at the rapidly fading colors on the horizon, the brilliance of the green flash now a distant memory. Cormac let the subject drop for a few seconds, but had too many questions to remain silent for long.

"Did your wife suspect anything?" he asked.

"Of course she suspected something! That's another reason I wanted to get the hell out to sea. She knew I hated her parents. In fact, she was on the verge of tracking down the men I'd hired, so right before I left town I hired hit men to kill the original hit men!"

Another long pause. "That's a lot of hit men," was all that Cormac could manage to say.

"You're telling me! And covering your tracks gets pretty expensive after a while! Hit men are barely affordable on a banker's salary, but on an unsuccessful whaling ship captain's? Forget about it!"

"You could probably afford one now," Cormac said knowingly. "In case you hadn't noticed, you're not so unsuccessful anymore."

Captain Anson laughed bitterly. "For Eleanor and her lawyer? Believe me, I've thought about it. But I swore off working with hit men years ago. It puts too much weight on the conscience. Too many sleepless nights. Also, the second pair of hit men I hired were not up to date with their union dues, so I've been blacklisted by the Hit Men's Union for working with scabs. Nobody will do a job for me if they value their pension plan."

Cormac stood there for his longest pause yet. "Well, sir, this discussion has been very revealing," Cormac finally said. What it had revealed, he could not exactly say. "How's your drink holding up?" Anson flipped his mug upside down to show that it was empty.

"Me too," Cormac said. "How about a refill?"

Captain Anson nodded, and they both started off toward the captain's quarters. Despite the captain's protests, Cormac insisted that they pick up some hardtack for Ziro on the way. Cormac fished two pieces out of one of the storage barrels. He took a bite from one and stuck the other in his pocket for Ziro as they continued on toward the quarters.

"So, sir," Cormac asked as he gnawed on the brick-like substance. "How does that joke end?"

"The whale and the nun?" Captain Anson said, a smile creeping back onto his face. He chuckled warmly at the thought of the filthy punch line. "Let's wait until Ziro is around. Ziro hates this joke."

* * *

Dean Frampton Q. Bickerstaff groaned in exasperation and hit the delete button on his phone yet again. A major aspect of his pre–Craymore Street life that he'd been neglecting was deleting emails without reading them. The dean was using the walk from the street back to the house as an opportunity to catch up with this burdensome task. As he slowly navigated through the drunken masses, he deleted unread emails regarding the budget, a threatened strike by the admissions office, and the crumbling infrastructure of the humanities building, which were marked as "Urgent," "Extremely Urgent," and "Several People Are Trapped Under Rubble."

Only one email did not get deleted unread, and as Frampton stepped onto the porch, he stopped in front of Cissy's new couch in order to read it. A rustling in the bushes indicated to Frampton that he should not consider actually sitting down on the couch, but at the same time the bandana men's omnipresent unseen threat kept the area clear of partying students, so he could read the email in peace. It was from one of Frampton's oldest friends, James "Jimmy" Chambers. Frampton hadn't heard from Jimmy in at least five years, but he always had time for a childhood friend who had grown up to become a powerful senator who served on the finance committee.

It turned out that in two days, Senator Chambers had a speaking engagement less than an hour from Harrington and he was very interested in stopping by to see this crazy whaling-portal kid he'd heard about on the news. A wide grin crossed Dean Bickerstaff's face as he read the email. At long last, the Harrington bad boys would be reunited.

Frampton and Jimmy had raised all sorts of hell together. They'd met in fourth grade when both of them turned up in the principal's office at the same time. Frampton was in for attempting to bribe a teacher, Jimmy for attempting to blackmail one, and they'd been fast friends ever since. They were an unlikely duo. Tall and handsome, Jimmy was able to charm his way out of just about any trouble with a flash of his winning smile. Strangers often stopped to help Jimmy search for the lost leash that they assumed Frampton was supposed to be attached to. But they'd bonded despite their differences, and it was trouble every time they got together. A host of schemes, scams, and charges that were suspiciously dropped at the last minute followed them from grade school to high school and then all the way to Harrington.

They'd started to drift apart toward the end of college when it became clear that their paths were diverging. Jimmy, by that point going by James, had been identified as an up-and-coming political star, and had his sights set on Washington. Suddenly he didn't have as much time for someone whose goals were as modest as simply taking control of an entire university. Still, Frampton had been a major fundraiser for Jimmy's first senate campaign, identifying alumni whose children would soon be applying to Harrington and shaking them down for donations regardless of their political affiliation. He'd even thrown the victory party the night Jimmy got elected. Jimmy had been unable to attend, but he had graciously sent a representative over in a pickup truck to borrow a few cases of champagne when the party he did end up at ran out.

Frampton was excited to see Jimmy, even if he was upset that his friend had learned about Cormac from an unauthorized news broadcast. Who knew what kind of half-truths and outright lies the news crews were spreading? Frampton wanted Cissy's half-truths and outright lies to be the only ones people were hearing! But Frampton had a more pressing concern on his mind: how to make sure that Jimmy had a good experience while he was here. He couldn't have his old partner in crime showing up only to watch Cormac sit around on the boat all day. Jimmy would think the whole endeavor was lame. Frampton and Vance would have to find some way to subtly suggest that Cormac provide a good show rather than a repeat of today's dismal affair.

Frampton thought back to earlier in the afternoon. If he had been stuck inside with George for just two minutes longer, the Astro van would currently be smoldering under a bridge somewhere. When the dean had finally managed to escape the house, he found G-Dimes slumped against the side of the van, even less conscious than usual. An extremely underdressed female student was smacking his face in a panicked attempt to revive him. In his right hand, G-Dimes feebly clutched a rubber hose whose path traced back to the van's gas tank. Evidently, his lady friend had suggested that they stop for a brief huffing break before continuing on to their planned van-sex rendezvous. G-Dimes had insisted on personally siphoning the gas for her by mouth. The bar was set low, but Frampton thought this was easily the most romantic gesture that had taken place during his time on Craymore Street. Who said chivalry was dead?

Even though Frampton would have bet his life savings that this was not the first time G-Dimes had siphoned gasoline from a vehicle, the drug dealer had apparently been confused by the process and ended up swallowing a great deal of it, hence his near-death state. But G-Dimes's body proved itself remarkably adept at processing noxious substances, and soon after the dean arrived he regained consciousness and resumed his progress toward his intended vehicular love den. Fortunately, by that point, a towel-clad Frampton had started to pointedly rummage around in the back of the van, negating whatever questionable sex appeal it ever had in the first place.

Frampton had waited until G-Dimes and his partner slunk off in search of another place to get busy, then locked up the van and started to walk across the street. To his dismay he noted that several TV news vans were parked about a block down the road. His mandatory blunt smoking had been able to deter reporters from infiltrating Cormac's bedroom, but the media vultures had comfortably settled into the public space, where the dean was powerless to stop their broadcasting. Frampton tried not to let it bother him for the time being. Much more pressing was the next item on his agenda: smoothing things out with the cult. Or, as it turned out, cults.

Evidently, earlier in the morning there had been a schism in Brock's congregation. Brock continued to present himself as the chosen one who would someday receive Cormac's true word, but a group of upstarts now believed that the chosen one might instead be this mysterious person who Cormac was jacking off on the boat. The splinter group had moved into a separate camp just a few feet over from Brock's original site, and tensions appeared to be running high between the two cults when Frampton arrived.

Brock was preaching fire and brimstone, branding the new cult as heretics and calling for a holy war to ensure their immediate extermination. Fortunately, all that this had led to so far was Brock getting caught trying to jack it in a tent belonging to one of the new cult's members. As dedicated as Brock's disciples seemed to be to their new religion, they appeared slightly reluctant to commit genocide in its name less than a week after it was formed. Everyone sort of just stood around, hoping that somebody else would start cleansing first.

Trying to play the role of diplomat, Frampton explained to the splinter group that Cormac had not actually been giving anyone a handjob back on the *Levyathan*. But the news that, in reality, he had been rubbing a barely conscious man's throat was evidently in line with one of their prophecies or some bullshit and it only served to

509

further solidify their faith. Brock's cult started to derogatorily refer to the new cult as the Throat Jackers, and the new cult responded by embracing the slur as a badge of honor and adopting it as their official name. At this point, the dean was sick of standing in the middle of the street wearing just a towel so he asked Brock and the leader of the Throat Jackerswhat it would take to get them to agree to an armistice. The consensus turned out to be a few pitchers of keg beer and a group discount rate at the hot dog truck.

Once they were chowing down on hot dogs and sipping beer, the two cults seemed much less likely to exterminate each other, at least for the time being. Tomorrow might bring about a horrific massacre, or perhaps the streets would run red with blood later that night after people got a bit drunker. The point was, Frampton had solved the problem in the most temporary and irresponsible way possible. It felt good to kick a can down the road. Kicking cans down the road had been a staple of his normal life as Harrington dean, and he hadn't had a chance to do it since he'd received the directive from the board to focus entirely on Harrington's X-Factor ranking. That still didn't change the fact that boring ear time, horny, gasoline-huffing drug dealers, and masturbating rival cults were not the sort of thing he wanted Jimmy to have to put up with when he graced Craymore Street with his presence in forty-eight hours.

At least it couldn't get any worse, Frampton thought, as he pocketed his phone, opened the front door, and immediately discovered the day's new low point. A dissatisfied customer had left a review of his Cormac experience in a tightly coiled pile in the middle of the living room floor. The dean was horrified, by both the floor dump and all the other partygoers, whose reaction had been not to immediately clean up the feces, but rather to just clear out a radius of about three feet. The effect was that the rest of the house was now even more crowded, while the poop occupied its own tranquil oasis of filth.

Frampton immediately marched down to Cormac's bedroom to confront Vance about the sanitation crisis. Not surprisingly, Vance seemed unconcerned.

"It was probably one of those dogs, Deano," Vance said. "They probably couldn't tell if they were inside or outside with those sunglasses on."

It took all of Frampton's willpower not to slap Vance for insinuating such vile things about the cool dogs. Instead, he bit his tongue and explained to Vance that it wasn't important *who* had crapped on the floor. What was important was that two days ago, they had not been throwing the kind of party where people took craps on floor, and today, this was sadly no longer the case. Things were trending downward, and in Dean Bickerstaff's opinion, it was all due to Cormac's yawn-inducing exploits on the *Levyathan*.

Vance just shrugged, and Frampton made a silent vow to never again partner with someone who got too high and drunk to care that a stranger was defecating on the floor of his house. When he walked out of Cormac's bedroom, Dean Bickerstaff was horrified to see that one of the cool dogs was eating the excrement. Frampton felt betrayed. He had thought the dogs were cool—how could they do this to him? He was on the verge of storming out of the party and locking himself in the van when he realized that a large, frenzied crowd was cheering on the dog as it went to town. People weren't disgusted, they thought it was awesome! The dean slowly cracked a smile, and by the time the dog finished, Frampton was cheering louder than anyone. Those dogs, Dean Bickerstaff thought with an admiring shake of his head. No matter what they were doing, they were the life of the party!

Feeling reinvigorated by the sight of a dog eating feces, the dean attended to the party with renewed gusto. He passed out extra blunts and took shots of cognac with the people waiting in line. He slipped the DJs a couple hundred bucks to really kick the music up to the next level. He even wowed the crowd on the dance floor with an impromptu shillelagh-twirling stunt that he made up on the spot. (Only a few people were injured, none of them seriously.) It didn't quite get a "dog eating poop" response, but the dean had heard plenty of people applaud out of pity before, and most of these people were not applauding out of pity.

When closing time rolled around, people were sad to have to leave and Dean Bickerstaff was exhausted. After making sure the cleaning crew paid extra attention to a key spot on the floor, he retreated to the van, where he now sat thinking back on the eventful day. The past few hours had renewed Frampton's confidence that he just might be able to show Jimmy a good time after all.

Frampton's phoned buzzed and he looked down. Another email subject line from a panicked board member scrolled across his notification bar. "Humanities building survivors resorting to cannibalis—" Frampton hit delete before it could finish. Whatever it was, it could most assuredly wait. He'd earned his paycheck today. Dean Frampton Q. Bickerstaff yawned as he lay down on the floor of the van. The last thing he heard before he drifted off to sleep was the gentle squeak of a clown nose that must have been beneath the pile of adult diapers he was using as a pillow.

DAY THIRTEEN

Cormac woke up. He didn't feel hungover, out of place, or terrified. This instantly terrified him. It meant that he'd actually grown accustomed to the fact that every night he was hurtling through time and space as he slept. This shouldn't seem normal! This was seriously fucked up in every way possible! Why was it happening? Why now? Why him? WHY!?

But these questions could wait. He was pretty hungry.

Cormac plugged his ears to block out Vance and Cissy's snores and shuffled into the kitchen to see if there was any cereal. His day on the *Levyathan* had ended in a pretty unspectacular fashion. By the time he stumbled off to the whalers' quarters, it was apparent that Pete was going to survive. The pirate captain had managed to sit up and drink on his own, and was eventually able to mutter a few feeble sentences. Well, technically he just stared at Captain Anson and repeated "Why? Why?" But Cormac felt that the obvious implication—"Why did you let me drink so much turpentine, you monster?"—qualified it as a sentence.

The kitchen was once again slightly cleaner than Cormac would have typically expected. But there was exactly one bowl of Lucky Charms left in the cupboard (and there were still marshmallows), so Cormac decided to ignore this for the time being. He poured the cereal into a bowl and was hunting for a clean spoon when he heard a strange sound emanating from his bedroom. It was similar to the sound his phone made when he received a text message, but longer and sustained. A chill shot up Cormac's spine as he realized what was happening: his phone was ringing.

This couldn't be good. None of his friends would ever call him. Emails and texts had been entirely sufficient to get him through three years of college. An actual phone call was a gigantic red flag that the person on the other end was somebody he didn't want to talk to. He was either in trouble with the law or somebody he knew was dead.

The ringing continued, but Cormac's ears soon picked up another ominous sound. Or actually, a lack thereof. The snoring from the living room had quickly grown half as deafening. Somebody else was awake.

Cormac set the bowl of Lucky Charms down on the counter and slowly walked out of the kitchen. When he entered the hallway, he turned toward the living room. A half-asleep Vance was standing there in his towel, trying to figure out what had woken him up. When he saw Cormac he wobbled back and forth for a second, not really sure what to make of his roommate. But then something clicked in Vance's head. His eyes went wide and he began to sprint down the hall toward Cormac's bedroom. "Mac, wait!" he shouted as he ran.

Cormac had no idea what to make of Vance's sudden movement, but he had no desire to be part of his roommate's erratic behavior this early in the morning. He darted across the hallway, slipped into his bedroom, and slammed the door shut. In the hallway, Vance came screeching to a halt just outside the door, and Cormac had to lean into it as he fiddled with the lock to prevent Vance from forcing himself in.

"Vance, what the hell are you doing?" Cormac asked as his roommate futilely twisted the knob back and forth on the other side of the door.

"Mac! Let me in! Don't answer your phone! You gotta trust me on this one!" Vance sounded panicked and incredibly untrustworthy. Cormac ignored his pleas and stepped back from the door. A few loud thuds in succession indicated that Vance was repeatedly slamming his shoulder into the door in an attempt to knock it down. Fortunately, it held fast, and after one particularly loud thud, Vance yelped in pain and the attempts ceased.

Cormac slowly walked over to his bedside table, hoping that if he took long enough his phone would stop ringing. When this strategy proved ineffective, he reluctantly reached out and picked up it up. Cormac realized he was instinctively wincing as he tilted the phone so he could see the display. It read "Mom & Dad."

Dammit. This was serious. Somebody was definitely dead. He crossed his fingers and hoped it was one of those elderly people at family gatherings who he had been instructed to call "aunt" or "uncle" even though they weren't really an aunt or uncle. Cormac thought he would be able to fake an appropriate amount of sorrow at the news of their passing and quickly get on with his day, no clarification needed as to what their actual relationship to him had been. As he hit the talk button, Cormac tried to remember the last time he talked on the phone with his parents.

The last time he could remember was when they had forgotten to pick him up from little league practice and he had to call them collect from a payphone. But that was when he was about ten years old. That couldn't possibly be the most recent time.

Cormac didn't have a bad relationship with his parents. It was just that over the past few years they had started disapproving of pretty much every aspect of his lifestyle and every decision he'd ever made. As his still-drunk, towel-clad roommate began shouting threats and banging on his door again, Cormac found himself empathizing with them.

"Hey, Mom," he said sheepishly into the handset.

"Oh, goddammit," Vance wailed from the other side of the door.

"Cormac, this is your father," came a gruff voice from the other end of the call. His father! This was even more serious than he'd feared. His grandparents might not just be dead, they might have been gunned down trying to assassinate the president!

"Dad!" Cormac said, futilely trying to conceal the surprise in his voice. "What, er . . . what brings you here?" What brings you here? Idiot! This wasn't fair, he was out of practice talking on the phone.

"What the hell are you talking about, boy?" Mr. McIlhenney barked. "We saw the news report about you and we want to know what in God's name is going on down there!"

News report? Cormac was momentarily speechless as he tried to process what was happening. Nobody was dead, but there had been a news report about him. It was hard to think with Vance pounding on the door, but Cormac quickly scanned his bedroom trying to make heads or tails of what his dad was talking about. He hadn't been doing anything newsworthy except for . . . Cormac's heart fell into his stomach as his eyes came to rest on the ukulele.

Oh God no.

Cormac's parents were severely technologically impaired. Their use of a computer was mostly limited to occasionally forwarding Cormac an alarming email chain that had been thoroughly disproven over a decade ago. Cormac had lived most of his life with the assumption that anything he did online would never be discovered by his parents' prying eyes. But if his ukulele video had gone viral enough to make the news, his secret might be out. His father, who had bought him his first guitar at the age of six and played in bar bands well into Cormac's teenage years, would never forgive him.

"Hello? Are you there?" came the confused, angry voice from the other end.

"Dad," Cormac stammered. "About the ukulele. It's not what you think. You see, I was—"

Mr. McIlhenney cut him off. "Ukulele? What in the name of hell are you talking about, Son?" Cormac heard a struggle on the other end of the line. Loud bangs and blasts of static forced him to pull the phone away from his ear. When he cautiously lowered it back to the side of his head, the shrill tones of his mother's voice were blaring out of it. "He's babbling about a ukulele!" Cormac could faintly hear his dad yelling in the background.

"Cormac, dearie, we saw the news," his mother said in a hurt tone. "Why didn't you tell us? How scary this must be for you!"

"Scary?" Cormac was still confused. "It's been kind of strange, ma, but everyone on YouTube has been surprisingly nice."

"Nice?" Cormac's mom sounded aghast. "Lining up to peer in your ear while you're unconscious? That horrible man in the towel charging admission like you're some sort of freak show act?"

"Freak show act? Mom, what exactly did you guys see on the news?" Under normal circumstances, Cormac would have assumed that his parents had been the victims of some sort of scam. After all, one time they'd nearly signed the deed to their house over to a guy from Nigeria just because he'd asked them for it. But the past two weeks had hardly been normal circumstances. Cormac looked over his shoulder at the door, where Vance had suddenly gone silent again. With his mangled left hand he reached up and rubbed his ear. Charging admission? Horrible man in a towel?

There was another struggle on his parents' end and Cormac's dad regained control of the phone. "Goddammit, son, whatever you've got going on down there I want you to cut it out. It's all over the news the way you're whoring yourself out to a bunch of degenerates while you're screwing around on that whaling boat. Someone was banging on our door today wanting to stick a camera in our ears to see if it was genetic! It's disgracing the family!"

Cormac was silent for a good ten seconds. Then all he managed to utter was, "What?" He was floored. Every other time in his life when he'd denied knowledge of something to his furious parents he had been lying. He was completely unprepared for the awkward sensation of actually not knowing what the hell they were angry about.

"I don't care how big of a cut those sleazeballs are paying you, or how you got hooked up with them in the first place," his dad lectured. "You tell them that it's over. Nobody's looking in your ear anymore, whether they're watching you catch whales, or hunt pirates, or build the goddamn pyramids for all I care. You've got your mother very worked up over here!"

"Ask him if he got those cookies I sent him!" his mother shrieked from what had to have been no more than three inches away from the phone.

"OK, Dad, listen." Cormac took a deep breath. "One, I have not received any cookies." From the other end of the line came a noise that was either Mrs. McIlhenney having a conniption about her undelivered baked goods or a very angry goose that had infiltrated his parents' house. Cormac ignored it and continued. "Two: yes, it's true. I have been waking up on a whaling boat in the 1860s for the past two weeks. And that's something I was totally going tell you guys as soon as I got the chance! But for now, I need *you* to tell me exactly what you saw on the news, because I seriously have no idea what you're talking about."

Mr. McIlhenney paused on the other end. He was obviously trying to decide whether he should believe his son. As far as his parenting experience went, this was also uncharted territory. It wasn't even a situation he had seen addressed on TV. "What to do when your good-for-nothing son has been keeping his time travel a secret from you" was not exactly a trope that kept popping up on your average family sitcom. But something, perhaps the uncertain tone in Cormac's voice or Mr. McIlhenney's petty desire to thwart his wife's attempt to seize control of the phone, convinced him that his son was telling the truth.

"Well," Mr. McIlhenney said. "The reporter started by saying that the news crew feared they'd be severely beaten if they brought any cameras inside your house." Cormac suddenly felt the need to sit down. He plopped himself on the corner of his bed and listened in horror as his dad started to explain what they'd seen on the news.

* * *

Dean Bickerstaff had slept fitfully. Throughout the night he'd been jolted awake by the slightest noise, believing it was a determined G-Dimes slinking back into the van to complete his unfinished dirty work. So he was already on edge when he heard the banging on the van's rear doors. He blindly began to grope around for his shillelagh, preparing to enact the scenario he'd rehearsed over and over in his head: wallop G-Dimes over the head, then immediately flee the country to avoid the severe retribution that would assuredly come from assaulting the top drug dealer on campus.

Finding his shillelagh was proving exceedingly difficult. Frampton kept grabbing floppy clown shoes. While they were quite sizeable, he doubted they would make an effective bludgeoning weapon. Meanwhile, whoever was outside banging on the door had started yelling something. Frampton couldn't make out exactly what the person was saying, but it was already more consecutive words than he'd heard G-Dimes utter the entire time he'd known him. It had to be somebody else. Frampton stopped moving and tried to concentrate on what the person outside was saying.

"Code green! It's code green, Deano!"

Code green? It couldn't be. Frampton had almost forgotten that they'd even established a series of code words. Vance had drunkenly cooked up the plan while Cormac was retrieving them drinks at Mickey's the other day. Frampton didn't remember the entire sequence, but he did know that code green was the one he most hoped never came up. The dean sprang to his feet and barged toward the rear doors of the van, banging his shin on his shillelagh in the process. Pain shot up his leg, but Frampton barely even noticed. He pushed the doors open and blinked into the morning light as he looked down at Vance, who was wearing just his towel and breathing heavily.

"Code green?" Frampton demanded. "Are you certain? How long ago did this happen? Have any of the board members discovered the antidote yet?"

519

"Antidote?" Vance looked confused. "What do you mean anti— You know what? I think I was confused. It may actually be code blue. "

"Code blue? I shouldn't go in the bathroom because there's a wolverine trapped in the shower?"

"Is that what code blue is?" Vance asked, sounding very uncertain.

"Code blue was *your* code!" Dean Bickerstaff sputtered. "You were the one who insisted we have a contingency plan in case that ridiculous situation ever happened!"

"Which is the code for 'Cormac has found out that we've been exploiting him while he's on the whaling ship?'" Vance asked.

"Code red!"

"Right," Vance nodded. "The most common code. Well anyways, it's that one."

"You're saying that he's on to us?" Dean Bickerstaff couldn't believe it. He slowly lowered himself out of the van and onto the ground outside. How had this happened? They'd taken every precaution in the book, other than the one about not introducing hundreds of drunken, unpredictable strangers into your tightly choreographed ballet of deceit. "What happened? Did he hire a private eye? Set up a secret webcam? Are there tracking devices planted under our skin right now?" Dean Bickerstaff started to panic at the thought, and began lifting and prodding the folds in his skin to examine for any such devices.

"Even more devious," Vance said grimly. "His parents called and told him about it."

Dean Bickerstaff dropped a roll of stomach flab that he'd been gripping with both hands and stared at Vance. "His parents," Frampton repeated to make sure he'd heard Vance correctly. "They just called him up and told him."

"That wily bastard," Vance added, averting his eyes to avoid looking at the dean's still-jiggling stomach.

"How did you let this happen?" Frampton bellowed. "We should have swapped his phone out for a dummy on day one!"

"Well, excuse me, Deano!" Vance sounded perturbed. "While you're basking in the lap of luxury out here in the van, I'm the one in there racing down the hallway to try and intercept the phone call! Which, I might add, is like the only one Mac has received all semester. The guy's not exactly calling up his parents three times every night to give them detailed reports about how his day went."

Vance lifted his hand to his ear to mime holding an invisible phone. "Hey, Ma. Yeah, just wanted to let you know how my day went. Skipped class and disappointed you. Got high and drank a lot with Vance. Yep, again. No, listen, Ma, you've got Vance all wrong! You'll never believe this, he's started wearing just a towel all day long, not just when he's getting out of the shower. I know, right? I'm really envious I didn't come up with the towel thing first, I really think it's got the potential to catch on. Ha, I was *just saying* that a MacArthur genius grant may be in his future—"

"I get it!" Dean Bickerstaff snapped.

Vance dropped his hand and stared at the dean, blinking as if trying to remember what they'd been talking about before he embarked on his little fantasy phone call.

"Look Vance, this is no time to play the blame game. Unless you can think of a way that we can blame it all on Cissy."

Vance shook his head no. "Dammit! Me neither," Frampton glumly added.

"So I guess this is it then?" Vance asked wistfully. "Well, I suppose we had a good run."

"A good run? What the hell are you talking about, Vance? We're not done here!" They couldn't be done, not now. Jimmy was coming in twenty-four hours and Frampton would be damned if a United States senator showed up only to find out that the buffoons in charge had been forced to close up shop the day before. They needed to give him the full red carpet treatment: music, booze, women, dogs in sunglasses, and an unconscious guy in his early twenties whose ear you could look into and see the 1860s.

"I'm not sure what you mean, Deano," Vance said. "How are we going to keep the operation going? I don't think Mac's going to be very happy about all this."

"What do you mean, you think?" Dean Bickerstaff asked, astonished. "You haven't talked to him about this yet?"

Vance shook his head no. "He was still on the phone with his parents when I came out here."

Dean Bickerstaff stroked his chin. Thank God Vance hadn't attempted to deal with this PR nightmare himself. If they went in together, as a unified front, they might be able to spin it in a way that made them look like slightly less horrible, narcissistic, sociopathic monsters. The dean was fully prepared to consider that a victory.

"OK, Vance," he said slowly, trying to make it seem like he was coming up with a plan as he spoke. There would be plenty of time for actually coming up with a plan during the walk from the van to the front door. "When we get inside, just let me do all the talking. If things go smoothly, Cormac's going to end up thinking we did him a favor."

"Roger that," Vance said, although Dean Bickerstaff could tell he was still on the phone with Cormac's mom in his head. Frampton walked back to the van and threw the rear doors open wide. There was no way in hell he was dealing with this situation shillelaghless. Once he'd retrieved his staff, he pulled a cigar from the waistband of his towel and lit up.

"Going towel on an off day, huh Deano?" Vance said, sounding very satisfied.

Frampton looked down. It hadn't even occurred to him that he should change out of the towel he'd slept in. Correction: the towel he'd slept in the back of an incarcerated pervert's van he'd retrieved out of a police impound lot in. Involuntarily, the dean flashed back to the moment twenty-two years ago when a fresh-faced Frampton Q. Bickerstaff received the phone call from the board informing him he'd be the next dean of Harrington. "Make us proud," they had instructed him. "And make Harrington proud."

Dean Bickerstaff might have found this memory crushingly depressing if he weren't so comfortable. As he debated whether or not the extra intimidation factor provided by a suit would outweigh the increased luxury of the towel, the dean looked across the street at the two cult camps for the first time that morning. He was relieved to see that neither camp was burning, and there did not appear to be any body parts mounted on sharp, pointy objects. A small golden calf had been erected during the night, but it appeared harmless enough. Perhaps the armistice truly was lasting. If he'd been able to negotiate peace with a bunch of religious fanatics, handling this delicate Cormac situation ought to be a piece of cake. He turned and looked back at Vance.

"Of course I'm going towel. It's important that we present a unified front," Dean Bickerstaff said through a cloud of cigar smoke as he patted his towel. Then, with a twirl of his shillelagh, the dean set off toward the front door, wondering just what the hell he was going to say when he got inside.

* * *

Cormac sat on his bed trying to comprehend everything that his father had just told him. In many respects, it sounded like a lot of the other crazy things his parents saw on TV and accepted as fact. Like the time his mom heard that microwaves could leak radiation and she burnt theirs in the backyard. Or the time his dad was convinced that the weatherman had told them to hoard dog leashes in preparation for an upcoming hurricane. Or the time his mom heard that dog leashes could leak radiation so she gathered all the ones his father had been hoarding and burnt them in the backyard. She then went around town snipping all the dog leashes people were walking their dogs with, creating a pack of dogs that ended up terrorizing the neighborhood for a solid week until they got swept away during the hurricane. Actually the more that he thought about it, Cormac wondered if both his parents were suffering from early onset dementia.

But their most recent report, as absurd as it sounded, made too much sense to be bullshit. All the little things he'd noticed over the past few days suddenly added up. Vance's strange behavior. The dean's sudden interest in his affairs. The stacks of cash and the random strangers showing up at the house only to be severely beaten and hauled away. They were all tied into the fact that strangers were willing to pay a bunch of money to see what he was experiencing back on the *Levyathan*. It was so much to process that Cormac temporarily forgot his parents were still on the phone.

"Hello? You there, boy?" his father demanded.

"Sorry, Dad," Cormac said, snapping back into the moment. "This is just a lot to take in. I thought I was having a weird month as it was, and now I learn that all this has been going on while I've been on the boat."

Mr. McIlhenney was not exactly sympathetic to the burden he had just unloaded onto his son. His concerns mostly seemed to be about what Cormac's mom would say as soon as a reporter stuck a microphone in her face. He also was not a big fan of what he'd heard about the towels.

"Listen, son," he said. "This woe-is-me attitude isn't going to get you anywhere. You've got to take responsibility for your actions. Do you still have those magnesium tablets I sent you? Whatever dosage you're taking, double it. That'll put a stop to these trips back in time."

"Oh God, Dad, not the magnesium again."

"Don't push that snake oil on our son!" Cormac's mom shrieked from the background. "I thought I burned all of that stuff in the backyard!"

"I've got magnesium hidden in parts of this house you don't even know about!" Cormac's dad shouted back at her. Cormac's dad had long espoused the beneficial properties of magnesium supplements. When Cormac graduated high school, he'd given his son a year's worth of tablets as a graduation present. Cormac had been stunned when his father inquired if he needed more just six days later. Apparently, what Cormac had thought was a year's supply was actually what Mr. McIlhenney consumed in a week. Cormac had never touched a single pill, a decision he now realized was all the wiser since apparently rampant magnesium addiction was present in his immediate family.

"Just try a few days of the increased dosage is all I'm saying." Mr. McIlhenney had stopped arguing with his wife and was now addressing Cormac again. "Your stomach probably won't be able to handle it at first, but you can crush them up, or snort them, or mix them with water and eat the resulting sludge with a spoon. Don't use a straw, you'll only tire yourself out trying to suck it through a straw." Cormac's dad chuckled, presumably recalling a fond memory of futilely trying to drink magnesium sludge through a straw.

Cormac had no idea how many magnesium tablets his father was adding to a glass of water to turn it into a thick enough sludge that he couldn't drink it with a straw, and he didn't want to find out. From the living room, he heard the distant sound of the front door slamming. That must be Vance. If his roommate was trying to leave, Cormac wanted to catch him before he got away.

"Sure, Dad, I'll see if that works," he lied as he got off the bed and started toward the door. "Look, thanks for calling, I really appreciate you guys filling me in on all of this, but I've got to—"

"Tell him about Gerald!" Cormac heard his mother yelling. "That's the whole reason we called in the first place!

"Right, right, Gerald. Cormac, your Uncle Gerald has passed away." Aha! Cormac knew somebody must be dead! He instantly felt bad that he'd felt good about this until he realized he had no idea who Uncle Gerald was. He couldn't admit this, in case it turned out Uncle Gerald was somebody his parents were close to, or more importantly, somebody who had mentioned Cormac in his will.

"Uncle Gerald? Oh no! I'll always remember the way he used to—"

"Cut the crap, boy, he didn't leave you anything," his dad said, bailing Cormac out before he had to finish his sentence. Which was good because Cormac's hastily improvised end to that sentence was going to be "the way he used to sort his collection of fingernail clippings while he watched *Wheel of Fortune*." He didn't need his parents thinking he was any weirder at this point in time.

"Whose side of the family was he on?" Cormac asked, straining to hear any indication of whether Vance was still on the property.

"Nobody knows. He just started showing up at Thanksgiving one year. I'm not even positive that Gerald was his real name. Anyways, your mother is very upset. She thought for sure he'd leave her some silver. But don't worry, son, your mom and I are healthy as horses over here. I don't think Uncle Gerald was taking magnesium, that's for sure!"

"That's terrific, Dad, I'm glad to hear it." Cormac paused for a second before quickly adding, "In the interest of full health disclosure, my pinky finger got severed. And I shot a pirate in the throat."

"His what got severed?" Mrs. McIlhenney shrieked.

"There are studies that show that in large doses, magnesium has the power to regenerate limbs!" Mr. McIlhenney enthusiastically offered as Cormac cut him off with the "end call" button. That had been uncomfortable, but as far as phone conversations with his parents went, it was one of the better ones he'd ever had. Sure, they'd informed him that he'd been unknowingly made the centerpiece of a gross and humiliating public spectacle, one that would likely define his life going forward. But, on the other hand, it hadn't lasted very long. He only wished he had more time now to process what his parents had told him. But he had to confront Vance.

After everything that had happened over the past two weeks, Cormac didn't think there was anything else that could take him by surprise. But if what he'd just heard was true, Vance was capable of even deeper levels of deceit and treachery than Cormac had ever thought possible. And Cormac had no doubt that it was true. What he found terrifying was that the news reporters were undoubtedly not privy to the most sordid, unspeakable details of what Vance and the dean were up to. Either that or they were forbidden from speaking about them on air due to their network's strict broadcast standards and practices.

Cormac paused for a moment to steel himself before he walked into the hallway. The bombshell that his parents just dropped had left him feeling kind of strange. In fact, it was an emotion unlike any he'd ever felt before in his life. Cormac was having trouble putting his finger on it. It wasn't anger. It wasn't betrayal. It was more of . . . a sense that as the primary person this operation depended on, he was probably entitled to at least 75 percent of the supposedly massive profits that the dean and Vance were raking in. Cormac unlocked the door and stepped out into the hall.

Still blinking the sleep out of his eyes, Cormac quickly made his way toward the living room. When the couches came into view, he realized that the door slamming that he'd heard had not been Vance leaving the house, but rather entering it. Even more notable was the fact that he was not alone. Vance was standing next to the front door whispering to the dean when Cormac stomped into the living room and cleared his throat.

Vance wheeled around at the sound and took a few steps back so he was standing next to the dean. Both of them gaped at Cormac, slackjawed, each hoping that the other would speak up first. The sight of the two idiots in nothing but towels almost made Cormac want to laugh. They looked exactly like the type of people who would plot a scheme this twisted, but be stupid enough to have the whole thing come undone by something as simple as a phone call.

They stood there, staring at each other, Cormac fuming, Vance and the dean looking like they'd just been caught in a freaky bathhouse sting. Cormac was finding it surprisingly hard to put his anger into words. Every time he opened his mouth to speak, he started to see red and choked on his own rage. But eventually, a flash of inspiration left him with the perfect quip on the tip of his tongue. Devastatingly harsh and impossibly witty, it would be the first and last word in the entire argument, and once it was spoken, his two adversaries would be reduced to quivering piles of deceitful goo. Cormac smirked, savoring the moment for a split second, then calmly began to quip with the steadied ease of a grizzled action hero.

Two words into the quip, Cissy emitted the loudest, longest, phlegmiest, most guttural snore the world had ever heard and would ever hear again. Cormac foolishly soldiered on, raising his voice in a feeble attempt to shout over the snore, even after he was forced to cover his ears with his hands about halfway through. Vance and the dean did the same, wincing at the physical blast of noise coming at them from the airborne couch.

The snore ended almost exactly as Cormac was done quipping. He stared at Vance and the dean with an eyebrow raised expectantly. They looked back at him as if he were an idiot.

"Did you . . . Did you get any of that?" Cormac eventually asked.

"WHAT?" Vance yelled. "MY EARS ARE STILL RINGING. I HEARD YOU SAY 'YOU TWO' AND THEN IT WAS ALL SNORING."

"DO YOU THINK SHE'S OK?" Dean Bickerstaff added. "IT SOUNDED LIKE SHE MAY HAVE SNORTED A LUNG OUT OF HER NOSE!"

"WHAT?" Vance shouted, turning to the dean.

"She's fine!" Cormac yelled back, determined not to turn this into a discussion about Cissy, who admittedly had very likely just dislodged something vital. "What I said was, you two sons of bitches had better . . . Wait, a second, how did it go again?" Dean Bickerstaff was twisting his index finger into his ear to try and remove some earwax that had shaken loose and Vance was hopping up and down to try and see over the back of the airborne couch to make sure Cissy was still alive. Neither of them seemed to be paying any attention to Cormac.

"Hey!" Cormac shouted. "Who the hell do you guys think you are?" The dean stop twisting his finger and Vance stopped pogoing up and down. Both of them looked at Cormac. His amazing quip completely forgotten, Cormac lurched forward without a plan.

"I talked to my parents! They filled me in on everything! You've been throwing parties here and lying to me about it? Printing decoy articles in the *School Paper*? Charging people admission to look into my ear while I sleep?"

"Easy there, Mac," Vance said, stepping forward with his palms spread in an "I come in peace" gesture. "Let's not be saying anything we can't take back here. This story of yours sounds pretty far out there. I mean, really? Looking in your ear? Are you 100 percent certain that those were your parents who called you?"

"Am I sure it was my parents?" Cormac sputtered. "Of course I'm sure! Who the hell would call me pretending to be them?"

"You can't be too certain," Vance said. "You probably made a lot of enemies yesterday. People who looked in your ear were not happy about that dullsville performance."

"Aha!" Cormac crowed in delight at Vance's tactical error.

"Dammit, Vance!" Dean Bickerstaff yelled.

"And you!" Cormac said turning to the dean. "How the hell did you get involved in this mess? You're the one who's been parking that pervy van everywhere I go, aren't you? I'm curious, dean, what kind of candy have you got in the back to lure the kids in? Twizzlers? Blow pops? Fun size Snickers?"

"Cissy actually ate all the candy the night we bought it," Vance said matter-of-factly.

"Vance!" the dean barked again.

"I ate what?" came a groggy, unseen voice from the airborne couch.

"Well, well, well, if it isn't the venerable fourth estate," Cormac said sarcastically. "Cooking up fake articles? That's a tremendous display of journalistic ethics, Cissy. That really ought to impress the awards committees."

Cissy poked the top of her head up over the back of the couch like a piece of Kilroy graffiti. "Hey, I lied in the real articles too," she yawned. "Like yesterday. I wrote that everyone was guaranteed to see pirates. It's not unethical if you balance it out."

While Cormac tried to parse Cissy's justification, Vance tried reasoning again. "Look, Mac, I know you think you've got the whole story. But I'm sure your parents didn't tell you everything." He started to move toward Cormac as he pointed a finger at his own chest. "I was looking out for you, buddy! Yeah, I bet you didn't hear that side of the story!"

Vance sidled up next to Cormac and attempted to sling an arm around his shoulder, an advance that Cormac deftly rebuffed. Undeterred, Vance continued to sweet talk him. "That guy Brock out there? I caught him trying to whack it while he looked into your ear. Kicked him out as soon as he started going at it!"

Cormac could only stare at his roommate in horror.

"I was vigilant, amigo! I stood guard the entire time! Who knows how many of those creeps me and Deano let into your room would have tried to whack it if I hadn't been there?" Vance beamed a self-satisfied smirk at Cormac. When it was not returned, it slowly faded from his face.

"Aren't you going to thank him?" Cissy asked as she lay back down on the airborne couch.

Cormac could only shake his head. "Unbelievable," he chuckled bitterly. "Just unbelievable." He stepped away from Vance and stared down the dean, who so far had mostly remained silent. "Well, Dean Bickerstaff, I hope it was worth it. Because I am going to sue the shit out of you. How much do you have in the bank, dean? I'm sure the invasion of privacy is worth at least five hundred grand. Maybe for the emotional distress I've suffered the jury will tack on that fancy Lincoln Town Car you're so proud of."

At the mention of his Town Car, the dean's face fell. As Cormac watched, his bewildered deer-in-headlights expression morphed into one of a grim singular purpose: to crush anyone who intended to separate him from his beloved luxury automobile. Frampton narrowed his eyes at Cormac as he tightened his grip on his shillelagh. He was so focused that he didn't notice the strange cracking noise it was making.

"I think you're gripping your stick a little too tightly," Cormac informed the dean.

"You shut the hell up!" Frampton barked. The sudden outburst disrupted Cormac's train of thought. He'd been ready to start laying out his grandiose plans to bring the dean to ruin through the legal system but now suddenly found himself on the defensive. Which was exactly where Dean Frampton Q. Bickerstaff wanted him.

"How dare you talk to me that way," Frampton hissed at Cormac as he attempted to relax his grip on his shillelagh. This proved surprisingly difficult. Enraged at being lectured by a student less than half his age, Frampton had clutched the stick so tightly that his fingers had made small imprints in the solid wood. The dean finally managed to pry his fingers off the staff using his left hand, but his right hand remained stuck in a claw-like grip. Frampton shoved the claw behind his back and walked toward Cormac, accusatorily brandishing the shillelagh with his left hand.

"You nearly tanked this entire enterprise yesterday you non-harpooning buffoon! A huge crowd turned out to see you catch whales and fight pirates and instead all they got was you rubbing some guy's throat. You made us look like fools. And nobody makes Frampton Q. Bickerstaff look like a fool!"

"Would this be a good time to ask why you're also wearing a towel?" Cormac asked. Frampton lashed out with the shillelagh and whacked Cormac on the ankle. Cormac yelped in pain and hopped up and down.

"Now you listen and you listen good," the dean said as he stepped toe-to-toe with Cormac. "Tomorrow's going to be a very important day for us. Senator Jimmy Chambers is going to be stopping by to look in your ear."

"Isn't he the guy who got in trouble for accepting a bunch of money from the horse meat lobby to try and legalize importing horse meat?" Vance asked.

"I don't know," said Dean Bickerstaff. "But probably. Actually, that sounds very much like something he'd do. The point is, he's a very dear friend of mine and I want to be sure that he has a good experience. That means you need to show him some action. We can't have a repeat of yesterday or he'll ruin us."

"Your dear friend will ruin you?" Cormac asked, prompting the dean to whack his other ankle with the shillelagh. "Ouch! Stop doing that!" Cormac knelt down to rub his sore legs. He shot the dean and Vance a reproachful glance and wondered how the dean had turned the tide so quickly. Cormac had gone from threatening to take everything the dean owned to cowering on the floor pretty quickly. Maybe he needed his own shillelagh.

"This is ridiculous," Cormac said. "You guys have been screwing me for weeks. Why should I do anything to help you?"

"Well, I'm afraid that you don't have very much say in the matter," Frampton smirked. "Once you go to sleep tonight, there's nothing you can do to stop us from charging people admission to look in your ear."

"What if I locked my bedroom door?" Cormac asked.

"He's got us there, Deano," Vance chimed in. "We better give him whatever he wants."

"Vance!" Frampton shouted. "Ignore that," he said as he turned back to Cormac.

"You know what? You two are unbelievable," Cormac said as he stood up again. "I don't know how you plan on spending your day, but I hope it doesn't involve me. I'm getting out of here." He brushed past Dean Bickerstaff and gave Vance the finger as he walked toward the front door.

"Where you going, Mac?" Vance asked.

"I don't care," Cormac replied, not bothering to turn around.

"And how are you planning to get there?" Dean Bickerstaff inquired. "I believe your car is still parked at Mickey's."

Cormac stopped in his tracks. Dammit, the dean was right. Well, he sure as hell wasn't staying here. He could walk to Mickey's, even if it took all morning. Anything to get out of this madhouse.

"I'll walk there," Cormac informed the towel-clad duo. "Some modern fresh air will do me some good." He reached out and gripped the doorknob.

"Mac, I don't know if you want to—"

The dean cut Vance off. "Let him go, Vance. He could use some time alone with his thoughts." Cormac pulled the door open and stepped out onto the porch. He slammed the door shut behind him and took a deep breath. Some time alone with his thoughts actually sounded pretty pleasant. It was a beautiful morning. There wasn't a cloud in the sky and some happy-sounding birds were chirping in a nearby tree. Cormac smiled and stepped off of the porch.

"There he is!" an excited voice called from across the street. Instantly the street was full of unshaven weirdos wearing obscene t-shirts. Someone started banging on a drum and the rabble started calling out to him.

"Cormac! Cormac! Give us the word and we shall smite the Throat Jackers!"

"Oh Holy One, don't listen to the heathens! Only through throat jacking can we follow in your blessed footsteps!"

"Cormac, I carved a hole in the rear of the golden calf idol. If you want a turn with it, I think that Brock is just about finished."

"One sec . . . Yep, I'm finished!"

The two mobs inched closer as Cormac stopped in his tracks. If yesterday's encounter was any indication, there was no way he'd be able to make it to Mickey's, let alone the next block, without something unimaginably objectionable happening to him.

"If I tell you to do something, will you do it because you think I'm the Second Coming?" Cormac shouted at the cults.

"Is it touch your wiener?" A voice yelled out in response.

"Throat Jackers must never touch the sacred wiener!" This second person sounded angry.

"What's all this about his wiener?" Brock shouted as he burst through to the front of the crowd in a panic, still pulling on his pants and fastening his belt.

That settled it. Cormac couldn't risk his desire to be left alone being interpreted as a holy writ to do obscene things to or around his person. Without a car, he was not going to be able to get by these fanatics. The taxi company certainly wasn't going to send any more cars in this direction after whatever had gone on during the cult members' ride two nights ago. Until he found another vehicle, it looked like Cormac was stuck in the house with his betrayers. It was just his luck that when he finally attained the loyal army of willing disciples he'd always secretly hoped for, he couldn't trust them to carry out his bidding without molesting him. Cormac turned around and started back toward the front door, but not before he noticed the dean pull back from the window where he had been observing him.

If Cormac had been inside moments earlier, he would have heard Vance shouting in amazement at Dean Bickerstaff.

"That was insane, Deano! You just went off on him!" Dean Bickerstaff ignored Vance as he walked to the window to keep an eye on Cormac. "You should have seen the look on his face," Vance continued. "We're standing there, totally busted, and you start laying into him like the whole thing's his fault! Oh man, I'm going to go make some Bloody Marys."

Dean Bickerstaff was unable to resist cracking a smile as Vance darted off to the kitchen. A few minutes ago, Frampton thought he was backed into a corner. Try as he might to justify his actions to the boy in his early twenties whose unconscious body he'd been selling to strangers, the words just wouldn't come. As Cormac grew bolder and angrier, Frampton, in his panic, had embraced a tactic he rarely ever used.

It was something that Frampton referred to simply as The Technique, and ironically, he'd learned it from one soon-to-be senator Jimmy Chambers. Well, he hadn't really "learned it from Jimmy" as much he "eventually picked it up after Jimmy had used it on him dozens of times." The Technique involved exploding in anger in order to intimidate an entirely justified victim of your actions into thinking they had actually wronged you. It was a crazy, desperate maneuver, and it almost never worked. The dean had attempted it only a handful of times in his career, and usually it resulted in him fleeing physical violence. But the few times he'd successfully pulled it off, it had worked wonders. The Technique had allowed him to turn a situation where charges were on the verge of being filed into one where the disoriented victim of The Technique would send him off with a nervous smile and a fine bottle of cognac.

Vance bounded back into the living room carrying two Bloody Marys. He joined Frampton at the window and thrust one of the drinks toward the dean. Unfortunately, Frampton was still looking at Cormac, and Vance, in his excitement, let go of the beverage before the dean realized it was there. The bright red contents spilled all over the dean's bare stomach and towel.

"Oh goddammit, Vance," Frampton said, staring down at the mess. "What the hell was that?"

Vance looked aghast for a split second. But with a clear of his throat, he straightened up and defiantly tilted his chin toward the dean. "How dare you talk to me that way!" Vance attempted to bellow.

"Vance, I know what you're doing," Frampton said as he tried to brush the liquid off his stomach and onto the towel. "You just saw me turn the tables on Cormac with The Technique; it's not going to work on me."

"That was perfectly good vodka you're brushing off your stomach you ungrateful bastard!" Vance's eyes were wild and he appeared not to have heard what the dean just said. He stepped in between the dean and the window and shouted directly in Frampton's face. "*Five shots* of vodka, to be exact! Where the hell are we going to get more vodka? I know I sure as hell won't be able to drive that junker of yours once I drink this Bloody Mary! And speaking of Bloody Marys, if those Bloody Mary stains don't come out of that towel, there are two kittens whose day at the beach is going to be ruined! *Ruined* you son of a whore!"

"Jeez, OK Vance, I'm sorry," Frampton found himself saying. Dammit! Why had he demonstrated The Technique in front of Vance? He couldn't be trusted to use it responsibly! It was as if Frampton had handed a stupid baby the remote control to an ICBM. Vance was still tense and breathing deeply, and the dean was relieved when he took a step back and gulped a big swig of Bloody Mary. Vance wiped his mouth with the back of his hand, and the booze seemed to quickly calm him down. After a few seconds, his normal expression returned and he smiled at Dean Bickerstaff.

"Hey, how about that, Deano!" Vance crowed. "It worked again!"

"Now Vance," Frampton cautioned. "What you just did is an old method of intimidation called The Technique. I learned it many years ago, you don't want to—"

"The student has become the master!" Vance stroked his chin as he pondered the implications of his newfound skill. "I bet I could use this to weasel out of bar tabs . . ."

"You're not the master, Vance. You just caught me off guard. The Technique is very dangerous, don't go using it at Mickey's. You'll get your dick cut off in a bear trap."

"I'll cut both of your dicks off if you don't keep it down!" Cissy hissed, unseen from the airborne couch.

Vance smiled and raised his eyebrows at the dean. He mouthed "she wants me" and pointed at his towel-clad crotch.

Frampton averted his eyes and looked back out the window, where he was surprised to see Cormac making a hasty retreat to the house. "Ssh, ssh! He's coming back!" he whispered to Vance as he pulled back from the window. "Act casual!"

Cormac pushed the door open, stepped inside and slammed it shut. "I changed my mind," he informed the room. "I'm staying here today."

"Scared of the cults, huh?" Vance said with a grin.

"No," Cormac lied as he turned to deadbolt the door. "What do you mean cults? There are more than one of them now? You're not covered in blood are you?" he asked the dean.

"There's been an unfortunate schism," Frampton said. "It's best not to worry about the particulars of their theologies. Neither of them have any plans for you that you'd want to be a part of. And no, it's not blood, it's a Bloody Mary."

"I gathered that they were bad news," Cormac said. He took another dismayed look around the home that for the time being was doubling as a prison, trying to think of how he might escape. For a moment he thought about sneaking out in the back of the dean's Astro van. But he didn't think he was that desperate yet. If the goal was to avoid masturbating perverts, stepping into that horrible van seemed counterintuitive.

"I guess I'm stuck here," Cormac said with a sigh.

"Join the club!" Cissy monotoned from the airborne couch.

"Why can't you leave exactly?" Cormac asked. When no answer came from the back of the couch, he turned his attention back to Vance and the dean.

"What would happen if I locked my door?" he asked. "Be honest."

"We'd kick it down," Dean Bickerstaff replied. "We have guys. Big guys."

"What if I checked into a motel?" Cormac countered.

"Bickerstaff's third law, my boy: 'As soon as you seize power, get the motel owners on your side.' They're doing indecent things they want covered up; you're doing indecent things and need a place with an ice machine to do them. One hand washes the other. Every motel owner in town owes me favors."

"What if I stay up all night and don't fall asleep?" Cormac was desperate.

"I wonder if either of those cults would like a tour of your bedroom," the dean mused aloud.

"Alright!" Cormac knew he was beaten. It hurt to be outsmarted by a man in a Bloody Mary–soaked kitten towel, and even more so to be outsmarted by Vance. But if he couldn't salvage his pride, or his dignity, or his privacy, or his sense of independence, or his . . . Cormac decided to stop listing things that he was unable to salvage and just demand a cut of the profits.

"I want half," he said bluntly. The dean and Vance stared at him, not understanding. Cormac even heard some rustling from the airborne couch. "I want half of all the profits from here on out," Cormac clarified.

"Listen, Cormac," Dean Bickerstaff said, attempting a warm grin. "You've got to understand. There are financial arrangements already in place! Cissy and Vance are full partners. There's a budget for the bandana men. Plus, G-Dimes and Mako take their cut for the mandatory drugs every customer is forced to ingest to keep out media spies."

Cormac wasn't going to be sweet talked. "You're looking in *my* ear," he said with determination. "You're watching *me* on the

Levyathan. You're sending people into *my* room. You're lucky I don't ask for more. Wait, what mandatory drugs?"

"Things got complicated fairly quickly," Frampton admitted.

"G-Dimes is part of this?" Cormac asked. "*The* G-Dimes? That guy is a maniac!"

Vance leapt to the defense of the dangerous drug lord. "He's actually pretty chill, Mac. Good weed too. Well, obviously."

Cormac felt everything slipping away from him again. He decided to pull out the big guns. "Look, Dean Bickerstaff . . . I want half from here on out. I don't care whose cut you have to reduce. Though I can think of a good place to start." He pointed at the airborne couch.

"Is he pointing at me?" came the unseen voice from the couch.

"But if you can't figure out a way to make that work, I'm going to call my parents back and tell them to come pick me up. They'll drop everything and be here in six hours, and there's no way they're going to let you two move this entire operation to their house." Cormac was not sure if either part of this last sentence was true.

Dean Bickerstaff was quiet for a few seconds as he mentally laid his cards out in front of him. He hated the old adage that you could lose a battle, but win the war. He preferred to win the battle, *and* the war, *and* salt the battlefield so that if a treaty decreed that the opponent maintained possession of it after the war, they would be unable to grow any crops on it.

"Alright, my boy," the dean said. "Fifty percent it is. Vance and Cissy, I'm sorry but we're going to have to make your full partnerships half partnerships."

"What the hell?" Vance was already starting to slur his words from the stiff Bloody Mary. "That's an outrage! We had a deal!"

"Alright, alright," said the dean, cutting off Vance before he had another chance to use The Technique. "You're still a full partner, but on half the share."

"That's more like it," Vance said, smiling a dopey grin. "Oh man, isn't it great that we're all doing this together? It's like we're all a big happy family!" Cormac rolled his eyes. Dean Bickerstaff dabbed at his stomach with the waistband of his towel. Cissy snored. Vance wiped a tear away from his cheek and retreated to the kitchen to freshen up his drink.

Frampton approached Cormac with an outstretched hand and a smile. "Well, Cormac," he said. "I'm sorry we kept you in the dark for so long, but I'm glad we were able to work something out. And I'm sure you'll try to have a more . . . *eventful* day tomorrow, won't you?"

Cormac looked the dean in the eye for a moment. Outside, he could faintly hear one of the cults chanting something. Cormac felt trapped, helpless, angry at himself for being so helpless, angry at the dean for manipulating him, angry at Vance for being Vance, and still pretty hungry. Reluctantly, he reached out and shook the dean's hand. For the first time in a week when he'd also killed half a dozen men, Cormac wondered if he was making a terrible mistake.

* * *

Captain Anson stood in the moonlight, staring out at the horizon. Just a few leagues past it lay St. John's. If the wind held, they'd be there shortly after sunup. The port would already be bustling, with fishermen and traders offloading their catches. Hopefully there would be an opening where they could dock, sell their wares, ransom Pete, and set back out to sea as quickly as possible. Any time wasted would increase the chances of discovery by Eleanor and her lawyer. There was also the chance that she might already be there waiting for him when the *Levyathan* docked, but the captain couldn't afford to dwell on this most dire possibility.

Anson was deep in thought when a voice from behind him took him by surprise. "What are you looking at, sir?" The captain turned and saw that Ziro was standing behind him, holding his mop.

"Oh nothing important, Ziro," the captain said. "Just my destiny."

"You're worried about what's going to happen in St. John's, aren't you?" Ziro asked.

Captain Anson nodded. "Who knows what awaits us on her shores. Fortune? Ruin? It's all straight ahead." He waved his hand majestically across the skyline.

"This is the stern of the boat," Ziro said. "We're moving in the other direction. Sir, how much have you had to drink?"

"I'm nervous, OK?" Captain Anson said defensively before hiccupping.

"I understand, sir, but you ought to go lie down. Tomorrow's going to be a busy day. You'll need your rest."

"Ha! I need my rest before my destiny. They should call it restiny, Ziro! Get it? It's just one word instead of a lot of words. Pssh, who cares?" Captain Anson wobbled and Ziro quickly dropped his mop and threw the captain's arm over his shoulder to steady him.

"That's great, sir," Ziro said as he started to lead the captain toward his quarters. "Come on, let's get you to bed."

"Where's Pete?" Captain Anson slurred.

"Pete's lying on the floor of your quarters, trying not to vomit up a thin mush of hardtack and water," Ziro informed him. "It's the first thing he's attempted to eat in days."

"Ha! That guy is crazy! What about Cormac?"

"Cormac's in the future today," Ziro said. "You know this, you complained that he wasn't here all day long because none of the other men could catch a single whale today."

"The other men are garbage!" The captain ranted. "Worthless durvy scogs! I mean, scurvy dogs! Especially Ziro! That guy's just a load!"

"I'm sure he's very fond of you as well," Ziro muttered. "Here we are at your quarters, sir. Do you need me to walk you to your bed or are you OK?"

"Where's Pete?" Captain Anson asked, his eyes attempting to focus on one of Ziro's shoes.

"I'll help you to your bed," Ziro sighed. He opened the door to the captain's quarters and, being careful not to step on the barely conscious pirate on the floor, carefully led the captain inside.

DAY FOURTEEN

Cormac's eyes popped open. The mattress on the bunk above his sagged down just a few inches from his face. It was stained and yellowed, sawdust spilled out of one hole, and what appeared to be a wriggling rat's tail protruded from another. Cormac had never been more relieved to see an object in his life. It meant he had fallen asleep and finally escaped the dean, Vance, and everything else associated with the house on Craymore Street.

After negotiating the uneasy partnership with Dean Bickerstaff, Cormac had endured one of the most awkward days of his life. Forced to stay at home because of the cults, he'd finally taken the opportunity to pick up the ukulele and attempt to craft a follow-up video to "Treasures o' the Sea." Unfortunately, the other three people in the house, who to the best of Cormac's knowledge were *not* being kept prisoner by warring religious factions, showed no interest in utilizing their freedom and actually getting the hell out of the house.

Vance, Cissy, and Dean Bickerstaff kept each other company in the living room all day long. Vance got progressively drunker, Cissy rolled another massive pile of blunts, and the dean, evidently for the first time, discovered their Netflix subscription. He spent the entire day thinking of a movie he wanted to watch, then getting furious when it inevitably wasn't available for streaming. Cormac found that their presence made it very difficult to concentrate on his music. It wasn't Vance's drunken boasts or excessive laughter, that sort of thing he was used to. It was just the unnerving sensation that they were keenly aware of what he was doing. Every time he left his room to get something to eat or use the bathroom, he heard all activity in the living room cease. Realizing how intently they were observing him made him very uneasy.

The result had been a follow-up song that was vastly inferior in just about every respect to "Treasures o' the Sea." It was called "I Love My Salty Lass." It had twelve verses, was somehow even lower brow than "Treasures," or even "Briny Bonin'," and made Cormac keenly aware of Ziro's talent for melody and rhyme. YouTube commenters were far less positive this time around. Many of them suggested that Cormac might care to rework some of the cruder rhymes, or perhaps never pick up an instrument again and kill himself. Less than ten minutes after he posted the video to YouTube, Vance knocked on Cormac's bedroom door and presented him with a dead fish that someone had left on their doorstep. They had carved "Salty Lass" into the side of it with a large knife that was still very much sticking out of the fish. Cormac changed the video's setting to "private" until he'd had a chance to think it over for a day or two.

After that failure, for the most part he'd spent the day waiting out the clock. He thought about tidying up his bedroom, making sure his underwear was not strewn about the floor, maybe clearing his web history. But after a few minutes of effort, Cormac wondered why he was bothering. By this point, hundreds of strangers had marched through his room. If they'd been interested in finding embarrassing skeletons in his closet, they'd surely have done so by now. He did take care to clean out his ears with a Q-tip, since people were staring directly into them. And after giving it some thought he decided to clear his browser history after all. There was no reason to have some of that stuff on there when a high-ranking government official was in the room.

Cormac had thought that maybe he could speed along the escape process by trying to go to bed early, and turned out the lights around 9:00 p.m. Sadly, a day of zero physical activity had not left him as exhausted as it apparently did Cissy. He lay in bed, staring at the ceiling, listening to Vance cackle, and trying to will himself asleep. The longer he stayed awake, the more frustrated he grew. He'd close his eyes, but nothing happened. Until just now, when he'd opened them up and realized he must have fallen asleep after all.

Cormac swung out of his bunk, careful to avoid the three or four whalers who were already milling about the quarters. The rest of the bunks were already cleared out. Arriving in St. John's meant rum, money, and freedom, possibly prioritized in that exact order. The whalers seemed excited, and Cormac instantly found it contagious. A whole day free of Vance and the dean! And also, an unparalleled opportunity in the history of human existence to experience what life was like over a century before he was born. Of course, he'd been doing this for the past two weeks, but the *Levyathan* was obviously a fairly atypical experience. It was going to be fascinating to see what the rest of the world was like.

This excitement was slightly tempered when it occurred to Cormac that some sweaty weirdo might be staring into his ear back on Craymore Street at this very moment. Determined not to let whatever was going on back there ruin the rest of his day, he pushed the thought from his mind and slipped past the still-groggy whalers, out onto the deck of the boat. Right away he was greeted by an unfamiliar sight: land.

It was off in the distance, perhaps a mile or so. Cormac could make out trees, the masts of other ships, docks, and faint curls of smoke rising from what must be factories. After weeks of nothing but uninterrupted ocean, it was quite the thing to behold. The *Levyathan* was moving very gradually. Cormac didn't see any of the other whalers on board and figured they must be in the galley, rowing the boat ashore. There was, however, one familiar figure standing off toward the bow, slowly pushing his mop back and forth.

"Morning, Ziro!" Cormac called as he jogged toward the former slave. "Looks like we're almost ashore, huh? What's the plan when we arr—GOOD GOD! What the hell is going on?!"

"Good morning, my boy!" Captain Anson said with a grin. He ceased his half-hearted mopping and awkwardly tugged at the collar of Ziro's shirt. "Did I surprise you? Guess I make a convincing slave. Ugh, that idiot Ziro wears some really uncomfortable outfits. Hold this, will you?" Captain Anson handed Cormac the mop and started messing with the waistband of Ziro's pants.

"Why are you wearing Ziro's clothes?" Cormac asked, still not recovered from the shock. When the captain had spun around to greet him, Cormac had nearly jumped out of his shoes. Before he realized it was just Captain Anson in disguise, he thought that some sort of curse, quite possibly related to the Chinese gold or the Black Barnacle's ghost, had somehow weathered Ziro's face, aging it a few decades overnight. He decided to keep this initial suspicion from Captain Anson.

"I'm taking every precaution," the captain said, hitching his borrowed pants to a level where they felt more comfortable. "If I go ashore dressed like this, I'll hopefully be able to slip past my wife and her lawyer while they go after the person who they think is the captain."

"So you're saying that Ziro . . ."

"Looks like a complete idiot in my clothes, yes."

Cormac heard someone clear their throat behind him. He turned and saw Ziro standing there. The captain had definitely meant for Ziro to hear his last remark, but Cormac didn't think he looked half bad. The captain obviously had much nicer clothes than someone who had been taken on board as a slave. The expensive fabrics, shiny boots, and especially the captain's spyglass actually suited Ziro rather well.

"I think you look pretty cool," Cormac assured Ziro, who fidgeted with the spyglass. He looked rather uncomfortable gripping something that wasn't intended to be used to swab a surface.

"I still think it's a mistake for you to not wear my earring," the captain said rather contemptuously. "It could blow this entire operation."

"I don't want to get my ear infected," Ziro said, in a tone that indicated they had already been over this many times. "And besides, your wife won't be expecting you to wear an earring! You've only been wearing it for less than a week."

"Yes, but it's quickly become a noted part of my persona," the captain countered. "I'm sure word has travelled far that Captain Anson is an earring guy these days."

"I'm not wearing the earring," Ziro said. Captain Anson didn't look pleased, but he didn't press the matter any further.

"What is our plan?" Cormac asked.

"Well, we're going to dock, sell our whale parts, auction off the pirate ship, and ransom Pete," Captain Anson said. "Hopefully the whole process will take five minutes, tops."

"It's going to take a lot longer than that," Ziro said. "There are so many whales down there."

"We're aiming for five minutes," Captain Anson informed Cormac.

"Merely tying the boat to the dock is a process that will probably take twice that long," Ziro said. "And there are dozens of hacked up whales we have to unload. The sheer tonnage of—"

"My point is, you shouldn't get too comfortable," Captain Anson cautioned Cormac. "There's a chance we will need to take off in a hurry. We've got to be ready to flee the scene if you-know-who shows up."

"What does your wife look like?" Cormac asked. "I'll keep an eye out for her."

"She's a dragon-faced harridan," the captain said, a dark cloud falling across his face. "You'll probably feel the chill of her presence before you even see her. She's a pinched, frigid ice queen. And just when you think you're about to turn to stone from simply gazing at her haunting visage, she'll peel her lips back into what she thinks is a smile, and the serpent's fangs that are her teeth may be the last sight you see."

"So like, are we talking five foot four? Five five?" Cormac asked.

"Five seven, I'd say," the captain estimated. "Slightly above average height."

"We're making pretty good progress," Ziro said. "Especially considering we're towing another boat. The men must be pretty eager to get ashore." Cormac looked toward the land, and indeed, it was much closer than it had been just a few minutes ago. The captain noticed as well, and tensed visibly when he saw how close they were. He instinctively reached toward his belt for his spyglass. When he came up empty, Cormac handed Ziro's mop back to him. The captain's expression indicated that he felt the mop was a poor substitute for his lucky spyglass.

As the *Levyathan* cruised into the St. John's harbor, Cormac found himself on the verge of sensory overload. There was so much to see and take in. Land extended out on either side of the harbor, forming a bay where the water was calm and flat. Docks jutted out from the shore, and there were boats of all sizes tied up. Cormac could see merchants unloading fish, livestock, and crates of fruit. Ramshackle huts and shanties dotted the shoreline, with cobblestone roads leading back to a more official-looking town.

The people he saw rowing boats and trading on the docks looked to be from all walks of life and all corners of the globe. There were the locals, Canadians who wore fur hats and animal skins. There were merchants from the Middle East in fancy robes and head wraps, selling spices and occult objects. Missionaries from Europe appealed to anyone who would listen about how to seek redemption for their immortal souls. Vendors roasted skewers of meat and fish on grills. Stray dogs fought over scraps that fell to the ground while boats were being unloaded. Drunks stumbled out of taverns and into other taverns. Everything buzzed with a palpable energy of excitement, adventure, and sleaze.

It was unlike anything he had ever experienced before and Cormac really wished he had his phone with him so he could take a few blurry pictures and add some crappy filters to them.

The rowers in the galley guided the *Levyathan* toward the largest dock in the harbor. Off the side of it hung an old wooden sign whose faded letters read "whale offloading." The dock was run-down and covered in barnacles. There were no other boats near it, and the workers milling about on it were indistinguishable from the drunks who had wandered there by mistake. Cormac figured that the lack of activity must be due to the whale shortage. If the industry was really hurting this badly, the captain and (theoretically) the crew stood to make quite the killing off the whales they'd hauled in these past few weeks. The relatively empty dock also meant they could see that Eleanor and her lawyer were not waiting for them, and Captain Anson exhaled in relief when he realized this was the case. There was still a chance she was laying low somewhere else nearby, but they'd have to take their chances.

The *Levyathan* slowed as it drew within a few feet of the dock. The whalers who had been rowing in the galley began to emerge onto the deck once they were no longer needed to propel the boat forward. They assumed positions along the port side, picking up coils of rope and prepping the gangplank. Ziro left Cormac and the captain and began walking among the men, helping them lift ropes and attempting to hail the attention of a dock worker. The pirate ship *Mongrel* floated behind the *Levyathan*. She would anchor in the harbor until a buyer was found on shore.

"I'm going to go see if Ziro needs any help," Cormac told Captain Anson.

"You do that," the captain replied. "I'll be here swabbing to keep up the ruse."

Cormac walked over to Ziro, who was leaning out over the railing, preparing to toss a rope to a dock worker. The worker had obviously used the downtime afforded him by the recent lull in the whaling economy to get in touch with his inner drunk, and he looked uncertain in his ability to catch the rope, let alone use it to secure an enormous ship. But Ziro tossed it with pinpoint aim, and after fumbling with the looped end for a few seconds, the dock worker secured it around a pylon, and the *Levyathan* began to slow to a halt.

Ziro barked orders at the dock worker, directing him up and down the dock to receive more thrown ropes from whalers. Once they'd secured the ship in three more locations, they dropped the anchor and two whalers extended the gangplank to the dock. Ziro, disguised as the captain, was the first across it. He was followed by a giddy stream of whalers, who pushed and jostled to take their first steps on dry land in months. One of the whalers was so moved that he knelt and kissed the dock over and over, cackling with mad glee. Only when a fellow whaler pointed out a sign above the section of dock he was kissing that read "DISCARD AREA: PLACE WHALE DICKS HERE" did he remove his lips from the wood surface and go off in search of the nearest jug of rum to wash out his mouth.

Cormac hung back and observed all this, as did Captain Anson. The captain was taking no chances that his wife had acquired some sort of ungodly shape-shifting ability and was going to materialize out of a vaporous mist at some point in time. They watched as Ziro explained to the longshoreman what they had on board, followed by a back-and-forth negotiation as they tried to settle on a rate for the cargo. The longshoreman seemed to be in over his head, and Ziro's frustration began to show as he tried to explain himself with increasingly exaggerated gestures. Finally, Ziro shook the longshoreman's hand, then turned and walked back up the gangplank toward the *Levyathan*. He rolled his eyes when he got closer to Cormac and the captain.

"Well, good news and bad news," Ziro informed them. "That longshoreman says we've got so much cargo to unload that they're going to need special authorization from the harbormaster to complete the purchase. I guess what we've got on board is worth more than the maximum amount of gold they keep on hand at all times. They're going to have to run to the bank or something. It's probably going to take at least two hours to get it all sorted out, but we can start unloading in the meantime. He also told me I was his best friend and then started weeping about a dog that ran away when he was a boy. I don't think he remembers what sober is anymore."

"Two hours!" Captain Anson was horrified. "Dear God, we can't take this kind of a risk! This is just spitting in fate's eye!"

Ziro ignored his panic. "Sir, if you want to minimize the amount of time we have to stay docked, you could handle our other business in the meantime. Take Pete into town and ransom him. Maybe you can find a buyer for the *Mongrel* while you're there."

"Yes, I suppose that's what I'll have to do," Captain Anson said. He turned to Cormac. "Well, my lad, you have a choice. You can either help Ziro orchestrate a major whale transaction, making sure you abide by all local tariffs, codes, and regulations. In between double checking the detailed customs forms, you'll be required to haul literally tons of blubber ashore. Or you can come with me to explore the seedy underbelly of this exotic island. We'll drink with swindlers. We'll encounter voodoo priestesses, musicians, dealers of rare animals, and black-market goods. We'll ransom a pirate captain and sell a pirate ship to the highest bidder, ignoring all local tariffs, codes, and regulations in order to maximize personal gain."

"I think I'll—" Cormac only got a few words out before the captain cut him off.

"Oh! There's also going to be prostitutes," Captain Anson remembered. "Lots of prostitutes."

"I think I'll come with you," Cormac said.

"I knew the prostitutes would sway you," the captain said with a sly smile.

"I was going to come before you mentioned the prostitutes," Cormac protested. "Your tasks sound like a lot more fun than unloading whales."

"Sure you were," the captain said, playfully nudging Cormac in the ribs and winking.

Cormac ignored the insinuation that the only reason he wanted to go ashore was to have sex with hookers. The truth was, he felt a strange compulsion to have a more interesting day now that he knew there was a different stranger looking in his ear every two minutes. Cormac knew that if he were paying good money to violate someone's privacy and the basic tenets of human decency, he would appreciate them seeking out adventures that were off the beaten path. Still, he deferred to Ziro.

"You need me to stick around and lend a hand here?" Cormac asked. "Or is it alright if I tag along with the captain?"

"Go ahead," Ziro told him. "I think our men are going to work fast. They're eager to get paid." Indeed, some of the whalers were already rushing past with whale bones, slabs of blubber, and baleen. Jugs of rum purchased on credit had appeared on the dock, and the whalers were already laughing and singing.

"Enjoy yourself," Ziro told Cormac. "We'll still be here when you come back."

"I'll fetch Pete," Captain Anson said, and darted off to the captain's quarters to retrieve the pirate captain.

Cormac walked over to the gangplank and stared down at the dock. Here he was about to set foot in a time that was not his own, an action that was uncharted in the recorded history of mankind. He would see sights and hear sounds that nobody else he knew ever had or would. Plus there were evidently women down there who would have sex for money, which sounded awesome. Tentatively at first, but quickly growing more confident, Cormac walked down the gangplank toward the dock. At that moment, he felt smaller than he ever had in his life, but also as if he was part of something unimaginably huge. It was a fleeting understanding of what it had always meant to be alive, a transcendental connection with the collective spirit of humanity. It quickly left him, but it had been an amazing sensation. His only hope was that the customer who was looking in his ear at that moment appreciated the enormity of what they were witnessing as well.

"Search for 'tapirs doing it,'" said the customer who was supposed to be looking in Cormac's ear at that moment. "I'm serious, it is absolutely disgusting."

Vance tapped the keys on Cormac's laptop as he entered the query into YouTube. The customer looked on expectantly. "You know this all counts toward your time," Vance informed him. Cormac's unconscious body lay in bed while a girl peered into his right ear, but the left ear was unattended. The left-ear customer had evidently seen this video at a party the night before, and now that he was sufficiently stoned, wanted to share it with other people.

"Is it any of these?" Vance asked as he scrolled down the list of search results.

"I don't see it there. Maybe it was 'tapirs mating.' Search for that instead."

"Time's up!" Dean Bickerstaff bellowed from the hallway.

Vance snapped the laptop closed. "You heard the man," he told the tapir fan.

"Aw man, what a rip! I didn't even get to look in his ear!"

Dean Bickerstaff leaned in from the hallway. "So buy another ticket and pay attention next time! Out!"

The tapir guy thought about protesting, but clammed up when he noticed the dean's shillelagh. He slunk past him into the hallway, presumably already trying to figure out a way to bring up the tapir video in his next conversation.

"You've got to help me out here, Vance," the dean said as he waved in the next person in line. "We can't be running a half-assed operation when Jimmy gets here!"

Vance rolled his eyes, and the dean bristled at his partner's insolence. Vance didn't seem to fully grasp how serious it was to have a visitor of the senator's stature. Frampton had been forced to look over his shoulder and micromanage him all morning. People had overstayed their ear time by thirty seconds, or left garbage in Cormac's room. It was as if Vance had decided that since their operation was no longer a secret, he didn't have to work as hard to keep it running smoothly.

Dean Bickerstaff, on the other hand, felt like he'd already put in a solid day's work and it wasn't even lunch time. He'd been rushing back and forth from the bedroom to the front door, determined not to let the senator arrive without a proper greeting. He'd also taken the time to sell admission tickets, force paying customers to get high, clean up a Bloody Mary that had fallen out of Cissy's hand when she nodded off, and silently admire an especially cool dog from across the room. The dean had hoped the sunglasses dogs might give the party a second chance, and had been delighted when they showed up at the door. He knew Jimmy would be impressed by their dynamic, room-altering presence.

On top of it all, it appeared that Cormac had taken his warnings to heart and was actually attempting to put on a good show today. Early reports rolled in that the boat had made landfall, with recent chatter indicating that Cormac was actually going ashore. Frampton was cautiously optimistic that he would run into some adventure. If word reached him that Cormac had detoured into a hospital to spend another day rubbing throats, he was not going to be pleased.

Frampton lit a fresh cigar and took a few mighty puffs, hoping the rich tobacco would calm his nerves. He looked down at his phone. Still nothing from Jimmy. Frampton had sent him a few emails earlier in the morning to try and pin down an arrival time. But all he received in return was a voicemail from someone claiming to be the senator's personal assistant. The voice sounded suspiciously like Jimmy doing an accent that managed to be both of indeterminate origin and wildly offensive. The assistant had informed him that "Senator Chambers will be there when he feels like it, so don't get your skirt bunched up about it, *Dick*erstaff." Then there had been a loud fart noise.

The cigar was not helping, so the dean decided to try and relax with a beer. Though a healthy stigma against pre-noon drinking might exist in the rest of the world, it disappeared once you set foot inside the Craymore Street house. Of course, the degradation and sleaze that took place in regular abundance on the property was as good an argument for that stigma as anyone would ever find. The dean didn't care. At the moment, with no cognac in sight, a beer sounded pretty damn good.

Frampton picked up a red plastic cup and waddled over to wait for his turn at the keg. The young woman who was currently pumping the keg turned to see who the newcomer was, and Frampton shot her what he intended to be a warm, reassuring smile.

"Oh God," she muttered, as she dropped the dispenser and made a beeline for the front lawn. Frampton looked down to make sure nothing that was supposed to be towel-clad had suddenly sprung free, but everything appeared to be in order. He shrugged and stepped forward, setting down his shillelagh so he could pick up the beer tap.

Dean Bickerstaff had never actually dispensed beer from one of these things before, but he'd seen enough people do it over the past few days that he figured he had the process down. He rapidly pumped the tap handle up and down. He wasn't sure how many times you had to do this, but figured there must be some sort of light that turns on to let you know when the beer was ready. The dean turned around as he pumped, smiling to anyone who might be looking to indicate that the beer pouring was going just fine, as it had every other time that he wanted you to believe he'd pumped beer from a keg.

Unfortunately, the only two people watching him were the girl who had been in line before him and a friend she'd recruited. "See what I mean?" the girl from the line said to her friend, who nodded in horror.

"We should make him do a keg stand," the friend suggested in a conspiratorial tone that made Frampton very alarmed. He didn't know what a "keg stand" was, but he suddenly wished he was holding his shillelagh instead of a plastic cup and a tap. Frampton chuckled nervously at the two ladies as they slowly began to approach him.

"Just pouring a beer," Frampton said as his eyes darted back and forth between the two women, trying to figure out what they were up to. "I hate it how much you have to pump these things, you know?" The ladies' blank stares gave the dean nothing to work with, so he stammered ahead. "Have you guys tried the ear thing? I hear it's pretty—WHAT THE HELL!?"

Before the dean could react, one of the girls darted behind him and shoved him forward. Frampton dropped his cup and the tap as the other girl deftly pinned his hands to the rim of the keg. He could only sputter in horror as he felt a pair of hands clasp around his ankles and start to lift his feet up off the floor.

"Dammit! Unhand me!" The strength of these two tiny young women was amazing. Frampton felt his body go horizontal as the girl behind him continued to raise his legs into the air. Now he was unable to let go of the side of the keg without toppling to the floor. "Stop lifting!" Frampton yelled, his voice raising into a high-pitched shriek that he was unaware he was capable of making. "I'm not wearing anything under that towel! Do you have any idea who I—"

Before he could finish his sentence, the girl he had scared out of her position in line shoved the keg tap into his open mouth. The dean went cross-eyed for a second as he tried to figure out what it was, then looked up in horror at the girl who was forcing it into his mouth. Her thumb rested on the tap, and she stared at the dean with a crazed, drunken expression. Unable to articulate himself with the tap in his mouth, Frampton could only grunt in protest, a sound that was drowned out by loud cheers from the suddenly formed crowd of spectators.

"On three!" yelled the girl who was holding the tap in the dean's mouth. "One!" The gathered crowd joined in on her countdown. "Two!" Unable to speak, Frampton shook his head no, but nobody was paying any attention. He squeezed his eyes shut and braced himself for whatever was coming at "three."

But three never came. Instead, a deep, booming voice called out "What the hell is going on here?" The spectators quickly went silent, and as Frampton felt his legs being lowered back to the floor, he slowly opened his eyes.

Looming in the doorway was the imposing frame of Senator James Chambers. The senator wore a sharply tailored suit and sported an impeccably styled haircut. His bright white smile revealed that the question had not been asked out of disgust, but rather excitement. The senator looked thrilled to be there, the two personal security guards who flanked him on either side slightly less so. They wore earpieces, gun holsters, and dark sunglasses, which they kept on even though they were inside. Dean Bickerstaff wondered how the cool dogs would respond to this encroachment on the style they had pioneered, but pushed the thought from his mind as Jimmy spotted him from across the room and started to walk toward him.

"I'll be damned!" the senator exclaimed in excited disbelief. "Dickerstaff? Is that you?" He strode across the living room floor to the kegs, where Frampton stood, still trying to catch his breath.

"Hello Jimmy," Frampton said.

"James," Senator Chambers corrected him. The tone and facial expression remained the same, but the sharpness of the correction took Frampton by surprise. "Can you believe this guy?" Jimmy asked the room. "I pay him a visit for the first time in years and he doesn't even bother to get dressed! What the hell are you doing, FQ?"

Before Frampton could reply, the girl who had been before him in line spoke up. "He was going to do a keg stand," she informed Jimmy.

"A keg stand? Really?" Jimmy looked slightly taken aback.

"No, not really," Frampton said, not bothering to disguise his irritation. He'd be damned if he was going to be debased in front of his important guest. "I wouldn't be caught dead participating in such a vulgar act, especially at the behest of two women of such questionable morals. Leave the dangerous and irresponsible stuff to the degenerates. Us adults will stick to fine cognac, right Jimmy?"

"James," Senator Chambers quickly corrected him. "Well that's too bad! I bet these kids would have liked to see their old dean do something cool . . . For once!" Jimmy was addressing the whole room more than he was talking to Frampton. The charisma that had allowed him to weather several scandals that easily should have been career ending was immediately apparent. The partygoers were hanging on his every word. "Am I right, kids?"

There was a somewhat enthusiastic response from the crowd, some light applause, and a few cheers. Most of them appeared not to realize that Frampton was their school's dean, and now that they knew it, they still weren't sure they wanted to watch him do anything that might reveal what was under his towel.

"I'll tell you what," the senator continued. "Your lame old dean probably wouldn't have made it ten seconds on that keg." The assembled crowd booed, and Frampton felt vaguely offended, even though he wasn't sure why. "But I bet there's a member of the United States Senate in this room that can pull off at least thirty seconds!" Jimmy continued.

The crowd looked around, confused, trying to figure out who this member of the United States Senate might be.

"Me," James clarified. "I'm a senator. I've been on TV like, a bunch of times." The crowd cheered in appreciation, and James pulled off his jacket and handed it to one of his security guards. He started to roll up his sleeves and walk over to the keg, and some students in the crowd began to chant "Sen-ate! Sen-ate! Sen-ate!"

Frampton fumed. He still wasn't sure what Jimmy was about to attempt to do for thirty seconds, but he did not appreciate the suggestion that he would be unable to do it for even one third as long. He'd been putting up with these drunken idiots all week long and wasn't about to let somebody else just waltz in and win their affection.

"Just a minute now," Frampton found himself saying as he stepped in front of the senator's path to the keg. "It seems our friend the senator has forgotten how the system of checks and balances works. The legislative branch is unfortunately limited by a certain power of the executive branch." He smirked at the crowd expectantly, but they all stared back blankly, with no idea what the hell he was talking about.

"The veto. I'm going to veto him doing a keg stand and do it myself. Do any of you know how our government functions? The president can veto a bill."

"Are you the school president?" someone called out from the crowd. "I thought you were the dean!"

"For the purposes of my analogy they're the same thing!" Frampton snarled. "President and dean, both are the most important guy! And I'm doing a keg stand, not the senator!"

The pronouncement was met by very light, scattered applause, another brief round of "Sen-ate!" chanting, and one guy in the back of the room who called out "Judicial! That's the other one!" when he remembered the name of the third branch of government. To top the whole thing off, Cissy emitted a strangled snore from the airborne couch.

"A keg stand?" Jimmy smiled at Frampton. "You sure about that, old buddy? You don't want to leave the vulgar acts to us degenerates?"

"Take a hike, Jimmy," Frampton hissed. "I'm going thirty seconds on your bicameral ass. You two! Hoist me up again!" The dean was surprised to hear the words coming out of his mouth, but Jimmy had always brought out Frampton's competitive side. For the time being, he chose to ignore the fact that virtually every competition he'd ever entered into with Jimmy had gone in his opponent's favor. He turned to the keg and furiously began to pump it.

The two girls who had attempted to force the dean into a keg stand moments earlier shrugged at each other and resumed their positions, one behind the dean, the other next to the keg in front of him. Jimmy just shrugged. "Good luck, buddy," the United States senator said. "By the way, I don't think you need to pump that thing any more."

"I know how an ale kegging system works!" Frampton snapped as he struggled to pump the nearly bursting keg further. "Let's do this thing."

Dean Bickerstaff rubbed his hands together as Jimmy led a tepid "Dean! Dean! Dean!" chant. He gripped the edge of the keg and nodded to the girl who stood in front of him. Once again, he felt the second girl's hands gripping him around the ankles, and the keg wobbled a bit as she raised his legs off the ground. Frampton balanced himself out as he was raised horizontal to the floor, but to his dismay, the girl kept raising him.

"Jimmy!" he yelled. "Man the towel! Don't let it fall!" Jimmy cupped a hand over his ear as if he couldn't make out what the dean was saying, and Frampton knew all too well what he wanted to hear. Desperate, he quickly relented to the senator's demands. "James! Senator Chambers! Get the hell over here before anything flops out!"

Jimmy smiled and strolled over to the dean, where he held the side of the towel against Frampton's knee.

"I'm pretty sure this is covered in my senatorial vows, FQ," Jimmy said. "These boys get out there, the nation's well-being might be at stake."

"Ha ha," Frampton said sarcastically. With all the blood that was quickly rushing to his head, it was the best retort he could manage. The girl behind him had been able to raise the dean so that he was now almost vertical, with his head at five o'clock and his feet at eleven.

"I think he's ready!" Jimmy announced to the crowd. The girl standing by the keg nodded her agreement and picked up the tap while Jimmy continued his carnival barker act. "Alright kids, let's see what your dean can do! Ready? Set? Go!"

On go, the girl thrust the keg tap into Frampton's mouth and pressed her thumb down. Ideally, this would have caused a stream of beer to pour into Frampton's mouth, and he would try to suck it down at the same rate it was pouring out of the keg. Unfortunately, all the pumping the dean had done over the past ten minutes had converted the entire keg of beer into one big foamy mess, and this foam is what shot out of the tap and into Frampton's mouth.

The dean immediately knew that something was wrong. The foam filled up his mouth but he wasn't able to swallow any of it. His cheeks quickly ballooned out like a chipmunk storing nuts as he tried in vain to swallow. Frampton panicked. His eyes swept to the left and right, but all he could see and hear were chanting idiots counting how many seconds had gone by. He tried to kick his feet free, but all this did was cause Jimmy to lend a hand and grip them even tighter. He had no way out.

The foam continued to shoot into his mouth and Frampton was nearing the bursting point. Red-faced and unable to breathe, he tried one final attempt at gulping some of it down. Finally, his natural swallowing reflex kicked in and Frampton felt the foam trickle down his throat. Unfortunately, the next thing he felt was the stinging in his esophagus from the bubbles of the super carbonated foam. This caused Frampton to do something that was in between a cough and a choke, which in turn caused the foam he had been trying to swallow to instead shoot out his nose.

The foam sprayed out of his nose and into the face of the girl who had been dispensing the beer from the tap. She screamed and dropped the tap, but the stream of foam kept shooting out of Frampton's nose. Upside down and unable to focus his eyes, Frampton assumed that her screams were due to his towel falling and exposing his naked lower half. Terrified and still choking on a mouth full of foam, he twisted his torso in an attempt to free his legs from the grip of Jimmy and the surprisingly strong college girl. All this did was cause the keg to become off balanced, and suddenly Frampton realized that he was falling.

His back hit the ground first. This sudden force had two effects. The first was to cause the stream of foam that was coming out of his nose to shoot several feet higher in the air, like Old Faithful. The second was to cause him to cough out the rest of the foam in his mouth, like a less popular, but no less voluminous geyser. As the beer foam rushed out of several of his orifices and Frampton struggled to draw a breath, he felt the grip on his ankles release, and his legs came crashing to the floor.

"Two!" he heard the crowd chant. He'd only been up there for two seconds? In a daze, Frampton slowly tried to sit up. Beer trickled down his chest and onto his towel. He gasped for air and tried not to pass out as all the blood that had pooled in his head rushed back out just as quickly. He heard a distinctive, booming laugh that after all these years he could still instantly identify as that of Senator Jimmy Chambers.

Dazed and dizzy, Frampton looked around the room. Almost everyone was laughing, and those who weren't were tapping out messages on their phones. Jimmy offered a hand to help him up, but Frampton ignored it in favor of making sure his towel was still in place. Then, slowly and unsteadily but without assistance, he got to his feet and waved to the crowd. The keg stand had not gone ideally, but perhaps he could still win back the crowd and triumph over Jimmy with a self-deprecating bon mot.

"Well," the dean said, in between deep breaths. "I guess that's what you call a—"

"It's still coming out his nose!" someone yelled from the back of the room.

Frampton wiped at his nose as the crowd burst out laughing again. Indeed, there was a steady trickle of foam still emerging from his nose. The crowd was now in an uproar; any chance of winning them back over to his side was gone. Fortunately, whatever the dean lacked in charm he could make up for in shillelagh beatings. He started over toward where he'd left his shillelagh, but before he could pick it up and dole out justice, Jimmy stepped in front of him.

"Man, that was great!" The senator was beaming. "Doing keg stands in the middle of the day! It's like we never left Harrington! Well, you actually never did leave, FQ, but you know what I mean." Jimmy slapped Frampton on the back, which sprayed beer and sweat everywhere and made an unpleasant squishy sound. Frampton rubbed beer out of his eyes and looked at Jimmy. He would have preferred to greet his friend on his own terms, but now that Jimmy was here, he remembered how excited he had been to see him. Frampton stuck his hand out and Jimmy clasped it and shook it enthusiastically.

"It's good to see you, Jimmy," Frampton said.

"James," Jimmy reminded him, as the rest of the party got back to whatever affronts to decency they had been committing. "It's great to be here, buddy. So this is the big shindig, huh? I'll tell you, this student of yours is getting a ton of press. I'm glad I was able to swing by and check it out." Jimmy's eyes lit up as he had an idea.

"Hey! What do you say we have a smoke, just like we used to do in school?"

Frampton smiled and nodded. He had hoped he'd have an opportunity to treat Jimmy to something from his private stash. He'd turned Jimmy on to the world of fine cigars toward the end of college. Jimmy had always been a casual smoker, but Frampton knew he appreciated having an aficionado for a friend. The dean rummaged through the waistband of his towel and eventually fished out two cigars. He smiled as he held one out for Jimmy, but the smile quickly faded when he saw his friend's face.

"What the hell is that?" Frampton asked.

"This?" Jimmy asked as he removed a pipe from between his teeth and looked at it admiringly. "It's my pipe. What do you think? It's meerschaum, handcrafted by an artisan in Sweden. One of a kind!" Jimmy looked down at the cigar in Frampton's outstretched hand. "A cigar? You're still smoking those, FQ? What year is it, 1993?" The senator laughed and slapped the dean on the back again. Frampton wordlessly tucked the cigars back into his towel as Jimmy filled his pipe with tobacco.

"Well, I suppose you'd like to see the main event," Frampton said. He reached out and picked up his shillelagh. "Just follow me, it's right down this hallway."

"Holy cow, you still carry that old thing around?" Jimmy reached down and rapped his knuckles on the shillelagh.

"This?" Frampton asked. "Rarely. Very rarely. Just need some support, I think my back is acting up from that fall."

"That fall just now?" Jimmy asked. "After the keg stand?"

"Yes," Frampton lied.

"So you brought your little stick with you so you could use it after a fall that hadn't happened yet?"

Frampton gripped the shillelagh tighter and fought every urge to swing it into Jimmy's shin.

"You're too much, FQ!" Jimmy laughed, punctuated by another back slap. Frampton raised a finger to remind Jimmy how much he hated and had always hated the undignified abbreviation "FQ," but Jimmy had already grabbed a passing student and was forcing them to listen as he reminisced about his old stomping grounds. "I still remember the day he got that thing. I told him, FQ, you let me burn that thing right now, or else there is not going to be a single Harrington lady that will come within ten feet of you. But I admit, I was wrong . . . They didn't come within *twenty* feet of him!" Frampton rolled his eyes and mouthed the familiar punch line along with the senator, who slapped the student on the back and laughed uproariously.

"There's still beer coming out of his nose," the student said.

Frampton blew out through his nose while simultaneously rubbing it to try and speed the rest of the foam along. It really seemed like it should have worked its way out by now, but there was still that telltale effervescent stinging sensation in the back of his nasal cavity.

As the dean wiped his hands off on his already soggy towel, Jimmy patted down his suit pockets in search of something. "Dammit . . . Hey, FQ," he said through teeth that were clenched around the stem of his meerschaum pipe. "I think I may have left my lighter in the Escalade. Do you have one on you?"

"Escalade?" Dean Bickerstaff snorted, this time unrelated to the beer foam in his nose. "Since when do you drive an Escalade? What happened to your Town Car?"

Jimmy threw back his head and laughed uproariously. "My Town Car! Whoa! I don't know, it's probably making the run from the Toledo airport to a Holiday Inn two dozen times a day. My Town Car . . . I swear, buddy, you can still crack me—Wait, you're serious? You don't still drive one, do you?

Frampton bristled and gripped his shillelagh tightly. "Of course I still drive one. They're the pinnacle of luxury."

Jimmy grimaced. "Aw, FQ! They're weird, man! The only thing they're good for is disappointing you when you thought you were getting a real limousine! You know Ford discontinued them right?"

This decision by Ford was still a fresh wound for Frampton, and he winced as Jimmy reminded him of it. "That just means it's a collector's item now," he said tentatively. "I was actually considering applying for a 'classic' license plate."

"It's garbage," Jimmy stated with finality. "Get an Escalade."

Frampton was glad that the Town Car was safely parked back at his home. Jimmy was so persuasive that if he had the keys on him, he probably would have considered trading it in right then. Instead, he tried to forget his friend's disparaging remarks while silently hoping that Jimmy did not find out who owned the Astro van that was parked outside.

A silence descended over the two old friends as Frampton scanned the room for something to show Jimmy that his big-city friend wouldn't instantly dismiss. As impressive as the stadium seating couches were, they wouldn't cut it. Jimmy undoubtedly owned several imported twelve-piece sectionals. At the hot dog stand outside you could get a pretzel bun for fifty cents extra, which the dean thought was pretty neat (and a good value), but Jimmy had surely been eating fancy buns for years.

Frampton was starting to panic, when suddenly, as if in answer to his prayers, a big, floppy golden retriever wearing sunglasses ambled into the living room from the hallway. It moseyed along with no real purpose, but its presence was immediately electric. Everyone it passed stopped dancing or making out with each other to stare in awe. Frampton pointed excitedly at the dog to get Jimmy to turn around and look at it.

"Look! Look!" Frampton immediately caught himself and dialed back how excited he sounded. He couldn't risk the dog overhearing him and thinking he was a square. "How about that, huh? It's no big deal, really, cool dogs just show up here all the time. I'm kind of used to it by now."

Jimmy stared at the dog for a solid ten seconds. Frampton was smiling expectantly when the senator turned around to face him again. "I've seen cooler dogs," the senator said witheringly. Frampton's face fell. They stared at each other again for what seemed like an eternity. Somehow, over all the other noise of the party, the dean was able to hear the golden retriever panting.

Jimmy eventually broke the silence. "Why are you wearing a towel?" he asked.

Frampton rolled his eyes with a knowing smile that said "I know, right?" "To understand that, my friend," he said to Jimmy. "I'm going to have to introduce you to Vance."

"Sounds good," said the United States senator. "But first, let me grab a beer." He slapped Frampton on the back and walked over to the keg. Frampton watched as his friend grabbed a cup, cut straight to the front of the line, and flawlessly poured himself a beer with a perfect half-inch head of foam.

* * *

"You're lucky I still had some Chinese gold stuck to my butt from when I dumped it down my pants," Captain Anson told Cormac. "You can't just go around haggling with merchants if you don't have the dough to back it up. If you think they're wasting their time, they'll cut your throat without a second thought!"

Cormac wasn't paying attention. He was too busy admiring his new harpoon gun. Sleek and shiny, it made the ones he'd been using on board the *Levyathan* look like pea shooters. The gun had caught Cormac's eye as they were walking through a seedy back-alley market. Nestled among the stands selling treasure maps, erotic scrimshaw, and opium paraphernalia was a discount harpoon gun/baked goods shack. The display case had been full of shoddy looking guns and shoddier looking cookies, but then Cormac had seen it, hanging on a special rack behind the shopkeeper. He could hear it calling his name.

Actually, it had been Captain Anson calling his name, trying to get him to help push Pete, who was slumped over in an old wheelbarrow. They'd traded for the wheelbarrow as soon as they got off the dock, once they realized how difficult it was going to be to transport the barely conscious pirate captain. Fortunately, there had been a swineherd carting a wheelbarrow full of dung to the harbor, where he intended to dump it. Captain Anson had quickly negotiated an exchange for some crummy ring that he had found in the pocket of Ziro's pants. Cormac intervened under the assumption that the ring was probably a family heirloom and potentially Ziro's only possession of value, and therefore, perhaps not a fair trade for a wheelbarrow full of pig shit. Captain Anson reluctantly agreed, and instead walloped the swineherd over the head with Ziro's mop, dumped Pete into the wheelbarrow, and made a speedy getaway.

Well, speedy was not entirely accurate. The wheelbarrow was technically more of just a "barrow" at this point. What was left of the wheel was wobbly and flat, and pushing it and its heavy load along the alternately cobblestone and mud paths of St. John's proved quite difficult. Cormac's frequent wanderings off to observe all the new sights and sounds of the harbor town hadn't helped matters, which left Captain Anson to struggle with Pete and shout at Cormac until he returned to help him.

But when Cormac saw the harpoon gun, all the cursing and shouting that Captain Anson could muster weren't enough to get him to move on. It was a thing of beauty, and Cormac knew that he had to have it. He'd immediately started negotiating with the proprietor, a hunched, wizened old prune with just a couple of teeth and one eye that was permanently squeezed half-shut. He looked like the kind of guy who would curse the object he sold you because you offended him during the process of buying it. Cormac ignored this and immediately set about trying to swindle him out of the harpoon gun.

The merchant seemed quite irritated once they finally settled on a sum and Cormac told him he had no money, especially since Cormac had assured him throughout the process that he had money on him. Cormac figured he could always run back to the ship for some gold once he'd completed negotiating. Fortunately, Captain Anson, in his boredom, had resorted to scratching his ass with Ziro's mop handle, and knocked loose a couple of Chinese gold pieces that had evidently been stuck there for the past few days. Just as the merchant was starting to mumble something ominous and waggle his finger at Cormac, Anson tossed the gold into his booth, Cormac snatched up the harpoon gun, and they gradually wheeled Pete the hell out of there.

"He was going to curse you," Captain Anson lectured, as he tried to navigate Pete around an enormous mud-filled hole in the street. "We got out of there just in time."

"Curse me?" Cormac snorted, not taking his eyes off his new toy. "The only thing he's going to be cursing is himself, for agreeing to toss in this sharp new harpoon for free!"

"It wasn't free," the captain snapped as the wheelbarrow hit a stone and Pete nearly toppled out. "I paid him twice what you agreed on because if I waited for him to give us change he was going to curse you!"

"Well, it's still a pretty sweet gun," Cormac said. "Those whales aren't going to know what hit them." Cormac raised the gun to his shoulder and closed one eye to look down the barrel. So far, this trip onto dry land had exceeded his expectations. He had a new gun, they'd had several pints of ale that you could just walk around the street with, and he'd even seen a monkey! Captain Anson had forbidden him from touching it, claiming the monkey was cursed, or that it would curse them. By this point, the only curse that Cormac believed in was the curse of the boring travel companion. He made a mental note to make this joke the next time the captain set him up for it.

Fidgety and nervous, Captain Anson had not settled down the entire time they'd been killing time in the streets of St. John's. At any moment, he expected that a shopkeeper or bartender or monkey would pull off their mask, revealing themselves as Eleanor or her lawyer. It was making it difficult for Cormac to do anything that might be considered a good show for the people looking in his ear back home. Any time they got close to something interesting or dangerous, the captain would hurry them along.

The whole time, they'd been keeping an eye out for any signs of where one might dispose of a notorious pirate captain, preferably for a large reward. Captain Anson was certain that there was a courthouse or town square where this type of thing happened regularly, but so far they'd seen no indication of where it might be. They'd been on dry land for nearly an hour. They had to find a way to ransom Pete quickly, or else they'd run the risk of the *Levyathan* being ready to set sail before they'd handed him over. This ticking clock did not make the captain any less jumpy.

Which is why he tried to hit Cormac with Ziro's mop when Cormac called out "I found one!" and it turned out he was just talking about a brothel. Fortunately for Cormac, the captain lacked Ziro's fine touch with the mop, and he swung the handle more than a foot over his head. Missing his target threw the captain off balance and he stumbled into the wheelbarrow, which upset it, spilling Pete and a large amount of pig manure out into the street. Captain Anson swore and went to right the wheelbarrow as Cormac wandered over to the whorehouse, still puzzling over why the captain hadn't let him dump out the pig manure back at the harbor.

Aside from a giant sign that read "PROSTITUTES – CHEAP!" the whorehouse was a nondescript brick building that was actually in much better shape than just about every other structure they'd seen so far. Every other building in St. John's looked ready to topple over as soon as there was a loud noise or a stiff gust of wind caused by an errant mop swing. The whorehouse, on the other hand, looked sturdy and well-maintained.

After just a few seconds of observing the whorehouse, it became clear why the owner was able to keep the building in such good shape. Men flowed in and out of the door at a steady pace. Watching them come and go, Cormac couldn't help but think of his own bedroom. He wondered whether there were more people coming and going here or there. Hopefully, scoping out this den of sin would provide everyone with enough of a vicarious thrill to satisfy the dean's violent temper.

Cormac's enthusiasm for actually soliciting prostitutes was dimmed by the fact that strangers back home would be watching. Killing a bunch of pirates who had been trying to surrender had been one thing. That was an act of heroism. Going ashore in the 1800s and banging prostitutes would just make him look like a lowlife. Plus he still wasn't clear on exactly how much the people looking into his ear could actually see. The last thing he wanted was anyone catching a healthy peek at his junk.

As Cormac worked up the nerve, the door opened again and a small Asian man walked out of the front door. He was middle-aged and wearing a sharp three-piece suit. Instead of hurrying away from the entrance with his head lowered, as every other customer had done, he stopped in front of the door and looked around, sizing up the activity on the street. When he saw Cormac gawking at him, he waved him over. Cormac broke eye contact and looked down at his feet, but it was too late. When he glanced back over, the man was still waving at him and smiling.

Cormac looked back at Captain Anson, who had propped Pete up against the side of the wheelbarrow and was for some reason scooping the manure back into it with his hands. Cormac figured that whatever the man had to say was better than helping with that. He walked over to him, nervous as hell about actually venturing inside, but trying to act like it was something he did all the time.

"Hello," Cormac said.

The man nodded, but remained silent.

"This looks like a nice place," Cormac continued. Still no response from the man. "I get prostitutes a lot," Cormac said, trying to come across as confident. He instantly regretted saying it and hoped that nobody had heard back home.

The man smiled and nodded, and Cormac realized about a sentence too late that he didn't speak a word of English. To try and make his point, Cormac pointed at the door repeatedly, and the man nodded in understanding. He reached inside his suit jacket and pulled out a thin leather binder with gold embossed script on the front that read "Bill of Fare." The man, who Cormac was just starting to realize must be some sort of pimp, stepped back and left Cormac alone to study the menu.

And study it he did. Cormac was amazed by the variety of vice that was suddenly at his disposal. The sex started fairly plain vanilla at the top and got dirtier and more difficult as he scanned down the list. Cormac noted that overall the rates seemed very reasonable. Back in the present day, he had paid more to get cheese added to a restaurant entrée than it would cost for some of these very hard-to-perform sex acts. Not everything on the list was something he was interested in, of course. Even fewer of them were things he was interested in letting everyone back home know he was interested in.

When he reached the end of the menu, Cormac froze. The last two items cost nearly twice as much as anything else on the list. They were simply called "Frog in Pussy" and "Rat in Pussy." On its own, this would be strange enough. But what really blew his mind was that someone had scratched out "Rat in Pussy" with a pencil to indicate that it was no longer available. All Cormac could do was stare. He re-read it several times to make sure it said what he thought it said, but there was no mistaking the elegantly lettered writing. He was still looking at it in stunned silence when Captain Anson walked up alongside him.

"Thanks for your help," the captain said sarcastically. "We lost a lot of manure."

"Look at this." Cormac demanded, thrusting the menu at Captain Anson. "Why is that last one crossed out? What the hell happened in there that made them have to take it off the menu? Why was it even on there in the first place?"

"Who cares?" the captain said. "Look, we really have to find someone to ransom Pete to. I don't want to have to take him back on the boat with us."

"Did the rat die? Did it bite someone? And where did the dying or biting take place? Was there really just one rat that performed every day? How often were people purchasing this?" Cormac couldn't let it go. He walked over to the pimp and pointed at the menu. "Why is this one not available anymore?" Cormac said slowly, pointing to Rat in Pussy. The Chinese man smiled and nodded, then pointed at it and shook his head no.

His congenial attitude on the matter flustered Cormac even more. "Are they getting a new rat? Is that why they didn't just print up new menus? How long has it been crossed out? Are there trainee rats? Trainee hookers? Which of those two has it worse?"

The pimp stuck out his wrist and tapped an expensive looking watch it to indicate that Cormac should hurry it up. Cormac still had a lot of questions, but this wasn't making for very exciting ear watching.

"Fine," he sighed. "I guess I'll take a Frog in Pussy." He pointed to it on the menu. The pimp looked, then smiled and nodded excitedly. He held up one finger to indicate just a moment, then darted inside to make some preparations.

"This better not take long," Captain Anson said.

"How could it possibly take long!" Cormac snapped back. He found the entire thing bewildering. He feared that not knowing why Rat in Pussy had been removed from the menu would haunt him for the remainder of his days. So it was much to his dismay when, a few seconds later, the brothel door flew open and the tiny pimp burst out of the door.

He ran over to Cormac and snatched the menu out of his hands. Then he produced a pencil from his suit pocket and hurriedly scratched off Frog in Pussy as well. He was breathing heavily and appeared very nervous. Cormac noticed that his shirt tail had come untucked.

"What just happened?" he asked the pimp, who forced a fake smile onto his face. "What did you discover in there when you went to go get the frog ready?"

Captain Anson placed a hand on Cormac's shoulder. "Let's get out of here, my boy. These are not people you want to antagonize." He pulled Cormac away from the whorehouse, back toward the street.

"What happened to the frog? Dammit, what happened to the frog!?" Cormac wailed as the captain led him back to Pete's wheelbarrow. The pimp tugged at his collar, obviously relieved that Cormac was not sticking around to ask any more questions.

"Let it go," the captain whispered. "Let it go." He reached out and grasped the barrel of Cormac's harpoon gun. The captain carefully pushed it down so it was pointing at the street. Cormac hadn't realized it, but he'd unconsciously cocked it and had pointed it in the pimp's direction. "Why don't you let me hold on to this for a second," the captain said in a calm voice.

"Why?" Cormac asked, reluctantly loosening his grip on the harpoon gun. "You don't think I'm crazy enough to shoot that guy over a frog?" he chuckled nervously while silently adding "and a rat" in his head.

"No," Captain Anson said. "I just want you to take a damn turn pushing the wheelbarrow."

* * *

Dean Bickerstaff led Senator Chambers down the hall to Cormac's bedroom. Jimmy smiled at the line of people they passed and even shook hands with a few terrified students. Frampton guessed that not a single one of them knew who Jimmy was, but they did sense that anyone with two armed bodyguards following a few steps behind him was probably not the sort of person they should be smoking weed in front of. People tried to hide the blunts behind their backs, but since they were standing in line, often the person behind them thought they were passing it back, and the drug use remained just as blatant.

Jimmy, however, seemed excited by the display of delinquency. "Harrington kids can still party, FQ! Not like we used to, of course, but I think they could at least hang with us for most of the night."

Frampton grunted in assent. Most of the parties they'd gone to in college had ended with Jimmy getting drunk enough that he ended up trying to ride Frampton like a pony. He wasn't surprised that Jimmy's memories of such nights were fonder than his own, and hoped that this afternoon wasn't headed in that direction.

They reached the end of the line and stopped outside of Cormac's bedroom. Despite Jimmy's assurances that he could look out for himself, his bodyguards insisted on verifying that the room was clear of threats before letting him enter. Jimmy seemed worried that this would make him look uncool, but Frampton insisted that the bodyguards had the right idea. Mainly, he just wanted to see what Vance's reaction would be when they burst into the bedroom.

It did not disappoint. Vance had his feet kicked up on Cormac's desk and was lazily instructing a customer where to kneel when the bodyguards entered. They weren't even able to get out the words "Secret Service" before Vance toppled over backwards in surprise.

He then scrambled across the floor toward the window, where he stood up and pulled a small, round object out of his towel.

"It was all Deano's idea!" Vance yelled as he attempted to light the object with a cigarette lighter. "I've got texts to prove it! He forced me into it at shillelagh point!" He kept flicking the lighter, but it was apparently out of fuel. Eventually he just hurled both the object and the lighter at the bodyguards, and started pushing the window open. The bodyguards, undeterred by the panicky guy in a towel, calmly began scanning the walls for bugs.

Vance was still struggling with the window when Dean Bickerstaff entered the room. "Vance, what the hell is going on here?" he asked. Vance stopped trying to force the window open and looked at the dean. Frampton walked over to the object Vance had tossed and picked it up. It was a small smoke bomb. How long had Vance had this exit strategy planned?

"These are bodyguards for Senator Chambers," Frampton explained. "They're not here because of you."

"Senator Chambers is here?" Vance asked, out of breath. "Is that what all that cheering and laughing was out there a few minutes ago?"

"I didn't hear any cheering or laughing," Frampton lied.

"It's all clear in here, Senator," one of the bodyguards said. Senator Chambers appeared in the doorway, grinning broadly. He'd gone back for another beer while his men were scoping the room out. "We'll be out here if you need us, sir," the bodyguard said. He waved Jimmy into the bedroom, then exited with his partner.

"So, this is where it all happens," Jimmy said. "He's really not going to wake up?"

"Wow," Vance said as he walked over to where the senator stood. "You're Senator Jimmy Chambers!"

"Vance, please," Frampton scolded. "Show some respect. It's James."

"Jimmy is fine," Jimmy said, smiling at Vance. "And you must be Vance. I hear you're the brains of this operation."

"Who said that?" Frampton demanded. "Nobody's saying that!"

Vance ignored the dean. He reached out and shook the senator's hand. "Sir, I'd just like to say that it is an honor to meet you. One day there are going to be enough votes to overturn that backwards horse meat law, and you're going to be fully exonerated."

"I fight the good fight," Jimmy said, looking Vance in the eye. "It's all I know how to do."

"How about a Bloody Mary?" Vance asked him.

"I'd love one!" Jimmy smiled.

Vance darted off to the kitchen to whip up a fresh batch of drinks. Frampton called in the next customer to show Jimmy how the process worked.

"So you look in the ear and you're in the past," Jimmy said dismissively. "I got it, FQ."

"Who's FQ?" Vance asked as he entered the room with three Bloody Marys.

"Nobody," the dean tried to say, but Jimmy overpowered him.

"FQ? Well he's right here! Frampton Q. Dickerstaff!"

"FQ!" Vance was delighted. "Deano, you didn't tell me you had a nickname!"

"Yes, well, nobody has called me that in over twenty years," Frampton said.

"I like it," Vance said. "Deano FQ Dickerstaff. It sounds like an acrobat's name."

"Cheers!" Jimmy said, clinking glasses with Vance and draining half his Bloody Mary in one gulp. "Wow, that packs a punch! A damn good Bloody Mary!" He slapped Vance on the back enthusiastically. Vance looked starstruck.

"It certainly does," Frampton said, setting his drink down untouched. "Now, James, if you want to take a look in Cormac's ear, you can just—"

Jimmy interrupted him. "So Vance is wearing a towel, too. I'm still waiting on an explanation, FQ."

"Ah yes, the towels," Frampton said. He walked over to Jimmy and assumed a condescending tone of voice. "The mastermind behind the towels stands right in front of you." Frampton gestured at Vance. "Makes all the more sense now, doesn't it? These ridiculous get-ups . . . So undignified . . ."

"You got any more of them?" Jimmy asked enthusiastically.

"I sure do!" Vance exclaimed. He bolted out of the room, while Frampton fumed.

"Jimmy!" he sputtered. "You are a United States senator! You can't just put on a towel and walk around a college party! Vance is a buffoon!"

"Yeah, a buffoon with another round of Bloody Marys!" Vance said as he hurried back into the room, a new towel draped over his arm and a fresh drink in each hand. Jimmy took a Bloody Mary and the towel.

"I think you're going to like that one, Jimmy," Vance said. "It's a special towel. I've been waiting to give it to someone important."

Jimmy unfolded the towel and looked at it in awe. It had four roly-poly panda bears turning somersaults while wearing party hats and blowing birthday party horns. The huge lettered caption read "Party Pandas."

"It's perfect," Jimmy whispered. Frampton hoped to God that he was hearing things, but to his ears Jimmy sounded a touch choked up.

Less than two minutes later, Jimmy had changed into the towel and was throwing back another Bloody Mary with Vance. Frampton sullenly waved customers in and out of the room as his friend and business partner laughed it up in towels just a few feet away.

"I'm surprised he went along with it," Jimmy was confiding to Vance. "He's not usually one to embrace the latest fashion trends. I mean, look at that stick he carries around. I still remember the day he got that thing. I told him, FQ, you let me burn that thing right now, or else there is not going to be a single Harrington lady that will come within ten feet of you. But I admit, I was wrong . . . They didn't come within *twenty* feet of him!"

Vance nearly choked on his Bloody Mary. "Oh my God, that is hilarious! Did you really say that?"

"Sure did!" said Jimmy.

"Oh my God, twenty feet. Classic!" Vance cackled and awkwardly tried to slap Jimmy on the back. He ended up missing by a wide margin and sort of grazing the senator's ear and shoulder, but Jimmy seemed to either not notice or not care.

"You sure you don't want to take a look, James?" Frampton asked. "From what I'm hearing in the hallway, Cormac's exploring some really seedy stuff right now." Frampton was pleased that Cormac was having a more interesting day, but was nervous that these reports might make their way to Brock's cult or the Throat Jackers. If either of them found out that Cormac was lurking around whorehouses, there might be riots, or even worse, orgies in the streets.

"Hey, Deano!" Vance shouted. "Go FQ yourself!" James guffawed at the clever word play as he and Vance slapped each other on the back and clinked their glasses.

Frampton clenched his jaw. The company was boorish, but at least Cormac was keeping people entertained. He tried to ignore the two braying idiots in the corner and waved the next customer into the room.

* * *

Cormac was terrified that he wasn't doing enough to keep people entertained. His attempt to let the audience back home experience the wonders of nineteenth-century prostitutes had been thwarted, and now here he was pushing a wheelbarrow of manure through the streets. The fact that the wheelbarrow also contained a notorious pirate captain would be of little excitement to any observers, unless they were taking bets on the length of the stream of drool that was gradually descending from the corner of Pete's mouth. The manure currently posed much more of a threat to Cormac's well-being than Pete did.

Well, it wasn't the manure itself that posed the threat as much as it was the pack of stray dogs that followed the manure, and thus Cormac, through the streets of St. John's. Attracted by the pungent smell, the rapidly growing pack trotted after Cormac wherever he wheeled Pete. Occasionally, when the wheelbarrow hit an uneven cobblestone, some manure would slop out onto the road. The dogs would make a break for it, snarling and fighting to earn the right to roll around in the pig feces. They were growing bolder and more aggressive, and Cormac feared that it wouldn't be long before the dogs decided it was in their best interest to remove him from the equation and gain direct access to the manure.

Captain Anson was of no help. Cormac attempted to call his attention to the grim situation that was developing at his heels, but the captain just ignored him as he darted from shop to shop, searching for one that had wanted posters on display. Most shopkeepers were put off by the captain's behavior. The natural inclination when a sweaty guy with a mop bursts through your door yelling about how he's got someone passed out in a wheelbarrow who's worth a lot of money is to assume that the sweaty guy is drunk, and likely intends to harm you. Quite possibly with the mop.

Eventually, one of the terrified shopkeepers shouted that they were going to call the constable if Captain Anson didn't leave them alone. That gave the captain an idea. He would harass the shopkeeper until the constable showed up to arrest him, then surely, as an officer of the law, the constable would know where to go to claim rewards for outlaws. Cormac pointed out that this was indeed a good idea, but perhaps it might be easier to just go to the constable's office and ask him for this information, instead of going to the trouble of getting arrested. The captain dismissed Cormac's idea as a needless handwringing and began to make menacing gestures with Ziro's mop at the shopkeeper. Cormac then pointed out that the constable's office was actually on the next block, that he could in fact see it from here, and maybe they should run right now because oh my God the dogs formed a semi-circle around us while we were distracted.

So they took off running, Captain Anson leading the way, while Cormac lagged behind with the wheelbarrow as the dogs nipped at his heels. Pushing the wheelbarrow at a normal pace had been difficult, but it turned out that once it got some momentum going, the thing could really cruise. Once it was going fast enough, Cormac was able to barrel over the uneven cobblestones. It probably wasn't good for the wheelbarrow—what was left of the wheel wobbled more and more with every stone it hit—but it wasn't long before Cormac passed Captain Anson and left the dogs in his dust.

As he neared the constable's office, Cormac realized he was going to have to put on the brakes. Unfortunately, now that it had finally built up some decent forward momentum, the wheelbarrow had no intention of stopping. Cormac made the split-second decision to angle to wheelbarrow toward the constable's office and let go. His aim was true, and within seconds the wheelbarrow crashed into the constable's door, sending up a spray of manure that hit the door and slowly started to trickle down. Pete did not wake up.

Cormac kept running, and got to the wheelbarrow just as the constable threw open the door. The constable was an older man, with a round belly and bifocals. He wrinkled his nose as he looked out at Cormac and the wheelbarrow over the rims of his glasses.

"Who the hell are you and what did you do to my door?" the constable demanded. He sniffed the air tentatively. "Is that manure?"

Cormac technically knew the answers to all three of his questions but didn't particularly want to answer any of them. Fortunately Captain Anson ran up at that exact moment. "We need to see your wanted posters," the captain panted. "This man in the wheelbarrow is an at-large fugitive!"

The constable looked skeptical. "OK, but leave the harpoon gun at the door. And you can't wheel that disgusting thing in here. Keep it out on the—" The constable stopped midsentence as the sound of angry, barking dogs grew louder.

"Get in," he said quietly.

Cormac was confused. "But you just said—"

"Get in, dammit!" the constable yelled. Captain Anson lifted the front of the wheelbarrow and Cormac hoisted it into the air by the handles. Together they pushed it up over the stoop and through the door into the constable's office. Immediately after they were inside, the constable slammed the door shut and locked the door knob, the deadbolt, and a sliding chain lock. He turned around.

"That was a close one," the constable said. "Those dogs are the real law in this town. We've lived in fear every day since some crazy lady got hopped up on drugs and cut all their leashes, and they formed their pack."

Cormac thought this sounded familiar. "Was she on magnesium?" he asked warily.

"No, whale dick pills. She wasn't popping magnesium like some sort of degenerate."

"It sounds like you need a dog catcher!" Captain Anson joked.

"A dog catcher?" The constable scoffed. "Like anyone's going to apply for that job after what happened to the last guy." He walked over to his desk and ruffled through a stack of papers. When he found what he was looking for he handed it to the captain. Cormac abandoned the wheelbarrow and sidled up behind the captain for a look. It was a handbill with a drawing of a large, shaggy dog and the words "WANTED FOR MURDER" printed at the top.

"They never found his body," the constable said.

"You mean *you* never found his body?" Cormac asked him.

"I'll be damned if *I* went looking for his body!" the constable said. "If the dogs wanted it found it would have turned up by now!"

"The dogs are really that violent?" Cormac asked. "They mostly seemed concerned with rolling in the pig poop."

"That's how it always begins," the constable cautioned.

"Always?"

"This is great!" Captain Anson chuckled.

"Try telling that to the dogcatcher's widow!" the constable said. He sounded like he was on the verge of tears.

"I don't mean the dogcatcher," Captain Anson said. "I meant that we finally found the place with the wanted posters. We've got another criminal here who I'm pretty sure there's a reward out for."

The constable looked at Pete. The unconscious pirate captain's arms and legs hung limply out of the wheelbarrow and flies buzzed around his open mouth.

"For that guy?" he said in disbelief. "I'm afraid we don't give out rewards for minor charges like vagrancy."

"Oh, he's no vagrant," Captain Anson said proudly. "Why don't you pull out your file for pirates."

The constable looked confused, but he did as the captain asked. He walked over to a file cabinet that was next to his desk, opened a drawer, and rifled through it until he came to a folder for pirates. He pulled it out and leafed through the papers inside, reading off ship names.

"Let's see . . . These are all the pirate ships we've got standing rewards out for. We've got the *Salty Dog*, the *Wavecrasher*, the *Scurvy Lady*, the *Mongrel*—"

"The *Mongrel*!" Captain Anson called out excitedly. "It was the *Mongrel*!"

The constable set the rest of the papers down and examined a wanted poster that had a drawing of the crew of the *Mongrel* on it. It had a list of their names, the crimes they'd committed, and the amount of reward that was being offered for their capture.

"And who might this be?" the constable asked as he ran his finger down the list. "Merrill, the ship bootblack, reward two dollars? Old Drunk Tom, the cook, reward fifty cents?"

"That's the captain," Anson said. "Pete."

The constable lowered the wanted poster and looked from Captain Anson to the wheelbarrow, and back to Captain Anson again. "Wait a second," the constable asked. "This is the fearsome pirate captain? The scourge who has looted and pillaged our ships unchecked for the past three years?"

"That's right," said Captain Anson.

The constable squinted at the wanted poster. "You're sure the captain isn't *this* guy?" he asked. He shoved the poster toward Captain Anson and pointed at a pirate in the background.

"Ah," said Captain Anson nodding knowingly. "That would be the late, great Black Barnacle. A common mistake, but no, Pete reigned as the *Mongrel*'s captain until Cormac . . . until *we* took him hostage."

The constable took another long look at Pete, then an even longer look at the wanted poster. "You're sure the Black Barnacle wasn't the captain? I mean that eye patch, the parrot . . ."

"You son of a bitch ..." Everyone turned and looked at the wheelbarrow. Pete's eyes were open and he was trying to push himself into a sitting position. His clothes and face were smeared with manure, but for the first time since he'd ingested the turpentine, he had a little bit of color in his cheeks.

"The Black Barnacle couldn't pirate his way out of a burlap gunny sack," Pete said, apparently finding new strength by the second. He swung his legs over the side of the wheelbarrow and gradually lowered them to the floor. "I'm the captain! Me, Pete!"

Pete slowly stood up out of the wheelbarrow. When he'd found his balance, he angrily pounded his chest, continuing his rant. "I'm the captain, dammit, not the Black Barnacle! I'm Pete!"

"You're Pete?" the constable asked. "The captain of the pirate ship *Mongrel*?

"That's right!" Pete smirked.

"Pete, you're under arrest for Grand Piracy. Deputies!" Two deputies emerged from a back office. "Lock Pete up until we're ready to hang him," the constable instructed them.

Pete's face fell as he realized he'd made a terrible mistake. "Wait, what the hell?" he stammered, looking around in a panic. "What's going on? Where am I?"

Captain Anson burst out laughing. "Ha! Suck it, Pete! This is the constable's office on St. John's!"

"Dammit," Pete muttered. "Oh well, at least it's not Greenland." The two deputies each gingerly grabbed one of Pete's arms, trying in vain not to get too much manure on their hands. Pete's passionate defense of his rank had evidently been all he had left in the tank, and he was powerless to resist their arrest. His shoulders slumped as the deputies led him down the hall. They shoved him into a cell and there was a loud metal clang as the door slammed shut.

"Why do all you captains hate Greenland?" Cormac whispered to Captain Anson.

"Really expensive prostitutes," Captain Anson whispered back.

"Alright you two," the constable said. "The reward for Pete is pretty impressive." He held out the wanted poster and pointed to the figure. Cormac whistled. Pete's reward made the Chinese whale dick money look like chump change.

"That's it?" Captain Anson whined. Cormac elbowed him in the ribs. Now was not the time to get greedy.

"That's more than enough," Cormac reassured the constable. "How long will it be until they hang Pete?"

"Oh, I reckon he'll be swinging from a noose before sundown. His crimes were pretty severe, and with that full confession he just offered up, justice will be swift. Oh, that reminds me!" The constable went over to his desk and pulled an official looking document out of a drawer. "If you two could sign this, testifying that you were witness to his confession, it will really help speed matters along."

"I'll sign anything," Captain Anson said. "Gimme a quill." The constable plucked a quill out of an ink bottle that sat on the corner of his desk and handed it to the captain. Not bothering to read a word of the document, Captain Anson signed his name with a flourish. He turned and handed the pen to Cormac.

"I'm not sure about this," Cormac said. "It feels like I'm signing his death warrant."

"Oh you are," the constable said. "See? Says it right here: Death Warrant." He pointed at the top of the form, just in case Cormac had missed it.

"Quit whining and sign it," Captain Anson hissed. "You're not even born anyways so it's not legally binding."

"What's that?" the constable inquired.

"Nevermind," Cormac said. He dipped the pen in the ink jar, and quickly signed his name under the captain's. He'd never written with a quill pen before. He enjoyed it, but doubted calligraphy was what the dean had in mind when he demanded Cormac provide more excitement. Time was running out to find some drama on St. John's.

"Can we have the treasure now?" Captain Anson asked, not taking any pains to disguise his impatience.

"Of course," the constable said. "Now this is a lot of money, so I can give you two options. You can have it all in gold right now, or we can give you a small percentage of it as a down payment and a promissory note for the rest. That's entirely backed and guaranteed by her majesty the Queen of England."

"We'll take the gold," Captain Anson said, not even bothering to consider the second option.

"It's an awfully large amount of treasure," the constable warned them.

"We've got our wheelbarrow," Captain Anson reminded him.

Outside, there was the loud sound of two dogs snarling and fighting, which abruptly ended when one of them emitted a final yelp of pain.

"You know what? We'll take the promissory note," Anson relented.

"It will be honored at any bank," the constable assured them. Cormac felt like this was the right decision, especially since he was pretty sure he was the one who would have ended up pushing the wheelbarrow.

"Give us a thousand pieces of eight, and a note for the rest," Captain Anson said.

"A thousand?" The constable asked. "Are you sure you want to carry all that money down the streets?"

"I don't see the problem," Captain Anson said. "It's not like the dogs want a bag of gold."

The constable looked nervous. "I wouldn't be so sure about that. There's been an uptick of canine purse snatchings lately. I'm not sure how much of the concept of economics they actually grasp, but really any amount is too much. It certainly doesn't bode well for us."

"Just give us the gold," Captain Anson said. The constable nodded and retreated to a back office. He emerged just a few moments later carrying two sacks of gold. He handed one to Captain Anson and one to Cormac. The constable had been right. Any more gold and it would have been difficult to manage. The sack was heavy enough on its own, and Cormac had to carry it plus his new harpoon gun.

"And here's the note for the rest of it," the constable said as he handed a piece of paper over to Captain Anson. The captain folded it in half and slipped it into his pants pocket.

"Don't let me forget about that when I give Ziro his pants back," he told Cormac.

"What's that?" asked the constable.

"I said thanks for the gold!" Captain Anson snapped. "And if this note gets turned down at the bank, I'm buying out all the sausage links from the butcher and then I'm going to tie you up with them!

This terrified the constable. "And then you'll open the door and unleash the dogs on me?" he whimpered.

"Er . . . Yes," the captain lied, trying to make it seem like that had been his plan all along. "Of course. It would be ridiculous if I just left you tied up in sausage, wouldn't it?" The constable nodded and Captain Anson laughed as he hoisted the sack of gold with one hand and grabbed Ziro's mop with the other.

"Let's go, Cormac my boy!" he said with the confident air of someone who just made the business deal of a lifetime. "We've got a boat to sell!"

A dog let out a bone-chilling howl from somewhere on the street.

"We'll take the rear exit," the captain declared as the constable nodded vigorously.

* * *

"Oh my God, that is so disgusting!" exclaimed Senator Chambers. "Play it again!"

"Hey, you're the senator!" Vance said. He hit reload on the "Tapirs mating" video while Jimmy cackled and slapped him on the back.

"A fourth time?" Frampton asked from the other side of Cormac's bedroom. Vance and Jimmy ignored him. They'd been over at Cormac's desk, cackling like idiots and swigging Bloody Marys for the better part of an hour now, leaving Frampton to manage the entirety of the operation. The dean lazily directed people in and out of the room with his shillelagh as his friend and business partner sat there in their towels, getting progressively drunker and louder, not bothering to even try and include him. Not that the dean really wanted to be part of the "Tapirs mating" viewing party. If it was getting this kind of reaction from someone as jaded and immoral as Vance, it must be really disgusting.

"How did you even find this?" Jimmy roared, pretending to shield his eyes, as he'd also done the past three times they watched the video.

"It's an old favorite," Vance lied. "I discovered it years ago."

"I'm sure that it is quite the spectacle," Dean Bickerstaff interrupted. "But maybe you'd like to take a peek in Cormac's ear? It's awfully impressive too, and after all, it is why you're here, Jimmy."

"Dammit, FQ, it is James," snapped the senator. "Don't make me lock you in a room with a horny tapir."

"Oh my God!" Vance roared. "I can totally picture it!"

Frampton wasn't a fan of Jimmy planting mental images in Vance's head, especially ones of him being violated by . . . What the hell was a tapir anyway? Some sort of weird pig? Whatever it was, he didn't like it being stored away up there, allowed to fester among the towel-based schemes and other sinister plans Vance had concocted.

The dean knew that if he left these two nitwits to their own devices, they might not progress past this point for the rest of the afternoon. If he was going to wow Jimmy with the Cormac's ear experience, he was going to have to drive a wedge between this burgeoning friendship.

"Vance," he called out. Vance chuckled, with a faraway expression on his face. The dean tried again. "Hey Vance. Vance! Dammit, Vance, stop picturing me and the tapir!" he finally barked.

Vance jolted in his seat like he'd just been awakened in the middle of a dream. "What is it, Deano?" he asked

"I think we're due for another round of drinks. What do you say? Nobody makes 'em like you."

The flattery had its intended effect. Vance smiled and folded the laptop closed. "I suppose it is about that time," he said. "Senator?"

Jimmy clinked the ice cubes in his empty glass. "Hell, I've got a driver," he said with a smirk.

"I'll be right back," Vance said. He darted out of the room, nearly colliding with the next customer on his way out. Frampton waved the customer over to Cormac's right ear, then walked over to talk to Jimmy.

"I tell you, Frampton, this Vance kid knows how to party," Jimmy said. "I may have to get him up on the Hill this summer. Our interns are the most uptight bunch of losers. I think he could really help relax the whole place."

A picture of the US Capitol building burning as Vance's Seahawks towel flew from the top of the dome flashed in front of Frampton's eyes, before suddenly disappearing in flames. "Please don't do that," he pleaded. Jimmy appeared to have already forgotten what he'd been talking about.

"Why don't you take some ear time?" Frampton offered, hopeful that this would be the moment. "It's a once in a lifetime experience. Word is that Cormac's being chased by a pack of wild dogs. You don't want to miss that, do you?"

Jimmy looked intrigued. "Wild dogs you say?" The look on Jimmy's face indicated that he was weighing whether getting up for a chance at the wild-dog ear time would be worth foregoing another viewing of "Tapirs mating." It appeared that the ear time was winning out, but only slightly, and mostly because Jimmy also had to go to the bathroom.

"Tell you what, FQ," Jimmy said, slowly rising from his chair and slapping Frampton on the back. "I'm gonna hit the can. When I get back, it's show time." Dean Bickerstaff silently hoped there would be something resembling show time. The morning's tapir-based entertainment might prove a surprisingly hard-to-top opening act.

Jimmy walked toward the bedroom door, the Party Panda towel doing nothing to diminish his impressive posture and presence. Vance met him at the doorway, carrying three Bloody

Marys. Jimmy plucked one out of Vance's hands. "Vance, it's time. I'm going in as soon as I hit the can!"

"Alright Jimmy! Once in a lifetime experience! You won't regret it!" Something in Vance's tone made the dean uneasy. Maybe it was the fact that Vance assuring someone that they wouldn't regret something was the easiest way to tell that an experience would be full of many and varied regrets. No, Frampton realized, that wasn't it. He was nervous because he had spent enough time around Vance that he was able to tell when his partner wasn't finished talking.

Sure enough, Vance had more to say. "There's just one thing," he informed Jimmy, who calmly sipped his Bloody Mary in the doorway. Vance walked over to Frampton and handed him his drink. Then he reached into the waistband of his towel and produced, to the dean's horror, the largest blunt he'd seen in all his time at the Craymore Street house.

"You've got to hit one of these before you take a look," Vance said, smiling as he waggled the blunt back and forth in the air like a conductor's baton. "House policy."

* * *

Ziro peered into the cold storage area. It was strange to think that just a few hours ago, it had been full of whale parts. It was even stranger to think that if Cormac could keep his rate of bagging whales at even half of what it had been, they might be offloading another full haul in just a couple weeks. Life on the *Levyathan* had certainly taken an interesting turn since the kid from the future had arrived.

Ziro left the cold storage area and walked to the deck, where he observed the whalers carousing on the docks. After they'd carried off the last piece of blubber, the whalers had descended into the crowd of vendors that flocked to the docks every time a new ship arrived. Based on the *Levyathan*'s sizeable haul, the harbormaster had extended them a generous line of credit, and the men took full advantage. They feasted on meat skewers, downed tankards of ale, and hoarded jugs of rum. Ziro would have loved to take advantage of the vendor who was offering mop head replacement and repair, but unfortunately, the captain still had his mop. He had instructed one of the whalers to pre-pay the vendor for a tune up, mostly because he felt sorry for anyone who had decided to earn a living offering such a strangely specific service.

Fortunately, amongst all the activity on the docks, Ziro had not noticed anything that made him suspicious that Eleanor or her lawyer had discovered their location. While this should have made him happy, he instead felt even more regret that he wasn't able to use the free time to have his mop tuned up. He only hoped that there was enough time once Captain Anson returned for him to let the craftsman change out the head. He'd already been paid, sure, but Ziro knew that as a true artisan, he would relish a chance to actually ply his trade. Gee, he sure looked lonely down there. Maybe I should go down there and just talk mops with him, Ziro thought.

He quickly dismissed the idea. As captain, or at least as the man disguised as captain, it was his job to see the transaction through to the end. The moment he abandoned his post, he opened the door to potentially getting swindled. Harbormasters were a notoriously unscrupulous lot, their longshoremen even more so. For now, Ziro needed to be vigilant. Mop talk could wait.

Fortunately, it didn't appear like he would have to wait much longer. Ziro noticed the harbormaster approaching, followed by a group of longshoremen carrying five extremely large treasure chests. That would be their payment, and it was more than even Ziro had hoped for. Three chests was an unheard of amount of riches, and even with his most optimistic calculations, he hadn't anticipated them getting more than four. Ziro walked over to the gangplank to observe their progress.

The whalers let up a rowdy cheer as the treasure chests passed by. Straining under the weight of the chests, the longshoremen looked a bit less enthusiastic. They temporarily deposited the chests at the foot of the gangplank, and sat down to wait while the harbormaster ascended it to take care of a few final pieces of paperwork.

Ziro reached out and shook the harbormaster's hand as he stepped onto the deck of the *Levyathan*.

"I hope that you're not coming back with a haul that size any time soon," the harbormaster said with a chuckle. "I'm not sure if the bank has anything left in their vault!"

"We'll be at least a couple of weeks," Ziro said.

The harbormaster thrust some papers and a quill pen at him. "Now, I'll just need you to sign these, saying that as the *Levyathan's* captain, you accept this gold as payment for all assorted blubber, bones, baleen, and other whale parts that do not begin with the letter B." The harbormaster winked, clearly this was patter that he was reciting from memory.

Ziro scanned the documents, making sure there was nothing the harbormaster had slipped into the fine print. He'd assigned himself a gratuity that seemed a percentage point or two higher than usual, but Ziro figured there had been more to carry than the average haul.

"You *are* the captain, right?" the harbormaster asked, in a skeptical voice that stood out to Ziro as not sounding like it was part of his usual patter. "Anson was the name? Because only the ship's real captain can sign these documents, and we can't load that gold on until they're signed."

"Yep, that's me," Ziro said. "Captain Anson."

The harbormaster narrowed his eyes at Ziro suspiciously.

"Got my lucky spyglass right here!" Ziro said, producing the spyglass and raising it to his eye.

The harbormaster instantly seemed more relaxed. "The spyglass, of course! I'm sorry, sir, I didn't notice it there. Just a precaution I have to take. Crossing T's and dotting I's, you know how it is."

Not wanting this interaction to go on any longer, Ziro signed each of the documents with a flourish and handed them back to the harbormaster. "That should settle it," Ziro said. "Have your men start loading those chests!"

The harbormaster saluted Ziro. "Aye aye, Captain!" he said. He shoved the paperwork into his pocket and gradually descended the gangplank. When he got to the bottom he clapped his hands twice and pointed toward the *Levyathan*. The longshoremen got to their feet, lifted the heavy chests, and one chest at a time slowly started to carry them up the gangplank.

Ziro exhaled a deep breath. He always hated pretending to be Captain Anson when they had shore leave, but all those other times he hadn't had to do any official captaining duties. The harbormaster had seemed suspicious, but then again, maybe it was just Ziro's nerves.

The longshoremen carrying the first treasure chest grunted as they set the chest down on the deck of the *Levyathan*. Ziro figured that the captain would want to keep at least one of the chests in his own quarters, and he walked off with one of the sweaty laborers to show them where to put it.

Down on the dock, none of the carousing whalers took any notice of the harbormaster having an animated discussion with the replacement mop head vendor. The harbormaster was nodding vigorously and crossing his heart as he swore that something was true. Only after he pantomimed extending a spyglass and lifting it to his eye did the peculiar vendor seem satisfied.

* * *

"Let's go, you booze hounds!" Captain Anson shouted. "We've got a boat to bid on!" A murmur echoed through the tavern as most of the drunks tried to figure out who this man was and what he wanted them to do. Sensing their uncertainty, Captain Anson started to shoo them toward the door with Ziro's mop. The barflies reluctantly took final gulps of their drinks, then wobbled out the door to avoid getting smacked with the mop.

Cormac stood at the entrance to the tavern with his harpoon gun, wondering if this was really the best method for finding a buyer for the boat. Captain Anson had insisted that when you were in a hurry, there was no better way.

"What you do is," he had explained to Cormac, "You find the dirtiest, sleaziest bar in town. Then you go in and tell all the bums who are sitting there piss drunk in the middle of the afternoon that you're going to sell them a boat. You round 'em up and lead them down to the harbor, where you show them the boat and start the bidding. They're drunk, so it brings out their competitive side. At the end, you tell each of them that they won, and you take off with their dough and leave them to sort out who owns the boat."

Cormac had remarked that this scheme sounded a lot more like a "robbery" than a "boat auction." And besides, how much money would these barflies really have on them? If they were better off financially, they probably wouldn't be in bar in the middle of the day. Captain Anson had snottily asked Cormac if he had a better idea. Cormac started to go down a list of them, starting with the suggestion that they consider stopping into the establishment directly across the street from the bar, a place called Big Clyde's Used Boat Emporium.

"A used boat lot?" The captain had snorted with contempt. "Speaking of robberies!"

"I *was* speaking of robberies!" Cormac protested. "The multiple robberies that you're willing to commit! Across the street they'll just buy the boat outright!"

But the captain wouldn't even entertain the thought, and Cormac now found himself posted as an armed sentry at the door in case any officers of the law wandered by, which further cemented what they were about to embark on as a crime in his mind.

"Let's go, all of you. Down to the docks!" the captain was calling as the drunks started to stream out of the bar. "A fine new boat to the highest bidder. No, I don't need your money now, you give me that after the auction," he told an especially generous drunk who was thrusting a handful of gold into his face.

All in all, about fifteen drunks wobbled their way out of the bar after the captain made his pitch. They spanned all ages and social classes, united only by their severe inebriation level and apparent desire to get a good deal on a boat. One of them started to tell Cormac an incoherent story about his grandson, and Cormac immediately felt his sympathy level for the drunks dropping.

It wouldn't even be good viewing for the people back home, Cormac figured. If they wanted to watch a bunch of drunks stumble around, they could do that in the living room or the front yard. It certainly didn't require them shelling out their cash to watch him do the same thing in the nineteenth century.

Captain Anson led the last drunk out of the tavern and tossed a piece of eight to the proprietor, who was none too happy with this pied piper figure who'd suddenly appeared and led all his customers out of his bar. The captain didn't give it a second thought, though. He had found his stable of patsies and was only concerned with how much more he could add to his already overflowing coffers.

"Let's roll, my boy!" he said to Cormac as he marched by. The captain held his sack of gold in one hand and hoisted Ziro's mop into the air like a drum major's baton as he led the funny little parade toward the docks. Cormac brought up the rear, the other sack tucked under his arm as he held the harpoon gun at the ready in case of any dog pack sightings.

That was the one nice thing about travelling with a bunch of drunk people, Cormac thought. It was like a variant on that old saying about outrunning a bear: you don't have to outrun it, you just have to outrun the other guy. But in this case, you didn't even have to outrun him. You just had to take advantage of his severe inebriation and knock him down, then make your getaway while the dogs do lord-knows-what to him.

Cormac decided that this slogan probably wouldn't look as good on a XXL T-shirt and pushed the thought from his mind as he made his way back to the docks.

* * *

"I dunno, Vance. It's been a really long time," Senator Chambers said as he eyed the blunt Vance was thrusting toward him.

"Oh come on, Jimmy," Vance replied. "You're telling me you've never burned one on the floor of the Senate? Got a little bipartisan buzz going?"

"I think that would be frowned upon," Jimmy admitted. He looked to Frampton for some help, but all Frampton offered was a shrug.

"I'm afraid it is a house rule," Frampton said in a helpless voice. Of course, the rule had been implemented to keep media spies from leaking information. Now that Cormac was fully aware of their plan, this precaution was no longer necessary. Plus, they knew that Jimmy was not a media spy. But truth be told, after the events of earlier in the day, Frampton was enjoying watching Jimmy squirm for a change.

Jimmy took the blunt from Vance and sniffed it, trying to size up what it would be like to actually light the enormous thing and smoke it. Jimmy's demeanor had noticeably calmed down in the past fifteen minutes, and he looked a touch pale. This was partly due to the blunt being produced, but mostly just the natural consequences of trying to keep up with Vance's partying. All those early-in-the-day drinks were taking their toll. As loathe as he was to admit it, Jimmy wasn't as young as he used to be. Not that keeping up with Vance was something he could have done twenty years ago, either.

"It really is a once in a lifetime experience, Jimmy," Frampton said.

Jimmy took a deep breath. "Maybe after a glass of water," he said. "Oh and it's . . ."

"James," Frampton said with a condescending smile. "I know. I'll fetch you one."

The dean walked out of the bedroom and into the kitchen, where he filled up a red plastic cup with water. Before he walked into the bedroom, he took a moment to address the line of people waiting in the hallway.

"Thank you all for your patience!" Dean Bickerstaff said. "Obviously, we have to take special precautions now that Senator Chambers has graced us with his presence. The senator's about to look into Cormac's ear, and we'll start the line up again in a few minutes just as soon as he's done!"

"Do another keg stand!" yelled a voice from the back of the line.

"Who said that?" Frampton snapped. He glared up and down the line, but nobody appeared willing to rat out the source.

"Just a few more minutes," Frampton repeated with a touch less enthusiasm. He walked back into Cormac's bedroom and shut the door.

"Here's your water!" he said to Jimmy, forcing a big fake smile back onto his face. Jimmy nodded his thanks, then took a small, tentative sip. Frampton noticed that beads of sweat were forming on the senator's forehead.

"Oh man, that's good," Jimmy said, a little bit of color returning to his cheeks. "I tell you, Vance, you make a damn good Bloody Mary, but I'm feeling a bit off right now. I think it could be my stomach, did you put anything spicy in there? Habanero garnish or anything?"

"A couple of the shots in the last one were pepper-infused vodka, but the other six or so probably balanced those out," Vance said proudly. "That's the mark of a true mixologist: balance."

Jimmy looked at the blunt and groaned. The color had drained right back out of his face, and Frampton gripped his shillelagh tightly as he tried to suppress his delight at the sight of it.

"What do you say, Jimmy?" the dean said as he thrust a lighter toward the senator. "It's a once in a lifetime experience."

* * *

Cormac, Captain Anson, and thirteen of the drunks they'd set out with arrived at the docks right about the same time that Ziro was signing the harbormaster's paperwork. One of the drunks had decided that he'd rather take a nap in the gutter than own a boat, and another had suspiciously gone missing right about the time the group passed by the whorehouse. Cormac learned, upon arriving at the docks, that he'd actually been dragged into an alley by the dogs, and his drinking buddies tearfully presumed him dead.

Damn, Cormac thought. If he'd shown up here after visiting the whorehouse I could have potentially gained some more information about the demise of the rat and the frog. Instead, Cormac was forced to stand by and witness Captain Anson's dog-and-pony show as he tried to encourage the men to bid on the *Mongrel*.

"There it is, men! Isn't she a sight to lay eyes on? The *Mongrel*, former ship of the notorious Captain Pete!" He paused to let this sink in, but the men were unimpressed. "Also a member of her crew, the legendary Black Barnacle!"

"The Black Barnacle?" yelled an impressed drunk. "I bid a hundred pieces of eight!"

"Two hundred!" yelled another.

"You'll see that it has a mast made of . . . I dunno, oak I guess," the captain continued. "I'm guessing the bunks are fully stocked with beds and stuff. I never went down there to tell you the truth."

"Three hundred pieces of eight for the Barnacle's boat!

"Technically Pete's boat, to be accurate," Captain Anson reminded them.

"Five hundred!"

"I bid one thousand! It will make a fine addition to my Black Barnacle museum!" bellowed another drunk.

"Not if I win it and add it to mine!" hollered another. "Two thousand!"

"Three thousand, you bastard," the first apparent curator of a Black Barnacle museum yelled at the second.

"I'm pretty sure the anchor is iron," Captain Anson said to nobody in particular. "Are standard anchors usually made of iron? It looked like a standard anchor."

By this point, the bidding had taken on a life of its own. Many of the drunks were taking all counterbids personally, and the entire affair teetered on the edge of exploding into violence. Captain Anson was wise enough to creep away from the rabble before any punches were thrown, as the chances of them hitting something other than their intended target were almost certain.

"What did I tell you?" he said to Cormac with a smirk. "Look at that passion. They're in a frenzy over this boat! None of them want to let it slip through their fingers!"

"If they're this belligerent now, what are they going to be like when they realize you've cheated them out of their money?" Cormac asked.

"I have no intention of being around to find out," Captain Anson replied. "Come on, this auction can run itself. Let's go sneak a peek at how Ziro's managing."

Captain Anson led Cormac down the dock, keeping a safe distance from any of the whalers and longshoremen they saw. Hanging back amongst the vendors, they managed to get close enough to the boat to have a view of the gangplank. Cormac bought a skewer of roast meat and a tankard of ale from a burly vendor using a piece of gold from his sack. The captain scowled disapprovingly, but eventually ordered one of the same.

They chowed down on the food and sipped the beer until the captain pointed out some activity on the gangplank. "There goes the harbormaster," he whispered to Cormac. "If everything is in order, they should start loading up our gold!" Sure enough, the harbormaster gave a signal and four longshoremen lifted the first heavy treasure chest and began carrying it up the gangplank.

"Do you see that!" Captain Anson sounded giddy. "It takes four men to haul that chest! Imagine how much gold is in there!" Cormac had to admit it was an impressive sight. The day's activities had made Captain Anson a very rich man. Cormac decided he could foot the bill for another skewer and beer combo.

The first group of longshoremen dropped their treasure chest off on the *Levyathan*, and once they'd made their way back down the gangplank, another group of four began to haul up the second chest. Captain Anson could barely contain his glee. He bounced from foot to foot like a little kid who couldn't wait to open his birthday presents. When the third group of longshoremen started to haul their chest aboard, he spun Ziro's mop around like it was his dancing partner. When he realized there was a fourth chest, he ordered a celebratory round of beers to be sent over to the boat auction, and when the fifth chest started up the gangplank he nearly fell to his knees and wept.

"Five chests! Five my boy!" He tugged on Cormac's pants leg and stared up at him with a dopey grin. "I'm as rich as Midas! And you know what they say about being as rich as Midas: There's literally no downside!"

Cormac was too busy staring intently at the gangplank to point out that this had never been an expression. There was something strange about this last chest. He pondered it as he took the last bite from his meat skewer.

"Sir," he asked Captain Anson. "Every other chest needed four longshoremen to carry it aboard. How come this one only needs two?"

Captain Anson sprang to his feet. He instinctively reached for his spyglass to get a better look at the distant gangplank, and cursed when he remembered that Ziro still had it. But even from a distance, it was obvious that Cormac was right. The previous four chests required one man on each corner to laboriously haul it aboard, but this one just had a man at the front and a man at the back, and they cruised up the ramp as if it was not a burden at all.

"Something's not right here," Captain Anson murmured. "Something's not right at all . . ."

"I bid ten thousand!" yelled a drunken voice from further down the dock.

* * *

Dean Bickerstaff flicked the lighter and Jimmy's eyes went wide as he inhaled. The end of the blunt blazed orange, and the air was quickly filled with the pungent scent of marijuana. Jimmy sucked on it for a couple of seconds, then quickly pulled it out of his mouth and erupted into a coughing fit. Vance grabbed the blunt from the senator's outstretched hand as Jimmy doubled over.

"Alright, James!" Vance said, raising the blunt to take a hit himself. "That's more like it! Now we know you're not a spy for the local news!"

"I'm not a what?" Jimmy wheezed as he tried to catch his breath. He looked up at Vance and Dean Bickerstaff, his eyes already bloodshot and confused.

"Never mind," Frampton told him. There wasn't any point in explaining it to him now. In fact, they'd be lucky if Jimmy lasted ten minutes before he entered into a Cissy-like state on the grounded couch.

"You're a lucky man," Vance informed Jimmy as he took another huge puff on the blunt. "G-Dimes rolled this from his private stash."

He passed the blunt back to Jimmy who stared at it for a few seconds before he raised it to his lips and took a wee little puff. "G-Dimes?" he asked. "Yeah, I'm cool with him. Is that the guy who . . ." Jimmy trailed off as he tried to impress Vance and at the same time remember who he was talking about.

"I don't think you've had the pleasure of meeting G-Dimes," Frampton said. "He was probably huffing something in a closet when you got here."

"No, I did, I did," Jimmy insisted. "Wait, is G-Dimes Vance?"

"I'm Vance, buddy," Vance said with a smile as he passed the blunt back to Jimmy. Jimmy put it to his lips and held it there for about ten seconds before he forgot what he was supposed to do with it and passed it back to Vance. Then he leaned over to Frampton and whispered "Vance thinks I'm cool!" loud enough to be heard in the hall.

"I'm sure he does, Jimmy," Frampton said. "Why don't you check out Cormac's ear now?"

"It's a once in a lifetime conspiracy," Jimmy said before bursting into uncontrollable laughter. Frampton helped the senator to his feet and walked him over to the side of Cormac's bed.

"Now what you have to do is close one eye, then put your other eye up to Cormac's ear, like you're looking into a microscope," Frampton instructed him. "No, Jimmy! Jimmy! Not *your* ear on *his* eye!"

"Ssshhh!" Jimmy said as he mashed the side of his head onto Cormac's face. "I think I can hear the ocean!"

Vance fell onto the floor in uncontrollable spasms of laughter as Frampton grabbed Jimmy by the shoulders and repositioned him. "Your eye on his ear, Jimmy," Frampton reminded him. "You're looking into his ear, not the other way around."

Jimmy flew into a panic upon receiving these instructions. "Frampton! Frampton!" he cried, turning around and looking up at the dean with terrified eyes.

"What is it, Jimmy?" Dean Bickerstaff asked.

"Do you think there's a panda out there with a 'Party Jimmy' towel?" Jimmy emitted an idiotic sounding stoned chuckle as Vance wheezed from the floor. Frampton scowled down at his friend.

"Let's not have any more jokes, Jimmy," he said, turning his friend around yet again. "There's a bunch of people out there who are waiting their turn. Now just close one eye and look into Cormac's ear with your other."

Jimmy nodded confidently, and gripped the side of the bed with both hands. He squinted his right eye shut and started to lean forward toward Cormac's ear. Then, all of a sudden he stopped abruptly. He turned and looked at Frampton again.

"Wait, what?" the senator asked.

"I didn't say anything, you buffoon!" Frampton screeched as Vance convulsed in hysterics on the floor.

Jimmy smiled a stoned smile at the dean, then turned his head, looking for Vance. "Hey Vance . . . Vance, where are you, man? You hear when I said 'Wait, what?' just then?"

Dear God, Dean Bickerstaff thought to himself. It gave him a second wind. Maybe Jimmy was more like Vance than he'd realized. He placed a hand on Jimmy's shoulder and guided him back over to Cormac's head.

"Let's try this one more time, Jimmy," Frampton said, talking to himself more than anybody else in the room. "It's a once in a lifetime experience . . ."

* * *

"Just right there, next to the other two," Ziro said, pointing to the two treasure chests with the spyglass. The four longshoremen slowly carried the treasure chest across the floor of the cold storage area, then with a grunt, set it down next to the other two. With one already stashed in the captain's quarters and three down here, there was just one more left to bring aboard.

Ziro walked to the cold storage area doorway and extended his arm to indicate that the longshoremen should go ahead of him. The surly dock workers shuffled past, shooting Ziro various forms of the evil eye as they went. Ziro had realized sometime during the second chest delivery that he had no idea what the protocol was for tipping these guys. They certainly seemed to be expecting something from him in return for their labor. Ziro, of course, had no money on him, and even though the men had just lugged what they all knew were untold riches onto what they rightfully assumed was his ship, none of it was technically his to redistribute. He didn't think it was worth explaining to them that he'd be happy to tip them, but unfortunately was just wearing the captain's uniform while the real captain was ransoming a pirate on the mainland with a guy from the future.

Even though the real captain most assuredly would have been just as stingy with the tips, it didn't make Ziro feel any better about the situation. "It's what the man who tricked me into slavery, then held me captive for five years would have done" was not a justification he wanted to start making with regularity.

Instead, he just smiled and waved to the longshoremen as they descended the gangplank. "Top-notch work, gentlemen," he shouted after them. "My compliments to your harbormaster. He runs a great facility here. Beats the hell out of Greenland!" He knew this last statement would make him sound more captain-like. Ziro personally had no problems with Greenland; he'd quite enjoyed himself every time they'd docked there. Between this out-of-character slander and the tipping issue, he didn't like the man he became when he put on Captain Anson's uniform. He hoped he'd get a chance to change out of it soon.

The longshoremen reached the docks, shooting Ziro a wide variety of obscene gestures on the way down. Many were ones Ziro had never even seen (though their intent was unmistakably obscene). Such was the wonder of a port town, he thought to himself. So many different cultures intermingling.

Longshoremen started to haul up the final chest, and before Ziro knew it they had reached the top of the gangplank. "So, that's the last of them!" he said. Ziro didn't realize it, but his tone was unmistakably that of the guy who thinks he can make up for not tipping by being extra friendly to the people he's about to stiff. The longshoremen grunted in response. "So, if you just want to follow me down to the cold storage area, it's right this way," Ziro said.

He turned to walk down to the storage area, but didn't hear the longshoremen follow after him. He looked over his shoulder, but they hadn't stepped away from the end of the gangplank. Ziro smiled and waved them his way. "Come on, just a few more feet, you two." It only now struck Ziro that there were half as many longshoremen carrying this chest.

"Oh jeez, I didn't notice there were only two of you," he said, quickly walking back toward the men. "That must be incredibly heavy, let me give you a hand with that."

Ziro reached out to grab a corner of the treasure chest, but without warning the longshoremen dropped it to the deck of the *Levyathan*. Ziro pulled back and winced as he braced himself for the sound of splintering wood that would surely accompany a chest full of heavy gold falling to the deck. But there was none to be heard, only a brief thump. When he looked back at the longshoremen, they were already hustling back down the gangplank. Ziro rushed over to the side of the boat, intending to chase after them, but the chest was blocking his access to the gangplank.

"Hey!" Ziro yelled over the side. "This is not where that chest goes! I am the captain and I command you to get back here and put it next to the rest of them!" When there was no response from the dock workers, he called out "Fine, you dicks! There goes your tip!"

Ziro forced himself to take a deep breath before he berated the longshoremen any further. "What the hell did I just say?" he mumbled to himself. "I have got to get out of this uniform . . ."

He took a step back and tried to figure out the best way to regain access to the gangplank. The chest was too large and unwieldy to move by himself, but there were large metal handles on each side of it. Ziro thought that he might be able to use a handle as a foothold and climb up on top of the chest, then jump down onto the gangplank from the top of the chest and recruit some of the whalers to lend him a hand moving it to the cold storage area.

Ziro was looking for a toehold with his right foot when he heard it: something inside the box had just moved. Ziro took a step back from chest and had a split second to try and process what this could possibly mean before the lid of the treasure chest flew open and a man popped up from inside.

He was dressed in a suit and tie with shiny cufflinks, and his hair was slicked back from his forehead. His appearance, though sharp and carefully attended to, was undercut by the fact that he was sweating as profusely as Ziro had ever seen someone sweat. He looked like he was continuously emerging from some invisible pool. His clothing was soaked through. It must have been incredibly hot in the treasure chest. Even though he was disgusted, Ziro found it hard to take his eyes off of him. He eventually forced himself to do so, because slightly more relevant than his copious sweating was the thick paper scroll the man held in his right hand.

"Captain Anson?" the sweaty man asked, not waiting for a response. "I have been retained as counsel for Mrs. Eleanor Anson. I'm here to serve you with papers for divorce." As the lawyer thrust the scroll toward Ziro, the sweat that had pooled in the arm of his suit jacket rushed forward as well. It made a sloshing noise as it flowed toward his cuffs and began to empty out onto the deck of the ship, as if the lawyer had just turned on a small faucet inside his jacket.

Ziro decided to wait until the sweat stopped pouring out before taking the scroll. Unfortunately, the sweat kept coming.

"You're legally required to take documents that you've been served with!" Eleanor's lawyer said testily, blinking as sweat ran down his forehead and into his eyes.

"I know, I know," Ziro said. "I just want to wait for . . ." He gestured toward the stream of sweat.

"For what?" the lawyer demanded.

"Well, for all that sweat to stop pouring off of you," Ziro said.

They both stood there and stared at the stream of sweat rushing out of the lawyer's sleeve. After about ten seconds, the lawyer started to look embarrassed. He attempted to bend his arm at the elbow to staunch the flow of sweat from it. After a few seconds, the stream was reduced to a mere trickle, and Ziro thought it was finally safe enough to move in and take the documents. But just as he was about to grab them, all the sweat that had backed up in the meantime began to rush out the lawyer's other sleeve at an even more ferocious velocity.

"Jesus!" Ziro yelped as he jumped back out of the way. "It must have been like a sauna in there! Was there any airflow at all? How long were you in that chest?"

"Mrs. Anson's council is not legally required to answer your questions," the lawyer said. "Just take the documents you've been served with."

Ziro couldn't help himself. "Was your hair . . . Did you slick that back before you got in the box or is it all just sweat from being so hot in there?"

"I slicked it back!" The lawyer sounded defensive. "Lots of lawyers slick back their hair!"

"What did you slick it back with?" Ziro asked. "I'm genuinely curious. Whale oil, pomade, gel . . .?" Ziro didn't think it was possible, but the lawyer had started to sweat even more under the stress of this interrogation.

"I've slicked it back with many things in my day," the lawyer said.

"But today," Ziro asked. "What did you slick it back with today, other than sweat?"

"Whale oil!" the lawyer said.

"I don't think people actually use whale oil to style their hair," Ziro said. "Did you actually use whale oil or are you just so dehydrated and confused from all the sweating that you repeated the first thing I said?"

The lawyer, both dehydrated and confused, again pushed the scroll at Ziro, who decided he had nothing more to gain from the sweat talk and took the soggy papers from his hand.

"These papers indicate a summary judgment of the divorce court of Nantucket ruling that 50 percent of all your current wealth and property shall be transferred to my client, Mrs. Eleanor Anson, as well as any future wealth earned by the use of your joint property, namely the whaling ship *Levyathan*." The lawyer looked as satisfied as somebody who had probably lost 10 percent of his body weight through sweat possibly could. Namely, not very satisfied and extremely lightheaded. He leaned out of the side of the treasure chest and waved his arms toward the dock.

"I did it!" he yelled. "I finally did it! I served him!"

Ziro didn't bother to unroll the scroll. He had no doubt that everything in it was by the book, except for it being served to someone who obviously wasn't the intended target of the lawsuit. Still, as long as Captain Anson remained on the mainland, they were far from in the clear. He leaned over in the direction the lawyer was waving to try and see who he was yelling at. Ziro winced as flecks of sweat flew off the lawyer's flailing hands and into his face. He raised a hand to try and protect himself and, though the sensation of the sweat striking his hand was still rather unpleasant, he was now able to focus on what was happening down below.

The mop head replacement vendor was ascending the stairs. Also, he'd thrown off his wig, fake mustache, and costume, and was actually a woman. Ziro had never felt so betrayed in his life.

* * *

Captain Anson was at his worst. Cormac was not sure he'd ever seen Captain Anson at his best. Actually, pretty much every time he saw him it seemed like he was at a new low. But this was definitely the lowest of the lows. When the chest on the *Levyathan* burst open and the man popped out, Cormac really thought that the captain was going to faint and a translucent, smoke-outlined version of his body would float up from his body clutching a ghostly flower.

Cormac couldn't hear what the man in the chest was saying to Ziro, but the captain had no doubts. "It's her lawyer," he gasped. "She's here somewhere . . ." Anson turned his head every which way searching for his wife, but to no avail. The dock was too crowded to get a good look at anyone more than a few people away from him. All they could do was watch and wait to see what happened next.

As it turned out, they didn't have to wait very long. A couple of minutes after the chest had opened, the lawyer inside turned around and started shouting "I did it! I finally served him!" to someone on the dock. Immediately, a sad-sack-looking mop head replacement vendor strode forward toward the *Levyathan*. He had been standing less than ten feet from Cormac and the captain. In fact, Captain Anson had been making fun of the vendor just a few minutes earlier, mocking his business plan and polling other people on the docks about when they thought he would be out of business. Now his jaw dropped as he realized who that vendor actually was.

As she walked, the vendor pulled off her fake mustache and wig. She shook her head, sending long blonde hair cascading down her back and shoulders. She pulled open snaps on either side of her mop vendor's uniform, sending the rough canvas apron falling to the floor and revealing a tight white dress that cut off well above her knees. Captain Anson and Cormac's jaws both dropped.

"Eleanor!" gasped the captain. "The mother of all harpies! The mop repair guy was really her!"

"*That's* Eleanor?" Cormac couldn't believe his eyes. The captain's ex-wife was easily the most beautiful woman he'd ever seen in person. "The foulest succubus in the universe?" Cormac asked for clarification. "The bitter hag? The gruesome hydra-headed serpent?" Captain Anson nodded.

"She's stunning!" Cormac was stupefied. "She's incredibly, incredibly hot! And not just like, hot for the nineteenth century!"

"What's that supposed to mean?" Captain Anson snapped.

"Let's not get into that now," Cormac said rather quickly. "But Captain! Eleanor is a goddess! She could be a movie star back where I'm from!" Cormac was just now realizing that he had even been slightly attracted to the mop repairman. He declined to voice this information in public. Instead, he looked at the captain, then Eleanor, then back at the captain again. "You want to divorce her?" he asked.

"It was hell!" the captain protested. "Every single day, with her whining. 'You look like you could use a backrub!' 'Which of these bras is sexier?' 'My twin sister is horny again, mind if she comes over?'"

"Oh my God!" Cormac threw his hands up. He couldn't believe that this was the woman who the captain had been obsessed with avoiding for the past five years. As Eleanor quickly walked toward the *Levyathan*'s gangplank, he regretted not having the captain's spyglass at his disposal just so he could keep basking in her radiance.

As much Ziro wanted to watch Eleanor gracefully glide up the gangplank, he forced himself to duck back behind the treasure chest. He wanted the reveal that he wasn't actually the captain to be a surprise. The excited lawyer hopped up and down in the chest, making tiny splashing sounds every time he landed. When Eleanor reached the top of the plank, Ziro turned to face the opposite direction and pressed his back up against the treasure chest. He crouched so she wouldn't be able to see him from the other side of the chest.

"I did it, Mrs. Anson!" the lawyer crowed. "Er, *we* did it! The papers have been served!"

"That's wonderful," Ziro heard Eleanor say. He tried to suppress a giggle. "And what do you have to say for yourself, *Captain*?" She seethed the word "captain" with utter contempt.

Eleanor waited for a response for a few seconds before speaking up again. "Is he there?" she asked the lawyer. "I can't see him over the top of the chest, pull it closed."

"Oh no, please don't, ma'am," the lawyer sputtered. "It's so hot in there! I've sweat so much I've already gone down three belt sizes today!" But Eleanor ignored his pleas and slammed the lid of the chest closed, re-imprisoning the lawyer inside. Ziro stood up, still keeping his back to the captain's wife.

"There you are, you cowardly little sea weasel," Eleanor said. "Hey, you know what? I think you're standing on my half of the boat! What do you think about that?"

Ziro decided that the moment was now. He turned around to face Eleanor, a huge grin on his face. "Oh, goddammit," Eleanor mumbled, lowering her face into her hands. She stomped on the lid of the treasure chest a few times. "You idiot!" she shouted to the lawyer. "That's not my husband! It's his slave!"

"Former slave," Ziro corrected her.

"So . . . hot . . ." came the muted, gurgled reply from inside the box.

Down on the dock, Captain Anson nudged Cormac. "I can't hear what's going on up there! Let's go get a closer look!"

"Are you sure, sir?" Cormac asked. "Do you really think that's a good idea?"

"Of course," the captain said, already confidently striding toward the gangplank. "She won't recognize us. She doesn't know who you are, and I'm disguised as a janitor." They took a spot about two or three people back from the foot of the gangplank and looked up at the ship. Cormac could hear Eleanor and Ziro talking on the boat, but with all the other noise from the people on the dock, he couldn't make out distinct words.

"Be quiet, everyone!" the captain requested. "We're trying to hear what they're saying on the boat!" All the vendors and dock workers shot the captain a vicious look, as if to indicate that asking them to be quiet a second time would be a good way to end up as part of the next batch of meat skewers.

"There's gold in it for you if you shut up for the next five minutes," the captain said. He reached into the sack the constable had given him and tossed a few pieces of gold at all the people around him. Immediately, they fell silent, and Cormac and the captain strained to listen to the conversation on the *Levyathan*.

"There he is!" was the first thing they heard Eleanor shout. "Right down there! About two or three people back from the gangplank, disguised as a janitor!"

"Crap," Captain Anson muttered. "I'm gonna need all of that gold back!" he announced to the crowd around him, who saw fit to disperse at that moment.

"We should probably run too, sir," Cormac whispered to him. Captain Anson nodded in assent. They turned to flee the docks, but standing in their way was the burly meat skewer salesman.

"You want anything for the road?" Captain Anson asked Cormac. Cormac didn't have a chance to answer, because the vendor reached out with both arms and grabbed Captain Anson by the shoulders. He spun him around and pinned both of the captain's arms behind his back. The captain struggled for about a second before he realized it was futile. The vendor had at least a hundred and fifty pounds on him.

"What the hell, man!" Captain Anson protested. "Cormac, did you not tip this guy or something?"

"I did," Cormac replied. "Did you?"

"I was going to!" the captain yelled, rather unconvincingly.

"Shut up," the vendor bellowed. "I work for your wife! Now hold still!"

"Your skewers were terrible!" the captain said to the man who held him prisoner. "I couldn't have choked a sixth one down if I'd been forced to!"

From the top of the treasure chest, Eleanor reached out and snatched the scroll of divorce papers from Ziro's hand. "I think I know just what to do with these," she said with a smile. Ziro was speechless. Was this really happening? The captain's past had finally caught up with him, and it was going to cost them all the boat that had been their home for the past five years.

Eleanor stomped on the chest again. "I'm serving him the papers myself, you worthless jackal!" she yelled at the lawyer inside. "You should consider yourself no longer held on retainer!" Inside the box, the lawyer just moaned. Eleanor hopped down from the chest and began to walk down the gangplank. Quickly, Ziro scrambled up over the top of the chest and down onto the gangplank behind her. He chased Eleanor for a few steps, but then stopped in his tracks. Ziro looked at Eleanor, then back at the boat, then at Eleanor once more. Not giving himself a chance to second-guess his kindness, he turned and ran back up the gangplank, reached up over the treasure chest, and pulled the lid back open.

The lawyer gasped from inside. "Thank you," he croaked. "It's up to my waist in here."

"Just stay in there for now," Ziro said. "If you climb out of there, I'm the one who has to swab up the mess." He jumped back down onto the gangplank, and ran after Eleanor.

"If it isn't the queen of the Gorgons herself," Anson bitterly chuckled at Eleanor as she descended the gangplank. "What tipped you off that it wasn't me? It was the lack of an earring, wasn't it?"

Eleanor stopped in her tracks, confused. "What? No! It was obviously an entirely different person in your uniform. Why, do you have an earring now?"

"That's right," the captain said. "Feast your eyes on what you're never going to get a chance to experience!" Captain Anson tried to turn so that he could thrust his ear toward Eleanor, but the burly vendor held him firmly in place. "Can you help me out here?" Captain Anson eventually asked. The vendor lifted him off the ground by his wrists and rotated his entire body a quarter turn. While he was still in the air, Captain Anson proudly jutted his chin out so his wife could take in the full spectacle of his earring.

"Eh? Eh? OK, starting to hurt my wrists now, you can put me down," he instructed the vendor, who abruptly dropped him to the ground with a thud.

"You've got good taste, *Captain*," Eleanor said, her voice thick with sarcasm. "Which is good for me, because since you bought that earring with proceeds from your whaling operation, half of it is technically mine!"

"Nice try, you freeloading remora!" the captain laughed. "But I didn't buy this earring! I'll have you know I looted it off a corpse before the body was even cold!"

"That doesn't surprise me at all," Eleanor said. "You're a terrible, immoral man." She turned and looked back up the gangplank at the *Levyathan*. Further up the gangplank, Ziro stopped in his tracks. "I'm not so sure that I want half a boat," she said, looking the ship up and down. "Maybe I'll sell my half off to a lumber yard. I no longer need the money of course, so I think I'll donate the proceeds to a 'save the whales' fund!"

The captain's face went white. "You wouldn't!" he gasped.

"I've been interviewing charities all week," Eleanor smiled. "There are several that have great plans for the money. It's so hard to decide, I may have to support more than one!" She threw her head back and laughed to herself as she started to walk back down the plank toward the dock. Cormac was dismayed that he found even her vindictive evil laughter to be quite sexy.

Enraged at the prospect of his boat being sold off for scrap wood to fund a whale charity, Captain Anson struggled mightily, but there was simply no escaping the vendor's grip. Cormac looked over at the captain. He watched him feebly kick his legs, trying to break free. Then he looked up at Ziro, and then at the *Levyathan*. Looking at her from the land, it was even more obvious how in need of repairs she was. Her wood was rotting, barnacles had aligned themselves so to spell out an incredibly obscene word just above the water's surface, and Cormac had never noticed it before, but the mast definitely rose out of the deck at an extremely crooked angle. There was one other thing he'd never noticed until he observed the boat from the dock.

Just under the railing of the *Levyathan*, there was a line of whale silhouettes, stenciled in black paint. Toward the bow of the boat, the whales were faded and flaking; you could only make out the first couple if you knew what you were looking for. The quality slightly improved as you went down the line until they started to appear jet black, the paint brand new. Cormac realized that the captain had been keeping a tally, one whale silhouette for every whale they'd killed on the *Levyathan*. The new marks were the whales they'd caught since Cormac was on board. His whales. Three quarters of all the whales the ship had ever caught.

"That's our boat," Cormac said to nobody in particular, his voice rising in anger. "She wants to take away our boat. That is *our* boat!"

"In a figurative sense," Captain Anson gently reminded him. "A very figurative sense—OW! Not so tight dammit! But still, I'm the only real owner of the boat."

Cormac didn't hear the captain. His head was spinning, so his actions were entirely dictated by muscle memory. Cormac raised his new harpoon gun to his shoulder, peered down the barrel, and pulled the trigger.

The harpoon flew through the air and struck Eleanor directly in the chest. The force of the projectile knocked her backward off the gangplank, where she fell into the harbor with a dainty little splash. Moments later, her body surfaced, floating lifelessly on her stomach, just the point of the harpoon sticking out through her back. Captain Anson stared, his mouth open in disbelief. The burly vendor released his grip on the captain's wrists. The lawyer fainted, collapsing back inside the treasure chest. From his position on the gangplank, Ziro scanned the dock for Cormac, but he was nowhere to be seen.

* * *

"Dammit, Jimmy!" Cormac heard a voice say. He opened his eyes and saw his bedroom ceiling.

"Uh, Deano?" This voice he recognized as Vance. "I think he's back."

Cormac turned his head to the right and cried out in terror. A grown man was kneeling on the floor next to his bed and had passed out with his head on Cormac's pillow. Cormac jumped out of bed on the other side from where the man lay. The sudden noise of Cormac landing on the floor disturbed the stranger, who slowly raised his head and squinted as he looked around the room.

The dean stood over the barely conscious man, slapping his cheeks with the back of his hand to try to revive him. Vance sat in Cormac's desk chair. All three of the men in his room were wearing towels.

"Cormac!" Dean Bickerstaff shouted. "What the hell are you doing awake?"

"I don't know!" Cormac shouted back. "I just . . . did something and the next thing I know I'm back here!" He was incredibly disoriented. What had just happened? It had been like waking up from a dream where you were falling. He'd instantly been very much awake in his bedroom, but he could still feel what it was like to be on the docks in St. John's. The taste of the salty air and the smell of the people around him, the sounds of the captain and Eleanor bickering, the feel of the harpoon gun in his hands. Why now? Why had the predictable pattern of the past two weeks suddenly ceased to function now?

Cormac couldn't concentrate. Vance and the dean were saying something to him, but he didn't hear a word. All he saw was their mouths moving. The third man, presumably the United States senator, was drooling on his pillow.

"I need to get back there," Cormac announced, interrupting whatever Vance and Dean Bickerstaff were saying. "The captain and Ziro need my help."

"Why?" the dean asked. "What's going on? Dammit, did we miss something exciting?"

Cormac paid the dean no attention. He climbed back into bed and pulled the covers over his body. Turning to the unwanted intruder, he gave his head an emphatic push off of his pillow, and the senator toppled backward onto the floor, where he resumed his drooling. Cormac flipped his pillow over, and was pleased that the drool had not yet soaked through all the way to the other side.

"I'm going back to sleep," he announced.

Dean Bickerstaff was tugging Jimmy's towel back down to an acceptable level near his knee, but he looked up at Cormac when he announced this. "Yes . . . Yes! That's a great idea! Get some more Z's, we've got a lot more people out there who want to see whatever it is you're doing."

"You need any pills, Mac?" Vance asked. "I've got some stuff that will knock you out like *that*."

For once, Cormac thought Vance had a good idea. "Definitely," he said, and made a "give them here" gesture. Vance pulled a pill bottle out of the waistband of his towel and tossed it across the room to Cormac. Cormac opened it and shook two pills into his hand.

"What kind of sleeping pills are these?" he asked as he popped them into his mouth.

"Oh, I don't think they're sleeping pills," Vance said. "And you'll want to crush them up and snort them. And I'd blow at least twice that many."

Cormac spit the pills back out into his hand. "Thanks but no thanks," he said. Vance walked back over to the bed and plucked the pills out of Cormac's hand. He rubbed them off on his towel, then plopped them back into the pill bottle.

"Whoa!" Vance exclaimed. "Good call, Mac! Bullet dodged. These are actually those whale dick pills I was telling you about a few days ago! You do not want to snort these, trust me on that one!"

Cormac felt his tongue trying to crawl down his throat and die, but he forced himself to stay calm. "Look, all of you just please shut up. I need to get back to sleep." He lowered his head to his pillow and closed his eyes. After thirty seconds, his mind was racing like he'd just pounded a bunch of energy drinks, so he decided to try counting sheep. The first sheep jumped over the fence without incident, but the next sheep that came by was wearing a towel. Vance was riding on the third sheep, and the fourth was unceremoniously harpooned while halfway over the fence. Cormac decided this method was not going to work. Frustrated, he popped his eyes back open.

Dean Bickerstaff's face was hovering six inches above his own. "Are you asleep yet?" the dean asked.

"Dammit, no!" Cormac shouted. The dean pulled back in surprise as Cormac furiously tried to think of another way to get back to the nineteenth century. He closed his eyes and tried to think of other ways to lull himself to sleep. Perhaps thinking the words to "99 Bottles of Beer" would work. He started reciting them in his head, but around the 97th bottle, Vance started pulling down three or four bottles at a time and chugging them. This wasn't going to work either.

Cormac was racking his brain to try and remember other sleep-inducing methods he'd heard of when he felt something tickling his ear. "Oh my God . . ." he heard an incredibly close voice say. "It's amazing!"

Cormac immediately sat up in bed and looked to his side. The senator was crouched over, still holding one eye shut and peering at where his ear used to be. Cormac would have felt no less creeped out if his entire body were covered in millipedes. He forced himself not to think about how many thousands of times this had happened in recent days.

"Dammit, Jimmy," Frampton said. "He's awake now, you didn't even . . ." He paused, reconsidering. If Jimmy was stoned enough to think he just caught a glimpse of the 1800s in Cormac's ear, why let him think otherwise?

"Pretty incredible, right?" Dean Bickerstaff said, quickly masking his earlier frustration. "What did you see?"

"I saw whales, and boats, and sharks jumping over the whales, and there were like three rainbows, and a griffin," Jimmy said, completely and totally awestruck. "Oh my God it was mind-blowing, FQ! A once in a lifetime experience!"

"You can open your other eye now, Jimmy," Frampton informed the senator.

"What do you think, Mac?" Vance asked. "You want to try the pills now? Look, you can take it slow. Just blow one, and after thirty seconds if you can't feel anything on the right hand side of your body, I'll help you blow another."

Cormac shook his head. It was pointless. Something had happened when he'd shot Eleanor. Whatever had snapped him out of the nineteenth century had also ended his time there. He wasn't going to be able to get back if he fell asleep now, or in two days, or anytime.

"It's over," he said to himself more than to Vance and the dean. "Whatever it was, it's over."

"The hell do you mean it's over?" Frampton shouted. "There's a whole house full of people out there who have already paid to look in your ear today!"

"I just have a feeling," Cormac replied. "It's hard to put my finger on it. This may sound silly, but I think it feels as if my very soul has—" Cormac cut himself off as a panicked thought occurred to him: there was a very good chance he was sporting morning wood right now in front of Vance and the dean. He looked down. Fortunately he wasn't, but when he started to continue his explanation, whatever he had been on the verge of articulating was gone.

"Just give them their money back," Cormac said. "Well, give me my cut, then give them their money back. It's not going to happen, Dean Bickerstaff. I can just tell."

Dean Bickerstaff watched Cormac swing his legs out of bed and stand up. His entire scheme had just gone poof right before his eyes. The dean realized that he had never thought about what might happen if Cormac eventually stopped going back to the 1800s. Would he really have kept coming over here and wrapping himself in a towel every day for weeks? Months? Even longer? Perhaps this was for the best.

"Well, at least there's a kick-ass party still going!" Vance said. "You gotta do a keg stand, Mac, there's no way you can be worse at it than—"

Cormac cut him off. "Tell everyone to go home," he said as he rubbed the sleep gunk out of his eyes. "I'm really not in the mood. And all of you get out of my bedroom. I need to take a shower and change clothes."

Vance shrugged. "I'll let you break the bad news, Deano!" he said, slapping Frampton on the back as he walked over to the door. Vance opened it and stepped out into the hallway. Frampton picked up his shillelagh as Jimmy sat on the floor, still marveling at whatever he thought he'd seen in Cormac's ear. The dean walked over to the doorway.

"You two!" he yelled at Jimmy's bodyguards. "Your boss needs a hand here." The guards quickly filed into the room.

"Oh no, sir, not again," one of them said. They helped Jimmy to his feet and each of them threw one of his arms over their shoulders.

"You guys gotta try this ear thing," Jimmy told them. "In the 1800s, there's always steel drum music playing and the sun has such a friendly face."

"Don't talk to anyone on the way to your car, sir," the other bodyguard said. "US senator coming through!" he loudly announced as they carried Jimmy out into the hallway.

"This was great, FQ!" Jimmy called back to the dean. "Just like old times! Come visit me in DC sometime! One night a year they let all the senators pee off the top of the Washington Monument! I'll sneak you in!"

"Sounds great!" Frampton called after him. It actually kind of did, Frampton thought as he followed Jimmy into the hall. The customers who had been waiting in line outside Cormac's bedroom looked impatient and frustrated.

"When is it our turn?" a girl near the front of the line demanded.

"Party's over!" Frampton announced, making sure the shillelagh was quite visible. "No refunds. Go home!"

Cries of protest went up from the people in line. "No refunds?" the guy at the front of the line yelled. "That's bullshit! Those were perfectly good Arts Dollars!"

"You're welcome to take it up with accounting," Dean Bickerstaff said as he raised two fingers in the air and whistled. Two bandana men silently appeared at the end of the hallway and the murmurs of protest went silent. "You've got five seconds," Dean Bickerstaff said, poking the guy at the front of the line in the ribs with the knotty end of the shillelagh.

The dean smiled as the entire line hurriedly dispersed to the living room. He followed after them, waving his shillelagh to clear the path in front of him. "Be sure to take a beer to go!" he cackled.

Vance popped his head out of the kitchen. "Whoa, easy there, Deano! Those kegs'll last us at least a couple of days!"

"Cancel the road beers!" Dean Bickerstaff called out. "Kindly pour them back into the ale keg!"

"That's not how kegs work, you idiot!" yelled an anonymous voice from somewhere in the living room.

"Who said that?" Dean Bickerstaff demanded, but it was no use. The guests were rapidly flocking out of the house, spurred on by the silent, intimidating presence of the bandana men. The dean stood and watched the exile for a few seconds, jabbing his shillelagh at anyone who appeared to by lollygagging. Eventually Vance appeared next to him. He held two Bloody Marys and offered one to the dean. Frampton eyed it warily for a few seconds, but eventually accepted it. Vance stuck out his glass, and the dean clinked it with his own.

"It was a good run, Deano," he said as they both watched the people file out of the house. "I feel like we really accomplished a lot these past two weeks."

"It's been . . . interesting, Vance," Dean Bickerstaff replied.

"You can't keep that towel," Vance informed him.

"Wouldn't dream of it, Vance. Come on, let's get these people off your lawn."

They walked out the front door and onto the porch. The people on the lawn were moving a bit slower than the people inside, but then again, they hadn't been threatened with immediate physical harm. The hot dog truck was preparing to drive off and the DJs were packing up their equipment. Dean Bickerstaff looked to his left and was stunned to see Cissy stretched out on her new couch. It still looked immaculate, another testament to the remarkable efficiency of the omnipresent threat of violence.

"I see you've already got the memo, Cissy," Dean Bickerstaff said.

"What memo?" Cissy asked with a yawn.

"We're shutting the party down, Cistress," Vance said with a funereal tone. "Mac woke up and doesn't think he's going back."

"Oh," Cissy said. "No, I hadn't heard that. I'm out here waiting for the couch movers."

"You're going home?" Dean Bickerstaff asked, trying not to sound too stunned.

"Kind of," Cissy shrugged. "I got offered a job at some gossip website. They read my articles about Cormac in the *School Paper* and were impressed by my journalistic ethics."

"Your ethics!?" Dean Bickerstaff blurted, making no effort this time to conceal how shocked he sounded.

"Maybe it was my *lack* of ethics," Cissy said as she rolled her eyes. "I don't care! They pay a lot of money and said I can make stuff up."

"But what about the Buckler Award?" Dean Bickerstaff asked. "The family tradition?"

"They pay . . . a lot . . . of money," Cissy repeated, emphasizing each word. "Now get out of the way, here come the movers."

Frampton and Vance stepped to the side as two large men in overalls walked up onto the porch. They looked displeased to see Cissy. "This couch again?" one of them said with a contemptuous snort.

"Not exactly," Cissy said, leaping to her feet. "Follow me," she instructed the movers. She disappeared inside, and the movers shuffled after her. Frampton and Vance shrugged at each other. A few seconds later, the movers burst through the door, carrying what was formerly the airborne couch. Cissy reclined on it, absentmindedly swiping at the screen of her iPad.

"My couch!" Vance cried.

"I'll trade you," Cissy said, pointing to the new couch on the porch as the movers kept walking. "I've gotten kind of used to this one. I do a lot of good thinking up here."

Vance tried to protest, but it was no use. Cissy had fallen asleep by the time the couch was ten feet off the porch. They watched as the movers loaded Cissy and the airborne couch into the back of a truck, and before they knew it, she was gone.

"It *is* a much nicer couch, Vance," Dean Bickerstaff reassured his crestfallen partner.

"I know," Vance said, sullenly kicking at the surface of the porch. "It just took like, a couple hours to get it set up." Then, immediately brightening he said, "Well, I better get busy!" Vance chugged the rest of his Bloody Mary, then grabbed a straggler who was just emerging from the front door and enlisted him to help him carry in the first piece of the sectional couch.

Dean Bickerstaff watched them struggle with it and considered lending a hand, but just then he heard someone call his name from the yard. He turned and saw that as everyone else was filing away from the house, George was striding toward him.

Frampton grinned. "Jorge!" he boomed, spreading his arms open in a welcoming gesture that also prominently displayed his shillelagh. "What brings you down here again?"

"What's happened to your little operation, Frampton?" George asked, ignoring being called the wrong name yet again. "Finally had a crisis of conscience and decided to shut the whole shameful operation down?"

"Of course not," Frampton said. "Cormac just woke up."

George looked disappointed, but continued on. "The board insisted I come down here and give you this news in person, Frampton." George took a deep breath and Frampton braced himself for bad news. A personal visit from a board member rarely meant anything but.

"We've heard from a source at the *College Review*. It turns out that an unprecedented amount of online attention has been paid to Harrington over the past two weeks. As a result, our X-Factor ranking has soared, all the way from last to fifth-to-last."

Frampton nearly dropped his shillelagh. Had he heard George right? They'd soared four places on the X-Factor list? His job was safe? The dean felt a gigantic grin creeping onto his face. He didn't want to let his emotions show in front of George; that would be unprofessional. So he masked it by taking a huge sip of his Bloody Mary, only dribbling a little on his bare chest and towel.

"So," Frampton said, wiping his mouth with the back of his hand. "It looks like my little 'operation' here was actually a tremendous success."

"A lab in the Harrington science department had a major breakthrough on a cancer prevention drug they've been working on, Frampton," George said with a sigh. "It's been written up in every scientific journal and blog there is. Harrington's name was everywhere last week because of their diligent work to make the world a better, safer place."

"A tremendous success," Frampton repeated, not listening.

"Plus, the student you've been exploiting this entire time uploaded a viral video that got Harrington's name out there as well. Even if the cancer breakthrough hadn't happened, the traffic from that video alone would have been enough to bump our ranking up one spot."

Frampton wasn't even trying to suppress his grin anymore. He got to keep his job. He pulled a cigar out of his waistband and quickly lit it in celebration. Jimmy could go to hell. Inhaling the smooth Havana flavors was the perfect way to celebrate.

"I hope you feel good about how you've spent these past few days, Frampton," George continued. "The board has voted to censure you, yet again. We were prepared to offer you a generous settlement in exchange for shutting down this blight on Harrington's campus, but it looks as if decency prevailed before we had a chance. You'll get to keep your job, but in the name of fairness, and in the best interest of the school, I'd like to ask you to consider resig—"

"Declined," Frampton interrupted. "Thanks for stopping by with the good news, though! Tell the board that I weighed the matter thoroughly, but I've decided to remain in power." He blew an enormous puff of smoke into George's face. "This school needs me."

George waved away the smoke cloud. He looked as if he were on the verge of tears. He opened his mouth to say something to the dean, but couldn't find the words. Without another word, he turned and quickly walked off to his car. Dean Bickerstaff grinned. He stepped down off the porch and walked across the lawn, shooing away the stragglers.

When he got to the sidewalk, he saw that a group of students had gathered there to discuss what to do with the rest of their day. In the center of them were Mako, G-Dimes, and the big, floppy, sunglasses-wearing golden retriever.

"This guy says the party's moving back to his house!" Mako announced to the crowd, who cheered appreciatively. "Lead the way, boy!" Mako said to the dog. As the dean watched, from out of nowhere a skateboard rolled down the sidewalk toward the dog.

When it reached him, he hopped on as it was still moving and, pushing with one of his hind legs, rolled down the sidewalk as the crowd followed after him.

"I'm going to miss those dogs," Frampton said out loud.

"What's going on?" someone shouted from the other side of the street. "Where's everybody going?"

Dean Bickerstaff looked across the road, where Brock's cult and the Throat Jackers stood assembled, keeping their distance from each other. Brock was standing in the middle of the street. Dean Bickerstaff gave his shillelagh a twirl, and silently hoped the bandana men hadn't wandered too far.

"Game over, Brock," the dean said. "Your messiah woke up. He says he's not going back in time anymore."

A buzz spread quickly through both cults. There were gasps and disappointed cries of "No!" Brock raised his hands for quiet. "How can we believe you?" Brock asked. "After all, you stand diametrically opposed to the philosophies of our organization. Should the dark ones speak, we must cast the light upon them to reveal the bitter falsehoods that they will—"

"Oh shut up, you crazy little perv," the dean said. "Get the hell out of here or I'm coming back with tear gas."

The cults went silent as Brock weighed the dean's words carefully. After a short period of internal reflection, he walked over to the leader of the Throat Jackers and whispered something to him. The Throat Jackers' leader nodded and Brock turned to address both cults.

"My brothers and sisters!" he announced. "We've heard that there is a guy over in the dorms who can eat a whole package of Oreos in two minutes! Let's go worship him!" Both cults murmured their assent to this idea, and they quickly packed up their tents and walked off down the road toward the dorms, chanting something that even the dean had to admit was pretty damn catchy.

Frampton turned and looked back at the Craymore Street house. The yard was littered with garbage and empty beer cups, but all in all it wasn't any worse for the wear. He walked over to the van and pulled the rear doors open with a horrible, rusty squeal. Frampton hopped in and quickly changed out of the towel and into his suit. He stepped back out of the van and walked up to the porch. He laid Vance's towel down on the porch, then pulled a piece of paper and a pen out of his pocket.

"Vance," he wrote. "Please split my share of the money with Cormac. Thanks for helping me keep my job. Your friend, Deano." He paused and re-read it once before adding, "PS – If any videos of that keg stand surface online, I will borrow the bear trap from Mickey's and personally cut your dick off with it."

Frampton set the note down on the towel, then folded half the towel over it so it wouldn't blow away. Giving his shillelagh a twirl, he walked back to the van, unlocked the door, and hopped into the driver's seat. It was going to feel good to get back to his own home, Dean Frampton Q. Bickerstaff thought as his puffed on his cigar. But first, he thought he might swing by a car dealership and check out one of these Escalades he'd been hearing so much about lately.

* * *

Cormac stayed in the shower for an hour and a half, just letting the water run over him and replaying the final moments of his time in the 1800s again and again. He'd pulled the trigger, seen the harpoon hit Eleanor, and watched her fall into the water. The next second, he'd been lying in bed with a senator drooling on his pillow. There hadn't been a crackle of light, or the sensation that he'd been whooshing through time, or anything out of the ordinary. One moment he was there, and the next he was here, and he was certain he could never go back.

He cranked the water as hot as it would get and stood there, breathing in the steam. Then he turned the faucet all the way in the opposite direction until the water was nearly freezing. Cormac stood there as long as he could bear it, which was only a couple of seconds. Then he jumped out of the shower, turned the water off, and dried himself off with his towel.

When he emerged from the bathroom, he was happy to see that the house was empty. He walked from the bathroom to his bedroom along the sticky hallway floor. He changed into clean clothes and took a moment to check the view count on "Treasures o' the Sea." Over 800,000. Not giving a damn what Vance might say, Cormac picked up his ukulele and headed for the living room.

He stopped in his tracks when he got there. Suspended in the air was an enormous sectional leather couch. It balanced on the same anvil and computer that had supported the first airborne couch, but Vance was now employing several kegs, a mini fridge, and a second anvil to support the extra legs.

Vance repositioned a beer keg a few inches and stepped back to admire his work.

"Pretty impressive," Cormac said.

Vance turned and grinned at his roommate. "What do you think, Mac?" he asked. "Cissy traded couches with us. It doesn't quite have the character of the last one, but I think it'll be pretty comfortable."

Cormac shrugged. He wasn't really sure what to say.

"You want to try it out?" Vance asked. "Strum that thing on some luxurious airborne cowhide?" Cormac looked down at his ukulele. He nodded without looking up. "Excellent!" Vance clapped his hands together a few times. "Now there are a couple of improvements to the system. One: keg access from this side of the couch. Just hang the hose over the arm of the couch and boom, you never have to get down. Two: this cushion right here is full of weed. Three: there does not appear to be anything living inside this couch at the moment, and I humbly request that you try to keep it that way."

Cormac nodded. "I'll do my best," he said. Vance vaulted himself onto the couch using the extension cord, then scooted over to the far end, where he lay down with his head on one of the arms. The couch was so big that it appeared both of them could lay on it fully extended and still have room for one more person to sit in between them.

"Pass me the uke, Mac," Vance said. "Don't want it to break on the way up." Cormac scanned his roommate's instructions for any hint of malice or sarcasm, and was amazed to not detect any. He handed the ukulele up to Vance, who studied it with amusement. Cormac then pulled himself onto the couch. It was a much more wobbly process than Vance's manuever, and took three times as long, but he finally made it without incident.

"You're in the beer seat, buddy," Vance said, passing the ukulele back to Cormac. "Feel like hashing out your day over a brewski?"

"I suppose so," Cormac was surprised to hear himself say. Vance had been here the whole time, maybe he'd have some insight as to whether something happened on this end that would have caused him to snap back to the present. Cormac poured two beers out of the tap that hung over the arm of the couch. It was a pretty convenient system, he had to admit. He handed one to Vance.

"So what happened just before you woke up?" Vance asked.

Cormac took a sip of his beer and thought about how best to describe to Vance what he'd done. Then he took another sip. Then he finished the entire beer, poured himself a new one, and described his entire day to Vance, piece by piece. Vance's jaw dropped when he heard about the whorehouse menu, he hissed when he heard about Eleanor's plans to divorce and ruin the captain, and noticeably crossed and uncrossed his legs a few times when Cormac described how unbelievably gorgeous she was.

When Cormac described pulling the trigger and shooting her, Vance tensed up. "You shot someone else, Mac? I thought that was just something you were doing to pirates."

"I couldn't help it," Cormac protested, pouring himself another beer. "I just thought about all that we'd worked for, and how crappy the boat was before I got there, and how we'd just started to turn it around. I couldn't let her take that away from us. Plus, it still seemed like . . ."

"Like it was just a video game," Vance said. "I get it." Vance sipped his beer and contemplated what Cormac had just laid out in front of him. "I guess my only question, Mac, is . . . did you get off a cool quip before you shot her?"

Cormac couldn't help but smile. He shook his head no. "I honestly didn't even think about what I was doing. Now I really wish I had, though."

"I'd have said 'See you in Hell-anor!'" Vance suggested. Cormac laughed and nearly spit out his beer.

"Wow," he said after he'd regained his composure. "Yeah, I definitely couldn't have topped that." Vance handed his cup to Cormac for a refill. They both sat sipping their beers in silence for a while before Vance spoke up again.

"Maybe you were back there for a reason," he suggested. "Maybe you went back because somebody needed your help."

Cormac looked at him. "What do you mean?"

"Maybe you took all those trips back in time in order to help somebody who really needed it! And then once you helped them overcome whatever they were having trouble with, you weren't needed anymore so that's why you came back so suddenly!"

Cormac pondered this for a little while. "So you're saying that my purpose was to go back and help the captain out by killing the woman who wanted to divorce him and take his boat?" Cormac asked.

"Hey, it makes sense, right? Someone needed your help, and you were there for him! You're a hero, Mac!"

"Maybe . . ." Cormac thought about it for another moment. "But the captain was a terrible person. He lied and cheated . . . He was a stingy coward. He enslaved Ziro!"

"Oh that's right, you did free a man from slavery," Vance said. "Maybe that was it?"

"Yeah, but I did that as soon as I got there!" Cormac said. "If that was the help I was supposed to provide, I wouldn't have kept on waking up on the boat."

"I dunno, Mac," Vance said. "Sounds like you were the guardian angel that this captain guy needed."

Cormac leaned his head back against the luxurious leather couch. Could that really have been it all along? He had been sent back to help the captain, a terrible person who didn't deserve kindness from anybody? And now the captain would be able to continue to live his awful life, rewarded for all the lying and cheating? All because Cormac had transcended time and space to help him do so? It kind of made sense, but it certainly didn't feel very rewarding to know that the purpose of the greatest adventure of your life had been to help out a total dick. The captain probably wouldn't even have thanked him if he were still around to be thanked.

"I suppose that's it," Cormac said. "I can't think of anybody else that I helped at that moment." Why? he wondered. Why on earth would that be the way the universe worked? It seemed like so much damn trouble just to reward evil.

"Oh, by the way, Deano said you could have half of his share of the dough," Vance said. "You probably earned like twenty grand this week, Mac! That'll buy a few pitchers at Mickey's, huh?" Vance cackled and flicked on the TV with the remote. "Twenty thousand bucks, straight A's for the rest of college, a hit video, a year's supply of weed, a brand new couch, and one hell of an adventure. Not a bad two weeks, was it, Mac?"

"No . . . No I guess it really has been pretty great," Cormac said, trying to sound enthusiastic.

"That actually sounds pretty good, Mac," Vance said. "Maybe the uke gets a bad rap."

Cormac looked down. He hadn't even realized it, but for the past thirty seconds he'd been strumming "Treasures o' the Sea."

* * *

The captain stared at the faint outline of St. John's as it disappeared behind the horizon. They'd pushed off a little over an hour ago, rowed for the first thirty minutes, then raised the sails once they were far enough out to sea. The wind was blowing in their favor, and soon the docks were left far behind.

The captain took one last look then walked to the bow of the boat. The sun was starting to sink in the west, and the sky was beginning to turn a brilliant shade of orange. The end of a crazy day was finally near. He placed both his hands on the railing and leaned forward, feeling the wind in his face, trying to remember all the little details and convince himself that they had actually happened.

"Captain?" came a voice from behind him. "Excuse me, captain? Sir?"

"Gah, I'm sorry," Ziro said as he snapped out of his daydream and turned around. "I'm still not used to being called that yet."

"That's not a problem, sir," said the whaler. "We were just wondering, now that we've got some wind . . . Well, where are we headed, sir?"

Ziro pondered the question. Amidst the frenzied excitement of the afternoon, where he was actually going to sail his new ship was a question that had not even crossed his mind.

Once Eleanor had hit the water, it had been utter chaos. Bodies surfacing in the harbor was not uncommon, especially since the dog pack had assumed power. But rarely were there murders witnessed by so many people, and even more rarely were the murder victims beautiful women. What made this event even stranger was that even though dozens of people had gotten a good look at the shooter, none of them could say where he had disappeared to immediately after.

Ziro had as good a look as anyone, standing on the gangplank just behind Eleanor. He'd watched Cormac pull the trigger and seen the harpoon hit. But as soon as he looked back to where Cormac had been standing, there was nothing there. It was as if Cormac had never been there in the first place. Ziro immediately figured that whatever had kept returning Cormac here had finally released its hold on him, just as mysteriously as it had brought him here in the first place. Even after he'd had time to think about it once the boat set sail, he hadn't come up with an explanation that he thought was more convincing.

Captain Anson hadn't wanted to think of one either. As soon as Eleanor's burly vendor realized that the person who was supposed to pay him was dead, he released Captain Anson and got back to selling his meat skewers. Anson had grabbed Ziro's mop and the two sacks of gold and darted up the gangplank. The crowd, who knew he hadn't pulled the trigger, had just let him go.

"Ziro!" he'd said as he handed Ziro his mop while they ran up the gangplank together. "I've got to get out of here! I'm not letting anyone pin this on me! Oh, and this is the greatest day of my life!" The captain jumped and giddily clicked his heels together, an incredibly awkward move that caused him to nearly tumble off the gangplank when he failed to stick the landing.

"Did you know Cormac was going to do that, sir?" Ziro asked as Captain Anson righted himself.

"No! He just muttered something about her trying to take away 'our' ship and pulled the trigger!"

The captain vaulted over the treasure chest that blocked the gangplank and Ziro followed suit. Eleanor's lawyer had crawled out of the chest and was lying on his back, breathing slowly and deeply. He'd finally stopped sweating, but there was a stain on the deck where the salty sweat had dried all around where he'd been lying.

"Dammit," Ziro muttered.

"Water," the lawyer begged.

"Take a hike, you vulture," Captain Anson said. "My beloved wife is dead. Go track down the slime who did it. Ziro, give me a hand here."

They lifted the lawyer off the deck and hoisted him by his pants waist up and over the treasure chest, then unceremoniously dumped him onto the gangplank. He rolled all the way down until he came to a stop on the dock.

"We've got to get a move on," the captain said, tossing the sacks of gold into the treasure chest, where they landed with a splash. "Help me move this chest, then go rally the men." Anson leaned into the chest and Ziro lent a hand. Slowly, they pushed it away from the gangplank, clearing the way.

Captain Anson was talking quickly. Clearly the adrenaline of wanting to leave before any more unpleasantness happened, combined with the ecstasy of finally being free of his tormenter, had left him super wired. "Which way is the wind blowing? We'll need to chart a course! Where's all the treasure? What are anchors made of? Dammit!"

"What is it, sir?" Ziro asked.

"The *Mongrel*," Captain Anson said, gesturing toward the pirate ship. "I started a drunk auction for it before Cormac shot Eleanor. They had bid it up pretty high, too . . . Dammit!" he repeated.

He paced back and forth rapidly for a few seconds before he stopped and looked up at Ziro. "How would you like your own ship?" he asked.

"My own . . ."

"Yes, your own ship," Captain Anson said. "I don't have time to sell it to any of those idiots. Take the *Mongrel*, Ziro. Consider it compensation for all those years of unpaid labor."

"Slavery," Ziro corrected him.

"Potato, po*tah*to," Anson said with a dismissive wave of his hand. "Now go tell the crew to get on board! We're pushing off in two minutes!"

Now it was Ziro's turn to feel overwhelmed. Had he really just been given command of his own ship? He walked toward the gangplank, his head spinning. Just before he set foot on it, he turned and faced Captain Anson.

"Captain Anson, sir," Ziro asked. "Would you mind trading clothes back with me? I just don't feel comfortable wearing yours."

"Sure, sure, anything you want, Ziro," Anson said, already unbuckling his belt. "Can't believe I nearly let you walk away with my spyglass!" He dropped his pants to the deck and kicked them over to Ziro. Ziro did the same, and they exchanged shirts as well.

"Now go, Ziro!" Captain Anson instructed. "Tell them that it's finally payday on the ol' *Levyathan*! And I'm not paying any interest on back wages!"

And that was the last thing Captain Anson had said to him. Ziro had descended the gangplank and informed the whalers of the recent developments. He put forward, just as a suggestion, that any of them would be welcome to join him aboard the *Mongrel* if they wanted to forego the money Captain Anson owed them. Roughly half of the crew had decided that no amount of money was worth another tour of duty on the *Levyathan*, and had decided to crew under Ziro.

They'd taken a few dinghies of supplies out to the *Mongrel*, and after making one slight cosmetic change, they started to row out of the harbor. Forty-five minutes later, Ziro discovered a promissory note for an utterly baffling amount of money in his pants pocket. He decided that despite the captain's last words, Ziro would count it as interest on back wages.

The whaler stood in front of him, waiting for a response. "Come here," Ziro said. "Let's see how it looks." He walked with the whaler back toward the stern. When they got there, Ziro leaned out over the railing and looked down at the rear of the boat. He waved the whaler over to do the same.

"What do you think?" Ziro asked. "I think it will do until we get someone to paint it professionally." Before they left the dock, Ziro had painted a large black X over the name *Mongrel*. Beneath it, in large hand-painted letters was the boat's new name: *Thank You Cormac*.

"It looks good," the whaler said, straightening back up. "But who is Cormac?"

"Who is Cormac?" Ziro shouted. "He was on the ship for the past two weeks! He shot all those whales!" The whaler stared at him blankly. "He killed the pirates! He saved all of us!"

"Was he the guy with the spyglass?" the whaler asked. "I've never been too good with names."

"That was Captain Anson!" Ziro rolled his eyes. "Look, it doesn't matter. He was my friend and he really helped me out. I don't know why he was here or where he is now, but I wouldn't be here without him. That's all you need to know."

"Sounds good," said the whaler. "When you pick a destination, let me know." He shuffled off to the *Mongrel*'s rum storage area. After a few steps he started whistling the opening notes of "Treasures o' the Sea."

"Hey there!" Ziro yelled after him. "What's that you're whistling?"

The confused whaler turned around. "Whistling? I wasn't whistling, sir. I don't even know how." He pushed his lips together and blew, pushing decidedly non-musical air and spittle out.

"Well where is that music coming from?" Ziro asked. "Listen!" They stood there in silence for a few seconds, but the whaler just shook his head.

"Sorry, sir," he said. "I don't hear anything."

"Huh . . . It must have just been me." Ziro said. But even then, he could still hear the faint strumming of the song coming from somewhere off in the distance. Ziro smiled, and the whaler started to walk away again.

"Wait a second!" Ziro called. The whaler stopped once more. "Where would *you* like to go?" Ziro asked him.

"I don't know," the whaler said tentatively, unsure if it was a trick question and the wrong answer would result in him being thrown overboard. "I guess I've always thought that Hawaii sounded kinda nice?"

"Then set a course for Hawaii," Captain Ziro said with a smile. "I hear they make some damn nice ukuleles down there."

EPILOGUE

The flash of lightning was barely visible through the low black clouds that permanently covered the sky. There was no thunder though. That meant it must be daytime. It only thundered at night.

Zi Rho stared out over the bow of the *Levy X-13*. So another day had dawned. He didn't know whether to curse God or give him thanks. That is, if there even was a god up there. The war with the Electrowhales had gone on for so long, Zi Rho wasn't sure anymore.

He strapped his surgical mask back over his mouth. It had been foolish to leave it off for this long. Perhaps the captain was right, perhaps he really did have a death wish. But really, anyone who got out of bed these days had a death wish. Odds are, if you got out of bed, you were probably going to die.

The Japanese were the lone holdouts defending the seas against the Electrowhales. Nobody knew where they had come from. Oh, there were rumors. Sinister lab experiments gone wrong. Americans dumping toxic waste off the coast of Alaska. Whales that mated with electric eels out of desperation due to their dwindling population, or possibly just sheer horniness. It didn't really matter where they came from. Mankind had been unprepared and they had taken over quickly.

Land became uninhabitable once the whales used their electro powers to cause a permanent electrical storm that prevented the sun from shining through. Crops failed, livestock died. Man took to the sea. Every boat became a whaling boat. Decades passed. New generations were born, knowing no other world than one where man was at war with the Electrowhales. This was the world Zi Rho was born into. This was why he had no choice but to fight.

He grabbed his mop and dipped it into the bubbling bucket of chemicals. He pulled it back out, careful not to let any drip on his boots, and began to swab the steel surface of the *Levy X-13*. Without hourly applications of protective chemicals, the surface of the boat would be eaten away by the acid in the atmosphere. Spring a leak, and the Electrowhales would be there within an hour to finish the job. Sometimes Zi Rho thought about missing a spot on purpose. Just one spot of unswabbed deck. Today was one of those days.

Zi Rho rarely saw the captain anymore. Years ago, he would stand in the crow's nest, shouting curses at the Electrowhales and damning them back to the hell that they had come from. That was before half the Japanese fleet was sunk in one day by the most vicious Electrowhale attack of the war. Now the captain just stayed in his quarters. He still cursed the Electrowhales. It was all his soul knew how to do.

The deck steamed as Zi Rho swabbed. One more hour until his shift ended and he could retreat to his bunk and enjoy a small glass of the ever-dwindling supply of rum. There were rumors that a rum storage facility still stood untouched on a small island near what used to be the Philippines. But there had always been rumors, the old whalers said.

As Zi Rho dipped his mop back into the bucket, he noticed something out of the corner of his eye. He nearly jumped out of his boots. There hadn't been another person on deck during one of his shifts in months. Unless there was an Electrowhale attack, the men just kept to themselves, drinking alone in their bunks and slowly going mad.

But this was definitely another person. Someone Zi Rho had never seen before. And all he was wearing was a towel.

"Holy crap," Vance said. "Mac said I would have bad dreams if I ate that ninth burrito, and he was right!"

Zi Rho didn't understand a word the stranger said, but against his better instinct, he removed his mask to speak to him. "Zi Rho," he said, pointing at his chest.

"Zi Rho," Vance said, sticking his hand out and speaking with the slow, loud voice people adopt for some reason when they're talking to someone who doesn't speak their language. "My name is Vance, and I'm having a bad dream!" Vance pointed at his chest and repeated his name. "Vance!"

"Vance," Zi Rho mumbled.

"Jesus, Zi," Vance said. "What the hell is in this air? My throat's all tingly all of a sudden." He coughed and pointed at Ziro's mask. "I think I need one of those!"

Zi Rho nodded. He kept the masks of fallen fellow soldiers in his bunk as a tribute. He would run and fetch one for this mysterious stranger. There was a prophecy about a stranger who would show up to deliver man from the menace of the Electrowhales. But there had always been prophecies, the old whalers said.

Zi Rho motioned for Vance to follow him. He'd get him some new clothes too—nobody should ever let that much skin be exposed to the air. But before he could take a step toward his quarters, he heard a low, loud hum. Zi Rho's eyes went wide with terror as the hum grew louder and louder, culminating in a deafening crackle of static electricity as an enormous Electrowhale breached two hundred feet from the starboard side of the *Levy X-13*. It landed with an enormous splash, sending lightning shooting through the murky water. Zi Rho was already running to alert the rest of the crew.

"Eight burritos," Vance muttered. "Definitely draw the line at eight burritos next time."

Acknowledgments

First and foremost, this book would never have been possible without Lauren. Not only your editorial expertise, but the encouragement and enthusiasm that you provided along the way. No matter what else happens, it was worth writing this book in order to hear you laugh at it.

Cason, it was great to collaborate again. Let's not go ten years between projects this time.

Adam, I will be honored if people judge this book by your cover.

Mike, who gave me a chance to write jokes for a living so many years ago, and who has graciously promoted and championed my work along with Kevin and Bill at RiffTrax.

And speaking of champions of my work, I would not be where or who I am today without my mom and dad, who have always been my two biggest fans.

For everyone who has pushed me in creative directions, who has let me make them laugh, and who took the time to read this book: Thank you. And now, it's time to get to work on the next one.

About The Author

Conor Lastowka has worked as a writer for RiffTrax.com, the web incarnation of Mystery Science Theater 3000, since 2006. In addition to writing jokes about modern blockbusters, old b-movies, and comically outdated educational shorts, he has been a writer-producer on several RiffTrax Live events broadcast nationwide and performs as the voice of DisembAudio on RiffTrax MP3s.

He is also one of the editors of the blog [Citation Needed], which collects the best of Wikipedia's worst writing. He has co-authored two volumes of [Citation Needed] books riffing on hilariously bad Wikipedia writing, and produced and written a season of podcasts expanding some of the all-time worst Wikipedia entries into skits.

He lives in San Diego with his wife Lauren. Gone Whalin' is his first novel.

Also by Conor Lastowka

[Citation Needed]: The Best of Wikipedia's Worst Writing

[Citation Needed] 2: The Needening: More of The Best of Wikipedia's Worst Writing